MOBILE SUIT GUNDAM

MOBILE SUIT GUNDAM

Yoshiyuki Tomino

Translated by Frederik L. Schodt
Introduction by Mark Simmons

Stone Bridge Press • Berkeley, California

Published by
STONE BRIDGE PRESS
P. O. Box 8208, Berkeley, CA 94707
TEL 510-524-8732 • sbp@stonebridge.com • www.stonebridge.com

CONTENTS

INTRODUCTION

"*THE GUNDAM MOBILE SUIT* is no ordinary three-volume science fiction series…" Thus began translator Frederik L. Schodt's preface to the English-language edition of Yoshiyuki Tomino's *Gundam* novels when they were first released in 1990. The purpose of Schodt's introduction was to explain the history of the *Mobile Suit Gundam* saga to Western readers. But ironically, those now long-out-of-print English-language novels have themselves become a landmark in *Gundam* history, as the first *Gundam* works to be officially released in English. Before the comics, before the animated shows, before the video games, these novels represented the first foray of Japan's beloved sci-fi franchise into the Western world. And in the subsequent decade and a half, that franchise has grown and expanded almost beyond recognition.

The *Mobile Suit Gundam* saga arose from humble beginnings. It began as an animated cartoon, or "anime," series which debuted on Japanese television in 1979. At first glance, *Gundam* appeared to fit safely within the genre of heroic "super robot" anime which filled the airwaves during the '70s. According to the formula, a young boy roughly the same age as the show's target audience would take the controls of an invincible humanoid fighting machine and use it to save the Earth from an invasion of monstrous bad guys. Gaudy colors, flamboyant poses, and

7

spectacular ultimate attacks were all hallmarks of the super robot genre, and its success was measured in terms of toy sales rather than artistic accomplishment.

Yoshiyuki Tomino, the director of *Mobile Suit Gundam*, was a veteran of the anime industry who already had a handful of traditional super robot series to his credit. Tomino's previous entries into the genre had drawn attention for their dramatic flair and unusually harsh storylines, but even so, *Gundam* came as a bold departure. Inspired by real-world space science, and literary sci-fi like Robert Heinlein's *Starship Troopers*, Tomino presented a near-future world of space colonies and high technology, in which humans struggled against each other for political and ideological reasons, rather than against comical space invaders. The super robot was re-imagined as a mass-produced weapon of war, based on consistent laws of physics. And instead of dauntless heroes and dastardly villains, Tomino populated his story with complex and troubled characters, who wrestled with moral conflicts and personal problems even as they struggled to survive amid the chaos of a catastrophic war.

Given the ambitious nature of Tomino's work, it's not surprising that at first the audience didn't know what to make of it. Thanks to its low ratings and the poor sales of its accompanying line of gaudy kiddie toys, *Mobile Suit Gundam* was canceled two months ahead of schedule, forcing the staff to hastily wrap up the story's loose ends. But when the series returned to the airwaves in a new weekday time slot, these reruns racked up two or three times the ratings of the original broadcasts, and a national craze was born. Six months after the end of the original run, a line of scale model kits was launched, and these detailed replicas of the show's robots and vehicles—aimed at an older and more sophisticated audience than the earlier toys—were likewise wildly successful.

As *Gundam's* popularity boomed, the show's staff were reunited to turn the television series into a three-part movie trilogy, which proved to be merely the first of many animated sequels and spinoffs. Director Tomino returned to helm new TV series—1985's *Zeta Gundam*, 1986's *Gundam ZZ* ("Double Zeta"), 1993's *Victory Gundam*—and original movies like 1988's *Char's Counterattack* and 1991's *Gundam F91*. New creators were given the opportunity to add to the saga of the Universal Century in video series like 1989's *Gundam 0080*, 1991's *Gundam 0083*, and 1996's *The 08th MS Team*. In the last decade, the *Gundam* franchise has expanded still further into a slew of alternate universes aimed at new viewers, which run the gamut from the martial-arts action of 1994's *G Gundam* to the traditional space opera of 2002's *Gundam Seed*. It was one of these alternate-universe series, 1995's *Gundam Wing*, which at last succeeded in winning *Gundam* a mass Western audience when it was broadcast on U.S. television in the year 2000.

In addition to the ever-increasing number of animated works—as of this writing there are some nine television series, ten movies, four video series, and a live-action TV special, to say nothing of the parody franchise known as *SD Gundam*—the *Gundam* franchise has spawned a dizzying array of products and merchandise. There are novels and comics, both adapted and original, and video games for a dozen different platforms. *Gundam* plastic model kits, or "Gunpla," are an industry unto themselves, with worldwide sales of over 300 million units to date; in recent years, their success has been rivaled by toys of similarly high quality. Thanks in large part to the popularity of *Gundam Wing*, this merchandise is now showing up in Western toy stores and bookshops as well, with the volume you hold in your hands being just the latest such offering.

So how do these novels fit into the larger picture of the *Gundam* saga? This story, written by director Tomino himself, is less a straightforward novelization of the original *Mobile Suit Gundam* television series than a radical re-imagining. It was originally published in three installments by Asahi Sonorama, with the first volume appearing in late 1979 some two months before the end of the TV series, and the last arriving in early 1981, simultaneously with the theatrical release of the first compilation movie. The novels were republished in 1987 by Kadokawa Shoten, and this English-language version is based on the later Kadokawa editions.

As the reader will quickly realize, these novels are aimed at a more mature audience than the animated series. There are a number of gory scenes, and the sexual relationships of the characters are explored in rather more detail than the animated shows. The novels also delve into the political and military history of the *Gundam* world, and the psychology of the story's principal characters. Considerable space is also devoted to philosophical discussion, especially as the characters begin to evolve into spiritually attuned "Newtypes." Much of the novels' enduring popularity among the saga's Japanese fans is due to this higher level of sophistication, but some of it must surely be due to the reckless abandon with which they depart from the narrative of the animated series and lay out an utterly different version of the *Mobile Suit Gundam* story.

The novels' recounting of the history of the Universal Century world—the early days of the space settlement program, the origins of the totalitarian Principality of Zeon, and the opening battles of the apocalyptic One Year War—serves to fill in gaps in the background of the animated story. As the earliest and most authoritative explanations of Universal Century history, these details have largely been accepted as canon by later creators. However, once the action begins, the storylines of the novels and the animation diverge almost at once. Here, hero Amuro Ray and his comrades are already uniformed cadets, rather than civilians who just happen to seize control of top-secret military equipment. Their battles take place entirely in space, and the voyage across Earth that takes up the middle section of the animated series is discarded outright. Amuro's encounter with enemy Newtype Lalah Sune, which represents the climax of the animated story, takes place at the end of the first novel, where it represents just the first step in the process of his Newtype awakening. Original characters are introduced, familiar faces reappear in new contexts, and the fates of the heroes and villains are often very different from those of their animated counterparts.

Despite the continuity differences, later entries in the *Gundam* saga have contrived to make reference back to these novels. Original characters from the novels, such as Zeon prime minister Darcia Bakharov and Gihren Zabi's secretary Cecilia Irene, were inserted into the compilation movies, along with new dialogue which refers to the background laid out herein. Later animated works, notably *Zeta Gundam* and *Char's Counterattack*, build on the novels' detailed discussion of Newtype phenomena. The gray Gundam codenamed "G3," the carrier *Thoroughbred*, Char's red Rick Dom, and other arcana from the novels regularly resurface in spinoff stories and toy lines. But no matter how often the novels are referenced in later works, their drastically different plot means that they can only be regarded as a story unto themselves, existing far outside the continuity of the animated *Gundam* saga.

Rather than recounting the events of the animated story, the novels provide a new perspective on the *Gundam* world, allowing us to see it as it might appear in the absence of the commercial constraints that govern the production of giant robot anime. Here, the characters are allowed to experience love and lust, ambition and despair. They inhabit a world of fantastic technology, in which soldiers grumble about dirty instrument panels and cramped cockpits, and even master warriors struggle against the limitations of their machines and their own flawed human psyches. Rather than a plot device to help the heroes win battles, the Newtype phenomenon becomes an avenue for exploring the nature of the human soul, and the prospect of a future in which humanity may yet evolve beyond the need for war and violence.

And that, as far as this writer is concerned, is the very essence of *Gun-*

dam in all its diverse forms and flavors. I'm delighted to see this landmark work made available once more to a new generation of Western fans, and I hope you find much enjoyment and understanding in it!

Mark Simmons

P.S. FOR THE SERIOUS STUDENT of the Universal Century world, a few technical notes . . .

First, *Mobile Suit Gundam* mavens will note that the vessel on which our heroes travel is herein described as the White Base-class carrier *Pegasus*, rather than the Pegasus-class carrier *White Base* featured in the animated story. This curious inversion has been faithfully retained from the Japanese novels.

There are also numerous differences between the facts and figures presented in these novels and those cited in other sources, including such matters as the heights of the mobile suits, the dimensions of the space colonies, the dates of historical events, and the ages of the characters. These discrepancies are likewise present in the Japanese editions of the novels, and it's probably best not to worry about them.

Lastly, a note regarding the space map that appears in this volume. Although several different maps have been published over the years, with different arrangements of the Sides, the version provided here is the one most commonly used for events of the original Mobile Suit Gundam story. This version of the map, in which Side 5 and its *Texas Zone* are located in front of the moon at Lagrange point 1, also matches the descriptions in Tomino's novels.

SPACE MAP U.C. 0079
(With Sides and Lagrange Points)

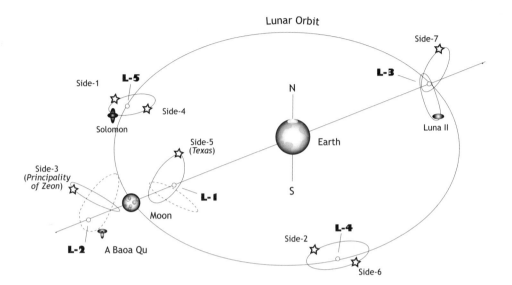

Lunar Orbit

Side-7

L-3

Side-1

L-5

Side-4

Solomon

N

Earth

Side-5
(*Texas*)

S

Luna II

Side-3
(*Principality
of Zeon*)

L-1

Moon

L-2   A Baoa Qu

Side-2

L-4

Side-6

AWAKENING

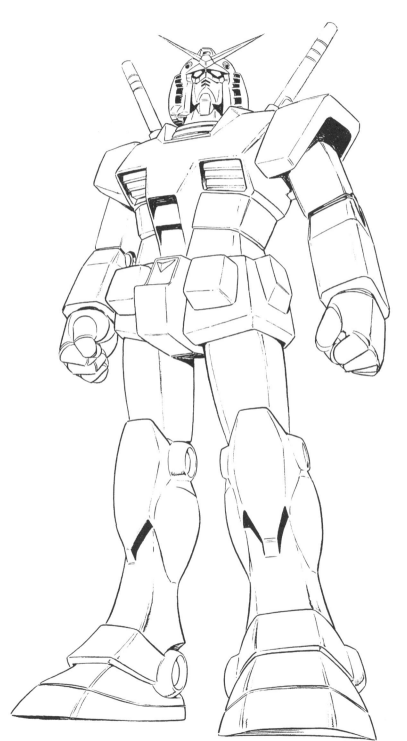

Volume 1

SIDE 7

"THE INSTRUMENT PANEL'S DECORATION—TO let you know if you're facing front or back. The only thing you can really count on is your eyes!! And they're useless unless you use your damned brains!! Understand?! God help you numbskulls when you become pilots!"

With spittle flying, Lt. (jg) Ralv thundered at the five young pilot cadets standing at attention in front of him, but they were having a hard time concentrating; their empty stomachs were making too much noise.

When the *Pegasus* entered inertial flight, the cadets were required to stand in the command center and observe the warship's seven regular pilots practice takeoff and landing in their Core Fighters. And they had to do more than just watch. When a Core Fighter was about to land, they had to yell out the correct landing procedure—before the pilot actually executed it. And if anyone failed to respond with the proper spirit, Ralv's left hand would let them know right away. Despite its realistic fuzz, the thing was artificial, and if it ever really connected in the weightless environment it could slam a cadet into a fixture in the command center and lay him out for three days. Unlike most warships, when last in port the *Pegasus* hadn't been fitted with protective padding.

The *Pegasus* was finally on a real mission, to proceed to Side 7 and

17

pick up the new mobile suits. It was time for Ralv to teach the newcomers about the ship, about the Core Fighters. It was time for young men to learn to submerge their wills to that of the ship. On the *Pegasus*, the best of the White Base-class, this was the way things were done.

The ship's seven regular pilots were lucky; they had already experienced real combat several times on the space carrier *Trafalgar*, and as a result they needed only three trial runs to learn the ropes of takeoff and landing on the new ship. For the five cadets, hell was just about to begin. First, they performed a textbook preflight check on five Core Fighters. Then they each climbed in one. It was their first time in a real Core Fighter. And it was their first time to attempt a takeoff.

"Follow me!" Ralv yelled.

The lieutenant was irritated, and he had a right to be; he was one of the regulars. If the ship picked up six mobile suits as scheduled, and if the higher-ups ordered them into action on a round-the-clock basis, even twelve pilots wouldn't be enough. The cadets were young and fresh out of training. The only way the regulars would be able to lighten their own load would be to make sure the boys could take up the slack.

Ralv's Core Fighter catapulted out of the ship's port hatch, and the cadets followed; Ryu Jose and Kai Shiden from port, Amuro Ray, Sean Crane and Hayato Kobayashi from starboard.

Ahead and to the left Amuro Ray could see the revolving red light on Ralv's machine. Using it as a guide, he twisted his Core Fighter's joy stick to the left—gingerly, like turning an egg in an egg cup. It was a good analogy, he thought, while marveling at the stars blazing silently all around. His sun visor had a reflective coating on the outside, but from his perspective it was colorless and transparent, and through both it and the fighter canopy he could sense the indescribable stillness of space. But inside his helmet his ears were filled with noise. Amid the static caused by Minovsky particle interference, he could hear the sounds of transmissions between Lt. Ralv and the *Pegasus*, and the calls of the other four cadets, echoing over and over again. Amuro thought about how Ralv always said that, "to be a real pilot, you gotta learn to sort the important crap from the noise." Ralv belonged to the amoeba-brain school and he wasn't into sophisticated logic. "Don't worry about your eardrums rupturing," he was also fond of saying, "your headphones've got an automatic volume control."

The six Core Fighters were now strung out in a curve like a strained fishing pole, as the lieutenant's machine led them back around to the mother ship. With the sun on his right, Amuro thought how fitting it was that the *Pegasus* was also known as the "White Base," for as it floated

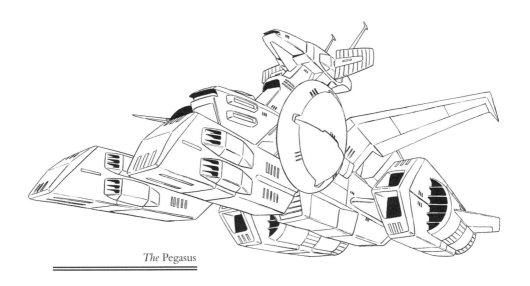

The Pegasus

to his left, lit up by the direct light, its body was a beautiful, pure white. But the ship's configuration was definitely complicated. The bridge was in the center of the ship. The prow was divided into two separate units for catapult decks, and the stern was similarly split into two units for the main engines. On the left and right sides, heat-dissipating panels with built-in solar batteries stretched out like giant wings. Viewed from one angle, the ship's profile could indeed look like the winged horse of its namesake, or at least a boxy wooden one. But it could also resemble a skinny sphinx, or even a dog lying prone with its front and back legs extended. In fact, Amuro decided, *Pegasus* was really too limiting a name for such a ship.

"Amuro!!" Lt. Ralv barked.

Amuro's Core Fighter had strayed two degrees off course. "Sorry, sir!" he yelled back with force, imagining how nice it would be if he ruptured the lieutenant's eardrums.

In front of him, Ryu Jose's fighter plowed into the arresting cables strung under the *Pegasus*'s port-side front hatch. Amuro, next in line, raised the landing hook behind his Core Fighter cockpit and sailed into the cables under the starboard hatch.

RALV ALWAYS SAID PILOTS should be able to spot the ship's arresting cables with the naked eye, but it wasn't that simple. In the vacuum of space, the resolution was too extreme, and even with the cables painted bright red it was hard to judge the distance to them relative to the rest of the ship. Landing manually, instead of on auto with the computer reading information from laser search-beams, was an art that would take over ten years to learn and then still be hard. On Earth all you had to do was hook the cables, and gravity would bring you down. Here in space you had to worry about the relative distance and speed of ship and Core Fighter, and hit the wires at just the right speed so they wouldn't snap, or else in an instant you'd shoot by the ship or smash into its walls. And even if the *Pegasus*'s arresting cables snared the fighter's landing hook properly there was still a risk. If they slowed you too fast, a fighter—worth its weight in gold—might flip and smash into the side of the ship.

The lieutenant always said the safest thing was to bring the fighters in by the book, following the digital read-outs on the instrument panel. "But remember," he would add, "if the power fails, your instruments are about as useful as sunglasses in a cave at midnight!" The analogy was a little oblique, but it got the point across.

Amuro felt the cables stop him with the same force as slamming on the brakes in a car on Earth, and when his fighter came to rest he felt rather proud of himself. There was a docking hatch above him that connected with the ship's catapult deck, and when the hatch opened, a crane arm with a giant hook emerged and hoisted the entire Core Fighter up to the deck. There, the fighter was reset on the catapult mechanism and made ready to launch again. The entire process took only twenty-five seconds.

"Core Fighter No. 4! Chief Petty Officer Amuro Ray, prepare for launch! You are cleared for takeoff!" The confident voice came through loud and clear from an officer in the command center. Inside the *Pegasus*, all communications were hard-wired to avoid interference from Minovsky particles, and even subtle nuances could be read in a man's voice.

"Ready for launch!!" Amuro yelled back with vigor, trying to sound like a proper pilot should. As a cadet, he knew that if he used the wrong language or tone it would be reflected in his grades. Then his Core Fighter soared once more into space.

THE CORE FIGHTERS PILOTED by Amuro and the other cadets were an integral part of a larger mission to pick up two new mobile suits developed by the Federation, models called Gundam and Guncannon. Mobile suits, or MS, were giant humanoid, heavy armor machines; a new type of weapon designed for close-quarter combat in outer space, and introduced for the first time in the current war. Externally they resembled "robots," but they were operated by human pilots in cockpits in their core modules. Unfortunately, Federation MS development had only begun six months earlier. The Zeon forces had already finalized their models the year before.

Core Fighters, as the name suggests, could be incorporated into the central core of a mobile suit, where they functioned as its cockpit, or, in emergencies, as a specially designed escape pod. They had heat-dissipating wings with built-in vernier jets that could fold up into the fuselage, and fairly powerful nuclear engines. They could perform a combat function independent of the mobile suit, but to call them true "fighters" would be stretching it.

BACK AT THE SHIP, Lt. Ralv continued doling out advice to his pupils. "The Gundam and the Guncannon mobile suits are even trickier to pilot than Core Fighters. Gotta handle 'em like a good woman in bed, with care. But what would you boys know about that?! This war's wiped out so many people, you'll never know unless we beat Zeon and you get to sow a few oats with their women!! Don't ever forget that!"

Amuro, standing at attention, stared at the lieutenant. He had an awful habit of waving his artificial left arm when he talked, probably to compensate for a complex about it.

He's probably right, Amuro thought. He couldn't help thinking of Fraw Bow, who lived on the Side 7 colony. He had lived there himself until enlisting in the Federation Forces, and for the first three months or so thereafter he'd received video letters from her on a regular basis. But then they had stopped. Now, on the *Pegasus*, he was headed back to his old colony.

"SWITCH TO THE NUCLEAR fusion engine the instant your Core Fighters connect with the Gundam or Guncannon," the lieutenant intoned, "That'll give you some *real* power . . . "

But then Ralv suddenly punctuated his monologue with a "Damn you!!" and his metal fist sliced through the air, barely missing Amuro's left temple. Amuro didn't mean to duck, but did so out of reflex when he felt the hand crease his hair. The lieutenant left the floor from the inertia generated by his hand's own swing.

"If that thing had connected," thought Amuro, *"I'd be a goner . . . "* But he had no time to feel relieved. The lieutenant quickly spun on his feet, and with his own weight and momentum regained his balance. Then he turned to Amuro.

"Not a bad dodge for an idiot with his head in the clouds . . . But not good enough! You two on either side of Mister Amuro! Restrain him!!"

As ordered, Chief Petty Officers Ryu and Kai reluctantly held Amuro's arms. Ralv then grabbed him by the collar with his right hand, and slapped him across the face four times in a row with his left.

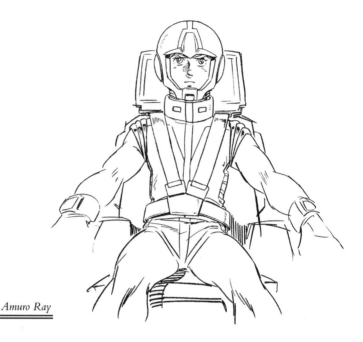

Amuro Ray

"Enough for now! It's chow-time!" he yelled. "You're all dismissed for an hour. We meet later in the briefing room. Hop to it!!"

None of the cadets needed to be told to hurry. They were gone in an instant. Twenty feet above the Core Fighter launch pad was a catwalk, and from there it was a short hop by lift-grip to the mess hall. Lift-grips were special moving handholds that ran on rails built into both sides of the ship's passageways, and the crew used them to move through weightless areas. When the cadets grabbed onto one they could zip along at speeds between six to twenty feet per second.

"Hey, Amuro!" said Ryu Jose, laughing at his friend's red cheeks. "Try a little harder to stay out of trouble next time!"

❏ ❏ ❏

ON THE ZEON *MUSAI* cruiser, Lt. Commander Char Aznable flexed the tip of his toes and floated up to the bridge. *Musai*-class ships were so quiet that when he landed the only audible sound was that of the Velcro of his boot soles meshing with the carpeting on the floor. Still, Dren, a junior grade lieutenant, had sharp ears. Turning, he said, "We'll reach Side 7 in fifteen minutes, sir."

Char grunted in acknowledgement and stared out the bridge window at the panorama unfolding before them. It was something he always enjoyed. There, down to the left, was Earth, an illuminated crescent floating in space. And next to it was the reddish rock crescent of *Luna II*, reflecting like a rusty little hand sickle.

Luna II was the nickname for Juno, an asteroid parked twelve years ago in a moon-like orbit around Earth. Originally from the area between Mars and Jupiter, humans had moved the asteroid to its present location, opposite the real moon, so it could be used to supply important minerals and landfill to over two hundred colonies. After years of mining, it retained little of its original shape and was now a lemon-shaped lump of rock less than eighty kilometers in diameter, floating in an area referred to as the Shoal Zone, heavily fortified by the Earth Federation Space Force since the beginning of the war. Zeon cruiser-class warships rarely attempted to enter the area, but that did not stop regular skirmishes between patrols sent out by both sides.

"Laser scope!!"

At Char's command, the monitor on the port side of the bridge displayed an image from the laser system; it showed the warship Char sought, floating in space between two asteroids on the other side of the Shoal Zone. But the image was not a true depiction of reality. The system detected what information it could, the computer analyzed it, and then, using inference and extrapolation techniques, finally output a detailed computer graphics image. Since the computer database did not yet contain specific information on such a new design of ship, however, the system could only display a silhouette of what looked like a resting, 180-meter-long wooden horse.

On first seeing this silhouette Char had remarked that it "looked like a Trojan horse," thus coining the name used for the enemy ship used on board the *Musai*. Unlike most Federation warships he had seen before, this one's shape also reminded him of an old-style navy landing or transport craft.

"Something about that ship worries me," Char muttered. Then he called out: "How far are we from Side 7?"

In response, an enlisted man stationed in front of the monitor typed in a command on a keyboard. Something about the torn seam on the man's left shoulder distracted Char, but the data he wanted nonetheless soon appeared on the lower right corner of the display, and he pored over it through his antiglare face shield. All the crew wore similar face shields on combat duty, but Char was unique because, beneath his, he had on another mask that he wore constantly. Technically allowed because of a horribly disfiguring facial scar, he had another, unstated, reason for wearing it; he didn't want the higher-ups in the ruling Zabi family to learn his true identity.

"How long has the Federation been developing Side 7?" Char asked Dren.

"About two and a half years, Lieutenant Commander Aznable, sir," came the response. Dren was a junior grade lieutenant ten years older than Char, and his reply was overly formal; rank was important, but last names were rarely used anymore. "They had only completed a third of Side 7's first colony when the war began," Dren continued, "so it's probably still a little primitive, sir."

"Hmm . . . And it's in the area controlled by *Luna II*, isn't it. . . ." Just as Char said this, something suddenly dawned on him. Ahead of them lay both the odd Trojan horse–shaped ship, and Side 7. It had to be more than a coincidence. "I bet it's Operation V!" he exclaimed. "Dammit! I bet the Feds have developed their own MS!!"

"Mobile suit? The Federation!?" said Dren skeptically.

Dren's stupidity irritated Char. But the man had begun his career as a civil servant. What could he expect? "Any troops occupying the Side?" he asked.

"Yes, sir!" called out the young crewman by the monitor. "A small unit under the Ministry of Colony Administration. According to information we received two months ago, it's Company No. 8 from the Third Sector Patrol Force."

"Two months ago?" Char thought out loud. "My God, that's already ancient information. Our intelligence forces must *really* be short-handed."

"Furthermore, sir," continued the crewman, "according to intelligence received seven months ago, there are 13,800 civilians . . . "

"Understood . . . "

The *Musai* cruiser had just completed a guerilla–style raid on Federation forces and was now headed home. It had almost no missiles left. Two of its four mega–particle beam cannons had been out of whack since the start of the operation, a single blast having fried the magnetic coating in their barrels and rendered them useless. The ship's three mobile suits—the Zakus—were usable, but there were only two cartons of ammunition left for their 120 mm rifles. There was only one way to find out if the Federation Forces were testing their mobile suits on Side 7, and that was by sending in Zaku scouts.

It was U.C. 0079, seventy–nine years since the start of the Universal Century. Year Zero of the new calendar system marked what had been mankind's first major movement into outer space.

At the end of the twentieth century (under the old system) Earth had plunged into crisis. Horrendous overpopulation had wreaked havoc on a civilization dependent on the burning of fossil fuels. It had brought out the worst evils of capitalism, aggravating a struggle for finite resources and exacerbating the "greenhouse effect." And when an attempt was made to switch to giant orbiting photovoltaic cells, transmitting the power to Earth had nearly destroyed the ozone layer, making radiation damage a serious danger. There had been only one way to avoid destruction of the planet's entire ecosystem, and that was through collective action on the part of mankind to manage its own population growth.

With Earth's very future at stake, a bold, massive program to colonize space was proposed and quickly adopted. In what seemed like a science fiction dream at the time, groups of floating colonies called Sides were constructed at Lagrange points; specific locations around the Earth and moon where the gravitational fields of the sun, Earth, and moon all neutralize each other. In the early days, individual colonies were giant floating cylinders three kilometers in diameter and thirty-eight kilometers long, but later they doubled in size. Emigration was made compulsory, and enforced by state mandate on a global basis, with no cultural or regional exceptions permitted.

The first group of forty colonies—Side 1—was constructed at the Fifth Lagrange point. It was followed by construction of another group called Side 4. Sides 2 and 6 were built at the Fourth Lagrange Point. Side 5 was built at the First Lagrange Point. And then Side 3 was built at the Second Lagrange Point—in an area colloquially known as "the back of the moon."

By U.C. 0045, *Luna II* had been parked in its moon orbit and emigration to Sides 1 and 2 had been completed. When construction on Side 3 began, the colonists on the first two Sides had already begun to think of themselves as somehow different from people on Earth. The construction of the subsequent Sides thereafter proceeded at an increasingly fast pace. By the time emigration to Side 6 ended and construction began on Side 7, a century-long colonization and emigration project was drawing to a close, and nearly eighty percent of mankind lived in space.

But on Earth more and more people began to rebel against the idea of emigration, and they petitioned the Earth Federation for permission to continue inhabiting the planet, to "preserve the native human stock," as they put it. As Earth residents, however, they still insisted on retaining the right to rule over all the space colonists. Inevitably, perhaps, a schism occurred between the Earth residents and the Colonists, or "Spacenoids," as they were sometimes called.

The most dramatic example of this occurred on Side 3. In U.C.

0054, a young revolutionary named Zeon Zum Deikun declared the colonies of Side 3 to be an independent republic. But four years later he suddenly died and was succeeded by Degwin Zabi, who resurrected an archaic concept of a sovereign state akin to an archduchy, established the "Principality of Zeon," and declared himself its absolute ruler, or "sovereign."

The men and women on Earth, needless to say, were in no mood to relinquish control to an upstart sovereign, and they remained determined to continue ruling the colonies from the home planet. But in their determination they ignored both the difficulties of remote rule on such a vast scale, and the realities of a changing era.

Matters came to a head when Degwin Zabi decided he would no longer be at the mercy of unilateral decisions made by a distant Earth Federation. Rallying the colonists of Zeon around him, he organized an independent military force and decided to resist by force. And thus mankind slid into its first war in space.

Two things made Degwin's audacious military stance possible. The first was the use of Minovsky particles, named after their discoverer. When several types of these infinitesimally small, charged particles were scattered in space, they fused with plasma and created an unstable ion state which absorbed rather than reflected radio and radar signals. Minovsky particles were short-lived, and limited by the fact that they had to be continually scattered in space, but they nonetheless fundamentally altered the rules of combat. For all intents and purposes they rendered radar-based weaponry unusable.

Then two grown children of Degwin Zabi's, Gihren and Kycilia, developed a new weapon that cleverly exploited the new situation. Called the Zaku, it was a mobile suit. Like warships of the time, it was powered by nuclear fusion engines and could therefore engage in long-term, sustained combat. But because it could use a variety of firearms interchangeably, it was also highly effective in close-quarter combat, even in the presence of Minovsky particles. This, combined with its maneuverability, hit-and-run attacks, and tactic of jumping directly into the middle of a battle, meant that one Zaku could singlehandedly destroy an Earth Federation *Magellan*-class battleship. Zakus, more than anything else, enabled the Side 3-based Principality of Zeon to embark on its War of Independence, and helped the opening rounds of the One Week Battle go more or less as Gihren and Kycilia Zabi had expected.

Zakus were not without their flaws. When armored with a compound triple honeycomb construction, a sixteen-meter-tall suit was said to be the maximum that a man could operate. And the pilots complained

Char Aznable

about the cockpits. The entry hatch was right in front of the instrument panel, and was difficult to get in and out of. Weightlessness usually made this no problem, but pilots griped that the instruments were often dirty.

The Zaku's 120 millimeter rifle, however, was exceptional. Only called a "rifle" because the mobile suit held it like one, in reality it was a cannon. When used in close-in fighting it enabled pilots like Lt. Commander Char Aznable to accomplish what had once been unthinkable. Piloting a single Zaku, Char had destroyed three of the enemy's *Magellan*-class battleships and seven *Salamis*-class cruisers. This feat had earned him both a special promotion to lieutenant commander, and the fear and respect of the Earth Federation Forces, who knew him and his red-colored Zaku as "the Red Comet."

AS ORDERED BY CHAR, Lt. (jg) Denim launched his Zaku fifty meters behind that of Ensign Gene. First, he detoured around the Side 7 colony and positioned himself with the sun to his rear. The cylindrical colony looked as bright as a full moon. Then, shielding himself with fragments of

Luna II drifting in the Shoal Zone, he led the way to the colony core.

It is hard to keep a cool head when closing in on an object three kilometers in diameter. The colony glared bright white in the sun, and the vacuum of space skewed Denim's perspective. Squinting, he could make out details on the looming walls, but his main monitor soon showed nothing but wall, making it even harder to keep a sense of relative distance. He stopped looking at the monitor, and fixed his eyes on the range finder beside it. Since the Zaku carried a 120 mm rifle in its right hand, he also made sure the gun sights were aligned with the mobile suit's mono-eye so he could fire at a moment's notice.

There was no response from the colony. Monitors on the left and right sides of Denim's cockpit displayed the colony's periphery and revealed its relative scale; a protruding framework of several hundred meters was still under construction.

Denim swore under his breath. "Gene's a lucky bastard. All *he* has to do is follow me. If I cream into something, I bet he'll turn tail and run."

Eventually Denim was so close to the colony wall that even the range finder was useless. He had to use the Zaku's orthoscopic monitor whether he wanted to or not. Just when it looked like he might smash into the wall, the details of a giant hatch used for entry and exit came into focus, as did what looked like human graffiti. He could make out phrases like *Toilet to the right,* or *I wanna do it with Hanes,* and worse.

He snorted, "Uh oh . . . " But he wasn't responding to the graffiti. He had spotted the cargo hatch in the colony's center module, and it was open. It might be a trap.

"It's a gamble," he muttered. "The moment I touch the wall an alarm might go off. But what can a few Federation clowns do right away against a Zaku?"

Denim maneuvered his Suit to touch the wall. Nothing happened. With Gene following, he entered through the first door on the cargo hatch and tried the inner lock hatch. Incredibly, the manual door was open.

This proves Zeon doesn't have a monopoly on idiots, he thought.

One by one, Denim opened the four layers of shuttered doors on the inner hatch. The last one was welded shut, but the laser burner built into the Zaku's hand took care of that. And then he and Gene emerged onto a deck that overlooked the inside of the colony. They were on the central axis of the cylinder, and had it not been for clouds that obscured their view, they would have seen a 360-degree panorama of "land" surrounding them.

From the inside, the colony cylinder wall, or "floor," was divided into six equal sections, which alternated between glass walled areas that let in sunlight, and "land" areas where people actually lived. As a result, the artificial land below the colonists' feet was their "earth"; the transparent wall section of the colony three kilometers directly above them formed their "sky." An enormous array of mirrors built outside the colony cylinder, next to the glass sections, distributed natural sunlight evenly throughout the interior, and by adjusting the angle of the mirrors to Universal Mean Time it was possible to create an illusion of day and night, even to generate a sense of seasons and regional differences.

Ensign Gene made his Zaku's left hand reach out and touch the shoulder of Denim's machine, initiating what was called "skin-talk"—a form of communication utilizing the voice vibrations that could travel through the Zakus' armor. Skin-talk could also be used when wearing the helmets that were part of "normal suits"—the term used for regular space suits ever since mobile suits had come into vogue.

"Look, sir . . . a spider web," Gene said.

Normally, Denim would have chewed out his subordinate for such an asinine comment, but this time he looked in the direction the man was pointing. To his amazement, in the corner of the deck above them there was a beautiful spider web. In the Zeon colonies insects were strictly regulated, and outside of the entomological rooms in museums no one ever saw them.

"Gosh, sir," Gene said, "I'd love to climb out of this Suit and see what that stuff really feels like . . . "

"Win the war," Denim retorted, "and you can play with as many spider webs as you want."

With that, Denim made his Zaku jump off the deck on which they were standing, into the mist. The pair had to drop 1500 meters from the core to the ground, or inner walls of the cylinder. But construction on the first Side 7 colony had stopped with only a third of it complete, and compared to Zeon colonies the clouds were still quite wispy.

So far so good, but if the enemy spots us we're goners, Denim thought. He noted that there seemed to be a fairly high concentration of Minovsky particles diffused throughout the colony, and realized Char's hunch had been right. *Something's going on here,* he concluded. Minovsky particles meant that he and Gene didn't have to worry about being detected by radar, but someone might still spot them visually. He'd just have to rely on the fact that it was early morning in the colony—4:30 AM, to be exact.

As Denim dropped closer and closer to the ground below, he was surprised. He had imagined that a colony still under development might look a little like this, but compared to Zeon's ergonomically designed, calculated environments, the area below seemed awfully primitive. Nonetheless, he soon spotted an open, undeveloped zone with what appeared to be some sort of military facility. While keeping the trajectory of his Zaku aimed at it, he noticed something flash in the corner of the site.

I wonder if it's their MS? he thought.

Ten seconds later, the two Zakus touched down in a pile of earth. Since they were still around three kilometers away from the military facility, Denim switched his main monitor to telescopic mode. In the distance, almost eleven kilometers away, he could see the colony's "mountain." This was an artificial construct on the central axis of the colony, on both ends of the cylinder. The mountain "peak" contained the colony's port facilities and industrial sectors, and from there the "ground" sloped into the colony's flat lands. As Denim watched, a giant elevator platform built into the side of the mountain began to slowly rise. There was no mistaking the exposed, red-colored machinery it carried: it was a humanoid mobile suit.

I wonder if they've actually completed the thing? he thought. The Suit on the elevator platform was still divided into a humanoid upper and lower torso. Even more interesting, it had what appeared to be missile or cannon barrels built into the shoulder sections. It was a rather crude design, but it made a lot of sense to Denim. *A design like that would free up the MS's hands. With a rifle, it'd be deadly!*

Then Gene initiated skin-talk. "Sir," he said, "look at that trailer down there on the left. The white thing on it might be another MS ..."

Sure enough, a self-propelled flatbed trailer was in the process of pulling another mobile suit, half-covered with a tarp, out of a gigantic building. But it was clearly a different model from the one on the elevator. Its "eyes" were in exactly the same place as a human's.

"Jeez, it looks uncannily human," Denim grumbled. "But makin' a weapon life-like doesn't always make it better ..."

Having confirmed the existence of two enemy mobile suits, it occurred to Denim that if, as it seemed, the Federation Forces were doing final operational tests on them, there ought to be two or three more Suits around somewhere.

"Okay, Denim," he said to himself, "It's time to make your move. What's it gonna be?"

The best plan would be to capture the two Federation mobile suits right in front of them. But this might also be the right time to show Lt. Commander Char Aznable—that young upstart so favored by the Zabi family—what a real combat veteran could do.

"Now, how many Suits have we really got here?" he thought out loud. . . .

THE *PEGASUS* GLIDED INTO the Side 7 colony port, and the instant the docking lock mechanism was activated, the crew opened the hatches on the front "legs" of the landing craft-style warship. The conversion system for the new model mobile suits was ready and waiting.

"Prepare to receive three Guncannons and three Gundams in three minutes! All crew to stations!"

With the announcement, Amuro and the other four cadets assumed their assigned stations on the left and right decks. At the same time, four of the regular pilots left the *Pegasus* and headed on lift-grips toward the port hatch that led to the inner colony. Being higher in rank, they would get to see the new mobile suits first.

"On the double, men! As soon as we finish loading the Suits we blast off from this Side. That *Musai*'ll be hot on our tail any minute now!!"

On the *Pegasus*'s bridge, Captain Paolo Cassius was worried. Twenty minutes ago in the Shoal Zone he had spotted a Zeon ship, but then lost sight of it. And he was bothered by the high concentration of Minovsky particles around the colony. Maybe it made sense for the mobile suit development team to scatter them in the area to confound enemy transmissions, but there was always a negative side to it. "If only they'd do things in moderation . . . " he grumbled.

From the bridge Paolo could see the module that formed the Side 7 colony's port. The central command section was built into a wall only a hundred meters away, and in the reddish glow of its lights Paolo could make out the forms of a few workers. Then, just as he was thinking that the facility seemed terribly understaffed, he heard an alarm sound. And at almost the same instant, one of his communications men turned around and suddenly yelled, "Captain! There's an attack *INSIDE* the colony!"

"An attack?!" *It must be a joke*, thought Paolo.

ZEON SCOUT LT. (JG) Denim had, after all, decided to demonstrate what sort of stuff he was made of. The two Federation mobile suits first sighted were temporarily hidden in mist, but there were four other flatbed trailers with heavy loads emerging from the shadow of an enormous building nearby. He waited a couple of seconds to make sure there were no more trailers, and then ignited the jump verniers on his Zaku. With the thrusters he could make his giant suit jump 800 meters in a normal gravity environment. Ensign Gene followed in his Zaku.

When his field of vision was free, Denim trained his gun sights on the mobile suit on the mountainside elevator, and fired in mid-air. Two shots hit their mark. The elevator platform crumpled and slid down the mountain slope, carrying the red mobile suit with it. Gene fired a volley at the base of the mountain and one of the flatbed trailers burst into flames. As he watched the column of black smoke that billowed from the site, Denim wondered if the Federation Forces were still using old-fashioned gasoline . . .

When the two Zakus touched down, their legs skidded in the soft earth of the colony floor, and they were immediately met by a wire-guided missile zooming toward them from off to the left (inside small colonies, guided missiles had to be wired to avoid Minovsky interference). Denim tilted the Zaku's upper torso a tad to let the missile zip by harmlessly, then slashed its guide-wire with his left arm. He hadn't expected any resistance from the Federation Forces, yet to his astonishment they actually seemed to have considered the possibility of an attack from inside the colony. Several enemy ele-cars with missile launchers appeared, but the Zakus picked them off like sitting ducks with their rifles. The Federation crowd didn't seem to have any idea how to properly use these slow, electrically-powered vehicles in combat.

FIVE HUNDRED METERS IN front of the *Pegasus*, over in the port area, a hatch leading to the inside of the colony opened and Amuro suddenly heard a roar from behind him. To his amazement, two Core Fighters launched from the ship and soared into the colony. Core Fighters weren't really designed as fighter planes, and it was sheer madness to take them into combat in the narrow confines of the colony. The Side 7 colony, after all, was only around twenty-five kilometers long and three kilometers wide. It would take all a pilot's skills just to avoid smashing into the colony walls that alternated between terrain and transparent sections bringing in sunlight. Intercepting the enemy would be almost impossible.

INSIDE THE COLONY, ZEON Lt. (jg) Denim was shocked by the sight of the two tiny craft bearing down on him out of a crack in the clouds. No one had warned him of fighters stationed inside the colony, so he could only deduce they were from that odd-looking "Trojan horse" warship spotted earlier in the Shoal Zone. But did the Federation pilots really believe they could destroy his Zaku with a simple strafing? If so, they were grossly underestimating his ability. He quickly had them in his sights, and fired. The 120 mm rifle wasn't equipped with diffusion shells, but Denim managed to pick them off anyway. The Core Fighters disintegrated in mid-air, fragments of them raining noisily down on the Zakus' armor.

IN THE PORT AREA, Amuro and the four other cadets quickly donned their normal suits, grabbed some recoilless rifles, and headed on lift-grips for the inner colony.

"I heard two companies of combat troops have infiltrated the Colony!" yelled Kai Shiden. He had a way of stating the outrageous, and no one could ever figure out where he got his information.

"We don't have any experienced combat troops on the *Pegasus*," Hayato Kobayashi muttered. "I wonder if we'll be all right inside the colony?"

Luckily, Amuro, standing next to Hayato, was the only one who overheard his friend's worried comment.

"One thing's for sure," said Ryu Jose, taking his hand off the lift-grip handle and sailing through the air. "The enemy's not gonna come running out to shake our hands." Ryu was big, and his body had a lot of inertia, but by grabbing on to the lift-grip on the other wall and using it as a brake, he was able to get to the "C" deck—the deck that led down to the section of the colony where the attack was taking place.

Explosions on the floor of the colony below reverberated through the air. And then two more Core Fighters took off from the central port entrance, and promptly disappeared into the clouds in the cylinder's atmosphere.

"Not bad," Sean Crane said. "Must be their small size that lets them turn on a dime."

With Ryu in the lead, the cadets approached one of the colony's giant elevator platforms and on the way got their first glimpse of a Guncannon mobile suit. The upper half of the machine, loaded on a trailer, was over eight meters tall, but it looked smaller than they remembered it from slides and videos. It was the massive twin 28-centimeter cannon built into each shoulder that really gave it a strange sense of power and enormity. Even after a month of field tests, the thing's shiny bright red body still looked brand new.

"Why don't they take the offensive with this thing?"

"'Cause it's got no legs yet, that's why . . . "

While listening to his companions' comments, Amuro noted the Guncannon's heavy armor and decided that, if given the choice, he'd prefer to pilot a mobile suit with *that* kind of protection.

On the elevator platform leading down to the colony floor, the power failed. The cadets therefore found an unused ele-car, piled into it, and began half-sliding, half-driving down the rest of the colony's central mountain slope. As they gradually entered the world of gravity, they again felt their flesh settle around their hips and their blood pulse toward their extremities. Try as they might, they couldn't suppress the knots growing in their stomachs. It was their first exposure to real combat, and the closer they got to ground level the louder the explosions sounded. Blasts from guns. Roars from missile launches. Even with helmets on, the noise in their ears was so deafening that they ducked despite themselves. Then, seventy or eighty meters away, the elevator platform they had just been riding on received a direct hit.

Their ele-car veered sharply from the shock waves, and then, with a *whomp,* its own metal frame buckled, white hot flames shooting in all directions. Another explosion, this time from slightly above them, tossed the cadets into the air and, aided by a gravity half that of earth, flung them against the foot of the mountain.

Amuro hit the ground just as he remembered that he should have fully lowered his sun visor, but it still caught enough of the shock to protect his face. The visor was made of incredibly tough bulletproof plastic, and any impact strong enough to smash it would probably have decapitated him.

"Everybody all right?"

At the sound of Ryu Jose's words, the cadets all momentarily took off their helmets and checked themselves. Luckily, no one was injured, so they picked up their rifles again and resumed scrambling down the mountainside on foot. Once below a layer of clouds, a flat expanse of ground—the battlefield—came into view. And in the midst of the growing "morning" light, they heard the roar of a Core Fighter approaching, its engine sputtering. It soared up over Amuro's head, creased the foot of the mountain with its fuselage, and exploded in flames.

Immediately, Amuro heard a scream. The automatic volume control on his headphones cut the top end off the decibels, but it nonetheless assaulted his ears. And he knew who it was.

"*Sean!*" he yelled. He spun to his right just in time to see Sean Crane's lemon-yellow combat normal suit fly into the air in an arc. The suit looked limp, almost empty, and fresh blood spewed from a huge hole in the side. It smashed into a big rock on the mountainside, and lay arched at an odd angle, what appeared to be a long cloth belt streaming out of the suit, apparently dyed bright red by blood. A piece of the exploding Core Fighter must have hit his friend, Amuro surmised, only to realize a moment later that the "cloth belt" was his friend's intestines, unraveling before him.

But there was no time to dwell on such thoughts. Still shaking from the Core Fighter explosion, the cadets resumed running. Behind them they could hear the battle cries of a combat company of thirty-some men from the *Pegasus*, charging forth.

I wonder if Fraw's all right, Amuro thought. Four years ago he had lived next door to her on Side 7. She was a year younger than he was, and since he had been living alone with his father, her mother had been sort of a surrogate for him. Like her mother, Fraw was kind and gentle. At the time he hadn't really been aware of it (and he still wasn't sure), but thinking about it now perhaps she had been his first real girlfriend. While still pondering this, he realized that he and his friends were headed for Block C in the colony, where he and Fraw had lived. *Wouldn't you know it,* he thought, *of all places, the military had to requisition my old neighborhood as a weapons test site!*

Then Amuro felt the shock of another thunderous explosion and hit the ground out of reflex. The others did the same, only slower. Something gigantic was skirting the base of the mountain, climbing toward them, and when it neared Amuro saw a huge machine with a seventy or eighty centimeter mono-eye in the center of a round "head," glowing as it scanned around one hundred and seventy degrees to the left and right. The machine kept coming, and it was walking. It was a Zaku, one of the Zeon Forces' mobile suits.

The *Pegasus* troops near Amuro began firing at the Zaku, but when their bullets merely bounced off its armor, their brave battle cries turned to groans of fear. Amuro felt a round from the Zaku zip through the air by his ear, and he shuddered. He began to run, heading straight for the metal monster's huge legs. He had no way of knowing exactly what direction they would move, but on a hunch that he could make it, he ran right between them and kept running, without pausing for breath.

To his rear, a Zaku shell aimed at the soldiers exploded on the ground, the blast from it sending rock fragments flying through the air. A boulder landed only a few meters below him, and a stone hit him in the back. He tripped, but got up and kept running. He hadn't fired a single round from his own rifle yet, but he already felt as though he had experienced more combat than he ever wanted.

With a *whommp*, another earth-shaking roar occurred, and Amuro saw the mountainside elevator-platform collapsing in flames. To no one in particular he yelled, "Hey, this isn't *fair!*"

In a few minutes he arrived in front of the military evacuation capsule, and he was joined there shortly by Ryu, Kai, and Hayato. The capsule was designed to be ejected with the aid of the colony's rotational force in times of emergency, but the cadets weren't there to escape. As one of the most conspicuous objects on the mountain slope, it was simply a natural place for them to regroup.

"I hear there's only two Zakus," reported Ryu with assurance, "but they already got three of our Core Fighters . . . "

"Nope," Kai replied. "Four."

The cadets looked out over the colony floor. A ball of flame was falling toward a river.

Amuro turned to Ryu. "Jeez, I wonder if the colony structure can hold up with this much fighting going on inside. If there are two Zakus here, that means there must be *other* Zeon forces nearby, right? Shouldn't we be even more worried about that *Musai*-class ship we saw?!"

One of the Zakus had by now stationed itself at the base of the mountain; the other was occupying the middle of the Federation's mobile suit test site. Together, they had more or less succeeded in suppressing their opposition.

At the first lull in the firing, a crowd of forty or fifty civilians rushed out from the right of the cadets toward an elevator platform. Almost all of them were women, children, and the elderly. Other groups were trying to escape to another section of the colony by crossing over one of the transparent sections of the colony floor. Still others headed for an elevator built inside the central mountain, for they knew it was one of the more sheltered spots in the whole colony and could take them to the port area for possible escape.

Amuro scanned the fleeing crowds hoping to see Fraw Bow, but with no luck. Over a kilometer away to his right, he saw a company of Federation troops rolling out five ele-cars equipped with anti-tank missiles, which launched with a roar. At almost the same instant, other soldiers on the mountain slope began directing their fire at the Zaku on the flat.

Seeing this fairly organized resistance, Amuro and the other cadets became acutely aware of how little they were contributing to the fight, despite the uniforms they wore. Hoping to locate more weapons, they dashed into a nearby military facility built into the mountainside, only to find that the guards had taken everything with them. But scrambling about, searching for something somehow made them feel better. At least they were involved in the action, if only indirectly.

An incoming round missed the building they were in, but shattered its windows. On the other side of a grove of trees they could see the legs of a giant Zaku, bearing down on them. It suddenly occurred to

Amuro that this might be the same MS they had seen higher up on the mountain slope earlier, and he wondered if it had somehow jumped down to where they were now.

"We'd better get out of here." Right after Amuro uttered the words, he and the other cadets all dashed out of the building, and just in time, for an enormous boulder came crashing through the roof. Outside, to their dismay, they found themselves directly exposed to a barrage of friendly fire aimed at the Zaku.

Hayato screamed in frustration, "Don't shoot! We're on your side!!" But Amuro knew that even if the Federation defenders could have heard his friend, they had only one thing in mind and that was to eliminate the Zaku, regardless of who was in the way. Sure enough, a volley of fire rained in the midst of some civilians who had taken refuge among the trees, scattering them. It was impossible to tell for sure where the fire was coming from, but it appeared that the Zaku had jumped in the midst of the civilians, and was trying to use them as a shield.

The cadets found an overturned ele-car, righted it, climbed in, and managed to start its engine. But just then a Zaku, only ten meters to their left, fired a burst. First the shock waves from the explosion reached the cadets; then empty cartridges the size of oil drums rained around them in a clatter. Ryu, in the driver's seat, tried to steer clear, but he suddenly yelled "Shit!!" as a cartridge scored a direct hit on the front of the ele-car and tossed the cadets from the vehicle.

Amuro, luckily, landed in a bomb hole, where his fall was cushioned by newly overturned earth. But on picking himself up, he looked at the bottom of the crater and shuddered. In the old days, colony floors had been built with a soil layer of around three meters. Nowadays the average was more like six. Nonetheless, the blast had exposed the basic structural elements of the colony cylinder's framework. "A few more explosions like this," he noted with a low whistle, "and the whole colony'll be destroyed . . ."

Superstitious soldiers always said that a new bomb crater was the safest place to be during an attack, so Amuro hesitated to leave. But when a fresh round hit smack in the middle of the road fifty meters ahead, he changed his mind fast. He saw a plume of smoke, and then a bloody human hand came flying through the air. It was small, its middle finger was still wiggling, and later he realized it must have belonged to a child.

THE SHOCK OF THIS sight triggered something in Amuro, for he dashed from the shelter of the crater with an idea. He knew there was still one undamaged Federation MS on a flatbed trailer at the test site. He wasn't sure why he knew, but he just did. He ran over three hundred meters, jumping over the charred bodies of several colonists, but then lost his footing when he stepped on what seemed a blackened log. On closer inspection, the blackened bark of the "log" had been stripped away, revealing salmon pink mixed with the bright red of human capillaries. Much to his horror, Amuro realized that the soles of his normal suit boots had literally skinned the flesh off a charred corpse. For a second he wondered how such a beautiful color could exist under a carbonized exterior, but then he felt nauseous. Steeling himself, he resumed running.

When he reached the site, sure enough, there was a Gundam model mobile suit on a trailer. Not only had the Zakus not yet captured it, but it was intact, and even configured with a Core Fighter. He hurriedly climbed up the ladder affixed to the trailer, and found the hatch used to enter the cockpit in the Gundam's midriff. Tearing away the canvas that covered it, he exulted in the fact that his hunch had been right: incredibly, the Gundam's engine was even idling.

Before actually entering the cockpit, Amuro scanned the surrounding landscape for the Zakus. One of them was still busy warding off Federation troops in anti-tank ele-cars, but there was no doubt about who was going to win. The other one had just downed its fifth Core Fighter, and was in the process of scrambling down the mountainside in Amuro's direction.

For the past three months Amuro had trained daily on a simulator for the Gundam model MS, so he immediately knew what to do, or at least thought he did. When he actually slid his slender frame into the cockpit and looked around inside, he realized he was in a machine with quite a few quirks. The instrument panel, for one thing, was covered with notes made during field tests and with corrections listed for numerical read-outs.

First, he checked to see if the control system had been switched from the Core Fighter to the Gundam MS, and then he stepped on the left and right pedals. The Gundam was powered by an ultra-compact magnetic confinement fusion engine, but it was said to overheat easily. It started up with a purr, but within seconds the indicators slammed into the red zone, and hot gas spewed from twin exhaust nozzles on the left and right side of the Gundam's chest area, filling the cockpit. Amuro quickly turned on the ventilator, but this was already more than he'd ever experienced in simulation.

When he closed the Gundam's triple-layered, armored front hatch, a central orthoscopic video monitor on the inside began displaying an image. Since it was linked to other screens on the left and right sides of the hatch, it could automatically convert the Gundam's "eye-level" view to a human pilot's perspective, and provide a sense of distance almost identical to what the pilot would have seen with his naked eye. Moreover, if the image happened to be a target registered in the mobile suit's data base, the computer system could accurately augment it with computer graphics, or provide a warning to the pilot if it was unidentifiable. Surrounding the Gundam's main screen, there were also eight smaller monitors providing a true 360-degree panorama; if needed, the image on any individual monitor could easily be switched to the main screen. In addition, although they often suffered from poor reception, there were two monitors used for communicating with close-by friendly forces.

Amuro quickly noted that there were eighty rounds left in the Vulcan cannons in the Gundam's head; good enough for at least two series of blasts. He slowly pulled on the left and right operating levers to start the Gundam. Sensors in the giant machine's legs took readings of the environment, and activated the system. The exhaust nozzles belched forth pent-up gas.

Where in hell's the beam rifle? While watching the monitors in the cockpit, he used the Gundam's cameras to scan the trailer and its environs, but he could see no sight of the weapon he wanted. Then, on one of the left-side monitors, he caught a glimpse of a Zaku at the base of the mountain. It seemed to hesitate, and he wondered if he had been spotted.

When the Zaku took aim with its rifle, there was no room for doubt. Amuro fired the Vulcan cannon on the Gundam's head, but the Vulcan had been developed for close-quarter combat and its barrels were too short to be very accurate; the shells exploded harmlessly around the Zaku. Worse yet, Amuro realized he'd forgotten to use the hinged sighting scope on the right side of his headrest. He quickly swung it around, positioning it in front of him, but while doing so the other Zaku—the one attacking through the trees earlier—turned toward him.

In haste, Amuro jammed the right lever away from him and twisted it into the third zone on the left. It took speed, a strong hand grip, and considerable pressure on the right steering pedal, but the Gundam's huge body did spin to the right. At the same time, the rifle aimed by the Zaku at the foot of the mountain flashed, and Amuro felt his entire cockpit reverberate from a near-miss explosion. His left upper monitor flashed pink and indicated the shock, but there was no time to look.

"Damn!" he cursed. "This thing's slower than the simulator!" He was stunned by the fact that the Gundam's entire control system differed from the one used in training, but he wasn't about to let it get the better of him. As his initial terror of combat gradually subsided, a newfound confidence welled up inside him and helped him transcend the craziness of what he was attempting.

Leaning the Gundam's upper torso forward slightly, Amuro headed straight for the Zaku at the base of the mountain, while dodging the attack of the other one further up. In the woods, the tallest conifers helped hide his machine. His main monitor began to display the Zaku. There were no civilian evacuees in sight.

"Hah hah! Now we're rolling!" He exulted in the thrill of the moment. He could tell by the way the Zaku on the other side of the woods was moving that its comrade on the slope above hadn't yet spotted him. But then he saw its legs crush the body of an earlier victim of the fighting. Blood spattered out onto a concrete surface.

Furious, Amuro yelled, "Let me at him!!"

Forgetting for the moment the other Zaku descending toward him from his left, he made the Gundam charge straight for the enemy. The hilts for the Gundam's twin beam sabers were stored in the Suit's backpack, so he simultaneously flicked a switch under the instrument panel to free up enough energy for them, and made the Gundam's right hand reach back to unsheathe one. The instant the giant hand connected electronically with the saber hilt, a particle beam nearly ten meters long stabbed forth to form the blade. Like beam rifles, beam sabers required an enormous amount of energy and could only be used for a short time, but their blades could slice through thirty centimeters of solid titanium in less than a second.

With his eye on the digital readouts from the MS computers, Amuro fired the vernier jets built into the Gundam's backpack, waist, knees, and ankles for 0.3 seconds. The resulting *g* force was mild, but it was enough for the Gundam to jump over the coniferous forest. The Zaku in front of him spun around, and its mono-eye flashed, as if in fear. But by the time it raised its rifle up it was already too late.

Screaming in rage, Amuro brought the Gundam's poised beam saber slashing downward in a blur of light. The beam-blade entered the Zaku's left shoulder and flickered for a second, but it had more power than in the computer graphics sequences Amuro had seen in training, and it sliced all the way through to the right side. The Zaku looked like a monster severed in half and spurting blood; sparks flew from its severed circuitry, and oil spurted out of its hydraulics.

But Amuro had cut too deep. Like the Gundam, the Zaku's main engine was in its waist and, as the training manuals noted, damaging it could be a fatal mistake for the attacking pilot. It was, after all, a nuclear fusion engine.

Damn! he thought, realizing his mistake. He turned the Gundam's chest verniers on full, and jumped backward. The Zaku descending the mountain slope tried to pick him off, but missed. Amuro cursed its pilot for even trying; the man must have known that his colleague had been mortally wounded, and that they both had to get out of the way of the nuclear blast that would ensue. It wouldn't go off like a normal atomic bomb, but it was far more powerful than normal explosives, and could cause contamination.

WHEN THE ZAKU PILOTED by Zeon Ensign Gene finally blew, it carved a hole in the base of the mountain and blew a hole in the nearest wall in the colony. The resulting blast of air even shook the *Pegasus*, docked way over in the colony port. Amuro, tossed backward in his Gundam, was able to slow his own speed by firing his vernier jets in reverse, but he was still tossed over four kilometers into the colony's B Zone residential area, where he finally came to rest on top of six smashed civilian houses. Lt. (jg) Denim's Zaku was blown in the opposite direction, into one of the areas called "rivers"—the glass sections of cylinder wall that let light into the colony—where it smashed over two hundred 50 cm square panels of glass.

"Jeez, what've I done?" sobbed Denim. In the space of a few seconds, he had lost a subordinate, and a Zaku, and losing the latter was regarded as far more serious. As his superiors always reminded him, even if it didn't have as much firepower, one Zaku was worth an entire space cruiser.

Denim cursed his bad luck. *But the Federation Forces weren't supposed to have an operational mobile suit yet!* And then he remembered the warning the normally daring Lt. Commander Char had given him when he left. "*Remember, Denim,*" he had said, "*it's a* scouting *mission . . .*"

Gnashing his teeth in frustration, Denim resolved to leave, alone.

ESCAPE FROM SIDE 7

THE ZABI FAMILY DOESN'T trust me, Lt. Commander Char Aznable thought, as light flashed from the Side 7 colony. Something had clearly gone wrong, and he knew he had only two real choices—to send in another strike team, or retreat—and given his reputation and character the latter was hardly appealing. It was he, after all, who had uncovered the information about the new Federation mobile suits in the first place, and he wasn't about to let anyone forget it. And a promotion, which it might lead to, was the only way he would be able to get closer to the Zabi family.

Char's father, Zeon Zum Deikun, had founded the original Republic of Zeon with the help of Degwin Sodo Zabi, the current ruler. But fourteen years ago, after Zeon Deikun's death, Degwin had repudiated the republican system of government and changed the country to a "Principality," purging it of all loyal republican elements. Char was too young at the time to have understood the difference between the two forms of government, but his foster father, Jimba Ral, believed—was, in fact convinced—that Zeon Deikun had not died a natural death, and had actually been assassinated. Jimba Ral had therefore raised Char with a single, burning obsession: to kill Degwin and topple the Zabi family.

At age fifteen Char had managed to infiltrate back to Zeon alone, and, with the help of a few loyal friends of his father, obtain papers identifying himself as Char Aznable. He attended a Zeon high school, and upon graduation entered the Military Academy. It was there that he became friends with Degwin's youngest son, Garma Zabi.

And then the war had erupted. Not surprisingly, Char saw it as an opportunity. It seemed mere training for his eventual mission, especially when what was supposed to have been a short, neat little victory for Zeon turned into a protracted conflict. Zeon had quickly fallen into the grip of Zabi totalitarianism, but a long, drawn out war, Char reasoned, would eventually rock the foundations of the system. In the interim, he could try to rally some of the old Deikun loyalists, and work to topple the Zabi family from within. It had to be done carefully. As much as Char despised the Zabis, he had no intention of letting Zeon slide back under the influence of the "absolute democracy" enforced by the bureaucratic Federation on Earth.

THE FATES ARE ON *my side,* Char thought with unshakable conviction.

Just then the crewman manning the laser search beams yelled, "*Lieutenant Denim's Zaku is returning, sir!*"

Char ordered, "Put out some covering fire!" and almost immediately, several missiles streaked out of the *Musai* cruiser toward Side 7.

"Take her forward," he directed. "We're going to do some scouting around Side 7."

The *Musai's* captain, Haman Tramm, frowned: "But Commander . . . er . . . don't you think that's a little risky?"

Char ignored him. The capillaries in the man's nose indicated someone too fond of the bottle, and Char despised anyone afraid to take a chance, simply out of fear of being demoted if he damaged his ship. And besides, the fact that Side 7 hadn't struck back yet seemed to indicate that Denim had at least accomplished something, even if he had gone on the attack without permission.

Five minutes later, when Denim docked in the *Musai,* Char could have called him on the carpet, but he didn't. Denim had, after all, brought back valuable information on the Federation mobile suits, including photographs and videos. Scenes of Ensign Gene's Zaku being destroyed, even if painful to watch, could provide rare, concrete information on the performance of the enemy's new weapon.

"We still need to do more reconnaissance," Char announced out loud on the bridge. "And if Side 7's as shaken up as it seems, now's the time to get the information we need. We'll infiltrate in normal suits instead of Zakus this time . . . "

SHORTLY THEREAFTER, CHAR TOOK off from the *Musai* with seven hand-picked crew members. "Sorry to make you shuttle back and forth like this," he said, touching his normal suit helmet to Denim's for "skin talk" while in transit, "but I've got to punish you somehow for disobeying my orders." Denim's face was hidden by his helmet's reflecting sun visor, but Char could sense the man's burning shame.

As the walls of the Side 7 colony gradually filled the men's frame of view, the *Musai* cruiser initiated a diversionary attack on the port side of the giant cylinder and finally met with some counterfire. With this as a cover, Char and his men one by one landed safely on the wall of the giant cylinder.

INSIDE THE SIDE 7 colony, despite the fact that the initial Zeon attack had ended, Amuro Ray still hadn't had time to climb out of his Gundam mobile suit. There was so much to do—help transport an undamaged Guncannon mobile suit to the waiting *Pegasus*, aid civilian evacuees, and carry heavy construction materials for the Side 7 repair crews. There were an infinite number of ways to put a sixteen meter tall giant to work.

To his surprise, Amuro found himself receiving orders transmitted from Warrant Officer Mirai Yashima and Ensign Bright Noa. They appeared alternately on the two-way communications display above the Gundam's main monitor, and told him what to do. Sometimes Chief Petty Officer Marker Clan also appeared. There seemed to be no senior officers left, at least not in the command center of the colony's port.

"What in the world happened up there?" Amuro asked Marker. They were on good terms and often spoke to each other.

"There was a direct hit right near the *Pegasus*, Amuro, and it took out the main bridge and almost everyone on it. Captain Paolo's been badly wounded, so Bright's taken command of the ship from the subbridge. Not a single man from the surface combat units that went down into the colony has come back up. But more than anything right now, we need you to help get whatever's left of the Gundams and Guncannons up here."

"What about the other pilots? Can't some of them help, too? Sean got hit down there, but Ryu or even Kai oughta be around!"

"Ryu's up on the main deck checking the one Guncannon we already recovered, Amuro."

"Chief Petty Officer Amuro Ray!" Mirai Yashima's image suddenly appeared on the screen, reading from a file in front of her, and telling him what he already knew. "According to this report from the colony,

Sketch of Side 7, *from port side*

there should be three Gundam models and three Guncannon models. We've got to get those other mobile suits up here!"

"There's only one other usable MS on this Side," Amuro answered her, "and that's the Guncannon being transported up to you right now." But he knew that there still might be some usable mobile suit parts and maintenance equipment left in the colony, and that he should haul them up to the ship as soon as possible. He wished his father, who knew something about these things, were around to help him decide what was important and what was not.

AT THE FOOT OF the colony's mountain-core, Amuro hoisted the other Guncannon's upper torso onto an elevator platform to send it up to the port area. As he did so, a van-style ele-car skidded toward him from Zone B, and a chorus of plaintive voices emerged from inside: "*You've got to help us . . .*"

There were around twenty civilians in the van—worried old people and women—who looked imploringly up at the Gundam. They, too, wanted to ride up on the elevator platform and Amuro didn't have the heart to say no. With the Gundam's left hand he signaled them to climb on board. Up to three humans could fit in the palm of a Gundam's hand, but if they fell out or were injured, he knew the military would be blamed, so he wasn't about to try that. He was more worried about the Gundam's beam rifle, which he still couldn't find.

When the elevator platform finally began its ascent up the side of the colony's mountain-core, it carried Amuro in his Gundam MS, the Guncannon, and over twenty people. It rose through the colony's cloud layer and then, another two hundred meters above that, it reached the port section, with its near weightless conditions. There, Amuro made certain that each of the civilian evacuees with him took firm hold of the lift-grips that would transport them through the port area to the *Pegasus*.

In another group of civilian evacuees in the port area he caught sight of Fraw Bow. She looked tiny as she drifted toward him on a lift-grip, staring up at his mobile suit with a worried look.

"*Hey, Fraw!*" Amuro called out, switching the Gundam's voice channel to external mode. "*You all right? Where's your mom? Why isn't she with you? What happened?!*"

At the sound of Amuro's amplified voice, the crowd of people moving on lift-grips toward the *Pegasus* all stared up at his mobile suit in shock. The Gundam had no mouth, but the bulletproof, heat-resistant, yellow glass panes covering its optical sensors resembled eyes and gave its face an uncannily human look. There was also something decidedly weird about hearing such ordinary, familiar language coming from a giant machine.

"*Er... excuse me, ladies and gentlemen ...,*" Amuro quickly announced, trying to explain. "*This is a Gundam model mobile suit, and I'm its pilot, Chief Petty Officer Amuro Ray.*"

Then he opened the hatch in front of the Gundam's cockpit and found himself looking down at the civilians nearly nine meters below him. True, he was now in an almost weightless environment where "falling" had little meaning, but even with his seat belt fastened, the ground seemed far enough "down" to make him feel giddy.

"Amuro ... Oh, Amuro ...," a stunned Fraw called up to him, her voice quavering. "Mom an' Gramps are dead...."

As if Fraw's words were a signal, the lift-grips transporting Amuro's group of civilians began to move through the port area. The grips were rubberized rings, two meters in diameter, that slid along rails built into the walls and transported people through weightless areas. But if anyone let go of his or her ring while moving, the inertia alone could easily send them flying over a dozen meters. Old people and little children often lacked the physical wherewithal to control their own momentum, so they had to cling desperately to the rings until they came to a halt.

"*Go with the other evacuees to the* Pegasus, *Fraw*," Amuro called out, trying to sound in control. "*I'll see you there later.*"

He made sure she got on the third lift-grip that came along, and then turned and hoisted the Guncannon's upper torso off the elevator platform. In the weightless environment this took a special technique; to counter the inertia created, he had to simultaneously exert a counter force in the opposite direction with the Gundam's other hand. Then he activated the electromagnets on the soles of the Gundam's feet and began walking through the port area toward the *Pegasus*.

Arriving at the ship's No. 1 hatch, Amuro found Ryu and several mechamen already working on the other Guncannon. As he lowered the Guncannon's upper torso he was carrying, the comm monitor in his cockpit flickered to life, and Ensign Bright's face appeared.

"Mister Amuro! We've got beta test reports on the Gundam from the Side 7 mobile suit test site! I want you to go over these and memorize 'em. Understand?! Better yet, copy 'em on your computer scanner!"

Bright's eyebrows were arched, and his voice high pitched. He was doing his best under the circumstances, but Amuro had never liked the man's overzealousness. Nonetheless, when Bright sent the documents to the Gundam's upper right monitor, Amuro scanned and copied them into the Gundam's main memory bank, and then began displaying them in enlarged format on the main monitor.

"I'm blowing up the specs now, sir," said Amuro. "Could you explain them to me?" Then, thinking of his father, he asked, "By the way, how'd you get these?" But Bright wasn't listening, and merely continued giving orders.

"The Gundam's spare armor plating's still at the main test site, and so are the magnetic control coils for the beam rifle . . . And finally, we've got to destroy whatever's left of the mobile suits that were hit inside the colony. We can't afford to leave anything behind!"

"Can't you let the other Guncannon help me, sir?! It'll take too long with just me in this Gundam . . . "

"Don't worry, kid. I'm not an idiot," Bright replied. "I'm gonna send Chief Petty Officer Ryu Jose out with you."

SAYLA MASS HAD JUST turned twenty. She had immigrated to the Side

7 colony voluntarily two years earlier, but it was rather unusual, since hardly anyone volunteered anymore. In recent years most "emigrants" left Earth against their will; the only ones able to remain on the planet were those whose political views were appropriately orthodox, or who had special connections to the Federation government. Sayla had nonetheless had her own reasons for coming to Side 7. The daughter of Zeon Zum Deikun, her real name was Artesia Som Deikun. Her brother was Casval Rem Deikun, otherwise known in Zeon as Char Aznable.

Sayla's father, Zeon, had died when she was three years old. One of Zeon's right-hand men, Jimba Ral, together with his wife, had taken in the two Deikun children and with them fled the collapsing republic, hoping to live in safety on Earth. To ensure success, the Rals took an enormous amount of money, with which they purchased the respected family name of Mass in Southern Europe. This had enabled them not only to pass as full members of Earth's elite society, but also to safely raise both children under the names of Edward and Sayla Mass.

Over the years, the Rals repeatedly told the two Deikun children that their father had been assassinated in one of Degwin Zabi's plots. When Char reached high school age, it was this, more than anything else, that fostered his unshakeable desire to return to Zeon, and destroy the ruling Zabi family.

But Sayla was different. She had grave doubts about her brother's obsession, and about the course of action he had chosen. Still, he was her only brother, he had always been good to her and she did not want to lose him. So when she finally found out that he had secretly returned to Zeon, she wept for three days and nights. She began to loath her foster parents' fixation with revenge, and began to hate them instead. She thought about running away from home, but upon hearing about construction of the new Side 7 colony, she hit upon the idea of emigrating. It took a year to persuade her aging foster father, Jimba Ral, to let her go.

"If a father truly loves his daughter," she had lamented one day, "why should he derive pleasure from her misery?"

"Artesia, dearest," Jimba had finally replied, giving up, "If you insist, you may go."

Sayla had once dreamed of becoming a doctor, but she instead enrolled in a school that trained mid-level technicians for the Side 7 project. And when construction began on the first colony she did emigrate. She wanted nothing to do with the Republic of Zeon or the Zabi family.

Unfortunately for Sayla, when war erupted between the Federation and the Principality of Zeon it became impossible not to be involved.

Along with other civilians on the Side 7 colony, she was pressed into working for the military, and when she qualified as a communications expert in six months they wanted her to formally enlist. The military were always looking for skilled people, and nearly a quarter of all personnel in both Federation and Zeon forces were now women, or Waves, as they were called. In some fields, such as supply, communications, and armaments, the ratio of women was even higher. Still, no matter how alien and despicable Zeon's social system, Sayla had no interest in going to war with it—especially when it bore her father's name. But then an event occurred that shook her beliefs.

As a comm tech on the Side 7 colony, Sayla had been assigned to work at the Gundam mobile suit test site. There she was given strict orders, in case of an emergency, to at all cost make sure that documents never fell into the hands of the enemy. As a result, after the first Zaku rocket attack, she had hurriedly collected and destroyed all the important-looking materials she could find, even if they were only simple code-lists for internal use, or work schedules.

When the attacking Zakus grew closer and closer, Sayla and the other comm techs left the test site and moved over to the Air Defense Capsule—an emergency escape system that could, in time of disaster, use the spinning colony's centrifugal force to escape from the Side. But when the Federation Gundam destroyed one of the Zaku intruders, the resulting explosion warped the rails of the escape system and rendered it unusable. The sergeant in Sayla's unit therefore issued the order, "Move to the *Pegasus*," and the group began to head toward the colony's port area.

Along the way Sayla occasionally spotted physical files that someone else had discarded, so she stopped to either pour acid on them or burn them. It was technically someone else's responsibility, but she didn't want to take any chances. If any documents survived and the test site supervisor found out, Sayla's entire unit could be slapped around, and she didn't want that. She wasn't about to give the military, which seemed to love corporal punishments like slapping and spanking, any excuse to apply its fetish to civilians like herself.

As a result of her diligence, Sayla lagged behind the rest of the group and had to dash alone across the area where the Zaku had been destroyed. She had been taught not to worry about residual radiation after the explosion of a mobile suit or even a warship's nuclear fusion engine, but she knew there were limits to this assurance. After all, if an explosion were big enough, and blew a hole in the colony's outer wall, even the *whoosh* of escaping air could kill a person. Luckily for Sayla, the hole from the Zaku's blast seemed to have already been blocked, probably by objects sucked into it, and the fierce wind had died down.

As she ran toward the elevator-platform at the base of the colony mountain, though, she spotted someone in a red-colored normal suit dash into the ruins of a building. How odd, she first thought, that a Federation unit would use red for their suits. There was also something odd about the way the man carried himself. She stopped in her tracks, picked up a revolver from the body of a fallen Federation soldier, and snuck back toward the ruins. To her amazement, the man in the red normal suit was pointing a camera at the wreckage of a Guncannon destroyed earlier by a Zaku, taking pictures. And then she remembered. She had recently seen a Federation report describing the uniforms used by the Zeon military. The man before her fit the description.

As a civilian, Sayla was theoretically under no obligation to engage a Zeon soldier in combat, but in times of stress theory does not always fit reality. Something about the red-suited man's bearing made her heart pound; implausibly, perhaps, she almost felt attracted to him. *I've got to capture him,* she thought, as her legs propelled her out from the cover of a shattered wall in the ruins.

"Take your helmet off and put your hands over your head!!" she yelled, as threateningly as she could.

THE MAN IN THE red normal suit—Char—was stunned. Why hadn't he sensed the approach of such an obviously rank amateur? True, he'd been preoccupied with collecting materials on the Federation's new mobile suit. But that was no excuse. Normally, his entire nervous system would have been scanning 360-degrees for anything unusual; after all, it was this ability, more than anything else, that made him and his Zaku feared far and wide as the "Red Comet." He stood stunned, as a young blond woman in double-handed firing posture pointed a revolver straight at him. Could the Fates have wanted him to meet this person, and deliberately created a blind spot in his consciousness?

Before completely recovering his senses, Char noticed that the woman's gun was shaking, and realized she'd never be able to hit him even if she fired. He jumped at her, and immediately heard the gun discharge, but he ignored it. The toe of his normal-suited foot connected with the gun, and sent it flying into the air. The woman staggered back, amazed. Then, the instant Char looked into her blue eyes, he knew. It was Artesia, his sister. She flinched, and then glared back at him. In her expression he read terror, and a defiant refusal to give in.

"Artesia!" he cried.

She looked at him, at first puzzled. Then she straightened, and looked again.

But just then Char felt the reverberations of giant footsteps, and knew they belonged to one of the new Federation mobile suits scrambling down the foot of the colony mountain toward him. He also knew he had to get out of the area immediately. By the time Sayla recognized him and rushed forward calling, "Casval!" he had already spun around, ignited the small vernier jets strapped to his back, and soared into the air. Maneuvering through the air to get out of the Gundam's field of vision, he heard his sister behind him exclaim "Casval!" once more, as she tripped and fell.

Moments later Sayla was still staring in the direction in which the man in the red normal suit had disappeared, thinking he might have taken refuge in some other distant ruin. To her surprise, behind her she heard the voice of a very young man say, "*Climb up on the Gundam's palm. I'm gonna raze this whole area.*" She turned and looked up, and saw a giant mobile suit kneeling next to her, extending its left hand.

"*Hop on board, but keep your head down,*" the voice said.

Immediately below the mobile suit's chest, in the area equivalent to the human solar plexus, a hatch opened and a young pilot peered down from it. As directed, Sayla climbed onto the mobile suit's hand, whereupon its fingers slowly but gently closed around her, as if forming a shield. It wasn't a pleasant sensation. She kept her head down and tensed, then felt a floating sensation as the Gundam stood up and began transporting her. The steel hand wasn't designed to carry people, so to avoid falling out she had to push as hard as she could with her arms against its sides. They were moving ten meters above the ground, so she also closed her eyes to avoid a sense of vertigo.

By now Amuro had found the beam rifle, and when the Gundam reached and boarded the elevator platform at the colony's mountain core, he turned and fired at the MS test site, scoring a direct hit with a napalm shell. *That fries the documents all right,* Sayla thought, astonished, *but it'll contaminate the remaining colony air.*

When the elevator platform reached the colony port level, a giant hatch opened to receive the Gundam, and Sayla saw the same red-suited man of her earlier encounter zip by in the air in front of them. He had his vernier jets on full, and roared through the hatch into the port's weightless environment. Sayla felt the hand of the Gundam that was holding her twitch. Its other hand rose up and pointed the beam rifle toward the port, but didn't fire. Using a beam rifle on a single man would be overkill, and might even hit the *Pegasus* moored two kilometers straight ahead. But just when the red normal suit disappeared from view Sayla heard gunfire coming from the direction of the ship. "Casval . . . ," she murmured.

The Gundam strode quickly toward the *Pegasus* in the docking bay, each footstep creating a loud echo. But then the sound of gunfire ended, and Sayla heard a small explosion from the direction of the port's exit hatch. When the Gundam reached the *Pegasus*, she heard one of the crewmen on deck running around yelling, "A Zeon infiltrator's blasted a hole in the outer air lock and escaped!!" No one paid any attention to Sayla as the Gundam gently lowered her to the ground.

Behind her, Sayla heard a nearly hysterical voice call out, "Over here! Please . . . You've got to help me treat some of these wounded!" Turning around, she saw that it belonged to a young female Colonist she knew, Fraw Bow, on a gangway two levels above her. She kicked off the floor and floated up toward her.

ON THE SUBBRIDGE OF the *Pegasus*, Ensign Bright ordered, "Have the Gundam MS precede us supported by the two Guncannons! And give me full combat speed as soon as we clear the colony's port!" Then, turning to the ship operators strategically seated above him atop a crane-like arm for maximum monitoring capability, he called out, "Keep me posted on every move the *Musai* makes!"

The operators, Chief Petty Officer Marker Clan and Petty Officer 1st Class Oscar Dublin were awfully young, but they were among the most dependable survivors on the bridge, and they had been formally trained. Mirai Yashima, the young Warrant Officer standing in as helmsman, was part of the same student group mobilized into military service as Bright. It was all she could do to cling to the ship's wheel.

Almost everyone on the *Pegasus* was inexperienced. The ship's normal chain of command had been wiped out earlier when the *Musai* cruiser had fired one of its four large Tam missiles at Side 7's core, piercing four layers of armor and nearly destroying the *Pegasus*'s primary bridge. With Captain Paolo and other officers gravely wounded, except for the men who had been in the ship's engine room, the rest of the surviving crew—including those now manning the warship's guns and the missile launchers—were almost all new recruits. The only mobile suit pilots left alive were all cadets; Amuro Ray would have to handle the Gundam with Hayato Kobayashi as a backup, and Ryu Jose and Kai Shiden would have to operate the two Guncannons.

THE GIANT FOUR-LAYERED AIR lock doors of the Side 7 colony opened, and the *Pegasus* sailed forth from the port. Mirai, manning the helm and looking deathly pale, bit her lip.

"You can relax a little now, Mirai," Bright said, tapping her on the shoulder, "the laser sensors'll help lead us out of here." He was so scared himself that unless he did or said something, he wouldn't have been able to stand the tension.

As the *Pegasus* emerged into the vastness of space, the shining orb of Earth came into view, fully illuminated by the sun. Sometimes it was possible to see little *Luna II* shining above it, but right now the asteroid was overwhelmed by the brilliance of the mother planet.

Bright called out to the operators, louder than need be: "Marker! Oscar! Where's that *Musai* cruiser!?"

"Must be in the colony's shadow, sir. We can't get a reading on it!"

"Mirai! How far out are we from the colony?"

"Th . . . Three kilometers, sir . . ."

On hearing Mirai's nervous reply, Bright inquired of no one in particular, "Think the mobile suits can keep up with us?"

There was no answer, because no one on the bridge knew. But just then the rear door to the bridge opened, and the ship's medic, Sunmalo, wheeled Captain Paolo into the room on a gurney. Beads of sweat oozed from Paolo's brow, as his eyes hurriedly scanned the instrument readouts. "Don't . . . don't worry about the performance of the mobile suits, Bright," he whispered between stabs of pain. "You've got to get that *Musai* off our tail first!"

"Maximum combat speed! Ready stern missile launchers!" Bright yelled, switching the captain's phone to ship-wide. "All crew double check the air in each section of the ship!"

IT WASN'T EASY TO move through space using a normal suit's vernier jets. Char and his men couldn't see their destination, their *Musai* cruiser, so they navigated using *Luna II* and the Side 7 colony as reference points. Checking them every once in a while to keep their bearings—the sun being their primary reference point—and taking into account their own speed, they calculated how many seconds to fire their verniers and in what direction. But they had to be careful to avoid the worst enemy of all free space walkers—panic. The physical sensation of floating in a weightless environment can psychologically resemble that of falling, and unless constantly reminded that one is positioned "above" Earth, or "above" a colony, it is all too easy to become totally disoriented.

"*Musai* . . . Do you read me?" Char spoke into his radio receiver while double-checking to see that his squad of seven men was still following him. The Minovsky interference was intense, but at close range radio communication was often possible.

"*Yes . . . we . . . read you . . . ,*" came the faint reply from the ship.

"Get my Zaku ready, and Denim's, too," Char barked. "The enemy's headed our way."

Char was determined to engage and fight the new Federation mobile suit he had just seen. From what he could tell, it was probably a high performance model, but he had no way of knowing how well it performed in the vacuum of outer space. After losing a Zaku to it inside the colony, he felt the least he could do would be to find out specifically how it operated. After all, he wasn't called the "Red Comet" for nothing.

IN CHIEF PETTY OFFICER Amuro Ray's Gundam, the far right corner of the main monitor indicated two enemy objects approaching. Laser sensors could be accurate on their own terms, even with Minovsky interference, but as Lt. Ralv had often said, until you confirmed something visually, it wasn't confirmed. But whatever this was, the monitor indicated it was approaching at high speed.

ON THE BRIDGE OF the *Pegasus*, operator Marker Clan read the same signals and yelled down from his perch at Bright. "Judging by the size, sir, it looks like Zakus, but one of them's closing in on us faster than I've ever heard possible!!"

"The other's speed matches a Zaku profile exactly, sir!" chimed in Oscar, the other operator. "I'm sure they're both Zakus!"

"Ready anti-aircraft guns!" Bright screamed, at the same time glancing behind him at Medic Sunmalo and Captain Paolo.

Thinking he had heard the wounded skipper say something, he went over to the man, who was still strapped in his gurney. He bent over and listened, and heard Paolo whisper, "If . . . if it's a fast red Zaku . . . , it's . . . it's *Char Aznable*. He's destroyed . . . over ten Federation warships . . . with his machine. They call him the 'Red Comet'. . . You've got to get the ship . . . out of here!"

Paolo's face looked contorted, not from the pain of his wounds, but from fear. And he said it again: "*Get out . . . of . . . here . . .* "

OUT IN SPACE IN the Gundam Suit, Amuro saw a reddish point of light weave through the stars toward him at high speed, and he felt a chill run down his spine. For a second he thought he was looking at a real red comet, but then his main monitor showed a close-up of a red Zaku. In the middle of its head, behind a panel that looked like the windshield of an ele-car, a pink-colored mono-eye flashed. And it was sighting down the barrel of a handheld rifle.

Amuro gently twisted the left and right joystick levers in front of him toward each other, and felt the sudden *G*-force as the entire Gundam spun sharply to the right. The Zaku fired and a tracer streaked brightly through the darkness. Amuro knew a single tracer meant that his opponent had actually fired a burst of five rounds.

With a horrible, sinking feeling, he remembered the way Lt. Ralv had lectured him and the others: "*You gotta watch out for the bastards who fire long bursts with rifles or machine guns, 'cause one of the rounds might hit you. But as long as you can still see the barrel of their guns, you're okay, 'cause it means you're still alive. It's the ones who never waste a shot that you really oughta be scared of. They'll really make you stay on your toes. What's that? You wanna know how to spot 'em? Lemme tell ya. In real combat, you'll just know. And when you know, you'll probably already be dead. So the first thing to do when you sight an enemy is to pray he's an uncoordinated idiot. That's your only hope.*"

Amuro felt lucky. He had managed to dodge the Red Comet's blast. The left and right monitors in his cockpit began displaying data, but he didn't have time to look. It was all he could do to track the enemy Zaku streaking across his main display. When the red machine seemed to hesitate, he pulled his beam rifle's trigger.

A multi-polar, super electromagnetic coil sucked energy from the engine in the Gundam's midriff, oscillated and accelerated heavy metal particles inside the beam rifle, and then blasted them out the barrel. Each shot was accompanied by an enormous burst of light which could reveal one's position to the enemy, so the rifle was best used only when in constant motion. But the magnitude of destruction a blast could cause more than offset the risk. Zakus were so well armored they could withstand a direct missile hit; the Gundam's beam rifle and beam saber were the only weapons that could take them out. And Zakus didn't have them.

The blast from the Gundam's rifle sliced through the blackness of space, leaving a trail of white light, but the Red Comet was already bearing down from another direction. If Amuro had kept his eye on the light, he would have completely overlooked the Zaku. But the moment he pulled the trigger he knew he'd missed, so he had deliberately broadened his focus. Like a real red comet, the Zaku bore down on him, and its mono-eye again flashed. Amuro fired the Vulcan cannon in the Gundam's forehead, knowing it couldn't destroy the Zaku but hoping to at least knock one of its camera eyes out of action.

The red Zaku swooped left, executing an almost perfect ninety-degree turn. Amuro maneuvered the Gundam to square off against it, and saw the small monitor on the left side of his instrument panel flash a warning. He jammed the joysticks to put the Gundam into an evasive maneuver and saw two bands of tracers. The Zaku had fired twice as many shells as the last time. It was trying for a death blow, but Amuro had managed to dodge it again. Amuro's reflexes were better than average, and the Gundam was responding to them instantly.

AGAINST AMURO IN HIS Gundam MS, any other Zaku would have seemed positively leaden in reaction. Char's Zaku had undergone fine tuning, it was true, but Char had really earned the name "Red Comet" for his unnerving ability to coax his machine into giving one hundred and ten percent of its potential performance, and to engage the enemy at breathtaking speed.

Nonetheless, even Char was amazed by the Gundam. As soon as he had obtained information about the new enemy Suits being developed, he had conducted mock battles once or twice using other Zakus as stand-ins. But that had been like child's play compared to this. The real Federation MS turned on a dime above and to the left of him, beams of light zapping toward him from its rifle. The beams seemed so powerful that Char's hair practically stood on end, and he at first thought they must have come from the big guns on the Side 7 colony itself. Then he realized that making a beam gun compact enough to carry as an MS rifle was a particularly diabolical act of genius. Whatever was sacrificed in destructive power was more than compensated by the MS's innate agility. And it would only take one blast to wipe out a Zaku.

The very thought of it made Char's blood boil. There had to be a way to put the white MS out of action. The Federation pilot was no doubt good but, although he couldn't put his finger on it, there was something about the slightly awkward movements of the Suit that convinced him the pilot inside was still a novice. This spurred him on, and he was seized by the same rush of adrenaline as in the past, when he had moved in on one of the Federation's *Magellan*-class battleships. The only difference this time was in the size of the target. But Char was too smart to judge an enemy by size. He had an uncanny ability to evaluate his opponent's total strength and weaknesses.

Turning his Zaku hard toward where he sensed his enemy would be in a few seconds, Char spotted the white Suit and exulted "Got him!" His main monitor displayed the crosshairs of his rifle scope. He lined them up with the gun sight, and then cranked his MS up to maximum combat speed. It wasn't a rash act, but a tried and true tactic used to overwhelm the enemy. Then he fired.

But something unexpected happened. Unlike the Federation forces Char had met in the past, the white Suit had somehow dodged his attack. What was going on?

It was then that Char thought the unthinkable: *Could the Federation pilot possibly be a Newtype?*

No one in the Federation, he was certain, was yet aware of the Newtype concept, which postulated the emergence of a "new type" of humans. After all, he himself had first heard about it a few months earlier, when he had contacted the Flanagan Institute. The last thing in the world he wanted to believe was that he was really confronting one now. He wanted desperately to believe that the Federation Forces were just using some uncannily skilled pilots. Yet as implausible as it seemed, the enemy pilot who had first moved like an amateur was already looking more and more like an expert. There seemed far more to the incredible leap in skill level than first met the eye.

Biting his lower lip in frustration, Char fired a burst from his rifle. The tracers from it left a trail of light that disappeared between the stars. And then, in the midst of the battle, he heard a brash voice cut through the static in his headphones: "*This is Lieutenant Denim. Do you read me?*"

"Watch out, Denim!" Char yelled back. "The white Suit's a tough customer!" he replied.

"*The fool,*" he thought, noticing a light on the top right of his instrument panel flash. Denim's Zaku was emitting its IFF—Identification Friend or Foe—laser signals, and in the presence of an alert enemy, that was tantamount to suicide. Denim obviously thought he should identify his position to his superior to avoid a case of mistaken identity, or to avoid getting in the way, but he was underestimating Char's ability. It was being overly considerate.

Char barked over the intercom: "Denim!! Turn off your damn ID signal!!" But it was too late.

Enemy fire streaked out of the area in space where the Federation warship—the Trojan Horse—was, and converged on Denim's Zaku. But Denim was a seasoned warrior, a veteran of the battle of Loum, and he wasn't about to let anyone turn him into space dust *that* easily. He skillfully evaded it, and continued in hot pursuit of the white MS.

AND THEN IT HAPPENED. A direct blast from a beam rifle pierced Denim's Zaku at its midriff. And it came, not from a Federation warship, but from the white MS. First the Zaku slowly scattered beams of light into space, and then it emitted an enormous flash. In an instant, it evaporated.

"D . . . Denim!!" Char screamed, hardly believing his eyes.

It was true. The white mobile suit's beam rifle did have as much power as a cruiser's main cannon.

AMURO HAD JUST DODGED a blast from the Red Comet above and to the right of him when he first detected an odd signal on his IFF monitor. The signal source was around four degrees above the Red Comet, and it was another Zaku, moving about half the speed of the Red Comet. *Just give me three seconds,* Amuro prayed, as he drew a bead and fired two shots so close together that they almost formed a single band of light. When the beams scored a direct hit in the Zaku's waist, his main monitor reacted to the burst of light that followed by instantly activating an automatic filter. Nonetheless, the screen showed a huge white, saucer-shaped orb of light gradually fading into the blackness of space.

One down, Amuro exulted to himself. But the next instant, he spotted the Red Comet bearing down on him straight out of the blast's residual light. And when his monitor returned to normal he saw—almost heard—the red Zaku's mono-eye flare. Instinctively, he pulled the trigger for his rifle. Another beam shot forth, and crossed in space with one of the tracers fired by the Zaku. On Earth, the sound of a 120 millimeter cannon merging with the super sonic roar of a beam rifle would have been unbearable. But this was outer space. The two mobile suits silently crossed paths in the vacuum. And with a shock, Amuro suddenly realized his Suit was running low on energy.

AROUND THE SAME TIME, Char began to curse himself because he had run out of ammo. In theory, Zakus were supposed to conserve ammunition so it would last until they returned to the mother ship, but something about the white enemy MS's humanoid face had irked him and made him squander his shells. Now, just when he had the enemy where he could polish him off, he was out of ammo. Glancing back at his opponent, he gnashed his teeth in frustration, convinced that he could have scored a direct hit.

"How could I be so stupid!?" he swore, as he pulled away from the combat zone at high speed.

AMURO HAD NO WAY of knowing the fight was over. He had six spare shells built into the Gundam's head, but once the beam rifle's energy was depleted it took thirty minutes to recharge. There was little he could

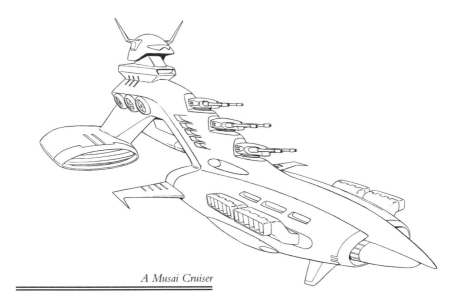

A Musai Cruiser

actually do, but he was too psyched-up to quit. He scanned the heavens 360-degrees several times, and wandered through the combat zone until the *Pegasus* finally issued an order to return to ship.

When he at last neared the *Pegasus* again, he opted for the safest docking procedure of all, he asked the ship to throttle its main engines back as much as possible so he could enter through the rear hatch. When guide sensors all around him went into action, all he had to do was to line up with them, and leave the rest to the computer.

"Good work, Mister Amuro," Bright said, ensconced in the Captain's seat in the middle of the subbridge. "Now that the *Musai* cruiser's lost two Zakus, they won't come after us for a while. And judging by the way the 'Red Comet' pulled out of the fray, I'd say he ran out of ammunition. In the meantime, I want you to work on getting the Gundam and the Guncannons ready again. Some of the mechamen on board were involved in testing on Side 7, and they can help."

Amuro formally saluted, and intoned: "Yessir! Chief Petty Officer Amuro Ray, descending to the second flight deck!" He noticed a young woman to his left on the bridge, with her back turned. It was Mirai Yashima, the warrant officer, who always had a friendly, gentle face. He wished she'd turn around and look at him. But she did not.

ON THE *MUSAI*, CHAR finally returned, and ascended to the bridge where he was greeted by an over-friendly Lt. (jg) Dren. "That white mobile suit's absolutely terrifying, isn't it, sir! Why those blasted Feds—"

Char held up his hand to stop the prattle. He stared out the window of the *Musai*'s bridge at the area into which the Federation Trojan Horse had disappeared. *Luna II* had moved out of the glare of Earth, and was visible on its own as a shining half circle.

There had been nothing wrong with his basic strategy, Char concluded, but Zeon's intelligence-gathering efforts clearly left much to be desired. And never, in his wildest dreams, had he expected to run into his younger sister Artesia on the Side 7 colony, of all places.

For a moment he started to feel a little sentimental, but he quickly collected himself. Forcing himself to reflect on the day's action instead, he muttered to himself, "I hate to admit it, but maybe I made a mistake. I'll just have to write it off to youthful inexperience . . ."

THE *CALIFORNIA* CRUSH

THE *PEGASUS* WAS HEADED for *Luna II*, the former asteroid *Juno*. Now a Federation base, it had a traumatic but pivotal history. The plan to move it into the Moon's orbit around Earth had been announced in U.C. 0035, but taken ten years to complete. First mainly mined and hacked at for resources, Federation forces had already begun fortifying it by U.C. 0067, when construction on Side 7 began. And then, in one week of January, U.C. 0079, when Zeon simultaneously struck Sides 1, 2, 4, and 5, and annihilated well over a hundred Federation colonies, *Luna II* was heavily bombarded with missiles and any and all surface construction was shattered beyond recognition. Largely because of this attack, Federation forces were deprived of one third of their entire fleet of ships before they could effectively resist.

There was one exception. General Revil's fleet, on Side 5 at the time, did manage to put up a fight. And because Zeon was unable to destroy Revil in its initial strikes, it was forced to throw much of its remaining forces into yet another attack. And this time the Federation forces rallied in a counterattack. The result was the first major fleet battle in outer space. The "Battle of Loum," as it came to be known, ended tragically in the nearly total devastation of Side 5, and the destruction of most warships in both Zeon and Federation fleets.

CHAPTER THREE

For over eight months afterward Federation forces frantically rebuilt *Luna II* and refurbished and expanded their fleet. Zeon, similarly, attempted to consolidate its hegemony in space by constructing its *Granada* fortress on the moon, and its *Solomon* space fortress in the area where Side 1 had formerly existed. Several smaller, strategic skirmishes continued throughout space, as both sides attempted to expand the territory under their control.

ONE OF ZEON'S STRONGHOLDS was a giant, ultra-advanced satellite called *California*, which orbited Earth on a thirty degree slant to the plane of the ecliptic. It served as base for a Zeon reconnaissance unit, and was primarily charged with scouting enemy movements on Earth and monitoring Federation activity on *Luna II.* To avoid direct enemy attacks from the latter, it moved constantly in a random orbit and sowed as many Minovsky particles as possible in the vicinity.

On *California*, a sallow-faced young captain, Garma Zabi, read an electronic message from Lt. Commander Char.

> *HAVE INFORMATION ON FEDERATION FORCES'*
> *"OPERATION V." WILL DRIVE TROJAN HORSE SHIP*
> *CARRYING NEW MOBILE SUITS INTO YOUR AREA.*
> *CAPTURE AND DESTROY THEM . . .*

"Not bad for the class valedictorian," Garma said, smiling and indulging in his habit of curling a lock of his bangs around his right index finger. "Sounds like Char's going to bring me a little present . . . "

GARMA, THE YOUNGEST SON of Degwin Zabi, had been eight years old when his father had crowned himself absolute ruler of the Principality of Zeon. Whether from upbringing or genetics, he grew up to be extremely indulgent of other people. If tolerance was his good quality, it also made him an ineffectual leader. Worse yet, he was far too immature for the level of responsibility he possessed as a result of his family connections. On *California*, instead of waiting for further contact, as Char had recommended at the end of his message, he excitedly ordered Rear Admiral Zom, the nominal base commanding officer, to immediately ready three Gaw attack carriers so he could take off and intercept the *Pegasus*.

TRAVELING AT FULL SPEED, the *Pegasus* would normally take over ten hours to reach *Luna II* from Side 7, so to divert the Federation ship from its course the *Musai* cruiser periodically fired blasts at it from its twin mega particle guns. In reality the *Musai* had only two of its large Tam missiles left, but Ensign Bright was no match for the more experienced Char, so the *Musai* cruiser's feints worked, with the result that both ships proceeded on a zigzag course just as Char had planned.

"IF CALIFORNIA WASN'T IN its southerly orbit now, we'd never be able to pull this off," Char said, laughing, to Dren on the bridge of the *Musai*.

"You really think it'll work, sir?" Dren asked, unable to conceal his nervousness about the plan. "They say the Federation ship has an awful lot of firepower . . . "

"Well, it's working right now, isn't it?!" Char retorted. Then, turning to the beet-nosed skipper of his ship for a change, he added, "Isn't it, Haman?" As long as there was no threat to his own life, the captain had no problem with diversionary attacks.

"Haman?!"

At the sound of his name, the captain blew his nose and laughed. But with Char's next words he fell silent, and the color drained from his face.

"We'll probably lose a *Musai*-class ship in the process of testing the Feds' new military capability," Char announced, "but it can't be helped. I want the crew's combat rations increased. We're going to try to catch the Trojan Horse at *California*."

THE *PEGASUS* WAS IN an unusual situation; in addition to its crew, it was carrying nearly a hundred and five evacuees from Side 7. Normally this would not have been permitted. Two or three holes blasted in a colony as big as Side 7 usually didn't mean the loss of the cylinder's atmosphere, or even require the total evacuation of its residents. Basic functions would continue. Total malfunction was almost inconceivable. Solar-powered colonies such as the one at Side 7 were almost perpetual motion machines, and once activated their ecosystems went through their natural cycles, and basic materials were largely recycled. Being man-made, they wouldn't last forever, but as long as the sun continued to shine they were exceedingly stable environments, especially compared to the state of permanent energy crisis on Earth. Their future was also guaranteed by the Antarctic Treaty, which both Zeon and Federation governments had signed after the carnage of the One Week Battle. The depopulation caused by the war had so terrified both parties that they had agreed to refrain from completely destroying each other's colonies.

FRAW BOW MOVED TO the rotating, artificial gravity sector of the *Pegasus* and busied herself treating the injured. She was becoming inured to it now, and open wounds and exposed organs were no longer a shock.

"Get me some Type A and Type AB blood for transfusions," Sunmalo, the nervous, bespectacled medic, said to Fraw. "There's got to be some left . . . "

Jumping over the bodies of several wounded soldiers, Fraw ran to the ship's blood bank as asked. Along the way, she couldn't help thinking what a horrible situation the ship seemed to be in. It was supposed to be a warship, but there were so few military men around in the sector that she began to wonder how in the world the Federation could ever win the war. And she was irritated by the fact that she had absolutely no idea where they were headed.

I wonder where Amuro is, she thought. It occurred to her that he might have been killed. She had known him, after all, not as a particularly strong boy, but as one who always needed someone to keep an eye on him. But she swept the thought out of her mind, remembering how he had looked when he opened the Gundam hatch to greet her back at Side 7. Amuro was now a full-fledged military man.

At the now half-empty blood bank, she picked up two bottles of the blood types requested and started to return to the room where the medic was. Along the way, among a crowd of civilians milling about, to her shock she heard children crying, and saw a young boy—certainly under ten—trying to calm two even younger children while sniffling himself.

"What happened?" Fraw asked.

"My mom. . . ." The oldest boy started to say something but began weeping uncontrollably. It was almost as though the gentle sound of Fraw's voice had broken the dam of his pent-up tears.

"Now you just wait here," Fraw soothed. "I'll go look for your parents later . . . "

She took the children into what seemed like an officer's vacant quarters, had them sit down, and, after comforting them again, started running back to the medic, with the blood. They bawled mightily when she left, but that somehow reassured her. If they had that much energy in their lungs, she knew they'd be all right. Besides, despite their own tears, the two older boys had tried to comfort the little girl. Somewhere, Fraw thought, she had seen the girl before.

ON THE SUBBRIDGE OF the *Pegasus,* Ensign Bright remarked to Sayla Mass, "You're just what we need. We're incredibly shorthanded. All you'll have to do is relay any messages that come in from *Luna II* or Side 7. I'll take care of most of the calls inside the ship, but I could sure use your help when things really get hectic around here." Bright should have been strapped in the captain's chair, but he felt better talking while standing.

Sayla answered, "Understood, sir."

Then she floated over to the comm panel on the right side of the bridge. An enlisted man drifted by her, his head covered with blood from a wound. For a second she thought he was smiling at her, but then she realized the expression was frozen; he was dead.

The comm panel had five monitors on it, and Sayla had no way of knowing which section of the *Pegasus* each showed. Nor, if there were any voice contact, did she know how to prioritize it. The main laser comm channel appeared open, but silent. Then she saw a close-up of a cadet's face on one of the right-hand monitors, and he seemed to be yelling. She pressed the button activating his voice channel.

" . . . I finished readying the Guncannon," yelled an awfully impatient young man of mixed ethnic background. "Now what!?"

"The . . . er . . . Gun . . . cannon, you say?" Sayla answered, tentatively.

"Yeah . . . This is Ryu Jose! Right, I'm talking about my Guncannon!"

Sayla turned and called over to Bright, standing under the Operator crane behind her. "Sir! A Mister Ryu Jose says his, er, Guncannon's ready."

"What?!"

Bright picked up the captain's phone, and curtly ordered Ryu to stand by.

"I don't mind standing by," Ryu snapped at Sayla from the little monitor, "but I wanna know what the hell's going on. How're we doing?"

"He wants to know how the battle's going!" Sayla relayed.

"Tell him we're sending the information to the control room, and for him to look at it there!" Bright screamed in reply, forsaking any politeness toward his newfound crew member. Turning to one of the operators perched on the bridge crane, he added, "I want you to compile information on our status and send it to each combat sector. On the double!"

"Yessir!" called out Petty Officer Oscar, with a gesture that almost looked like a salute. Watching the exchange between the two men, Sayla sensed things weren't going very well.

Ryu Jose laughed bitterly in the monitor in front of Sayla, and said, "Well, I guess I just learned what I wanted to know by overhearing Bright's scream. By the way, I'm Chief Petty Officer Ryu Jose. I'd sure love to take *you* out on a date sometime . . . "

Rather than being put off by such forwardness on an official comm channel, Sayla found herself staring at the image in the monitor in front of her. Was he half Black and half Caucasian? Or was he part Arab? She couldn't really tell, but when he smiled, his white teeth flashed beautifully against the dark tone of his skin. "Well," she replied, flirtatiously. "*Maybe*, if I have the *time* . . . By the way, my name's Sayla Mass . . . "

Why did she say that? She was shocked by her own friendliness to a total stranger.

Ryu's image said: "We know you're a newcomer, Sayla, but hang in there!" Then his monitor went blank, and as if on cue a close-up of a different enlisted man appeared on a monitor on the far left of the panel. It was Chief Petty Officer Marker, the other operator, calling out to Bright.

"*Musai* approaching at 7 o'clock, below us at an angle of 25 degrees! It's coming at us at maximum combat speed, sir!"

When she heard Marker's voice, Sayla looked up. Both the main and subbridge ceilings had displays built into them showing a three hundred degree panorama of the heavens. The balance—sixty degrees—could be seen on another monitor to her rear.

"You absolutely sure, Marker?!" Bright questioned.

Images generated from laser sensor readings were useful even when there was a heavy Minovsky concentration, but they were only a simulation; a computer graphics model created by extrapolating from prior data corrected for Minovsky induced errors. They were far less precise than the three dimensional displays used in the days of uninterrupted radar, but they nonetheless gave an idea of what was going on. Without these models, a skipper like Bright—a rank amateur—would have been completely helpless.

"Launch mobile suits!" Bright yelled into the bridge phone. "Anti aircraft units stand by! No, wait . . . Prepare for a direct ship attack . . . "

"Looks like they've launched one of their mobile suits, sir," said Marker. Then, interpreting his own reading, "It's . . . a Zaku . . . the Red Comet!"

"You absolutely sure?!" said Bright, again feeling a tinge of embarrassment because he kept asking the same question. He scanned a multiscreen display in front of him that monitored the inside of the ship. In the left corner screen he could see the two Guncannons being loaded into the catapult mechanism. The Gundam was already poised for ejection. Bright grabbed the bridge phone and barked.

"Amuro! Char's on his way! Get ready to . . . "

Before Bright could finish his sentence, he heard a "Yessir!" and saw the Gundam blast across the screen of his launch deck observation monitor. The mere sight of the MS, fully equipped with its beam rifle and shield, made him feel better. The others were next.

"Chief Petty Officer Ryu Jose launching, sir!"

"Chief Petty Officer Kai Shiden taking off!"

As the two red-colored Guncannons soared out of *Pegasus*'s portside hatch, Bright felt a lump form in his throat. Here he was, using trainees—*teenagers*—as mobile suit pilots, sticking them in cockpits the mechamen called "coffins," entrusting the defense of the *Pegasus* to them.

Through the static, he heard a fragment of a message from Amuro: "Gundam intercepting Char! *Musai* heading straight under me. You'd better ready your stern missiles . . . "

The *Musai* cruiser was on a course that would take it beneath the *Pegasus*. Char, approaching ahead and slightly above the *Musai* in his Zaku, apparently intended to take on all three Federation mobile suits.

Bright yelled out a command: "Elevation minus 2.5 degrees. Launch missiles in a fan pattern! Two barrages!"

Mirai, gripping the ship's helm, glanced over and commented, "I hope our boys are a match for the Red Comet . . . "

Bright stared at her, and said nothing. *Why*, he wondered, *do women always say things best left unsaid?*

Then Oscar's yell assaulted Bright's ears from above: "Our stern missiles missed, sir!!" Eight precious missiles had vanished into space.

"What about scattering some mines?" Bright asked Oscar. "Think it's possible?"

"We're outside the Shoal zone, so it's a little hard to hide them. But if we use Model 2's they might not spot 'em . . . "

"Model 2's, eh? Those won't work against the *Musai* . . . "

Model 2s were contact mines with a diameter of ten centimeters, and when dispersed in space they were almost undetectable, but they wouldn't even put a dent in a cruiser.

Then Oscar let out what sounded like a wounded cry. "A heat-emitting object's headed straight for us!!"

"Missiles?" Bright instinctively clutched the armrest of his captain's chair and looked up at the ceiling display screen.

This time Marker answered, with a strained voice: "Looks like a Tam, sir!"

"Just one?!" Bright demanded, immediately learning the answer. One of the multi-screen displays to his left clearly showed a computer generated image of a single large Tam headed toward them, along with its estimated course and time of arrival.

"Mirai!" he barked out. "Initiate evasive maneuvers! Angle the ship up nineteen degrees. Hard starboard!"

The *Pegasus's* emergency alarm sounded, and the crew first felt the *g* force with their legs. For humans used to weightlessness it wasn't a pleasant sensation. The blood drained from their heads and those with low blood pressure felt dizzy. The instrument monitor went into countdown mode, ticking off each hundredth of a second. When the readout reached 1.5 seconds, Bright looked out the window of the bridge and saw, with the naked eye, a bright white light bearing down on them. The sensors built into the bridge window detected the light, and automatically activated a protective filter shutting out much of it, but it was still too bright to look at directly.

The next moment the entire *Pegasus* was suddenly tossed violently upward, and its metal frame screamed as it twisted. The crew on the bridge wearing seat belts hung on for dear life, and prayed their bodies wouldn't be severed at the waist. Mirai, standing at the helm when the blast hit, ricocheted back and forth between the ceiling and the floor three times, and, had she not been wearing her normal suit, would have broken several bones. As it was, the shock was enough to kill some of the wounded soldiers on the ship. They had had no protection at all.

Before the ship stopped shaking, Bright grabbed the phone built into the armrest of the captain's chair and yelled, "Main engines! Give me every ounce of speed you have! Maximum acceleration!"

Mirai, wincing from a blow to her chest, carefully monitored the gauge for the ship's main engines. It read ninety percent of the way to red-line, but could conceivably go thirty-five percent higher. She realized what Bright was trying to do—to use the force of the blast to help accelerate the ship and escape from the combat area.

"WONDER HOW OUR MOBILE suits are doing out there?" Bright said, half to himself. To his surprise, a voice behind him rasped in an almost scolding tone, "*Don't . . . don't worry about them . . .*"

It was Captain Paolo again. Fortunately, his gurney had been secured to the bottom of the bridge crane when the blast occurred, but the restraining straps had ripped open his wounds and the blankets covering him were now soaked in blood.

Turning to the ship's medic, Sunmalo, Bright yelled, "See to the Captain!" Then, speaking over the phone he bellowed an order to the entire crew of the ship to inspect all stations for damage. A computer-generated image on a screen to his left displayed potential problem areas.

The ship's external skin looked all right; besides, "wall film"—a viscous, plastic film which could seal off most holes—would automatically go into action. But only humans could restore the equipment inside the ship, and any that had a direct effect on the ship's combat status would have to be fixed right away.

Bright asked Marker, "How many Tam-class missiles does a *Musai* cruiser normally carry?" and felt a chill run up his spine when he instantly received the answer: "Four, sir . . . "

OUT IN SPACE, LT. Commander Char had one weakness in the way he attacked; right after he fired his rifle, he usually made his Zaku run in a straight line for two seconds. Lucky for him, however, Amuro, Kai, and Ryu were too inexperienced and too busy fighting for their lives to take advantage of the opportunity presented them.

Amuro would spot the comet-like streak of Char's Zaku in his center monitor, fix him in the sights of his rifle scope, and then . . . *fire!* But the instant the beam left the gun barrel, his foe was nowhere to be seen. Instead, Char kept firing at him. Like the Guncannons, the Gundam wielded a shield for protection, but it wasn't armored heavily enough to withstand direct hits from a Zaku's 120 mm rifle forever. It had already absorbed several rounds, and one more direct hit would render it useless. And Amuro's brain was reaching a state of overload. At one point, Char's Zaku came so close its red mono-eye seemed to fill Amuro's entire scope, and he reflexively screamed in terror. But then a miraculous thing happened—the Gundam moved with the agility of a judo expert.

Amuro kicked the Gundam's left leg forward, and felt the impact as it connected with something. If he had had time to look, he would even have seen a readout on the instrument panel showing the force of the impact.

CHAR WAS ELATED BECAUSE he had caught the white MS within a one kilometer range. If he could just destroy its head, he could knock out its main TV camera. He confidently fired again, but the catlike MS somehow managed to evade the burst. He cursed under his breath.

At almost the same instant he felt the impact above the ceiling of his cockpit. His center monitor went blank for a second, and the *g*-force threw him back into his seat. Incredibly, the white MS had kicked his Zaku and smashed its head camera. The Zaku spun backward.

"And they call me the Red Comet?"

Char felt humiliated. Mobile suits hadn't been in use very long but

his Zaku was certainly the first to ever be physically kicked by the enemy. Smoldering anger erupted into fury. "You won't get away with
this!" he screamed.

His center monitor automatically switched over to an auxiliary camera and came to life again. Fifteen kilometers ahead, he could see the
white MS. Its beam rifle flashed again, but as usual missed.

"Even a cruiser's beam cannon won't do you any good if you don't
know how to aim," he yelled.

But then a barrage of fire swept between the two dueling mobile
suits. Kai and Ryu, in the Guncannons, had started firing in support
of Amuro's Gundam. Outclassed in fire power, Char initiated a zigzag
evasive maneuver. He knew he had to close in on the white MS fast, but
he also knew that his opponent was no sitting duck. With his ammunition running low, he started to feel impatient.

"INCOMING TAM!" YELLED MARKER, the operator on the *Pegasus*.

"Launch AMMs!" ordered Bright, suddenly remembering the ship's
Anti-Missile-Missiles. They might not hit the target, but they were better
than nothing.

ELSEWHERE IN THE *PEGASUS*, Fraw Bow's back throbbed in pain as she
headed back to the officer's quarters where she had earlier deposited
the three young children. When the Zeon missile explosion had rocked
the ship, she had been tending the injured with Sunmalo. One of the
wounded had not had a restraining strap on him, and had bounced back
and forth several times between floor and ceiling, splattering the room
with blood from his wounds. She had grabbed him and tried to restrain
him, and she was now covered with his blood. Her blouse soaked and her
hands still slippery, she drifted along on the ship's lift-grip. Her own pain
paled in the memory of it all.

"Well, you've been fine, haven't you?!" she said to the children when
she reached them.

"Yeah ... um ... but ... "

The oldest boy started to say something through his sniffles when the
ship's alarm sounded again.

"Hurry! Put your seat belts on," Fraw urged, seating the three children on the sofa in the officer's cabin and strapping them in.

Then the *Pegasus* shuddered again. This time the explosion seemed
even closer than before. The covers on the bunk in the room, normally
fastened with Velcro, flew off, and the three children screamed in terror
and pain. Seat belts, even if made like restraining harnesses with two or

three straps, dug deep into flesh. The younger boy's body slipped and the strap around his chest pressed hard against his lungs; he began hacking. Then, as Fraw and the children exclaimed in surprise, the emergency combat room lights went out.

The little girl wiggled out of her seat belt, crawled into Fraw's lap, and clung to her in fear. She still had the softness of an infant, but Fraw hugged her as hard as she could. In the semi-darkness of the room she made a mental note of the emergency oxygen source, the video monitor that connected them to the bridge, and the ship-wide phone.

"Everyone stay still now. . . ." Fraw took off her seat belt, and tried to stand up, but the little girl wouldn't let go. Feeling indulgent, Fraw carried the child as she felt her way along the wall to the officer's desk. With a little light leaking in from the hallway, she could barely make out objects in the room, but she needed a flashlight. She searched the desk, wondering who normally used it; there were only two ring binder notebooks in one drawer. Another contained the flashlight she sought, and a gun.

Maybe I'd better take it with me, she thought for a second, looking at the gun, then realizing she'd never have an opportunity to use it. She picked up and switched on the flashlight, turned, and spoke to the boys on the sofa.

"You know?" she said, "I forgot to ask your names."

"My name's . . . my name's Katz. Katz Hawin . . ." said one.

"I'm . . . um . . . Letz Cofan . . ." said the younger boy. Then, squinting in the glare of the flashlight, he asked with a worried tone, "Did you find my folks?"

Fraw, at a loss for an answer, felt herself panic. Ignoring him for the moment, she turned to the little girl and asked, "And what's your name, honey?"

"Kikka. Kikka Kitamoto," the girl stated. "You said you'd look for my *mom* . . ."

"I'm sorry," Fraw apologized, trying to be as gentle as possible. "I haven't searched the whole ship, but when the fighting's over I can look some more." She wondered if there weren't some easy way to disengage from the kids. She'd already looked through several of the ship's civilian areas, but hadn't run into any parents searching for these children.

"THEY'VE MADE QUITE A nice course correction," said Lt. (jg) Dren, watching the Federation ship through binoculars from the bridge of the *Musai* cruiser. One more blast from a Tam missile would have made things perfect, but there were no more left.

"'Guess we'll just have to threaten them with our mega particle cannon," Dren ventured.

"You're entitled to your opinion," the red-nosed Captain Haman Tramm replied in a mocking tone. "But Captain Garma's part of Rear Admiral Kycilia's Space Attack Force. If we drive the Trojan Horse toward *California*, we'll have an argument on our hands with Vice Admiral Dozle later."

"That's Lt. Commander Char's problem, not ours," Dren retorted.

"No, it's a problem for *me*. I'm captain of this ship," Haman said.

"Well," Dren countered, "then why did you agree to go along with this plan?!"

Dren knew that correct protocol required obtaining some sort of permission from Dozle Zabi's Mobile Assault Force before Char contacted *California*. But they were in the Shoal Zone, and Dozle was on the space fortress *Solomon*, which was now blocked by Earth. Laser transmission was impossible.

"It all depends on how much one of those new Federation Suits is worth . . . " Haman added. "If it's really so important to snare one, all arguments over turf will be irrelevant. If not . . . "

Then Dren replied, "I guess we'll just have pray its performance knocks our socks off."

Against this, Haman was at a loss for words. In a huff, he turned his gaze to a computer display beside him.

How about that, Dren thought. *He hates Char even more than I do.* In war there were always brave young men who distinguished themselves and soared in the ranks, and it wasn't easy to serve under them, especially when they were like Char Aznable, a young Lt. Commander, overly talented and overly deferential to his superiors. Social class had little meaning in the young Zeon hierarchy, but Char's attempt to reach *California* and deliver a "present" to Garma Zabi, his classmate from the Military Academy, was nonetheless the act of an overly ambitious ingrate. Someday Char would probably slip and show his true colors. Someday, Dren thought, Char's luck would surely run out.

IN HIS GUNCANNON, IT was all Kai Shiden could do to maintain his balance. The Suit's left leg had taken a direct hit and thrown off his sense of equilibrium. Then, through the static, he heard the faint voice of Ryu Jose in the other Guncannon, saying, " . . . *That's enough . . . withdraw . . .* "

"Withdraw?! Where the hell to?!" Kai screamed to himself in his cockpit in frustration. He had no idea where the *Pegasus* was. All laser search beams had been turned off because they were in an area where

Char could attack at any moment. And Kai couldn't very well leisurely wander around in open space looking for the mother ship.

Ryu, for his part, tried to support Amuro by training his sights on Char's Zaku for the third time. He knew it was risky since the "Red Comet" tended to move in close to Amuro's Gundam, but he fired anyway. Three times the 28 centimeter twin cannon on his Suit's shoulders flared. Nothing happened, but at least he didn't hit the Gundam. Then he took his eyes off his gun sight, and to his surprise Char had disappeared. He activated his 360-degree monitoring camera and had his laser sensors trace the heavens. Thirty seconds passed and nothing happened, but then something giving off an IFF signal approached. It was the Gundam. Amuro's static-filled image and voice appeared in Ryu's cockpit.

" . . . to . . . the *Pegasus* . . . " it said.

Ryu tried to query him: "What happened to the Red Comet, Amuro? He turn tail?"

He knew it was a dumb question. Three state-of-the-art Federation mobile suits, after all, had gone after one Zaku, and hadn't even scored a single near-miss.

Amuro made the Gundam hold up its shield so Ryu could see.

Ryu whistled low in appreciation. "He did *that* to you?" One quarter of the shield was gone, revealing a cross section of its honeycomb construction.

Ryu was impressed not only by the accuracy of Char's attacks, but by the fact that Amuro had been able to ward them off with the shield. To himself he muttered a word he had heard recently: "Maybe the guy's a Newtype."

❏ ❏ ❏

"CHAR ONLY RETREATED BECAUSE he ran out of ammunition." Mirai's statement was delivered with such conviction Bright felt compelled to ask how she knew.

"Sure, Char lives up to his reputation of being a fearless pilot," she explained, "but I think he's a lot more than that. He's also a brilliant tactician. Look how he made those mincing little attacks on the Gundam. Seems to me he wasn't even trying to destroy it. I think he's just trying to gather information on it."

As Mirai spoke, it dawned on her that even if Char *had* run out of ammo, his decision to about-face had been too sudden.

"You mean he seemed *too* in control?" pushed Bright.

"Well, yes," Mirai said, hedging. "Seems odd, doesn't it?"

Returning her gaze, Bright was impressed by how intelligent and perceptive she suddenly seemed.

Then Marker, perched above on the operator crane, announced something that gave Bright a chill. "Sir," he said with urgency, "if we continue on our current course, we won't be able to descend toward *Luna II.*"

Ever since loading the mobile suits back on Side 7, Bright and the others had had no way of knowing the *Pegasus'* s true assignment because most of the ship's key officers had been killed in the initial attack. And now Captain Paolo was fading in and out of consciousness from loss of blood, and unless he came to and told them, they would never know. Given his condition, returning to *Luna II* seemed the only logical choice, but every time the *Pegasus* tried to head toward the base, the *Musai* unleashed another beam attack. Unless they were prepared to directly confront the Zeon warship head on, they would never make it.

"Well, Miss Sayla," Bright called out across the bridge. "Any communication with *Luna II*?" For the first time, he noticed how pretty she looked. When the light was from behind her, her medium-length blond hair almost seemed to glow.

"Something's creating interference," she ventured. "I think it's an enemy ship . . . maybe the *Musai* cruiser. There's a horrible distortion in the laser oscillation."

"Hmm," Bright said, pondering a minute. "I think we've been led into a trap, by Char."

Then a voice came from near the entrance to the subbridge: "What's happening, Mister Bright?" It was Amuro Ray, but he wasn't alone in wondering. The fifty-odd crewmen already assembled in the room were all looking at Bright with the same worried expression on their faces.

"For the last three hours," Bright explained, "we've been traveling at full speed but we haven't been able to shake the Zeon ship. If, as it seems, they're trying to prevent us from landing on *Luna II*, I had planned to take the *Pegasus* into a broad loop around it, turn our prow 180 degrees, and approach from the opposite direction. But I just remembered something—Zeon's base, *California*, is in the way."

Hayato shouted out the next question: "You mean they might send some Gaw attack carriers after us?!"

California wasn't a particularly large base, but to the inexperienced crew of the *Pegasus,* if it could dispatch two or three Gaws after them, it was terrifying.

A crewman then mentioned, "I heard Garma Zabi's in charge of *California*." And at that point, a commotion ensued among the rest of those assembled. If they had been forced in range of Zeon's *California* base, and if Degwin Zabi's youngest son were there, it had to have been part of a master plan by Char.

Bright spoke bluntly: "We're all in this together, crew, and I need your opinion. Should we turn around and attack the *Musai* head on, or try to scrape by *California*, use the Earth's gravity to boost our speed, and make it back to *Luna II*?"

The first answer came from Mirai. "Let's turn around and face the *Musai*," she said. "If *California* hadn't been in Char's plans from the beginning, he wouldn't have attacked like he did earlier. And if the *Musai* had had enough fire power on board, it would have come at us a lot more aggressively."

"I agree with Mirai," Ryu Jose said, "the *Musai*'s probably out of ammo, and probably outgunned by us, in which case we should attack it. And who knows how many Gaws they have on *California*?"

No one seemed to take issue with Ryu's assessment, so it appeared a consensus had been reached. After a brief pause Bright turned and announced, "All crew don normal suits again! We'll reverse course and destroy the *Musai*. Then we'll head straight for *Luna II*." The crowd assembled on the subbridge scattered.

Next, Bright broadcast an appeal throughout the entire ship: "Some civilians on board have had prior military training or are former military personnel. All of those to whom this applies, whether male or female, are hereby ordered to help in the defense of the ship. Infants, children, their adult guardians, and any wounded troops must immediately move to Ward E in the gravity sector. We will engage the *Musai* in fifteen minutes!"

The subbridge fell silent. Taking advantage of the moment, Sayla Mass turned and looked up at Bright. "Excuse me, sir, but isn't there a map of the layout of the *Pegasus* somewhere? I'm having a little trouble understanding what's going on."

"We can display one for you on one of the top screens," said Bright, "but maybe Marker knows where there's a printed version."

"There should be one in the right-hand drawer over there," Marker replied. "Take a look."

Following his directions, Sayla finally found a document that graphically showed both the ship's layout and its internal communication channels.

"Anyone want some coffee?" asked Bright.

At the sound of the word, Sayla realized how parched her throat was, but it was Oscar who replied.

"Good idea," he said. "Let's send Seaman Tamura down to the galley to bring us some."

As if this were a signal, the crew on the bridge stopped talking and returned to their assignments. But before Sayla had time to digest the new information she had been given, the comm monitors in front of her all suddenly sparked to life with questions, requests, and protests from people stationed throughout the ship. There weren't enough normal suits to go around. What station to proceed to? Where was an assigned gun turret? The questions were all new to Sayla, and more than she could possibly have handled. All she could do was relay them to Bright.

"The rule of thumb on this ship," he explained, "is that the officers stationed on each deck make those decisions. Tell them not to bother us with stuff like that."

In the end, the only job Sayla could perform with confidence was to check the monitors and oversee the movement of civilians and wounded troops throughout the ship, and then relay the information to Sunmalo, the medic.

"Five people in Sector 24 being moved to Ward E," she announced. "No wounded among them!"

Immediately afterward, a young civilian woman appeared on a screen saying, "Hi, I'm Fraw Bow. I've got three kids with me. How do I get to Ward E?"

"Where are you currently located?" Sayla asked, thinking the woman looked awfully young to be their mother.

"I'm in an officer's cabin," Fraw reported. "Number 16, I think …"

In the midst of all this confusion, a gray-haired old man suddenly rushed into the subbridge area, yelling, "Where's the Captain?! What the hell's going on?!"

"What do you want?" Bright asked.

"Hmph. I asked to see the *captain*, not an ensign," sniffed the intruder.

"Captain Paolo's in a coma right now, sir," Bright replied. "I'm standing in for him."

"*You're* taking over for Cassius Paolo, as skipper?!" The man was incredulous.

"Yes, I am," Bright said, feeling irritated. "What can I do for you?"

"Listen," the man huffed, "I hope you're not serious about that earlier announcement—about taking on an enemy warship! In the condition we're in, it'd be madness!"

"We've no other choice, sir," Bright retorted. "If you've nothing further to say, I'd appreciate your leaving the bridge."

"I'm Jarma Amov, son," the man said, drawing himself up. "I may not know much about this ship, but I once commanded the heavy cruiser *Buchanan*. I'm here to help you."

The graybeard did look like he might have been a military man in his day, but he also looked like he could cause trouble. Bright surmised that he was probably a by-the-book ex-officer, who had left the *Buchanan* after ten years of service, unable to advance in the ranks beyond commander.

"Times are different now," he said to the man. "The combat tactics we use these days are more like those of the pre-radar age. It's a whole new ball game."

"I know that," Amov protested.

"Well," Bright sighed. "I don't have the time to explain the *Pegasus* to you, but we've got twenty-four missile launchers up in the fore of the ship. Why don't you take charge of those for us."

"Where's the command post for them?"

"On the deck below us. Petty Officer Dublin should be down there. Take over from him, and tell him to move forward to the launch tubes."

"Er . . . understood, Skipper." Reluctantly, the former commander turned around and started to leave.

"There's a radar display in the command post," Bright called out after him, "but it's useless."

The old man said nothing. He was wearing a normal suit, and tottered as he reached out to grab the lift-grip. For a moment it looked like he wouldn't make it.

Bright got Dublin on the ship's phone immediately. "Dublin. A former ship commander named Jarma's on his way to your area. I want you to pretend to let him take over. But you'll actually be in charge of all missile launch tubes from one to twenty-four."

"B . . . but skipper," Dublin answered, confused, "what should I tell him?"

"Just say the comm channels are out, or something. He's one of these radar-age military men, you know. Let him think he's still in command."

Bright put down the receiver, and congratulated himself on having handled a sticky situation well.

"Now, who's in charge of the stern missiles?" he asked.

"Seaman Torkum, sir," replied Marker. "And he's a veteran, so he's no problem." As operator for the ship's internal operations, Marker had an uncanny ability to remember every last detail, all the way down to the number of shells left.

"Understood," said Bright. Then, turning to Mirai, he added, "Okay, let's turn this ship around."

He switched his comm link to ship-wide, and wondered why the coffee was taking so long to arrive.

ON THE *MUSAI* CRUISER, Lt. (jg) Dren announced, "Captain Garma's leading three Gaw attack carriers, sir, and he'll be in firing range of the Federation ship ten minutes from now."

"Sounds like Garma," Char answered. "The guy'll never grow up."

"I think he wants to distinguish himself in battle, sir. You know how he always says he doesn't want to be a desk-jockey type of leader."

Something about Dren's know-it-all look, Char realized, rubbed him the wrong way. He blurted out to the older man, "And that's why Zeon'll never win this war against the Federation. Understand, Lieutenant?"

The instant Char uttered the last two words he knew he'd gone too far. Dren turned his back on him, as if saying in silent accusation, "You're just as young and inexperienced as Garma, Lt. Commander."

The younger a man, the more sensitive he is to perceived slights. If Char differed at all from other people, it was in his normally superb self-control. Despite the fact that he was exceedingly young for his rank and responsibility, he possessed a type of maturity which gave him a powerful advantage in dealing with others, and was especially useful in the Zeon forces. Garma Zabi, on the other hand, had the typical psyche of someone his age, and it showed in his actions.

"If Garma's leading three Gaws," Char continued smoothly, ignoring the overtones of the conversation with Dren, "it means he has eighteen Dopp fighters. Here's hoping he can pull it off."

Dren suddenly turned toward Char again, smiled, and said, "So if Captain Garma spots the Trojan Horse first, he ought to be able capture it, right?"

"Sure," Char answered, deliberately being affable. "By the way, I've got a hyper bazooka with my Zaku, right?"

Dren punched a couple keys on a terminal in front of them and displayed an answer. "Yessir. But it only has three shells available. And all three are refurbished duds from the battle the day before yesterday. . . ."

"That's enough," Char announced. "I'm going out to help him."

When he estimated that Garma's Gaw attack carrier had launched its Dopp fighters, Char took off in his Zaku.

A GAW WAS FIFTY meters long by sixty meters wide and looked more like a fat rounded "aircraft" than what used to be called a "carrier" on earth. The main fuselage carried five mobile suits; the front part of each wing section had bays containing four Dopp space fighters. The aft part of the wing section flared into giant nozzles, which, when the twin nuclear fusion engines were on full power, could propel the ship at twice the speed of a normal cruiser. The ship was also equipped with two mega particle cannons.

The Dopp carried by the Gaws was one of the first fighters developed by Zeon, and first put into operation when Minovsky particles were still largely a rumor. It bore a slight resemblance to twentieth century military craft of the same category. The cockpit was stacked on top of the engine, giving the fighter a rather awkward silhouette, but providing the pilot with a superb field of vision in dogfights, where it was generally believed Dopps easily outclassed the Federation Flying Manta fighters. But in terms of modern firepower, the Dopp was pathetically under-equipped, for it had only Vulcan guns and small missiles.

DREN HAD TRIED TO stop Char when he first announced he was going to help Garma. If there was a heavy concentration of Minovsky particles in the area, he feared friendly machines might misinterpret Char's Zaku's IFF signals. There was a real danger, in other words, that he might be blasted out of the picture by his own forces.

But Char had sniffed at the idea, saying, "How can I possibly play the coward now, Dren, when Garma's always been my friend? I want to help him out by ramming as many bazooka rockets as I can into the Trojan Horse. I want to make the guy look good. . . ."

Char realized that the crew of the *Pegasus* had resolved to turn about, take on his cruiser, and break through to *Luna II*. Oddly, however, he found himself sympathizing with the enemy ship's captain. *You're too late,* he thought. *Thirty minutes earlier and you would've only faced the* Musai *with its single MS, and you might have had a chance.*

THE EIGHTEEN DOPP FIGHTER-BOMBERS from the Gaws, each equipped with four Lim anti-ship missiles (two classes under a Tam), could turn on a dime. With them dodging fire from the *Pegasus*'s gun turrets while boring down on the ship, and with blasts from the twin mega particle cannons on each Gaw carrier, it should have been easy to deliver a fatal blow. But ten minutes later the error in Garma's carefully laid plans was revealed. Six particle beams from the three Gaws streaked toward the *Pegasus* but somehow, with stunning agility, she managed to evade them all.

EVEN MIRAI, MANNING THE *Pegasus* helm, couldn't explain it. She hadn't relied on directions from the ship operators, Marker or Oscar. To her surprise, she had merely noticed a strange feeling piercing her body, and piloted the ship as if to avoid it. But even Bright, watching the enemy's particle beams zap by on either side of the ship, marveled at the speed with which she reacted. It occurred to him then that if she could just keep it up, they might even be able to trick the enemy into blasting each other out of the sky.

The three mobile suits launched from the *Pegasus*—the Gundam and two Guncannons—squared off against the Dopps attacking from the *Pegasus*'s port side. If used right, the explosive shells fired from the Guncannon's shoulders could take out more than one Dopp, and sure enough, when Ryu fired he turned three of them into star dust.

"Hooray!" Ryu yelled, having scored the first kill.

Hayato Kobayashi was standing in for Kai Shiden as pilot of the other Guncannon. Like Ryu, rather than use its handheld beam rifle, he chose to fire the cannons built into the MS's shoulders, and immediately knocked out two more Dopps. The Gundam, for its part, destroyed another two.

FORTUNATELY FOR CHAR, HIS Zaku managed to approach the *Pegasus* without being hit by friendly fire. Weaving through blasts from the Federation ship, he executed his famed multiple "S"-shaped maneuver, and then headed straight toward the ship's blind spot—its "underbelly."

He held his fire. Federation ship bottoms were built with reinforced armor which no Zaku bazooka or rifle had ever managed to pierce. He therefore moved around from the ship's belly, almost creasing the side of the ship, trying to head first for the bridge, then the main engine's magnetic core. Both sections were practically devoid of armor, and two blasts from his bazooka could put the entire ship out of action.

As soon as he was in position, Char trained his sights on the bridge.

Then something impossible happened. Just as Char had the bridge in his rifle scope, a white Federation MS slipped into view like a dog following a scent. Stunned, he felt a moment of real fear, but he wasn't a Zeon ace for nothing. Fear became anger. He yelled out loud from inside his cockpit: "What the hell do you think you're doing here?!"

It wasn't supposed to have happened. He had closed in on the ship's blind side and maneuvered his red Zaku into striking distance so fast no one should have noticed. By the time they did see him, they should have been pulverized. But here was his nemesis, the white MS, again.

It caught the first shell he fired with its shield, and appeared to shake violently, but that was all. Then it lifted up the beam rifle it had in its right hand, and moved as if to draw a bead on his Zaku. Char gritted his teeth and fired his bazooka again. The white MS's beam rifle also flared.

It must have been sheer luck, but the beam from the enemy rifle vaporized the rocket Char fired, and merely creased the top of his Zaku. A few particles diffusing on the edge of the beam burned part of the shield on his Zaku's left shoulder. It still looked fine but he knew it was useless; millions of tiny holes invisible to the naked eye had been blasted in it.

Only one more shell left, Char thought to himself. He felt the same fear he'd felt the first time he'd gone into combat, when he had narrowly missed a Federation Flying Manta fighter-bomber.

THE SIXTEEN METER GIANT white MS came at Char at high speed, and he could almost sense the war cry of a seasoned pilot radiating from inside it. Had he known that the pilot of the MS—the Gundam—was a youth named Amuro Ray who had logged a grand total of two hours flying time, he would have again suspected a true Newtype. But he had no way of knowing.

The white MS unleashed one more blast from its beam rifle. Char managed to evade it, but then saw the enemy MS's left arm (which carried a half-destroyed shield) reach behind its back. Something flashed and for a second he thought he saw an explosion. But he was wrong. The flare of light from a beam saber swept toward him, aiming for a point right between his eyes. Under his face mask, he felt as though cold ice had been shoved against his brow. The main orthoscopic monitor in front of him automatically filtered out the overexposure, and there, on the darkened display, the white MS's eyes appeared to glare at him in mockery.

ZAKUS DIDN'T HAVE BEAM sabers, although a month earlier Char had observed a test of a new Zeon MS model—a Rick Dom—which did. When its hand had connected with the saber hilt, a direct link was formed to the main engine and the hilt then emitted particle beams, which, when focused, formed a beam of mega particles over a dozen meters long—the "blade" of the saber. But in the demonstration Char had seen, the Rick Dom's saber had lacked a filter of sufficient precision to contain the

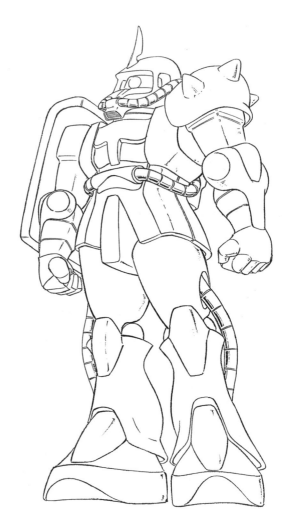

Char Aznable's Zaku

particle diffusion. The final beam blade was too broad. It still needed more work to be practical.

The sixteen-meter-tall white MS now in front of him was far beyond the experimental stage, and looked like a human fencer with a saber in its hand. The beam blade had a sharply defined edge, and it was coming right at him.

CHAR STARTED TO UNSHEATHE the heataxe on his Zaku's waist, knowing full well that although it, too, was made for close-quarter combat, it was like a toy compared to the destructive power of a beam saber.

Then he put his Zaku into reverse, and not just because he was outclassed by the enemy's weaponry. Despite the heavy Minovsky interference, he heard Garma's voice issuing orders, saying, "*Dopp fighters pull back. Gaws, start count down for the mega particle cannons!*" Char wasn't dumb enough to let himself be blasted to smithereens by a barrage of friendly fire. Following a few surviving Dopps, he quickly steered his Zaku out of the area.

And then the impossible happened again. Two of the Gaw carriers were destroyed. With its mega particle cannon, the Federation ship scored a direct hit on the main engine of one, and the ensuing nuclear fusion explosion incinerated the entire ship, creating an enormous fireball that temporarily enveloped Garma's command ship. When Garma's Gaw emerged from the inferno it looked like a giant fire-spewing bird-monster, the jets on both wings on full thrust for maximum speed. Nose first, it plunged forward toward the Federation Trojan Horse, looking for a moment as if planning to ram it.

Char, watching from far off, felt helpless. He knew Garma was personally manning the helm. Only Garma, the brash young Zabi kid, would do such a crazy thing. His mind screamed, *Garma!! Stop!!*

But at the same instant, another, utterly different thought flashed through his consciousness. Garma was, after all, one of the Zabi family. So what if he died? The Federation ship was merely aiding his own quest for revenge. He should feel lucky.

He looked over toward the *Musai* cruiser. He couldn't make out his own ship's shape in the darkness between the stars, but he knew Dren was doing his job. One after another, blasts from its mega particle cannon streaked toward the Federation Horse. Still, to his amazement, the Trojan Horse never received a single direct hit, despite being in the line of fire of both the *Musai* and Garma's Gaw. Perhaps, he thought for an instant, the Horse was possessed by demonic forces.

Yet another, even more chilling notion then occurred to him: Perhaps the entire crew was a specially formed unit of Newtypes. No, he reminded himself again, that would be impossible. The only people in the world who knew about Newtypes were himself, Rear Admiral Kycilia, and Dr. Flanagan Rom of the Flanagan Institute.

Suddenly, a beam of light pierced the prow of the Horse. Even Char could see the ship shake violently. And as if on cue, the white MS that had been dogging him reversed course. Char knew it was a useless gesture, but he fired his last bazooka rocket at it anyway, and the enemy pilot dodged it with ease.

Even though the area was heavily saturated with Minovsky particles, Char miraculously heard a transmission. It was intermittent and hard to make out amid the static, but it sounded like the voice of young Garma Zabi shouting, "Glory to the Principality of Zeon!"

"Glory to the Principality of Zeon"? That's Garma all right, Char thought,

now convinced that his former classmate was at the helm. Twenty kilometers out from the Trojan Horse, Garma's Gaw carrier caught three
blasts from the enemy's mega particle cannon and turned into a ball
of light. The image of a young man teasing a lock of his bangs with
the fingers of his right hand flashed through Char's mind. Now, he
realized with a twinge of sadness, Garma Zabi would carry that trait to
his grave. In war, it occurred to him, the only reward for Garma's type
of overzealousness was death.

CHAR SIGNALED THE ORDER to retreat with his laser oscillator, and began
heading back to his ship. Six Dopp fighters fell into line behind him, but
he wondered if any of them would be able to make it to the *Solomon*
base. It was odd how little he felt about Garma. He never would have
made lieutenant commander without Garma's string-pulling, but that
was Garma's problem. At the Academy, where Char was always head of
his class, Garma had often said, "*I want you to be my staff officer in the future.
I need you to stay alive till then, so don't do anything rash.*"

With a growing sense of unease, Char thought: *Vice Admiral Dozle
Zabi won't be happy about this.*

NEWTYPES

"I'M AMAZED YOU ALL made it to *Luna II* alive . . ."

The lips that formed the words smiled. They were a little full, but well shaped. Lt. (jg) Matilda Ajan, their owner, was about the same height as Amuro, and tall for her sex. If she had any flaw, it was the way she wore her reddish hair cut short. Nothing in Federation regulations specifically said that officers had to wear their hair short, but among military people who spent a lot of time in a weightless environment it had become a de facto rule, and they often kept it in place with a stiff gel. Matilda Ajan's hairstyle was one thing. Her almost transparent blue eyes, her lips, reddish hair, and low, lustrous voice were another. For Amuro, it was love at first sight.

Amuro had never met a real officer of the Supply Corps, especially one like Matilda Ajan. She was the skipper of the *Medea*, a *Luna II*-based transport belonging to the 28th Division, and was normally out supplying the front lines. Since she was currently on *Luna II* preparing for the next offensive, she had been ordered to supply the *Pegasus*.

AMURO AND THE OTHER *Pegasus* cadets had been on *Luna II* once before during their training period, but this time when they arrived they were handed a manual and expected to perform maintenance on the mobile suits. Ever since the Battle of Loum there had been a chronic manpower shortage in both military and civilian sectors of the economy, and double duties were the order of the day. Only absolute rookies were exempt, but as soon as they learned their way around they, too, were put in charge of any and everything. Amuro was now a combat veteran.

A flurry of activity swirled around the *Pegasus*. First, Lt. Matilda's unit deposited repair parts anywhere they could on the *Pegasus*, and left for more. Then men from Lt. Woody's Engineer Corps arrived on the ship, and the *Pegasus*'s hangars echoed over and over with arguments between his men and the ship's own mechamen over correct procedures. Because it was the first time for most of the mechamen to work on a completed mobile suit, far more than were actually needed milled around the machines.

Inside the crew's normal suit helmets, all was bedlam. In theory, of course, one could tune out the racket and enjoy some silence by simply switching off the mike, but that was only in theory. In reality, if a mike wasn't set to a specific frequency for a specific job, it was impossible to know what was going on, and one might be accidentally clobbered by an object being moved about the site. The trick, as usual, was to be able to isolate the voices needed from among all the others echoing inside the helmet. Except for emergencies, within the teams most people found that it was easier to use skin talk, and send voice reverberations directly through touching helmets.

Seaman Maximilian put his normal suit helmet against Amuro's and laughed scornfully: "Hah! At least our team's had three chances to practice before with the MS blueprints. Can you believe they call this a combat ready deployment?"

Following proper procedure, Amuro quickly checked the places the Gundam had been hit, and busied himself reloading its Vulcan guns. Compared to Amuro, Hayato Kobayashi seemed to perform a better overall inspection. He scurried back and forth among the two Guncannons and the Gundam, helping the mechamen at each stage of their work.

"Amuro," Hayato advised his friend, "it looks to me like you depend on the Gundam's armor too much. Look at the effects of all those near-misses on its skin. Don't forget the Gundam's designed mainly for movement. It's not as well protected as the Guncannons."

Amuro threw in a bit of flattery to reward Hayato for his consideration. "Hey, you're my buddy out there in space, aren't you? I know you'll keep me out of trouble."

"Don't hold your breath, pal," replied Hayato, as he drifted over to the Guncannons. "Our future assignments haven't been finalized yet, and they won't be 'til Bright comes back from the General Headquarters."

Watching his friend in action, Amuro marveled at what a skilled, dedicated worker he was. Then, noticing that everyone around him had moved on to other chores, he floated over to the floor next to the hangar, and called up to the ship's bridge on the internal video system.

The blond comm tech, Sayla Mass, appeared on the display, and answered with a "Yes?"

"Er . . . ah . . . I was wondering if you could tell me where the civilian evacuees are located?"

"They're still in the ship's gravity module."

Amuro couldn't help thinking her voice had a rather unfriendly tone, as if she wanted to ask why he wanted to know. And there was something else about her, something he sensed she was holding back.

"Could you switch me over there? I can't contact that module from this monitor."

"Wait a second . . . I think so . . . " She tried to lighten up, and with feigned laughter said, "Did you know in the old days there actually used to be a job like this called 'telephone operator?' Hang on. Here we go. Sorry, but I can only reach Ward E in Sector 28 . . . "

Before Amuro could finish telling her that was fine, Medic Sunmalo's face appeared on the screen, demanding, "Whaddyou want?!"

"I'm calling from the No. 2 deck, sir. If there's someone named Fraw Bow there among the evacuees, could you get her on the monitor for me?"

"This some kind of emergency, or what!?"

Sunmalo looked angry, but he didn't wait for an answer. His face disappeared, and in its place Fraw Bow drifted into view. Since docking in the *Luna II* port, the *Pegasus*'s gravity gondola had been deactivated, and Fraw almost couldn't stop in time. But she righted herself and peered into the camera.

Remembering that he still had his helmet visor filter on, Amuro quickly deactivated it and put his face close to the monitor-camera, saying, "Fraw, it's me . . . Amuro."

"Amuro?! Where are you calling from?"

"The mobile suit hangar. . . . You all right?"

"I'm . . . I'm fine, but. . . ." She looked pained, and tears began welling in her eyes, but she continued, " when the Zakus attacked Side 7, Mom and Gramps were . . . " That was as much as she could get out. With her face in full display, Amuro watched her break down and cry.

"Fraw! Fraw! You'll be all right. I know you will!"

AMURO HAD BEEN EXTREMELY close to Fraw's mother, Fam. Separated from his own mother, Kamaria, at age six, when his father, Tem, moved to Side 7, he had only been down to Earth two or three times after that to see her. She had always spoiled him with kindness, but never agreed to go to Side 7, and Amuro's father never demanded it. In reality, his mother's refusal to leave Earth was a convenient pretext for his parents to separate. His father used his fame as a colony architect to make a deal with local officials, and obtained special dispensation for her so she was spared the forced emigration to the Sides. His own philosophy was simply expressed as, "I want Amuro to see the construction of the new Side. The experience will make him strong, the kind of man we'll need in the new century."

After arriving at Side 7, Fraw Bow's mother, Fam, had shown enormous sympathy for the single-parent family next door and, in effect, become Amuro's surrogate mother. She was just being kind, of course, but her affection had helped assuage his longing for his own mother.

"FRAW," AMURO CONTINUED, "YOU'VE got to get hold of yourself . . . think of all the other people . . . "

"Amuro . . . I need to see you so bad . . . Where are you, Amuro?"

Right on top of Fraw's words, a general summons was suddenly announced for Amuro and the other cadets: "*All pilots named report immediately to the subbridge!*"

"Fraw . . . Fraw!" pleaded Amuro. "I've got to go—they've called me! Listen, if you move or transfer stations, make sure you leave a message for me! Understand?! I know you'll be all right. You're stronger than you think." He wished he could wipe the tears from his own eyes, but in order to do so he would have had to enter an airlock and take off his helmet.

CAPTAIN WAKKEIN, IN COMMAND of the Federation base on *Luna II*, had his office in the centrifugal gravity core. The only decoration on the wall was a copy of an abstract painting by Jube Blanc. Ensign Bright, Warrant Officer Mirai, ship's engineer Ensign Sem Dowai, and Chief Petty Officers Amuro, Ryu, Kai, and Hayato—all told to wait by the soldier on duty—stared at the painting as if trying to find some clue to the captain's personality.

They heard the gentle laughter of General Revil approach from the hallway outside, and then Wakkein opened the door and ushered his superior in, still chuckling.

"Sorry to keep you waiting, troops."

Wakkein said it in a rather curt, almost cold way, but Amuro had read a review of his poetry in the local newsletter, *Luna II News*, and knew the man also had a sensitive side to him. As for General Revil, while he had never met him in person before, he had seen many TV broadcasts of his famous *Zeon is Exhausted* speech, delivered after his escape from captivity in Zeon, during negotiations on the Antarctic Treaty.

The still-smiling general returned the salutes of Amuro and the others and performed a cursory review. When his expression turned more stern, Amuro recognized in it the same power he had felt at the time of the TV broadcast, and felt a chill.

Then the general turned straight to Amuro, grinned, and said: "And are you Chief Petty Officer Amuro Ray?"

WARFARE BETWEEN THE PRINCIPALITY of Zeon and the Earth Federation had first erupted in January, U.C. 0079, when—three seconds after issuing a formal declaration of war—Zeon threw its entire military might into an attack on Sides 1, 2, 4, and 5. Each Side was composed of about forty colonies which collectively held up to a billion people, so in one audacious move the Zeon fleets nearly accomplished the unthinkable, slaughtering four billion people, annihilating the entire Federation Forces, and forcing the Earth government to capitulate. Survivors later sarcastically referred to having received a "Three Second Warning."

The tactic used to destroy the colonies was horrifyingly simple. The colony cylinders had a sealed atmosphere, so the Zeon military simply injected GG gas into them. Poisonous, colorless, and odorless, it took only fifteen minutes to inject ten tons of the gas and, in five hours, kill nearly twenty-five million people. Had Zeon forces managed to continue at this rate for twenty hours, and then immediately demanded the unconditional surrender of the Earth Federation Forces, they probably would have triumphed. But two factors worked against them.

First, General Revil put up a courageous struggle around Side 5 (known as Loum), and successfully held off the Zeon forces there. Second, immediately after the first gas attacks, the Federation Government on Earth began to put up a fierce resistance of its own. It wasn't merely because nearly four billion of its fellow citizens in outer space were being killed. Human psychology reacts to more directly perceived danger.

It was because Zeon also implemented its diabolical "Colony Crash Strategy," which consisted of maneuvering the "dead" colony cylinders into earth orbit, and then decelerating them until they plummeted toward targets on the ground. When the first colony fell on New York, the horrified people of Earth were driven to action. Taking advantage of the fact that the Zeon forces required considerable time, energy, and large numbers of Zakus to prepare for such a massive undertaking, the Earth Federation Forces regrouped and counterattacked. Unfortunately for Zeon, large numbers of Zakus were destroyed.

For once, both Gihren Zabi and his sister Kycilia were in fundamental agreement on the correctness of the "Colony Crash Strategy." They believed that true victory in war could not be achieved solely by slaughtering innocent millions with gas attacks; rather, because they saw war primarily as a psychological process, their plan was to crash colonies into Earth's major cities until the arrogant ruling Federation elites trembled in fear. And to a certain extent they achieved their initial objective.

A month after the "One Week Battle," as this first stage of the conflict came to be known, Zeon launched another attack. But General Revil had consolidated the surviving Federation ships and was again able to effectively resist. As the opposing fleets clashed in a fierce struggle between the Earth and the moon around Side 5, the Zeon forces were disadvantaged in terms of the absolute number of ships, but they put their new mobile suits—the Zakus—to superb use, and managed to annihilate most of the Federation ships. Revil's flagship was destroyed by a special team of Zakus called the Black Tri-Stars, and Revil himself was taken prisoner. It was in this same Battle of Loum that Char Aznable first distinguished himself as a Zaku pilot.

Zeon's Supreme Commander, Gihren Zabi, then issued an ultimatum to the Earth Federation government, threatening to crash *Luna II* into their headquarters at Jaburo unless they surrendered unconditionally. Jaburo was the central command post of the Earth Forces, located deep underground in South America, and if it were destroyed the planet clearly would have to capitulate. Shuddering in fear, high-level Federation officials began negotiating with Zeon representatives, including Supreme Commander Gihren and Rear Admiral Kycilia, at a site in Antarctica. While most felt unconditional surrender was unavoidable, they asked Gihren for ten days to debate the issue among themselves.

Without waiting for their decision, Gihren returned to Zeon, entrusting the rest of the negotiations to Kycilia with the advice: "*The Earth Federation leadership is spineless. Be sure to take advantage of that.*"

Three days later, the day before the surrender treaty was to be formally signed, General Revil managed to escape and return alive to Earth. And from Jaburo he broadcast his speech, *Zeon is Exhausted.*

Fellow Earth Federation citizens! Fellow survivors! I appeal to you all. Zeon is exhausted! It is low on troops! Low on ships, weapons, and even ammunition! Why then, I ask you, should we surrender? Dear fellow citizens, our true enemy is no longer Zeon, but our own weak-kneed civilian leaders. Hiding behind some notion of "absolute democracy," they are reduced to absolute indecision. Why should we, the survivors of this horrible war, entrust them with the power to make decisions for us!?

How can we forget the arrogance of Degwin Sodo Zabi, when he usurped power in Zeon? He claimed that the people of Zeon are a "chosen people." That we of the Earth Federation are hidebound by archaic ways of thinking, and incapable of realizing the new potential for an expanded human consciousness in outer space. That there is no need for the people of Zeon to obey an "Earth Federation" run by outmoded human relics! Well, fellow citizens, even though I am a member of our armed forces, I have to admit that if Degwin was referring to our corrupt Earth Federation bureaucrats, he was correct.

But, fellow citizens, we must not be deceived by Degwin Zabi simply because part of what he says is true. Zeon may be the Side farthest away from Earth, but that is no reason to believe its leader's prattle about communing with the universe!

Degwin Zabi must not be allowed to justify his version of Zeon because of corruption in one part of our Federation. His words are dogma, the dogma of a man plotting a dynasty of Zabi dictators on Zeon. Even if we do the unthinkable, and recognize the existence of the Zeon dictatorship, that in no sense means we must also sink to our knees before it! The Earth Federation is a government, founded on the premise of sovereign individual rights. Mankind, furthermore, was able to advance into outer space as a result of the Federation government, which is itself a crystallization of all mankind's accumulated knowledge and experience.

Now, Degwin's son, Gihren Zabi, says it is the weak and inept Earth Federation itself that must be destroyed! Well, let him go ahead and try. Strike at the heart of our weakness! But what right does he—who has slaughtered four billion innocent people—have to strike such a righteous pose?

Gihren Zabi tells us that mankind has violated the laws of nature by reproducing more than any other species. He tells us that mankind's population growth must be managed, because mankind must learn to inhabit the universe in harmony with nature. He tells us that the death of four billion people was merely expiation for our past sins against nature.

Is Gihren mad? What does he possibly think the human race—an entire species—could gain by exterminating itself?! There is nothing to gain! No! Gihren is a despot trying to exterminate the very source of life that has supported and nurtured him. We, of the Federation, shall never comprehend the monstrosity of his actions.

And now Gihren threatens to crash Luna II onto Earth unless we surrender to him. What basis does he have for his demands?! Is he in possession of some sort of absolute truth? No!! He possesses nothing more than his own demented dogma. Is the entire Federation completely enfeebled, corrupt, and degenerate? Again, the answer is no. Many good, capable citizens have fought bravely against the threat from Zeon, and we are still strong and alive!! So, then, does Zeon actually possess an overwhelming military superiority over the Federation? Again, the answer is NO!

Fellow citizens! Listen to what I say! Gihren's threats are a mere bluff. Unworthy as I am of my good fortune, I was captured rather than killed by Zeon forces, and thus was afforded the opportunity to see the Zeon nation firsthand. I therefore can assure you that the people of Zeon are exhausted, and there is no way they can possibly strengthen their forces enough to carry out their threats. So I say to you, Gihren Zabi, if you think you can send Luna II crashing to Earth, well then, go ahead and try!

When General Revil said this on television, it was almost as if he were staring Gihren Zabi straight in the eyes.

Zeon's strength was expended in the Battle of Loum. There is no way they can create new soldiers overnight, and Gihren Zabi knows it. I therefore appeal to all the citizens of the Earth Federation, to each and every one of you. Zeon is exhausted! Now is not the time for us to kneel before Zeon. It is time for us to rise! Now, more than ever, is our chance to defeat Zeon!

After hearing General Revil's speech, Rear Admiral Kycilia was said to have been so enraged that she tried to smash the negotiating table. An explosive shift in public opinion occurred throughout the Earth Federation, with the result that the Antarctic negotiations concluded, not in surrender, but in a treaty that merely banned the use of chemical and nuclear weapons, and attacks on the transport ships both sides used to ferry critical resources, particularly helium from Jupiter.

After his speech, not everything went well for General Revil. Rumors swirled of a possible demotion by the Earth Federation government, but he had already become a global hero and there was little they could do.

An opportunity was thus lost. The inability of the Federation government to come up with any bold initiatives, combined with the uncompromising stance of Zeon, led to the continuation of the war, and it quickly slid into a protracted stalemate. It was almost as if too many people had already died in the conflict, almost as if, out of resentment, their souls had enveloped the world and tried to ensnare the remaining survivors.

GIHREN WAS SAID TO have once had the following conversation with his father—the Sovereign—Degwin Sodo Zabi.

"We've killed off too many people, Father. We need a certain number of people in the solar system just to keep the infrastructure of civilization going."

"You know, son, Zeon Zum Deikun once prophetized that someday mankind would undergo a transformation. Should that come to pass, mankind may give birth to new race of men who by themselves will rule the universe."

"Mankind will give birth to a 'new race'?"

"Yes. What he called a 'new type' of human."

"Well, surely he must have been talking about us, on Zeon."

"Your arrogance is showing, son. That is not what Zeon Zum Deikun was thinking of when he founded the Republic of Zeon."

"But *we're* a superior race, father. Surely we're good enough to rule over mankind, solve its overpopulation problem, and then—after achieving a proper balance in accordance with the laws of nature—forever prosper?"

"But we're not good enough. Men who lust for power are doomed to become relics of an obsolete age."

"Father, are you including me?"

"You've heard of Adolf Hitler, haven't you? Well, son, you're following directly in his footsteps."

"Father! How can you say that?"

"You're not what Zeon Deikun meant by a Newtype."

From that moment on, Gihren began to have murderous thoughts about his father.

BACK ON *LUNA II*, General Revil was saying, "At ease, troops." He then made himself comfortable on a sofa and lit a cigar. "Sorry this thing makes such a stink," he added, glancing at Warrant Officer Mirai.

"It doesn't bother me, sir," she reassured him.

Mirai decided she liked this general, who seemed as shy as a boy in front of her, and she knew she'd have no problem whatsoever following his commands. It was clear that he possessed a quality as good as gold in an officer—the ability to inspire confidence. Come to think of it, when he'd mentioned the cigar smoke, maybe she should have told him what she really thought. She had never smelled tobacco smoke before, but she already knew she didn't like it.

Revil continued. "Even though you young men and women were only able to pick up three mobile suits from Side 7, I can't thank you enough. We've just begun mass producing the GM model mobile suit, and currently only have thirty or so machines. That means your three mobile suits are even more important, and for the time being will have to form the core of the Federation Mobile Suit Corps."

"The problem is that some top officials in our Federation government have been tentatively discussing an attack on Zeon's *Solomon* base. To get to the point, I know you're all a motley crew of inexperienced officer trainees, thrown together by accident, but I find it extremely interesting that you nonetheless managed to bring back a damaged warship like the *Pegasus*, to successfully operate the mobile suits, and to win two battles with the enemy. Now, I fully realize that both the *Pegasus* and its mobile suits can technically outperform anything the Federation's ever had in its arsenal before. So maybe your success shouldn't surprise me. But it does."

The general looked around the room at everyone's face once more. Then, turning to Captain Wakkein he said, "They *do* look awfully young, don't they?"

"Yessir. Absolutely right," Wakkein replied, glancing coolly at Amuro.

Revil continued: "I first heard the word Newtype when I was a prisoner on Zeon. It refers to a new breed of human, part of a new space generation with enhanced mental powers. But these are not super powers—they're just what in the old days might have been casually called intellectual awareness, or even 'consciousness,' but on a higher level, I suppose. The basic idea seems to be that the traditional type of man, the earthbound variety, will evolve into something different in a space environment. Unfortunately, if I may say so, the old earthbound type of consciousness is still dominant in the political structure of our Federation, so this idea obviously hasn't gained much credence there. Even the Zeon government—or the Zabi family, as the case may be—still officially denies the validity of the Newtype concept, but select circles in academia have already advanced theories to support it."

Finally pausing, the general stared straight into Amuro's eyes for the first time. Returning his pensive gaze, Amuro again felt a chill. He sensed he was in the presence of a man with enormous insight.

"Having learned of the accomplishments of you youngsters," he said, still looking at Amuro, "I'm almost ready to believe in Newtypes."

Then he smiled and gazed at everyone assembled.

"Although the Zeon government has formally rejected the Newtype theory, I have come to the following conclusion. I think they have a plan to actually deploy Newtype humans in combat, or that they are already using them, and that their public negation of the theory is really a ruse."

This elicited immediate questions from the group. "You mean they're going to deploy some sort of a Newtype corps?" and "Is this a group of people with super powers?"

"Of course they don't have true super powers," Revil replied. "We live in a real world. And real people don't undergo dramatic physical evolution overnight. But take Zeon's Lt. Commander Char—the 'Red Comet'—for example. Now, he could conceivably be a Newtype. His performance in combat has been extraordinary. That's probably the level of ability we're talking about. He's not a superman in the traditional sense of the word. The best thing about the Newtype theory is that it predicts that the entire human race will eventually shed its collective skin, so to speak, and experience an expanded consciousness. This seems even more fantastic than science fiction, don't you think?"

The general stubbed out his cigar on an ashtray balanced on his knee.

"On a long shot," he said, "I took the liberty of checking into your past records. I may be going senile, but my idea was that if there are such things as Newtypes, we'd better take full advantage of them. Much to my regret, I have to tell you that by military standards none of you have particularly spectacular grades. On the contrary, they've been terrible."

The general smiled when he said this, and Amuro and the others couldn't help but laugh. Amuro actually hadn't had *bad* grades in the past, but he paled in comparison to someone like General Revil, who'd been at the head of his class all the way from kindergarten to military academy.

"Now, of course I realize," the General explained, "that your performance may simply have been heightened by the crisis you were in. Nonetheless, I find the fact that you operated at high levels in *all* areas—from operating the *Pegasus* to piloting the mobile suits—to be astonishing. For rank amateurs with poor grades, frankly, I find it incredible."

Bright interjected with an overly serious, "Yessir!" making the group once again burst out into laughter.

"But I want to believe in the existence of Newtypes," added the General. "And I want you yourselves to test the theory."

Mirai was quick to answer. "'Test,' Sir? We only did our best given the situation. And we were lucky. Like you said, our performance was probably heightened by a sense of crisis. Who knows, maybe the planets were all in alignment or something astrological. We've no way of knowing if we're Newtypes or not, and frankly I don't see how we can test ourselves, anyway. You surely don't mean in combat, do you?"

"Warrant Officer Mirai Yashima, isn't it? Let me tell you, young lady, I think the way you handled yourself through those two battles was most impressive. But let me also make an announcement here and now. The *Pegasus* and its crew have been formed into the 13th Autonomous Corps, under the command of Junior Grade Lieutenant Bright, and you'll all be participating in Operation Star One."

"B . . . but sir, I'm only an ensign."

General Revil ignored Bright's protest and stood up. "I believe I've made myself clear. Everything is now up to you people. We'll all get together again some time soon, and have more discussions on the future of mankind."

As he started to leave the room, Bright commanded the others: "Attention! Salute!"

AFTERWARD, WAKKEIN BEGAN HANDING out written commissions to everyone present. "Hmph," he muttered, "I'd like to boost you all up a few more notches, but the Federation Forces are so rank-inflated that you'll just have to be patient for now. We could only promote you enough to bring your rank in line with your level of responsibility. Wouldn't look right otherwise."

Looking at his new papers, Amuro couldn't help but exclaim, "An ensign, sir? *Me?*"

"Hell, even an ensign isn't enough. They oughta make you a lieutenant commander. After all, you're gonna be using a beam rifle with as much destructive power as an entire warship."

And with that, everyone assembled had reached officer rank. Wakkein laughed and said, "I know it's going to be hard for four pilots to operate three mobile suits, but you'll just have to work things out among yourselves for now. It's not easy to locate potential Newtypes!"

Amuro, for one, wasn't ready to believe for a minute that he had some weird new type of blood circulating in his veins. He was mostly worried about Fraw Bow.

SAYLA MASS, PERHAPS BECAUSE of her military-related training, and the fact that she had volunteered for service on Side 7, was granted the rank and uniform of Petty Officer 2nd Class in the Federation Forces. She'd always tried to avoid anything directly connected to the war, though, so the commission hardly made her happy.

After all, although her companions were unaware of it, her father had been Zeon Zum Deikun, one of the first persons to advocate the independence of space colonies, the leader of the revolution on Side 3, and founder of the Republic of Zeon. If he hadn't died, the Zabi family never would have been able to seize power and pervert the revolution. But be that as it may, the rebel Principality of Zeon now existed, it bore her father's name, and it was supposed to be her enemy.

Sayla's adoptive father, Jimba Ral, had always told her, "Your real father was a Newtype. He was a great man who showed us how we should live in space, and while still young he had millions of followers, some of whom spoke of him as though he were the second coming of Christ or Buddha. Degwin Sodo Zabi helped him form the Republic of Zeon, but that was really part of a scheme on the part of Gihren, Degwin's son. Gihren was responsible for everything that went wrong after that, including your father's assassination . . . "

At that point, Sayla usually grew tired of the old story and cut off her foster parent, saying, "We're living on Earth, Father, and we're just ordinary citizens now . . . "

To avoid the war and all its unpleasant associations with her family, Sayla eventually emigrated to the new frontier of Side 7, where she hoped to live in peace. Her brother Casval, on the other hand, became so completely obsessed with their foster father's story that he infiltrated Zeon (using the alias "Char") to "kill Gihren Zabi and restore Zeon to its true glory." Although Sayla had always been very close to her brother, and although he had always treated her with great kindness, she frankly felt he was too rash, and too obsessed. Before he had left Earth, she wished she had asked him how in the world his military exploits were going to avenge their father's death, for their father would surely have disapproved. Even now, she dreamed of somehow meeting her brother again and changing his mind. It was highly unlikely, but at least joining the Earth Federation Forces would increase the odds of being able to do so. No Federation civilian, after all, would ever be able to travel to

Zeon. This thought, more than any other, helped Sayla overcome her inner resistance to wearing a military uniform.

"WELL, WHAT'RE YOU GONNA do?" Amuro again asked Fraw, while glancing over at the three noisy young children playing with computer games in the corner of the mess hall.

"I'll work here on *Luna II*, Amuro." she said, her mind apparently made up. "There was some talk of sending me back to Side 7, but there's no one I know there anymore. Look at these poor kids. Luckily, the nursery's agreed to look after them till their parents can be tracked down."

"But what if *you* have to start taking care of them?"

"Because their parents are dead?" Fraw finally uttered the words she had been afraid to speak. "Oh, I don't know. I'm tired, Amuro. I've never seen so many seriously wounded people, or so much death."

Amuro then realized how badly Fraw had been shaken by events. It also explained why, in retrospect, when Fraw, Amuro, and the children had eaten together earlier, she hadn't taken a single bite of the meat on her plate.

"So, where are you going to live?"

"In Karol; Sector No. 32, South." She was referring to the *Luna II* refugee camp.

"I know they'll try to draft me into doing things like tightening bolts on an assembly line, Amuro, but I'm no good at it. I should probably try to get an ele-car mechanic's license, or something, so I can at least support myself. So much for my dream of becoming a fashion designer, huh?"

"Really, Fraw, I think you ought to continue studying design. This war won't last forever, you know." Amuro meant what he said. He could easily imagine her as a fashion designer, but not as a grease monkey.

"I hope so, but how many years do you think I'll have to stay here on *Luna II*?"

"This is a military base, and heck, Fraw, it could be attacked any day. And if Gihren Zabi ever makes it here, and gets his way, he'll carry out his threat to crash the entire asteroid onto Earth, with you on it . . . "

He said the last sentence half in jest, but Fraw took it seriously, and nodded.

Then a child's voice broke the ice. "Can you gimme some more coins?" It was Kikka, the youngest. She ran over from the video games and clung to Fraw's legs, hungry for any kind of affection, while at the same time keeping up a guard against Amuro. Amuro later heard that she had said that he looked "scary."

A crowd of forty or fifty crewmen poured into the mess hall, so Fraw and Amuro stood up from their table to leave. They knew there was nothing they could do about their future, that they were at the mercy of their own fates.

"Amuro . . ." Fraw started to say something, but paused and reached out to take his hand. An awkward silence ensued. She'd never done this before. On Side 7, she'd always acted like an older sister, or even a mother, always telling him to eat properly, take a bath, wash his clothes, or wipe the sleep from his eyes.

"Can I count on you?" she said.

What a silly question, Amuro thought. Here he was, talking like this with her, and depending on her friendship as much as she on his. But there was something vague and sweet about the way she said it, and the way she had reached out to hold his hand. He knew they weren't meeting because they were in love or anything like that, or at least he thought so. But neither, then, were they just getting together for an idle chat. It was more like meeting someone really close, like a family member, even a sister.

"Heck, Fraw, you know we're both in this together . . . "

Fraw smiled happily, showing her beautiful white teeth. Then she whispered, "I love you Amuro."

And he knew they were more than just friends.

ZEON

SOVEREIGN DEGWIN SODO ZABI, the nominal ruler of Zeon, looked far older than his actual years. For nearly ten years, real power had rested in his eldest son, Gihren. After seizing power from the revolutionary, Zeon Zum Deikun, Degwin had successfully reigned for a while by appeasing the former members of the Deikun faction. But then some of his own more hard-line supporters had accused him of being too idealistic and out of touch with the real world. They formed a separate faction in the Zeon Assembly—which supported not Degwin, but his son, Gihren—and they succeeded in reducing Degwin's role to that of a virtual puppet.

Three days before the death of his youngest son, Garma, Degwin Zabi received a video letter. "Father," Garma said in it, "I'd hate to have my countrymen laugh at me if I someday become general or supreme commander, and say it's just because I'm the son of the nation's leader. Be patient, Father, and I promise I'll distinguish myself in war, and achieve the rank of admiral on my own merits." It was a message from a pure-hearted youth, and it warmed Degwin's heart. Garma, it seemed, had inherited many of the virtuous qualities of his gentle mother, Naliss. How different he was from his brothers and sisters.

Out of concern for Garma's development, Degwin had kept the

Zeon media away from him until he could enter the Military Academy. But when a news tape was finally released announcing his matriculation, Garma had been catapulted into the limelight, and become a national idol overnight. His delicate, almost nervous features conveyed great nobility. The tone of his voice sometimes made him seem a little aloof, but he chose his words carefully, and he always addressed his countrymen with kindness. No matter what the situation, his public speeches began with the sentence, "Thank you, friends, for giving me the opportunity to address you." And as almost everyone on Zeon seemed to know, he was fond of saying in private that, although he was the baby of the Zabi family, he wasn't going to let anyone take him for granted.

Needless to say, Garma's public popularity gave his father immense, almost childlike pleasure. Degwin had become a mere puppet on Zeon, but through Garma he secretly hoped to control his eldest son, Gihren. It was the vain hope of an overly doting father, and it was dashed with Garma's death.

"FATHER, WHAT ARE YOU doing?" It was Degwin's daughter, Rear Admiral Kycilia. "Please get up. The people are waiting for your appearance at the funeral ceremonies."

Degwin muttered, "Why . . . of course . . . " and slowly stood, feeling as if an enormous weight had descended on his shoulders. He looked at Kycilia, and she seemed to read his thoughts.

"If you don't perform your duties as the Sovereign of Zeon today, Father," she said icily, "we'll lose control over our subjects."

It was hard for Degwin to get up and walk out there, but he had to if he didn't want to hear any more snide reminders of his figurehead role from his own daughter.

The crowd began to chant, "*ZABI! ZABI!*" and the roar of their two hundred thousand voices shook the air. Funeral cannon were fired, and then the chants were suddenly accompanied by the thunder of the crowd stamping their feet. The enormous vibrations shook the colony's artificial earth and, for a nanosecond or two, skewed the axis around which it revolved. Looking out over the crowd from a giant center stage, Degwin noticed how young most of them seemed, and he began to grind his teeth in frustration. With this kind of support, and with Garma's help, he thought, he would surely have been able to depose Gihren. If only Garma hadn't died, that is.

A fifty-meter-square portrait of Garma had been placed atop an altar in the middle of the stage, and it was surrounded by cascading flower arrangements on either side. Degwin strode forth, sat down in

Degwin Sodo Zabi

the throne reserved for him, and gazed out again at the giant assembly before him. At least two hundred thousand people were gathered, with twenty million more watching the speech televised. "Garma, my son," he whispered, thinking again that if only his youngest were still alive, they might really have been able to counter Gihren. It was a good thing Garma's mother Naliss had passed away before all this happened. If she had been alive, she would probably have gone insane.

As the nominal ruler of Zeon, Degwin sat at the center of the stage. To his right and below him were arrayed his remaining children, Gihren, Dozle, and Kycilia, in that order. Below and to his left were top government officials and other Zabi family members.

WHY DID THE CITIZENS of Zeon support Gihren Zabi and his evil ways?

One reason was that he was always careful to appoint people unrelated to the Zabi family to positions of power in the government and military. Many were pure Zabi puppets, but some were also talented, brilliant men with Newtype potential, such as the forty-two year old Darcia Bakharov, the current prime minister of Zeon. Now delivering the opening address to the assembly, Darcia was perfectly suited for his job, and beloved by the people of Zeon. He was also a perfect example of the success of Supreme Commander Gihren Zabi's strategy to preserve his own power.

On stage, Dozle Zabi whispered bitterly to his elder sister, Kycilia, standing to his right. "I hear you're planning to take Char Aznable under your wing, sister. Well, I don't like it. I cashiered him as an example to my men, so if you back him it won't look good."

"Well, you kicked him out, didn't you?" Kycilia defiantly hissed back. "Why should it concern *you* what I do with him? There's no problem with it legally. So what if he wasn't able to protect Garma? You've punished him enough."

"But . . . but how do you think Garma would feel?"

"That was then, and this is now. Lt. Commander Char has extraordinary abilities. We can't afford to waste them."

While this interchange took place, their father, Sovereign Degwin Zabi, publicly expressed his profound sadness at the death of his beloved son, and noted his gratitude to the Zeon citizenry, who so clearly shared his sentiments. Then representatives of each sector of society read seemingly endless speeches of mourning.

And the whispered spats among the Zabi siblings continued.

"DOZLE, YOU'VE MADE YOUR point with Kycilia," Gihren said, with an utterly expressionless face. "If you're really worried how Garma would have felt, keep your nose out of this business. Remember, Garma was also one of those naive enough to have actually believed Zeon Zum Deikun was mankind's savior."

"I know. I know. He was an idealist," Dozle replied. "But frankly, he was the type of person even I would have felt honored to serve under. I was even hoping he'd rise to the rank of General or Admiral. Understand how I feel, Gihren? You're a politician. A schemer. But Garma wasn't like that. He could have become a *real* military leader."

"My, my, how blunt you are, brothers," Kycilia whispered, laughing softly. "And how *respectful* of your brother's spirit."

SOVEREIGN DEGWIN ZABI SAT down on his throne and resumed staring vacantly out at the crowd before him. From a distance this gave him the look of a rather dignified father figure, but in the eyes of his son, Gihren, Degwin was already lower than human scum; he was a constant thorn in his side. Gihren had heard a rumor that Prime Minister Darcia had been talking with his father, and if it were true, it meant that his father could become a major obstacle to his plans. Things would go a lot better, it occurred to him, if only the funeral ceremony were being held for his father, Degwin Sodo Zabi, instead of his brother, Garma.

Then the crowd of two hundred thousand began chanting "Gihren Zabi! Our Supreme Commander!" and stomping with their feet. It was Gihren's turn to express his thanks for the statements of mourning delivered by the people's representatives. He stood up straight and walked over to the podium on the stage, his tall, erect bearing giving him an air of nobility. And he spoke: "*Honorable citizens of Zeon! Listen!*"

Gihren's words cut through the air, and the two hundred thousand in the audience plus the twenty million watching a live broadcast of the ceremonies waited hungrily for more. One out of every five Zeon families had lost a member in the war, and now their suffering was shared by the Zabi family. Now the Zabi family would be able to understand their loss. This, they appreciated. The Supreme Commander would give them an uplifting speech about the responsibilities they all shared, and a goal to pursue. He would give them a sense of direction, and, at least for the time being, help them forget their pain and suffering.

> *. . . I know you have all lost friends and lovers, parents and children, in the war, and I know you mourn your loss. But let me ask you. Since the Battle of Loum, is it not possible that we have all become too soft? Is it not possible that some of us have secretly begun to believe there is nothing wrong with submitting to the Federation, given their size and overwhelming material superiority? Well, it is time to reaffirm our convictions! We, the people of Zeon, are a chosen people, and we must never even consider giving into Federation corruption! Never forget what Zeon Zum Deikun, the heroic founder of our nation, taught us!*

IN REALITY, IT BOTHERED Gihren to have to use Zeon Zum Deikun's name. Zeon Deikun had been a revolutionary, and one of the first to advocate the right of the colonies to govern themselves. Now that he had been enshrined as a near-deity by the people, his name was essential in public speeches like this.

The people of space have always looked upon Earth as the birthplace of all mankind, as a sacred place that needs careful protection. In order to save it, it was necessary for us to leave it. But some of the older generations refused to leave. They continued to try to control and rule us, the Space People, from Earth. They do not realize that the vastness and infinite nature of the universe works to expand our awareness, and that it teaches us we no longer need to be connected to the old Earth-bound generations. What, after all, can we, the new Space generations, do under the control of the old Earth generations? We need to remove the Earth generations, to protect the sacredness of Earth, and to lead mankind into eternal prosperity. We may dwell in a solar system that is only a remote speck in the galaxy, but we are nonetheless the torchbearers of civilization. As you know, this is the reason the Zeon nation was founded. Why, then, do some of you, merely because of your personal difficulties, or the death of your relatives, even think of submitting to the old Earth generation? Remember the spirit in which the Zeon nation was founded!

Side 3, the frontier most distant from Earth, is the Side your mothers and fathers elected to live on! It is here that mankind's chosen race began! We must never forget Zeon Zum Deikun's most powerful speech, 'To the New People,' in which he said, "Never forget!! The people of Zeon are a chosen people! It is our destiny to forever protect all of mankind!"

Lt. Commander Char Aznable, unable to protect his superior, Garma Zabi, incurred the wrath of Vice Admiral Dozle Zabi and was cashiered from the Mobile Assault Force. But sure enough, shortly thereafter he received a visit from an officer in Rear Admiral Kycilia's Royal Guards, who offered him the rank of Commander.

"Rear Admiral Kycilia," the officer had said, "is extremely interested in the fact that you have had contact with the Flanagan Institute about Newtypes. She wants you to proceed immediately to the Balda colony on Side 6, and initiate talks with them for her."

The same officer then added that a new mobile cruiser, the *Zanzibar*, had been readied for Char, and, he proudly noted, it was vastly superior to the standard *Musai*-class cruiser in both maneuverability and power. Compared to the uneven, protrusion-covered surface of a *Musai*, its smooth outline also allowed for greatly improved armor.

"Is there a time factor involved?" Char asked.

"Yes, sir. For the last six months or so Rear Admiral Kycilia has been receiving some very specific information from the Flanagan Institute, and she has used it to help develop what we call the psycommu, sir."

"The psycommu?" Char feigned ignorance but he already knew about the weapon interface. He didn't particularly care for the young officer's overly obsequious manner.

"I can't discuss the matter here with you, Commander, sir," the officer replied. "You'd best ask Dr. Flanagan directly at the Institute."

Char thought to himself: "*Commander" is nice, but everyone's so protocol-obsessed around here I wish they'd only made me a Captain instead.* He almost said it out loud, but thought the better of it. He had other reasons for accepting this assignment besides the promotion, and one of them he wouldn't have admitted, even under the pain of death. By going to Side 6, he would get to see Lalah Sune again.

"We also have some mobile armor we'd like you to deliver to the Flanagan Institute, sir. An engineer on the *Zanzibar* will brief you on it."

"Mobile armor?" It was a term Char had never heard before.

"Yes, sir. It's different from a traditional mobile suit. It replaces Suits that rely primarily on traditional means of delivering their firepower. In this case it's composed of two components: the Elmeth and its support units, Bits."

"Hmph." Char nodded. How interesting, he thought, that although Dozle Zabi seemed to have absolutely no interest in the Newtype theories, his sister Kycilia appeared to already be thinking about forming an operational combat corps of potential Newtypes.

AFTER FORMALLY ACCEPTING HIS new commission and his new orders from this exceedingly polite, cautious officer, Char boarded the *Zanzibar*, and took off from Zeon's Zum City colony for Balda Bay on Side 6.

During the trip, the ship's engineer, Lt. Muramasa, showed him the Elmeth. It was stowed in the *Zanzibar's* hangar next to his beloved red Zaku, which Kycilia had somehow been able to retrieve from Dozle. To Char's surprise, the Elmeth was utterly unlike any mobile suit he had ever seen. It had no arms or legs, and bore a faint resemblance to an old-style aircraft. And it was equipped with only two mega particle cannons. Even so, Muramasa boasted, "If everything goes according to plan, this thing'll be one hell of a weapon."

"Even better than the Red Comet?" Char asked sarcastically.

"Well, it depends on the pilot, of course. But I don't see why not."

As Lt. Muramasa filled Char in on the specs of the new machine, he spoke persuasively and with conviction. But even more than the hardware itself, Char again found himself awed by the Newtype concept of humans that the machine relied on. The pilot scheduled to first use the Elmeth-Bits system would have to be a truly extraordinary person.

SIDE 6, OR REAH, as it was also known, was governed by the Rank administration and generally regarded as neutral territory. But the truth was far more complex. If Zeon prevailed in the war, it would need a safe base from which to control the defeated Federation territory. Gihren, Kycilia, and the other Zabi leaders had therefore deliberately spared Side 6 from destruction, and coopted the supposedly autonomous Rank administration. Side 6 was in reality a Zeon puppet.

"AND HOW IS LALAH Sune?" Char asked in the lobby of the Flanagan Institute.

"Aah, a wonderful girl. The best, in fact," replied Dr. Flanagan, with a slight grin.

As when he had first met Flanagan, Char felt a negative reaction. For a seventy year old engaged in the supposedly noble profession of science, the man was far too worldly. But, as Char had to admit, it was probably this same quality that had enabled him to ingratiate himself to Kycilia and achieve recognition for his organization.

"Well," Char said, "that's good to hear." He'd had a strange feeling about Lalah Sune when he had first encountered her as a newly orphaned young woman on this strange place some time ago. Something about her had made him think she might have some sort of Newtype potential, and now that he sensed he'd been right, he could already see new possibilities emerging. It always made him feel good when his hunches played out, and now, with Kycilia Zabi backing the Flanagan Institute, the wheel of fortune might slowly be turning in his favor.

"In looking at your combat record, Commander, it's even occurred to me that *you* might have Newtype potential. . . ."

"I'm a down-to-earth type of man, Doctor, and frankly, I don't believe in supermen or Newtypes. I'm just bringing you the Elmeth-Bits system from Rear Admiral Kycilia Zabi for testing. I want to meet the Elmeth pilot and run the tests, that's all. We don't have much time."

"Commander, I must say I'm surprised by your words."

"That I don't believe in Newtypes?" Char repeated the statement for effect, and felt Flanagan's doubting eyes trying to probe through his face mask. The man clearly had his own agenda and Char had resolved to never fully trust him. But that didn't mean Char had abandoned hope for the research the scientist's team was doing. If Newtypes ever went beyond the theoretical stage and proved practical in the real world, Char knew they could be used as a weapon to topple the Zabi family, and even to control the Earth Federation. If not, he never would have entrusted Lalah Sune to a man like Flanagan.

Newtype humans were still a vague idea, but if they possessed even limited special powers, it was only a matter of time before someone would deploy them in actual combat. With individually piloted mobile suits now the centerpiece of modern warfare strategy, there would be plenty of places to apply their talents. The Flanagan Institute, a "think-tank" or intelligence organization, could be put to great use performing needed research. Char would use the worldly Flanagan, and in turn be used by him. He would simply have to deal with the man carefully, from a position of strength.

Then Char heard the sound of silk brushing against silk. He turned and saw Lalah Sune.

"Well, if it isn't Char Aznable!!"

Lalah's clear voice resonated pleasantly in his ears. She wore a pale yellow one-piece outfit, with long billowing sleeves trailing in the air as she walked, and it made her tawny skin appear almost glistening black. There was something quite incongruous about the sight of her in the impersonal lobby of an institute charged with developing new fighters for the Zeon forces. Smack in the middle of her forehead, almost like the light-emitting third eye of a Bodhisattva, was a beauty mark. Her real eyes were emerald green, and hinted at an ancestry more complex than that of most Asians. Her limbs moved with grace as she glided directly up to him. She lacked any natural fragrance and had an altogether ethereal quality about her.

Turning to Dr. Flanagan, a shocked Char exclaimed in spite of himself, "This potential pilot you've been talking about for the Elmeth–Bits system . . . You meant Lalah, didn't you?!"

"Correct."

When Flanagan replied, his eyes probed the proper-looking Char with a lecherous look, as if to ask, "*Well, don't you think she's developed into a fine woman in the six months since you last saw her?*"

"Now about the performance of Newtypes, Professor . . ." Char looked into Lalah's eyes and wished he hadn't started to say it, but it was too late, and besides, he couldn't restrain the impulse to mock Flanagan a little. As he paused, Lalah laughed as if she understood, and seemed to urge him on. "Do you think it makes a difference," he continued, secretly thrilled, "if they're virgins or not?"

Caught off guard, Flanagan looked away in embarassment. Perhaps, he thought with fear, Char could read his thoughts. He had spent too much time studying people with paranormal abilities—from potential Newtypes to those purported to have real super powers—not to be suspicious.

"That's . . . that's . . . *er* . . . a difficult question," he answered, flustered. "We really don't have enough test samples to yield solid data yet."

"Hmph. That's no good," Char said. "Everyone's always making such grandiose claims about the Flanagan Institute, I wondered how thorough you really are."

"Please, Commander, spare us your sarcasm. Newtypes haven't been clearly defined yet. It would be far easier if we were dealing with garden-variety paranormal abilities."

"Well, how about starting out by showing me some of the more simple tricks they can do?"

"My dear Commander, I don't know what type of relationship you have to Her Excellency Kycilia, but you should know that the Flanagan Institute is an organization under her direct control. Please cease this mockery of yours and get to the point."

"Mockery? Heaven forbid. I just wanted to help clear your mind of some depraved notions, and have you show me what you've been able to actually accomplish with the Newtype idea," Char said with a grin.

It then occurred to Flanagan that Char himself might be a true New-type. Newtypes generally had remarkably refined insights, which they often referred to themselves as "hunches." Until he knew exactly what sort of ability Char had, he would have to engage him with extreme care.

"Well?" Char said, as if further confirming Flanagan's suspicion. "How is she?"

"There's no doubt about it, Commander. You were absolutely on target in recommending Lalah Sune. She's a second generation space colo-nist, from Side 5, or the Loum colony, and although her family was killed later in flight, the very fact that they were spared *during* the Battle of Loum, may, in large measure, be due to Lalah's own considerable abilities."

Char could tell from the way Flanagan was talking that Lalah had been forced to retell her own history more than once. *The poor kid*, he thought, with a twinge of guilt. He knew such painful memories were normally best left alone, but he also knew that he himself was partly responsible for their being dredged up.

"You've done well, Lalah," he said.

"Thank you, Commander," she replied clearly, looking up at him.

Somehow their exchange left Dr. Flanagan with no doubts—he knew he wasn't witnessing any ordinary flirtation. The relationship between Char and Lalah seemed characterized more by a type of tension, of the type that occurs when two psyches suddenly click together perfectly. It was a powerful bond.

IN A LABORATORY, ONE of the Institute's younger scientists gave Char a formal presentation on the progress of their research. There was some machinery and, somewhat distanced from it, a ten-cubic-meter transparent glass enclosure with around twenty mechanical manipulators inside. Standing before the machinery, the researcher first noted how honored he felt in the presence of Zeon's famous Commander. Then he began his explanation. His cheeks were flushed with excitement.

"First of all," he said, pointing, "this mechanism, which we call the *psycommu*, is used to conduct brain waves. The extremely weak electrical signals emitted by a human brain are detected by this receiver, amplified, and transmitted to the controls that operate the power manipulators. We say transmitted, but in reality the brain waves themselves become an integral part of the electrical oscillation that drives the manipulators."

"Can't you just show us how it works?" Char asked.

"Er . . . why, yessir!"

On Dr. Flanagan's order, the young researcher began to double-check the connections on the machine. As he traced each lead wire running into the amplifier, his cheeks reddened even more. The whole process took so long they could easily have had a cup of coffee.

"Lalah," Char asked. "Tell me. Does this thing always take so long to set up?"

She laughed, and replied in the affirmative.

Turning to Dr. Flanagan, Char asked, "Does a fear coefficient, or any type of negative coefficient adversely effect the device's operation?"

"It does. And we know this for certain. For example, if Lalah were to use the system to handle dead animals, she would emit only a negative reaction. In fact, her negative reaction would be even stronger than that of the average human."

"Hmm," Char said, "that makes sense, I suppose." Then he suddenly asked Lalah: "What kind of corpses did they make you handle?"

"Frogs, rats, rabbits, horses, and humans." She replied so matter-of-factly that Char decided not to pursue the matter any further.

When the young researcher resumed his presentation, he noted that the manipulators in the enclosure could theoretically move faster and with greater precision than a human hand.

"I'm now going to release one fly and one mosquito," he announced. "Lalah, I'd like you to catch them as soon as you can."

He then inserted the insects into the enclosure from an opening on one side. They were so small they were hard to see, but Char could tell something was definitely flying around inside. Lalah donned a special cap containing the receiver circuitry, and stared inside the glass enclosure. Seconds later, one of the manipulators in the case suddenly moved.

The researcher announced, "Both of the insects have been caught," then adding in a somewhat disappointed tone, "but crushed."

Char had to ask. "You mean sometimes the hands don't crush them?"

"Yessir. The flies, at least."

The manipulators had responded almost instantly and precisely and demonstrated the psycommu system's astounding ability to amplify brain waves. Lalah had been able to operate the manipulators without having to move her hands or feet.

Char stepped closer to the enclosure. He turned around and looked at Lalah, seated several meters away. Then he inspected the manipulators she had operated. Sure enough, between the fingers of one of them was a fly and a mosquito. "Well, I'll be," he muttered to himself. Turning to Lalah, he smiled and added, "This is incredible."

"In the beginning it used to wear me out. Now I can do it any-time."

"But isn't operating mobile armor a lot harder than this?"

It was Flanagan's turn to make an icy comment, "Her Excellency Kycilia loaned the Institute a simulator, Commander, sir. Using it, Lalah has already become an expert pilot of the mobile armor, sir."

"Dr. Flanagan. Forgive the way I acted earlier. I was out of line. But do me a favor. I may be a commander in the Zeon forces, but you don't need to be so formal with me—I'm almost young enough to be your grandson, after all. Can we agree?"

Flanagan uttered a strained laugh, and said, "I didn't mean to sound too obsequious, Commander. I'll try not to be _overly_ polite."

"Good. Let's get back to business, then, and attach this psycommu device to the Elmeth-Bits system. We have to let Lalah get used to it."

"Understood, Commander," said Flanagan. "We'll speed things up." He extended his right hand, and for the first time the two men shook hands.

WHEN THE TEST WITH Lalah and the psycommu was over, Char invited her to join him in the Institute's dining room. She was now formally under his command, as he carried a commission for her (signed by Rear Admiral Kycilia) which made her an ensign. His real task was to introduce her to actual combat, and turn her into a true soldier for Zeon. Right now she still looked too much like an innocent young girl.

There were only four or five of the Institute's off-duty researchers relaxing in the room, all engrossed in a video broadcast of the speech Gihren Zabi had given at Garma's funeral.

> *The old generations of the Earth Federation have no vision, and if we place our trust in them mankind is doomed. They speak only of a vague notion that, somehow, their system of government by "absolute democracy" and a "perfect parliament" will result in peace and happiness for mankind! But their system leads only to more incompetence of every sort, and to continued overpopulation. And the result? Instead of an enlightened civilization, the Federation is producing a race of incompetents who will multiply out of control, upset the balance of Nature, and defile our Universe!*
>
> *History shows that when the members of any given animal population—be it rats, locusts, or ants—increases too much, and reaches an abnormal level in the natural order of things, that species instinctively knows enough to commit mass suicide or abandon itself to the gardener of natural selection. This is the most virtuous, altruistic act any form of life can perform for the good of Nature. Yet what of mankind? Simply because he has intelligence, he insults Nature with his arrogance. And he becomes lazy. The Zeon nation, however, with your united support, and your powers of perception, has struck a blow for Nature. For the last eight months we have helped atone for the sins of Mankind against Nature. I know you all remember why!*

"Well?" Char asked Lalah. "What would you like?" He handed her a menu, knowing she probably had it memorized from eating in the same place so often. She merely glanced at it and said, "I'm not hungry. I'll just have some juice."

"I hope you don't mind if I go ahead and eat, then."

"No, of course not. Please, be my guest."

Their table was in one of the best spots in the dining hall, bathed in natural sunlight beamed in from outside the colony. Since the atmosphere of Balda City was kept at the same temperature as the 45th parallel on Earth, it felt like spring everywhere. Gihren's speech continued.

> *Remember, honorable citizens of Zeon, that our beloved Garma has joined your departed friends and relatives and died for the cause! Why did he sacrifice himself?*

Char muttered to himself: "Because he was a naive kid."

"Did you say something?" asked Lalah, unable to hear him clearly. She showed absolutely no interest in the broadcast and had been gazing outside the dining hall. There were so many things she wanted to ask him, but she didn't know where to begin. She was beginning to get irritated with herself.

"No," Char replied with a gentle smile. Gihren's speech was just reaching its climax.

> *Garma Zabi died to spur those of us who have tired of fighting to greater effort! Garma—the Garma you loved—died crying out to us not to let our warriors die in vain! He died shouting "Glory to Zeon!" Why?! Because he knew that you, the wise people of Zeon, are the true people, the chosen race in this world! Yes, he died shouting "Glory to Zeon!" Open your eyes, fellow citizens! Now, more than ever, we must unite and strike at the enfeebled Federation!*

"Lalah?"

"Yes?"

"I know the researchers at the Institute must have inspected every pore in your body, and analyzed every memory you have. I want to apologize."

"You don't need to, Commander," she said, placing her hand on top of his and shaking her head. "When my parents died I was devastated. You gave me a reason to go on living. And I'm grateful for it. And besides, this assignment means I'll be with you. I'm happy."

"That makes me feel better, Lalah."

"I was picked up by a Zeon warship after I lost my mother and father, and I did whatever I had to to survive until I arrived here at Side 6. I had no choice. And it was the same after I got here. I'm just grateful that I met you as soon as I did, before I became a physical and mental wreck. Now I'm going to be working with you. Just think of it. Suddenly, I've even been made an *ensign!*" Somehow, Lalah managed to laugh.

"Funny how fate works, isn't it?" Char said, smiling with her. He could imagine what she'd been through in the two months before he had met her, and he knew it must have been rough. She still had the look of a young girl, but her face was almost too beautiful. She was the type of woman who drove men crazy.

"I'm . . . I'm no saint, or even a gentleman, Lalah. I'm just like other men. And I've no right to criticize the way you've lived. But I keep wondering what your life was like before this all happened."

She said nothing, and merely stared at Char's mask. He looked into her eyes, and saw something terribly honest. He knew there was more he had to say, but also that he'd have to take off the mask in order to continue. He was silent for a second, and then looked around the dining hall. The broadcast of Gihren's speech was over, and everyone else had left. He removed his mask, and turned to Lalah.

She squinted as if staring at something bright. "How did . . . how did it happen?" she asked, referring to the deep scar that ran diagonally across his forehead.

"In a fencing match with a man called Garma Zabi when I was in Military Academy."

It was a lie. Char had deliberately done it to himself before even entering the school. It had been part of his oath of revenge and a ploy. In order to get close to the Zabi family in the future, he knew he would have to hide his real identity. An ugly scar would help distract people from noticing any trace of his father's features, and even give him a pretext to wear a face mask. But the pain was something he would never forget.

"Frankly, Lalah, I nearly managed to forget about you on a personal level over the last six months. But now, seeing you again, I like what I see. Tell me, what do you think of me?"

Lalah stared at Char. His eyes seemed so clear.

"This is about as romantic as I ever get," he said. He suddenly felt very young. It was sad, but at the same time his rational mind was warning him to be careful.

"I . . . I'll do my best for you, Commander. . . ."

Lalah chose her words very carefully, but tears began to well up in her eyes. "Right now, I'm very, very happy."

THE *TEXAS ZONE*

"Hail Zeon! Hail Zeon! Hail Zeon!"

The roar of two hundred thousand citizens capped the end of Garma Zabi's funeral in Zeon's Zum City. Amuro, watching the ceremony on a Federation news broadcast thousands of miles away, heard his video speakers vibrate, and was taken aback when the cameras zoomed in on the giant photographs of Garma Zabi displayed on the altar. They showed the face of a decent, gentle man, utterly lacking in the qualities one would expect of an evil "enemy." It had never occurred to Amuro when he had tried so hard to knock out the Gaw carrier, that it had been commanded by Garma Zabi.

The Federation announcer continued:

> *. . . And that was the face of Garma Zabi, the young Zeon officer who recently met his demise at the hands of the new Federation warship, the* Pegasus. *If Zeon, in order to incite its citizens to further slaughter, must stoop to portraying the ignominious death of one of its ruling family members as a glorious event, then its days are clearly numbered. The cries of "Hail Zeon!" are the last flicker of light for the Principality of Zeon, before total darkness descends!*

CHAPTER SIX

"Hah!!" Lt. Bright muttered to anyone in range. "I'll say. And did you get a load of Gihren Zabi's speech? The man who hijacked Zeon and turned it into a Zabi dictatorship?" Then he turned to the crew of the *Pegasus* around him and spoke in a louder voice:

"We launch from *Luna II* in two hours, so there'll be no time for rest. The good news is that we've got twenty GMs, our new mass produced MS, on other ships in the fleet. The bad news is that they're pretty useless compared to the three mobile suits on our ship. So that means that *we're* the main force going up against the enemy. Understood?"

The Federation's Operation Star One was finally being put into action. The *Pegasus*, as part of the 13th Autonomous Corps, was a key player in the strike force because of its three mobile suits. Before embarking, Amuro called Fraw Bow on the vid-phone to bid goodbye, but he was a loss for the right words. All he could think of was, "They say it's a big operation, Fraw."

"I know this is a weird thing to say to someone going out to defend us with his life, but do be careful, Amuro."

"Don't worry, Fraw . . . I'm not going to die."

"What'd you say?"

"I said I'm not going to die. I promise I'll come back alive."

"Good. That's the right attitude, isn't it? I'll be waiting for you, Amuro."

"Thanks."

Just then Kai Shiden came by and thumped Amuro on the back. "Well, what're you waiting for, Ensign?! You've got equipment checks to perform, don't you? Let's get with it, man!!" And then he zipped off on a lift-grip.

"I'll . . . I'll see you later, Fraw." Amuro grabbed one of the lift-grips, but as he did so, out of the corner of his eye he saw the expression on her face on the video screen. He knew she wanted to talk more. The vid-phone was coin operated, and he probably had another thirty seconds left. But there was too much to to be done to engage in small talk.

Because of the chronic labor shortage, none of the Federation warships carried the required number of mechamen, and as soon as the supply or maintenance personnel finished one task they were off in a flash to another. As a result, even pilots like Hayato Kobayashi and Ryu Jose often had to go haggle with the Supply Department for spares to ensure the three mobile suits were always operational. On the *Pegasus,* even mundane chores like cleaning up and putting away tools were left up to the pilots. This was simple work but it had to be done right, for while a mobile suit might not overheat if a screw were dropped into its

Bright Noa

exhaust system, a single loose bolt could wreak havoc on the catapult mechanism used to launch it. To prevent any such accidents the pilots had to carefully wipe everything in the area clean with rags.

It seemed as though the *Pegasus* would never be combat ready. Not only was she understaffed, but on Luna II ten or twenty new mechamen and gunners had joined the regular crew, and they were still utterly disoriented. Once Bright accidentally left the switch on the captain's phone on "ship-wide," and the entire ship had the chance to overhear an interchange between him and one of the newcomers. "What the hell's taking so long?!" yelled Bright, his voice booming throughout the ship.

"Jeez, how should I know?" the crewman answered. "I'm not here 'cause I wanna be. I don't even know where I've been assigned yet!"

"State your name and rank before you gripe, Mister!"

"Hey, not so loud, man. I'm Sleggar Law, lieutenant junior grade. I came here with the Gunnery Corps. I'm gonna be in charge of the anti-ship cannon!"

"I'm the captain of this ship, Sleggar. Don't forget, I make the decisions around here, and I want you to watch your language!"

"You?! Lieutenant!? You're the ship's captain?! You gotta be *kidding*!"

To the disappointment of those eavesdropping, some idiot do-gooder switched off the phone so no one else on the ship could hear. As far as anyone knew, Bright probably slugged Sleggar for insolence.

FIFTEEN MINUTES BEFORE THE ship's scheduled departure time, some critically needed parts arrived from Matilda Ajan's unit in the Supply Corps. And then the 13th Autonomous finally sailed out of the *Luna II* port. The *Pegasus* was preceded by a *Magellan*-class battleship, the *Hal*, and followed port and starboard by two *Salamis*-class cruisers, the *Cisco* and the *Saphron*. Six smaller *Public* attack ships were deployed in a defensive perimeter around the entire strike force.

Kai Shiden joked weakly to anyone in sight, "Hey, tell me I'm hallucinating. This has gotta be just a routine exercise, right? It can't be for real."

"The goal of Operation Star One," Bright finally and confidently announced to the crew, "is the destruction of Zeon's most powerful moon base, *Granada*. Once this is accomplished we can easily take Zeon's heartland. Our forces—the Federation Forces—are several times larger than those of Zeon, so if we knock out *Granada* and get past *Solomon* they won't stand a chance. The fleet we're part of, the 13th Autonomous, will enter the Texas Zone and draw out Zeon's *Granada* fleet. Then the main Federation force under the command of General Revil will attack both *Granada* and *Solomon*. I expect each and every one of you to be fully aware of the importance of the role assigned us, and to put the training we have received to maximum effect."

Kai, irreverent as always, whispered to his friends, "Amazing, isn't it? Give the guy a promotion, and he suddenly starts to sound like a real skipper."

Amuro wondered out loud: "But do you really think we'll be able to pull it off?"

"It won't be easy," said Ryu. "We're the decoy in this strategy—the bait."

AMURO ENVIED THE CALM way Ryu said it, as though he were already prepared for the worst. He wasn't so sure about himself; he'd already accomplished more than he'd ever hoped as an MS pilot, but he still had a reservoir of fear. He clung to the precious hope that he might survive, and he let his confidence be boosted by a new anger he was starting to feel—directed not only at the Zabi family, but also at the whole trail of human sins and failings that had led to their emergence.

Until the end of the twentieth century, the history of mankind—the "progress of civilization"—had really been nothing but an endless series of wars. When the world had converted to the new universal century calendar it therefore had done so not only to commemorate its advance into space, but also to help usher in what was hoped would be a new era of peace. And for over seventy years it had seemed to work; man did almost forget war. But then fighting had erupted again. For all their fancy statements about being a new, chosen people of space, Amuro knew that the Zabi were trying to dominate their fellow men with violence, and that they were really no different from their rapacious, power-hungry ancestors throughout the ages.

Gihren Zabi, the de facto ruler of Zeon, always claimed that a new type of humans with an expanded consciousness—the Newtypes of Zeon, presumably—should "manage" the rest of mankind. But there were competing ideas of what Newtypes really were, and it seemed to Amuro that if Gihren's notion of them was the true one, then Newtypes were indeed a barbaric crowd and he would rather have nothing to do with them. As he told his friends, "General Revil's gotta be mistaken, don't you think? If Newtypes are anything like the Zabi family, then they'll treat the rest of us like the lowest form of life imaginable." It was a point on which everyone seemed to agree.

WHEN LT. BRIGHT FINALLY finished briefing the crew, Hayato wryly commented, "Damned if I'm gonna let Zeon blow me up in the *Texas zone*. I'm gonna go all the way to *Granada*, and nothin's gonna stop me!" Without missing a beat, Kai chimed in in agreement.

ONCE THE *PEGASUS* WAS clear of *Luna II*'s jurisdiction, Amuro and his fellow pilots began intensive practice of takeoffs and landings with the three mobile suits. They missed the jeers of Lt. Ralv, who had first trained them, but the four of them were no longer cadets. They were now regular MS pilots. They knew their shared experiences had bonded them together like brothers, and they also knew that in actual combat that wouldn't be enough. At first they rehearsed in formation around Ryu Jose, who was technically the senior pilot by virtue of his age, but somehow things didn't come together quite right. The true state of everyone's feeling was hinted at by Ryu, who said he was more interested in becoming a Guncannon specialist and not really that eager to be the point man. And by Hayato, who said he wanted to pilot the Gundam, but was told by Kai it was Amuro's role, as Amuro was already twice combat tested in the machine.

THE FLEET ITSELF NONETHELESS went ahead with a relentless training program, and Amuro found himself having to perform mock space duels with two GM suits from the flagship *Hal*. To his shock, he realized for the first time that a GM actually outclassed the Gundam in firepower at close range. Like Guncannons, a GM had a single panel of glass where its "eyes" would have been, which gave the sighting monitor a clearer image. The Gundam designers for some reason had felt it necessary to make their machine look much more humanoid, and had installed two cameras, linked to the system's sight-scope, to appoximate a human face. The result, it seemed to Amuro, was that the scope tended to cloud over more easily and was often a tad out of synch. He believed the simpler a mechanism was designed, the better. But the Gundam had far more power in its vernier jets and could outperform the GM in almost every other aspect.

Supported by Kai and Ryu in the Guncannons, the Gundam and two GMs practiced making mock attacks on the *Cisco*. They practiced attacking simultaneously, first in a lateral, then vertical formation. They practiced timing their attacks and staggering their approach. It was Amuro's first formal training in tactics, and it seemed to him that they practiced everything possible, repeating moves over and over again until he just wished it would all end. His throat was starting to feel parched, and the undergarment he wore under his normal suit was soaked with sweat.

Then the order finally came to return to the flagship *Hal*. It was time for a critique of the mock combat sessions and further study of formation tactics. The Earth Federation Forces had only a rudimentary, almost primitive, combat manual for use with the mobile suits, and it had been written by officers with no actual combat experience who could only imagine how Zeon's Zakus actually operated. Rumor had it that the manual was really patched together from a surreptitiously obtained Zaku manual and from information on old-style fighters. An enormous number of errors needed to be corrected as a result. The Federation MS pilots were clearly in an awkward position. They were inexperienced and vastly outnumbered by Zakus. They would have to rely instead on a great deal of creativity.

Lt. Commander Rudolph Ramski, who led the sessions in the ship's mess, announced, "We don't have a lot of time, men, so I'm going to talk while you chowdown." He was popular, an engineer involved with mobile suits since they were first developed. "Mock battles are good training for novices," he said, "but you all tend to rely too much on the performance of your mobile suits. Don't expect them to always compensate for you."

His little audience groaned.

"I say this," he continued, "because I want you to *stay alive*. Keep in mind that what I say is true of almost all weapons systems while they're being developed. Think of yourselves as test pilots. 'Course you've probably never heard of test pilots going into combat, have you? Well, the big shots in the Federation don't fully realize what they're asking you suckers to do, so you don't even get a special test pilot bonus. 'Course you're all free to step down from the Mobile Suit Corps if you so decide, but your pay'll also be taken down a few notches . . . "

Ramski's forthright manner made Amuro and the others like him even more, but they knew that there was a big difference between his theoretical approach and the reality of combat.

"One point the comm techs on all our ships have stressed in their group meetings is that all you pilots are slow in transmitting your call signs. It's hard for them to track you in battle with radar. Laser signals work better. And it's especially important to get those calls out promptly when the warships go into action against each other—unless you want to be hit from behind by friendly fire!"

The pilots were aware of the flaws in this logic, of course. Both the comm techs and the navigators on *Pegasus* were inexperienced. Would they really be able to properly read the call signs even if issued? When the area was heavily saturated with Minovsky particles, radio broadcasts were only effective up to twenty kilometers, and the Petty Officer in charge of wireless communications was Sayla Mass. She was a rank amateur, and there was an awful lot of communications jargon and terminology she didn't yet understand.

"SAYLA'S GOT A LOT to learn, but I love the sound of her voice." Kai whispered to Amuro. "It gives me goosebumps."

"Sayla?!" When Amuro had first glimpsed her on his display monitor, it was true she had looked beautiful, but she had a habit of jutting out her lower jaw that made her seem a little too nervous for his tastes, and he hated the formal, prissy sound of her voice. "*If I say anything incorrectly,*" she always said, "*please let me know. I'll soon learn the right way.*"

Amuro hissed a reply to Kai's comment: "She tries too hard to be like us."

"Of course, stupid," Kai said. "That's what makes her so cute!"

The lt. commander interrupted them: "Ensign Amuro—you're the Gundam pilot, right?" And when Amuro answered in the affirmative, he continued. "The Vulcan cannons built into the Gundam's head are auxiliary weapons, for close-in fighting. You rely on them too much.

And you're not using your throttle properly. You should be able to control your vertical roll better."

After critiques of each MS pilot's performance, lectures followed: first on the various types of Zeon warships and the specific formations in which they flew; then on Zaku combat flight patterns. To be truly useful, the lt. commander's theoretical approach had to be augmented by comments from the MS combat veterans. But since the pilots tended to articulate their experiences in a limited, fragmented fashion, the lt. commander tried to help them mold their impressions into a larger conceptual framework that described Zaku tactics.

"I wish I could show you how Char operated," Amuro said apologetically, as the rest of the pilots listened intently, "but I can't. When I was engaged with him, I wasn't even aware the Gundam had special combat sequence video recorders. But I can tell you that Char Aznable is unlike any other MS pilot. I know this sounds incredible, but he almost seems to see the beams coming at him and then find a way to initiate evasive maneuvers—in *advance*. I can frame him in the crosshairs of my beam rifle scope when he's moving laterally, but the instant I pull the trigger he's gone."

Then someone asked the question: "Think he's one of these Newtypes we keep hearing about?"

"I don't know. I was too busy trying to stay alive to think about that. If I hadn't put the Gundam through evasive maneuvers at top speed, though, Char's rifle blasts would have pulverized me. Both the Gundam and the GM seem to have enough armor to withstand about two hits, but not by a marksman aiming directly at the same place twice."

During the nearly six hours that the discussion and critiques took, the Gundam and Guncannon mobile suits were transported from the *Hal* to the *Pegasus*. Amuro and the other pilots followed later in a space launch.

PEOPLE ON EARTH REFERRED to the moon's invisible half as its "dark-side" or "back-side," but from the perspective of the Principality of Zeon it was the "front-side." They had a major moon base, *Granada*, located at the southern tip of the Soviet mountains, from which their warships regularly landed and took off, and to counter increasing Federation intrusions into the area, a Zeon fleet under Rear Admiral Kycilia's command had begun to reinforce its presence there. It included Captain M'quve's squadron, with its single heavy and three light cruisers, which was assigned to defend the *Texas Zone*.

The "*Texas Zone*" was an area in space around the Lagrange point where the Battle of Loum, the last major conflict between Zeon and the Federation, had taken place. It got its name from the sole surviving Side 5 colony in the area—*Texas*—which had once been used exclusively for sightseeing and large-scale cattle ranching. An old-style colony only three kilometers in diameter and thirty-two in length, *Texas* had been built to simulate the mountains and plains of the Western regions of the North American continent. It was equipped with cowboys, herds of cows, and covered wagons, and people had come from throughout the space colonies to *Texas* to enjoy camping, horseback riding, and the experience of rafting down a replica of the Rio Grande. Although the colony had been attacked several times during the Battle of Loum, it had never been completely destroyed, but the motors that drove the mirrors used to radiate sunlight into the colony had been wrecked, leaving them stuck perpetually in a sunset mode. The colony still had air, but humidity had fallen so low that, eight months after the Battle of Loum, *Texas* had become a near desert. The livestock had all been seized by Zeon forces, and the former residents had either escaped to Federation territory or surrendered to Zeon. The colony was now totally deserted.

The space around the colony was filled with remnants of other Side 5 colonies destroyed in the war, creating a shoal region even more dangerous than that around *Luna II*. When a heavy concentration of Minovsky particles was used, the combination made the region almost impenetrable. Both Zeon and Federation forces feared entering the *Texas Zone* because enemy ships were too hard to spot, and ambushes were too easy.

CAPTAIN M'QUVE, TO WHOM the defense of the *Texas Zone* had been en-trusted, enjoyed the full confidence of Rear Admiral Kycilia because of his political position, rather than his military skills. Should Zeon triumph over the Federation, he was destined to become her right-hand man; for now, however, he had to bide his time. But there was one thing that bothered him about his superior's actions.

"Char Aznable," he muttered, while admiring one of his prized white china vases from the Northern Sung dynasty. "I don't like the idea of that kid working with the Flanagan Institute on Side 6 to form a Newtype combat unit. How can someone who couldn't even protect Captain Garma possibly be qualified to lead Newtypes? Seems like he's up to something behind our backs. And Dr. Flanagan can't be trusted. Look who he's hooked up with. Her Excellency is far too impulsive for her own good. How can she place her faith in a lowlife like Flanagan when the existence of Newtypes hasn't even been fully proved?!"

Until Kycilia declared her intention of rehabilitating Char, M'quve had planned to cut off all payments to the Flanagan Institute. Why waste any more money on research that produced no results? Why not spend it instead to improve the Zaku design, or further development of the new Rick Dom suit? Surely the Zeon auditor general wouldn't like the idea of wasting precious research money on some unproven mobile armor—the Elmeth or Bits or whatever the thing was called.

Moreover, M'quve had learned that before Char left Granada, Kycilia had given him command of a new advanced mobile cruiser, the *Zanzibar*. Coming on top of that, a formal decision to use the Elmeth-type weapons was like a stab in the back. He remembered with bitterness the words Kycilia had laughingly tossed out at him: "*You worry too much, M'quve . . .*"

But there was something else M'quve was also worrying about. He knew a man like Char, who obviously had talent running out of his ears, could be dangerous and would eventually become his enemy. There was something too calculating about the man's overly proper behavior, and the way he cozied up to authority. First he had leeched on to Vice Admiral Dozle, and then to Her Excellency Kycilia.

Why, he thought, *the man acts like he's Kycilia's favorite pet.* He liked this idea, and subtly began popularizing it with the help of his men. It caught on among the troops, who soon began joking among themselves that Char was "*Kycilia's pet, cause he's got a nice ass.*"

MEANWHILE, CHAR, ON THE *Zanzibar,* had left from Side 6's Balda Bay and was himself proceeding to the *Texas Zone*; he planned to test the new Elmeth-Bits mobile armor, now equipped with the psycommu interface, inside the deserted *Texas* colony. It would have been possible to conduct the tests in open space, but Char didn't want to take any chances. Lalah Sune would be operating the system, and he wanted to avoid exposing her too fast to what was essentially a vast battlefield. Newtype-operated weaponry, he sensed, had to be handled carefully. Newtypes, after all, possessed nothing like the "superpowers" of comic book heroes and merely had a finely honed sense of intuition. As for the psycommu, it was part of a system; a system that amplified the Newtype operator's intuition and both projected and fed off an expanded consciousness. It was itself an astonishing device, especially since its signals, unlike normal electromagnetic waves, could overcome any Minovsky particle interference. But the system was not without its problems. It was still unclear what kind of person was really capable of projecting clearly defined brain waves—"willpower waves," for lack of a better term—that could be amplified. Char and Dr. Flanagan's discovery of Lalah Sune had been a fluke. To isolate and quantify the characteristics required for an Newtype mobile armor pilot would require testing of far more potential candidates.

ON THE BRIDGE OF the *Zanzibar*, Char turned and looked at Lalah Sune, seated deferentially in a chair in the corner. He smiled, and whispered to himself, "I wonder if I'd be able to pilot the Elmeth-Bits system?" She was seated too far away to have been able to hear him, but to his astonishment she replied.

"You, Commander? Why of course . . . and much better than I, I'm sure."

Char's eyes widened. He hadn't even fully verbalized his statement. "You . . . understood me?" he asked.

"You think very logically, so it's fairly easy to deduce what you're thinking."

Lalah giggled softly as she said this, almost reflexively. It was one habit of hers he didn't care for. He suddenly announced, "I'll see you later, Lalah," turned away, and began walking in the direction of the captain's quarters.

She let her eyes follow him out the door and was suddenly seized with melancholy. She wasn't sure why. She imagined herself in the embrace of his arms and broad shoulders and reminded herself that he was everything she had ever hoped for. But she knew there was something else. The coldness he sometimes exhibited stemmed from the fact that his goals in life were very different from hers. Whatever those goals might be, they were clearly a vital component of his being, and they would make it impossible for him to ever lead a normal life. When Lalah used her Newtype intuition to try to probe the core of his consciousness, she could feel him try to shut her out, and she then knew he was almost a full Newtype himself. But in the unformed thoughts she contacted, in the depths of a mind trying to conceptualize its surrounding reality, she sensed dark, brooding hatred. It was this hatred, she knew, that manifested itself in his detached manner, and explained why, when she was talking alone with him, that his mind always seemed elsewhere.

To the Commander, I'm a means to an end.

It was something she had only realized recently, and one of her greatest fears. It wasn't that he had no love for her. She knew he did. Love was a solid reality in the swirling interface of their shared consciousness. But it was here that Lalah's femininity exerted itself in a grand compromise; if she loved him and she could help him, what could possibly be wrong with being a tool for him?

ON THE PEGASUS, OFFICERS and enlisted men normally ate in separate mess halls. Since Amuro and his colleagues had just been promoted, he could have eaten with the officers, but he still felt more comfortable with the enlisted men. He got his meal tray from the mess hall self-service window, and proceeded out of habit to a table in the right hand corner of the room, only to find it occupied. Ensign Mirai Yashima, having finished eating, stood up to leave when he approached, but her companion, a Wave petty officer, did not.

"Nice to see you, Ensign," Mirai said with a smile as she walked by him. He stuttered a pleasantry in response, thinking how pretty her eyes were. Her full figure was apparent beneath the sharp lines of her uniform.

Mirai acted like an older sister to the younger men, and it was no wonder she was one of the ship's most popular Waves. Amuro recalled Kai having once said, "*Wife material. That's what she is. Two years older than me . . . but, yep, I like that idea.*" And of course Hayato had agreed wholeheartedly. But Mirai was also as smart as a whip and had another side to her. She had an uncanny ability to discover shoddy work, and more than one young crewman had had his ears boxed by her. It was this dual personality, perhaps, that made her so attractive. Once Ryu had once boasted, "*Hell, I never screw up, so she never slaps me,*" whereupon someone else chimed in, "*Hey, when she does, it feels* good!*"

Amuro was about to seat himself somewhere else when he realized he had seen the other Wave at Mirai's table before. Then he remembered her name, and blushed to the tips of his ears. Sayla Mass, having finished her meal, was savoring a cup of coffee and reading what looked like a manual. Amuro and the other young pilots knew her only from the three inch image they saw on their MS cockpit monitors. It was hard to connect that to the real thing.

Everyone knew Sayla Mass was technically ill-suited to be the ship's "communications" specialist. Most of the crew weren't about to follow an order telling them to move from Sector A to D if it was simply parroted by someone relaying it from above. They wanted to know why they were supposed to do something, and even if no one could tell them, they still wanted to hear something, anything. It didn't matter if it was true or not. If told something as simple as "Keep up the good work," even a stubborn idiot would happily run to perform his task, his head full of sweet thoughts for the pretty face that gave the order. This fact of male psychology was the main reason Waves were regularly used to transmit orders throughout the ship.

But whatever reason, Sayla couldn't bring herself to act this way, with the result that crewmen often ignored her messages, and chaos resulted. She became known, therefore, as "the Bungler."

Standing in front of Sayla with his meal tray in hand, Amuro knew that as an ensign he now technically outranked her. But he also knew she was older than he was. With one factor offsetting the other, he figured they ought to be on equal ranking. Gathering up his courage, he ventured, "May I join you?"

"Oh . . . uh, of course, Ensign . . . er . . . "

Amuro knew she was having trouble remembering his name—an automatic demerit for a comm specialist. She glanced at his tray, and looked up as if to say, "*What are you doing here?*" Looking down at her, he instantly cursed himself for having addressed her. His heart started pounding again, and he felt his attempt to act like a sophisticated ensign collapse in ashes. He accidentally put his tray down on the table too hard, and to his embarrassment it clattered.

"Er . . . excuse me . . . " he said, thinking for a second perhaps he'd better move to another table, then realizing it was too late to turn back. He knew he should say something else before he started into his meal . . .

" . . . I used to see you at the Zeravi library on Side 7," he ventured, hoping this was a good approach.

"You were there, too, Ensign?" Sayla said, with a thin smile.

"Uh . . . yeah . . . I . . . I lived on Side 7 for two years before I joined up."

"Really?" Her overly formal smile suddenly brightened.

The Federation military was a collection of so many types of people that when a crewman ran into anyone from the same Side it was like meeting an old acquaintance. If it was someone from the same colony, it was like meeting a bosom buddy. Amuro felt ecstatic. Here was Sayla, smiling, really smiling, not on a display monitor, but right before his eyes.

"When you were in the library," he said haltingly, "uh, I . . . actually I didn't go there very often, but once, ten days before I signed up, I thought I'd say hello to you, and actually I started going every day, but . . . uh . . . I . . . uh."

"You should have said something. But please, go ahead before your food gets cold."

"Uh . . . thanks." He picked up a forkload of noodles and began shoveling them into his mouth, but his mind wasn't on the taste.

"When I used to see you in the library, Sayla, I only knew of you as the, er—'scuse me—the 'Blond.' It was a nickname I gave you."

"Well, gee, I'm awfully glad to know you're from Side 7, Ensign. I'm the only one of us Side 7 folks on the *Pegasus* bridge. I didn't join the military through normal channels, and there's an awful lot I don't know yet, so if it wasn't for Mirai's help I don't know what I'd do. I can't tell you how happy I am to know there's somebody else from my Side, 'specially when it's an ace pilot like you!"

Amuro was in seventh heaven, but Sayla was shocked at herself for the way she had spoken to him. In her communications with the MS pilot over the video monitors, she had always sensed something in common with him, and now, meeting him in the flesh, it was almost as though she couldn't stop herself. The guy stammering in front of her was younger than she was, and cute, and hardly resembled the ensign she'd been seeing on the comm monitors.

Something about the way he transcended his age reminded her of the talk going around the bridge about Newtypes and made her wonder if he might really be one. It was a quality Amuro shared with her brother, Char, aka Casval. Her foster father, Jimba Ral, had often told her that her real dad, Zeon Zum Deikun, had been a Newtype. "*It's an expanded consciousness resulting from mankind's leap into outer space,*" he would say. "*A New Type of human. Your father was a great man, Artesia. And you are his offspring. Someday you must realize your own Newtype potential, destroy the Zabi family, and help lead mankind back to a world of peace!*" In the end, Jimba Ral always came back to the same point: the need to overthrow the Zabi family on Zeon.

Sitting and talking with Amuro, Sayla began to sense that the Newtype potential mentioned by her foster father indeed might appear in other people as well. It was a far-fetched notion, but when she thought of the millions who had died in vain in the war, it made her hope it was true.

"Ensign . . . ," she began, as Amuro suddenly looked up. "Have you ever heard the word, Newtype?" Something about the fact that he was younger made it easier for her to talk freely.

"Well, I've heard General Revil use the term," Amuro answered, "but, hey, I don't believe in Superman or anything with superpowers."

"Still, you've heard the Zabi family thinks they're Newtypes, haven't you?"

"Are you kidding? If they're what Newtypes are all about, then what's the point of staying alive? I heard Gihren Zabi's speech the other day, and the man's a maniac. His idea of paradise is to enslave the peoples of the Earth Federation, and frankly, I don't like it. . . ."

When Sayla heard blunt talk like that from Amuro, it made her feel even happier. "I agree," she said, "but have you ever read about the legend of Zeon Zum Deikun?"

"I only know what I read in my school textbooks. He's the man who claimed that in order to feel truly at home in the solar system, mankind would have to start thinking differently. And didn't he also say man shouldn't cling to his home planet? I understand all that, but it hardly seems to apply to the Zabi family. Don't you think they're living anachronisms from a feudal past, to say the least?"

Sayla had to restrain a smile of satisfaction. The shy, stammering youth of a few minutes ago was turning rather eloquent.

"When men get into positions of power, they always seem to forget about people, even the people who helped put them there. Heck, look at the Earth Federation government. 'Absolute Democracy' sounds great, but the parliament can't do a thing without a two-thirds majority, so the politicians spend all their time scheming, and nobody thinks about the people anymore. No wonder the Zabi family calls them spineless. The Federation government's ruled by bureaucrats and incapable of change. As far as I'm concerned, I don't care if it collapses."

"So why are you fighting in this war, Ensign?"

"Mainly because I don't want to die. War's about people killing each other, right? But to get back to your Newtypes, I'm willing to believe in the idea if it means a type of person capable of putting the Federation organization back in the hands of the people. I mean, sometimes people have an almost intuitive understanding of each other. If that kind of awareness could link not only individuals, but all of mankind, well, then maybe we really could all live in harmony. If that's what 'Newtypes' are all about, I'm all for them. Heck, I'd even like to be one."

"That's exactly the kind of person Zeon Zum Deikun was talking about when he used the term Newtype; people with that sort of consciousness."

"Really?" Amuro looked at Sayla and saw what looked like sadness or loneliness. "You seem to know an awful lot about this Zeon guy. . . ."

"Why . . . no . . . I really don't." For a second Sayla panicked, and she knew Amuro had noticed.

"Newtypes . . . hmm," he said. "Well, it's an interesting idea, but I don't see how people can change so easily."

"Yes . . . yes, you're quite right, and even if real Newtypes did appear among us, well, it wouldn't be easy. Giving birth to something totally new is usually painful."

Suddenly Amuro had a powerful, subjective understanding of what she was trying to say. "Sayla, you're really convinced Newtypes are going to appear soon, aren't you?"

Almost reflexively, she responded to his sudden question with a smile. He stared at her. For a second the two of them interacted on a new, emotive level, but then she shifted the focus. It made her too nervous.

"I just think it would be nice," she said.

In reality, she yearned to meet a real Newtype if they did exist. She wasn't exactly sure why, but being separated from her brother, and having no close friends to speak of, she found herself more fascinated by people than ever before. If she could be sure that, as she earnestly hoped, true Newtypes possessed some intangible essence of humanity, she might be able to use this knowledge to change her brother's mind. Jimba Ral had always said that her father, Zeon Zum Deikun, was a Newtype and that he had referred to a sort of future renaissance among humans that would help propel them into a true space-based existence. If he was right, perhaps in some odd way the huge conflagration now taking place in space between the Federation and Zeon was a prelude to it. Perhaps it would provide a catalyst, allowing mankind to collectively shed its old-type skin.

Sayla looked deep into Amuro's eyes, and tried as hard as she could to project a thought: "*If you're really a Newtype, Amuro, give me a sign. Show me if there's any hope for us!*" She knew he wouldn't understand something so desperate. And she was right. Her earnest look registered on him, but he interpreted it in an entirely different manner, as unsettling evidence of something terribly powerful in women in general. Amuro Ray was still a virgin.

THE ZEON SQUADRON LED by Captain M'quve in the heavy cruiser *Chivvay* was on patrol, making a wide sweep around the *Texas Zone*.

"There's the *Zanzibar*, Sir!" yelled one of the men on watch.

M'quve automatically sprang out of his captain's seat. He knew the *Zanzibar* had left Side 6, but no one had informed him of its movements after that. Sure enough, there, looking as though it would practically slice off the starboard-wing of his bridge, he could see the enormous shape of the *Zanzibar* silently drifting by, blinking out a signal.

"What're they saying?!" he demanded of Uragang, the junior grade lieutenant on the bridge. M'quve couldn't read old-fashioned Morse code.

Uragang's hoarse, subdued voiced slowly responded: "*TO-THE-M'QUVE-SQUADRON. GOOD-LUCK-IN-BATTLE!* sir."

"Hmph. I'll bet."

Keeping his eye on the brightly-lit bridge of the *Zanzibar* as it drifted by, he ordered Uragang to reply: "Tell them, 'We await the triumphant return of the Red Comet and the Elmeth. Go in Glory! M'quve'"

"Did you say Elmeth, sir?"

"That's right. And don't forget the 'Go in Glory' part, either."

M'QUVE'S MESSAGE WAS FLASHED from the *Chivvay* over to the *Zanzibar*, where it was deciphered by a Lt. Muligan and conveyed to Char, who frowned and remarked, "The man's like a rose with too many thorns." He knew that if he ever had the opportunity, he should do something about M'quve, and groused aloud that as far as he was concerned, "the man would be far better off chasing skirts." He had no way of knowing, of course, that at the same time his rival was calling him "Kycilia's pet."

M'quve's ships and the *Zanzibar* then silently went their different ways in the darkness; the *Zanzibar* to dock at the *Texas* colony, the M'quve squadron to eventually encounter the Federation's 13th Autonomous Fleet under Captain Wakkein's command. The rendezvous between the two fleets came much earlier than anyone expected.

"ENEMY SHIP ABOVE THIRD combat line!!" called out Chief Petty Officer Marker Clan from the operator's boom chair suspended on the *Pegasus's* bridge.

"But we're in the *Texas Zone*!!" yelled Lt. Bright. "Are you positive?!"

"The computer database readout identifies it as the *Chivvay*, a Zeon heavy cruiser, sir! It's too close a match in weight and size to be an asteroid!"

From the ship's helm it was Ensign Mirai's turn to comment: "We've got a message from the *Hal* requesting us to assume level 2 battle stations!" she yelled.

Bright reached for the captain's phone, and switched it ship-wide. *"All crew! Assume level 2 battle stations!"* He repeated the announcement twice. Ensign Gilal, Petty Officer Sayla, and the other communications crew would make sure that everyone moved to the proper sectors and took up the right positions.

Sayla announced: *"Decks One and Two, open launch hatches! Mobile Suits stand by for takeoff!"*

Before she could get all the words out, a response came from Amuro. "All systems are go on Gundam!" he yelled. "Beam rifle ready! Catapult set!" He was ready thirty seconds faster than Ryu and Kai in their Guncannons.

Marker, the operator, shouted from his perch: "The enemy will reach second combat line in one minute! One heavy cruiser, two regular! Estimated number of Zakus . . . eleven!"

After Sayla relayed the information to each pilot, what sounded like a wail came from Kai in his mobile suit: "Jeez! We're outnumbered more than two to one!"

"Sayla!" called Bright, angry. "Tell Kai to cut the personal chitchat!"

"Yessir," she replied.

Marker started counting aloud as if to confirm the number of enemy mobile suits. "Four . . . Five . . . Six . . . Ten! Eleven!"

Bright looked up at the display on the ceiling of the *Pegasus*'s bridge, where computer graphics showed a simulated model of enemy ship locations. "Launch mobile suits!" he ordered.

Just before the radio link to each mobile suit was severed, Sayla's final communication reached the pilots. "Marker's estimate was correct," she said. "There are eleven Zakus."

ON THE FEDERATION SIDE, the six *Public* attack ships were not designed like fighters, but they were still more maneuverable than cruisers or other warships. Six of them deployed themselves in a wedge formation facing the direction of the Zaku approach, and were followed by the mobile suits; the Guncannons, the Gundam, and the two GMs from the *Hal*.

As soon as the lead *Public* fired two large Lim missiles at the oncoming formation of eleven Zakus, it peeled away from the main force. The timed missiles then went on to explode in the general area where it was assumed the Zakus would be. It was a crude method, one that would have surely puzzled a military man from the old days when radar-linked, computer-controlled weapons were taken for granted.

Two bursts of light appeared to swallow the Zaku formation, but it was only an illusion. Before the light had completely dissipated, several darkened shapes—Zakus—came into view. The five remaining *Publics* in the Federation formation, rather than waste their Lim missiles, launched a barrage of smaller ones, and some seemed to hit. Two enormous balls of white light mushroomed in space with a shape unique to an exploding nuclear fusion engine. They overwhelmed the visual spectrum; in the mobile suits, even with the orthoscopic monitor's automatic exposure control on full, the light was blinding.

"Here they come!" Amuro cried seconds later, spotting something bright soar toward him from the upper right corner of his field of vision. It was a single Zaku, and if the earlier explosion hadn't diverted him, he never would have noticed it bearing down on him. Then he saw something flash in the area of its torso. Simultaneously, he pulled on the Gundam's control levers and jammed his feet on the pedals, dodging a blast from the Zaku's hyper-bazooka with only about ten centimeters to spare.

Damn! he thought, trying to aim with his beam rifle. The enemy Zaku wasn't as fast as the Red Comet, but almost. Their relative speeds made them cross paths before the Zaku had a chance to fire another blast. Amuro tried to spin his Gundam around in time, but gave up. From now on the battle would be a free-for-all. The same Zaku would either spot another target, or become a target itself. Amuro checked the upper left display in his cockpit, then switched to orthoscopic monitor and spotted another Suit. It was a Guncannon.

Amuro pushed the swivel-mounted gun scope away from his face, realizing that his trajectory was taking him away from the enemy. In relation to the plane of the elliptic, he was too far north, or above them. For a moment he wondered if he might have opened the Gundam's throttle too much, perhaps out of fear, or even a subconscious desire to avoid the enemy. He began a broad curving maneuver to his right, hunting for enemy Suits. The light of the earth passed over his monitor and for a second he thought it was an attacking Zaku. He felt a shiver run down his spine. *It's going to take me over ten years to really get used to this*, he thought, and in the same second he spotted a real Zaku.

Incredibly, it was only five kilometers to his right, descending parallel to him and seemingly oblivious to his presence. In hot pursuit of some other prey, it was already sighting down the barrel of its bazooka rifle. Amuro swung his beam rifle around ninety degrees and pulled the trigger.

For a fraction of a second the entire Gundam shook, as heavy metal particles bundled by a laser beam were blasted out the gun barrel. Even with a shock absorber system built into the beam rifle and into the Gundam's shoulder, it was impossible to avoid some sort of kick. But by the time Amuro felt it, the enemy Zaku had already been blown several kilometers away, with the initial explosion colored by the residual light from the beam. Then came the main blast, as the Zaku reactor went. Averting his eyes, Amuro spun the Gundam around a hundred and eighty degrees, and as he did so he suddenly spotted several other mobile suits in the area, illuminated in the light of the blast. There were a lot fewer Zakus than he had expected. For a moment he wondered if the other Federation pilots had been able to take out the Zakus, but he knew that was too much to wish for; all of them, including the GM pilots, were essentially still novices.

Then, just as Amuro had always feared, several Zakus began closing in on the four Federation warships under Captain Wakkein's command. The ships began evasive maneuvers and unleashed a barrage of anti-air fire in all directions, but Amuro knew the Zakus were cannily taking advantage of the fleet's feeble defensive perimeter. He cursed them for trying to make fools out of him and his friends, and then, spotting a flash from a Zaku bazooka far off to his right, he put the Gundam into a high-speed swoop toward the Zakus around the ships, careful at the same time to avoid friendly gun and missile fire.

"I know we all have to die sometime, but God help me, 'cuz here I go."

Amuro didn't vocalize the words, nor is it likely that he remembered them later. His action was an intuitive response to the fact that the Zakus were perfectly positioned for him to attack. Zaku squad leaders were normally identified by a decorative antenna-like rod protruding from their machines, and sure enough, Amuro immediately spotted one. The enemy assumed a defensive posture as Amuro closed in, and raised its bazooka as if to fire, but Amuro fired his beam rifle first and scored a direct hit. A ball of light mushroomed from the exploding Zaku and nearly enveloped Amuro's Gundam, which flashed by without a second to spare.

"Two down . . . " he exulted.

MS pilots wore helmets wired not only for radio transmissions, but also for localized sounds. As the Gundam shook violently from the Zaku's explosion, Amuro heard a crackling sound, as though something was burning inside the cockpit. He let his body roll with the MS, and checked around him. He wasn't expecting to find any major damage; if a critical condition warranted abandoning the MS a computer readout on the upper right instrument panel would notify him and the escape mechanism in the Gundam's Core Fighter system would be activated—assuming, of course, that the system survived an attack.

THE TWO OR THREE seconds Amuro used to check the inside of his cockpit nearly cost him his life.

"Jeez!" he suddenly yelled in terror. From the bottom of his monitor, he saw a third Zaku soar up toward him and almost overwhelm the screen.

Thanks to automatic avoidance circuitry in the Gundam, which mercifully worked properly, the Zaku's heataxe slashed through empty space rather than hacking off one of the Gundam's legs. The Zaku's first attack thwarted, it next fired a laser burner built into its left hand. Using the Gundam's shield, Amuro managed to deflect what would otherwise have been a direct hit, but the blast nonetheless struck his Suit with an inaudible *whomp!* and a burst of light. And then the Zaku sliced through space again with its heataxe.

Amuro felt something like a spark deep inside his brain, and a rainbow of light shot through his consciousness. He knew that unless he acted the Gundam's head section would be split open like a watermelon. The instant the light in his own brain turned to blackness, he found himself staring into an abyss in his own consciousness, confronting a force that transcended all time and tugged on him like a magnet. It was colorless, transparent, and utterly black. And then he felt it. He felt a leap in his awareness.

Amuro's right arm moved so fast it threatened to overwhelm the Gundam's safety mechanisms; the Suit's arm, moving in response, groaned. Wielding the magazine of the beam rifle, Amuro intercepted the swing of the Zaku's heataxe and stopped it with only a millimeter to spare. He could see the blade of the heataxe glowing bright red, almost screaming. Sparks from the severed laser oscillator in the Gundam's beam rifle sprayed light between it and the Zaku. And then suddenly, as if confused, the Zaku's mono-eye flickered and seemed to go out.

Something in Amuro yelled, "*I did it!*" It didn't come from his conscious mind. It came from whatever had caused the leap in his awareness. He felt as though he had been guided by some external force and led out of a crisis. It was almost as though the scream came not from within him at all, but from a larger, independent consciousness.

Amuro made the Gundam discard its now-useless beam rifle, and used the freed right arm to reach back over the Suit's shoulder and grab the hilt of one of the beam sabers. When the Zaku's mono-eye flashed again, he slashed downward through its head, driving the glowing pink saber blade all the way through to its chest. The Zaku, nearly severed in two, collapsed forward at the waist, molten metal fragments spraying from its innards like magma spewing from a volcano. Amuro turned off the saber's oscillation and put the Gundam in reverse to get away from the explosion he knew would occur. And then he was enveloped in the light of another nuclear fusion blast.

"Three down . . . " he said to himself.

Then Amuro turned the Gundam toward the remaining Zakus attacking the Federation ships. Luckily, almost all of the Zakus would have already exhausted their supply of bazooka rockets, because without his beam rifle he would have no choice but to use the beam saber in close-quarter combat.

At exactly the instant the Zakus changed course to avoid a barrage from the Federation ships, he plunged the Gundam into their midst. The fourth Zaku he severed in two before it had time to draw its heataxe. The fifth tried to parry with its heataxe, but the Gundam's beam saber melted it in an instant, and sliced diagonally down through its shoulder to its waist.

"Five down."

THAT WAS THE END of the fight. Ryu's Guncannon had bagged one Zaku. A GM had finished off another. The remaining four retreated. Federation losses included two *Public* attack ships destroyed, and four ships slightly damaged. Or so it seemed.

WHEN AMURO RETURNED TO the *Pegasus*, Sayla's face appeared on the miniature monitor in his cockpit. The few words she uttered were so official and shocking that he forgot to release his seat belt, and sat temporarily speechless. Of the *Pegasus*'s MS team, only Amuro's Gundam and Kai's Guncannon had returned. "You must be kidding." he groaned.

"No. It's true," she said. "I just received confirmation from the bridge."

The hatch on the *Pegasus*'s catapult deck was still open, as if waiting for Ryu Jose to return in his Guncannon any minute. Death in battle, it seemed to Amuro, was too sudden. It had happened to Sean Crane, and now to Ryu. One instant they were there, and the next they were gone. And they would never come back. That was it.

When Amuro climbed out of the Gundam and made his way to the briefing room, sure enough, there was the chair Ryu had been sitting in before they had all taken off. The original five pilot cadets now had been reduced to three.

Kai Shiden entered the room, looked at Amuro, and merely shrugged his shoulders. Hayato Kobayashi, who had stayed behind on the ship during the battle, turned to Kai and exploded with grief: "Why?! Why couldn't you protect him?!" he yelled.

"Who the hell do you think I am?" Kai retorted. "Some kind of invincible veteran MS space ace?!"

Hayato said nothing, and when Amuro turned and stared at him, he started to leave the room with an expression of utter despair.

Kai yelled at his back, "Next battle, you're ON, partner! You were brought along on this ship as a backup for Amuro! He knocked out five Zakus! And you're telling us we should have saved Ryu?!"

"Okay, enough!" Hayato broke under Kai's blast. His anger spent, he turned around, slumped into a chair, and exclaimed "Dammit!" in frustration. Instead of Hayato, it was Kai who left the room.

Amuro walked over to one of the recliners in the room, eased himself into it, and strapped on the seat belt. If they were going to be on round-the-clock stand-by for combat, he thought to himself, they should at least have two more alternate pilots. His pulse was still racing from the adrenaline of combat, but he knew he was exhausted. He wouldn't have time for a good sleep, but he would at least try to take a short nap. He popped a tranquilizer and called out to Hayato, "Wake me up if anything happens."

BECAUSE OF THE BATTLE between the 13th Autonomous and Captain M'quve's fleet, Zeon might decide to send out reinforcements, but by then General Revil and the main Federation force should have started closing in on Zeon's *Solomon* fortress in the area around Side 1. Any Zeon reinforcements coming to the *Texas Zone* would have to leave from either Zeon's *Granada* moon base or *Solomon*, and General Revil's fleet might be able to respond accordingly. It was too early to tell if the final showdown would take place around *Granada* or *Solomon*, but either way, the accomplishment of the 13th Autonomous—especially the *Pegasus* and the *Hal*—had opened the door to a major battle.

IMMEDIATELY AFTER RECEIVING HIS letter of commendation for downing five Zakus from Captain Wakkein, Amuro had to go out again. An enemy fleet had been detected coming out of *Granada*, so if at all possible, in advance of its arrival at the *Texas Zone*, the 13th was to destroy Captain M'quve's Squadron and then wait for a major fleet offensive to shape up. Unbeknownst to Wakkein and the other Federation commanders, however, Commander Char and the *Zanzibar* were already on the *Texas* Colony.

LALAH SUNE

"JUDGING BY THE DAMAGE the Federation pilots inflicted on us," Captain M'quve said as he sifted through reports from his men, "we're dealing with a fairly powerful opponent."

"Yessir," replied Lt. (jg) Uragang. "We have reason to believe there were over ten enemy mobile suits, but it is possible that the count was slightly inflated, if, for example, two of our pilots reported downing the same machine. Still, I agree we shouldn't have lost seven Suits. An enemy MS can't possibly be more powerful than a Zaku."

"Hold your tongue for a second, Lieutenant," M'quve said. Uragang always talked too much, which irritated him. He wished he'd brought along his little white marble Tang dynasty statue of the Goddess of Mercy. Its gentle expression could soothe the spirit of any who gazed upon it, and he often used it to help collect his thoughts. Right now he was also disgusted by his own carelessness. Who would have dreamed he'd run into a Federation fleet on what was supposed to be a routine patrol mission?

"How many mobile suits do you think the Federation 'Trojan Horse' can carry?" he asked, referring to the *Pegasus*.

"Well, er, according to information from Lt. Commander Char, sir . . . "

CHAPTER SEVEN

"He's a full commander now, Uragang," said M'quve, interrupting.

"Yessir! General Staff Headquarters, based on information from the Commander, has determined it can hold between six to eight Suits."

"Well, that's the number we're looking at then. Even if their mobile suits perform twice as well as ours, they still don't have any veteran pilots. It seems to me, that we're looking at no more than eight. Don't you agree, Uragang?"

"Why, yes . . . *yessir!*"

"I don't know what Commander Char and the *Zanzibar* are up to at the *Texas* colony, but send an emissary requesting they go into action to support us. The Federation Forces will make the next move."

Sure enough, M'quve was right.

TWENTY MINUTES AFTER AMURO received his commendation from Captain Wakkein, Sayla broke the news to him over the video link that he had been ordered on a scouting mission. "You all right, Amuro?" she said softly. "Bright tried his best to get Wakkein to rescind his order, but we lost track of the Zeon fleet that launched the Zakus earlier, and . . . "

"Bright? Bright did that for me?"

As far as Amuro was concerned, Bright was usually preoccupied with yelling orders from the bridge, and it was hard to imagine him looking out for any of his pilots. As it turned out, however, at first Hayato had been scheduled to launch in Amuro's stead, but Bright had refused. And his refusal had angered Wakkein.

"Why can't Hayato go?" asked Amuro. "What's wrong with sending him out?"

Sayla answered lightly: "I think the skipper trusts you, Amuro." And then, "We can see asteroids from the bridge. Be careful."

SINCE THEIR CONVERSATION IN the mess hall, Sayla had begun to let down her guard with Amuro. He, for that matter, had been unable to forget the strangely beautiful blue color of her eyes. There was something in them that hinted of a great personal burden. There was something different about the woman he had always thought of as "the Blond," and he knew it was more than his imagination.

Later, while doing a preflight check on the Gundam, he wondered to himself if *she* might even be a Newtype . . .

After checking the signal shells, the beam rifle, the bazooka, and its spare rockets, he called out: "Gundam, ready for takeoff!"

Sayla wished him luck over the video link, and then he felt the *g* force of the launch. It felt better than he remembered.

"Hey, Hayato!" Kai called out to his friend, watching the Gundam launch on the monitor in the *Pegasus*'s briefing room. "Be thankful it's Amuro! It lessens the odds we'll buy the farm!"

"But I'm a full ensign, just like him!" Hayato exclaimed. "How come I'm still just an alternate Gundam pilot?"

"Tough luck. We're not Newtypes. We're Guncannon specialists now, Hayato."

"What are you getting at?"

"Well? Don't you think Amuro's a little different than we are?"

"Nope. I still don't have the foggiest idea what people mean by 'Newtypes.'"

"Well, since we're just average joes, they're basically telling us to take a back seat. Nothin' wrong with that, as far as I can see. Heck, I don't want to meet the same fate Ryu did."

Hayato, his eyes glued to the video monitor, said nothing. On the launch deck the mechamen were scurrying about, doing last minute maintenance on the Guncannons. This time there was nothing for the pilots to do but wait. Noticing after a while that Kai had fallen silent, he turned and looked at his friend, and found him sound asleep in his recliner.

Pilots were specially chosen officers, and Hayato had no reason to think he was incompetent, but when he thought of his peer, Amuro, carrying out such difficult and dangerous assignments, he couldn't help feeling a trace of self-disgust. If, as General Revil had suggested, Newtypes symbolized a transformation of all mankind, then they clearly weren't mere comic-book style supermen. And if, as implied, a human "consciousness raising" was going to herald a new stage in man's evolution, well, that would be almost too good to be true. In the past, man's progress had always been dependent on his periodically destroying the very civilization he had built; if that could be changed, who would need something as terrible as war?

Still, it seemed to Hayato that something about all this smacked of nonsense. If the Zeon government was really planning to form a special Newtype Corps, its members could hardly represent a total transformation of humanity. Surely they would simply be a group of murderous supermen, even super-butchers. Weren't Newtypes just some freak-mutants? Hayato had never heard of any people with special powers—at least not with the type of powers currently being whispered about—who had made so much as a dent in history. Newtypes, Hayato concluded, were really just deviant personalities. There was no other way he could comfortably compare himself to Amuro. His pride wouldn't allow it.

Lalah Sune

WENDING HIS WAY AROUND asteroids up to two kilometers in diameter, Amuro traced his way in the Gundam over the Federation squadron's planned course. Captain Wakkein wasn't so foolish as to leave the advance scouting to the Gundam alone; the four surviving *Public* attack ships were deployed in a supporting role, above, below, and to either side of him.

As the formation navigated past another asteroid, Amuro encountered a giant piece of wall panel over a kilometer long, a remnant of one of the Side 5 colonies destroyed in the Battle of Loum. Sensing something odd, he tilted the Gundam forward and started to maneuver around the wall. Far off in the distance to the left, he could see *Texas*. The moon, as usual, appeared so enormous that it nearly overwhelmed his optic nerves. If the enemy was lying in wait on the other side of the wall, he realized they would be in the perfect position to ambush the Federation fleet when it came by.

Just as he was puzzling over what he sensed, a corner of the wall seemed to ignite, and a group of particle beams stabbed through space toward his Suit. He responded reflexively and the incredible speed of his movements was transmitted to the Gundam, which creaked and groaned as if tortured. The core of the enemy beams missed, but a few diffused particles on their periphery pierced the Gundam's armor; the bazooka fastened to the machine's back was blown to smithereens.

"What the hell happened!?"

When his guard was down he had been hit by a particle beam attack! He had evaded it. And that was that. He knew an enemy MS could easily have been waiting to ambush him from behind the wall, but the beams aimed at him were far too powerful.

Putting his MS through a wide evasive maneuver, he slipped around to the other side of the wall and found himself staring at a small squadron of Zeon ships—looking up at their bottoms, from his perspective. Scattered smaller fire—both particle beams and missiles—streaked toward him, missing but nonetheless unnerving him. No wonder he had sensed something odd. One heavy cruiser and two *Musai*-class ships had been lying in wait for him, and the first blasts that had zapped out at him through the darkness had come from their main cannons. The thought made his flesh crawl. It was a miracle that he hadn't been pulverized.

Without hesitating Amuro moved into action. The *Musai*-class ship immediately in front of him blocked his view of the heavy cruiser *Chivvay*, making a direct hit on the latter with his beam rifle impossible. He therefore trained his rifle sights at the *Musai*-class ship, and pulled the trigger. Three beam blasts pierced the engine on one side of the vessel, but just before the entire craft blew the *Chivvay* and the other *Musai* cruiser accelerated forward, and two Zakus that been hiding behind them came toward him, firing rockets from their bazookas. One smashed into the Gundam's right arm.

"Damn!"

The Zakus had seized the perfect moment to attack. Amuro was still drunk with his own success at bagging the *Musai*. He cursed his foolishness.

Luckily, although his Suit's right arm had received a direct hit, the joint had been spared and the arm still functioned. But the power lines connecting the main engine to the beam rifle mechanism had been damaged, leaving it unusable, and there was no time to switch the rifle to the Gundam's left hand, which was holding the shield. Amuro tried to ward off attacking blasts with the shield while bolting the rifle onto a restraining fixture on the Gundam's hip. Then he unsheathed the beam saber hilt from his back pack. Positioning himself between the two oncoming Zakus, he thanked the stars the Gundam's beam saber and rifle had independent power lines; if not, he would have been a goner.

With a *zap!*, the saber hilt projected a blade of beam particles over ten meters in length, which sliced into the left shoulder of one of the oncoming Zakus. Amuro knew he had connected with the enemy MS but he didn't have time to check if he had delivered a mortal blow; they were both streaking toward the giant cylinder of the *Texas* colony, and unless he was careful he himself would crash into its walls. Turning and accelerating the Gundam way into the tach red-line, he swooped right in front of the Zakus. Carefully avoiding the colony's giant extended mirrors, he glanced at his rearview monitor and for the first time saw concrete proof of his kill in the form of a fading burst of light from an explosion. But what about the other Zaku? He would have to be extra careful; it had had the insignia of a squad leader on it.

He badly needed to check the damage to the Gundam's right arm. As he soared alongside the colony, he spotted its docking bay and decided to enter and take cover. It was on the "sunny side" of the huge cylinder (having been abandoned by the Ministry of Colonies, its rotation was now one-fifth slower than normal and its axis was permanently skewed), but at least he would be temporarily out of sight of the Zakus.

The Gundam mobile suit, as Amuro found once he parked in the bay and took a close look, could withstand a lot. The armor in its damaged right arm was constructed of a triple-layered, compound honeycomb material, and had a four- or five-centimeter dent, and what looked like a hole in it. The arm would still work, but using it to hold the beam rifle was out of the question. What he really needed at this point was a bazooka. Beam rifles were formidable weapons but they taxed the concentration of already overburdened pilots because they required great marksmanship; unlike bazookas and other old-style weapons which created a more diffused explosion and required a less precise aim, with a beam rifle anything less than a direct hit was meaningless. And as Amuro's earlier skirmish had proved, MS pilots had to operate on a hair-trigger basis, with no room for mistakes. During the two or three seconds of exultation over hitting a *Musai* his overconfidence had almost led to disaster; he had let down his guard and let a Zaku blindside him.

Now, parked inside the *Texas* colony docking bay, he had no idea where the enemy, especially the surviving Zaku, was. Nor did he know who its pilot was. He knew he wasn't dealing with the Red Comet, but judging by the earlier action, he felt certain its pilot was a veteran of more than one battle.

ON THE ZEON CRUISER, *Chivvay*, Captain M'quve was livid. "What?!" he said. "No response from Commander Char?!"

A Federation squadron of four ships had already arrived on the scene, and his ship, as well as the cruiser *Kwamel*, had come under fire. True, like him, the Federation forces didn't have much firepower. But the mobile cruiser *Zanzibar* Char was on, now supposedly docked on *Texas*, was far more powerful and agile than any *Musai*-class ship, and should have been able to arrive on the scene in a few minutes. If it would only come to his help, he thought, he could hit the Federation ships broadside and destroy them all.

Now here he was, in the midst of a battle, with particle beams from cannons on both sides crisscrossing through space, unable to deliver fatal blows but pulverizing several small asteroids in the process. Luckily for M'quve, his men were brave. Two of his Zakus even courageously managed to approach the Federation fleet flagship, *Hal*. If only that white enemy MS hadn't appeared on the scene so fast and spoiled his surprise earlier, M'quve was convinced his carefully planned ambush would have wiped out the Federation's entire 13th Autonomous Fleet.

Perhaps he had given away his position by being too hasty to attack the Gundam, but he wasn't the type to dwell on the pros and cons of past decisions. His was a simple philosophy. If a crisis arose, it had to be solved. He was also pragmatic enough to put his personal grudges aside for the moment, and he really did wish Char were around to help him now. After all, he'd lost the *Tolmeth*, a *Musai*-class cruiser, and eight Zakus. He had an account to settle.

M'quve's *Chivvay* concentrated a barrage of fire on the Federation's *Magellan*-class flagship, *Hal*. Dodging blasts of friendly fire, the two Zeon Zakus also contributed their own firepower. Under normal circumstances this would have been an absurd strategy, but M'quve knew he had no other choice if he wished to get the upper hand.

"Lieutenants Rolm and Zerol are piloting our Zakus, are they not?"

"Yes, sir." Uragang wondered why his captain would ask such a question at a time like this.

"Well, I certainly feel proud of those men today!" M'quve exclaimed in his subordinate's face, just as a shout went up from the other officers and men on the bridge. The main engine on the *Hal* had turned into a ball of light.

"That's the way!" exulted M'quve, standing at attention on the bridge and urging on his forces, while the mushrooming orb of light threatened to envelop him. "Now go for the Trojan Horse! Turn your guns on the Horse!"

BUT ZEON GUNS WEREN'T the only ones capable of hitting their targets. Several blasts from Federation beam-cannon also scored direct hits on the *Chivvay*. Then eight missiles struck home. Then two more. The main foredeck cannons were knocked out of action, and to use the aft cannon to maximum effect M'quve had no choice but to swing his ship around, exposing his right flank to the enemy.

Lt. Uragang yelled out a report: "Lt. Rolm's Zaku has reached the cruiser on our port side, sir!"

"Excellent!" exulted M'quve. "Steady your aim!!"

Beams streaked forth from the *Chivvay*'s three linked aft cannon as the Federation cruiser *Saphron*, on the right wing of the formation, suddenly pulled in front of the *Pegasus*. It looked unscathed. An intense barrage of mega particle blasts followed.

OVER ON THE *PEGASUS*, Bright was livid. "What? Hayato's taken off on his own?! The kid's crazy to go out there in the midst of a battle between fleets! Order him back at once!"

Sayla knew the best way to get her skipper to calm down was to let him rant and rave. With the loss of the flagship *Hal*, the *Pegasus* was more exposed than ever, and Bright was understandably upset. She acknowledged his command and radioed Hayato's Guncannon, knowing full well her message couldn't reach him.

"*Pegasus to Guncannon! Ensign Hayato, return to ship immediately! Return to ship!*"

IT WAS MADNESS FOR Hayato to have taken off in the middle of the cross fire between enemy warships, but once outside the immediate area, the incredible latticework of light he saw looked like beautiful shining threads. It was hard to imagine being hit by them. It made him realize why, in the vastness of space, it really was difficult to achieve a direct hit on anything.

Homing in on the beams of light coming from the enemy, Hayato could see that the Zeon cruiser *Chivvay* was half-destroyed but still pursuing the attack. As he trained his sights on its aft deck cannon, he marveled how calm he felt. Indulging in a little self-satisfaction, he congratulated himself on having finally become a seasoned combat veteran. He pulled the trigger, and the two cannon built into the shoulders of his Suit belched forth flames.

"Three . . . two . . . one . . . " he did a countdown by himself, while putting the Guncannon into a broad curve to the left, and training his sights on the other *Musai*-class cruiser on the other side of the *Chivvay*. And just then the aft deck cannon on the *Chivvay* exploded.

"Bull's Eye!" Hayato yelled.

M'quve's ship gave its last, final gasp, and then a ball of light equal to that of the *Hal* earlier highlighted both the asteroids and the surviving warships in the area. In the midst of all this, the *Kwamel*, the last *Musai* cruiser in the Zeon squadron, heeled about sharply, desperately trying to escape.

"Can't let them get away," Hayato swore to himself in the narrow confines of his Guncannon cockpit as he swooped after the *Kwamel*. The *Pegasus* fired a signal flare indicating all forces should regroup, but Hayato was too preoccupied to notice.

OVER BY THE *TEXAS* colony, the Zeon Zaku squad leader following Amuro closed in for the kill outside the docking bay. Since the colony port was nearly four hundred meters in diameter, he fired two rockets from his bazooka as cover before entering and then, without waiting for the explosion to clear, plunged inside.

Amuro quickly retreated behind an old transport ship scuttled in the center of the colony's port. He could physically sense the intruder's presence—he was learning to "sense" things from inside a cockpit—and he was seized by a crazy idea. He would try to grab the bazooka from the Zaku.

And then he saw the girl.

It was such an odd sight that for a moment he wondered if he was seeing things. She was standing in a corner of what used to be the colony's control core, behind the multi-layered glass of its observation window. And from his perspective she was upside down. Despite the distance her emerald green eyes were strikingly beautiful, almost transparent and glowing, and he sensed something indescribably powerful and vast in them. Remembering what he had sensed in Sayla once before, he felt a vague sense of déja vu. What could it be? he wondered. Even more important, was the girl real?

The control core of the abandoned colony was unmanned and the lights should have long ago been extinguished. The girl was standing in darkness yet there was a faint glow around her. The notion that she might be a "ghost" crossed Amuro's mind, but it was soon canceled by a powerful realization that this girl actually existed, that she was *there*. Without knowing exactly where this realization came from, he wondered if she was projecting her own conscious thought on him, even deliberately creating an awareness in him.

Without verbalizing, something in Amuro's mind nearly screamed: <Who are you?!?>

And again: <Who are you?!>

The question was pleading, almost desperate, and almost a physical yell.

"What do you want from me?!"

Could she hear him? She appeared to smile, and when a transparent light seemed to pierce the center of her forehead, he hoped it was all an illusion. But then he understood it was real. She had parted her jet black hair in the middle of her head and gathered it in buns on either side of her head. Her skin was a glistening tan, and the contrast made her emerald green eyes seem almost transparent. Her dress also surprised him. It was nothing more than folds of cloth hung over her neck and draped around her body, an awfully mature outfit for someone so young. But then another realization welled up inside him. She was the same age as he was! It was a physical sensation, and undeniable. It was incredible.

Then he felt a growing awareness of a new sensation—a darker force, like a shadow—run through his cerebral lobes. He sensed Z-A-K-U.

An enemy had brazenly managed to sneak up behind him and was now so close he could have finished the Gundam off with a bazooka blast. But he didn't. Instead, the Zaku swung its glowing heataxe toward the Gundam's hips in an attempt to connect with and destroy the Gundam's power train. But Amuro forced his Suit to move so fast its metal nearly screamed, and dodged the blow in the nick of time. Like a knife slicing through butter, instead of Gundam armor the Zaku's heataxe sliced through the wall of the abandoned transport.

Seizing the moment, Amuro raised the beam rifle in the Gundam's functioning left hand and slammed its stock into the Zaku's left shoulder, sending it smashing into the side of the transport. The ship's framework shook, and as the Zaku rebounded from it, Amuro jammed his rifle muzzle into its cockpit area. He knew there was a human pilot inside, and when he pulled the rifle trigger it felt colder than normal. The beam from his gun pierced the Zaku, sliced through the wrecked transport, and even reached the Control Core on the other side of the port.

Heaving a sigh of relief at his narrow escape, Amuro shoved the fallen Zaku out toward the colony port exit. It scraped and bounced on the deck once, spun crazily, and then drifted out and off toward the sun. Somehow, Amuro didn't want the girl to see what he had done. The fight with the Zaku had only taken a few seconds in all, and he hadn't even glanced at the monitor that earlier had showed the girl, but he was afraid she might have become frightened, and disappeared. For him that would have been a disaster. He had no idea who she was, but she had seemed eerily capable of understanding his intentions. And he was terrified by the implications of losing contact with her. She had made him realize something profound; that he was not alone, that she was a kindred spirit he must meet.

It was an intuitive realization, the recognition of one Newtype by another, yet even Amuro himself was not yet fully aware what was happening. While pushing the Zaku corpse out the docking bay, fearing she was no longer there, he suddenly sensed her presence. He mentally "saw" her. He *knew* she was still there. He knew her name was Lalah Sune. And he knew she was real.

Unable to stand the idea of looking at her over a video monitor, Amuro yanked the lever for the Gundam's main hatch. The orthoscopic monitor lowered and the double-layered hatch door opened up and outward. He unbuckled his seat belt, stood up, and looked straight at her. If he hadn't still been in the vacuum of space in the colony's docking bay, he would even have removed his normal suit helmet. And if he could have, he would have smashed the glass panels of the Control Core window that still separated them. There was too much between them. He could sense her physical presence, but visually she was still too unclear, too unstable. With her still standing upside down from his perspective, he stared straight into her eyes and asked: "Lalah, what are you doing here?"

He knew there was no voice channel available. But she responded anyway, as if she had physically heard. Her hands floated up to her cheeks, and her nearly transparent, emerald green eyes seemed to cloud over in sadness.

He knew her spirit was wavering. He knew she was afraid but he couldn't tell why. He cursed the limitations of trying to understand her mind. But then he clearly sensed a thought from her directed at him, assaulting his brain like a wave. It was a perception so powerful it threw his mind off balance for a second and allowed her to connect directly with his consciousness.

<You're too late!!>

<What do you mean?!>

<I've already fallen in love with *Char!*>

Amuro felt like a hole was being bored in his brain, splitting his nervous system in two. What did she mean? Who was the Char she spoke of? Who was too late? "Love"?! All he could think of was "Who are you?"

<Why?>

Suddenly, as the girl gradually began to express herself, several thoughts struck the confused Amuro simultaneously. And behind them he could still sense sadness and anxiety.

<Why are you so late? It took you too long to get here!>

The thoughts were clear, and filled Amuro's awareness.

<I had no idea you existed!>

"What are you talking about? What has all this got to do with me?" Amuro tried to answer but then stopped. She had mentioned Char! Could she possibly mean the same Char he knew as the "Red Comet"? Char Aznable?

This time Amuro's words were not received by Lalah Sune. Their form of communication was unlike telepathy, which never needs spoken words. Nor was it triggering some sort of leap in consciousness. As impressions were traded back and forth, an awareness that transcended conscious thought was built up. What seemed like an exchange of fragmentary ideas created the context for understanding another person. It was not a simple means of communication. It was more like a weaving together of two minds.

And it allowed Amuro to feel the sadness behind Lalah Sune's words.

<You are too late. I just realized now that you are the one I was waiting for. But you are too late . . . >

<My name's Amuro Ray. I'm from the Federation. I don't understand why you'd be waiting for *me* here, in *Texas*, of all places. Do you mean you were waiting here for some sort of kindred spirit?>

<Yes, and it was a new person. . . . It was you, and not the commander. This is too cruel.>

Amuro's next thought was like a dagger to Lalah's heart.

<I don't think a true Newtype . . . would make a mistake like that.>

<How can you say such a cruel thing?! Why didn't you contact me?!>

With that, Amuro had a profound realization of his own basic weakness. And he lamented it deeply.

<Because. Because I don't think I'm really a Newtype.>

<We . . .we are both imperfect, Amuro.>

<Maybe. But listen, Lalah Sune. What can we do about it? We're supposed to be enemies!>

<I don't know. I just know I'm supposed to be the pilot of this mobile armor. I'm the first pilot in our Newtype Combat Unit, but I can't believe this is my only mission in life. Meeting you has convinced me. But that said, I'm . . .>

<I get it.>

Amuro had a powerful, sudden insight. Newtypes might be real after all. And it just might be possible, as he and Sayla Mass had once discussed, that people *could* learn to communicate on a new level. It was an incredible idea, but perhaps hundreds, thousands, even millions of different levels of awareness *could* overlap, and perhaps mankind *could* one day finally leave its prejudices behind and achieve a universal wisdom.

Amuro had to believe in the idea. He had no other way of comprehending the thoughts flowing back and forth between him and Lalah Sune. But he answered based on an objective reality.

<I hope you're right!>

Lalah sensed his meaning and the implications of what failure would mean, and fell deeper into despair.

Amuro, for his part, realized that he just might have a spark of Newtype insight within him, pointing the way toward his own destiny.

<Amuro! It's too cruel. Amuro! You've got to stop me!>

<What?!>

He didn't understand. He saw her emerald green eyes, her tawny skin that seemed to melt into the surrounding darkness, her long, supple limbs, and her beautiful hair. She appeared to waver and then tried to smash through the glass barrier that separated them. He was taken aback by her abrupt change in behavior, and completely at a loss how to respond.

Then a door opened behind Lalah, and through the light it let in, Amuro made out the shadow of a quickly moving man. A sound like static violently intruded on his and Lalah's thought communication. There was a perceptual spark, and then a fragmentary interruption by a third thought form overlaid on his and Lalah's. It was not words. It was a ruptured type of noise, and it assumed an aura of hate.

The man was wearing a red-colored military uniform with a platinum-colored helmet and face mask, and he appeared to be an officer of the Zeon forces. A cape fluttered from his back. It was Commander Char Aznable, a.k.a. Casval Rem Deikun, of the Zeon forces.

"*So this is the Red Comet!*" thought Amuro to himself.

WHEN CHAR SPOKE, THE words were real. "Lalah!" he curtly ordered. "Get out of here! *Now!!*"

"B . . . but Commander," she started to say, as if afraid.

The interruption resulted in confusion in all three's consciousness, but the confusion was soon transformed to an instinct common to all mammals—a fighting instinct.

Through the windows of the Control Core, Char saw the object of Lalah's attention—a young Federation pilot dangling out of the cockpit hatch of a Gundam MS. Lalah, glancing at Char, was unable to hide her panic. She saw in him a lovable quality to which she was powerfully attracted, but she also saw emerging in him one of man's most despicable traits. She knew that that combination, in this situation, would be a disaster for her.

Amuro, for his part, mournfully watched the couple in the Control Core. Too young and inexperienced to understand all the ways of men and women, he watched Lalah tremble and thought: *So that's what she meant about being too late.*

As Amuro watched, the red-uniformed Zeon officer floated across the room and out the door with Lalah in his arms. The door slammed shut, and the Control Core command center was again deserted.

AMURO INSTINCTIVELY CRAVED MORE contact with this mysterious female, Lalah Sune, but he had just seen what seemed to be incontrovertible evidence of her physical love for his archenemy. A thought suddenly ran through his brain in a way he himself didn't fully understand. It was more than a sixth sense; it was subtle proof that he was developing an expanded awareness and power of insight. It said, <Time to scram!>. He was in real danger.

Quickly shutting the Gundam hatch, he checked his beam rifle. It was low on energy, so he maneuvered the MS to pick up the bazooka left behind by the Zaku he had earlier dispatched. It still had three rockets left in it. Then he moved over toward the colony port exit, where the Gundam's instruments detected the *Pegasus* and its two accompanying cruisers nearby in space. Even the Guncannons were close enough to be identified. Amuro should have felt overjoyed, but he couldn't suppress a basic animal instinct welling up inside him. "Lalah Sune . . . " he whispered. He wanted to see her close up. He wanted to touch her. He wanted her. His perception of danger was already beginning to fade, and he had no way of knowing what kind of enemy was really lying in wait inside *Texas*.

When encountering a member of the opposite sex with whom one has a powerful, intuitive understanding, physical desire can sometimes be masked. But when the actual thought waves of both individuals are almost perfectly entertwined, the encounter can be a powerful aphrodisiac. Amuro was far too young to understand what was happening to him, or to restrain himself. Instead of launching into space toward the *Pegasus*, he spun the Gundam around and walked toward the series of hatches at the other end of the colony port. Opening them one by one, he stepped through the last door that led inside *Texas*.

It was impossible to see the inner surface of the colony from the final hatch. Giant external mirrors normally reflected sunlight inside the colony, but their automatic control mechanism was broken, and for the last few months they had been stuck on something equivalent to dawn or dusk. Atmospheric conditions inside the colony had deteriorated into violent wind storms, with sand-colored tornadoes often occurring around the colony's central axis.

Keeping his eyes on the Gundam's main monitor, Amuro watched a small whirlwind form next to him and twist through the air. Wondering where Lalah might be in the 360-degree panorama in front of him, he tried to rely on his intuition. He closed his eyes and tried to focus his mind, to no avail. It was frustrating. Only a few minutes ago he had been so close to her that he could almost have physically called out to her. He asked himself: *What to do?*

The next instant, he barely dodged an incoming bazooka rocket. But a fraction of a second before it burst next to him with a leaden *whomp!* he put the Gundam into a jump maneuver toward the direction of its origin, somewhere above to his right. He soared to an elevation of nearly five hundred meters off the colony floor, right through the middle of a brown twister cloud. There were fierce winds blowing throughout the colony but luckily a true greenhouse effect had not occurred; without the cooling effect of the external walls the place would have been an inferno.

As Amuro made a rapid descent into a corner of the *Texas* colony, for the first time he saw the grand scale of the place. Although he had spent the first few years of his life on Earth, his father, a construction engineer, had taken him into outer space almost as soon as he could remember, and he had only returned to Earth three times after that, always to visit his mother. He was only familiar with the gentle mountains and temperate climate of her home and had never experienced anything like the wild environment of *Texas*.

The people who designed *Texas* had done their best to represent nature in all her glory, and paid special attention to visual effects. Rivers and streams wound through steep canyons that appeared to have been carved by ancient glaciers; forests of evergreens spread on the foothills. The environment was totally artificial, but the scenery was more than enough to evoke images of the ancient reality on which it had been modeled. Although the plains were now desert, tourists had once delighted in the sight of hundreds of cattle herded by cowboys, imagined campfire smoke in the distance to be signals from Indians, crossed the colony's glass sections on giant bridges made to look like natural rock formations, and experienced a simulation of the Wild West on Earth's North American continent.

THE GUNDAM MS DROPPED out of a dust-cloud on the verge of forming a vortex and sailed into a roaring wind. With his attention diverted by the scenery unfolding before him, Amuro nearly made a fatal mistake. But as before in the colony port area, a cool light-like sensation seemed to bore into his forehead. His awareness expanded to 360-degrees, and he sensed a specific direction, just in the nick of time to dodge another incoming enemy round.

"Where are you?" Amuro muttered, scanning the area around him. He knew it might be overconfidence, but he somehow felt he was better positioned to deal with the enemy—even if it were Char Aznable, the Red Comet—than the enemy was to deal with him.

"Where are you?" he growled again, frustrated by the fact that his new awareness couldn't help him pinpoint a distant target. Perhaps, he thought, it was because of the turbid atmospheric conditions. But unknown to Amuro, Char Aznable was already retreating with Lalah Sune to the port on the opposite end of the colony cylinder, where the *Zanzibar* was anchored.

EARLIER, INSIDE THE COLONY, Dr. Flanagan and his team of assistants had performed the first successful feasibility tests of the Elmeth-Bits mobile armor system with Lalah. The Bits, equipped with beam-cannon and explosive charges, were operated remotely and made to attack when her willpower was channeled and amplified through the psycommu interface. From the cockpit of the Elmeth, without using its own beam cannon, she had simultaneously mobilized and fired the cannon on eight out of ten Bits, effectively destroying the test targets. It was after completing this test that she had wandered on her own to the Control Core of the colony's other port and encountered Amuro. When Char took her away from the Control Core, he had put her under the care of the Flanagan team in the mobile trailer used to launch the Elmeth-Bits system, and immediately moved to attack the infiltrator MS—Amuro and the Gundam.

Char's mood had plunged to near despair.

The pilot's a Newtype. He may not be as advanced as Lalah, but there's no other way to explain the way he parries my attacks.

His worst fear on first encountering the white enemy MS—that there were Newtypes among the Federation pilots—had been born out. He knew mankind might be in the midst of a transition, even a new type of evolution, but it was wartime. If there were to be a genesis of Newtypes, the real question was, When would the fetus begin quickening, and what kind of labor pains would result? He himself might have Newtype potential. He was at least capable of one form of insight that the older, conservative, earthbound generations were not; he was able to recognize a true Newtype when he saw one. And this time he had to believe his opponent was one. After all, a terrified young Federation recruit had named him, Char, the "Red Comet." If he weren't up against a true Newtype, he felt as though his pride would crumble simply from the shame of failing to beat his opponent.

Damn! he thought. Making his way in his MS through the colony's evergreen belt, he checked all monitors for any sign of the enemy. After parrying Char's second barrage, the white MS had looked as if it would make a steep descent and come in for a hard landing on the colony floor. But the pilot might have anticipated his movement.

Char began to doubt himself. Had he ordered too high a concentration of Minovsky particles scattered in the area for Lalah's test earlier? The scan lines on his MS radar display had turned to static.

THE BEGINNING

AFTER ORDERING THE TWO cruisers, *Cisco* and *Saphron*, to stand by outside, Lt. (j.g.) Bright moved the *Pegasus* inside the *Texas* colony port. The four layers of giant air lock doors in the port were all operational, and the second and third already open. When the fourth and final hatch opened, the *Pegasus* passed through into the murky twilight of the colony's inner environment and was immediately enveloped in a cloud of swirling sand.

"SAYLA!" BRIGHT YELLED. "DETECT any signal from Amuro's Gundam yet?!"

"No, not a thing," she replied, haltingly. "There's . . . there's an extremely high Minovsky level in here, sir."

She looked pale. Turning around, she slowly stood up and asked, "Could someone spell me?"

As far as Bright could tell, she wasn't faking it. She looked bad. "Vammas!" he ordered a petty officer on the bridge. "Relieve Sayla. And I want Ensign Kai to take over from Hayato in the Guncannon and to launch a search for the Gundam immediately. Get Hayato up here on the bridge with me." Hayato had escaped punishment for his earlier escapade only by virtue of successfully downing two Zeon cruisers, but Bright wasn't anxious to turn him loose again.

"Do you think we're safe anchored here, skipper?" Mirai queried, still manning the helm. "It might be dangerous. There's no way to tell what's going on at the port on the other end of the colony cylinder."

"Hmm . . . maybe you're right." Bright found himself agreeing with her once again.

"Lift off!!" cried Mirai.

"*Mirai?*" Bright was so stunned by the way she had unilaterally initiated the order that he forgot to countermand her and just stared. She was right, though. If any enemy forces were at the colony's other port, they would be directly opposite the *Pegasus* in the cylinder; firing straight down the colony cylinder would be like shooting fish in a barrel.

"Hmm . . . I wonder if we should . . . ?" he wondered out loud.

"It's worth it, skipper," Mirai replied instantly. Bright didn't have to complete the sentence. She knew exactly what he was thinking.

He turned and barked: "Prepare a barrage of Model Six missiles in the fore section! Fire when ready!!"

The *Pegasus* moved out of the core of the port area, and began descending to the colony's outer walls, firing groups of twelve missiles at three-second intervals. With a diameter of two hundred meters, the port on the opposite end of the cylinder was hard not to hit, and sure enough, the atmosphere inside the colony soon reverberated with the sound of explosions and torn metal.

MIRAI AND BRIGHT WERE right; a Zeon ship, the *Zanzibar*, had been moored directly opposite them. But they had no way of knowing that two layers of hatches saved it from final destruction, or that firing one more volley of missiles would have done the job.

On the bridge of the *Zanzibar*, Captain Burman immediately ordered his four Zakus to go into action inside the colony and resolved to follow them with his ship. If the enemy forces were merely remnants of the Federation fleet encountered by Captain M'quve earlier, he was convinced he could destroy them with his Zakus. M'quve, as far as he was concerned, was a rank amateur when it came to fleet battles.

His own ship, the *Zanzibar*, was no ordinary warship, but a state-of-the-art Mobile Cruiser equipped with four regular Zakus piloted by combat veterans. If he had to, he could rely on Char's Red Comet, and if worst came to worst there was even the new Elmeth-Bits system. Its true capability was untested, but he was sure at the very least it could outperform the Federation's mass-produced tanks in the colony.

INSIDE THE *PEGASUS*, SAYLA began running down a corridor, seized by an

Sayla Mass

overpowering, growing feeling that if she moved fast, she might somehow
be able to contact her brother, Casval. She knew it was now or never.

Normally she never suffered from headaches, but she had a fierce
one now. Pressing her palm against her head, she tried to restrain the
growing pain, and just when it seemed to hurt so much she felt nauseous,
the *Pegasus* rocked. She stumbled, cried out, and fell. Picking herself up
and resuming running, she wondered if the ship had touched down on
the colony floor or been hit by enemy fire. She ducked into an air lock
and started to don a normal suit. The door from there led into a hanger
where she knew there was a dune buggy. *I just hope the ship's actually
landed,* she thought between stabs of pain as she struggled to put on the
suit. She had only experienced two trial ground landings before. Cursing
her poor coordination and bad memory, she used her now-gloved hands
to pull her sweat-soaked locks away from her face.

With the *Pegasus* still hovering forward around five meters off the
ground, Sayla punched the accelerator on the dune buggy and flew out
of the *Pegasus* hatch, hit the ground and bounced, kicking up a cloud
of sand. If she hadn't been wearing a normal suit she would have been
rendered unconscious by the shock. Luckily, the colony had enough atmosphere left to breathe, but she still had to keep her helmet visor down

to keep the dust out of her eyes. Somehow, she knew which direction to go.

CHAR, MEANWHILE, SENSED DANGER approaching and felt a shiver run up his spine. If the white Federation MS was about to emerge from the evergreen forest to his right, he wasn't sure if he could stop it. He was a realist, and he knew his limits. He never hesitated to confront an enemy when he had to, but he never let his ego get in the way when prudence called for a retreat; he knew he could figure out a way to come back and destroy him later. But the opponent he now faced was different. It wouldn't let him get away. It had become too powerful.

Then, to his astonishment, he heard the missiles explode in the port where the *Zanzibar* was moored. He refused to believe that an enemy warship had infiltrated the colony, but there were too many blasts to have come from a mobile suit. *Besides,* he thought, *the pilot of the white MS wouldn't waste its ammo like that. He's too smart.* In his mind the white MS would act like a lion obsessively stalking a lone rabbit. It would train its sights on him—Char—first, even if it knew the *Zanzibar* was in the colony. Yes, that was the way a true opponent would surely act, especially if he were a Newtype. Char had great faith in his ability to out-think his opponents.

LALAH SUNE WAS RIDING with Dr. Flanagan in the cab of the mobile trailer carrying the Elmeth-Bits system when the Federation missiles exploded. Turning to him, she suddenly pleaded: "Doctor! Stop! We don't have a minute to lose! Let me take off in the Elmeth and attack the enemy!"

"What are you talking about? You know it hasn't been perfected yet!!"

"It doesn't matter! The enemy in here's too powerful! We can't afford to lose a single mobile armor machine, and if we don't do something we might even lose the *Zanzibar*!"

Her last words made Flanagan tremble. If the *Zanzibar* were destroyed, they might be stranded on *Texas*, and that was a thought he couldn't bear. "Well . . . " he said, hesitating, "I . . . I did adjust the psycommu in the test earlier. I guess we've no choice, have we? But you've got to wear your normal suit." Flanagan was, after all, a scientist, and when he had to, he could rationalize anything.

Ignoring him, Lalah jumped down from the cab of the trailer and, without bothering to don her normal suit, climbed into the Elmeth cockpit. The Elmeth had two mega particle cannons and fin-like protrusions on both sides and the top and bottom which acted as antennae, projecting her amplified consciousness from the psycommu interface.

From the front it looked like a trifurcated projectile, but because the fuselage contained a disproportionately large and powerful engine, from the side it had a silhouette rather like that of a yellow-crested cockatoo. Using the psycommu interface Lalah could operate the engine by will, and she could also remotely control up to ten armed Bits—miniature flying orbs—that normally flew behind the Elmeth.

The four Zeon pilots dispatched from the *Zanzibar* performed low altitude jumps in their Zakus, moving toward the colony port where the Federation forces were believed to have infiltrated.

Amuro, crouching low in the forest with his Gundam, let them go by. Char, he deduced, would expect him to attack them. Then a vague sensation flared in a corner of his brain. It seemed to indicate a direction, and he gambled on it. A few heartbeats after the Zakus passed by, he ignited the Gundam's backpack jets and jumped. As he rose into the air his field of vision automatically expanded, and on the other side of a river he spotted a different Zaku turning away from him. There was a cloud of sand between them but he could tell the Zaku was red. His hunch had been right. Fearing he was too late, he fired. The beam from the Gundam's rifle streaked straight toward the red Zaku, particles from it scorching the earth below and then whooshing into a ball of flame.

"Wha?!" Amuro gasped. The Zaku's right leg was gone, severed below the knee, but, incredibly, it still managed to soar like a red comet into the air just in the nick of time. Amuro shuddered. Even as his own powers of perception seemed to be increasing, Char's ability to avoid his attacks seemed to be increasing, too. *Maybe General Revil was right*, Amuro thought. *Maybe Char really* was *a Newtype.*

Unfortunately for Amuro, he didn't see Char put a spin on his Zaku in midair; he barely had time to maneuver his shield into position, when he saw a bazooka blast, and then—*wham!*—it was blown to smithereens.

"Whoa!" he yelled, as the Gundam fuselage shook violently and the immense force of multiple *g*'s bore down on him. Somehow managing to keep his eyes wide open, he fired a blast from the Vulcan cannon in the Gundam's head as a feint and increased the power in the backpack jets. He knew he had to get above the Zaku. To attack, to even threaten an enemy required gaining some tactical advantage. No matter how weightless an environment, it was still important to get above the upper limit of the enemy's field of vision.

The Gundam still had a lot more power than any Zaku, perhaps, but to Amuro's distress it now had nowhere near the amount he wanted. Losing faith in his machine, he thought, *I'm a goner.*

UNBEKNOWNST TO AMURO, CHAR was feeling exactly the same way.

"Damn!" he cursed, as he made his Zaku utilize the force of the blast to soar into the air. "This MS's no match in power for the white Suit...." He was climbing four times faster than he normally would have, but it still wasn't enough. The enemy MS rose toward him fast enough to pass him and launched another attack. Within seconds the shield on the Zaku's left shoulder had been blown away, and if Char hadn't had his safety harness on, and if there hadn't been an air bag in his cockpit, the shock would have snapped his spine in two. Then a whirlwind enveloped the battling Suits, and both pilots took evasive action.

"Only two rounds left?!" Char checked his magazine indicator, and gnashed his teeth in frustration. If only his Zaku had a beam rifle.

NOT FAR AWAY, SAYLA gripped the wheel of her dune buggy even tighter and cursed her brother. If his goal was to avenge their father's death, what good would it possibly do him to die in this worthless, out of the way *Texas* colony? She kicked herself for not having spoken more frankly to him when they had met accidentally on Side 7, for not having tried to steer him away from his crazy obsession. Neither she nor Casval could know what their father really would have thought, but given his idealistic view of the world, she was absolutely certain revenge wasn't part of it. "Casval," she lamented, "can't you join the real world?"

In the distance she saw flashes of light. Slamming the buggy accelerator to the floor, she steered toward them.

WHEN THE FOUR ZEON Zakus finally closed in on the *Pegasus* at the other end of the colony, Kai turned his Guncannon around, and abandoned his search for Amuro and the Gundam. He didn't know if Amuro was still alive or not, but he knew what he had to do—defend his mother ship.

Fighting inside a cylinder only three kilometers in diameter is no ordinary feat, and neither the Zaku pilots nor Kai could maneuver their machines with anywhere near the skill of Char or Amuro. They were used to the vastness of space, but now sand and dust obscured their field of vision, and gravity forced them to adopt what amounted to old Earth-style hand-to-hand combat techniques. The Zaku pilots, maneuvering on the ground, couldn't just slip in to attack the *Pegasus*'s underbelly. Nor, for that matter, could the *Pegasus* easily repel the Zakus. Missiles and shells fired by both parties missed their mark and wreaked havoc on the colony's artificial ground cover.

When the Federation forces stationed outside the colony learned of the assault on the *Pegasus* they immediately sent in reinforcements, but the colony environment exacted a toll on them, too. Two of three *Public* attack ships promptly became disoriented in the dust clouds and smashed into the colony's earthen floor. Similarly, when a GM Suit followed the ships into the colony, it crashed into a Zaku, and both machines vanished in a swirl of dust.

In the midst of all this, Kai spotted a flare from a Zaku bazooka and immediately put his Guncannon into a two-hundred-meter jump, swinging behind the enemy just as he was about to pump another round into the *Pegasus*. Kai knew it was a gamble—under normal conditions a Zaku would have easily anticipated his move—but he went ahead anyway. Poor visibility affected them both equally, and he might as well put it to work for his own advantage.

His tactic worked. Two shells from the Guncannon scored a direct hit on the Zaku, instantly pulverizing its upper torso. Miraculously, the engine didn't blow; since the *Pegasus* was maneuvering only five hundred meters above, a nuclear fusion blast might have mortally wounded her. Flush with success, Kai moved on to his next quarry.

BURMAN, THE SKIPPER OF the *Zanzibar*, was far less lucky. Twenty kilometers ahead, he saw flashes of defensive fire put up by the *Pegasus*, and when the clouds of sand parted he suddenly spotted the ship itself. He unleashed a barrage of mega particle beams from all four front cannon and scored direct hits on the *Pegasus*'s port and starboard foredecks, causing the ship to shudder violently. But then Burman made a fatal mistake. Instead of firing more blasts to polish off the enemy, he waited for another break in visibility and thus gave Bright the opportunity he needed. Bright ordered all his surviving guns fired in the direction of the flashes. In a showdown between a brash youth and a cautious veteran, youth won out. Two particle beams, along with three volleys from the main cannon and three missiles, streaked forth from the *Pegasus* and smashed directly into the *Zanzibar*.

Both ships were heavily damaged, and—needless to say in a colony three kilometers in diameter—there was no room for either to take evasive action or make an easy escape. Although holes had been blown in the colony walls, none were yet large enough for an entire warship to slip through.

IN THE ELMETH, THE instant Lalah Sune saw the *Zanzibar* burst into flames she knew her commander was in mortal danger. She had no way of knowing for sure, but she surmised the Gundam had jumped into a trap Char had laid and proven more difficult to handle than anticipated.

In her mind an awareness of two people appeared and became entangled; the thoughts of one, Amuro, turned directly into a white light and began to destroy the other—Char. Shuddering, she recalled her shock and sadness on meeting the young Amuro earlier. She knew he might be a Newtype, too, and she was seized by a sudden desire to abandon the Elmeth. *Why couldn't I have met him earlier?* she lamented, but it was too late. Her consciousness was already linked to the psycommu interface, and while her confusion might prevent her from properly controlling the remotely operated Bits, she was the pilot of the Elmeth and, as such, already an integral part of a highly sophisticated weapons system.

The surviving Federation *Public* attack ship spotted the Elmeth through the sand clouds, approached, and unleashed four missiles. Horrified, Lalah automatically began evasive action in her Elmeth and concentrated her thoughts on the missiles. The danger level she sensed automatically triggered subconscious self-preservation instincts and further stimulated her latent powers of perception. Waves emitted from her brain were sensed by the psycommu interface and amplified. When this neural information was transmitted to the remote Bits carried on the Elmeth, they went into action.

BRAIN WAVES ARE ESSENTIALLY electrical signals, and Dr. Flanagan had developed a computer-based system that converted them into pulse signals for amplification. But from his research into people with paranormal abilities, he knew that human consciousness was comprised of far more than electricity, and that it included other waveforms such as the Psycho Wave. Using new bio-computer technology, he therefore succeeded in creating a device—called a psycho-communicator, or *psycommu*, that could interface with a brain-wave amplification apparatus. As it turned out, the total system failed to function properly with human operators of average paranormal abilities, and worked only with those who possessed unique, expanded powers of insight or intuition.

Early experiments proved problematic for Dr. Flanagan and his assistants. They demonstrated the existence of mysterious different "types" of humans and the wide range of their abilities. But categorizing these abilities proved infinitely more difficult than first anticipated. Clearly, the psycommu interface worked best with subjects who had enhanced powers of intuition—with the so-called Newtypes—but that only led to the question of how to define, or for that matter how to even find, Newtypes. There was no guarantee of identifying them in any great number among the truly gifted members of society—the geniuses in the arts and sciences. Nor were average persons with superior intuition always Newtypes. Newtypes sometimes even existed among extremely ordinary, conventional people with a rigid sense of self and relatively little heightened awareness.

Lalah Sune was herself a case in point, as the Flanagan team realized from the moment she joined the project as a subject. She had no higher education to speak of. Nor was her I.Q. particularly outstanding. But her ability to activate the psycommu interface was so unusual that they could scarcely believe their own data.

What, they then began to wonder, was a true Newtype? Unable to come up with a single, concrete definition, they were forced to conclude merely that Newtype subjects were characterized mainly by a power of insight greater than anything ever before recorded in research on human consciousness. Newtypes were different from ordinary geniuses or the highly gifted, and different from people with already identified extrasensory powers, such as telepathy, prescience, psychic photography, teleportation, or even channeling. Newtypes were also capable of simultaneously addressing multiple problems and of projecting their thoughts externally.

Dr. Flanagan's greatest scientific achievement came when he realized that the Newtype concept symbolized not just a unique, individual ability, but a positive transformation that all mankind could potentially achieve. This was an idea with universal appeal, but in Zeon it especially caught the attention of Kycilia Zabi, who immediately realized that the psycommu interface could be utilized for military ends and therefore banned any public mention of the Newtype concept. Human nature being what it is, however, people tiring of the war nonetheless began to whisper in wishful terms about a Newtype transformation of all mankind. In reality, of course, nothing had changed at all yet.

YET NOW, ON *TEXAS*, a young woman—a true Newtype—was going into action. Controlling four Bit modules from the cockpit of her Elmeth mobile armor, she destroyed each individual incoming missile, as well as the *Public* attack ship that had launched them. It was more than just a demonstration of Newtype potential. It was a terrifying testimony to the abilities of the developers of the Elmeth-Bits military machine—the scientists of the Flanagan Institute and the weapons experts under Kycilia's command. Lalah had simply sighted the incoming missiles and their mother ship, and willed an attack on them from her Elmeth. The mega particle cannons in each Bit—a six meter diameter machine composed primarily of a small nuclear fusion engine—had automatically trained their sights on the targets, and destroyed them all.

Perhaps because thought waves flowed in reverse from the Elmeth's psycommu interface, the action also served to heighten Lalah's awareness. Through the psycommu she became aware of the presence of Amuro and Char in the area, and of something terrifying. Something screaming, symbolizing man's basic fighting instinct, rushed toward her like a dark wall of water. There were no audible words, nor describable sounds, but she knew what it represented. It was the yells of two men locked in mortal combat, the war cries of two independent conscious beings merging in screams, anger, and fear.

Lalah was no stranger to the horrors of war, yet she was horrified. In the past, when two Federation warships had raked the colony she lived on, she had trembled in fear of her own death, only to experience true horror and despair on learning that her parents, from whom she had become separated, had been killed. But these were memories, and something experienced on the periphery of battle. She had imagined before what it would be like for two people to deliberately try to kill each other in combat, but the reality of what she now faced was far more frightening. A torrent of conscious thoughts rushed toward her, thoughts trying mightily to dispel fear of death, trying at all costs to avoid being killed. They seemed like a maelstrom; a dark, foreboding image like that of ancient Japanese Hell scrolls, of two demons locked in mortal combat, devouring each other's flesh.

She glanced out her cockpit window and beheld a Federation Gundam MS and a Zeon Zaku, with weapons, clashing. The Gundam's beam saber slashed, and the Zaku's heataxe seared the air. The Zaku was clearly outclassed.

Lalah screamed, "Commander!" But then she sensed yet another thought emerging from the two men's blurred consciousness. It was sharp, and clear, like a bright, beautiful light; something that could only involve skill or art. How ironic, she thought, that killing could only be perfected by something so beautiful! From the terror of two men trying to slice each other in two came a force that penetrated right through her. With a sense of sadness tinged with despair, she realized that it was in fact the very same mental quality required to vanquish an enemy in combat.

IT OCCURRED TO CHAR that he had made an unforgivable error, trying to be a Newtype when he wasn't one. He cursed his carelessness, but had no time to dwell on it, for the Gundam never gave him a chance.

Victory in combat can only be assured by taking advantage of every possible opportunity. History at the very least teaches us that the best warriors never leave victory up to their own fighting spirit, or to mere chance. When outclassed by an opponent, an appropriate strategy is all the more essential. Only in comic books are battles determined by brute strength alone.

I should never have let this business about the Red Comet go to my head, Char thought. The Gundam's beam saber had him completely on the defensive, but he wasn't ready to concede victory yet. "You may be a Newtype," he screamed in the direction of the Gundam pilot, "but you don't have a psycommu interface . . . "

The Gundam, he realized, was without doubt a mechanical marvel, but therein also lay its biggest weakness. There was no evidence that the Federation had developed an MS with anything like a psycommu interface. While parrying yet another blow of the Gundam's beam saber, Char swung his heataxe at the enemy's extended right arm.

AMURO SWORE. THE GUNDAM'S drive system was already at breaking point, but it worked well enough to avoid the Zaku's thrust one more time. Leaning his machine forward and to the side, Amuro brought the MS's right leg up in a kick to the Zaku's right wrist, and sent the heataxe flying into the sand. And then he heard what sounded like a moan or gasp. It didn't come from Char. It was a sensation that surged through his brain, from his frontal lobes to the rear, creating an almost audible <S-t-o-p> and forcing him to rivet his attention to it.

A thud brought Amuro back to a more immediate reality. Much to his horror, the Zaku had crashed into the Gundam, and the laser burners in its left fingers were already burning deep into his Suit's back pack. Cursing, he countered by smashing the Zaku's mono-eye with the Gundam's left hand, and then using the right, which was holding the beam saber, to try to slash down through the base of the Zaku's neck in a diagonal trajectory.

AS THE GUNDAM'S BEAM saber zapped and flickered, sparks showered on Char's head inside the Zaku cockpit from severed coils and circuitry. He cursed in frustration. Then, while marveling at the performance of the enemy weapon, he quickly activated his auxiliary camera-eye, and with the laser burners in the Zaku's left fingers took aim at the Gundam's "eyes" and fired. With a *whoosh,* the blast made a hole between the Gundam's eyes and nose. Next Char took aim at his opponent's neck. If he could, he wanted to fire a direct laser blast into the MS torso. But then the Gundam's right hand pulled out the beam saber and tried to thrust it through the Zaku's left side.

Char yelled in surprise. His Zaku's left arm was no longer usable. And then he heard something that shouldn't have been physically possible; he heard Lalah scream, "Commander!"

Frantic at the plight of her superior, Lalah's thoughts had turned in wrath on the Gundam, thereby activating and sending the eight remote control Bits on the attack. But Amuro, in the Gundam, had already sensed the presence of another enemy. Disengaging from the Zaku, he ignited the Gundam's verniers and jumped high into the dust-clouds, thus completely avoiding the beam blasts directed at him from the Bits.

Lalah shuddered in terror. The Elmeth-Bits combination was supposed to have been invincible, yet the Gundam had easily out-maneuvered her.

MEANWHILE, THE *PEGASUS* AND the *Zanzibar* were about to cross paths in the middle of the colony cylinder. Although few direct hits had been scored, barrages of fire had heavily damaged both warships, and the intense explosions had created enormous cracks here and there in the colony walls. On the *Pegasus*, Lt. (jg) Bright and Ensign Mirai had decided that for their final gamble they would try to cut the enemy off inside the colony. Outside the cylinder, the *Pegasus's* consort ships, the *Saphron* and the *Cisco*, trained their beam-cannons through the largest holes in the colony walls and waited.

Because both *Pegasus* and *Zanzibar* were in such close proximity, Bright knew his opponent would either try to knock his ship out with a single blow or try to increase speed and avoid him. To preempt either action, he immediately tried to destroy the *Zanzibar* bridge. The more rounded *Zanzibar* was better armored than the complex *Pegasus*, but it nonetheless had its weak spots.

First, to avoid crashing into the enemy ship, Mirai steered the *Pegasus* so low it nearly creased the colony floor, and then she brought the *Pegasus's* foredeck main cannon level with the *Zanzibar's* bridge. When fired, the cannon blast smashed straight through it. Crippled, the ship crashed into the colony's central "mountain," and then rebounded, floating back in the opposite direction.

Firing retrorockets, Mirai braked the *Pegasus* and narrowly steered her through the five-hundred-meter space between the drifting *Zanzibar* and the colony floor. Then she swung the prow of her ship toward the *Zanzibar's* aft mega particle cannon. Ensign Hayato, waiting on the bridge for this very instant, directed a blast that smashed the Zeon ship's remaining cannon, leaving it a drifting metal hulk with only a few remaining operational missile launch tubes and ship guns.

Bright flashed a "V" sign at Mirai and called out, "Good work!" But just then the *Zanzibar* fired her main engines and the force of the exhaust struck the *Pegasus's* starboard prow, driving her skidding into the colony floor. The *Zanzibar* sliced through a cloud of dust on the parched plain, crashed again into the central mountain, and came to a halt. The entire colony shuddered as if an earthquake had struck.

As PETTY OFFICER 2ND Class Sayla Mass raced across the Texas plain in search of her brother, she saw the flash from the firing of the *Zanzibar's* main engines, but she couldn't feel the tremor that followed; her dune buggy was bouncing too wildly.

And then she finally located her brother's red Zaku. It had made an emergency landing and appeared heavily damaged, but the hatch opened and out slid a red-suited young pilot in a platinum-colored helmet with the visor up, revealing an unforgettable face mask. Hitting the ground, he knelt and hunched over and appeared to be coughing, but on second glance Sayla realized he was readying an oxygen tank. She checked the air pressure gauge on her own normal suit and saw to her horror that it had dropped dramatically. Too many holes had been blasted in the colony walls.

Jumping out of her dune buggy and switching on the voice channel in her normal suit, she cried out. "Casval! It's me, Artesia!"

The red-suited pilot looked up in surprise and reached for his side-arm, but then, as recognition sunk in, he yelled, "Artesia! What in the world are you . . . ?!" There was no point in completing the sentence.

"Casval!" Sayla cried. "Listen, what good is it going to do you to fight on Zeon's side? Why can't you just forget about avenging father for once?!"

"Artesia . . . You've got it all wrong. Times have changed, and I didn't just join the military for revenge . . . But this is no time or place to argue. We've got to get out of here!"

"Can't you return to the Federation?"

"Return to the Federation?! Are you crazy? I'm Char Aznable now, a commander in the Zeon forces! And I'm in love with a woman in the force. Her name's Lalah Sune."

"Well, can't you at least leave the Zeon military?!"

"There's no guarantee either of us'll get out of here alive, Artesia, but the answer's no."

"Why?"

"Because we've finally proved Newtypes exist, and there's so much to be done as a result . . . "

"Proved Newtypes exist?"

"That's right. You know how people always said Father was a prophet of the first Newtypes? Well, you're his daughter, so you ought to be able to sense it—there are two Newtypes here in this colony, right now . . . "

"Are you talking about Amuro, Casval?"

Even as she spoke, Sayla wondered if some Newtype potential might not be stirring in herself. Otherwise, she didn't see how she could possibly have made it safely this far.

"The Gundam pilot? Probably so . . . " Then, fastening the air tank to his belt, and putting on his oxygen mask, he asked in a muffled voice: "Artesia. Are you coming with me, or not?"

"To . . . to Zeon?" Her voice revealed her scorn.

"If not, sister, be a good girl and quit the Federation Forces. And don't ever show your face in front of me in uniform again! The military's not for you. "

"Casval . . . "

It was too late. He had already jumped in her dune buggy. Roaring off into a billowing cloud of dust, he yelled, "You've got to go back, Artesia! I'm sure a Federation ship'll pick you up . . . "

"Casval, wait!" she yelled. Ever since she was old enough to remember, it seemed she had yelled the same thing after her brother. And he had always left her behind.

STANDING ALONE BESIDE HER brother's abandoned red Zaku, Sayla felt a tingling sensation inside her head. It wasn't a result of meeting him again. It wasn't pain. But it was nonetheless a physical sensation, and it pervaded her entire brain. She looked up at the sky. The voice channel inside her normal suit activated and, amidst the static, she heard the order, "*All hands abandon ship!*" It was the *Pegasus*. The ship had finally been dealt a mortal blow.

MEANWHILE, LALAH SUNE HAD entered maximum combat mode. The remotely controlled Bit units, oblivious to any and all obstacles, began to randomly attack the Gundam. One self-destructed on the MS's left leg and partly pulverized it.

Even strapped in his seat, Amuro's body was being tossed around. His collarbone felt as though it would snap and he groaned in pain, but he remained aware enough to sense the remaining seven Bits streaming toward him from Lalah's Elmeth.

He saw no physical trail but rather the stream of consciousness that connected the Bits and Lalah. It was like a trace of light reflected through his own brain. He knew they were coming, and he knew this time he had to wait. One more high-speed, high-*g* dodge would destroy the Gundam's already overloaded power train. He would have to gauge the angle of attack from the trace of lights he sensed, and try to blow the Bits out of the air. *Here goes nothing,* he thought, knowing it was a gamble.

A narrow beam of light flashed out of the Gundam's rifle and miraculously knocked one Bit out of the air. Normally, concentrating so hard on one target would have left Amuro blind to another's movement, but when the other Bits attacked this time it didn't happen. Just as his awareness of the first trace seemed to peak, he sensed others headed toward the Gundam's other leg and its back. Infused with new self-confidence because of his growing powers of perception, he exulted, *I can do it!*

His attention quickly turned to the mothership controlling the Bits. He had no way of knowing about the psycommu system, but he knew it was theoretically impossible to use radio-controlled weaponry in an area where there was such a high level of Minovsky particles, that somehow the attacks were originating from the mother ship. It could present him with an opportunity.

The Gundam creaked badly but still managed to evade the other six attacking Bits. Amuro destroyed one, and while his MS swayed from the aftershock the Elmeth mother ship fired a blast from its mega particle cannon. And this time a clear thought pierced Amuro's brain like an exclamation mark; it was born of a hatred so intense it revealed to him the beam's angle of impact before he could even see it. He easily evaded the attack.

Why?! he thought. It was a double-edged query. Why, he thought angrily, was he being attacked like this? And why, thinking of himself, was he able to able to anticipate the angle of attack in advance? He spun the Gundam toward the direction where he sensed the Elmeth was and plunged through a cloud of sand.

As the rounded, flame-shaped Elmeth grew larger and larger on the Gundam's orthoscopic monitor, Amuro saw beyond its physical armor and wiring. He saw an image of grief.

SIMULTANEOUSLY, FROM THE ELMETH, Lalah Sune sensed the same thing in Amuro; she saw the grief that lies opposite hatred on the spectrum of human emotions.

AN IDENTICAL STREAM OF thought linked two physical, flesh and blood forms.

<Lalah! What are you doing here?> Amuro thought.

<Why did you attack. . . .?!> Lalah started to add the word "Char" to her demand but never completed the thought. She liked Char a great deal, was even in love with him. It was a young woman's private, almost secret infatuation, the type tinged with melancholic yearning. Amuro's answer would be too obvious; they were at war.

But now a stream of Lalah's thought was linked with that of Amuro's, and growing, expanding rapidly. When both streams fused completely into one, it seemed they would explode, and soar forever. To her, at least, the experience felt as if it held the potential for the universal trans-formation, even resurrection, that mankind seemed to be yearning for.

Then Amuro remembered the reality of their situation.

<Stop, Lalah! It's not you I'm fighting! Stop!>

<Amuro, I made a mistake! My feelings for Char made me do it! And now it's too late! I can't stop this process!>

<You what?! What do you mean you can't stop?!> A scream from Amuro soared into the ether. <That's crazy! I'm here! Lalah, I'll help you! I'll do anything!>

<Amuro! I love you!>

In the midst of despair, Amuro saw an image of Lalah Sune; her emerald green eyes widened, and the Bodhisattva-like beauty mark in the middle of her brow flared into light.

<Amuro, I see you, too!>

There were no words spoken. Amuro simply knew. His thoughts were hers. Hers were his. They had fused together; a direct line of pure thought flared and soared straight into the heavens. It was perfect; two separate individuals had experienced a perfect empathetic communion.

Amuro and Lalah's fused consciousness ignited, expanded, and journeyed far into space. Before returning to lodge in human form, it presided over a world where chaos and confusion continued to reign and where a drama continued to unfold.

SAYLA MASS MANAGED TO use her normal suit vernier jets and escape through a hole in the colony, eventually alighting safely on the Saphron, waiting outside.

Mirai, with Bright holding her hand, ran full speed toward the Texas colony's port, as did Hayato, leading a group of the surviving crew from the Pegasus. Kai, piloting the Guncannon, destroyed yet another Zaku and then blasted into space.

Char Aznable resumed command of the Zeon fleet, with images of his smiling sister Artesia still in his mind.

OTHER IMAGES AND SENSATIONS fused into one, of Mirai, Bright, and Fraw Bow *buffeted by wind; of the spirits of Lalah's dead father and mother soaring through the heavens, of her mother smiling. . . . Of tears in Lalah's emerald green eyes . . . Of the sound of crying . . . Of the sound of a life force from a woman's womb, crying its lungs out. Whose voice could it be? Mirai? Sayla? Fraw Bow? Matilda Ajan? Who was it? Lalah? No, the Lalah of the fused consciousness could only scream in grief. . . . But somewhere there was an embryonic life, surrounded in warmth, with heart beating . . . A new life. Thump thump thump. A strong, steady pulse. A vital pulse. The sound of life itself—beautiful and all-enriching.*

Lalah and Amuro's fused consciousness flowed out in a wave of light over a panorama of earth. Metamorphosing through the colors of the spectrum, and finally becoming gold, the light passed by the Zeon fleet that had left from the Granada moon base. Passed by the fierce fight that had ensued between it and the defensive wing of General Revil's main fleet. Passed by before it was clear if Revil would get by Solomon and attack Granada directly.

The light, in a torrent, somehow testified to the fact that the Pegasus would survive. The sound of the heartbeat. The symbol of life, of survival.

Amuro and Lalah's fused consciousness sensed beyond. The dark force of the Zabi ruling family . . . flowing into and disappearing in an instant of light . . . The light, without which no one would know how long mankind's future would last; no one would know . . .

The physical Lalah tried to abandon herself to the flow of light . . . The fused part of her consciousness knew that once the two of them were no longer joined, they would no longer be able to see the flow of light. Would other Newtypes emerge in Lalah's place? Were not she and Amuro gazing into the infinity of future precisely because history promised the appearance of Newtypes?

All thoughts transpired in an instant. All thoughts transpired in an eternity.

THE GUNDAM, UNDER FULL power, smashed into the Elmeth.

Amuro's conscious mind awoke with a shock, and at the last minute he tried to deflect the Gundam's beam saber from its trajectory. But it was too late. The saber connected directly with the weakest section of the Elmeth—its cockpit. In an instant, it incinerated Lalah's young flesh and spirit and penetrated all the way to the engine. The Bits began flying madly and randomly in the colony air, and smashed into its floor. Lalah disappeared into a torrent of light and dissolved into the flow-of eternal time.

Amuro had killed the person he needed more than anyone else in the whole universe. He screamed a scream of despair: "*My God! What have I done?!*"

In wretched disbelief, he put the Gundam in reverse, and the instant he did so he saw the fuselage of the Elmeth suddenly mushroom in size. A second later, his Gundam was blown by the fusion blast into the colony wall; the wall warped, ruptured, and then the Gundam was tossed into outer space. In a ball of light, the Gundam's cockpit escape mechanism went into action. The mobile suit's upper and lower torso separated and the cockpit module transformed into the Core Fighter.

"*Lalah!*" Amuro screamed, half-delirious. "Lalah! Was it all a dream?"

As his Core Fighter was tossed from the area by the blast, he mercifully slipped into mumbling unconsciousness. But the fused awareness he had shared with Lalah was not a dream. They had seen a future, and the future was one of promise. It was real, and it was burned into Amuro's mind. He knew that although only he and Lalah had seen it, it did not belong only to them. It was vast. It was universal. And now he could rest. Sleep would be but a brief respite before he emerged from the depths of despair to fulfill his final destiny.

Mankind still was not aware that Newtypes had awakened. But a new future had already begun.

It was U.C. 0080. And the war was still not over.

ESCALATION

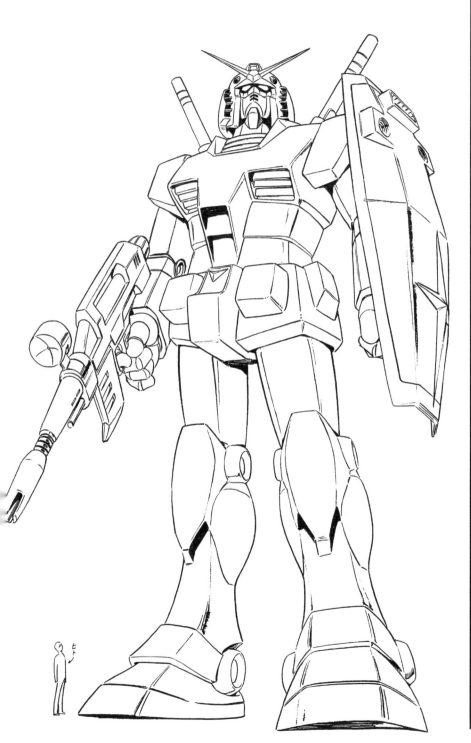

Volume II

ESCAPE

SEVERAL SMALL NUCLEAR EXPLOSIONS occurred, and the *Texas* colony began to self-destruct. Two Federation cruisers standing-by outside, the *Saphron* and the *Cisco*, boldy ventured into the vast interior of the cylinder in a desperate attempt to rescue survivors from the Federation assault landing ship, *Pegasus*, and the Zeon mobile cruiser, *Zanzibar*. With luck they hoped to be able to save at least thirty percent of the crews, but when the port modules on either end of *Texas* showed signs of rupturing out of the colony cylinder framework, they were forced to evacuate the area.

First, the huge external mirrors normally used to reflect sunlight inside the colony were blown far into space. Then, when the final blast came, an enormous ring of light spread out from the colony, overtaking the mirrors and illuminating the drifting debris and fragments of other old colonies throughout the entire space shoal region known as the *Texas* Zone. The light was visible far away, and seen by both the forces of Rear Admiral Kycilia Zabi of the Principality of Zeon and General Revil of the Earth Federation.

Commander Char Aznable survived, but his Zaku mobile suit was destroyed inside *Texas*, as was Zeon's state-of-the-art mobile armor, the Elmeth-Bits system, and its Newtype pilot Lalah Sune. In the Elmeth, Lalah had willed the remote-controlled Bit units to attack and annihilate

CHAPTER NINE

175

the pride of the Federation—the Gundam mobile suit—but merely succeeded in inflicting heavy damage on it. Its pilot, young Ensign Amuro
Ray, managed to flee the narrow confines of the colony in the Gundam's
escape capsule, the Core Fighter. After achieving inertial speed, he soared
through the danger zone and made a beeline for outer space.

"THESE GIZMOS ACTUALLY WORK . . . "

G-i-z-m-o-s. If the power failed on a Core Fighter, Amuro's instruc-
tor, Lt. Ralv, always used to say, its instruments would be about as useful
as sunglasses in a cave at midnight—they would let you know if you were
facing front or back, but that was it. To survive in space *real* pilots relied
on their eyes and their gut instincts.

" . . . *if the power fails, your instruments are as useful as sunglasses in a cave
at midnight . . . "*

How nostalgic the words now seemed.

*"Lieutenant Ralv . . . look . . . the gizmos are working . . . Look how well
the Core Fighter's made . . . "*

Amuro knew he had performed the right check procedures before
escaping from *Texas.* The *Zanzibar* and the *Pegasus* had both blown their
main engines, and the Elmeth had been destroyed, and in the ensuing explosions the Gundam's main fuselage had begun to melt. He had
instinctively activated the Core Fighter escape mechanism, but he wondered if some residual consciousness from Lalah Sune might not have
affected his judgment, even his mind. He remembered the colony walls
flashing by on either side the instant his Core Fighter had exited *Texas.*
He remembered the blurred shape of either the *Saphron* or the *Cisco.*
He remembered seeing the actual moment of escape, and the system
operating as it was supposed to. And he remembered Ralv's comments
about the instruments. But that was all.

AMURO RAY SANK INTO fatigue-induced unconsciousness, but among
his feverish thoughts there gradually appeared another, more assertive
awareness. His deep subconscious was awakening, and normally dormant
functions of his cerebral cortex, now activated, were rising to the conscious level of his mind.

*Lalah . . . What happened? It was a ten- or twenty-minute encounter . . . and
it all happened so fast . . . You showed me so much. But there's something that
bothers me. There's something that bothers me terribly. We were strangers. Absolute
strangers. You weren't supposed to mean anything to me . . . So how could we
possibly have understood each other so well?*

Is it because you were a Newtype? A new human? Someone supposed to

Amuro Ray

symbolize mankind's potential for a universal "renaissance?" And me? I may have better than average intuition, but I hardly think I'm a real Newtype—I'm hardly some sort of new species that's going to transform humanity. Frankly, I don't believe that stuff for a minute. Lalah, the whole thing's crazy. I don't know you any better than my childhood friend Fraw Bow, or even Sayla Mass, but our minds seemed to fuse . . . to resonate . . . It felt as if we both glimpsed a way man-kind could possibly evolve . . . But wait . . . no . . . maybe it wasn't just us . . . Maybe it really was part of that universal awakening people talk about, the new human renaissance that's supposed to happen someday . . .

It makes me exhausted just to think about all this . . . I'm tired. I don't need anything now. I'm just going to sleep. That's all I want—to sleep . . . to sleep . . . The whole thing was too painful . . . I know you felt the same despair I did. Look what happened to us!

THE NEXT STEP IN Amuro's awakening was triggered by anger.

WHY, LALAH?! WHY WERE you on Char's side?

That alien presence I felt . . . that presence that interrupted us when we first met in the docking bay of the Texas colony port module . . . That was Char Aznable, wasn't it, Lalah? I felt static—painful static. But the expansion in awareness we experienced then . . . the leap in our ability to understand each other . . . it was amazingly powerful even if it was interrupted by hatred or an awareness of danger. Was it some sort of "thought transmission!?" I know we're not the only ones capable of this . . . I'm sure we're not . . . But something still bothers me. Lalah, why were you in love with Char? Why were you on his side? Just because you love him? It seems beneath you, Lalah . . . You must have been deluding yourself . . . To tell you the truth, I find it hard to believe . . . Nothing makes sense . . .

ENSIGN AMURO RAY WAS comatose, his thoughts a series of illogically structured, overlapping ideas that slid through his brain over and over again. The eight-meter-long Core Fighter carrying him continued in inertial flight, with no destination logged, streaking past the outer reaches of the *Texas* shoal zone toward the beckoning stars of an expanding universe. Behind it, the ball of light from the exploding *Texas* colony, once bright as a star between Earth and the moon, slowly faded from sight. The little craft had used up almost all of its fuel in escaping from *Texas*, and it now had only enough left for a few attitude corrections with its vernier jets, but the soft glow of the instrument panel testified to the fact that the fighter continued to function. In reality, however, the only operation regularly executed was an intermittent oscillation of a 360-degree identification laser-sensor. And the time limit was slowly running out on the pilot life-support system.

AFTER LEAVING *LUNA II*, the Federation fleet led by General Revil had headed toward Zeon's front line moon base, *Granada*, arriving at the third combat line above it around the same time Amuro's ship, the *Pegasus*, was destroyed in the conflagration inside *Texas*. The surviving ships in Amuro's unit, the 13th Autonomous, somehow managed to link up with other Federation units and execute their assigned feint maneuver, approaching *Granada* counterclockwise against the plane of the ecliptic while the main force closed in from the opposite direction. When all fleets reached their assigned stations, Revil's *Magellan*-class flagship, the battleship *Drog*, used a series of laser signals and rocket flares to transmit the following code to all ships in the armada:

BUTTERFLIES IN THE DESERT.

With these words the Federation Forces finally received their long-awaited instructions: to attack and occupy *Granada*. But it was not going to be easy.

The Federation armada was huge, but its size hid the limitations in its actual fighting capability. The fleet led by General Revil was grouped around the space carrier *Trafalgar*, and consisted of two battleships, seventeen *Coral*-class heavy-cruisers, twenty *Salamis*-class regular cruisers, and sixty-five *Public* attack ships. Vice Admiral Karel's detachment was grouped around the space carrier *Garibaldi*, and comprised of one battleship, seven heavy and eight regular cruisers, and thirty *Public* attack ships. Both the *Garibaldi* and the *Trafalgar* each carried sixty cosmo fighters, for a combined total of 120.

In the old days an armada with so many cosmo fighters would have been more than adequate for the task at hand, but cosmo fighters had been designed for the radar age. Widespread use of Minovsky particles had made radar ineffective, and rendered former tactics obsolete. Instead of hit-and-run attacks, true close-quarter combat had become the norm. Even homing missiles were nearly useless. As a result, when the Principality of Zeon had first developed its Zaku model mobile suit, it had gained an overwhelming advantage. The Earth Federation Forces continued to manufacture and deploy cosmo fighters only because they had no choice; their development and production of mobile suits had lagged too far behind that of Zeon.

Unlike Zakus, most mobile suits carried by ships in the Federation armada were still relatively primitive. There were ninety of the VX-76 model—an early MS prototype nicknamed "Mister Balls" because of their rounded shape. They lacked legs, but had vernier jets in a 360-degree configuration for attitude control, and had a pair of rudimentary manipulator arms. The arms were incapable of holding anything as sophisticated as a beam rifle, but a hyperbazooka was built into the top of its spherical hull. In addition, there were forty GM model Suits, a mass-produced version manufactured while the Gundam and Guncannon were still in prototype stage. Instead of the stereo-binocular design of the Gundam's head, the GM had a simplified glass front panel for a broader field of vision. And it had reinforced armor.

WHEN GENERAL REVIL ISSUED the final burst of laser code from the *Drog* to the rest of the armada to initiate the attack, he chose the words *Tora Tora Tora*—the same phrase used in another age by the Imperial Japanese

Navy when it had attacked Pearl Harbor and ushered in World War II on Earth. Although General Revil did not lack conviction in the justness of his cause and his certain victory, his choice of the words was a gross error bound to elicit criticism from future military historians. Japan was an upstart Far Eastern nation which, without warning, had suddenly attacked a territory of the superpower of the day, the United States of America, yet eventually lost the war (at least technically). It would have been far more appropriate to use "Overlord" or "Neptune," names which the true victors in that conflict had used in their Normandy campaign.

THE MAIN FEDERATION FORCE under General Revil's command accelerated to maximum combat speed, followed 8500 kilometers to the rear by Vice Admiral Karel's detachment, which entered moon orbit from an angle of sixty degrees and began descending toward *Granada*. The route of attack for the fleets had led through two difficult space shoal regions filled with the remnants of former colonies; *Texas* Zone and the area where Side 1 had formerly existed. By taking advantage of the cover this debris provided, and by scattering a heavy concentration of Minovsky particles to render enemy radar useless, the armada had been able to approach the third combat line above *Granada* without being detected. But from that point on it was necessary to use brute force. Using laser search beams, the Zeon defenders on *Granada* had already detected the armada and gathered their forces in near the moon base. They were prepared to make a major show of resistance.

REAR ADMIRAL KYCILIA ZABI, the commander of the *Granada* moon base, was worried.

"Still no further word on reinforcements from Supreme Commander Gihren?" she asked the Vice Admiral next to her.

"Er . . . no, Your Excellency," he replied. "I've been trying to get word from our *A Baoa Qu* space fortress for the last three days, but they keep saying they can't spare any forces until they know Revil's exact route of attack." Technically, the flag officer outranked Kycilia, but he had to be circumspect. She was the daughter of Sovereign Degwin Zabi, the nominal ruler of Zeon, and thus had absolute decision-making authority as far as he was concerned.

Kycilia tugged on her veil-like mask. "Well, what about Dozle on *Solomon*?! Revil's obviously going to ignore *Solomon*. Have Dozle muster his forces and attack him from the rear!" Her mask was made of a rubberized material that fit like a second skin, but she normally wore it down around her neck like a scarf, only raising it above her nose before going into battle. She was a woman of considerable vanity who liked to pretend it helped preserve her complexion, but in reality she hated the smells of battle. In the past, the only time she had not worn it in battle, a supposedly inactive shell had exploded, killing a soldier next to her and overpowering her with the stench of death.

The Vice Admiral lied in response to Kycilia's query. "I've already asked Dozle, too, Your Excellency . . . " Then he took his leave.

AND THEN IT HAPPENED. The sixty-five Federation *Public* attack ships under General Revil's command blanketed the space over *Granada*, firing missiles that emitted a powerful electromagnetic field capable of diffusing enemy beams. It was an extension of the same technology in radar-absorbing Minovsky particles. The field remained effective for several minutes and, although incapable of diffusing one hundred percent of all beams fired from the ground, for all intents and purposes neutralized and scattered the electrons in them. *Granada* was thus forced to abandon its beam-cannon defense and resort to barrages of anti-air weaponry using conventional explosives.

Sixty Federation cosmo fighters next slipped through *Granada*'s defensive fire and began their attack, while the *Public* attack ships assaulted the base with air-to-ground missiles. Then, as the *Salamis*-class cosmo cruisers in the Federation fleet's vanguard engaged their Zeon *Musai*-class rivals in skirmishes, the ninety Federation VX-76 "Mister Balls," supported by GMs, broke through *Granada*'s southern defense perimeter. Simultaneously, Vice Admiral Karel's forces attacked the eastern perimeter of the base.

Because the Zeon ships defending *Granada* had been dispersed in local space, they were forced into a purely defensive role for the first thirty minutes of the assault wave. But then Rear Admiral Kycilia Zabi, who was in charge, made a quick decision.

"Give the order to retreat!" she commanded. "But let it be known this doesn't mean Revil's beaten us. Tell headquarters Granada was lost because Gihren vacillated in sending reinforcements. One more division and we could have easily repulsed the enemy!"

Thus absolving herself of all blame, Kycilia boarded the *Zanzibar*-class mobile cruiser *Swamel* and abandoned *Granada*. Under normal Zeon military tradition, she would have been required to defend the base to the death, but both she and her brother, Supreme Commander Gihren Zabi, had agreed in advance on secret fallback plan. And in reality, her immediate decision was influenced less by this plan than by the emotions of the moment—by a burning desire to live, and eventually confront Gihren.

On the Federation side, the conquest of *Granada* was only part of a much larger strategy. The captured base gave their forces a beachhead on the back of the moon from which to attack the heartland of the Principality of Zeon. Appropriately, they renamed it *FS*, or *First Step*.

❏ ❏ ❏

A HIGH-PITCHED SOUND STABBED through the darkness, expanded, and then suddenly transformed into a flash of light. It was not a horrifying flash, such as might accompany a nuclear explosion, but the gentle brilliance of a flare in blackness, the type of light that penetrates to the corners of the mind and then quickly fades into nothingness. Every time a sound arose from the distance the light would flare in the darkness again. It was like the light a new life might encounter on emerging from a long period of gestation in the womb.

Amuro Ray's consciousness was slowly awakening.

Why, of course . . .

Mother, you were really unlucky . . . I know you were one of the privileged few to obtain permission to live on Earth. And I know it was mainly 'cause Dad was a well-known Side architect. But living on Earth spoiled you. It made you unable to adjust to the idea of living in space . . . and it made you refuse to join us . . . I wish you could have joined us . . . I don't know anything about marriage, but couples are supposed to help each other, right? Maybe Dad didn't love you enough, Mother. Maybe he really just lived to build more Sides in space, and maybe he treated you like his personal maid, or something. . . . But Mother . . . what about me? I was your son! I was involved in all this, too . . .

I remember it as clear as day. I was five, and it was Fall. October 28th, to be exact. That's when Dad took me away from you. . . . You kissed me on my left cheek. And I started to hate you. I didn't want to be a little boy anymore. I wanted to be a grown man. I hated Dad, too. I hated Dad for not being nicer to you. But if you had kissed me for just a few more seconds, Mother, I would have loved you. You were so stiff and formal . . . It made me think it was better to be with Dad . . . Why couldn't you come with us into space, Mother? Was it just because you didn't like the idea of living there? Or were you in love with another man? You were, weren't you? That's why I left with Dad, and didn't cry.

ANOTHER FLARE OF LIGHT followed a far-off high-pitched sound. For a minute, it seemed to Amuro that it was Lalah Sune's voice. But then he couldn't hear it anymore.

KUSKO AL

THE FIRST SOUND AMURO HEARD was that of someone chuckling. It seemed to continue forever, but he could also make out the words, "*You mean the kid?*" He had no idea what was so funny, but in the process of trying to figure it out he began to regain consciousness. It helped, perhaps, that the voice belonged to a woman. It had a rather suggestive sound and was infinitely more pleasant than the gruff tone of the man who interrupted her. His words were hard to make out, and merely part of a whispered conversation in the darkness.

"*Why not?*" said the woman, giggling, but using a different tone. "*Don't you think he's kind of cute?*"

"*Because we have rules against it . . .*" The man seemed to be cautioning the woman against something. . . .

Amuro tried to open his eyes, and watched a light fixture directly above him gradually come into focus. It was the type of light he'd seen a lot of in the last two years—a fluorescent panel covered with the protective mesh favored on military space craft.

I wonder if this is a military ship? he thought, as his conscious mind began to reassert itself. He blinked several times. Aware of a woman's presence, he felt a little shy, but he wanted to know where he was. He tried moving his body for the first time, and a face peered down at him, blocking the light.

CHAPTER TEN

"Can you hear me?" The voice that sprung from the lips was bright and unaffected.

"Yes. " he answered, hoarsely. For a moment he wondered why he had replied so readily. He had no way of even knowing, after all, if the woman was from the Earth Federation. But any resistance faded with the sight of her smile.

"You've been asleep a long time," she said, "but you should be all right now. It must have been rough . . . " Then, turning from Amuro, she called for a doctor.

Amuro liked the way her jaw looked when she spoke.

She turned back toward him again. "Understand everything I say? My name's Kusko Al. *Kus-ko- Al.* You're on the *Kasetta III.*"

"Kusko Al? Are you the one who rescued me?"

"Well, quite frankly, Ensign," she said, with a toss of her long chestnut hair, "I don't know if 'rescue' is the right word or not. Our transport just happened to be the first to spot you, that's all."

"Thanks. . . . I think I'm getting sleepy again . . . "

"You should rest then, Ensign. You're safe now."

Amuro began sliding into sleep once more, but before losing all consciousness he heard a doctor enter the room and exchange words with Kusko Al.

" . . . *because he's an officer in the Federation Forces. . . .*"

The way it was said gave Amuro a vague sense of unease. But he trusted his own instincts. He detected no basic danger. And then he blacked out.

LATER, AMURO WOULD ONLY remember a dream of his mother, Kamaria Ray. She was still living near his old home on Earth, but the war had involved her, too. She was lying naked in bed, wearing a Red Cross armband, next to a man he had never seen. Amuro, wearing his pilot suit, was standing and staring at both of them. He felt strangely dispassionate, but since his mother was married to his father, he wondered why she felt no shame.

"You shouldn't wear a cross on your bare arm like that, Mother," he said. "It doesn't seem right, somehow."

His mother's eyes showed no sign of anger, but her lips formed a little smile that seemed say he was an unwelcome interruption.

It's your life to do as you please, Mother, but you ought to listen to your son once in a while . . .

He turned his back on her and the man, and began walking away. His pilot's suit seemed heavier than ever. His boots had lead in their soles, and with each step they felt heavier and heavier. Five . . . six . . . seven steps . . . twelve, thirteen . . . when he reached twenty-three, he was no longer able to raise his feet off the ground. And then it happened. From his mother's bed in the shadows behind him came a scolding voice.

"What an ungrateful child you are! I didn't raise you to talk like that to me!"

"What do you mean by 'raise,' Mother!? You didn't raise me! Even Dad was too busy with his work to raise me! I raised myself!"

Amuro wasn't really sad when he said it, but he wept anyway.

Then he was hundreds of kilometers away from his mother, but she came running naked after him, her hair all disheveled.

"Don't come near me!" he yelled, trying to flee, *"You're unclean!"*

He began running again, but the more he ran the more leaden his feet became. He donned his pilot helmet and activated the sunvisor in an attempt to block out all sight of her, but when he did the sound of his labored breathing became a roar in his ears. *"Help! Help! I can't breathe!"* he screamed, groping desperately with both hands at the surroundings he could no longer see.

Then someone's hand took his. It was warm, and he somehow knew it belonged to the blond comm tech recruit who had been with him on the *Pegasus*. *"Sayla, is that you?"* he asked.

"ENSIGN! ENSIGN!"

At the sound of the words, Amuro's eyelids fluttered open. It wasn't Sayla, but Kusko Al. His guard instinctively up, he cursed himself for having fallen asleep again without verifying his rescuers' real identity.

"Thanks," he said, smiling. "I feel better now . . . "

At Amuro's confident reply, Kusko Al tossed her long chestnut hair again and smiled. But Amuro detected another, wavering thought behind her surface expression, and sensed danger. She responded to him too quickly, too precisely, as if she already knew too much about him. *What am I feeling?* His mind began groping for an answer, but he tried to tone down his impulses. He would have to be careful. He knew nothing about her, and it would be better to feign ignorance if there were a threat.

"I was dreaming," he said. "It was frightening. And it was obscene ..."

"'Obscene?'" Her pretty gray eyes narrowed as she stared down at him.

It worked! he exulted. The word "obscene," with all its physical implications, had caught her off guard emotionally. He had pierced her emotional barriers and aroused her basic feminine curiosity.

"My mother was sleeping with another man," he said.

Kusko Al was at a loss for words. The peach-fuzzed, innocent-looking young ensign in front of her was certainly not yet twenty, yet he spoke in a self-confident manner that belied his youth. No ordinary Federation pilot would speak in such casual terms about their mother to a virtual stranger. He was either an utter fool, or . . .

"You've been through some hard times, Ensign," Kusko said. "You'd better forget the nightmares."

"Thanks. Actually, I'd like to speak to the ship's captain, if I may. Would you call him for me?"

With the aid of the doctor, Amuro checked himself from the top of his head, down his neck and back, all the way to the toes of his feet. He was all in one piece, and he felt no pain. For a moment he wondered if his memory was intact, but then he began to remember what he wished he could forget—the entire battle on *Texas*. What of his fellow crew members on the *Pegasus*? What had happened to them? It was too painful to think further, so he brought his attention back to Kusko, in front of him, just as she put down an intercom phone and said, "The captain will be here to see you any moment, Ensign."

After muttering his appreciation, Amuro gingerly raised himself up on his elbows. Luckily, the *Kasetta*'s artificial gravity was only one third that of Earth's, for when he moved he felt enormous fatigue throughout his body, especially in his joints. He had worn his pilot suit too long.

"Where's this ship headed?" he asked.

"Side 6. We're scheduled to dock at Balda Bay. But be careful when you move like that. You okay?"

He couldn't tell if the concern expressed was real, or merely a technique to get him to let down his guard, but the tone of her voice had suddenly changed.

"I'm fine. It wasn't a direct hit. By the way, what happened to my capsule?"

"Your 'capsule'? You mean that thing that looks like a light plane? It's moored on the ship's deck . . . "

Amuro said nothing. He knew he had made a major mistake in letting them get hold of his Core Fighter intact. He had referred to it as a capsule because he didn't yet know who Kusko Al really was and needed to hide its true function from her. The "escape capsule" was far more than it seemed. It could operate as the Gundam's cockpit module, but when configured independently, the dozens of vernier jets on the winglike protrusions on its top, bottom, and sides made it highly maneuverable; it was called a Core Fighter because it could also function as a fighter. The problem was that there were several exposed joints on its external skin—joints that connected to the Gundam's control system. An expert seeing these would instantly realize what the capsule's true function was.

An unknown ship picked me up while I was unconscious . . . For Amuro, the unthinkable had happened. What would he do if his rescuers were really flying a Zeon flag and his Core Fighter had already fallen into enemy hands?

As Amuro watched, the door to the room opened and in walked a man on the cusp of old age, with deep wrinkles around his eyes. The gold braid on his uniform suited him well and implied that he was the ship's captain. He was followed by another man in his mid-thirties, who appeared to be some sort of aide. While pondering the second man's role, Amuro stood up and saluted, and noted for the first time the pain in his right upper arm.

"Ensign Amuro Ray, of the Earth Federation Force's 13th Autonomous Corps. Thanks for rescuing me, sir."

"You're more than welcome, Ensign. I'm Famira Ashul, the skipper of this ship, and this is Isfahan, my aide."

While nodding in greeting to both of them, Amuro indicated with his eyes to the captain that Kusko should leave. A perceptive man who seemed to be aware of the ways of the world, the captain immediately understood.

"Kusko," he asked, "would you mind leaving us alone for a minute?"

With a smile in Amuro's direction, she left.

Amuro addressed the captain. "I have two questions, sir."

"Fire away, Ensign."

"First, I need to dispose of the escape capsule you found me in. Can you do it for me? Second, what do you plan to do with me?"

"Relax, Ensign. Since your capsule's already tethered to the deck of the *Kasetta*, we cannot, unfortunately, allow you to dispose of it yourself. But the *Kasetta*'s registered to Side 6, so when we arrive your capsule will be handled according to the terms of the Neutrality Act that Side 6 has signed with the Earth Federation. That means that after going through immigration inspection at Balda Bay, it will be turned over to the Federation consulate. As for yourself, we'll hand you over to the Federation consulate, too."

"That creates a problem for me, Captain . . . "

"Well, I'm sorry, Ensign, but regulations are regulations. Had you first abandoned your capsule and then requested rescue, the means of disposal would be your prerogative. But at this point the capsule is technically *our* cargo."

"How do you have it tethered?"

"Shall I show you, Ensign?"

"Captain Famira," ventured the aide, "er . . . are you sure it's all right?"

"It used to be the Ensign's capsule," snapped the Captain. "We have no reason to refuse his request." Then, to Amuro: "Think you can walk?"

LIFT-GRIPS WERE USED IN weightless areas of the *Kasetta III* to transport crew members. Handholds moving on guide rails built into the ship's walls, they could transport a single person at speeds from two to seven meters per second, but it took quite a knack to use them. One had to start "swimming" horizontally parallel to the grips, and then grab on to one with the right arm to be pulled along. In places where there was a break in the guide rails, transfers were tricky. It was necessary to slow down two or three meters in advance, minimize all inertial movement, and then—after double-checking the position of the next grip to be grabbed—make the body swim straight toward it through the air. Accidentally bending a knee would create a different movement vector and make the connection impossible.

Amuro hadn't used a lift-grip for weeks. He grabbed the third grip after Captain Famira, following Isfahan and Kusko Al. For the first time he noticed Kusko's shapely figure. She was wearing denim pants, and she turned and smiled broadly at him.

"You can see your capsule out the hatch window over there, Ensign," Captain Famira said.

Amuro's view was blocked by the Captain's enormous rear end in front of him, but he took his hand off the grip and let himself float up by the man's left side. Sure enough, through the thirty-centimeter-square hatch window he could see the expanse of the ship's upper deck and, on the starboard side, his Core Fighter tethered with wire cables. The canopy was bent and the right wing almost destroyed. The fuselage seemed to have cracks in it.

While checking his craft visually through the narrow window, Amuro also scanned as much of the *Kasetta*'s deck as he could. In the shadow of a container on the left side of the deck he saw several people dressed in normal suits (the term used to describe space suits ever since mobile suits were developed). Since the ship was a transport soon to dock at Side 6, there was nothing intrinsically odd about a few workers outside, but the fact that there were so many of them, and that they were in the same area of the deck where his Core Fighter was tethered, confirmed his worst fears. They were either Zeon military men or somehow connected to the enemy, he concluded. And one of them might have already entered his Core Fighter cockpit.

Pretending to be greatly relieved, Amuro turned to Famira and smiled broadly. "I can't thank you enough, Captain. I can't tell you what it means to me to be able to tell my superiors in the Federation that my capsule's right next to me."

"Well, I frankly feel as relieved as you do, Ensign. As soon as we disembark on Balda Bay, someone from the Federation forces normally comes to interrogate us. It'll make it a lot easier for me if someone like you can vouch for us."

Amuro smiled in response.

"If the Federation consulate requests it," the captain continued, "I'm sure Side 6 will turn over your capsule right away."

"How long does it normally take to clear customs on Side 6?"

"With luck, two days. Without it, five days to a week. You've got to be prepared for the worst. Bureaucrats are the same all over the solar system . . . "

Amuro gazed out the hatch window again, and over the ship's prow saw two bright lights in space in the distance. They were clearly Side 6 colonies, and one, he deduced, contained the port called Balda Bay. A military ship could reach it in fifteen minutes, but the *Kasetta* was a transport and might take another two hours.

"Take a look at this monitor, Ensign," Kusko said, pointing at a screen next to her. Like most space ships, the transport had remote control external security cameras monitoring its outside decks, giving Amuro an even better look at his Core Fighter. The system worked well, and the screen showed a high resolution view of the Core Fighter from above. When the cameras zoomed in for a close-up, shadows cast by the blazing sun were displayed with the proper exposure, and even details such as individual welds in the armor plating were clearly visible. Thankfully, there were no normal-suited shapes meddling in the cockpit. But still, Amuro sensed that something was wrong.

He commented with veiled sarcasm: "The *Kasetta*'s certainly well equipped to handle my capsule . . . " The eyes of Isfahan, the aide, flashed angrily, and Amuro then knew that the true nuance behind his remark had registered. He looked back at the screen.

As a neutral territory aligned with neither the Earth Federation or the Principality of Zeon, Side 6 had been spared the ravages of the war, but its government leaned heavily toward Zeon. Its president, Rank

Kiprodon, was widely rumored to be collaborating with Kycilia Zabi. Amuro sensed, moreover, that the *Kasetta III* was in the enemy camp. And he also sensed that were it not for Captain Famira's personal good-will toward him, he definitely would have been treated as a prisoner of war. But where, he wondered, did Kusko Al fit into all this?

"THANKS FOR YOUR HELP," Amuro said to the Captain. Then he started to grab onto a lift-grip. He knew the aide was secretly laughing at him, so he deliberately turned to Kusko Al and said, "Mind telling me where I can get some coffee around here?"

"If you'd like," she said flirtatiously, "I'll bring some to you in your quarters, Ensign."

"You . . . you would?"

"Sure. You mind?"

The conversation was a ploy. Amuro had asked Kusko Al because he wanted Isfahan to think he was personally attracted to her, and the strategy seemed to work—Isfahan smiled a thin smile as if to say, "good luck, sucker . . . " and went off with the captain. But what really surprised Amuro was that, although he had decided to use Kusko Al as a shield, she seemed to have sensed his intention and even tried to help him. For a second he wondered if she might even be a Newtype. Unlike Lalah Sune and Char Aznable, he felt no spark of intuitive understanding with her. *I'll just have to see what develops, and act as naturally as possible,* he thought, resolving to keep his guard up.

AS A CARGO SHIP, the *Kasetta III* had a rather rudimentary self-service mess hall with around twenty tables. A large counter protruded from the kitchen into the hall, with trays and utensils piled on it. Coffee was served from a coin-operated vending machine stuck against the far wall by the counter.

"Well, what'll it be?" Kusko asked.

"How about some mocha mattari or mandarin-flavored American coffee?" Amuro asked teasingly, looking up at her bright gray-tinted eyes. She was a tad taller than he was.

"Let's not be too picky, Ensign," she bantered as she deftly filled two coffee cups.

After moving over to a table beside the vending machine and sitting down, he asked her, "Do you understand my situation?"

"No, not totally, but the worried look on your face gave me a pretty good idea of what's going on. One thing's for sure. You'd never make a good spy."

Amuro chuckled, and took a sip of some of the worst coffee he'd ever tasted.

"I have to get my capsule off the *Kasetta*, Kusko," he said. "If it's inspected on Side 6, my superiors'll have my head."

"That's what I thought. But if you're going to do something, you'd better hurry. We're docking at Side 6 soon."

"Soon?"

"Very soon. Want me to help you, Ensign?"

She looked straight at him when she said this, and her gray eyes flashed. She seemed to have the ability to instantly establish rapport with men, and the positive first impression she gave off must have unhinged more than a few. What was it about her, Amuro wondered, that gave her such absolute confidence in her own femininity?

SEVERAL MINUTES LATER THEY were standing in front of a desk manned by the crewman in charge of the ship's normal suit lockers. Kusko Al turned and deliberately said to Amuro: "I feel like taking a walk. Want to join me for a look at the Side 6 colonies from outside the ship? We dock in thirty minutes, so we have to be back inside within ten." Then, turning to the young crewman and keeping a perfectly straight face, she said, "We just want to take a souvenir photo. No problem, right?"

Sure enough, after cautioning them to strictly observe the time limit, he handed over two normal suits.

FROM THE DECK OF the *Kasetta III* Amuro could clearly see all eight colonies that comprised Side 6. The eighth, which held Balda Bay, was one of the largest structures ever created by man. Its enormous cylinder, with giant reflecting mirrors unfolding on three sides, slowly rotated in space and was home to over ten million people. He could already make out a string of lights forming a circle around the colony, much like lights around an Earth city at night, and he knew he was looking at the colony's industrial belt; each light represented a module positioned out in space around the central port area, and was either used for repair and maintenance of ships or for the manufacture of goods. Having been raised in space, there was nothing particularly remarkable about the sight for him. His immediate concern was to find some way to dispose of his Core Fighter.

They walked several paces forward, hugging shadows cast by the cargo containers lined up on the ship's deck. No one on the bridge could see them directly from this angle, but Amuro also wanted to avoid anyone who might be snooping around his fighter.

Kusko Al put her helmet to his to initiate "skin talk"—the low-tech form of communication preferred by normal-suited people in space, which relied on transmitted voice vibrations. "Relax," she said, "there's no one else here. . . ."

Already sensing the same thing, he kicked off from the deck. In the weightless environment, his body floated in a straight line away from the direction of the kick, toward his goal—the Core Fighter cockpit canopy. Reaching it, he opened an emergency hatch under its frame and yanked on a lever. The entire canopy popped open and, just as he had feared, he saw that someone had removed the self-destruct explosive charge under the seat.

"Damn Zeon spies!" he cursed. Hastily, he opened a cover on the back of the attitude control computer module behind the seat. What looked like part of the computer was really a dummy box stuffed with a full complement of emergency explosives, ones that could be used for everything from flares to demolition. He proceeded to attach three units of explosives to the cables tethering the Core Fighter to the *Kasetta*'s deck, and then started walking backward away from the fighter, unraveling a remote control wire that terminated in a pull-ring safety switch.

And then it happened. A searchlight suddenly stabbed out at him. An alarm had probably sounded inside the ship, but in the vacuum of space he couldn't hear it. Instead, the wide-range receiver headset inside his normal suit helmet suddenly picked up the overlapping sounds of several voices barking, "*Who goes there!? Don't move!*"

But it was too late. Amuro pulled the pin on his switch, and with a flash the cables restraining the Core Fighter were blown apart, allowing it to slowly drift off into space. Kicking off the *Kasetta*'s deck, Amuro propelled his body toward the container where Kusko Al was hiding, and as soon as he reached cover, the fuselage of the Core Fighter suddenly swelled around the canopy, and then exploded with a *whomp.* Fragments rained down on the deck of the *Kasetta*, showering several normal-suited crewmen who had dashed out of the bridge area in response to the alarm.

Amuro put his helmet next to Kusko's and, although he couldn't see her expression because of her sunvisor, he could imagine the twinkle in her eyes when she clearly said, "Congratulations, Ensign . . . "

"Thanks. Now I don't have to worry so much."

"I'm happy for you. To tell you the truth, it was kind of exciting. But now comes the hard part."

"Like the Captain said, it was my capsule, and I had a right to do what I wanted with it . . . "

He felt her gently rest the left arm of her normal suit on his shoulder. Again, he couldn't see her expression, but there was definitely something suggestive about her gesture.

"Tell me, why'd you help me?" he probed.

She answered, laughing with the same tone he remembered hearing when he had first regained consciousness on the *Kasetta*. "Because you're cute," she said.

It was the last thing in the world he expected to hear from her. She was clearly no Lalah Sune. Brushing her arm off his shoulder, he stood up. Some of the *Kasetta* crew were already running over.

❏ ❏ ❏

"PLEASE GO IN, COMMANDER," said the round-faced secretary with the charming smile outside Kycilia Zabi's office on *A Baoa Qu*. Char stood up, wearing a brand new red uniform delivered only two hours earlier. Save for the fact that it was a little tight in the chest, it was quite acceptable. Given that it had been made by military tailors on a frontline base, it was nearly perfect.

"Hmph." He turned his head to see how the collar fit around his neck.

"It suits you very well, sir," the secretary remarked. She seemed unusually interested in the masked officer.

Just before Char stepped inside Kycilia's room, another officer exited. He passed Char, audibly hissing, "So it's the masked young hot shot again," and Char made a mental note to never forget him. Then, through the still-open door, he saw Kycilia, her back turned toward him, standing and admiring her tropical fish in an aquarium one-meter tall by three-meters wide. The tank held several varieties of fish, but it was dominated by a school of red sword tails, their scales flashing in the light.

"You must be tired, Commander," Kycilia said as he entered.

He walked directly over to the chair in front of her desk. As always, he kept his mask on. Ostensibly, it was to hide the disfiguring scar on his forehead and to protect his eyes, but he had an additional reason to wear it in front of her. He was afraid of being recognized because his foster father, Jimba Ral, had often told him that when he was an infant, Gihren, Dozle, and Kycilia Zabi used to play with him. Enough time had since elapsed that he was probably safe now, but he knew that any sudden change in his habits would only serve to arouse Kycilia's suspicions.

"I read the combat report on the Elmeth," Kycilia said. "Both you and many of the *Zanzibar* crew were lucky to get out of *Texas* alive."

"It's thanks to the people who built the colony, Excellency. It took quite a beating before it blew."

Kycilia moved away from her aquarium. "It's too bad the Zeon patrol ships in the area weren't doing their duty," she grumbled, "or we might have rendezvoused earlier."

"It's too bad *Granada* couldn't have held out for a few more hours," he replied, carefully. "If it had, I could have joined you in the fight."

Just before the *Texas* colony had exploded, he and several other *Zanzibar* crew members had escaped in launches and been picked up by a *Musai*-class cosmo cruiser in the area on its way to participate in the defense of *Granada*. But on learning of the premature collapse of the base defenses, the cruiser had changed course. Making a broad detour around the moon, it had instead headed for Zeon's *A Baoa Qu* space fortress, arriving only the night before.

A Baoa Qu shared the same gravity-neutral Lagrange point as Side 3, which also held the Principality of Zeon itself. Constructed of two giant asteroids transported from a remote belt, fused together, and fortified, it had the horizontal profile of an umbrella and was sometimes affectionately referred to as such, but the designers intended it to create a deadly crossfire. Like *Solomon*—another man-made space fortress orbiting around Lagrange point 5—it formed Zeon's final line of defense. After fleeing *Granada*, Kycilia had managed to reach *A Baoa Qu*, obtain the use of part of it for herself and her surviving troops, and immediately begin reforming her forces.

"So you're another one who thinks we should have held out longer," Kycilia said, her eyes narrowing.

Char was at a loss for words, but he understood her frustration. If only *A Baoa Qu* had been able to spare some of its forces, Granada might have been saved. The implication was clear. Gihren Zabi, the supreme commander of the Zeon forces and her brother, had conspired with her other brother, Dozle, and deliberately refrained from mobilizing to help her.

Rumor had it that Kycilia had learned of Gihren's secret plans in advance and deliberately fled *Granada* before it fell, rather than be trapped into defending it to the end. Kycilia's reaction to Char's statement seemed to verify the rumors. And, if they were true, Char realized, the Zabi ruling family was in even greater disarray than he had imagined. With luck, it occurred to him, it might eventually collapse without his having to lift a finger against it.

"It's the sort of thing that can't be helped, Excellency," he said, as if to console her.

It was such an obvious statement that Kycilia laughed bitterly. "I just can't believe the way they treat us here at *A Baoa Qu*," she said. "Like total outsiders. And although it's not like Dozle, something's making him act awfully nervous here, too."

A Baoa Qu was under the direct jurisdiction of Gihren Zabi, and not Kycilia. Dozle Zabi had come from *Solomon* to *A Baoa Qu* to attend reorganization meetings begun the day before.

"And how is the plan to reform your forces proceeding, Excellency?" Char asked.

"So-so. My dear brother, Gihren, isn't easy on defeated commanders. But I'll show him. I've decided to form a Newtype Corps."

Char was suddenly uneasy. Kycilia was acting impetuously. "A Newtype Corps?" he probed.

"Gihren may be Supreme Commander, but he has no idea of what's really happening here on the front lines. All he thinks about is what he's going to do after we win the war."

"He's quite confident, I'm sure," Char said, empathizing. "But do you really think his new strategy will work?"

Kycilia looked both puzzled and shocked.

"I've heard it said," Char continued, "that he plans to lure the Federation forces to a point directly between *Solomon* and *A Baoa Qu* and destroy them in a single strike."

"Are you talking about the 'System' plan?" Kycilia's words suddenly had a hard edge to them.

"Er . . . yes."

"Garma told you about that?" Kycilia's younger brother, and Char's former classmate at the Zeon Military Academy, had only recently been killed in action, and mention of his name was still awkward.

"I leave that to your imagination, Excellency. But I don't think the Supreme Commander's goal is moving any closer to reality . . . "

"I quite agree. Nor does it seem likely that any single plan would be enough to end the war. We might succeed in annihilating most of the Federation forces, but still be unable to alter the course of history in favor of the Zabi family. I say that because I've heard that the Earth Federation Forces already have a Newtype unit of their own under development. I'm of the opinion that the coming age may well belong to Newtypes. Don't you agree, Commander?"

Char was temporarily at a loss for an answer. Since directly confirming the existence of Newtype individuals through Lalah Sune, he was no longer cooperating with Kycilia simply out of revenge and a desire to destroy the Zabi family. He was, in fact, in utter agreement with her comment about the next age belonging to Newtypes—making it come true had become his personal goal and ideology, but for different reasons. History clearly showed, he knew, that ordinary people were capable of resolving serious disputes only through war. Newtypes held out new possibilities.

He answered slowly: "A Newtype age. . . . Yes, I think I can agree with that."

What he meant and what Kycilia was thinking were totally different, but that wasn't his concern. It was currently in his interest to use Kycilia and the Flanagan Institute she controlled. It was to his advantage to go along with her for the time being.

"I thought you would," she said. "That's why it's imperative for us to form a Newtype Corps as soon as possible."

"I understand, Excellency, but I thought Ensign Lalah Sune was the only true Newtype we had available . . . "

"Don't worry. I didn't pour all that money into the Flanagan Institute for nothing. It just so happened that when you visited them you only encountered the girl. In reality, they have other Newtype troops fully capable of operating in combat situations."

Kycilia pressed a button on her desk intercom and asked her secretary to send in a Commander Garcia Dowal of the Flanagan Institute. Then she stood up and turned back to Char. "I understand you were on extremely good terms with Ensign Lalah Sune . . . "

"Excellency?" Just like a woman, Char thought. She would have to bring up exactly what he didn't want to hear. "I was a little carried away by my youth, I suppose," he said in self-deprecation.

"Youthful ardor and kindness, Commander Char, are the very qualities which suit you least as a professional soldier."

He replied with a wry, forced smile. He recalled Lalah and how, from the very beginning, he had never really thought of her as a military person. How, through a series of coincidences, she had accidentally encountered the pilot of the Federation mobile suit, Amuro Ray, and how her mind had reached a mysterious harmony with his even in the midst of a duel to the death. Had she not been doomed, Char knew her consciousness would have fused with that of the young MS pilot and reached even higher levels. The memory made him jealous; maybe, he reflected, it was a good thing she had been killed. But he was also man enough to realize that if she truly represented the emergence of Newtypes people had long talked about, then there might indeed be hope for mankind. The emotion that had surged between Lalah Sune and Amuro Ray had transcended normal love between men and women. Their fused awareness had expanded and strengthened into a type of universal wisdom. It held out the potential of a unification and purification of human desire and intelligence, all at the same time. *If only*, he thought, *if only it could happen to everyone.*

COMMANDER GARCIA DOWAL WAS explaining to Kycilia: "Lieutenant Challia Bull commands a fleet of ships that transport Helium 3 from Jupiter. When he returned to the Fatherland two weeks ago we had him investigated. He appears to be extremely promising."

"But why," asked Char, swirling the ice cubes in a glass of scotch an aide had handed him, "would a man of his caliber have been employed away from the front lines?"

"Perhaps because he has some sort of prescience unique to Newtypes. Perhaps it was thought he could cause problems at the front."

Garcia flipped through the file he held and began to read from another page, but Char stopped him.

"Don't you think it's a little odd? That the Flanagan Institute, er, excuse me, I mean you, managed to stumble across him, out of all the others being considered for investigation?"

"'Challia Bull'? Why, he came to my group on the direct recommendation of Supreme Commander Gihren Zabi . . . "

Char was stunned. If, as he understood, Kycilia seemed to think that forming a Newtype unit was exclusively her own idea, here was Gihren directly sending his own Newtype candidate—one of the most promising so far—as if to warn her. He didn't know what to say.

Garcia continued reading from his file. "And then we have junior grade lieutenant Cramble Karela. He's a former Zaku pilot . . . "

"And is he at exactly the same level as Challia Bull?" Char asked without waiting for Garcia to finish.

"Yes, the same as I mentioned earlier," Garcia answered, suddenly serious now. "But then there's also junior grade lieutenant Kusko Al. She has such extraordinary abilities that the Flanagan Institute had to put together special tests just for her. They even took her to Earth this week, at great risk, to see if normal gravity would cause any changes to Newtype brain wave patterns."

"To Africa, right? I heard about that. Tell us the result."

"We haven't received any information yet, but we should have some communication today."

"And where is this Kusko Al now?"

"She should be at Balda Bay, on Side 6 . . . "

SIDE 6 HAD BEEN designed with a temperate climate. There were some inconveniences associated with having four delineated seasons, but the

Rank administration believed people needed variety and stimulation. As a result, while no annual rainy seasons or typhoons were programmed into the climate patterns, heavier-than-usual rains and snow were randomly scheduled every five years or so. It was a humble human attempt to approximate the natural environment on the home planet, Earth.

The first day Amuro visited the Earth Federation consulate on Side 6, a Lt. List Hayashida offered him coffee and strawberry shortcake. One of twelve military attaches assigned to the consulate, List's job was to gather information, and he was more than willing to fill Amuro in on the details of the colony.

"We even had a flood here not too long ago," List said. "I think it was in June the year before last. Twenty houses were swamped. It became something of a political problem."

"Houses swamped?" It was an utterly alien notion to Amuro.

"Sure. It never even happens on Earth anymore, but basically, rivers overflow their banks and water inundates the houses."

"Really?"

"Really. Doesn't bother me, though. I've got a great life here. All I have to do is check on the people who visit the Flanagan Institute. I spend about four hours a day monitoring the Institute entrance, compiling names and taking photographs of those who go in and out. Then I forward the info to Staff Headquarters at Jaburo on Earth. That's it."

"What's the Flanagan Institute?"

"You don't know?! I didn't realize you were *that* green, kid. It's where the Zeon forces train their Newtypes. Surely you've heard of Newtypes?!"

"But I thought Side 6 was neutral!" Amuro stabbed a strawberry with his fork and popped it into his mouth. "That's a violation of international law, isn't it?"

"Hah! Where've you been?! Welcome to the real world! You can't be blamed for your ignorance, though, I suppose. Nowadays they put you kids into the Force before you've even had the chance to chase a few skirts."

Picking up another piece of shortcake, Amuro weakly countered, "My superior officer used to say the same thing. But frankly, I don't think experience with the opposite sex has anything to do with it. Seems like an awfully jaded way to look at things."

"You know, I bet you drive some women out of their minds. You're the good-looking, innocent kind of kid they just love to mother to death. But enough of that . . ."

List had apparently concluded Amuro was something of an idiot. He took a gulp of coffee and stared out the consulate window at the colony's expanse of artificial hills and greenery. "Ah, the ways of the world," he sighed, before continuing. "Lemme tell ya something. When I leave the consulate I put on a disguise. Sometimes I wear a fake beard. But someone from the Zeon side always tails me and watches when I photograph stuff from hotel windows or gather information at coffee shops. And when my four hours of work are over, the Zeon spy follows me back to the consulate. He works longer hours than I do. Understand? That's what being a spy is all about . . . "

"Seems a little devious."

"That's the way the real world is. I've never had a gun battle with an enemy spy, or anything exciting like that. That stuff only happens in the movies."

Amuro nodded, and sipped his coffee.

BECAUSE OF THE SABOTAGE of the Core Fighter on the _Kasetta III,_ Amuro had arrived at Balda Bay under a cloud of suspicion, and he therefore anticipated a rough time with immigration and customs. Lt. List Hayashida had of course gone to bat for him, but that was expected, since he represented of the local Federation consulate. The real surprise had been Kusko Al. She had turned out to be his biggest ally of all, speaking vigorously in his defense and even creating an alibi for him, testifying that he had been in her room when the Core Fighter exploded. When the immigration officer had asked Amuro point blank if her statement were true, he had of course replied in the affirmative. It was an outrageous lie, but her stubborn adherence to her story had proved pivotal. It also enraged Isfahan, the aide on the _Kasetta,_ who had exclaimed, "_She was sleeping with an officer from the Earth Federation?!_"

Hayashida had initially taken the story at face value but, as befits an intelligence officer, he had eventually realized that Amuro was for all intents still a babe in the woods when it came to women. He had no idea of what had really transpired between Amuro and Kusko Al. It was a mystery to him, but it was not his main concern. He had been specially commanded by General Revil, who had just occupied Zeon's _Granada_ moon base, to take good care of the young ensign.

AMURO STARED AT THE bluish tone of List's freshly shaved chin, and decided to change the subject: "Um, may I assume I can return to my unit soon?"

"Sure," the lieutenant muttered, pulling a photograph from his vest pocket and tossing it down on the table between them. "But take a look at this first . . . "

Amuro was stunned. It showed Kusko Al, of all people, running up a flight of imitation stone steps. She seemed to be looking at the camera. Her full lips were formed in a smile.

"This isn't a one-time thing, pal. I wouldn't show it to you unless I knew what I was talking about. I saw her enter the Institute three times, and just to make sure—since I've only been on the job here for a little over a month—I even checked my predecessor's records. Except for the last ten days, she's been visiting the Flanagan Institute almost daily for over six months. She's officially on the Institute's staff, but she's not a regular employee. She's a Newtype."

"You must be kidding," a shocked Amuro whispered, picking up the photo and scrutinizing it. "Is this building the Flanagan Institute?"

"Hey, the photograph's yours. Use it for reference."

"I . . . I didn't know . . . "

The lieutenant smiled weakly. Amuro looked up at him.

"So tell me," List said. "What's a Core Fighter?"

"It's an escape capsule for a mobile suit. It contains the entire cockpit."

"Of a GM Suit?"

"Yes."

"Something stinks here, Ensign."

"What do you mean?"

"Listen, don't take it personally, but from my perspective you don't know zip about the ways of the world. Still, there's something else I don't understand going on here. I don't think you're leveling with me."

"Really?"

"Really."

"I know maybe you're thinking I'm a Newtype, too, but I'm not. I haven't had any special training at all."

"Well, then how come I received a direct order from General Revil concerning you? I even heard your name from the Immigration office. Ordinarily Federation military people are just checked for their identity and the unit they're attached to, and then cleared. All I usually do is greet them at the port area. Don't you think it's a little odd that Revil would personally order me to look out for you?"

"Maybe it's because my unit was annihilated on *Texas*."

"Don't play me for the fool, kid." List was getting visibly angry.

"No, it's true. I don't have any of the traits associated with Newtypes, and even if someone told me I was one, I wouldn't believe them. But . . . " Amuro seemed to suddenly recall something. "But what if I were?"

List stood up, and informed Amuro that a Federation transport was scheduled to depart from Balda Bay the next morning at five. Then he announced in a flat voice, "Kusko Al's a Newtype. Her I.D. number's J6159. She'll leave the Flanagan Institute at six tonight and return to her quarters . . . "

Amuro smiled. "Really? Thanks for the information." It dawned on him that he was being set up.

THE FLANAGAN INSTITUTE HAD an official-sounding name, but it was housed in a nondescript building identified only by a worn, scarcely legible nameplate at the entrance. In front of the building there was a broad flight of "stone" stairs of over a dozen steps—the same stairs Amuro had seen in the photograph. The building was bordered by Himalayan cedar trees on a property facing a four-lane highway. It was a typical colony office building.

In an ele-car borrowed from the Federation consulate, Amuro stopped in front of the Institute's parking lot. He knew List was probably tailing him, suspecting him of being a Newtype, but he didn't even bother to turn around and check—List wasn't the type to blow his cover that easily. He gazed at the entrance to the building. It was long past normal closing time. Two or three people emerged and walked over to their cars in the lot, without paying any attention to him. Then, suddenly, he saw a female figure exit, dressed in a knee-length skirt that fluttered as she walked. It triggered an odd reaction in him. On the *Kasetta III*, he had only seen Kusko Al in slacks. Her chestnut hair bounced off her shoulders as she skipped down the stairs and came over.

"'You wait long for me?" she asked.

"Less than thirty minutes," he answered, turning the key in the ignition. She sat in the seat next to him and he sensed the power of her presence. It was a warm sensation, and he liked it. He had planned to check his rearview mirror before pulling out but he was so distracted by the sight of her hair that he forgot. To his surprise, she said, "Don't even bother. Someone'll follow us anyway." He stepped on the accelerator and spun the ele-car onto the highway in front of the Institute.

"Sorry," he said.

"Sorry for what?"

"Sorry if it seems like I was lying in wait for you here like this."

"I saw you through the glass doors of the building entrance. What were you doing?"

"Lying in wait for you . . ."

"I knew you'd come. I knew if you were at the consulate you'd learn about this place. It's been three days, hasn't it? I knew you'd come. That's why I wore this skirt."

"This some sort of female intuition, or what?"

"Probably. I knew I'd never see you again if I suddenly had to go to Earth, or relocate to the front lines. But I also knew if you were still on this colony you'd come today."

Kusko smiled happily as she said this, but Amuro sensed something else, something indicating she was playing with him. Was it an illusion? He imagined her saying something like "*you really are kind of cute, aren't you?*" Tensing slightly, he smiled back and said, "Mind if I ask you something else, Kusko?"

"Sure, go right ahead."

"Are you using some special kind of psychology to figure out what I'm thinking?"

"I don't know anything about psychology, but we've been attracted to each other since we first met. Hey, isn't that enough?"

She didn't call him "baby," but Amuro sensed that she wanted to. She was only a little older than he was, but something made her sound like she was talking down to him. What was it? He wondered.

"No, I . . . I . . . uh . . . I don't think you understand . . . " he stammered, quickly regretting that he had ever come to meet her.

"You really are kind of cute, aren't you?" she said. And then she giggled.

Amuro stopped the ele-car. Kusko stopped giggling and stared at him. He stared back at her gray eyes. In his peripheral vision he noted her beautiful skin and the lines of her body. "Get out," he said.

"But . . . I . . . " Kusko, taken aback, was at a loss for words.

"Hey," Amuro said. "If you think I'm such a cute kid, then I'm not the man for you. Get out."

"Listen, Amuro, I'm sorry. I didn't mean it at all. I was just happy to see you. I . . . I didn't mean to offend you. Really."

"Don't worry. I'm already taken. I already have a girlfriend—Fraw Bow . . ."

"I . . . I didn't realize," she stammered. "I'm really sorry."

And then she got out of the car.

"Sorry, Kusko," Amuro said, as he punched the ele-car's accelerator to the floor. He didn't understand why he was so angry. In reality, he had hoped to eat dinner with her and even go dancing. It all could have happened. Better yet, they might even have wound up sleeping together. He knew all he had to do was to turn the ele-car around.

While Amuro was still debating whether to pull over to the side of the road, two ele-cars passed him on the left. He straightened his steering wheel and drove straight ahead. In his rearview mirror he caught a glimpse of Kusko Al, standing, still waiting. Then he saw her turn around and start walking the other way. *I've got to go back for her,* he thought, knowing it was already too late.

Why had he mentioned Fraw Bow's name? He couldn't understand it himself. Fraw, his former neighbor on Side 7, was now a refugee on *Luna II.* In spite of being younger than he was, she had always tried to mother him. She was more than his first love. She was almost like a sister. It was true Fraw was waiting for him. He clearly remembered her telling him when they had parted. But he never should have blurted it out.

Why had he let Fraw get in the way of things? If he really took his mission seriously, he probably should have had more contact with Kusko Al. He tried as hard as he could to calm his mind, but found himself thinking things he had never thought of before. *Why did I act that way? Kusko Al was right. I* was *interested in her* . . .

The day was over, and darkness was slowly falling on the entire colony in accordance with its design. The tail lamps on Amuro's ele-car streaked through the night, and the street lights diffused into geometrical patterns of light on either side as he passed them by. He cursed himself and stomped on the accelerator.

PRELUDE

AFTER THE FEDERATION FORCES took over *Granada* and renamed it *FS*, for *First Step*, they were careful to deploy only enough forces to secure it as a beachhead—the former Zeon base was located at the southernmost tip of the Soviet mountain range on the far side of the moon, and was thus directly exposed to Zeon's *A Baoa Qu* space fortress. The Federation continued to keep its main forces on the other side of the moon—the side facing Earth—at a base code-named *LH*, for *"Look Home."*

THE *TRICHIGEN*, A *SALAMIS*-CLASS cruiser, slowly descended to the No. 6 deck on *LH*. A standard Earth Federation warship, its basic shape conformed to that of the floating vessels that had once plied Earth's seas, yet because it was designed for a weightless environment it had subbridges protruding from both port and starboard sides that could also be used as decks. Warships only needed true "bottoms" for docking and coming alongside space piers.

Ensign Amuro Ray stood and watched from the bridge. After leaving Balda Bay on a civilian transport flying the Earth Federation flag, the *Trichigen* had come alongside specifically to take him on board, and for the duration of the flight he had been assigned a private room with a Chief Petty Officer ten years his senior to care for him. It was VIP treatment normally only extended to senior officers and it should have made him feel at home, but it didn't.

Like many combat-seasoned lower-ranking officers, Amuro had a rebellious streak in him, and it tended to manifest itself in the regular military heirarchy. He quickly became suspicious of his assigned aide, who followed him around like a shadow and liked to proclaim, "*I'm under strict orders to take good care of you, sir!*" From Amuro's perspective, the man's expression really said the opposite, that if he, Amuro, so much as tried to leave his "prison," he would have his teeth knocked in.

Amuro knew that Lt. List, in accordance with his duty, had probably filed a report on his meeting with Kusko Al in front of the Flanagan Institute. Given that he and Kusko Al had separated so soon after meeting, he also knew hardly anyone would believe he had only gone there in an attempt to date her. It would definitely look like he had been furtively meeting her to exchange information. He knew he could never explain it, but at the same time he hoped it would be overlooked. He had been picked up by the *Trichigen* and was now docking at *LH* because he had General Revil's special protection. And the Federation military, he suspected, now had far more pressing matters at hand than his encounter with Kusko Al.

On the bridge, at least, the officers and crew treated him normally, but he nonetheless got the feeling that everyone, from the ship's captain on down, was keeping him at a distance. Perhaps they did not suspect him. Perhaps, since he was only with them for the duration of the voyage and unlikely to be assigned permanently to their ship, they had merely decided not to waste their energy in befriending him.

The *Trichigen* bridge communicated with the *LH* control tower one last time on docking procedure, and then a giant hatch opened over a huge shaft leading from the fortress's ground level to the underground decks of its port. The shaft extended over a kilometer deep into the moon's surface and could hold up to eight *Salamis*-type ships; descending all the way required passing through three different hatches. As a frontline base, the area was poorly maintained and often had unsecured materials that easily floated free. As scrap metal bounced off the bridge, someone yelled, "What's the matter with this place? Don't they have any gravity on the moon?"

If Kusko Al were really a Newtype, it occurred to Amuro, he probably would never see her again. In fact, if they were both sent into combat, the odds that they would meet again in the vast theater in which the war was being played out were surely less than one in a million. But if that were the case, he wondered why he hadn't spent more time talking with her the night before. Why had he suddenly become so angry? *I just hope I don't meet her the way I did Lalah Sune*, he thought, regretting his impetuousness all the more.

Just when he was deciding it was all Kusko's fault, his eyes widened. The *LH* docking pier below seemed to rise up to meet them, and the *Trichigen* quickly decelerated to reach its assigned mooring spot. There were people in civilian clothes on the pier rushing about in preparation for the landing, and several military ele-cars zipping in and among them.

Amuro instantly forgot about Kusko Al. "*Hey, look!*" he excitedly exclaimed to anyone in earshot. "I'll be damned! My crewmates are there! There's Bright, my old skipper who's always flying off the handle! . . . And Mirai, the ensign with the maternal instinct . . . And Kai . . . Kai Shiden . . . And look there . . . that's Hayato. They've all come to greet me! Hey, and there's Chief Petty Officer Marker! And Oscar! And that big heavyset man . . . That's Sleggar Law, the gunnery officer . . . And Ensign Ram Dowai, the engineer, with the big laugh. And wait a minute . . . that pretty blond . . . that's Petty Officer Sayla Mass!"

Two weeks had elapsed since the destruction of *Texas*, and during that time Amuro had assumed that most of his friends had been killed. Now, seeing so many of them alive, he felt as though an enormous burden had been lifted from his spirit. *So many had survived!* But one memory suddenly moved into his mind like a dark cloud on a sunny day. *Ryu* . . . Ryu wasn't there. Ryu, who had begun pilot training at the same time as he had, but been destroyed in a mobile suit battle. If only Ryu were there to meet him, too.

When the *Trichigen* finally docked, the ship's captain turned to Amuro and said, "Congratulations on a job well done, Ensign. We look forward to hearing about your further success in the new 127th Autonomous Squadron."

"The 127th?" Amuro queried.

The skipper grinned and said, "Well, it's just a rumor, but we hear it's an elite combat unit, handpicked from the Federation Forces. If General Revil thought enough of you to have us give you VIP treatment, I'm sure you're among the pilots selected. And I'm sure you'll perform superbly, Ensign."

"Thanks, sir . . . " he answered, resisting the impulse to tell the man that he also knew the negative implications of any such assignment. He shook the captain's hand, feeling terribly adult about the whole matter, and said, "Here's wishing the *Trichigen* good hunting, sir . . . "

Then, as soon as he disembarked onto the pier, Amuro heard a familiar voice cry out, "*Way to go, Amuro . . . Our star pilot . . . We knew you'd make it! Now tell us you're surprised to see* us *alive!"* It was his old comrade, Kai Shiden.

Amuro laughed. "Surprised? Hey, I'm amazed . . . especially to see *you!"* he said. The crowd on the pier burst into laughter at the goodnatured exchange, and he felt himself drawn into the mood of the moment. The informality of it all was perfect, and nothing could have pleased him more. He was reunited with his friends, with his old crewmates, and filled with a profound sense of relief. It was almost like being reunited with a family.

"Good job, Ensign!" said Bright, his skipper. "A lot of cheers went up around here when we got word you'd made it to Side 6 alive. We've been waiting for you a long time."

Amuro looked around at everyone again and again, still not completely believing his eyes. And then he caught sight of a familiar blond young woman standing behind Petty Officer 1st class Howard. He smiled briefly, and she smiled back. Her mouth seemed to form the words, "Welcome home, Amuro," but she was drowned out by the rest of the crowd.

"General Revil's waiting to see you," Bright announced, letting Amuro know he wasn't supposed to dawdle too long. There would be time to socialize later.

Mirai began hustling everyone toward four ele-cars standing by. Amuro noticed a new, confident air about her, and wondered if it could be simply a result of having survived the ordeal on *Texas*. Sayla jumped in Kai's ele-car behind Hayato. Ram Dowai, sitting next to Mirai in the back of Bright's ele-car, yelled out for Amuro to join them, and he eagerly jumped in the front. It was hard to contain his enthusiasm. "Yahoo! Step on it!" he yelled gleefully. First Kai, and then Bright accelerated forward, and the others followed.

The engines of the huge moored *Trichigen* slowly shut down. When the boisterous former crew of the *Pegasus* left the giant domed underground port, the entire area was finally enveloped in silence.

ALONG THE WAY, AMURO's crewmates began to fill him in on what had transpired in his absence. "I'm sure you know," Bright said, "that the 13th Autonomous was completely successful in its feint maneuver. Despite losing our ship, we managed to lure several of Kycilia's ships out into the open, and that helped the main force achieve a total victory in Operation Star One. Goes without saying, of course; we wouldn't be here on this moon base if we hadn't won. All-in-all, things don't seem to be going well for the Zeon side."

"Think they're having some sort of internal power struggle, sir?"

"You could say that. Relations between the Zabi family members seem a little strained, to say the least."

"Really?"

"It's just a rumor, Amuro," Mirai added from behind him, "but people say there's a power struggle going on between Gihren, Kycilia, and Dozle—the three surviving Zabi siblings."

"By the way, Mirai," Amuro suddenly turned and asked her, teasingly, "did you gain some weight?"

"Me?!" She gasped and covered her cheeks with her hands, her small round eyes practically popping out of her head. "Er . . . well, I guess I *have* put on a kilogram or two in the last ten days."

"I'll bet the military hasn't been giving you guys enough to do, that's what," Amuro said with a grin. "The Force is famous for poor horizontal communication in the ranks, right? They've probably forgotten all about you folks!"

"Sorry to disappoint you, Amuro, but things have been so busy here on *LH* recently you'd probably wish you were off fighting instead."

"And that, kiddo," Bright injected with a mischievous grin, "is why everyone *really* wanted to come see you. They figured they could get out of a day's work. . . ."

AMURO WAS PUZZLED. BRIGHT seemed to have matured by at least ten years. Was his extra confidence simply that of a survivor?

"To tell you the truth," he said, "you all seem different to me somehow."

"Different?"

"Different. Maybe this is a weird thing to say, but everyone seems to be getting along so well now, almost like a family. I never sensed that before. Even Sayla, the one everyone used to tease and call the 'bungler,' seems to be doing great."

"Maybe you're right," Mirai said. "Maybe it has something to do with having survived *Texas*. As for Sayla, some of us did used to feel she was different, and didn't really fit in. But it turns out she's the one who helped us all escape *Texas*. She's the one who showed us the way out of the colony before it exploded. It was like there was a mysterious voice leading her, that none of the rest of us could hear."

Bright interjected: "You mean she might be sort of a Newtype, right?"

"Well, maybe not as much as Amuro. Say, not to change the subject, but look at Kai and Hayato in the other ele-car, both jockeying for her attention . . ."

"I'd say that's proof that she's finally been accepted," Ram Dowai said, seated next to Mirai.

"Amuro," Bright asked, "You're from the same Side as Sayla, aren't you?"

"Yessir. Side 7."

When Amuro's ele-car finally arrived at the _LH_ Operations center, the other three vehicles were already waiting. Instead of getting out, their riders called out, "Go to it, Amuro!" "Good Luck!" and "See you back at the _Pegasus_!" and then took off again. Sayla smiled and waved and, after having seen the way both Kai and Hayato had acted around her, there was something reassuring to Amuro about that.

Amuro and Bright got out of their ele-car and Mirai took the wheel. "I'll see you both later," she said. "We're going to have a little celebration afterward on the _Pegasus_—another excuse to take a break from work."

As they entered the Operations center, Amuro turned to Bright and asked, "Did I hear right, skipper? Did she say '_Pegasus_'?"

"She did. But it's really the _Pegasus II_. Turns out the Federation fleet had a second White Base-class warship, and we've all been reassigned to it. We're apparently going to form the core of the 127th Squadron."

Amuro fell silent for a second, realizing that he was the only one who had absolutely no idea of what was going on. Then he asked: "We're shipping out again soon?"

"We sure are," Bright replied. "Time's apparently running out. Word is that Zeon's cooking up something a lot bigger than a little skirmish on the other side of the moon."

Inside Operations, General Revil took a puff on his cigar and let his eyes follow the trail of smoke. "I'm speaking to you, Ensign Amuro Ray, on the assumption that you may be a rare find—a true Newtype. And I expect you to hold what I say in the strictest confidence."

"Yessir. "

"Zeon forces have been lying low the last two weeks, but there's a reason. And it's not simply because they lost _Granada_. They're apparently developing a new secret weapon, one with awesome destructive power, and they're stalling for time."

Bright blurted out, "You mean they're going to put a Newtype unit into action, sir?" When Revil ignored him, he stepped backward and looked down at the floor sheepishly.

"No, I'm talking about a weapon capable of directly hitting the moon from Zeon territory."

"A direct strike?" Amuro felt a chill run down his spine. That would be no easy feat. He had never heard of a beam weapon capable of inflicting direct damage from tens of thousands of kilometers away. In theory a long-range missile might work, but even if it emitted Minovsky particles to confuse local defense radar systems it would never be able to break through a defense perimeter of contact space mines. It was precisely because of these limitations that current military strategy still dictated the use of battleships for such attacks.

Revil laughed at the sound of Amuro's shocked voice. "I'm exaggerating, Ensign. I'm exaggerating." He shot a glance at Bright, as if to scold the overly-young lieutenant for his earlier remark, and then continued. "But not totally. Ever since the end of the twentieth century people have talked of a weapon that could instantly annihilate an entire fleet—talked of using an entire space colony to create a colossal laser cannon. It's exactly the sort of madness Zeon would seriously consider."

"Sir," Amuro said, "are you saying Zeon might use one of its sealed-cylinder colonies for that?"

"Exactly."

Bright interjected again: "But wouldn't they have to build a new colony cylinder specifically for the cannon?"

"Not necessarily. Don't forget Gihren Zabi's an absolute dictator. All he has to do is evacuate the residents of one of Zeon's existing cylinders and then reinforce its structure. It's probably not as difficult an engineering feat as it sounds. We have information they've already begun evacuating one."

Revil said it casually, but Amuro knew the scale of the operation would be mind-boggling. Even compact colonies were now being built to house up to five million people. Large ones could hold ten to fifteen million. "I find it hard to believe anyone could carry out an operation of that size so fast, sir," he said, staring at the General.

"You'll find it easier to believe when you learn more about the political intrigues the human mind delights in, young man. Don't forget that in the old days people used to take summer vacations in space—up to five hundred thousand people a month used to visit the *Texas* colony. We're only talking about Zeon mobilizing ten or twenty times that number. It's not impossible. And by the way, Ensign, to get back to the point your skipper made about Zeon forming a Newtype fighting unit...."

"Sir?"

"That rumor may also be true. It's why we've decided to form one of our own, with you at its core. It's what the 127th Autonomous Squadron's all about. We want you to be in the vanguard."

"*Me*, Sir?"

"Surely you're not surprised? You must have been expecting it. After all, the Zeon mobile armor you destroyed on *Texas*—the Elmeth—was clearly a weapon developed specifically for Newtypes. I know the general public would've been more impressed if you'd destroyed the Red Comet, but we in the military know what a terribly important service you performed."

"Er, thanks, I guess."

"I've made arrangements for your promotion, Ensign, but our staff seems a little bogged down with paperwork these days, so it might take a while for it to formally come through." Revil then picked a letter of commission up from his desk and handed it to Amuro, who stood up to receive it.

Amuro started to read aloud to himself from the paper, "*You are herein re-assigned to the 127th Autonomous Squadron. . . .*" when he was interrupted.

"That's correct," Revil said. "The performance of the *Pegasus* and its crew under the command of Bright Noa here has convinced me we should take a chance on *all* of you being potential Newtypes. There's no sense waiting for the desk jockeys at headquarters in Jaburo to understand something like this. They've been working in their underground complex on Earth so long, they'd never believe that merely living in the vastness of space could alter human consciousness the way the Newtype theory postulates."

The general ground out his cigar in an ashtray and stood up. "It's good to see you again, Ensign. I know you won't disappoint me."

"Er, th-thank you, sir. I'll do my best." He shook the general's hand, and despite the powerful grip, he could tell the man was tired. It was no wonder.

"The general put his career on the line and fought tooth and nail with the General Staff to get us assigned to the *Pegasus II*," Bright explained as they left the office. "It seems like the Jaburo desk jockeys are an even bigger problem than Zeon . . ."

Amuro pondered the meaning of Bright's words.

IN THE DISTANCE, COMMANDER Char Aznable could see *A Baoa Qu*, the odd, umbrella-like shape of the floating fortress backlit by the rays of the sun. But he was more interested in what was going on inside the cockpit of his new model MS.

The accelerator peddle beneath his right foot was divided into three main stages, each of which could be precisely modulated. He stomped

Mirai Yashima

it to the floor and noted that the entire MS cockpit, including his seat and the control panel, acted as a 360-degree shock absorber, canceling out much of the *g* force that would have normally born down on him. He was delighted. The new model—a Rick Dom—would perform even better than his old Zaku. It was larger in girth, and its armor was twice as strong, but it could turn on a dime. The handheld beam bazooka, moreover, was directly linked to a highly efficient accelerator built into the arm, giving the MS the firepower of the main cannon on a *Musai-*class cruiser.

With this thing, he exulted, *I might be able to bag that White Federation Suit.*

Then a voice came over his receiver, so garbled by Minovsky interference that it was nearly unintelligible: "*Here comes the target, Commander!*"

He barked into his mike in verification, and his message was transmitted to the *A Baoa Qu* operators by both radio and laser transmission. Several seconds later, when he was able to visually identify the target, he lined up the mono-eye sight of his MS with the bead on the beam bazooka barrel in its right hand. Then he pulled the trigger on the control stick, sending a laser-simulated beam streaking toward the target, and awaited a signal telling him if he had hit home or not. He had complete faith in his aim, and used the intervening seconds to check the five Rick Dom Suits deployed on either side of him. They had not even sighted the target yet.

"Suits 2, 3, 4, 5, and 6!" he yelled. "Look above and to your right eighteen degrees! If this were real combat, you'd all have been pulverized! You've gotta do better! Let's run this one more time!"

How many times had they performed the same maneuver? Char was beginning to lose faith in his men. In the last three or four moves executed they had always been too slow. None were new recruits. All were veterans, survivors from the beginning of the war, and all were skilled marksmen. Four had even bagged the ultimate prize—Federation battleships. Perhaps, he thought, the difference between himself and them was that he had more Newtype potential. The futility of forming an effective, coordinated combat team with them grated on his nerves.

Another target appeared to streak out of the fiery sun, attacking the Rick Dom formation in a zigzag maneuver, and Char pulled back to see how the others performed. He had to laugh at himself a little for even believing that humans could improve dramatically overnight or suddenly become "Newtypes." Perhaps, he thought with a tinge of bitterness, there had only been one real Newtype: Lalah Sune.

Then the garbled voice of the operator on *A Baoa Qu* said, "*An Elmeth will be part of today's mock combat.*"

"I thought that wasn't in the schedule today," Char griped.

"*Her Excellency, Kycilia, specifically asked to see your team's performance against it, sir.*"

"Very well," he replied, "but it means we have to stay out here and practice for another five minutes . . . " Before he could finish the sentence, he saw the flare of the Elmeth streak through the blackness. *I wonder if the thing's piloted by a human,* he thought. If so, no one had informed him.

"Formation G!!" he yelled out to his men, initiating a defense tactic that had been devised to take on the white Federation MS—the Gundam—on the assumption that its pilot was a Newtype. It involved deploying the six Rick Doms in an enveloping circle over an area five hundred kilometers in diameter. It was impossible to get a good look at the Elmeth itself at that distance, but the computers in their Suits would put them on a course calculated to bring them into contact, and the rest would be automatic. They would gradually close the noose around the enemy machine, and try to sight it as soon as possible visually.

That was the theory, at least. Ten seconds later the Elmeth had slipped through their net and was closing in on one of the Rick Doms, attacking it without the aid of its remote-controlled auxiliary Bit units, instead using its twin particle cannon with devastating, though simulated, effect. When the fourth Rick Dom in his formation had been "destroyed," Char knew what was happening.

"The Elmeth's not on remote. The pilot's real!" he yelled.

In the same instant he spotted the machine streaking above his own line of fire. He slammed his MS into an evasive maneuver and reflexively pulled the trigger on his beam bazooka. The shot was wasted. Then came another attack.

He aimed, thought he had the Elmeth in his sights, but it outmaneuvered him and dropped below his field of vision.

Char yelled. He heard the simulated sound of something slamming into his Rick Dom and his fuselage creaking. Could he have been hit in the split second his mind was diverted? The readout below his main monitor indicated the left leg of his MS had been "shot" off. He put his machine into a retreat.

As he watched, in the next few seconds the Elmeth polished off the remaining two Rick Doms. The Elmeth's smooth skin swept upward in the rear, from the front giving it the rather charming silhouette of a tricornered hat, but its performance was far from charming. The Elmeth was deadlier than a humanoid-style mobile suit, and not because of its shape (which had little advantage over old-style space fighters), but because of its Newtype pilot.

I bet they've found another woman to pilot the damn thing! Char fumed. He sensed a unique presence emanating from the machine, something female yet unlike that of Lalah Sune. Whatever it was, it possessed a defiant, abrasive quality. Could it be Kusko Al, the junior grade lieutenant candidate that Garcia Dowal had mentioned? He feared a repeat of what had happened with Lalah. He didn't want to see another woman piloting the Elmeth.

The Elmeth floated right in front of his Rick Dom and then suddenly changed course. And sure enough, he caught a glimpse of a woman in a normal suit seated in an illuminated cockpit. He couldn't recognize her, but he knew the unusually large helmet of her normal suit was designed for a Newtype. *Looks just like the one Lalah wore,* he bitterly noted.

He barked out the order to reform, and the other Rick Doms fell into their conventional flight formation around him. He could see the rear of the Elmeth right in front of him.

Laugh at us if you want, he thought, as he put his MS into second level combat speed and soared past the Elmeth, his five comrades trying hard to keep up. For a second, he imagined he heard the Elmeth pilot giggle. But in an instant a trail of light streaked across his main monitor and disappeared into a corner of *A Baoa Qu*. It was the Elmeth.

"*Damn woman!*" he muttered. And then he heard—or thought he heard—a reply:

<*I'm not a 'damn woman.' I have a name . . . Kusko Al . . .*>

There was nothing audible. There were no words. A thought had simply slipped into Char's mind.

"IT'S TRUE WE'RE PUTTING a prototype into action, but we're not compromising on performance. We're talking about something fundamentally different from the new GM Suits. *Understand!?*"

In the mobile suit development hangar on the Federation's *LH* moon base, Amuro listened as Professor Mosk Han lectured him on the latest improvements in MS designs. Mosk was one of the most talented mobile suit engineers in the Federation, but Amuro found that his authoritative, macho demeanor was belied by an almost feminine tendency to over-excitability. He tried to interpret the man's behavior in the best possible light, and write off his outbursts as the product of an overly-intellectual orientation to life.

"But Professor," he said, "if you use a prototype MS design, I don't see how you'll be able to exploit the strengths of the magnetic coating . . ."

"Hmph. You're not trained to think, but just to sit in your cockpit and attack the enemy, so I guess it's *beyond* your comprehension, but the magnetic coating practically eliminates all the mechanical friction normally occurring in the MS power train."

"You mean it functions sort of like oil?"

"Oil?! Did you say, *oil*, lad?!"

Amuro realized he had used the wrong word. Oil was an archaic term, and that apparently had raised Mosk's hackles. "Well," he said, "I'm trying to understand, sir. I know this prototype Gundam is the third model produced, and that it's been put through a pretty strenuous test period. But as the person who has to pilot the machine, I'd just like to make sure every potential problem is eliminated in advance . . ."

"Well, that's clearly impossible. We've painted every single point of physical contact in the power train with magnetic coating. The positive and negative fields of the coating repel each other, thereby completely eliminating any mechanical friction. That's the theory. Understand? This is supposed to eliminate mechanical interference, no matter what amount of force is applied."

Amuro wanted to say something, but he held his tongue. He knew that eliminating mechanical friction would also eliminate the natural braking effect it could provide. And although the new MS body should be able to withstand almost any degree of stress—even when its engine ran into the red zone—he knew it still wouldn't have the speed or agility of movement he really wanted.

"But we still haven't solved the power problem, have we?" he ventured.

"Of course not. What do you think I am? An engine specialist? But listen, since the resistance has dropped in the drive chain, the Gundam's actual overall mobility has increased between 120 and 130 percent. That's almost like installing a new engine that's twice as powerful . . . "

"Oh, I see . . . "

"Try it out. You'll be pleased. If we improved the MS performance much beyond this point your body wouldn't be able to keep up. You'd be constantly buffeted by enormous g forces, and in four or five minutes your insides'd be Jello. But I agree it's an area we've eventually got to address. We've got to find a way to create a cockpit that cancels out the g forces, or else do something to your body so it can withstand them better."

"Oh."

"You're a clever lad. Keep me informed of the test results. And when you write up your reports, don't forget I'll be reading them, too."

"Yessir."

It was awfully difficult, Amuro realized, to judge people by first impressions. Those who seemed pleasant at first, usually were good people. Professor Mosk wasn't particularly pleasant, but the instant Amuro had changed his attitude to one of deference, the man had become so friendly it was uncanny. Perhaps, Amuro thought, it was a characteristic of technologists in the field.

WHILE STILL PONDERING THE professor's personality, Amuro kicked off the hangar deck and sailed up through the low gravity air to the new Gundam's cockpit hatch. He was relieved that the Suit's basic humanoid design hadn't been tampered with, and that, unlike the GM models, it still had two "eyes." If the machine was functionally going to reflect the pilot's will—his will—he wanted it to have some sort of expression. It needn't be able to frown or raise its eyebrows like the crude pneumatic-powered Marilyn Monroe humanoid robots popular in shows in the last century. The two "eyes" were enough to create the emotive quality he wanted.

As always, the Gundam cockpit was encased in a cold, steel-like material that felt like coffin walls. He shut the front hatch, whereupon the sound of the idling motor faded, leaving him enveloped in the Zen-like nothingness of total darkness. The instrument panel was inactive. Something about the air in the cockpit reminded him that maintenance people had been working on it only a few minutes ago, but it was freshly vacuumed, and spotless. The pilot seat was as hard and uncomfortable as ever, but that was to be expected. Everything was more or less as he was accustomed from his last MS. The main control levers were on either side of him, and the foot pedals were in their appropriate locations. Even in pitch darkness he knew exactly where the twenty-eight switches of the control panel were. It was a relief. Switches, levers, pedals. All he had to do was stretch out his arms and legs, and everything was where it was supposed to be. *This should do fine*, he thought, *for the time being, at least.* He wasn't really sure where the thought, "the time being" came from, or what he really meant.

Peering around him, he knew it wasn't true, as some people said, that total darkness was frightening. He let his pupils dilate, and still couldn't see a thing; in fact he could hardly tell if his eyes were open or shut. He looked straight ahead, and let himself relax. He listened to, and counted his breath. He became more aware of being alive, and felt incredibly peaceful.

Then he heard, or sensed, a pinging noise. It was faint, but soon accompanied by what felt like a tiny thread of light streaming out from the center of his brain into the darkness before him, through the hatch of the Gundam cockpit, through the surface of the moon above him, and into the vastness of the surrounding space. The light was sharply defined, but had a warm, reassuring glow to it.

"Lalah . . . ?"

Amuro shifted in his seat. He wanted to see where the light was headed, but it was already gone. It hadn't been a hallucination. He knew it had continued on into the black space before him. But he felt confused. *Lalah Sune . . .* An indescribable aching sensation welled in his body, irritating and then destroying his earlier tranquility. A chill slowly crawled up his spine and spread out through his flesh until the ends of his limbs quivered.

Lalah Sune . . . is it Lalah Sune? Something in his mind nearly screamed the thought. He felt even more anxious and annoyed. *What are you trying to tell me? Lalah . . . or whoever you are. What is it?*

He knew he had to do something. He put his hand on one of the Gundam's control levers and squeezed it. Then he turned the key in the ignition, and through the floor of the cockpit felt the engine groan before fully igniting. When the instument panel sprang to life, its lights nearly blinded him with their sudden brightness, and instantly banished the entire black universe before him. They had two stages of intensity, and when they reached the second he knew the main engine had fired. With a *VROOM*, the Gundam revealed its inner power.

Then he knew part of the source of his frustration. The machine enveloping him was a weapon. *Are Newtypes*, he wondered, *merely extension of weapons? Just tools of destruction? Is that what Lalah Sune was? Is that what the "Red Comet" is? Is that all I am?* He was flesh and blood. Not a machine. He wanted desperately to refute such a repulsive idea and assert a higher purpose in life for himself. But a swirling undercurrent of self-doubt undermined his ability to do so.

Newtypes are humans . . . He pushed the right hand control lever forward, and the Gundam's right arm rose with a burst of energy, far faster than the old model, with enough force to make the entire MS fuselage recoil. But with that movement Amuro's own reflexes also came alive, and his limbs began moving the other controls in the small cockpit, working rapidly to keep the Gundam properly balanced.

A TEAM OF MECHAMEN who had just finished a job in another corner of the hangar turned and stared at the Gundam. It was standing with its back still attached to a maintenance fixture, but its limbs began slicing through the air. One man yelled to his comrades: "Hey, get a load of that, will ya? That shows what magnetic coating can do!"

The new Gundam was infinitely more maneuverable than either the original model or the mass-produced GM Suits currently in use, and its next maneuver was truly astonishing. Its left arm slowly rose in the air, paused for a few seconds, and then slammed downward, but the body of the machine scarcely twitched, despite having moved off the supporting fixture. By slightly shifting the Suit's hips, Amuro had perfectly canceled the weight of the mass in its arm. To the cheers of the mechamen, he then began moving the Gundam with such speed and grace it looked more like a human boxer than an inorganic machine. In theory, it shouldn't even have been possible.

An order then issued from the control room. "*Number Six hatches will open shortly. All personnel in hangar area must move to the air-lock!*"

The mechamen in the maintenance area ran for cover to the air lock room, and clustered around its one-meter-square blast-proof window, transfixed. The new Gundam began striding forth.

AFTER PASSING THROUGH THE double-layered hangar hatches, Amuro entered the vacuum area of the moon base. On the cockpit's displays he saw a sliver of Earth shining in the distance, surrounded by stars blazing in the heavens. He announced into his mike: "Ensign Amuro Ray in G3, ready for launch! Now commencing practice flight!"

The base flight control officer's voice crackled in his headphones, stating what they both already knew: *Take it away, Ensign. Remember, you're going out there to get used to the Suit's flight characteristics.*

Amuro double-checked his radar and laser sensors. Neither would be much good with the high Minovsky concentration in the area, but the lasers could at least act as an Identification Friend of Foe, or IFF, signal, and there was something reassuring about having radar, even if it didn't work. He looked up at the heavens through his main display, double-checking the area in space from which his computer was registering information. Somewhere out there he knew a space-beacon would delineate the practice area for him.

"Blast off!"

He said it half to himself, half as a formality to inform the flight officer. He fired the main rockets in the Gundam's backpack, and to his astonishment the Suit soared nearly ten thousand meters in seconds. The new model was far faster than he had expected. The laser accelerator in its nuclear fusion engine had been improved, theoretically yielding only twenty to thirty percent more power, but when combined with the new magnetic coating on the power train, the resulting synergy seemed to have nearly doubled the MS's power and speed.

Yet he was still bothered by one thought: *If only the armor had been reinforced, too.* The engineers had improved the machine's performance without improving his personal protection and there was something disturbing about that. He understood the logic behind the changes made, but he was the pilot and the one whose life was on the line. Perhaps he was asking too much, but he was human. Perhaps, he imagined, it was even something Lalah had tried to warn him about earlier.

He was sure of one thing—this talk of Newtypes and their future transcended concerns over his personal safety. He knew the leap in consciousness, the sense of prescience he had experienced with Lalah Sune was not limited to them alone. Their special communion had heightened their five senses, and expanded the fundamental communication of which *all* humans are capable. And in the end it had generated a mysterious compound, universal wisdom. It was an experience, he was convinced, that led beyond personal oblivion.

But if Amuro was a potential Newtype, he was also an ensign in the Federation Forces, a military pilot. And military pilots were not supposed to ponder the future of mankind. They were supposed to kill, and survive to kill again. To stay alive and develop as a true Newtype he would first have to conquer the vast obstacle unfolding before him, the battlefield of outer space. It seemed like a cruel fate, but whether military pilot or Newtype, his fundamental emotional makeup was the same. He knew that he would just have to wait and see what happened.

THE NEW GUNDAM MOBILE suit was a deep gray color and therefore harder to visually spot in space, but it had also been designed to be even more invisible to radar. To make certain accidents didn't happen during training flights, the Suit had running lights for identification on its shoulders and toes. To Amuro's left and right, the lights streaked through space among the stars.

ON THE BRIDGE OF the *Pegasus II*, Chief Petty Officer Marker Clan suddenly sighted a unique laser oscillation on the computer-generated model displayed on the ceiling and called out, "*It's the new Gundam!*" The computer system was even less reliable than radar, but it was at least capable of detecting and encoding laser signals.

"*Three degrees to port! Elevation 36 degrees! Distance 180 kilometers!*" barked Petty Officer Oscar Dublin, perched opposite Marker on the bridge's boom crane.

Bright scrambled down from the captain's seat at the base of the crane arm, ordering, "Sayla! Open a radio link! The Gundam's coming in for a test landing on Deck One."

"*Gundam! G3!*" Sayla announced, her eyes intent on the comm panel in front of her. "*This is* Pegasus II. *Can you read us? Over.*" She sounded so professional it was hard to believe that she had once been a raw recruit derisively referred to as "the bungler."

Amuro's voice burbled up through the static. "*This is G3! I read you! My instruments confirm the Pegasus II . . .* " In a heavy concentration of Minovsky particles, it took a highly trained comm tech to fully understand what he was saying.

"Pegasus *to Gundam,*" Sayla replied. "*We have opened the hatch on Deck One for you. You are cleared for landing!*"

"*Understood! Landing at third combat speed. Incoming!*"

Bright turned and nodded at Mirai, standing with her hands on the helm. She switched it to automatic and ran to the bridge window to see the Gundam.

"He came into view awfully fast, didn't he," she said.

"That's Amuro for you," Bright replied.

"I'll say. The ace of the 127th . . . "

PEGASUS II, THE SECOND White Base-class cosmo cruiser in the Federation arsenal, was an assault landing ship but from certain angles it resembled a giant winged horse. In the vacuum of space, the wings performed no aerodynamic function but instead acted as heat dissipation panels and held the ship's solar energy cells and many of its vernier jets. The wings were so huge that on Earth the ship would have seemed capable of leaping through the stratosphere. As with its predecessor, the main bridge of the craft, protruding forward near the prow, truly looked like the head of a horse, which was of course why the first ship of this class had been called *Pegasus*. Federation Forces had christened the second ship with the same name as the first, not only because of the physical resemblance, but because the original crew had been transferred to it, and because General Revil believed it would bring them good "luck."

With the officers on the bridge marvelling at the sight, the Gundam approached the *Pegasus II* and logged the correct coordinates for landing on Deck One, on the ship's right front "leg."

The upper and lower hatch doors of Deck One opened, exposing the landing floor and its approach lights. The Gundam moved straight toward them, a line of horizontal green lights on either side of the deck blinking in confirmation of its course. Simultaneously, indicators showing horizontal status, attitude, and speed relative to the ship blinked in synch on Amuro's console—laser sensors were accurate at distances under two thousand meters, even with a heavy Minovsky concentration. The hatch quickly looming into view was huge, but the landing site still wasn't an easy target. The Gundam sailed toward the center of it, streaking by painted white guidelines. Then, with a *whoosh*, retrorockets fired, the Suit's knees bent to absorb the shock, and both of its legs hit the ground simultaneously. Amuro had made a perfect single-point landing.

"*Congratulations, Ensign!*" Kai Shiden's voice echoed from the upper left three inch mini-monitor in Amuro's cockpit. "*It looked beautiful!*"

Amuro grinned bashfully at the image on the screen. As he released his seat belt, he replied, "I used to be able to fly by the seat of my pants, but I think I forgot how. I broke out in a cold sweat a couple times back there!"

On the next monitor over, the face of the flight deck supervisor appeared, yelling, "*G3! Stand-by for thirty seconds. Do not open your cockpit hatch until air intake is completed on Deck One!*" It belonged to a young recruit Amuro had never seen before, who immediately introduced himself with loud enthusiasm. *"Petty Officer First Class Callahan Slay, sir! At your service, sir!"* He seemed so overzealous Amuro wondered if he would be able to stay calm in times of a crisis.

"Glad to be working with you, Callahan. Twenty seconds have already elapsed!"

"Twenty seconds . . . Yes, sir! Go ahead and open the hatch, sir!"

Amuro pulled a lever and opened the cockpit hatch. It shared space with his main display, which meant that to exit he had to use a foot rest built into the far right side of the console panel, and then ease his torso out. A ramp from the right wall of the flight deck extended out to his cockpit.

"Well, how was it?" It was Lt. Seki, a technical officer Amuro had known ever since his days on *Luna II*.

"No problem, sir! The magnetic coating seems to work perfectly."

"Well, I'll still give it a once-over to check for anything unusual. You know how it is. I've got to compensate for those scientists and the top brass. They always tend to rush these things."

"You think there might be problem with the coating, sir?"

"If there is, it's a relative problem. The structural materials used in the Gundam design aren't going to get any stronger. In some ways it's safer if you can't move the thing too fast."

"Sounds to me, sir, that you're saying we need to compromise on speed for safety's sake."

"Exactly. But we're talking about a *combat* Suit here, so combat performance gets priority. The brass apparently assume anyone operating this thing has the skills of a test pilot."

Amuro laughed despite himself. There was more than a little irony in Seki's words. After all, the *Pegasus II* and its entire crew were part of a grand experiment. They were all, in a sense, test pilots.

"Basically, Ensign, I want to keep you alive as long as possible."

"The sentiment's shared, sir," Amuro replied, removing his helmet and starting to walk down the ramp to the flight deck.

Then he heard a *"Yo,"* and saw a smiling face in a lemon yellow pilot's suit. It was Kai Shiden.

"Hey, Kai," he asked, pointing at a new red MS to the rear of Deck One, "you piloting that Guncannon over there?" Guncannons, like the Gundam, were of humanoid design and had two arms capable of holding a beam rifle, but they weren't as suited for close-quarter combat as the Gundam or the GM models. Instead, the twin 28 centimeter cannons built into their shoulders were used primarily for long-range support.

"Yeah," Kai answered without enthusiasm. "That's the C108. It'll do the job, maybe."

Kai didn't have the type of positive personality Amuro normally admired, but the two of them had begun their pilot training together, survived combat together, and now were linked by a bond different from friendship but just as real.

"Everyone's waiting for you, partner," Kai said.

Since being reunited with his comrades on the *LH* docking pier, Amuro had spent two days alone working with Mosk readying the new Gundam. Now he would finally, hopefully, be able to spend a little time relaxing with them on the ship. Just thinking about it made him feel flush with anticipation, but there was still an enormous amount of work to do. The *Pegasus II* carried five mobile suits including the Gundam, and several hours would be required to train the Suit pilots to work as a team, in formation. Amuro's first assignment was to lead a special training session on the ship's bridge.

The moment he stepped into the room, he was warmly welcomed. Bright, in the captain's seat, saluted and barked, "Congratulations, Ensign!"

"Well, how was the flight?" Mirai asked.

"You looked great out there, Amuro. Well done. . . ." Hayato added.

Amuro first noticed the new faces among the group, including Ensigns Sarkus McGovern and Kria Maja, both new MS pilots. But he also saw some old ones. Marker Clan and Oscar Dublin grinned at him from their operator seats on the bridge boom crane. And when Sayla Mass turned around and smiled at him, he nearly choked.

With her blond hair and nearly perfect posture, she looked more beautiful than he remembered. Perhaps, he suddenly thought, she really *was* the woman of his dreams. He felt a little confused. Before taking off in the new Gundam from the *LH* moon base, when sitting in the pitch blackness of his new cockpit, he had experienced a sort of intuitive communion with the memory of Lalah Sune. But there had been something missing with Lalah. And here it was. For the first time since parting with Kusko Al, he felt physical desire.

"Congratulations, Ensign," Sayla said. Her clear voice was music to his ears.

I never realized how much I wanted her . . .

Amuro, surprised at himself, decided to invite her to join him that very night.

PEOPLE

"FOR THE LIFE OF ME, I can't understand why Gihren would call me back to the Fatherland on the eve of our showdown with the Federation."

In the vast hall of the Zeon War Council, Vice Admiral Dozle Zabi deliberately blurted out the words loud enough so that his father, Sovereign Degwin, seated on his throne, could easily hear them. Dozle's elder brother Gihren, the Supreme Commander chairing the Council, did not react at all, and merely continued to lord it over those in attendance. He was flanked by both Dozle and his sister, Rear Admiral Kycilia, and a bevy of ranking Zeon officers under Zabi family control.

Technically, a civilian government ruled Zeon, but even the layout of the room reflected a bargain struck between image and reality. Prime Minister Darcia Bakharov, along with several ministers under his influence, was one of the few civilians to rise to power through the ranks of the bureaucracy and was thus supposed to have been given the seat of honor near Sovereign Degwin Zabi. Since the Zabi family depended on the military, however, he was seated the farthest away. One third of his cabinet ministers were controlled by the Zabi family. Degwin, nominally an observer at such meetings, had already been reduced to a puppet. True power lay in the hands of his son, Supreme Commander Gihren Zabi.

CHAPTER TWELVE

THE PRIME MINISTER'S OCCASIONAL reluctance to conform had created a suspicion in some quarters that he harbored a desire to depose Supreme Commander Gihren and restore Degwin to power. Gihren was fully aware of the rumor, yet prepared to tolerate it. He was accustomed to scheming minds, and knew intrigues were a normal part of human nature. He knew, moreover, that as long as the rumors were not an overt threat, there was no use in trying to suppress them completely, and that doing so would only be counterproductive. As long as Darcia was restrained, therefore, Gihren would not take action against the man. All he had to do, he believed, was to tighten the reigns of control and make him subtly aware of the futility of his scheming. That was the type of man Gihren was. He would let his brother Dozle raise as much fuss as he wanted. As long as there was no major change in the overall picture, he knew his position was secure. He could trust his sister Kycilia to keep the rest of the situation under control.

"VICE ADMIRAL DOZLE," KYCILIA began, replying to her brother's earlier comment, "if, as we suspect, the Federation Forces have detected what we are up to, then I respectfully submit that there is only one issue that must be urgently addressed today, and that is the state of progress on our System project. We must keep our perspective!"

Gihren noted that, as he had hoped, Kycilia was working to keep Dozle in line.

Kycilia glanced at Gihren after her statement and then turned to Prime Minister Darcia. "We need you to give us an overview of the System project as proposed by the Supreme Commander."

Darcia thereupon launched into a prepared presentation. For most of the officials present it was the first time they had heard of the plan, but the principle behind it was elegantly simple. Zeon's older colonies consisted of sealed cylinders six kilometers in diameter by thirty kilometers in length. One of these would be evacuated and the inner walls coated with aluminum. Solar energy would be stored and concentrated in a powerful electromagnetic field inside, and then released by suddenly opening one end of the cylinder. It entailed a massive construction project, and would thus take time, but if all went as planned the result would be a weapon of unprecedented destructive power, a giant laser cannon six kilometers in diameter. If properly aimed, an entire battle group, perhaps even half of the Federation Forces, could be instantly annihilated. For the Principality of Zeon, whose forces were from the beginning limited and now nearing the point of exhaustion, the "System," as the project was code-named, was an extremely attractive strategy.

"The cabinet," Darcia announced, "wishes to keep Zeon's civilian casualties to a minimum, and to do this we must bring the war to its earliest possible conclusion. We therefore have resolved to endorse the System project."

The prime minister's announcement was important, as without a national consensus the project could never be completed. The System required not only a massive budget, but also the evacuation of over three million people from an older existing colony, and the cooperation of a wide variety of industries.

"Hmph," Dozle sniffed. "What do we need a cabinet resolution for?"

"Hold your tongue, brother," Kycilia hissed, again acting just as Gihren had hoped.

Darcia raised his voice another notch and continued. "Accordingly, given the nature of this measure, we wish to propose that it be seriously discussed by all parties in attendance today, and then, in order to obtain the final authorization of His Excellency, Sovereign Degwin, that it be submitted for formal approval."

Two or three questions then followed, all of which revolved around the prospects of total victory. There was no need to debate anything else. Unbeknownst to most civilians present, the project was already well under way, and the evacuation of Zeon's third colony cylinder, *Mahal*, was proceeding under the supervision of a high ranking Zeon officer.

The council fell silent for several minutes. All present sensed the tightening web of Gihren's total control. But distracted by all the attention to a single grandiose strategy, or by the fate of this or that Zeon warship, few truly realized that the Zeon nation had begun to move in a direction of its own. It was, needless to say, a totally different direction from what they suspected.

Prime Minister Darcia took the cabinet's written proposal, placed it in a black leather file with the Principality of Zeon seal, and walked toward Degwin. No one in the hall spoke. Gihren kept staring at the long table top in front of him, and his face took on an ashen hue. Darcia ascended the three steps in front of Degwin's throne, placed the file on a stand next to it, and stiffly slid it toward the sovereign. And then he heard words that made him doubt his own ears.

"My eldest son is a blot on my honor," Degwin whispered. "Do with him as you please ... "

Zeon's sovereign had never uttered such a thing, even behind closed doors. *Perhaps he's going senile*, Darcia thought for a second. He stared at

Degwin's spectacles, trying to fathom the expression in the eyes behind them, but the man had already reached out for a pen to sign the document and his face was turned away. Darcia hoped the words he had heard were a figment of his imagination. He was a civilian, with precious few connections in the military elite. His real role in the government was to provide a civilian face to the Zeon people. Like Degwin, he was really only a puppet, and what could a conspiracy between two puppets possibly accomplish?

Degwin put down his pen, smiled, and whispered words unrelated to his expression. "*It's Kycilia, isn't it?*"

What did he mean? Darcia wondered. Was he trying to say that he should use Kycilia to crush Gihren? As far as Darcia was concerned, Kycilia was just as formidable a threat as Gihren.

"Thank you, Your Excellency," he nonetheless replied, returning Degwin's smile. Then he turned around and walked over toward Gihren. When viewed from behind in his military uniform, Gihren's neck looked as thick as a log, invulnerable even to a beam saber blade. Darcia opened the file and showed Gihren his father's signature.

"Well done, Darcia," Gihren said. He normally looked at people with a cold, piercing expression, but his mouth was now formed into a thin smile.

"Thank you, sir," Darcia answered. Then he turned to either side, showed the same file to Dozle and Kycilia, and after receiving their acknowledgement returned to his own seat, the lowest in the hierarchy.

Gihren next rose and addressed the Council:

"One hour from now we shall hold a comprehensive strategy meeting at the Joint Chiefs of Staff Headquarters. Let me humbly express my appreciation for the time and wise counsel you have all invested in this issue. Like us, the Federation Forces are nearing exhaustion. But a new element has been introduced into the balance of power. Now that the System plan has been authorized, what we have gained in strength is equivalent to between five to ten new divisions! I am proud to say, frankly, that our decision has altered the odds of victory in our favor. It is an accomplishment that every citizen of Zeon should take pride in, for the System project is a crystallization of all of our labor and sweat. The System strategy will henceforth be the centerpiece of our operations. I ask now that each and every one of you take this fact fully to heart, to exert your utmost to destroy the Federation Forces as soon as possible, and thus gain honor for the Principality of Zeon. May you and your families prosper. *Death to our enemies!*"

In the midst of Gihren's speech, Degwin Zabi stood up and left.

It was already past seven o'clock mean time when the *Pegasus II* and its five mobile suits finished practicing combat formation flight and returned to the *LH* moon base. In the base docking bay, several *Salamis*-class cruisers were already moored, and preparations for the upcoming mission were proceeding at a feverish pitch.

Before leaving the bridge, Amuro loosened his pilot's suit and turned to Bright in the captain's seat. "When do we ship out next, skipper?" he asked.

"How the hell should I know?! You think they'd tell me? All I know is that we have to perform all preflight maintenance within twenty-eight hours."

"And we take off right after that?"

"I doubt it. We're talking about the military here, remember? But there's always a possibility we'll have to leave even earlier, so just in case you'd better get as much sleep as you can tonight. My gut feeling is that we'll be here another two nights, but who knows?"

"Understood, sir. Do you think my stuff has been delivered to officer's quarters on base?"

"Your stuff?"

"Just one duffel bag, that's all."

"Probably . . . "

A "duffel bag" was military slang for a waterproof denim sack that held a single standard-issue military uniform. It was an anachronistic term in the space age but still popular, a holdover from naval traditions of a bygone era.

Turning to Petty Officer Sayla Mass, Bright said, "He doesn't seem to know his way around this place. Show him to his quarters . . . "

"Yessir," she replied. Still engrossed in her work at the comm console, she quickly added, "Just give me two or three minutes, okay?"

While waiting, Amuro watched Bright monitor the pre-flight checks on the bridge displays and bark orders throughout the new ship. Things seemed to have changed so much, he noted, and so fast. The bridge was bustling with activity and alive with a new energy he did not recall from before. Was it because many of the crew were potential Newtypes? There was no way of knowing for certain, but there *was* a palpably different, though intangible, aura about them. He sensed something unlike the emotive communion he had had with Lalah Sune, and for a moment he wondered if the difference was simply because he wasn't properly attuned to his crewmates, but he decided it was more than that. There was something clear, soft, even reassuring in the atmosphere. It was a peaceful feeling, almost like home. There was no point on dwelling on the reasons. Had it not been wartime, with all its attendant tensions, he would have abandoned himself to the sensation and been lulled into a deep and restful sleep.

"Sorry to keep you waiting, Ensign . . . "

At the sound of the overly polite voice, Amuro turned around to see Sayla. She was carrying a thick file, which reminded him of the studious young woman he had first encountered on Side 7's Zeravi library. But she seemed tired. It was odd, because she had been so energetic when working earlier. And standing close to her, he sensed more than fatigue, something closer to melancholy, for lack of a better term. For some reason, he was suddenly also acutely aware of the fact that she was of the opposite sex. He wondered what was troubling her, and what to do, but he decided not to dwell on it. Her mood was probably just a normal part of her overall emotional makeup.

"This way . . . " She turned away from him, and walked toward one of the two hatches in the rear of the bridge. He followed, watching. She was a year or two older than he was, but a tad shorter. As usual, he admired her pretty blond hair. When they reached the elevator that would lead them out to the docking bay, he asked: "Well, have you finally gotten used to life on ship?"

"Why, yes, thank you," she replied. "At least I don't get in everyone's way anymore. And by the way, I'm glad you made it back okay, Ensign."

"Whoa . . . please, let's cut out the rank. You'll embarrass me . . . "

"Well, I'm a petty officer second class; you're an ensign. This *is* the military, isn't it?"

"Well, yes . . . but dammit . . . Don't be that way with me, Sayla."

"Just between the two of us, then, what should I call you, Ensign?"

"Er . . . um . . . " Unable to answer properly, Amuro began to grind his teeth. It was weird. Here he was, a seasoned combat veteran. Somehow he had assumed that would help him relate to her on a more equal, adult basis, but so much for that idea. He was stammering away, another naive delusion shattered. He fell silent.

Twenty seconds later the elevator stopped at the ship's upper deck and the instant the door opened they were enveloped in a cacophony of sound. *They oughta let the air out of the hangars when they do pre-flight maintenance and supply operations,* Amuro thought reflexively.

The upper deck was at the base of the ship's bridge, and from it one could look out the open hatches of the starboard and port leg-like extremities. The hangars of the *LH* docking bay were on two staggered levels, and on the lower one a transport ship that had moored was busy unloading ammunition and weaponry. On the upper level, work crews Amuro had never seen before were engaged in a flurry of activity, and clearly a source of most of the noise. They were already welding parts of the *Pegasus II* deck, and even stripping off parts of its armor.

Amuro tried to cross over to the mooring pier but tripped on a ladder. He grumbled despite himself at an officer in front of him holding a transceiver. "What the hell's going on?"

"What's the matter? The repairs bother you?"

The officer turned around and Amuro had to stifle a gasp. It was Matilda Ajan, the pretty junior grade lieutenant from the 28th Division whom he had met once before on *Luna II*.

"Ensign!" she said, as surprised as he was.

As when they had first met, he noted her auburn hair. It was a shame that she kept it so short.

"I . . . I'm sorry . . . I spoke out of line," he mumbled.

"Never mind, Ensign . . . Ensign Amuro Ray, isn't it? I remember you. Lt. Woody Malden's in charge of the repairs and you can trust him one hundred percent. He says the *Pegasus* needs a more consistent thickness of armor plating."

"Lt. Woody Malden?"

"An officer from the Armory . . . " She pointed with her chin in the direction of an officer engineer with a powerful physique, who turned around as if on cue.

Amuro silently mouthed the name "Woody," and for a moment couldn't think of anything else to say. The timing between Matilda and Woody could have been accidental, but then again it probably wasn't. The officer had responded in a special way to her. He was a handsome man with heavy eyebrows and full lips, twinkling eyes, and an active demeanor, exactly the type Amuro suspected Matilda would go for. And he was in a unit with which she would naturally have a lot of contact.

"You say something, Matilda?" Woody asked, walking over toward them. He seemed to have absolutely no trouble handling moon gravity. *He looks and acts like a real combat veteran,* Amuro thought.

"No, sir," Matilda replied. "This is Ensign Amuro Ray. He was just asking what you're doing . . . "

Amuro heard a slight quaver in Matilda's voice, and turned away from the pair in embarrassment.

"Some problem?" Woody asked.

"No, *sir!*" Amuro fired back. "Just an opinion stated without knowing the facts. I'm sure the *Pegasus* is in good hands!" He saluted, and jumped off the ladder toward the pier itself.

"Amuro!" Sayla called out after him as he sailed through the low gravity air.

When the concrete surface of the pier filled his vision, Amuro flexed his knees, and landed. To his surprise, Sayla landed beside him only seconds later.

"*Amuro!* What's the *matter* with you?" she cried, regretting her choice of words before she had completed her sentence. She felt flustered herself.

He sensed her emotion, but he wasn't ready to think of its implications. He was still preoccupied with Matilda Ajan and the sudden realization that she was in love with someone. He had no idea why it bothered him. He didn't have a crush on her or anything like that, he told himself, although he knew his reaction spoke otherwise. Maybe, it occurred to him, he was simply too immature and inexperienced around women. But maybe he was just too self-critical. Just having a woman like Sayla or Matilda stand in front of him was enough to overload his brain and paralyze him. He knew he could never compare himself favorably with Woody, for example. If Matilda so much as tossed her auburn hair in the direction of Woody, for example, he knew the confident officer would grab her right away. Just thinking about it made him feel all the more humiliated.

"*Amuro!*" Sayla said, grabbing his left arm.

"What?" he said, noticing her blond hair again. She was so different from Matilda.

"That building over there . . . that's the quarters you've been assigned to!" she said, with an official tone. Most men would have detected a tinge of jealousy in her words, but Amuro was oblivious to it.

She helped him check into the facility, where he was assigned his private quarters. As an ensign, he was on a different floor than Sayla, who was housed with the junior officers. As he was about to step into the elevator to go to his room, he turned to her and asked, "Will you join me for dinner tonight?"

"But Amuro, you're probably busy, and tired, right?"

"Uh . . . no . . . heck . . . Besides, I don't get the chance to eat with you very often. I'd love it if you'd join me."

She nodded an "okay," and they agreed to meet in the mess hall in fifteen minutes. He then proceeded up to his room, where he showered and changed and wished he had time to polish his shoes. Something about way she had agreed to join him seemed a little vague, and bothered him.

Sayla showed up a few minutes late, apologizing, and looking different. To his surprise, she had put on a touch of lipstick. Their eyes met and he realized she really had been looking forward to their date, but he also recognized something in her that *did* remind him of Lalah. Perhaps Sayla really was a Newtype, too. There was only one reason he suspected so. There was something in her eyes he had never noticed before, something subjective, something that couldn't be explained logically. It was as if she had another aura about her; one darker, more ponderous. He knew it wasn't malevolent, but whatever it was, it made Sayla seem different. Perhaps he had been blind all along, blinded by his impression of her as the "bungler" on ship, blinded by the childlike interest he had had in her ever since Side 7. He knew she had managed to lead the *Pegasus* survivors to safety before *Texas* had blown up. He knew that whatever image he had had of her in the past, it was time to revise it.

"Something the matter, Amuro?" she asked, looking at him oddly.

"Nothing . . . uh . . . I . . . " He started to say something, but stopped. The most important thing at this point was just to sit down and calm down, but he was in a self-service dining room, with all the bothersome procedures it always entailed.

"Congratulations on your escape from *Texas*," he said as they started eating. "I heard all about how the *Pegasus* was put out of action."

"Thanks. But I wasn't on the ship at the end. . . ."

"You weren't?!"

"That's right. "

It had never occurred to him before. Did she mean that she had abandoned her post and fled? The rules were sometimes bent for the Waves in the military, but desertion was an offense for which men and women were judged equally.

"What happened? Some sort of Newtype impulse grab you?" he feebly joked.

"I could *feel* the enemy," she said, hesitatingly. "It felt like a powerful force. I knew the whole crew would be in danger, so I left to locate an escape route from the colony."

"Wow . . . "

Sayla was feeding him a half-lie. But it was true that after parting with her brother Char Aznable she had worked feverishly to help rescue the crew of the doomed *Pegasus*. In fact, as some of the crew had later told Amuro, they had heard her voice mysteriously come out of nowhere.

"Did you know where the crew were when the ship finally went down?"

"No. I didn't know where *they* were, but they apparently knew where *I* was."

"See, you must be a Newtype . . . "

"I can't believe it myself. Do you really think this is the way Newtype powers appear in people?"

"I did some research on Newtypes when I was on Side 6, Sayla, and they're not supposed to be able to do anything supernatural. But if many people can do what you did, the scientists'll probably have to rethink the whole concept."

"Don't read too much into what I did. The Newtypes Zeon Zum Deikun spoke of were supposed to symbolize something much more universal, something that applies to all mankind."

"So?"

"They're not supposed to be people who dash off on a whim, like me." She put her fork down on the table. "You know what? It's a one-sided affair for me . . . "

A one-sided affair? What on earth did she mean? His ears immediately pricked up. Was she trying to tell him she was in love with someone?

"I have an older brother, Amuro. Someone I haven't seen for years and years. I've got a bit of a hang-up about the whole thing. Sometimes I have something like a seizure when I'm near him. I'm sorry, I know this all sounds weird . . . "

An older brother? A seizure? Amuro was perplexed. What in heaven's name was she talking about? What did this have to do with their discussion of Newtypes?

"It's like something suddenly goes off in my mind sometimes. Maybe in this case it helped me save the others. . . ."

"Sayla, when you say 'seizure,' do you mean something that might conceivably happen between two Newtypes, if, say, their minds were on the same wavelength? The sort of thing that might suddenly expand their consciousness, even project it?" Amuro chose his words carefully, thinking of Lalah Sune.

"You've quite a way with words, Ensign," she said. Then she looked into his eyes, and added, "and you may be right . . . "

"Think so?"

"Yes . . . "

"I know you used the word 'seizure,' Sayla, but I think you're really referring to a special ability, something dormant until activated by a sudden stimulus. Right?"

"Right. It's sort of like when . . . "

Amuro didn't need to hear the rest. He completed the sentence for her: " . . . *like when you met your brother . . . your brother Char Aznable . . . "* It was incredible, but he knew exactly what she was trying to say.

Sayla blanched.

"Forgive me," he quickly added. "Just my imagination running wild."

"No," she replied hoarsely. "It's true. How'd you know?"

Now it was Amuro's turn to feel shocked. It wasn't the sort of connection, after all, that could be easily deduced. "That's a good question," he replied. "I don't know. I wish I did, but I don't."

Sweat started to bead on his brow, and he raised his hand to wipe it. How the hell could he know? He didn't have the faintest idea. The whole conversation was starting to confuse him enormously. He looked at her. Maybe she had the answer. If anyone did, it would have to be her; he was sure she had something to do with what he had just sensed. Come to think of it, there was something similar about the aura he sensed around her and that which he had once sensed in Char Aznable. But it was easy to make a logical connection after the fact. He waited for her to say something.

"As long as we're on this track," she continued, haltingly, "you want to know something else? Char's real name is Casval Deikun, mine's Artesia Deikun, and we're the children of Zeon Zum Deikun. Sayla Mass is the name I took after my brother and I fled from Zeon to Earth. Well? How's *that* for a shocker?"

Amuro was stunned by her words. He glanced around the room, and his nervous system went on a 360-degree alert. If anyone overheard their conversation, there would be hell to pay. "This is not the place for that sort of talk, Sayla . . . " he cautioned in a low voice.

"Maybe I made it all up," she countered with a weak smile.

"Sayla! I honestly don't know if you did or not. But to me it's got to be real. It's the only way I can understand what I've been sensing in you."

"You think we're kindred spirits, Amuro?"

"For lack of a better word, yes. I've felt the same way with Char, with Lalah, and even with Kusko Al . . . "

"*Lalah? Kusko Al?* Who are they?"

"They're Zeon Newtypes. I had to fight Lalah on *Texas.* And Kusko Al's probably the next one I'll face. I got to know her through the intelligence organization on Side 6. She's a Newtype."

"So Zeon's really deploying Newtypes in combat?"

"Right," Amuro sighed, "while the Federation still thinks they're some sort of joke . . . "

KAI SHIDEN SUDDENLY ENTERED the dining room with several mechamen, heading for the tables in the corner. "Yo, Ensign Amuro!" he called out.

"Having a good time?! And the Petty Officer? How about a date with me tonight, sweetie?"

"Too bad, *Mister* Kai," Sayla bantered back, her clear voice echoing through the dining hall. "I've already got one ensign here, and he's more than enough to keep me company . . . "

Amuro's jaw dropped in amazement. He stared at her, feeling terribly self-conscious, while Kai's table erupted in laughter and wolf whistles. "Yo, Don Juan, the irresistible!" someone said in his direction. "It's no fair! You join our new ship late, and then walk off with one of our prize Waves! What've you got to say for yourself, man?!"

In the midst of the teasing, Sayla turned and with a twinkle in her eye whispered, "Don't make me lose face now, Amuro. . . . Go along with me and make it up to them later. You know, buy them a drink or take them out to dinner."

"Go along with you? Me?" Amuro gulped.

"Sure. You. You *are* irresistible, you know. . . ."

Something about the way she said it bothered Amuro. It reminded him of the overly-flirtatious Kusko Al. And when he thought of Kusko, the memory of Fraw Bow washed over him. When he looked back at Sayla, she was already standing up to leave, expecting him to follow.

"I THINK IT'S A little dangerous to write off the Supreme Commander as a mere fanatic," Lt. Challia Bull murmured to Char Aznable. "He does have some leadership qualities." The two men, along with Kusko Al, had gathered in an officer's music listening room on *A Baoa Qu*. It was soundproofed, but they kept their voices low anyway.

"I agree," said Char. "We can't overlook the fact that there is genuine support in Zeon for the dictatorship."

Challia nodded, but seemed to be pondering something else.

Char was beginning to rethink his opinion of the lieutenant. A New-type candidate who had arrived on *A Baoa Qu* only six hours earlier, he was of medium build and height, and not the type that stood out in a crowd. But there was something about the way he carried himself, and the slightly hollowed look in his cheeks, that spoke of extraordinary endurance. His resume said he was twenty-eight yet he looked far older. He seemed awfully cautious, but for someone in charge of the Jupiter transports that was probably an important quality to have.

"If you ask me," Kusko Al interjected, "the real tragedy of our Supreme Commander is that his ambition exceeds his ability. Don't you think so?"

Kusko was striking in her military uniform. She wore it well; so well in fact, that it almost looked as though Zeon's rather fashionable officer's uniforms had been specifically designed for her. But Char was unimpressed. Something about her always irritated him. He had no problem with women in the Force acting a little different from the men—there was certainly no need for them to be exactly the same—but Kusko tended to ignore even the basic protocols of military hierarchy. And it wasn't just because she was something of a free spirit. Her parents had come from some place called Argentina on Earth, but had divorced. She had moved to Side 3 as part of the forced emigration program to the space colonies. There was something self-destructive about her.

"Listen, Kusko," Char cautioned, "we have to be careful not to speculate too much on his character." He wanted to put her in her place, but her eyes flashed in defiance. "We've got to keep track of what he's doing," he continued, "and collect more hard data on him. But we have to be careful. One wrong move and the people who're supposed to be our allies will do us in . . . " He added the last statement because more than anything else he feared that she would leak word of their conversation to the wrong party. It seemed to work, for she fell silent.

"I may not be subordinate to Kycilia forever," he continued, "but for now remember that we're under the command of Her Excellency, and that without her we're doomed. Understand?"

Challia softly asked, "You mean you'll follow her as long as it fits in with your personal plans. Correct, sir?"

"Let's be blunt," said Char. "I'll say yes, and you'll believe me, right?"

"Why are men always so power-hungry?" Kusko interjected again.

"Be careful, Kusko," Char cautioned again. "We didn't invite you in on this discussion."

"Maybe," she retorted with a laugh, "but you haven't asked me to leave, either. And I know why. Because you'd feel guilty if you did, right?"

"No, we're letting you stay because you're a Newtype and we've got no choice. But there's no time to argue that point. There's something very important I've still got to confirm with Challia."

"Go ahead. You've already said enough to make me a co-conspirator."

To Char's surprise, Challia laughed. "She's right, Commander."

Char and Challia had originally planned to meet alone in the officer's private music listening room, but Kusko had somehow sensed their plans. Char knew she had come out of curiosity more than anything else, and he felt obliged to let her stay, but it made him feel uneasy when Challia talked about Gihren Zabi in her presence. Challia was a Newtype candidate, and he had been specifically sent under Gihren's orders. There was a distinct possibility that he might be a spy, planted by Gihren.

"I need some sort of guarantee from you," Char said, turning to Challia. "Since there's a strong possibility that you may represent Gihren's interest in all this, how much can I trust you?"

"You have my word. Isn't that enough?"

"Perhaps yes. Perhaps not."

"The real reason I came here, Commander, was to confirm for myself that Newtypes actually exist. Frankly, I don't fully believe I have any Newtype potential myself."

"You wanted to 'confirm for yourself' . . . ?"

"That's right, sir. Personally, I find the original theory of Newtypes espoused by Zeon Zum Deikun very appealing."

"He was an idealist, Challia."

ZEON ZUM DEIKUN HAD predicted that mankind would undergo a revolutionary transformation in outer space; that as men and women broke the boundaries of the planet earth and moved further and further out into space, living throughout the universe, their consciousness would also expand and become more universal. The further they went, he believed, the more they would develop a powerful bond among themselves independent of physical distance. It would be an inevitable change, and a logical step in the evolution of the human psyche.

The original Newtype concept was simple and idealistic, but when war erupted it took on an utterly new meaning. Perhaps because the military authorities of the Principality of Zeon were so embroiled in war, they were the first to interpret it in their own way, latching on to the notion that Newtypes could be used for more specific, immediate purposes—as humans with paranormal powers, as pilots with prescience, as weapons of war.

"I GREATLY ADMIRED ZEON Deikun," Challia said, continuing. "It's a shame he didn't survive long enough to become more than just a revolutionary propagandist and visionary. He might have become the type of politician we really need today."

"No one can be everything," said Char. "Besides, politicians with too much personal ambition make me nervous."

"True. That sort of thing can shorten a person's life. And if you always have a hidden agenda, people start to distrust you, too . . . "

Char's hands suddenly turned clammy. Challia couldn't possibly know his real identity, but he might have sensed something. His words were getting close to the danger zone. He was, without a doubt, a man with considerable intuition.

Char replied as tactfully as possible: "I may outrank you, Challia, but you're older than I am, and more experienced. I think I have a lot to learn from you." He didn't like saying it in front of Kusko Al, and it made him resent her presence all the more. Even before meeting Challia, he had noted an obstinate masculine pride in himself.

Kusko spoke up, as if sensing what the two men were thinking. "I know my being here probably bugs both of you. But, hey, you won't find much double-talk from me. Unlike you men, there's no hidden agenda in *this* girl." She meant to be sarcastic, and help break the tension in a loopy sort of way, but her words didn't quite have the effect intended.

"All well and good," Char said icily, "but put your curiosity on hold, okay? Sometimes it's better to be in the dark about these things. Sometimes it's dangerous to get hooked up with people in a situation like this. Be realistic about what you're getting into, and conduct yourself in as responsible a fashion as possible . . . "

"Hmph," she replied petulantly. "I can hardly change my personality, can I? In any case, I wouldn't want to. I like the way I am, thank you very much."

"In that case," Challia said, "you have to accept us the way we are, too, and be a good girl and occasionally leave the room. Frankly, I prefer women who don't pretend to be so intelligent."

"*Lieutenant!*" Kusko exclaimed.

Char couldn't help smirking. Challia was capable of a more barbed tongue than he would have ever imagined.

"We're not asking you to change your personality, Kusko," Challia continued, "but it does create problems for us. We have to be careful. We might say something you don't like. How do we know you won't betray us to the Zabi family?"

"Well, if that's the way you feel, why'd you say all that stuff in front of me?"

"You gave the answer earlier. We set you up as a coconspirator. Char Aznable has accepted me, Challia Bull, a spy sent by Supreme Commander Gihren, as a partner in his plans. In the future he's going to destroy Kycilia Zabi, and eventually the Supreme Commander himself."

"You both must be *dreaming!*"

"If you think so, Kusko, keep your nose out of it," Char said. "This is our business. The fact that Challia came as Gihren's spy to find out what Kycilia's up to, the fact of my plotting . . . forget everything you heard. Understand?!"

"I can't *believe* you two," Kusko retorted.

"We're at war, Kusko."

Kusko kicked off the floor, and left the room upset. Challia turned to Char. "Let's head over to the base bar," he said with a smile, "and have a drink to clear the air a bit. Some of the girls over there are a little less trouble."

"Sounds great to me. To tell the truth, I'm not even sure myself why I have such a hard time getting along with her."

"It's just the way people are, Commander. You said it yourself earlier. No one can be everything to everyone."

The two men turned off the lights and left the listening room. From outside the window, the moonlight streamed inside. Earth was out of sight.

IT WAS A GOOD thing women had such warm, smooth skin, Amuro thought, as he spread his right hand over the gentle mound of Sayla's breast. Then he remembered what someone had once told him—that sleeping people have nightmares if something weighs upon their chest—and removed his hand, reluctantly letting it drift down to her side. His eyes lingered on the gentle shape of her breasts, and the delicate outline of her nipples.

It was a violation of military regulations for a woman to be in a male officer's quarters at night, but it happened all the time and was never punished anymore. Nearly thirty percent of the Federation Forces were now Waves, and liaisons were overlooked as long as the following basic guidelines were observed: Trainees could not be involved, the interaction could not be during a time of combat and had to take place in a private room, and everyone had to be in their original assigned quarters for lights-out and reveille. The last rule was one of the reasons that, in some areas of the ship, there was a considerable amount of coming and going ten minutes after the official lights-out time.

Attitudes toward sex had changed radically in the Space Age, but most people still looked askance at those who engaged in promiscuous sex or changed partners too frequently. Inappropriate behavior could result in harsh criticism from fellow crew members and accusations of being a "playboy" or "playgirl," both terms with highly negative overtones. When Sayla had first entered Amuro's room, she had grinned and said, "I passed Mirai on the way here but she doesn't suspect anything. Some of your pals back there in the dining hall probably feel jilted, though, so don't forget to be nice to them."

"Oh." That was all Amuro had managed to say. After that he remembered little. She had received him, and he had felt vaguely dissatisfied after it was all over. Then she had said with a giggle, "*If I'm ever assigned a private room, you can come visit me . . .*" That was ten minutes ago. Now, he could tell by her breathing that she was fast asleep. It was strange. At first he had thought that she had come to him specifically to talk about Char Aznable. But to his surprise, it seemed she had just come to sleep with him. She had wrapped him in her exquisitely long limbs, and not even mentioned her brother's name once.

There was definitely something unnerving about the ways of women, Amuro thought, wondering if Fraw Bow were the same way. Then the fatigue from a long day caught up with him, and he fell asleep in the warmth of Sayla's body, marveling at how complex humans are.

AMURO AWOKE ABRUPTLY TO the sound of Sayla sobbing quietly, her face buried in a pillow, her shoulders shaking. "Sayla, what is it?!" he asked.

"Amuro . . . " she sobbed almost inaudibly. "I'm sorry . . . I'm sorry . . . "

He gingerly placed his hand on her back and, as she kept weeping, began gently massaging her. Then, to his surprise, she suddenly rolled over, jumped out of bed, and ran naked to the shower. It happened so fast that he only saw her white limbs flash for a second in the darkness.

He roused himself, shocked. From the shower he could hear the water blasting her skin, and knew she had the pressure on especially high. With nothing to do but wait, he placed his hand on the impression her body had left on the bed and enjoyed the residual warmth. And as he occasionally did when frustrated, he began biting his right thumbnail.

Ten minutes later the sound of the shower stopped. The door to the bathroom opened and Sayla emerged, a bath towel wrapped around her torso. She walked straight over to him and announced, "Well? Think I'm pretty?"

"Very," he said.

"Thanks." She sat down next to him and added, hesitatingly, "Listen, on a totally different subject, about tonight . . . "

He was absorbed in the beautiful lines of her neck and back, but he thought he knew exactly what she was going to say—that they wouldn't be able to sleep together again. To his amazement she suddenly announced, "I love my brother, Amuro, but he's gone too far. He's got some crazy ideas about what he can do with Newtypes, and I'm afraid he'll do something horrible. If you meet him, I want you . . . I want you to kill him . . . " Then, seeing Amuro's shock, she added, "It hurts me to say it, but I mean it. I can't stand to think of my brother playing God. I'd rather see him dead."

"I don't go around killing people for personal reasons," Amuro replied, his voice rising in anger. "Is this why you slept with me?"

"No, no . . . " she moaned softly. "It doesn't have anything to do with it."

"Listen, Sayla. You're a complicated person. I've known you as the young blond girl on Side 7, as the *Pegasus*'s communication's officer, and now even as Artesia, daughter of the late Zeon Zum Deikun. But there's only one real Sayla as far as I'm concerned, and you'll always be that Sayla. I don't like the Sayla I see now. . . ."

"I'm sorry, Amuro. But I almost never have a chance to talk to you, so when I'm with you like this, everything gets mixed up and you wind up misunderstanding me. It's not the way you think it is!"

"Maybe not. Maybe I'll never meet Char again in combat. Who knows? Maybe I'll be killed first. Either way, in my book what you just said is *taboo*."

"Amuro, I don't think you can understand because you've never had a brother you really love!"

"Well, I sure hope I never love anyone so much I want them dead. . . ."

He suddenly felt thirsty, and stood up and walked to the bathroom to get a drink. He was stark naked but he didn't care. He wished Sayla would leave, and decided to kill some time by taking a shower, but minutes later, when he finally turned off the water, he could sense that she was still around. Sure enough, when he emerged, she was wrapped in a blanket on his bed, lying face up, her eyes open, staring at the ceiling.

"I'm sorry," she said. "Let's go back to sleep . . . "

He thought about sleeping alone on the sofa in the room but her warm body was too tempting and, besides, it was *his* room and *his* bed. He lay down beside her, and before he slipped into sleep he felt her hand reach out and gently touch his waist.

CONTACT

EARTH FEDERATION SCOUTS HAD detected a significant change in Zeon activity. Kycilia's forces, the survivors of the *Granada* battle, and support warships had previously been observed converging around *A Baoa Qu*. But now there were also ships from entirely different units moving under full speed in the opposite direction, toward *Solomon*. General Revil and his top officers puzzled over the new information.

"SIR, IT LOOKS LIKE Dozle Zabi's Mobile Assault Force is trying to link up with the Zeon reserves on *Solomon* and stage an attack on *LH*."

"What should we do, sir? We don't have enough ships to divert some to another position."

"Are you absolutely certain Dozle's headed for *Solomon*?"

"Yessir, and if he links up with the other ships there, they'll form a force that could easily take on *LH*. That means the *A Baoa Qu* forces will also probably come out in a feint maneuver, and try to take *LH* in a pincer attack."

"We've got to be able to support *LH* somehow. We've got three divisions on *Luna II* that could help."

"Yes, sir."

"It's a tough call. We don't have any solid proof Dozle will attack

CHAPTER THIRTEEN

242

LH. But on the other hand, the Zeon forces are as much in the dark about our plans as we are about theirs. This is where the Zabi family rivalries could get interesting. It looks like the Zeon high command has equally divided their forces between Dozle and Kycilia Zabi so neither loses face. . . ."

General Revil made light of the situation, but he was troubled by the lack of information on the true extent of the Zeon forces converging on *LH.* The whole business was distracting him from his own plans. The twenty-square-meter 3D display projected on the ceiling above him showed the estimated positions of both enemy and friendly forces in red and green flashing lights, and did a particularly good job of representing the moon. He looked up at it and muttered: "Where's the focus of Zeon's military strength now? *That's* what I need to know. Where's their Newtype unit?" He was convinced Zeon hadn't yet totally committed its Newtype unit, and he was certain it wasn't the centerpiece of their current strategy. He even suspected that much of the talk of Zeon Newtypes was simply rumor, perhaps intentionally planted by spies.

"*A Baoa Qu* . . . ," he whispered to himself. "Hmm. And we know that several ships from Side 6 have recently docked there."

Revil was even more worried by some new intelligence he had received about Zeon's *Mahal* colony. There appeared to be a flurry of activity taking place there, and one report said it had something to do with a plan to evacuate the entire cylinder.

"Any evidence an evacuation has actually occurred?" he asked his men.

No one yet knew.

WHEN SAYLA FINALLY WOKE up next to Amuro in the morning, the first thing she said was, "If you're a real Newtype, it's a dream come true for me. Maybe you wish I'd never said what I did about my brother last night, but it's too late. I said it, and I can't help it if you hate me for it."

He was already sitting up on the bed with his back to her, but he replied, "I just don't understand it. I don't have a brother. But I don't think it's the sort of thing anyone should ever say. It sure as hell isn't anything I want to hear."

"Maybe so," she said, suddenly gloomy.

She had just finished fastening her bra when Amuro turned around and looked at her. *How beautiful she is,* he thought, whereupon she smiled faintly as if sensing him. He stood up, hugged her, kissed the nape of her neck, and drank in her scent. He had already concluded that there was always something vague and unsettling between men and women, and that was surely the problem between him and Sayla now. Her earlier statement was so outrageous, he could only understand it if it really stemmed from a twisted desire to save her brother. That was the only way he could possibly interpret it. As for her remark about him being a Newtype, the connection was simply beyond him. She probably just needed a man to help her forget the whole unpleasantness with her brother, and if that were the case, nearly any man might do. Given his own tender age and inexperience, though, Amuro wasn't even sure if he fit the bill on that score. The more his Newtype potential developed, the more prone to self-delusion he seemed to be becoming.

Sayla sighed deeply and embraced him. He held her tightly around the waist, and marveled how slender and delicate she seemed. He wished he were more experienced, more of a man, and knew better what to do. She groaned, and then he realized that he had squeezed her too hard. "Sorry," he muttered, cursing his clumsiness.

"ENEMY FORCES AT ONE hundred and sixty degrees, ten minutes! Elevation thirty-three degrees, twenty-six minutes! Stage One Alert!"

Speakers blared throughout the Federation's *LH* moon base, letting the defenders know that Zeon ships would enter missile and beam cannon range within ten minutes. Amuro and his fellow pilots had just returned from a second training mission when the next announcement came: *"Open launch deck doors! All crew don normal suits!"*

The *Pegasus*'s giant deck hatch doors opened. Amuro hooked a lift-grip, sped along at maximum speed through a passageway leading directly into the deck, and then used his inertia to leap up to the new Gundam model mobile suit. The moon had gravity, but it was easy to jump four or five meters. He knew the *Pegasus* was already moving, because through its open front hatch he could see the walls of the *LH* moon port slide downward.

From inside the Gundam cockpit, he yelled into his microphone, "This is G3! Ensign Amuro Ray, ready for launch!"

The comm monitor above his main display flickered to life and Sayla's voice emerged from its speaker: *"Pegasus exiting port area in twenty seconds. Launch after confirming clearance!"*

"Roger! G3 now launching!"

"Amuro??" Sayla was so surprised that she unintentionally violated takeoff protocol by calling his name out informally—there was a strict rule against launching mobile suits before the *Pegasus* completely cleared the port area, and it looked like Amuro was about to break it.

Through the open launch hatch in front of the Gundam, Amuro watched the walls of the port slip by faster and faster. He waited for the right instant, and then yelled, "Enemy approaching! G3 now launching!" He fired the main engine under him and it responded with a roar that reverberated through his spine.

"G3! Ensign Amuro launching!" He heard Sayla confirm his launch and relay the information to Bright. In the background, he thought he heard the skipper say something negative, but he wasn't about to dwell on it. He stepped down on the middle launch pedal and felt a mild *g* force as all sixteen meters of the giant Gundam mobile suit surged forward on the launch catapult. The instant it kicked off the catapult, he fired the backpack verniers on full thrust, and the Suit began a slow climb, squeezing through the eighty meter gap between the *Pegasus* and the inside walls of the moon base. In seconds, he had checked his ceiling display and confirmed that he had the correct attitude and trajectory to clear the port. Then he checked his beam rifle and the arm that held it for full range of movement, and double-checked the integrity of the energy circuits. Then he released the safeties on his weapons systems. When he next glanced at his main monitor, he had cleared the moon surface.

"Godspeed, Ensign Amuro!" Sayla's voice came through loud and clear, but when Amuro turned to look at the mini-monitor where her face normally appeared, Minovsky interference had already broken up her image. Her next words were unintelligible, but he didn't have time to listen anyway. The static was so distracting he turned it off. From this point on he had to locate the enemy with the naked eye. He switched the cockpit's eight observation displays to maximum telescopic mode for a 360-degree panorama.

What the?!

To his horror, what looked like an enemy mobile suit was rapidly descending from his rear left toward the moon's surface, but the *LH* base hadn't yet fired a single cannon or missile in defense. A cardinal rule of military strategy was that once a lone MS broke through a defensive perimeter it was almost impossible to stop, yet none of the Federation forces seemed to have even noticed!

He spun the Gundam around and gave chase at high speed. The *g* force pushed him back into his seat, and the thought of an impending fight made his spine tingle. He eased off on the left and right levers and told himself to slow down, to be careful. The enemy Suit swung into view directly in front of him and it was definitely a Zaku, but it was faster than any he had seen before. To his dismay, it was still plunging unchallenged straight toward a corner of the *LH*. Worse yet, it might only be a decoy. The enemy sometimes deployed Zakus at this stage of attack, but rarely sent out only one.

There was not a second to be wasted. Amuro fired a single blast at the enemy Suit from his beam rifle. It was too far away for a direct hit, but the beam would at least help alert the Federation defenders. As he expected, the Suit returned his fire, but he ignored it. He twisted his MS ninety degrees and checked the heavens unfolding above him. Amid the static from Minovsky interference, he could overhear panic in the communications transmissions from *LH*. The people down on the base had never in their wildest dreams imagined such a sudden attack, even from a scout unit.

The two Guncannons from the *Pegasus* finally caught up with him, but he groaned with frustration because the new GM pilots—Ensigns Sarkus and Kria—were late. In mobile suit battles, machines normally advanced in formation until the enemy was directly engaged; from then on it was essentially every man for himself. There were, of course, some basic tactics employed (most of which were based on conventional dog-fighting experience), but there were no hard and fast rules. MS combat was a relatively new type of warfare, with no real military model to follow, and it tended to quickly devolve into close-quarter combat.

Amuro slowed down when he finally saw the *Pegasus* pulling along his port side. He wanted at all costs to avoid becoming separated from his own forces and accidentally destroying a friendly ship. As he watched, a *Salamis* cruiser rose up on either side, and the lead one moved straight ahead. Its goal was clear: to protect the heart of the *LH* moon base.

"Don't overexpose yourself!" he yelled at the lead cruiser over his mike, but it was too late. He sensed a light ahead of them, coming faster and faster, almost leaping out toward him. It was a light he had experienced before when fighting Char's Red Comet, and when fighting Lalah Sune in her mobile armor. It was a thin, glowing beam of light, traveling at great speed. Then he saw the flares of five or six rocket engines, spinning, coming closer and closer.

"*Damn! I've seen this before! I know what this is!*" He swore under his breath, leveled his beam rifle in front of him, and fired. He knew the blast was wasted. It scorched through the blackness of space, but he was aiming at things that were far too fast. They leapt out of the way, and continued to plunge toward the lead *Salamis* cruiser.

The next blast from his beam rifle finally struck home—one of the attacking objects burst into a ball of white light in the blackness. But only then did the lead *Salamis* cruiser seem to realize it was the target of the attack and commence defensive fire. The rocket-propelled objects easily evaded the barrage and beelined toward the ship.

One of the easiest ways to overwhelm a defense is with numbers.

Amuro picked off another of the objects, but that was as much as he could do. Several missiles plunged into the cruiser's bridge and, after a few paralyzing seconds of nothingness, it was enveloped in flames. Then the flames mushroomed into a ball of white light that illuminated the surface of the moon below.

Amuro knew he was confronting the same weapon that Lalah Sune had used—the Elmeth and its Bits. The weaving engine flares were from the system's multiple supporting units, armed with either a beam cannon or nuclear warheads, and remotely controlled from the Elmeth—even in the midst of heavy Minovsky concentrations. Amuro knew from prior experience that the Bits were not radio-controlled, that somehow the pilot was able to control them with his or her brain waves. What neither he nor the Earth Federation Forces knew yet, however, was that the system depended on a new interface device called a psycommu, which magnified and projected pilot's will.

Another Lalah Sune! Amuro remembered what Lt. List had said about Zeon's plans for a Newtype unit. The Flanagan Institute had clearly been more successful than the Earth Federation had ever suspected.

They can't possibly have very many of these things, he thought, trying to reassure himself. He strained to see better in the area of space where the flares had appeared, but unlike the time he had encountered Lalah, he still couldn't "feel" anything from the pilot of the system's main unit. After pondering for a second, he decided it must be because of the distance involved. There was one other possibility, but it was almost too terrifying to consider.

When Kai, Hayato, and the two GM pilots deployed their Suits in a horizontal formation on either side of *Pegasus II*, Amuro yelled into his mike as loudly as possible at the two Guncannons: "We're under attack by enemy Newtypes! Make sure GMs 324 and 325 stay to our rear!" Almost immediately, he heard Kai echo his words in shock. *"Enemy Newtypes?!"*

There was no time to reply. Amuro had already spotted Zeon Suits above and to his right—six of them, all a model he had never seen before, deployed in what he recognized as a "spear" formation. There was no sign of the Elmeth-Bits system. Before he could get a good look at the Suits they plunged forward, attacking a squadron of *Salamis* cruisers to the *Pegasus's* starboard that were riding cover over the Federation's third White Base-class ship, the *Thoroughbred*. Six Federation GMs came soaring up in the *Thoroughbred's* defense, but their pilots were obviously green and outclassed. Worse yet, Amuro could tell that the new model Zeon Suits were even faster than Zakus.

"Kai! Hayato!" he yelled. "Don't leave the *Pegasus* unprotected!" He spun his Gundam to the right and put it into a dive. There was no way to save the cruisers and at this point he wasn't even certain he could help the *Thoroughbred*, but he had to try. His gray Suit streaked through the black space above the moon, as he desperately attempted to cut off the enemy.

The new model Zeon Suits had flared waists that gave them a less threatening, skirted appearance, but Amuro knew it was an illusion. The new design merely shielded the nozzles of new, even more powerful rocket engines, which in turn accounted for the increased speed over the old Zakus. When he saw a ball of white light flare in space again, he realized one of the enemy Suits had already scored a direct hit on a *Salamis* cruiser.

"You'll pay for that," he yelled, lining up the sights on his beam rifle with the crosshairs on his main monitor. But in an instant, the lead Zeon Suit changed its course slightly.

"Sensed me, eh?" he muttered, realizing that he had lost the element of surprise. In a fraction of a second, he shifted his aim to the next Suit in line and pulled the trigger. A narrow band of light streaked out of his gun barrel toward the enemy Suit, still illuminated by the earlier *Salamis*'s explosion. But at the same time, yet another, equally large ball of light mushroomed in the same area, and the enemy formation shifted to a course that took them below it, out of Amuro's view. As he watched, the *Thoroughbred* emerged shuddering from the light, dropping in altitude toward the surface of the moon.

"You're too slow!" he yelled at the Federation ship. The *Thoroughbred* had almost met the same fate as the cruiser earlier. At the rate things were going, the enemy Suits would continue their hit-and-run tactics, swoop close to the surface of the moon, dodge *LH*'s air defenses, and then disengage. And in the interim they would destroy a couple more Federation ships.

Amuro nonetheless chose not to pursue the formation. He was more worried about the Elmeth he had encountered earlier; it was a far more formidable rival. He turned the Gundam around and positioned himself under the left wing of the *Pegasus*. Kai, in his C108 Guncannon, moved in to initiate "skin talk" with him.

"I can't see any enemy above us, Amuro," said Kai. "What's going on? What's with these Newtypes, anyway?"

"They're incredibly fast. And they've got new type of Suit! I think they're using beam rifles!"

"Did you see them?"

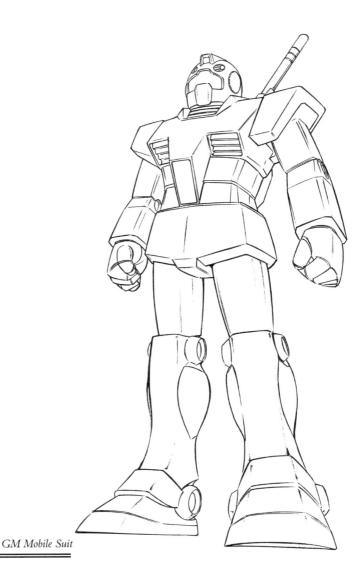

GM Mobile Suit

"Hell, yes!"

"Well dammit, I couldn't. I saw something that looked like a Zaku, but it was gone before I could be sure."

"Kai! What am I gonna do? I depend on you! Your Guncannon's supposed to play the main role in long-range support."

"Go easy on me, pal . . . "

"Whoa!" Amuro suddenly exclaimed. He felt a ricochet-like sound. It was distinct, but not physical, and neither discernibly high nor low in tone. It seemed to reverberate, not in his ears, but directly on his brain stem. And he wasn't the only one to sense it; Kai, Hayato, and all the

others in the area apparently did too. Then it happened again. It was powerful enough to make all who heard it tremble in fear.

SAYLA WAS MANNING THE comm panel on the *Pegasus* bridge when she heard it. Fearing her headset somehow prevented her from telling where the sound was coming from, she tore it off her head and stared around the room as if looking for the source. Bright, in the captain's seat, turned around and gaped at her.

"Was that caused by a failure in the comm system?" he asked.

"I can't tell, skipper . . . "

When Mirai, manning the helm, turned to Sayla and revealed that she had heard it, too, both women simultaneously arrived at the same conclusion: "It's coming from outside the ship!"

"Outside?!" Bright, following their gaze, stared through the bridge window at the space in front of them. All he could see was the usual; millions of stars staring back at him. Then he noticed the two GM mobile suits attached to *Pegasus II*. They had moved two thousand meters out in front of the ship, apparently anticipating trouble.

Sayla couldn't sit in front of the comm panel any longer. She stood up, kicked away her chair and ran over to the bridge window. Because the sound she "heard" seemed to trail off in a specific direction, she looked upward.

"Ensign Mirai!" she exclaimed. "There's a light . . . " She knew none of the others would be able to see. She wasn't even a hundred percent sure she hadn't imagined it herself.

"What are you talking about?!" Bright demanded.

"Mirai! It's coming at us . . . at about one o'clock!"

Mirai immediately spun the helm in response, but in acting unilaterally she violated a basic rule of the ship. Bright was technically only a junior grade lieutenant but he was still captain of the ship, and *he* was the one supposed to issue orders.

But that same instant Bright saw the Gundam and Guncannons swoop into view, firing their beam rifles and twenty-eight centimeter shoulder cannons. And then he saw the light of three explosions mushroom in the area Sayla had pointed to earlier. The filter on the shell-proofed glass of the bridge windows automatically activated, and in the reduced light he finally spotted something else—what looked like six homing missiles—streaking toward the *Pegasus*. "So *that's* what you were talking about!" he exclaimed.

"Hard to starboard!" he yelled. "Give me a curtain of defensive fire!" He knew there was no time to properly execute his orders, but luckily sniping blasts from the Gundam's beam rifle took out three of the objects bearing down on them. The bridge rocked from the closest explosions and special protective barriers were activated on all ship windows. With the main bridge window view now blocked, Bright concentrated his gaze on a large horizontally elongated, rhomboid-shaped monitor above it, which now displayed the same view. On it he saw the immediate light from the blasts diffuse in the heavens, and residual particles flash and fade.

"Think they were homing missiles?" he asked Sayla. They had seemed to cut an arc through space.

"I don't know, sir," she replied. "But I don't think so." Before the window barriers had completely retracted, she began to visually scan the heavens in front of the ship.

"The Gundam's moving out, sir!" she announced.

"Good! Let him!" Bright replied. "But tell the Guncannons and the GMs to strengthen their defense of the ship!" Something was happening that he didn't understand. Amuro, Sayla, Mirai, and the others were reacting on their own. He was the skipper, but as frustrating as it might be, he knew for the sake of the ship's survival he would have to go along with what they did.

Sayla relayed the orders and felt a new respect for her commanding officer. He was the ship's captain and she was only a relatively raw recruit, a lowly second class petty officer. He could have thrown the book at her for acting on her own but he seemed to take it all in stride. Things were happening beyond his immediate comprehension, but he was nonetheless capable of sensing the proper response. He was either a man with enormous leadership potential, she thought, or possibly someone with Newtype potential. General Revil had overcome considerable opposition in the civilian and military hierarchy to appoint Bright skipper of the *Pegasus II*, but his performance now, Sayla concluded, more than justified the effort.

Twelve small monitors on her comm panel were dedicated to mobile suits in the area. As she relayed Bright's orders to the four Suits still hugging close to the *Pegasus*, she kept an eye on the one that normally showed Amuro. He was so far away it was filled with static, but sometimes for a few fleeting seconds she could distinguish his form in the darkened Gundam cockpit. She knew she was probably the last thing on his mind right now, as that was the way men had to be in combat. But *she* was thinking about him. Not because she had more time on her hands than he did, but because of a strange tension she felt. The image of him on her screen was always the same size, but he was physically rapidly distancing himself from her, and she could *feel* the increased separation. Was she being oversensitive? She didn't think so. It was simply that every once in a while she couldn't help thinking of him hurtling through space, hunting for the *thing* that had targeted them. What was it? She recalled the mysterious sensation she had felt earlier—first as an indescribable tone that had pierced her brow, then a glowing streak she could "see" deep in her mind. The line of light it had formed still lingered, and she felt she could almost trace it back to its source in space. And she knew that was where Amuro was headed. He was plunging into the unknown, doing something terribly dangerous, but terribly important. The more she thought about it, the more she admired him. He had the same mysterious inner strength she had observed earlier in her captain.

Bright's next command interrupted her thoughts: "Sayla! Tell everyone manning laser sensors to ignore the others for the moment and concentrate on Amuro!"

"Yessir," she replied. Bright clearly seemed to know what was going on.

Mirai, at the helm, turned and queried: "What do you think's out there, skipper?"

Staring straight ahead, he answered without hesitating: "A real Newtype. Mirai, Sayla . . . you both saw something earlier, didn't you?"

Sayla felt she had finally become a true member of the *Pegasus II* core crew. And despite everything else that was going on, she felt happy.

As with many regions near Earth, the area surrounding the moon was contaminated with debris from the ravages of war. Chunks of landfill and sections of former colony structures—objects often over a hundred of meters in diameter—floated incongruously, randomly, in orbit.

Amuro Ray skillfully made his Gundam leap over one such obstacle, and then finally spotted what he was looking for—the same machine Lalah Sune had once piloted, an Elmeth. He swore under his breath, trying not to think how many more of the things he might soon confront, and then he saw something streak toward him. But it wasn't the flare of a rocket. The Elmeth had fired its beam-cannon at him. Without bothering to line up his sights he squeezed the trigger. Several bands of light from his beam rifle converged on the enemy machine, but it leapt effortlessly out of the way. He had no time to try and establish any empathetic communication with the pilot; the waves of thought he felt streaming toward him were too unidirectional, too powerful, too insistent, and too unyielding.

Concentrating his mind, he squeezed the trigger again, hoping for a single knockout blow. He had already learned enough about the Elmeth's performance from seeing its reaction to his first blast to know that he had to act fast or it would kill him. To his dismay, it evaded his second attack, too. And his third. The enemy pilot appeared to possess a mysterious, latent power.

Two more beams streaked out from the Elmeth, toward him. Thanks to the Gundam's new magnetic coating he was able to evade them but he knew he was being outmaneuvered. A new, unfamiliar anger suddenly welled up inside him. He raged against the faceless Elmeth pilot for cooperating with Zeon. It was because of such cooperation that military men on both sides were starting to consider Newtypes instruments of war. He wanted to scream: *Newtypes aren't weapons! They're humans! You're supposed to be like Lalah Sune, capable of a new communion of thought!*

The more emotional Amuro became, the faster he wanted to move, and the more he wanted to close in on the Elmeth and destroy it. He slipped by some more space debris, slid sharply to the right, and there it was again. With his left monitor clearly showing the rear of the enemy machine, he kept it in his line of fire, and the instant it seemed to notice him he pulled the trigger. First he thought he had scored a direct hit, but after the initial whoosh of light he realized with disappointment that the Elmeth had only been grazed, and probably only received minor damage. It seemed to stagger in the light, but then proceeded to hide itself in the remains of a destroyed colony.

Amuro knew it was time to abandon his pursuit. A heavy, oppressive sensation was forming in his subconscious, quickly transforming itself into physical fear. Something was coming at him from behind. *He* was coming! There was no mistaking it. It was Char—the *Red Comet!* Sure enough, he glanced up at his left rearview monitor and saw readouts in both corners indicating relative distance and estimated point of contact with an approaching object. But this was no video game. He needed more than numbers. He needed visual confirmation. He spun the Gundam around 180-degrees and spotted the enemy Suit. But Char wasn't piloting the red Zaku he expected. This was a new model MS with a flared skirt-like construction, painted a dark color to blend in with the blackness of space. Its mono-eye flashed as it plunged straight toward him.

Amuro swore softly: "*Don't underestimate me, Char . . .* " He adjusted his sights and felt a renewed sense of pressure. His opponent was angry and—he realized with some surprise—probably as desperate as he himself was. But Amuro didn't realize his own emotions were being triggered by a type of empathy, that he was already unconsciously adapting to his enemy's mood, and that if he weren't careful, the empathy itself could cause his destruction.

The skirted Zeon Suit proceeded in a straight line and then, as if sensing Amuro's weakness, suddenly fired its beam rifle. A cluster of beams streaked toward Amuro, but he had already shifted his own Suit to the right and positioned his shield in front of him. The next nanosecond, the main beam creased him and the glowing particles on its periphery blasted thousands of invisible holes in his shield. The Gundam body shuddered, its mechanical components strained to the limit.

EVEN IN HIS NEW Rick Dom MS, Char still relied on his old hit-and-run tactics. Seconds later he slipped by the Gundam's left side and fired. But Amuro fired at exactly the same instant. Incredibly, particle beams from the two men's respective rifles collided head on. A ball of white light equal to that of an exploding warship mushroomed in space, and then faded.

"He's faster than I thought," Char swore. He knew that if the Gundam had been caught in the middle of the light, all the armor in the world wouldn't have saved it. He had visually sighted and attacked the enemy Suit, but it had demonstrated astounding speed and agility with its evasive action and counterattack. For a second he wondered if the Gundam before him were really the same one he had encountered in battle before. Its fuselage was no longer white and now had a light gray look that made it seem more formidable than before. He grinned despite himself at the psychological effect a mere color change could create. And the pilot? He considered the notion that it might be the same young kid he had faced before on *Texas*, but quickly abandoned the idea. There was no way of precisely knowing the final outcome of the Gundam's showdown with Lalah's Elmeth on *Texas*, but there was also no way, he told himself, that its pilot could possibly have escaped the subsequent explosion of the colony cylinder. He himself had only escaped by the skin of his teeth, and at that point he had already intuitively known that Lalah Sune was dead. He recalled the whole affair with particular bitterness, for during her last moments he knew she had someone other than him in her heart. Her death also made the idea that the enemy mobile suit and its pilot might have survived almost too cruel to contemplate, for it would mean that she had fought and died in vain. Except for the pilot of the original white mobile suit, he had received no intelligence information on the existence of any other Federation Newtypes. Now he desperately wished he knew exactly what had happened.

In the meantime, he shielded his Rick Dom behind some floating debris and checked for any movement to his rear. *"Where's Challia Bull?"* he muttered. He trusted the lieutenant and was convinced he was the real thing. The man's ability to fly in formation, and the way he had evaded the Federation beam blast earlier, made it entirely possible he possessed even greater skills than he, Char—the seasoned combat veteran—did.

Just as he feared, less than forty kilometers to his rear he saw several streaks of light in the blackness. He put his Rick Dom into a jump and sprang from his cover. To his astonishment, he nearly collided with the Gundam, whose pilot was just as taken aback as he was. It all happened so fast that as the two Suits slipped by each other neither pilot had time to properly aim his beam rifle or bazooka. Char swore and fired even though he knew it was useless, and the Gundam pilot did the same. But then something different happened to the Gundam. As Char watched, beams fired by Challia Bull rained down on the Gundam from above and to the left, but when he turned back to look at the Federation Suit it had already evaded them by slipping sideways and taking cover behind a hundred-meter-long rock. The rock caught a beam blast and exploded in fragments, but that didn't help Char, for in the explosion the enemy Suit suddenly vanished from his view.

He swore again. *"Where in the hell's Kusko Al and her Elmeth?!"* She had always seemed overconfident.

He had no way of knowing she had been hit by the Gundam earlier.

AMURO RAY WAS GETTING nervous. There were two skirted Zeon Suits after him, and something made him suspect both of their pilots were Newtypes. He had to make sure they didn't get near Kai and Hayato, and if at all possible destroy them before his comrades entered the combat zone, but things weren't going in his favor. He turned away from the moon, scanned his observation displays, and saw two more mushrooming balls of white light from exploding Federation ships in the area. It was hard to believe that only four or five enemy Suits could wreak so much damage.

He knew what he had to do, and that only he could do it. His ego was egging him on, but he also knew he would need every ounce of overconfidence he could muster simply to confront the pilots in Zeon's Newtype unit. Keeping one eye on Char's skirted Suit below him, he turned and saw the Suits which had rained beams on him a second earlier. To his horror, instead of two, there were now three. Where had he miscalculated?

He pulled the trigger and the muzzle of his beam rifle flared, but the result was unexpected. He had aimed at the lead Suit, but it had executed a perfect evasion maneuver, and his beam had scored a direct hit on the second Suit in line instead. His elation with a hit was quickly tempered with fear. Why, he nearly screamed aloud, had the lead Suit been able to avoid him?! Who the hell was piloting it? It certainly was no ordinary person, and it might be an opponent even more formidable than Char Aznable.

He fired two more bursts of beams. Incredibly, the lead Suit evaded him again. What on earth was its faceless pilot trying to do? He wanted to scream *"Stop!"* He wanted, desperately, to tell him true Newtypes wouldn't lend their powers to an enemy as detestable as the Zabi family. He was furious.

As his Gundam streaked through the void, he saw fire below him from Kai and Hayato's Guncannons converge on the skirted Zeon Suits. It was ineffective, and he knew it would only make things worse. Sure enough, both the Federation fleet guns and the ground-based defenses below suddenly concentrated a furious barrage of fire right on the area he was in.

He yelled, *"Hey! Don't forget I'm here!"* but knew he would have done the same thing in their position. Within the space of a dozen minutes nearly ten Federation ships had been incinerated. The junior officers manning the moon base missiles and the ships' guns were almost duty bound to fire if they so much as thought they saw the enemy. In the midst of the barrage, he strained to keep an eye on the Rick Doms and hoped he wouldn't be hit.

Char finally gave the order to retreat. His men had done enough fighting for the day. They had obtained valuable data on the performance of the Elmeth and new Rick Dom machines in combat, and both Kusko Al and Challia Bull had managed to get in a little on-the-job training. To stay longer in an area so clearly controlled by the enemy would be tantamount to suicide. He pulled out of the area, and the surviving Zeon Suits followed him, fire from the Earth Federation Forces merely illuminating the blackness of space behind them.

THE ATTACK ON THE Federation's *LH* moon base finally over, *Pegasus II* returned to port where, to the crew's surprise, they found they had all been promoted an entire rank. General Revil, acting on his own conviction, had decided a promotion was necessary for them to function as an official Newtype Corps, and the General Staff at Jaburo on Earth, realizing that he was staking his career and life on the new strategy, had decided to humor him. They had apparently even considered advancing the crew two ranks, but Revil had disagreed.

"If we don't promote them," the brass reportedly had said, "their ranks'll be out of synch with those of the crews on other warships. How can Bright Noa possibly function as skipper if he's only a lieutenant?"

"They're all too young," Revil had replied. "It'll go to their heads. They know what they're in for, and I need them to think clearly."

At around eleven o'clock mean time, Bright returned to the *Pegasus* from a war council on the base. Although none of the core crew members had been ordered to do so, they had gathered in the armory as if on cue, and were waiting for him.

Bright, now a full lieutenant, turned to Amuro and joked: "If it gets too hard for us to synchronize our activities with you, Mister, we might have to put you in charge of Tactical Operations, eh?"

"Only if you think I've got the appropriate qualifications, sir," Amuro grinned back. Along with Kai Shiden, Hayato Kobayashi, and Mirai Yashima, he, too, had been promoted to junior grade lieutenant.

Sleggar Law, the gunnery specialist who was already a junior grade lieutenant, griped, "Am I the only one who didn't get promoted just 'cause I joined later than the rest of you?"

"It's all a fluke, Sleggar," Bright answered, as if consoling him. "They only did this to make my job easier as skipper of the ship." Then, turning to Sayla, he said, "And you, you're a petty officer first class now, so have a seat along with the rest and listen to what I'm about to say. The General was extremely interested in learning more about the enemy's raid on *LH* today, but I couldn't fill him in on the details at the meeting because so many others were in attendance. One thing's clear though. The Gundam probably moved out too fast."

Bright sipped on a cup of coffee while he said this, and glanced at Amuro. "It's too bad we can't depend on radio transmissions," he continued, referring back to his earlier comment, "because then we on the ship actually could have received directions from Amuro, riding point out there in his Gundam."

Sleggar leaned forward and practically thrust his large chin in Sayla's face. She made as if to move away but he ignored her. "Well, Sayla," he said, "how'd *you* know the enemy was approaching?"

"I didn't really 'see' them. It was sort of like there was a flare of reddish light inside my head" Then, turning to Mirai, she asked, "Isn't that the way it seemed to you, too?"

Mirai had taken her boots off and was relaxing in an almost disheveled pose on a sofa in the room. "It sure did," she said. "It was almost like seeing them, though. But that was just this one time. It's not always like that. Maybe the enemy *wanted* to make sure we spotted them today."

Kai glanced at Hayato, grinned, and commented, "Beats me whatever these fair damsels are talking about."

"Maybe it's like the sparks you see when someone slugs you," his friend joked.

Then Kai turned to Amuro: "It's sort of a white light, isn't it?"

Amuro loosened the collar of his uniform and responded in a weary tone, "Maybe you guys were slugged by Lt. Ralv once too often during training . . . " But sensing Sayla's gaze on him, he fell silent.

Mirai, for her part, had already realized there was something different about Sayla the moment she entered the room. She knew Sayla had been out the night before, but she never would have imagined that she had been with Amuro. When she reflected on it, though, she realized it was possible. She knew Amuro had once had a crush on Sayla, yet something in the way the two were acting with each other now suggested a much deeper bond. Was it, she wondered, some sort of Newtype psychic affinity?

"I agree with Mirai," Amuro said. "I think the enemy *wanted* us to see the light. I felt some sort of weird psychic pressure directed at me, something telling me it was coming. We know the pilot of the Elmeth on *Texas* was a Newtype, right? But there was something different about today." He wasn't being fully honest. He had no intention of telling anyone—even Sayla—exactly *how* different Lalah Sune had been.

"What do you mean," Sleggar suddenly asked, "by 'psychic pressure'?"

"It was a menacing sensation," Amuro answered. "And it was projected right through the mobile armor fuselage. It was the sort of thing you might feel if a sworn enemy was standing right in front of you."

"'Menacing,' eh?" Sleggar was awed.

"Shit," Kai said, sounding almost jealous. "I never felt anything *that* specific . . . "

"See?" Sleggar said, turning to Hayato. "Even a cat with nine lives wouldn't stand a chance against an enemy like that."

"What bothers me," Bright added, "is that if anyone told this kind of story to the other pilots in the Force, they'd probably quit right away."

The skipper had a point, Amuro realized. It was probably the reason Newtypes weren't officially recognized in the Federation Forces yet, and probably the reason their deployment in combat was still top secret. "You know what I think?" he said. "If Newtypes're really all they're cracked up to be, there oughta be a way to use them not just to wage war, but to *stop* it, too."

"You must be out of your mind," Bright shot back. "It's hopeless as long as Zeon's under the thumb of the Zabi family."

Salamis *Cruiser*

"Besides, Amuro," Kai added, "look at the Federation. The war'll never stop as long as the government brass, the Earth faction or Natives or whatever they call 'em, insist on controlling the space colonies from their 'home' planet."

That was more than Bright could let go by. "*Mister* Kai Shiden," he said deliberately, standing up, "we don't allow talk like that around here. And it's not the kind of language I expect to hear from a Federation officer, involved in a holy crusade to defend our sacred Mother Earth."

"The skipper's right, Kai," Sleggar added with a sly grin. "You'd better be careful, 'cause for all you know I could be a spy sent by the Jaburo bureaucrats. Hell, I might squeal on you, pal."

There was actually something plausible about what Sleggar said, if for no other reason than the fact that there were many murky aspects to his resume. He had been bounced from unit to unit for bad conduct, but here he was, still stationed on the front lines of the war. And none of the core crew on the *Pegasus II* seemed to think much of him, either. He had a reputation of being a womanizer and an officer incapable of controlling his troops, who tended to be as undisciplined as he was.

"Who gives a damn?" Kai retorted. "The skirted Suits we let get away today are totally different than the old Zakus we're used to. And what about the new mobile armor we encountered that Amuro says sank one of our cruisers? I don't care if you rat on me or not, Sleggar. I stand a lot better odds than you do of buying the farm out there in space."

Sleggar stopped leaning over Sayla, and stared at the floor for a second. Kai had clearly spoken for all the core crew members. Everyone felt a new sense of danger.

"Tell me, Amuro," Sleggar asked softly, "what are those units that accompany the main mobile armor?"

"I don't know exactly," Amuro replied. "I've never been able to get a close look at them."

"Can you can spot one close enough to shoot it down?"

"You're the gunnery officer. Have you ever tried shooting down a missile? It's like that."

"I guess you'd just have to put up a defensive barrage and hope for the best."

"Imagine you're dealing with a conventional homing missile," Amuro explained, "but the thing's a hell of a lot faster. And it has an ability to slip up on you from your blind spot. *And* it's carrying a beam cannon."

Sleggar, impressed, looked over at Kai and said, "Well, in that case it evens the odds between us on the ship and you guys out in the Suits, doesn't it?"

Kai turned to Bright and asked with a grin, "You got anything for us to drink, skipper?"

"Some Newtype candidate you are!" Bright retorted. "Find it yourself! And while you're at it, think of this as your last night on the moon. If we embark tomorrow on a new mission, we're headed straight for Zeon!"

Amuro looked at Sayla when he heard Bright's words, but she avoided his glance and started walking away, which made him uneasy. He started to follow her, but as he passed Sleggar the gunnery officer slapped him on the rear end and chortled, "Way to go, playboy!"

"I do something wrong, sir?" Amuro bantered.

"Nope, not a bit," Sleggar grinned in reply. "Be my guest!"

It was only a momentary interchange, but it made everyone in the armory burst out laughing. When Sayla, almost out the door, turned around and realized what was going on, even she blushed.

Bright, in an admonishing tone, said, "*Mister* Sleggar Law, mind your manners, please. You'll be a bad influence on the lad."

"Er, sorry, sir." Sleggar looked sheepish when he said this, but still, when everyone had filed out of the room except himself, Bright, and Mirai, he had the temerity to turn to Mirai and brazenly inquire, "Well, ehem, in that case, what about you, mademoiselle? Free tonight?"

"Unfortunately for you, sir," she answered curtly, "the answer's an emphatic *no*."

Ignoring the banter between the two, Bright called up to the ship's bridge on the comm monitor. "This is the skipper. I'll be down here in the armory another thirty minutes or so."

Sleggar glanced quizzically at his superior and shrugged his shoulders. Then he finally stood up and left Bright and Mirai alone in the room seated together on the sofa.

"Can you get some rest, skipper?" Mirai asked.

"I hope so. I'm off duty at one o'clock," he answered.

Mirai made no attempt to leave. Bright looked at her and said nothing. He knew it might be their last chance to relax together like this.

"Something you wanted to tell me?" she asked.

"No. I just wanted the chance to look at you a little. You don't mind, do you?"

"No, but it makes me feel a little awkward. You want to talk?"

"Not particularly. I'm worried about our mission, but there's nothing unusual about that. I just hope everything goes the way it's supposed to. You know, I kind of appreciated the way the crew all gathered together here earlier. Something about it made me feel a little calmer."

"Everybody's used to the way things work around here now."

Bright toyed with the idea of asking Mirai to sleep with him but decided not to. It didn't seem right in their present situation, and the last thing he wanted to do was to complicate things before they went into combat. And Mirai clearly felt the same. A feeling of peace came over both of them, and for several minutes they said nothing, merely enjoying each other's presence.

"Maybe when the campaign's over," Mirai said, in her only hint of intimacy, "we could put some pictures on the wall in this room. I'll buy some for you . . ."

"A good idea," he replied. "It does look a little barren in here . . ."

SAYLA AND AMURO ALSO found they needed few words. They embraced in silence, their young bodies craving each other, but Sayla had a deep, unspoken regret and Amuro knew what it was—the remark she had made earlier about his killing her brother. Still, he didn't mention it, and neither did she. In the silence of their embrace they fully accepted and understood each other's differences, and not just because they were Newtypes.

Amuro stopped thinking about his childhood sweetheart, Fraw Bow. And he realized that sometimes the hunches he experienced were wrong. And for some reason that made him feel good.

PREMONITION

"BOTH YOU AND YOUR unit performed admirably, Commander," Kycilia Zabi commented to Char Aznable. "I must say, destroying nine enemy ships in a matter of minutes was quite a feat. I understand Junior Grade Lieutenant Kusko Al was piloting the Elmeth . . . "

Char was glad that Kycilia was pleased, but he knew her position in the Zeon hierarchy was eroding. He had no idea what had happened in his absence, yet she and her brother Gihren Zabi, the Supreme Commander, were clearly on even worse terms than before. Perhaps, he thought, she had deliberately antagonized Gihren by placing the Newtype Corps under her direct control.

Kycilia turned to the other officer in the room, Commander Garcia Dowal. "I want you to give top priority to locating more Newtype candidates," she said. "Things are going so well, I might just make the Newtype unit the centerpiece of our Space Attack Force."

Kycilia's statement, Char realized, was symbolic of a larger problem. She was a military leader who had once possessed considerable insight into problems of strategy and tactics, but now she was beginning to lose her perspective. The attack on the Federation's *LH* moon base had been a highly useful test of the Newtype Corps. It had been important to use the unit in actual combat and assess its potential. But the most surprising discovery of all had been that the Federation's Gundam model mobile suit was back in action and more powerful than ever. Char had, in fact, been grateful that Lt. Challia Bull was on his side. The man was a godsend, even if he was a spy sent by the Supreme Commander. He was mature, awesomely aware of everything around him, and the test sortie had proved he would stand firmly behind Char as long as he understood his goals and deemed them worthy.

"Kusko Al," Kycilia continued, addressing Char again, "has proven quite a successful graduate of the Flanagan Institute, hasn't she?"

"Indeed she has, Excellency."

"And your future plans for her?"

"It's simple. We'll put her out in front in the Elmeth, and myself and the other Rick Dom pilots will support her. She's highly capable."

"Good! As long as you have faith in her, Commander, I'll leave the immediate combat decisions up to you. Our next mission starts in twenty-four hours. As you know, in some of our other operations the regular military hasn't done as well as they should have, and we can't leave everything up to them, which is why I'm asking you and your team to make an extra effort. You understand the situation, of course . . . "

"Er . . . yes . . . " Char was beginning to regret some of his own words. Kycilia was Kycilia. And perhaps because she was a woman, she was quite capable of seeing through his own plans. Women often seemed to have a way about them in that sense.

"I want you all to get some rest tonight," Kycilia said. "From now on, the Newtype Corps—the 300th Autonomous—will be the center of our operations."

Char knew there was an element of sarcasm in the way she said "center of our operations." In the final master plan, conceived of by Zeon forces and code-named *Revol I*, the *A Baoa Qu* forces would be used as a decoy to draw out the Federation fleets so Dozle's forces from *Solomon* could destroy them. Kycilia's warship, the *Swamel*, would then lure the surviving Federation forces into position so they could be annihilated in the Solar Ray attack being developed in the System plan. There were still several hurdles to be overcome before the plan could be properly initiated, but Kycilia's impatience was evidence that it would soon start.

Among the problems, the "Newtype Corps," while possessing a name, was still a combat unit based on an as yet vague, unproven concept. If each member's unique abilities could be fully exploited in combat, the overall military gains might be enormous, but one Elmeth had already been destroyed and the third had still not been delivered. According to the original plans, Challia Bull was supposed to have been the new Elmeth pilot, but the mechamen in charge of the project had refused to accept him. The psycommu interface, they claimed, had already been specifically adjusted and set for Kusko Al, not him.

Turning to Commander Garcia, Kycilia anxiously asked, "We currently have six Rick Doms and only one Elmeth. What happened to the plan for reinforcements?!" She had gained a great deal of confidence in her Newtype unit and already wanted to strengthen it. Her logic was simple: the greater number of people and machines, the better.

"Excellency," Garcia replied, "it's a matter of what level of performance we want to maintain. We have about twenty potential candidates for the Corps."

"Why not enlist them all?" she demanded.

Char interrupted: "Excellency. Allow me to be frank, but we should be careful here. The issue's not the *number* of pilots we have. Even at our current strength, if we just refine our teamwork we can completely annihilate a large enemy force. The most important thing is to have experienced, seasoned pilots. For now, I strongly recommend against a hasty increase in the unit."

"Hmm. I think I understand what you're trying to say, Commander, but it certainly should be possible to train other candidates in combat as part of a separate, detached force. But don't worry, I'm not asking *you* to undertake their training."

"Thank you for you consideration, Excellency," Char answered. "I'll try to ready my own unit as fast as possible." He saluted, did an about-face, and started to leave. Kycilia said something to Garcia on his way out, but he wasn't listening.

Outside the office door, Kycilia's secretary promptly rose to her feet and greeted him with an "Always pleased to see you, sir." Something about the way she said it surprised him and temporarily put his mind in a different mode.

He knew he had other business to attend to. Kusko Al, for example, was upset, and he should be trying to calm her down. But he went ahead and said what he wanted to, anyway. "You have plans for this evening?" he asked, his face mask glinting in the light.

ALL SIX RICK DOM pilots in Char's unit had returned from the attack on *LH* with a kill to their name, and all were relieved because the new Suits performed better than the old Zaku model. And the members of the unit had functioned superbly as a team. No one made any snide asides about having such a young leader. These were all battle-seasoned veterans, and they were perfectly capable of recognizing and appreciating Char's skills, and his remarkable ability to calmly appraise even the most desperate situation (his choice of route to attack the Federation *LH* moon base, for example, had seemed treacherous at first, but it had allowed their hit-and-run strategy to succeed). All of them, including Lt. Challia Bull, had also been brought closer together by the mutual realization that they might have something *profound* in common—that they might be true Newtypes. The result was an unprecedented sense of solidarity and trust, a feeling that they could always depend on each other during combat, and that as long as they worked together as a team, as comrades in arms, they might avoid death in battle. It almost seemed as though they were connected by a thread of consciousness, as if instead of six individuals, they were a single unit with six sets of eyes watching out for the enemy. Although physically unable to see what each other observed, they knew how the team was moving and positioned, and when one team member felt the shock of sighting an enemy the others could sense it, too. And when their Rick Doms returned to base and they looked up at each other's Suits, they felt a union of spirits. It was a good feeling.

There was only one qualifier to this sense of solidarity. It did not guarantee that the pilots liked each other as individual humans outside of the team context.

"Commander!" Challia announced to Char. "Kusko'll be all right. She's calmed down now. She's a pretty tough Wave." He grinned and started walking toward the briefing room.

"She's with Junior Grade Lieutenant Cramble, right?" Char asked.

"Yessir."

"I think they're a little too similar in personality, don't you?"

"Maybe it's better that way if they have to work together. Sometimes Kusko's a little high-strung and strong-willed at the same time, and she has trouble controlling herself as a result."

"Think she'll work out?"

"She's certainly got the potential to . . . "

Char and Challia entered the briefing room together and found Cramble refilling Kusko Al's coffee tube.

"You come here to make fun of me?" she asked.

"This isn't the time or place for that, Kusko," Char said. "How do you feel?"

Cramble deferred to both Char and Challia, offering them a seat.

"Everyone's *so* considerate around here," Kusko said. But the bitterness in her eyes told a different story.

"We're only being nice," Char confessed, "because we're thinking of our own skins. Cramble here's probably the only one being nice out of pure altruism." He glanced at the man, and then added, "We're worried about the *team*."

"Think you can sleep tonight?" Challia added. "That's our concern now."

"'I'm sorry about all this. I'm sure I'll be able to go out again on a mission again tomorrow. I swear I'll do my best."

"We heard you were having headaches and nausea and we were worried. I know it's rough working with the psycommu interface."

"I'll be fine."

From behind Kusko Al, Cramble piped up, "We rechecked the Elmeth system, sir . . . "

DURING THE EARLIER FRAY in space with the Federation forces, only Kusko's Elmeth had taken a hit from the Gundam and survived. The beam had in fact been a near-miss, but the diffused particles on its perimeter had caused more than minor localized damage. The blast, equivalent to a direct hit with conventional explosives, had momentarily knocked Kusko unconscious and left her in a state of shock. She had never been hit before and, even more disturbing, she had been hit by a far-off marksman.

Until hit, she had easily detected the Federation ships deploying themselves around the *LH* moon base. They were far easier prey than the remote-controlled target ships on which she was used to practicing; she could practically see the curdling waves of fear emitted by terrified crews inside the metal hulls. But her basic temperament made her take combat too lightly. It had allowed another flare of consciousness—a narrow thread—to infiltrate her mental space, and allowed an enemy to snipe at her from far-off. To her, the talk about a Federation Newtype unit had been just that—talk—so that when the alien thought waves came toward her, she had had no idea what was happening. No one had ever told her she might have to fight another Newtype. Not even Char. He had never fully comprehended the battle he had witnessed between Amuro and Lalah on *Texas*, and even if he had, it was doubtful that he could have explained it to Kusko. Newtype battles were far too new a military development.

If Kusko was too ignorant of Newtypes on the Federation side, she also had too much confidence in her own Newtype potential. She had forgotten that people are often controlled by their immediate emotions, but that there is a time lag between emotional response and one based on rational thought.

KUSKO HANDED HER COFFEE tube back to Cramble. She looked at Char and Challia and said, "Guess I'm not as smart as I thought."

It was a spontaneous remark, but both Char and Challia knew it was spoken from the heart.

"Nobody knows everything, Kusko," Char said, as if to console her. "That's why the teamwork's so important. Remember what I said earlier about being nice to you to save our own skins? That's what it's all about. About helping ourselves by helping the team. That's all it takes to make the team concept work."

"The commander's right, Kusko," Challia added. "If you'd just reign yourself in a little, we'd all get along better and work together better. It's important not to overestimate yourself in this business. And by the way, the final maintenance check on the Elmeth's scheduled for tomorrow morning, so we need you to get some shut-eye. Let us know if you need any pills."

"Thanks, but I think I'm fine."

"Of course you are!" Char replied deliberately, with a smile.

Kusko removed a pin from her chestnut-brown hair, and in the weightless environment it fluffed, framing her face. Then she stood up, grabbed the nearest lift-grip, and left the briefing room area, her long, attractive legs flowing behind her.

Cramble turned to his two superiors and remarked with a smile, "Not a bad girl, eh?"

"She'll be useful in battle," Char said, "but the Federation's rapidly acquiring the same sort of capability. It's safe to assume their Gundam model MS—probably piloted by Amuro Ray—is back in action. Don't forget that he's the one who destroyed Lalah Sune. The leaps in ability he's making suggest a powerful Newtype."

Challia added: "And don't overlook the mobile suits they're deploying around the Gundam, including the Guncannons and the GMs. They're formidable foes in their own right."

"Still, the Elmeth is what gives us the advantage," said Char. "Without it, we'd be exactly matched in strength. I just hope we can become the core fighting unit Her Excellency expects."

AFTER TAKING OFF FROM *LH*, the *Pegasus II*'s unit gradually linked up with the main forces around the Federation's *FS* beachhead on the back side of the moon. Every conceivable type of supply and repair unit was involved in the operation in a supporting role. Even elite reinforcements from *Luna II*—the Federation's ace-in-the-hole—joined the growing fleets, leaving almost no effective reserves in the entire Federation. Yet not a single ship in the vast armada had received concrete word of its final destination.

AFTER A MEETING ON *FS*, Lt. Bright Noa returned by launch to the *Pegasus II* and summoned all pilots.

"Thanks for coming," he began. "Within eighteen hours our unit—the 127th Autonomous—will move from its present position toward Area 365, so all preparations must be completed by then. We'll be supported by two squadrons of cosmo fighters whose ETA is 2000 hours. At 2100 we'll have a joint operations strategy meeting with their pilots. That's it for now."

The MS pilots looked around at each other, knowing their time had finally arrived. Hayato Kobayashi had the honor of speaking for the rest.

"What's going on, skipper?" he said. "I know you can't tell us our target yet, 'cause you probably don't even know yourself, but the *Pegasus* is basically a MS landing craft. We're not designed to be a full carrier for fighters."

Bright stepped up to the captain's seat on the boom crane in the middle of the bridge area and sat down. "How the hell should I know what's going on?" he said, as he began to check the ship's internal communications system. "That's why I called you all here. Lt. Commander McVery, of the 203rd Squadron, is in charge of the cosmo fighters. He's a veteran combat pilot and I know he won't get in our way."

"I bet we're gonna attack *A Baoa Qu*, right?" Kai said.

"Yeah," Hayato chimed in. "I bet General Staff thinks they can get us to do whatever they want."

"Think they're just using us?" Amuro asked.

"Yup," Kai answered, emphatically.

As if supporting Kai, Ensign Kria Maja, the GM 325 pilot, commented, "Seems like they just shift us around from one battlefield to another every week."

Kai, making as if to leave the room, couldn't help adding, "Sure seems that way, doesn't it? Damned if I understand what's going on. What the hell's the General thinking, anyway?"

"Having us spearheading the attack, that's what," Amuro shot back. "Probably capture *A Baoa Qu* and plunge into the Zeon heartland." He looked up at the ships in the Federation armada displayed on the ceiling screen above him and began counting. To the untrained eye, the armada would have been more than adequate for the job, but the rules of modern warfare had changed.

Sayla also glanced at Bright and asked, "Can't you at least tell us the code name of the operation, skipper?"

"*Cembalo* . . . It's an archaic type of musical instrument, sort of like a piano."

"What's that got to do with what *we're* doing?"

"Probably nothing. Somebody in General Staff probably just liked it. Maybe it's like the time part of a poem was used as a code name in a campaign. I think it was the poet Paul Verlaine's line, *With long sobs the violin-throbs of autumn wound my heart . . .* "

"When was that, sir?" Amuro asked, suddenly impressed with Bright's erudition.

"During an old global war in Europe, if my memory serves me correctly."

Mirai glanced at Amuro, but first addressed Bright. "There's something about all this that bothers me. When I read Amuro's combat report, it almost sounded like he's some sort of esper or something. I bet Headquarters is relying on that, and on using all of us on the *Pegasus II* as a sort of secret weapon. What do you think, Amuro? Do you think if this war's ever over we'll be able to lead normal lives? Think Newtypes'll ever be accepted back in society?"

"You're jumping ahead way too much, Mirai," Amuro responded. "Do you really think we're true Newtypes? I'm still not sure we've done anything to deserve that label." He leaned back against one of the windows on the bridge and glanced up at Bright in his captain's perch. Having checked the ship's intercom system, the skipper was sipping coffee from the tube used in weightless environments.

"Wait 'til the media gets hold of the idea," Bright said in between sips.

"But skipper," Amuro responded. "Nobody's really even come up with a precise definition of what a Newtype is yet. It's too early to even think about how people will react to them, let alone whether they'll discriminate against them."

"Amuro," Sayla said, "don't forget what happened to Zeon Zum Deikun. He advocated the Newtype concept and wound up being persecuted by the Earth Federation. And people knew a lot less about Newtypes then than they do today."

Everyone on the bridge knew Sayla was right, and Mirai summed it up for all of them: "No kidding. Just wait and see if the *Pegasus* survives this war. For sure, Amuro'll be treated as an ace. A *Newtype ace.* The mass media'll have a field day. And for better or worse, Newtypes'll be presented as something they're not."

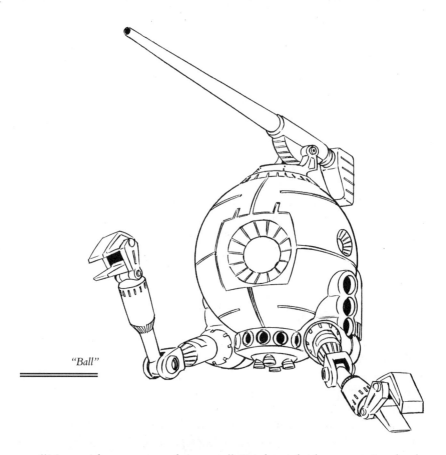

"Ball"

"Man with supernatural powers," Bright sighed, tongue in cheek. "A telepathist. I can see the headlines already: '*Lt. Commander Amuro, the Federation ace who can read your every thought!*'"

Bright was joking, but Amuro knew he and Mirai were probably right. He tried to imagine how he would respond if it all ever came true, but it was too depressing. But by the time Mirai's fears were realized, he and all the other core crew on the *Pegasus* would hopefully be a lot older and wiser and better able to deal with it. "You surprise me, Mirai," he said. "I always thought you were more of an optimist. I'm sure it'll work out."

"I hope so," she responded. "But something about it all bothers me. I just can't help worrying . . . "

"Maybe you're worrying *too* much," Sayla interjected. "You *have* been working awfully hard recently."

"Well, in that case," Mirai joked, turning to Bright, "maybe I could get a break after this meeting . . . "

"I think we can arrange that," he replied with a grin.

"All right, Sayla," Mirai said with a conspiratorial wink. "What do you say the two of us go out for a drink tonight?"

"Now hold on!" Bright shot back. "You're not serious are you? There's no liquor on board . . . Is there?"

"Of course not, silly."

Amuro couldn't help but laugh at the way Mirai bantered with the skipper. "I'd love to join you both," he said to the two Waves.

"Enough out of you, *Mister* Amuro," Bright retorted. "You can go below immediately! There's a strict ship rule against private chitchat when on duty . . . "

The captain was right, of course, but the chitchat was a welcome relief to the tensions building on board. And it was a reflection of a new camaraderie developing among the core crew, a closeness based on more than the mutual tolerance and affection implied by friendship, and supported by a growing Newtype awareness. But the crew had few chances to talk in terms that all understood and appreciated, and it was precisely opportunities like these, however fragmentary, that they needed. Most of the crew were not yet evolved enough to experience the extreme understanding and psychic harmony that Amuro and Lalah had experienced. They still needed more peak experiences of communication.

CHAR AZNABLE SOMETIMES FELT the same way. And perhaps this was one of those moments. Still, he had nothing so specific on his mind now. He was proud, even vain, but he wasn't arrogant enough to give priority to such personal, philosophical questions, especially not when lying next to Kycilia Zabi's secretary for the first time.

"My name's Margaret Ring Blair, commander," she said with a smile. "And it's my real name."

Char had a naturally suspicious mind, but with one sentence Margaret had managed to disarm it. She laughed, let her full-bodied hair fall over her face, and then looked up at him. "You look *awfully* scary," she said, not looking at all as if she meant it. She kept giggling, as if somehow able to see through the serious facade of his life, and even laugh at it.

There was something about her innocent mannerisms that he liked, something about the way she could see through people yet not offend them. It occurred to him that he might even be able to fall in love with her, in a way that was uncluttered with the sort of savior complex he had felt with Lalah Sune. Deep down, he was an extraordinary idealist. And because of his idealism, he was normally incapable of totally trusting or loving any individual. Incapable even of making his only sister happy. Love, he believed, was an ideal, and it should be perfect and pure. Physical love condemned a man to a physical level. In the case of Lalah Sune, only his desire to save her had helped elevate his love to a higher plane.

"Does the, er, scar on my forehead bother you?" he asked, tentatively. He was bemused by his own tongue-tied manner. Shyness was something he could scarcely imagine, especially when he was in his normal military persona. He couldn't recall ever having asked Lalah Sune what he had just asked Margaret.

"Well, it *is* rather ugly," she bluntly replied. "Not a pleasant sight at all. But frankly I think it looks rather good on you, Commander. Forgive me for saying so," she hastened to add, "but I just want to be honest. It doesn't bother me. Really."

"Thanks," he replied, "for being kind. You're everything I imagined when I first met you." He cursed himself for phrasing it that way. It seemed like that was the only sort of thing he was ever capable of saying. *I want to love her, and tell her so,* he thought, *but I don't really know her well enough yet.* Perfectionism was a tragic shortcoming in his romantic character, and it always seemed to get in the way at times like these.

Char liked the way she interacted with him; he liked her sincerity, and the way she didn't pressure him. She gave him such a sense of relief that all of his senses—normally so taut—relaxed. As long as he felt her body next to his, it seemed there was nothing to worry about. *Who cares about Newtypes?* he thought, turning around as she moved slightly next to him. Her cheeks had a glow to them and her full lips were formed into a smile. With his left hand he traced the lines of her full waist and suddenly, spontaneously, wished she could bear his child. It was something he had never dreamed of with Lalah Sune. Perhaps, it occurred to him, humans often acted on impulses like this, and then spent the rest of their lives trying to reconcile them with reality. There was something interesting about that idea, something to savor.

He could hardly remember what it was that had attracted him to Lalah Sune, and why he had tried so hard to look after her.

It was time to sleep.

Lt. Commander McVery's 203rd Squadron, with its twelve Tomahawk cosmo fighters, was stationed on the upper decks of the *Pegasus II*'s "leg" sections. With the addition of the squadron and its support units, the *Pegasus* had finally taken on the organized hustle and bustle of an active warship. It was a new ambience that helped offset both the basic manpower shortage on the ship and the extremely informal atmosphere that existed among the original crew.

McVery, a dyed-in-the-wool space pilot, epitomized the change. He had the type of personality that had to be experienced to be fully understood; an informal manner that coexisted with a cautious approach bordering on nervous obsession. Wherever on board, he liked to yell out, *"This thing's not a warship! It's a den of disorder and poor training. I feel like I'm off to play war with a bunch of kindergarteners!"*

Sleggar Law and other *Pegasus* crew members often made cracks about McVery, accusing him of "riding awfully high on his hobbyhorse for a newcomer to the ship." McVery would then immediately do an about-face and always claim his willingness to defer to the *Pegasus* crew. Then in the next breath, since the mobile suit unit had been ordered to form the Tomahawk Squadron's rearguard, he would threaten to shoot down anyone who moved into his field of fire.

"Poor McVery," Kai liked to say with a laugh, "he's just upset 'cause he's stuck in the cosmo fighter ranks an'll be there forever."

Kai and the rest of the crew had a tendency to belittle the ability of both McVery and his squadron, but in reality cosmo fighters still played an important support role for warships. The crew took McVery more seriously when he pronounced that no one would likely survive the coming mission.

They knew the 127th Autonomous—the *Pegasus, Cyprus*, and the *Greyden*—was headed for Area 365, and that it had been assigned such scant protection because that was all the Federation was willing to spare until the fleet reached its as-yet-unknown staging point for Operation Cembalo. Once in Area 365 they would have no contact with other ships in the armada. Area 365 formed one point of a triangle completed by Zeon's *Solomon* and *A Baoa Qu* space fortresses. To venture into this area meant that the 127th was being used as a strategic sacrifice. Put more politely, it was a decoy, or at best a feint for the larger Armada operation. They were, in other words, on their own.

McVery put it in his typically eloquent fashion: "The brass obviously have a hell of a lot of faith in this 'Newtype' stuff. I think me and my men were dealt a lousy hand when we were assigned here. But lemme tell ya. I won't be easy bait. I'll take out at least ten or twenty Zakus . . . "

THE 127TH AUTONOMOUS LEFT the sunlit moon behind it and sailed toward Area 365 at primary combat speed. Bright, the skipper of the *Pegasus II*, had a special operations file with information on their exact destination, but the file's lock was programmed not to open until twelve hours had elapsed.

Along the way, the Gundam, Guncannons, and GMs 324 and 325 (piloted by Ensigns Sarkus McGovern and Kria Maja), practiced flying in attack formation, accompanied by four "Ball" machines from the other two warships. The exercises had no real strategic value but helped keep the MS pilots in a state of readiness.

When Zeon's MS unit had attacked the Federation's *LH* moon base, few of the Federation pilots or crew members had even spotted the Elmeth, and fewer yet had realized it was being piloted by a true Newtype. Some crewmen listening to friendly radio reports had detected a mysterious, dissonant sound that seemed to reverberate deep in their brains before the Elmeth fired its first blast, but those, like Sayla, who realized what the sound meant, were a rarity. Only Amuro had intuitively known the enemy machine was part of a Newtype combat unit and deduced its true strength. And only he had understood that its destructive power exceeded that of Lalah Sune. His main regret was that he had been unable to confirm the exact number of attacking Suits—they had simply been too powerful for him to worry about counting, and they hadn't been fooled for a minute by an attempt to divide their forces. When up against an enemy like that, he wondered if it was really fair to rely on Kai and Hayato in their Guncannons. He was encouraged by their performance. They had increased the speed with which they could come to his support and the level of their teamwork. With them, he knew wouldn't have to worry so much about being caught with his rear exposed. Still, he hoped that he had acted correctly, for he was plagued with doubts at the thought that he might be subconsciously trying to maximize his own chances for survival at the expense of his friends.

His desire to survive the war had suddenly been strengthened by knowing Sayla intimately. It was odd, because the notion of fighting for the chance to sleep with a female—even to "protect" her—somehow skewed whatever sense of ethics or propriety he felt should exist on the field of battle. He was still naive enough to believe that fighters should be inspired to risk their lives for more noble causes such as overthrowing dictators or preserving democracy. Yet somehow his experience with Lalah Sune had hinted at an entirely different possibility. It was a possibility he believed existed in his new relationship with Sayla, too. It transcended physical sexuality. Men and women. Women and men. Amuro was becoming aware of a potentially new world.

"AMURO RAY IN G3! Ready for landing!"

"Go ahead, G3! But be careful!"

As he closed in on the *Pegasus II* after practice, Amuro saw Sayla appear on his three-inch comm monitor, almost as if she were right there talking to him. Then he heard First Deck Petty Officer First Class Callahan Slay energetically giving directions: *"Two minutes on the horizontal axis! Correct to the right!"*

"Roger!" he called back, keeping a careful eye on the flight floor of the First Deck looming up at him. He imagined Callahan watching wide-eyed, checking the Gundam's entry into the ship, probably reacting the same way others had when he had first piloted the Gundam on Side 7.

"I CAN'T BELIEVE THIS . . . "

Lt. Commander McVery's eyes flashed under his thick eyebrows when he first saw the sixteen-meter-tall Gundam mobile suit parked in front of the MS elevator.

Amuro removed his helmet and held it by his side, and tried to change the subject. "It wasn't a very useful practice, sir," he said.

"I don't care what anyone says," McVery sputtered, "b . . . but that *thing* still looks like a giant toy robot to me. Landings and takeoffs must be hell, no?"

"Not particularly, sir," said Amuro, ignoring McVery's astonishment. "I was trained for Suits from the start."

From his reading of history, Amuro knew that at the beginning of the twentieth century, under the old calendar system, the battleship faction in many navies had often been unable to adjust when aircraft were first introduced. Similarly, as a seasoned veteran, McVery was probably still attached to the "good old days" when cosmo fighters had been in their primacy. Of course, if he had problems adjusting it was understandable, for the mobile suit concept had only taken root about five years ago, and it had only been proven feasible in combat with the development of Zeon's Zaku model. It was no wonder McVery still thought of mobile suits as giant toy robots.

Without waiting for Callahan to officially announce the safe return of the other Suits to the ship, Amuro swigged a bottle of liquid vitamins and floated up to the briefing room. Bright was already there, and the rest of the MS pilots slowly drifted in, one after another. Then McVery entered with all of his cosmo fighter pilots.

"What are they doing here?" Amuro whispered to his skipper, feeling inhibited.

"I wanted them to hear your debriefing," Bright announced. "You're the leader of our MS unit, after all, and we may be involved in a joint operation with them."

Amuro didn't like the idea. He was still in the process of learning himself, and the idea of giving a presentation in front of McVery and his men—all older combat veterans—would be like the pupil lecturing the teacher.

"Don't worry," McVery said with a grin. "We won't get in your way." He was chewing gum, and the noise irritated Amuro.

Like Amuro, Kai, Hayato, Sarkus, Kria, and the pilots of the four "Mister Balls" were young, and nervous with McVery present. Amuro opened his flight notebook and looked at it. Then he addressed his unit. "Well, based on what I saw during practice," he said, "in real combat you guys'd all be dead ducks. But we've gotta be confident of our ability as Newtypes. Senior, more experienced military officers may put pressure on us to do things differently, but it's important to ignore them." He looked McVery straight in the eye when he said this last sentence. Then he continued.

"You probably don't understand everything I'm talking about, so let me explain. It's one thing to be aware of the physical conditions and environment you're operating in, but there's something important beyond that. Recognize, be aware of what you see, store it as knowledge, and remember there's a lot more out there to look out for. Your senses have got to be wide open, reading information from every direction to catch it. Sure, you need the instruments in your cockpit. But remember you can't always rely on them. Mostly, you've got to ignore them because the enemy isn't gonna jump out at you from inside your instrument panel. He's gonna come at you from outside your Suit. The moment you forget this, he'll take you by surprise. Now maybe what I'm saying sounds like a contradiction, but anyone who doesn't understand the logic behind it sure as hell isn't a Newtype, and probably isn't even qualified to be a regular pilot. Wouldn't you agree, Commander McVery, sir?"

The sudden question caught McVery by surprise, but he grinned and said, "They'll never understand it that way. You're making it, how shall I say, a little too *conceptual*. For a lad like you teaching your peer group you've got to make things more concrete, specific, down-to-earth. Understand?"

"Yessir." Amuro replied. Out of the corner of his eye he saw Sayla enter the room, apparently off-duty.

McVery continued: "I think you're talking about something like the *ki* or 'spirit' that martial arts people refer to. You're saying we can detect this and we'd better not forget it, right?"

"Exactly, sir," Amuro replied. Then he continued. "And when we face an enemy Newtype unit, the *ki*, for lack of a better term, is transmitted in an even more clearly defined form. It's sort of a situational 'pressure' you can sense, an almost 'evil' force you can feel coming toward you. Being able to sense this in a way makes it easier to confront the enemy, but the problem is that he's faster than most normal opponents. Infinitely faster. Which means that there's only one way to respond, and that's by operating almost reflexively, by anticipating the enemy's moves in advance. Judging by everyone's performance today, though, you guys would all have been blasted to smithereens."

"Even me?!" Kai asked, with a quaver in his voice.

"Even you," Amuro said gently.

"What about me?" Hayato next asked, plaintively.

"Sorry . . . "

"You're being a little tough on us, aren't you?" Hayato complained.

"Sorry, but the important thing is to figure out what to do about it. Remember, I'm assuming a Zeon Newtype unit attacked our *LH* base. As I mentioned yesterday, I think the pilot of the Elmeth mobile armor's a Newtype, and even more advanced than the one I encountered on *Texas.* I say that because there was even more interference with radio transmissions around *LH* than we'd normally find with Minovsky particles. That's why some people claimed they actually 'heard' something inside their heads, and that's why it should be clear to everybody that we're talking about something totally different from normal radio waves. Whoever or whatever is out there emitting those waves, is our enemy."

Amuro knew he still wasn't explaining things very clearly, and it irritated him. He wasn't used to standing in front of people and lecturing. But while talking, something completely different occurred to him. During the confrontation with the Elmeth over *LH*, he had suspected its pilot was a highly evolved Newtype whom he would face again soon. But he had also sensed more than a simple desire to kill him; he had sensed something dark, brooding, and ominous directed at him, a personal hatred with a masculine edge. For that reason, perhaps, it hadn't occurred to him at the time that the pilot might again be a woman. Now, suddenly, for some reason he couldn't fully understand himself, he wondered if it might have been Kusko Al. Perhaps everything was all a matter of fate. That notion had occurred to him once before when confronting Lalah Sune. But the here-and-now transcended fate. He had to live in reality.

The presentation continued for over two hours, but when the discussion turned to close-quarter combat tactics McVery and his men finally left the room. In parting, the Lt. Commander said, "We're obviously living in different worlds because, frankly, I can't understand this stuff. As far as I'm concerned, this Zeon Newtype unit you're describing is still just a bunch of men in giant robots. And I don't intend to let them get me."

Combat veterans tend to be conservative and to cling to whatever methods worked for them in the past. They see little merit in adopting other tactics. In warfare, if a new, unknown tactic is adopted and fails, there is no second chance.

As the other men left the room, Amuro wondered out loud, "How many of us are really ready for what we're going to encounter?" He loosened his pilot suit and sat down, wondering when on earth the Federation would develop the perfect suit. His undergarments were cold from his own sweat and even his socks were damp. His toes felt like they were swimming. Only Sayla was still left in the briefing room.

"You know, Amuro, as long as you're leading the MS team, I'm sure things'll work out," she said, as if to console him. She was still intensely bothered by the fact that she had mentioned killing her brother, Char Aznable. Ever since leaving Side 7 she had felt a tension inside her, but during the short time she had spent with Amuro in his room the other night, it had left her. Perhaps, she worried, she had opened herself up too much to him. She had spoken impulsively, and created a chasm between them. If Amuro were a real Newtype, she thought he would have been able to deduce what she had really meant and not dwell on the words themselves. But she knew she had made a mistake. She had been too naive. If anyone could really read another's mind, know their history, and always know why they had said something, that person wouldn't be a Newtype, he'd be God.

Newtypes were distinguished by a superior intuition and their re-markable "hunches," but they were not mind readers in the true sense of the word. If anything, they were distinguished by a superior ability to read their *own* minds and understand information ordinary people might overlook. But if one could know one's own mind, would that extend to the spirit? If so, might it not be possible to extrapolate the truly universal aspects of oneself to others, and through this "bridge" truly read another's mind? Unfortunately, such a feat would probably require that both parties be similar Newtypes, and Sayla and Amuro were fundamentally different.

"I grew up with a complex about my real family, Amuro," Sayla said. "And because of that I sometimes don't trust people." She knew he was probably too naive to understand what she was trying to say. But in order for him to expand and grow as a Newtype, she felt it was important. She looked at him, unable to apologize or retract her statement about Char. If she did, she knew he'd feel attracted to her for all the wrong reasons.

Amuro, for his part, didn't press the matter. He was fiercely attracted to her, but on the eve of a major battle he wanted to keep his emotions in check. Still, it was hard.

He looked up at her with a tired expression and said, "Sayla, can't you feel it?"

"Feel what?"

"When I was talking here a minute ago, I felt something. Char's on his way. And so's Kusko Al. It's almost like I can feel the weight of their presence."

"Weight?"

"It feels sort of like a wall of pressure, I guess, and it's spreading out toward *Pegasus II*."

Sayla thought she finally understood what he was saying. The "weight" he referred to *was* something spreading, and menacing.

"I thought maybe it was just the normal stress before battle, Amuro . . . "

"No, it's more defined than that. This may sound crazy, but you know what I think? I think we've got to put a stop to this operation somehow. I know that alone won't stop the war. There'd still be thousands of people killed in other areas of the solar system. I can't stop the war myself, but I think somehow the strongest people, the best fighters, have to get together and destroy whoever's causing this war to drag on."

"Destroy them? You must be dreaming, Amuro."

"Maybe. But listen, Sayla, let me ask you. Do you really think your brother—Char Aznable or Casval Deikun or whatever his real name is—*likes* this war? I bet he doesn't."

"No, I'm sure you're right . . . "

"He's got his own goals and dreams, right? He's older than me, and he's been around more. I'm sure he does."

"Well, maybe . . . "

"That's why he mustn't be killed. And as long as he isn't too self-righteous about what he's doing, we ought to cooperate with him."

"*Cooperate*? With my brother?"

"It's only an idea. But if he's the type of person I think he is, maybe we ought to cooperate, as Newtypes."

"Amuro, you're talking about people *causing* the war, but things aren't so simple. The Zabis aren't the only ones to blame. Nor is our crazy mixed-up Federation government. It's the whole system."

"I know. I know. That's why we've gotta find a way to end the war as fast as possible. Then we can work to eliminate the root cause of it."

Sayla was afraid of what Amuro was saying, but she knew he was right about her brother. It was probably why Char had always avoided confronting her directly when she tried to stop him.

"Amuro," she said. "I always wanted Casval to be my brother. I never wanted him to be Char Aznable. . . ."

"Listen Sayla, I don't know your brother at all, but as long as he's the 'Red Comet,' he's the enemy, and if I meet him in combat I have to fight him. I have to protect myself because I don't have any guarantee he thinks the way I think he does. But you know what? There's something about him I kind of admire. And I think a lot of other men in the Forces feel the same, too."

"That's just because you never had an older brother."

"Maybe. It's true I always wanted one."

Amuro's voice betrayed a trace of resentment. Sayla was surprised at his emotion. It had never occurred to her how hard it must be to be an only child.

"Sometimes I think it's easier being alone, Amuro," she said, suddenly feeling like a little girl. "It's a lot easier than having a brother you love, and then losing him."

Amuro said nothing. He stood up and left, slamming the door behind him. *What should I do?* Sayla thought. The room felt suddenly chilly. Monitors on the wall showed scenes of each launch deck. Everything was quiet. She knew it was dangerous to have illusions about what Newtypes could or could not do, yet she was seized by the desire to follow both Amuro and her brother, no matter what happened.

THE ATTACK

"AMURO RAY?!"

Lt. (jg) Kusko Al was so shocked when she heard the name that she repeated it out loud.

"That's right," Challia Bull said, looking at her curiously. "We have information that he's the same pilot who destroyed the first Elmeth model, and that he's headed in our direction."

Kusko felt suddenly naked, embarrassed before Challia, but she feebly tried to respond to his unvoiced questions. "I . . . I've met him before," she confessed, hesitatingly. "On Side 6. I . . . I never realized he was capable of anything like that. He seemed so young . . . "

The instant she heard Amuro's name a vivid image had popped into her mind. He was waiting for her in front of the Flanagan Institute with the nervous look of a youth with more on his mind than just a platonic meeting. And there was something she had found rather charming about that, so much so that she probably would have gone along with whatever he was thinking. After all, she had helped rescue him when he had drifted near the *Kasetta III* in his escape pod, and she had even helped him destroy it later. It wasn't as if they were total strangers. She had intuitively liked him, and that made her feel good. She had enjoyed the almost-Newtype sensitivity of his character, and toyed with the idea of getting to know him even better, but that was all. Perhaps it had been a mistake not to bring the escape capsule back to the Flanagan Institute for a more thorough investigation, but she knew the Federation had no weapons system that could compare to the psycommu and, following that logic, she didn't see how the capsule could have been all that important. It was only one part of the new mobile suit. Besides, she had liked Amuro, and sincerely wanted to help him.

She turned to her commander, Char Aznable, and asked: "Did you have a chance to see how developed he was as a Newtype?"

"No," Char answered, fidgeting with the collar on his pilot suit. "But I can tell you this. During the attack on *LH*, we're almost positive your Elmeth was hit by a blast from Amuro Ray's Gundam."

Kusko Al couldn't help muttering to herself, *Of all people, it would have to be Amuro Ray in the Gundam . . .* She was a woman with strong likes and dislikes, but she had never dreamed that she might develop strong feelings for an officer in the Federation Forces. Especially since he had reddish hair. That was normally enough to make her want to laugh. But there was something about the way he had regained consciousness on the *Kasetta III* and instinctively dealt with the crew in such a cautious manner. Something about the way he had been so perceptive about his environment. More than anything else, she realized, it was the fact that he was a sensitive person that had made her first like him. Then, when she had learned that he was also intelligent, and the sort who did what he said he would do, and had enormous strength of character, well, that had made her positive first impression escalate to another level. Federation troops might have burned her parents to death, but Amuro Ray was different, so she would forgive him for being with the enemy. That was the way her femininity asserted itself. *Perhaps,* she thought, *I can even contact him through the psycommu interface and let him know I'm piloting the Elmeth.*

What Kusko Al did not know was that her naive sentimentality would be first swallowed and then crushed by the overwhelming reality of war.

WHEN THE 127TH AUTONOMOUS reached Area 365, it immediately came under observation by Zeon scouts, from both *Solomon* and *A Baoa Qu*, as the most advanced, exposed unit in the Federation armada.

On *Solomon*, Dozle Zabi told his men, "Ignore it. It's just a feint. Revil bypassed us to take *Granada* before. So now he's coming to get us. Get our forces out in position and keep them together."

General Revil, meantime, hoped Kycilia Zabi would overestimate the importance of the 127th, so he could flush her *A Baoa Qu*-based New-type unit out in the open. "After the fight on *Texas*," he told his staff, "Kycilia will suspect we have our *own* Newtype corps. It doesn't matter if the *Pegasus II* is really manned by true Newtypes or not. The important thing is that she *believe* the 127th is a true Newtype unit."

"Do *you* believe it, sir?" an aide asked.

"Depends on their performance in battles to come," he replied. "At this point, they look pretty good."

General Revil personally commanded the main Federation fleet centered around his flagship, the *Drog*, and the carrier *Trafalgar*, yet even this fleet was but part of a giant armada of over three hundred and twenty Federation ships. After leaving the moon, the armada had appeared positioned to strike *A Baoa Qu* directly. In actual fact, however, neither the Zeon forces nor the crews of the Federation ships themselves knew where the armada would finally converge, for it was not just dispersed along a single plane, but within a three dimensional spherical area over ten thousand kilometers in diameter, nearly the same size as the planet Earth. In this vast space, three hundred and twenty ships were like floating specks of dust in a cavernous hall, so dispersed they presented little immediate military threat. But when collected together at their final rendezvous point, they would constitute an awesome destructive force. Mankind was standing on the brink of yet another bloody power struggle.

A single red light suddenly winked on the ceiling display over the *Pegasus II* bridge, and Ensign Marker Clan yelled, "Enemy ships sighted!"

The first Zeon force encountered was not a Newtype unit but a special task force of three *Musai*-class cruisers from *Solomon*, carrying a total of six Zakus.

The order immediately went out: *"Launch Tomahawk Squadron!"* The twelve cosmo fighters under Lt. Commander McVery's command were released from their moorings and floated off the *Pegasus II* upper deck. With verniers deployed on a wing-like design, they resembled fat spears. Referred to as "fighters," they had far greater firepower than old-style heavy bombers. Rocket trails flared from them as they launched, and then they were followed in loose formation by the ship's five mobile suits.

Bright next issued a series of commands: *"Enemy has penetrated the second combat line! Ready main cannon! Missile elevation zero point three degrees! Launch nine! Two volleys!"* From twelve missile tubes on either leg of the ship's front section, two volleys of nine missiles each instantly streaked forth, leaving a trail of light among the stars.

"Initiate evasive action! B formation!"

"B formation!" Mirai yelled in response, flicking a switch in front of her and putting the ship on an auto pilot. If she had to maneuver quickly to evade an incoming missile or an attacking Suit, she could manually override auto, but as soon as the maneuver ended the guidance system would default back to auto and thus keep the ship in formation. The warships following the *Pegasus*, the *Cyprus* and the *Greyden*, began criss-crossing back and forth around her in an evasive maneuver, preparing for enemy missiles.

"Incoming at twelve o'clock, two minutes!"

From the bridge of the *Pegasus II*, the crew suddenly spotted two bands of light from missiles streaking toward them, but in almost the same instant they exploded. A Federation Suit had picked them off.

"I think it was Amuro," Sayla said softly.

"Lower protective shutters!" Bright yelled.

Shutters immediately descended over all the windows on the bridge, but the crew never lost their view, for the inside of the windows now functioned as display monitors.

"Second wave incoming!" called out Marker Clan, the operator, in a tense voice, as he spotted a dozen streaks of light from new approaching missiles.

"Ready ship guns!" Bright barked. "Fire at will! Fore missiles, raise vertical elevation point six degrees! Launch three volleys of twelve missiles each!"

It was the sort of missile defense that was nearly futile in three dimensional space. The *Pegasus*'s anti-missile-missiles streaked forth in what looked like a single band of light, but some of them had apparently been launched too close together, for they soon collided with each other, mushrooms of light flaring not too far from the ship. Luckily, the incoming Zeon missiles were no more successful.

In telescopic mode, one of Bright's displays showed three enemy ships among the stars, and he knew they were close enough for his main cannon.

"Target in range! Fire main cannon!"

Brilliant beams of light, far more dense than the trails left by the missiles earlier, belched forth from the *Pegasus*'s two mega particle cannons and pierced the blackness, stretching for what seemed like an eternity. The beams emitted sparks on their periphery, probably from contact with comet fragments or "star dust," but neither appeared to hit the enemy. It had long been rumored in the Federation Forces that Zeon's *Musai*-class cruisers were adept at evasion, and the *Pegasus*'s difficulty hitting them confirmed it. Twenty seconds after the *Pegasus*'s cannons fired, beams from the Zeon forces streaked back in retaliation, suggesting that they had a less sophisticated telescopic mode on their gun sights and thus took longer to aim.

"Tough luck about the lousy optics, guys," Bright yelled at the Zeon ships on the display monitor in front of him. "Just try an' hit us!!"

And then it happened. A beam fired from the *Pegasus* struck the *Musai* cruiser on the left, and an enormous burst of light flared in the darkness. But the explosion did not appear to have been fatal.

"Give the left one two more blasts!" Bright barked. "McVery's squadron'll be there in five more seconds!" He knew that from then on it would be too dangerous to support McVery with either beam cannon or missiles. And he also knew that the enemy Suits would soon be on top of the *Pegasus II.* It was critical that Amuro and his men destroy them before they could wreak any damage.

In the distance he spotted the telltale fatal mushroom of light from the *Musai* just hit.

"One *Musai* cruiser destroyed, sir!" Oscar yelled. "But I'm picking up what looks like Zakus at eleven o'clock, elevation minus three degrees!"

Bright prayed that Amuro's unit would be able to intercept the enemy Suits. If the Zakus followed normal Zeon tactics they would try to slip under the ship's defenses. One never knew what would happen in a combat situation, but he had faith in Amuro.

The *Pegasus II* and the other three ships in the 127th group continued to close in on the enemy. When it appeared that Lt. Commander McVery had finally reached the *Musai* ships and commenced his attack, Bright couldn't help thinking, *I wish he had more than twelve fighters . . .* No matter how seasoned a warrior McVery might be, the odds against him were steep.

AMURO AND HIS MEN steadfastly approached the six enemy Zakus.

"Give 'em hell, guys!" he yelled into his mike, knowing that with the Minovsky concentration they were encountering it was probably his last radio transmission for a while. "And don't forget we're better than they are!"

Sarkus and Kria had both been in combat before, but they had originally trained on cosmo fighters and the new GM Suits were harder to handle. For example, the GM's electronic 360-degree display system was nice, but it was initially unnerving to a pilot used to making direct visual sightings through the Plexiglas canopy of a fighter.

Then they met the Zakus. Sarkus took on the first one, which unfortunately had the colored antenna-like rod of a squad leader. He fired his beam rifle. The Zaku easily evaded it and closed in. Sarkus yelled in terror, but in the same instant a beam pierced the Zaku and it vanished in a ball of light. Amuro's Gundam had slipped up on Sarkus's right side.

"Sarkus!" Amuro barked into his mike. "Don't just fly with inertia! You've gotta be more proactive!"

"Ye . . . *yessir!*" the GM pilot responded.

Sarkus's GM was nimbler than a cosmo fighter, and he was trying to operate it as confidently as possible, flying in a zigzag pattern above the assumed line of combat. Then he heard Amuro's voice call out again, "*Ten o'clock, up fifteen degrees!*" He looked up and spotted the glowing mono-eye of a Zaku. In rapid succession, several blasts creased his GM's armor. Cursing, panicking, he got the Zaku in his sights and fired a volley from his beam rifle. With a *whoosh*, one blast hit home. The Zaku began spewing beads of light from its back and then raised both hands as if clawing in desperation at the heavens. Sarkus fired another beam. The Zaku's limbs disintegrated and the entire Suit turned into a ball of light.

"*Sarkus! Don't waste your fire! Conserve your energy!*" It was the scolding voice of his unit leader—Amuro—again.

AFTER KAI AND HAYATO had each made one kill, Amuro bagged one more. Then he led his entire unit in pursuit of the sole remaining Zaku, as it tried to flee back to its mother ship.

"Kria!" Amuro commanded, "I want you out in front!" He wanted to present the ensign with an easy target, but the man still managed to bungle it, and took two shots to finish off the retreating Zaku.

By the time the MS unit caught up with McVery's Tomahawk Squadron, the last remaining *Musai* cruiser had been badly damaged, but it was still putting up a fierce resistance. Since McVery had already lost four of his fighters, Amuro's unit helped him out by slamming several beam blasts into the ship's prow and finishing her off.

Only thirteen minutes had elapsed between the moment of initial contact with the Zeon task force and its annihilation. In terms of fire-power, the *Pegasus II* and its accompanying ships had had a slight advantage over the Zeon squadron, but in reality the battle had been determined by the tactics employed. Not a single attacking Zaku had been able to penetrate the 127th's defense.

BACK IN THE BRIEFING room on *Pegasus II*, Amuro stated his opinion emphatically: "That was nothing. We haven't even seen the real enemy yet. And I don't mean Kycilia or Dozle's regular forces. I mean Zeon's true Newtype unit."

Lt. Commander McVery, still preoccupied with the last battle, couldn't resist a dig at Amuro's MS unit. "If you'd reached us earlier, Mister Amuro," he caustically commented, "I wouldn't have lost four of my fighters!" Everyone knew the criticism wasn't fair and that he was just letting off steam. In reality, he had been amazed at the speed with which Amuro and his men had joined the fray. He had heard that MS battles were essentially chase-and-be-chased melees, but in the entire war he had never witnessed such a feat. Six enemy Zakus had been unable to sink a single Federation ship, and had instead themselves been annihilated. He knew the 127th had achieved a phenomenal victory, but on a personal, emotional level he couldn't ignore the fact that several of his own men had been lost.

McVery still had enormous pride in the vanguard role of his cosmo fighter unit, but out of pique he couldn't help sarcastically commenting, "Next time, maybe you'd prefer it if we formed the rear guard . . . " And he wasn't ready for the answer he received.

Amuro took his words literally. "Well, if that's what you'd prefer, sir," he said, "maybe we can try it next time."

"Whoa. wait a minute, sonny," McVery answered in a quick about-face. "Let's be serious here. I'm a *Tomahawk* man. That's not funny."

"Well, sir, we'll eventually be confronting the same Zeon Newtype unit that attacked our *LH* moon base. Frankly, I don't think there's any reason for you to do anything suicidal. The most important thing, it seems to me, sir, is to defend the *Pegasus*. Don't you agree?"

"What are you talking about? Hell, the Red Comet or whatever he's called isn't some sort of supernatural character. Just because he's destroyed a few Federation ships doesn't mean he can destroy the whole Tomahawk squadron!"

"I'm sorry to differ with you, sir. But the unit on its way here's far more powerful than the old Red Comet."

"You're talking about that Elmeth thing, right? Who knows what the hell those mobile armor contraptions really are, anyway? Right now we're just dealing with prototypes!"

"Maybe," Amuro replied, standing his ground. "No offense intended, sir, but in the interest of saving as many of your men's lives as possible, I honestly think it'd be better if your squadron did take the rear."

THE 127TH AUTONOMOUS CONTINUED along its assigned course, but a turning point had been reached. General Revil's flagship, the *Drog*, fired off a blue signal flare that was observed far off on the Federation's *FS* moon base. *FS* then transmitted a coded laser message to each of the Federation fleets in the armada—*Proceed at third combat speed!* Each unit commander was thus finally permitted to open the secret file delivered on departure, and to learn that the armada's ultimate target was Zeon's space fortress, *A Baoa Qu.*

Bright Noa, for his part, finally learned that the 127th's true mission was to use all means available to destroy Zeon reinforcements from *Solomon.* He knew that *Solomon* forces would not sit by idly during the ten hours it would take for the dozen or more Federation fleets to form a virtual wall between *Solomon* and *A Baoa Qu.* He also knew that if the armada was not careful, it would be constantly harassed from the rear by *Solomon* forces as it closed in on *A Baoa Qu.* The 127th, at the highest elevation relative to the plane of the ecliptic, would act as a shield for the armada. And it would be the first unit attacked.

"Here we are," Bright grumbled from his captain's seat on the bridge, "the decoy, the bait, the sitting duck. If I understand this right, it looks like Revil's ships'll take on the main force from *A Baoa Qu*, while we hold off everyone else from *Solomon.*"

"But that at least means the 'Red Comet' won't come after us, right?" Kai seemed relieved when he said it.

"He's right, isn't he?" Amuro asked, glancing at Mirai.

After pondering a second, Mirai answered, "I don't think so. We've won enough skirmishes to attract attention from all over. We'll be targeted by both *Solomon* and *A Baoa Qu* forces, but since we're too small a unit for them to waste a large fleet on, I bet the special unit led by the Red Comet *will* eventually come after us."

SAYLA, MANNING THE COMM console on the bridge, removed her headset to better hear the conversation taking place around her. Could her brother really be coming after them? Mirai seemed to think so. Sayla felt trapped in a web of fate. In her heart she knew he was on his way.

ON VICE ADMIRAL DOZLE'S flagship, the *Gandow*, the comm techs quickly noted the increased activity of the Federation Forces, and the fact that they appeared to be converging around a single area in space.

"Don't they regard *Solomon* as a worthy enemy?" Dozle wondered out loud. He felt oddly slighted by General Revil. But when he heard the news that three of his *Musai*-class ships had just been destroyed in a fray with a Federation unit he was enraged.

"*What?!*" he yelled. "They annihilated our cruisers in only ten minutes?"

"Er . . . Yessir," a junior officer replied nervously. "One of our patrol ships in field 550 sighted the explosions and went straight to the area, but it was too late. Our ships had already vanished, sir."

"Even though they had Zakus protecting them?!!"

"Yessir . . . six of them, sir."

"That should've been plenty! What the hell went wrong?!" Dozle's face was beet-red with anger, and he had to restrain himself from striking the officer giving the report.

"The Federation force appears to be centered around a White Base-class ship, sir. We understand there may be a Newtype unit involved."

"Who says so?"

"The skipper of the patrol ship, sir, No. 600."

Dozle slowly lowered himself into a chair and commanded an orderly next to him to bring him some coffee. "Well," he said, "we certainly don't need the captain of some little patrol ship to engage in speculation, do we? That won't do when we're trying to formulate a coherent strategy. Our main battle isn't going to be with some fuzzy 'Newtype' unit or whatever it's called. I want our observation of the entire Federation armada beefed up. I want to know what route of attack Revil's going to take to *A Baoa Qu*. We'll leave behind the minimum number of ships needed to defend *Solomon*. All others will launch with us."

After Dozle barked out his orders, he reached out for his coffee tube and took a sip. *Just wait, Revil,* he muttered. *I'll teach you a lesson you won't forget.*

ON *A BAOA QU*, Kycilia Zabi couldn't help smiling when she heard of the change in the Federation movements. Technically speaking, she wasn't responsible for *A Baoa Qu*. It was under her brother Gihren's jurisdiction and she was merely using it temporarily.

"Gihren should fly here and defend the place himself," she snapped.

But could he arrive in time? It would still take several days before the System project could be completed. The real question was whether or not her own forces on *A Baoa Qu* should move out to strike the Federation armada. And if so, how she could inflict maximum damage on them with her limited strength.

"There won't be time for us to try and wipe out the Federation units one by one," Char Aznable said. "We should wait until they come closer and converge."

"Why do you say that?" Kycilia demanded, noting that his view was at odds with the strategy put forth by the Zeon General Staff.

"Because the forces coming at us aren't omnipotent. I think we should draw them in closer and then crush them right in front of *A Baoa Qu*. And I think Your Excellency's forces should lead the attack. If we try and hit their fleets individually, we might accidentally disperse them. That might gain time for the System project to be completed, but it would indirectly aid your brother, the Supreme Commander."

"I won't let him use the System. I'm going to show him what we can do without it."

"Your brother's an extremely ambitious man, Excellency. Remember, this is war. But I understand your wishes. I'll take my unit out to meet the enemy, and hope Vice Admiral Dozle comes through to help us."

Char turned and started to exit Kycilia's office. He felt angry. He wanted to tell her that in order to survive politically they should abandon *A Baoa Qu* and flee. But he didn't. He knew she was obsessed with the idea of staying and destroying the Newtype unit on the Federation's White Base-class warship.

MARGARET RING BLAIR WAS standing and waiting nervously for Char outside the door to Kycilia's office.

"Are you really taking off?" she asked when he emerged.

"It looks that way," he said. "I think this is it. Take care of yourself, Margaret."

"Thank . . . thank you, Commander."

There were other secretaries and aides watching in the reception area, so he merely touched her elbow. She immediately sensed his meaning, and moved to open the door for him. Once outside he turned to her.

"At this point, Margaret," he said, "the most important thing is to survive. Don't do anything rash. It's better to be a coward in this business. Look out for yourself."

"But . . . " She started to say something, but stopped.

"Don't worry about me," he said, placing his lips on hers. "I'll come back alive."

THE ROUNDED SHAPE OF the *Madagascar,* a *Zanzibar*-class cruiser, lay at rest on the darkened flight deck of *A Baoa Qu*, ready for launch. The mobile suits and the Elmeth that made up Commander Char Aznable's Newtype unit had already been loaded.

"Well," said Lt. Challia Bull, turning to Char with a grin, "where do we rendezvous with our Federation date?"

"The enemy White Base ship's apparently in field 660. We don't know where one other ship in the unit is, but we'll aim for field 600."

"Why?" Kusko Al chimed in.

"Because that's where the Gundam apparently sank a *Musai* cruiser," said Char.

"Was Amuro Ray the pilot?"

Challia laughed. What had once seemed a game to Kusko Al was clearly turning very real. "Who cares what his name is, Kusko?" he asked.

"I don't know. It just seems a shame to kill him. He wasn't a bad kid."

To Challia, her attitude had overtones of feminine sentimentality, and he decided to rectify it: "Well, don't let your own abilities go to your head," he said. "Judging from what the Commander has said, the 'kid' is a crack MS pilot, and there's a strong possibility he may kill us, instead of the other way around."

Kusko was taken aback. She knew Challia was right but she had a competitive streak in her. She had been raised to ignore the differences between men and women, and she believed people should be judged on the basis of talent and ability, not gender. But war tended to wreak havoc with everything. And that was another reason she hated it.

"It's not like you, Kusko," Challia continued. "You, of all people, should have a healthy respect for Newtype abilities. After all, you're the one this Amuro Ray character nearly vaporized earlier, right?"

CHAR AND CHALLIA LEFT for the *Madagascar's* bridge, and Lt (jg) Cramble came over to console Kusko. She tried to avoid him by climbing in the cockpit of the Elmeth, but he called out after her, "Don't take it to heart. Challia's just being his usual pompous asshole self. He's just trying to make himself look like a Newtype."

"Thanks, Cramble. But don't worry. I'm okay."

She didn't think much of Cramble. And she never could understand why he fancied himself a ladies' man. To her he was just another over-sexed male. As for herself, she knew she attracted men, but she wasn't going to exploit that; she believed she had a responsibility to improve whatever talents God had given her. She knew she had some, and she was proud of it. And Amuro Ray? His naiveté clearly came from his youth. That she had liked him showed she was a woman, and as far as she was concerned there was nothing wrong with that. She also liked the fact that he had been broad-minded enough to have been attracted to a woman like herself.

Kycilia Zabi

In battle, however, she knew Amuro Ray might be entirely different, and that combat might drastically transform his otherwise innocent personality. This logic, in turn, allowed her to realize that Amuro indeed probably had been the one who had nearly killed her. And from there her own acute intellect quickly led her to a radically new conclusion: *I liked you, Amuro. But I have to kill you.*

Shortly thereafter, the *Madagascar* took off from *A Baoa Qu*, supported by two Gattle fighter-bomber squadrons.

IN THE MEANTIME, ON the Federation side, the 127th Autonomous had detected a second enemy force approaching. It was no surprise. The officers on the bridge of the *Pegasus II* had known they would run into more and more resistance the closer they got to the heart of Zeon territory.

"It's been only six hours since the last attack, right?" Amuro said. Twenty-five degrees below the ship's starboard wing he could already see the shapes of six or seven enemy ships.

"Know what I think?" Lt. Commander McVery said. "I think there's finally been enough killing. When this campaign's over, the whole god-awful war's finally gonna be over, too." Then he laughed and added, "But don't worry, this time, my men and I'll form your vanguard again, Mister Amuro!" and hurried out of the room.

Amuro glanced up at Bright in the captain's seat above him on the bridge. "Is McVery becoming a philosopher, or what, sir?"

"Well," Bright replied. "Over five billion people have died in the war, and that puts a little brake on the population explosion. Maybe it's just McVery's backhanded way of saying that mankind may yet manage to overcome the biggest crisis of all time."

"Are you trying to say this war's just another form of population control?!"

Bright looked at Amuro with an amused expression and said, "I suppose that's one way of looking at it."

Unable to believe his skipper's words, Amuro's anger showed. "You've gotta be kidding, sir. That's not what *I'm* fighting for. . . ."

"You wanna stop?"

Stunned, Amuro just stared back at Bright.

Mirai answered instead, coolly: "While you're both philosophizing, the enemy's on his way here to kill us."

Amuro's anguished voice rose in volume in response, "I don't care if the skipper's joking, Mirai. I think that sort of talk's an insult to all the people who've given their lives in the war. Don't you? We're not living in a video game world, are we? How many points to kill another human? One? Two? How many points was Lalah Sune worth?"

Bright signaled Sayla. She quickly read his meaning, stood up from her seat in front of the comm console and came over to Amuro. Taking him gently by the arm, she whispered, "*You've got to calm down . . .*" Their bodies swayed in the weightlessness, but the pair reached out and grabbed a fixture, and pushed against it.

As they floated out the bridge exit, Sayla said, "You don't really believe they're serious about people killing each other for such a crazy reason, do you? Just think, by building the space colonies we created room for billions more people to live. And life on the colonies has now stabilized. History can't go backward."

"I don't know, Sayla. There *was* a weird logic behind what Bright said. It's based on the idea that man's fundamentally rooted to the planet Earth, and that his population should be tied to it, too."

"But Newtypes are supposed to transcend all that, right? They're not bound by archaic ways of thinking that force them to kill each other, right?"

Amuro headed for the flight deck, and Sayla followed him. When they boarded the flight deck elevator they were at last alone. She suddenly turned and kissed him.

"Amuro," she whispered, "unless we somehow stop this war, Newtypes'll never really come into their own. You've got to fight in order to end it. If someone like you dies, the old ways of thinking are going to last forever."

"You mean we've got to win over the 'Old Types,' right?"

"Over the land-based faction. The Earth faction. The Natives. Whatever you want to call them. Newtypes have to win over the people who don't realize that this war has become a habit, a collusion on a grand scale. I know what I'm saying's even more difficult than winning the war we're in, but Newtypes are going to have to *fight* for a world *without* war."

"Listen, Sayla. Do you think your father really believed what you're saying now?"

"He never specifically told me anything like this, and I wouldn't have been old enough to understand it even if he had. But I do know our world's changing, Amuro."

"What you really mean is that *we* have to change it, right?"

"Yes. I don't know anything about Lalah Sune, but maybe she was related to it all. Maybe Newtypes *can* transcend normal empathy among humans, even normal modes of human communication. But they're still human. You follow me?"

"I know. Newtypes aren't espers. I know *I'm* just an ordinary human. If there's any difference between me and the people on Earth, it's—how should I say it—it's that the light of the stars is just as important to me as the Earth's air is to them. For people to understand each other in the vastness of space, we're going to need a *lot* more intuition and insight, and a hell of a lot more patience."

"We need those qualities all the time, but you're saying that in space they're especially critical, right?"

"Right. But most people are still locked into old ways of thinking and don't understand that yet."

Sayla suddenly looked at him, smiled, and said, "You know, Amuro Ray, I think you're just the man to teach them . . ."

He looked her in the eye and smiled back. "Sayla . . . pretty Sayla. Tell you what. I'll launch from the *Pegasus* and go fight today. Not for some high ideal. But for you. To protect you. How's that?"

She giggled. "In this day and age, words like those seem a little *too* romantic, but I'm not complaining. Go out and do your best, Amuro.

For me, if you want. And when you come back let's talk some more about what we can do."

Then, without saying a word, he bent his head and gently placed his lips on hers again.

THE SECOND ZEON TASK force sent to destroy the 127th Autonomous consisted of two *Chivvay*-class heavy cruisers, four *Musai*-class regular cruisers, three Zakus, and one squadron of small, minesweeper-like Jicco attack ships. Although the 127th was outclassed in number and firepower, McVery and Amuro's units lured the enemy into a well-defined combat zone and annihilated them. Incredibly, the entire action took less than fifteen minutes.

Two of McVery's Tomahawks were heavily damaged, but much to his relief Hayato and Kria had managed to rescue the pilots with their mobile suits. "In times like this," McVery later admitted, laughing loudly, "I guess those damned robot arms come in handy sometimes after all!! And as for you, *Mister* Amuro Ray, well, let me congratulate you on the fine job you did of training your men. From now on, lad, we'll work together like hand and glove!"

After returning to the *Pegasus* bridge, Amuro quickly spotted Sayla. They winked and jokingly flashed each other the "V" for victory sign. They did not know that with every victory the 127th was attracting an ever more powerful enemy.

"WE'RE DEALING WITH SOME full-blown Newtypes here," Char Aznable said, after demanding more speed from the *Madagascar*. "They're steadily increasing their level of performance, and aggression."

With the Minovsky level rising and radio transmissions no longer practical, laser communications were the only means the *Madagascar* had left to track the Federation fleet movements, and even lasers required predicting in advance approximately where the target was going to be.

"It's going to be hard to find them," Char said, "but we've got to. If we don't stop them soon, Zeon's entire line of defense'll be compromised."

"I know you're right, sir," the *Madagascar*'s captain agreed, adding with what sounded like a groan, "but you don't seriously believe it's the same unit that wiped out our two task forces, do you?"

"Who else could it be? We're better off assuming the worst. That way, if we survive, we can at least break out the liquor and celebrate. By the way, any shoal regions ahead?"

"Only one, sir. Corregidor."

"Does it cover a wide area?"

"Yessir. Looks that way."

"Good," replied Char, turning to leave the bridge area. "We'll try and ambush them there."

Now things get serious, he thought. Thinking about what his unit faced, he was both tense and exhilarated. Normally he just wanted to survive the war, but this time he knew there was far more at stake.

Later, in the *Madagascar's* briefing room, Char privately addressed the MS pilots in his unit.

"Times are changing," he began. "I first began to believe in the Newtype theory because of the Gundam pilot. And I now know Newtypes aren't just a mutant form of humanity. Nor are they just a weapon. Let me confess to all of you right now—and to hell with my own personal goals in all of this—I think we're on the brink of a new era, a Newtype era. And because of that, it's important that none of you be killed! Understand? The Earth Federation has formed their own Newtype unit to use as a weapon against us. We will annihilate them. But beyond that, I want you all to refrain from senseless killing. Concentrate on destroying the weapons of war, and not the people. Too many people have already been slaughtered, and we need to end the war, not prolong it. I want you all to go out there and fight bravely, but stay cool, and keep your wits about you at all times."

Kusko Al was moved by Char's last words. She knew she would use whatever powers God had given her, to their fullest extent. That was simply the way she was. As the pilots all headed toward their mobile suits, she donned her helmet and thought to herself, *Amuro, if I run into you, I'll have to kill you, because by the time you realize who I am, it'll be too late—you won't be able to stop fighting. It's too bad, but that's just the way things are.* She climbed into the Elmeth cockpit and frowned, for she knew her thoughts were only a means of covering up the growing nervousness she always felt before combat. It was true that if it weren't for the war she would never have met Amuro Ray. But she had no time to think of that. With a growing sense of rage, all she could think of was that if it weren't for the war, she would never have been placed in such a wretched position.

THE *MADAGASCAR* ENTERED THE Corregidor shoal zone. While its Gattle fighter-bombers took cover behind the huge rock fragments in the area, the seven new Rick Dom Suits in Char's unit deployed themselves with the Elmeth in the lead.

Char's red Suit came up alongside Kusko's Elmeth and plunged ahead together with it. Challia Bull's Rick Dom formed the rearguard. If the Elmeth's remotely-controlled Bit units could just destroy the Federation's "Trojan Horse," their work would be half over.

"Kusko!" called Char. "Do you read me?"

"Loud and clear, Commander," she answered.

"The enemy'll direct cannon fire and missiles at us before we visually sight them. Don't just rely on your intuition to evade them at first. Follow me until you get the hang of things. Then, when we catch up with the warships, they're all yours. Challia, myself, and the other Rick Dom pilots'll take care of the enemy Suits."

"Understood, sir," Kusko answered, and her face began to set itself in a mask of intense concentration.

THE ELMETH

LUNA II CONTINUED CIRCLING Earth in its orbit 180-degrees opposite the moon. In addition to functioning as a Federation fortress, the former asteroid now also housed several thousand civilian refugees from colonies, most of whom had been mobilized to work for the various supply units or local military factories. Among them was Fraw Bow, Amuro Ray's former neighbor on Side 7.

Although still in her teens herself, Fraw was in charge of three young war orphans named Katz Hawin, Letz Cofan, and Kikka Kitamoto—the oldest of whom was nine. Because they had refused to enter the local orphanage and instead insisted on staying with Fraw, the officials concerned had reluctantly granted her custody. With the war still raging, and with her new situation and the need to earn a living, she abandoned her long-held dream of becoming a fashion designer and decided to pursue a mechanic's license. Aware of her plight, some friends with connections helped her obtain work at the local military vehicle maintenance plant. Life on *Luna II* was hard, but by no means miserable. Fraw was young, with a body resilient enough to recover when overworked, and her three young charges loved her as if she were their own mother.

"*WE BROUGHT YOU LUNCH, Fraw!*" Kikka's high-pitched young voice

298

echoed through the maintenance area where Fraw worked. Over a dozen mechamen, most graying at the temples, crawled out from under the vehicles they were working on to greet her.

"Well," said one worker, "if it isn't little Kikka again! We've been waiting for you, sweetie . . . "

"Hey, Kikka!" added the foreman, doffing his military helmet and wiping his brow, "what's up? You're three minutes early today!"

"You guys make Fraw work too hard!" Kikka retorted, sticking out her tongue, "she needs an early break!"

Chuckling at the little girl's impudence, the workers in the plant gathered together, opened their lunch pails, and began eating.

"Kikka, where're Katz and Letz?" Fraw asked.

"They're coming. They're still playing Space Invaders."

"Video games? Well, tell them to get here on the double! It's time to eat!"

"Roger-Dodger!" Kikka said, happily running off to fetch the others.

As Fraw watched her little charge disappear, she realized how long the girl's pretty blond hair had become. She loved the sight of it, and was even a little envious, but she also knew she should cut it soon. She reached into her purse and fished out a compact. It was military-issue and utterly lacking in any esthetic quality but she treasured it nonetheless. In the little mirror she saw grease smeared on her cheeks. She took out a handkerchief and, while wiping them clean, resolved to buy some lipstick when she got her next month's paycheck. In the Force, the more mature Waves often scorned those who wore lipstick or makeup but Fraw didn't care. She was still in her late 'teens and she had rights of her own. She would do it for Amuro.

For Amuro. The moment the thought formed in her mind, tears welled in her eyes, and as she watched in the little compact mirror, began rolling down her round cheeks. *Amuro.* She didn't care if he came back missing an arm or a leg, or even if he fell in love with another woman. She just wanted him to come back alive. The thought grew louder and louder in her mind. If only he would survive. In the future he could make her cry or even make her angry, and she wouldn't mind. But if he died there would be no future. Only memories. And her last memory of him would be their brief exchange over a vid-phone as he departed from *Luna II.* That was a possibility she couldn't bear to think of. Fraw again resolved to buy her lipstick. To buy it for Amuro. She slowly closed the lid on her compact.

"Hey, I was just about to break three thousand points!" Letz complained to Kikka as the two of them ran over to Fraw. "Let's eat!" they yelled.

"Well, if you're going to bring us lunch, you guys should at least be here on time!" Fraw gently scolded.

"Hey, it's Letz's fault . . . " Katz whined, nonetheless taking out a paper napkin and wiping the hands of the younger two.

Noting Fraw's face, Letz suddenly piped up, "You've been crying, haven't you?"

"Now why would I do that, silly?" Fraw answered, opening up the lunch rations the children had brought.

"Oh no! Not *hamburgers* again!" they all chimed.

"We're at war," Fraw said, again in a scolding tone. "Think of all the poor soldiers out there who'd love to eat something as nice as this . . . "

"You really think Zeon's that clever, eh?" Bright asked the pilots assembled on the *Pegasus II* bridge. "We've arrived at our rendezvous point ahead of schedule, so I say we ought to stay here till we can hook up with the other fleets. The Corregidor shoal zone's an ideal place for us to hide."

"Well, the same's true for Zeon ships," Amuro answered. "Do you really think we can avoid being ambushed?"

"Why would they ambush us now? We're the only squad in the area, and the Zeon warships coming out of *Solomon* now are ignoring us. The Principality wants to take on the entire armada, not just us. That's the way they think. And that means they don't want to waste a single ship on us."

"That's assuming a lot, skipper," said Lt. Commander McVery. The performance of the young MS pilots seemed to have impressed the veteran fighter pilot mightily, for he rested his arm on Amuro's shoulder and continued, "With all due respect for your own Newtype potential, I disagree with your analysis, and I'm inclined to agree with young Amuro Ray on this one. Personally, I think there are enemy ships waiting for us."

"You really think an ambush is possible?" said Bright.

"You said it yourself, skipper," Hayato interrupted, speaking with far more conviction than usual. "We got here early. That'll bring the enemy out after us. Especially the Red Comet. I bet he wouldn't pass up an opportunity like this. I think we oughta get through the Corregidor area as fast as possible, and then wait to coordinate our movements with the others somewhere else."

Bright finally caved in. "All right, all right. Looks like nobody has an absolute majority here, but you've convinced me. I'll buy your ambush idea. We'll go through the shoals, but on one condition. McVery, I want you to agree to the lineup I've decided on."

McVery grinned sheepishly, then turned to look at Amuro quizzically.

"The skipper's known us longer, sir," Amuro. "So he's putting us out front . . . "

"'Looks that way, doesn't it?" said McVery.

"He's deferring to you in a way, sir. I'm sure you can understand. He knows you've already lost four of your men."

"I know, _Mister_ Amuro. 'Deferring' has a polite ring to it, but what it all boils down to is that the lieutenant doesn't trust me and my men."

Amuro laughed. "Sir, don't you think you're being a little too sensitive?"

"Hell, yes. But in the Tomahawk squad we have to be sensitive. We have to be on our toes at all times."

"I know what you're saying, sir. But I've gone up against the Elmeth once before and I think it's better that I go up against it again."

"All right. All right," said McVery. "In front of you, my fair-haired lad, I'll skip the bravado." He gave Amuro's rear end a light slap, turned and walked over to where his men were standing on the bridge, the magnets on the soles of his boots making a pleasant clicking sound.

Amuro shrugged, and as he turned back toward the captain's seat he saw Sayla behind Bright. She had been watching his interchange with McVery, and smiled.

Next, Bright formally announced the lineup. "Junior Grade Lieutenant Amuro Ray's G3, the Guncannons, and the GMs will lead the _Pegasus_. Lt. Commander McVery's Tomahawks will assume positions to our stern, starboard and port. The _Cyprus_ and the _Greyden_ will follow. And the four VX-76 Balls will form our rear guard."

McVery saluted with a forced smile and left the bridge, his men following without protest.

There was something about the way McVery handled himself that Amuro admired intensely. He had a masculine, charismatic quality that made men want to follow him. It involved principles and ideals, individual goals and a plan to attain them, and it all seemed like a mysterious art to Amuro. The only excuse he could think of for his own lack of leadership was his youthful inexperience, and the more he thought about that, the more inferior he felt. At least, he secretly prided himself, pretty blond Sayla had finally introduced him into the ways of manhood.

That Amuro could congratulate himself on such a simple matter in itself revealed his immaturity, for although youth does mature quickly through direct experience, a further test of maturity is the way the experience itself is interpreted—whether it is glorified, or accepted as a natural part of growing up. In his belief that his relationship with Sayla had turned him into a more sophisticated adult, and in his growing conviction that nearly anyone could easily evolve into a Newtype, he was still frighteningly naive.

TO THE OTHER FOUR pilots in his mobile suit unit, Amuro announced, "Once we get through the Corregidor shoals, we'll be resupplied. We take off in an hour. I want everyone to go out there and do their duty."

He tried to choose his words carefully, but he noticed Kai and Hayato had smirks on their faces. They weren't deliberately trying to insult him, but he didn't like what he saw.

"Dismissed!" he barked, immediately remembering he should have first asked them if they had any questions.

Kai Shiden, always the jokester, couldn't hold back a laugh. "Hey, Amuro! You don't have to get so uppity just because you're our unit leader! We'll still respect you!"

Amuro ignored his friend's remark and turned on his heel. Why was he so tense? He wasn't experiencing a Newtype premonition, or it would have manifested itself in a far more distinct format. But if this was a way for his musculo-skeletal system to deal with pre-combat stress and anxiety, it wasn't doing him any good, either. If Kai, Hayato and the others hadn't been there, and if he hadn't been on duty, he would have liked to spend some time with Sayla. But that wasn't possible now. The *Pegasus* was on a maximum combat footing, and plunging straight into the Corregidor shoals.

ALONG WITH THE OTHER MS pilots, Amuro climbed into his Suit and performed a final check of his cockpit instrumentation. Then the face of Sayla Mass appeared on his three-inch communication monitor.

"G3," she first announced. "*Junior Grade Lieutenant Amuro Ray. Are you ready?!*"

"All systems are go," he replied over his mike. "Currently at launch point."

That was all Sayla needed to hear, for her image immediately disappeared from his monitor. Faster than normal, it seemed. Was she deliberately ignoring him? *Didn't women feel any special emotion at a time like this?* he wondered. Then in the next instant he heard Petty Officer 1st Class Callahan's high-pitched voice. "*G3! Stand by for launch! Ready . . . three . . . two . . . one . . .*"

"G3 now launching!"

The catapult mechanism beneath the Gundam's feet surged forward with a roar. He felt the *g* force, and a second later all manmade objects disappeared from view on his main screen and he found himself looking at millions of stars in a jet black universe.

"*C108! C109!*" Over his receiver, Amuro heard the call signs of the other mobile suits behind him mixing with a rising level of static. The Gundam's auto-pilot system established the correct distance to precede the *Pegasus*, and the other Suits fell into formation. "Secondary combat speed," he called out.

He fixed his gaze on his main screen. A huge boulder loomed before him, and then vanished to his rear. They were in the Corregidor shoal zone.

THE ELMETH COCKPIT WAS roomier than that of a mobile suit, and Kusko Al rather enjoyed sitting in it, waiting. Her instrument panel glowed faintly in the darkness, and outside the only light was that of the stars around her. With the sun out of sight, they seemed to be burning brighter than ever, densely matted in a world of black.

She saw the faint red shadow of Char's Rick Dom next to her appear to drift slightly. *I wonder if he's noticed?* she thought, but decided not to dwell on it. In the weightlessness of space it seemed absurd to perfectly position anything.

"*The universe would be a lot nicer place if men weren't so power hungry,*" she muttered to herself. She hated it when Char and Challia Bull started talking so righteously about the Zabi family and their own plans. It made her want to throw a monkey wrench into their schemes. She smiled at the thought. Perhaps, subconsciously, *that* was a reason she had taken a liking to Amuro Ray. It wasn't just because she had sensed Newtype potential in him. She really had thought he was cute.

As if triggered by the association, she suddenly sensed something. With her right foot she gently pushed down on an activator pedal, and aligned her Elmeth with Char's Rick Dom. He seemed to have sensed something, too. Amid static, she could make out his fuzzy image on her comm monitor.

"*Twelve o'clock, Kusko! Elevation zero!*"

"Understood!" she replied curtly. She yanked back on the left and right steering levers, and the Elmeth rose steeply, bursting from its hiding place in the shoal zone. The six Rick Doms followed. Simultaneously, the *Madagascar* readied its cannon for attack.

Kusko gradually accelerated her Elmeth, cursing the men around her:

"Politics, politics . . . ! They ought to think more about what it means to be a Newtype!" Then she released the twelve remote-controlled Bit units carried in the Elmeth's fuselage.

As if on cue, beams began stabbing toward the Elmeth from in front of her. For a second, Char's Rick Dom was highlighted by the glare. "*Kusko!*" his voice barked over her speaker, "*Concentrate on operating the Bits! I'll cover you and the Elmeth!*"

"Thanks!" She had registered the relative position of the Bits in her mind, and they were already charging forth toward the enemy she visualized. Bits were configured with either a mega particle cannon or a nuclear warhead, and operated under a system of remote control that used brain waves amplified and projected by the psycommu interface. Since Minovsky particle interference had made radar-based guided weapons impractical, they were the only remote-controlled weaponry that worked effectively in space.

As Zeon and Federation forces converged at high speed, all thought of Amuro Ray disappeared from Kusko's mind. The twelve Bits headed for their targets, and their built-in video cameras recorded images that were amplified and projected by the psycommu directly back to her brain, where they became an integral part of her vision. It wasn't hard to control the Bits. Humans easily recognize and act upon visual information from multiple sources simultaneously—Kusko Al merely demonstrated this ability on a more advanced level, controlling the Bits through the psycommu interface. There was a linear order to the visual information from each of the Bit units, and her cerebrum merely had to reflexively differentiate and exert control over it.

Then Kusko saw the Federation's Gundam model mobile suit.

In the same instant suppressed thoughts barged back into her consciousness. Was the Suit really piloted by the young man she had found so attractive? By Amuro Ray?! She hadn't really received any solid information to that effect, but she felt somehow certain it was true. And during her seconds of confusion, one of her Bit units was destroyed. A light stabbed deep into her cerebrum, and she knew that the Gundam had taken a shot at her.

She swore. She knew she was in trouble if she had to directly confront the Gundam. Her survival instincts—and the primeval fighting instincts that had qualified her for combat in the first place—would automatically assert themselves over all other thoughts. She began to feel pure hatred. For the Federation. For Zeon. For the war. For the male society that caused it. She was ready to fight.

As Char watched, a rocket *whoosh*ed out of the Elmeth into the darkness, leaving a long trail from the blue-white cone of light billowing around its nozzle. It happened so abruptly that even he was shocked. "Kusko!" he shouted into his microphone, pushing his red Rick Dom to catch up to the Elmeth, "Don't rush yourself!"

As if the Elmeth's actions were the trigger, Challia Bull led the other Suits forth. Huge flares spewed from their skirted cowlings, for Rick Dom engines were said to be equivalent in power to those of cosmo cruisers. And at the same time, the MS unit's mother ship, the *Madagascar*, sailed out from the shelter of a huge asteroid, firing both cannon and regular missiles in the anticipated direction of the enemy approach. The ship's massive *Fife* nuclear missiles, mounted both port and starboard, possessed such awesome destructive power they had to be used before the opposing fleets of ships actually came into contact. Crewmen often claimed they could shake the whole universe, and when the first one launched even the *Madagascar* seemed to shudder. In a blaze of light, a Fife soared up past Char and his men toward the enemy.

AMURO RAY SENSED SOMETHING coming straight for him, and during a second of confusion he wondered if it were an auxiliary remote unit, or an incoming missile. Then, as his mind suddenly cleared, he intuitively knew: *It was a missile!* Unlike the leaping, relentlessly advancing impression generated by an Elmeth's remote units, missiles normally created a linear pressure in his consciousness and were thus easier to deal with. But if this were a missile, it felt unlike anything he had ever before experienced—it seemed to possess far more power.

He knew his comrades couldn't hear him, but he shouted out, "Kai! Hayato! Leave this one to me!!" Then, lining up the sights on his beam rifle with the crosshairs on his main monitor, he shifted his aim 0.3 degrees to the right. And in that instant several bursts of light erupted around his Gundam. Kai and Hayato had destroyed a couple of the attacking remote units from the Elmeth for him. He gave silent thanks and knew they were buying him time to concentrate his entire being on the incoming missile. And then he knew it was a *Fife*.

The first shot from his beam rifle hit home. The Fife exploded and blossomed into a giant, roiling inferno. The blast occurred in the middle of the two approaching fleets, but it was still powerful enough to make the mobile suit units of both forces shudder. The light from the explosion was sighted by Federation and Zeon warships several combat zones removed.

Amuro, furious, drove his Gundam forward toward the enemy at full speed, but as he did so he saw the unique leaping light of several more

Elmeth Bits bearing down on him from both sides. He wasn't in the mood to put up with any more attacks. He swung the Gundam fuselage left and right, and fired two blasts from his beam rifle. Light from the exploding units streamed toward him, and he aimed the Gundam in a downward trajectory in their direction.

With a shock, he instinctively realized that whoever was piloting the Elmeth this time was even faster than Lalah Sune had been. He was awed by the way the attacking units slid toward him, and the way they timed the blasts of their mega particle cannons. And he felt an intense mental pressure when they approached.

While Amuro had no way of knowing, the thought waves amplified by the Elmeth system's psycommu interface originated from Kusko Al's subconscious fighting instincts, and were projected in all directions. They appeared inside his own cerebrum like a moving black shadow, creating a powerful "force," a wall of sensation.

What is it? A chill suddenly ran down his spine.

AT THE SAME INSTANT, Kusko Al yelled, "What's going on?"

Commander Garcia Dowal of the Flanagan Institute had once confidently said, "*The Earth Federation putting Newtypes to real use? Total fantasy. Don't worry about it. Ensign Lalah Sune's Elmeth? That was just a prototype. It was just bad luck that the enemy attacked when the system hadn't been perfected yet, when she was in the middle of a test flight. She was killed in the line of duty, but it was practically an accident.*" It was amazing, Kusko now realized, how different reality appeared to combatants on the front lines and theoreticians in the rear. Survival required an utterly different mentality from that of the desk jockeys. On the battlefield, nothing was constant, nothing was certain.

She had closed in on the Gundam enough to clearly make out its form. But to her horror, before she could get a good look a force screamed through her mind. It wasn't light. It wasn't an audible voice. And it wasn't the force from a nearby explosion. But when it hit, it felt as though the skin and the hair on her head were being ripped off by a gale force wind. It seemed like a hallucination but it felt real. It *was* real. And it enabled her to avoid the next threat. She saw a light from the direction of the force and she made her Elmeth soar upward, just as several beams nearly zapped her from below.

She willed her seven remaining Bit units to attack the Gundam MS, and at the same time aligned the sights of her Elmeth's twin mega particle cannons. And then she saw Char streak by her in his red Rick Dom—*just in the nick of time!* she thought. Char, too, began firing his bazooka at the Gundam, and a light from an explosion even greater than a Fife missile overwhelmed her main monitor.

She wondered if it were all over. *Was that Amuro?* she thought, feeling suddenly detached. *If so, well, that was it. Too bad, Amuro, but it was your fault. You were shy and cute, but you treated me like dirt. If you were really the Gundam pilot, the slate's wiped clean now. Come to think of it, there's something nice about that idea. I guess we might have been together, but it just wasn't in the cards.*

But the battle was not over. Another powerful force roared through Kusko's mind. She opened her mouth wide and screamed.

"*Kusko Al! Pull back!*" She heard a voice loud and clear in the midst of the roar; it was her commander, Char Aznable. "*Pull back immediately!!*" Without thinking twice, she put the Elmeth into reverse so suddenly that—despite triple shock absorbers in the cockpit—the *g* force slammed her body toward the instrument panel in front of her. But she was well trained, and never once took her eyes off her main screen.

Is that . . . is that really the Gundam?! Her eyes widened. She could clearly see the enemy MS, illuminated by the light of an explosion, charging straight toward her, its gold-colored eyes flashing, glaring menacingly right at her, through her main monitor, through the sunvisor on her normal suit.

In a twist of logic, her fear was canceled by rage. The mysterious pressure in her mind earlier had been like a shock wave, a form of mental rape that altered her thought patterns and rattled her psyche. And if such an unwanted, unpleasant sensation happened to have come from the Gundam, well, she was not about to forgive anyone. She turned the Elmeth's twin mega particle cannons on the charging Suit and fired, but to her astonishment it skillfully dodged her attack with a movement uncannily like human body english. Her chestnut hair practically stood on end, as she screamed: "It's a two-way street, Gundam! You tried to kill me. Now it's my turn! I'll turn you into dust!"

INSIDE THE GUNDAM, COLD, oily sweat beaded on Amuro Ray's brow and soaked his flight suit undergarments. If he were going to die, he thought, he wished it could be under more comfortable conditions. The Elmeth quickly filled his field of vision, and each time it fired its cannons he was surrounded by light from heat-emitting particles. That it was an oddly beautiful sight bothered him—it was absurd to feel beauty in something so deadly. He had no idea how he managed to avoid the beam blasts. He just knew that to escape from the force trying to envelope him—the force being projected at him from the Elmeth pilot through the psycommu interface—he had to close in on the Elmeth itself. It was a realization that spurred him on, for with it, and with a little faith in his Suit, he knew he could survive the attacks.

"*You won't be able to use the remote units this time!*" he yelled inside his cockpit. He fired his rifle three times, and each time powerful beams of light scorched through the blackness toward the Elmeth, but each time it "leapt" out of the way. He spun the Gundam fuselage, trying to keep on top of the weaving enemy machine, and in the process its metallic green image shifted from his left monitor to the main display. He was now directly opposite it. He pulled the trigger of his rifle and fired. The Elmeth started to swoop below him, but he had anticipated the maneuver and brought up the Gundam's left leg, smashing it into the Elmeth's prow. Under normal conditions what he had done would have appeared comical. His MS was humanoid, and he had in effect "kicked" the enemy. But his MS was also a weapon of war, to be used as he saw fit.

The shock of physical contact reverberated through the Gundam cockpit, and Amuro saw the Elmeth shudder. And in the same instant he felt a powerful "force" bearing down on him simultaneously from both his front and rear. Could it be the Elmeth's remote units? Since he was attacking their mother machine, they were surely out to get him. In the "force" pressing on him, he could detect a single thought: *Kill him!*

Could the pilot again be a woman?! Several beams stabbed toward him from behind, but he anticipated them. Putting his Suit through an ear-grinding, bone-jarring maneuver, he managed to absorb the brunt of the attack directly with the shield in the Gundam's left hand.

WHOMP! The Gundam shook violently and the impact nearly knocked Amuro unconscious. He kept his eyes open but realized he hadn't been looking at his monitors or instrument panel. When he did, he saw glowing beams. And he saw an interaction among them—some sort of wave force controlling the beams. The waves created an undulating arc in space that quickly seemed to envelop the Gundam. He tried to scream but couldn't. His physical body wouldn't cooperate, and only an inaudible breathless cry erupted from the depths of his spirit.

The Vulcan cannon in the Gundam's head belched, and destroyed an incoming Bit with a nuclear-tipped missile. Both the Gundam and the Elmeth were swept along by the blast.

He cursed, but kept his eyes open and again saw the flow of waves he had noticed earlier. He knew he was up against a formidable enemy. Staring straight at the Elmeth remote units weaving toward him, he fired three shots from his beam rifle. With the light from the earlier nuclear blast still illuminating the area, three more explosions occurred in a clump.

The Gundam and the Elmeth were now locked in a close-range duel that quickly became a raging inferno. In a matter of seconds, the battlefield was transformed from a conventional one, where isolated beams stabbed back and forth in the darkness, to a spectacular light show. The firepower was so awesome that to both Federation and Zeon warships in the area it looked as though not two machines, but the entire mobile suit units of both forces had smashed into each other. Challia Bull, with a direct view from the rear of the action, could only whisper in awe, "The Elmeth and the Gundam . . ."

The two machines clashed again and again, and explosion after explosion occurred, but as with fencers in ancient times, whose supporters would stand by and watch them duel to the death, at first none of the other Suits in the area dared intervene. Both Zeon pilots in their Rick Doms and the Federation pilots in their Guncannons and GMs held back, perhaps fearing their Suits would instantly be destroyed if they jumped into the fray.

But Kai Shiden and Hayato Kobayashi knew what sort of battle Amuro was engaged in, and both had the same idea in mind—to make sure no one else interfered and thus give him time to dispose of the Elmeth. Taking the initiative, they boldly plunged ahead of the other Federation Suits, Kai yelling, "Don't let the fireworks distract you! More Zeon Suits are on their way—the ones with flared skirts!" Hayato gingerly maneuvered his Guncannon below the battle zone while Kai took the higher position. But someone had already snuck into the area.

As far as Char Aznable was concerned, he was already too late. When a missile-bearing Bit unit took a direct hit from the Gundam, he was too close to the explosion and was temporarily disoriented as a result. "*Damn!*" he swore, reminded again of the frailty of human flesh compared to machines. Kusko Al was locked in close combat with the Gundam and appeared to be determined to destroy it at all costs, even if it meant her own destruction. Incredibly, she had even involved the remaining remote Bits in the close-in fray. The blasts from the particle cannon in the Elmeth were like screams of her frenzied fury.

"*Kusko! Stay calm!!*" he yelled, training the sights of his beam bazooka on the Gundam. But he couldn't keep his aim steady. The enemy Suit, moving with blinding speed, was locked in a weird acrobatic dance with the Elmeth and two Bit units, firing beam blast after beam blast, and giving him no room.

Char then realized that he was witnessing what he had seen once before with Lalah Sune, only this time the effect was even more powerful. It was as though the two combatants, their mutual wills locked in mortal combat, were exuding a force powerful enough to physically shut him out. Perhaps, he thought, it was because of the psycommu interface. Perhaps it could not only amplify human will, but even project it as a type of "power."

He knew he had no choice—he had to act to save Kusko, even if it resulted in the destruction of the Elmeth itself. Beams from a Bit unit were already being deflected by the Gundam and striking the Elmeth. He had to get the Gundam away from her. He let the energy collect in his Rick Dom's beam bazooka. The Elmeth crossed in space above his trajectory. Then the Gundam. Then the two of them crisscrossed vertically at blinding speed. He fired, and saw an explosion. He blinked, wondering if he had scored a direct hit, but then he saw the Gundam's smashed shield and watched the enemy Suit slide back behind the Elmeth. With a yell, he fired a second, then a third blast. The powerful verniers in his Rick Dom helped him twist and turn in space, and for a moment it looked as though the three machines—the Gundam, Elmeth, and his own Rick Dom—would smash into each other.

The next moment Char swore at his carelessness. The Gundam's left arm, which normally held a shield, reached over its shoulder toward its backpack beam saber hilt and swooped forward. In an instant, a saber blade formed and connected directly with his Rick Dom's left leg. For half a second, the Rick Dom and the Gundam were physically joined, but then the saber sliced into the leg like a sword into flesh and bone, particles from the beam exploding in light.

Char groaned, his lips curling in a unvoiced curse. He lowered his beam bazooka and fired blindly at the Gundam, but it had already begun to move out of his line of fire, toward the rear of the Elmeth. Reluctantly, he eased off on his trigger finger, and then heard a *WHOMP!* as an explosion thrust him upward. He looked up at the upper left instrument panel in his cockpit, and to his dismay saw that an explosion had occurred in the damaged portion of his Rick Dom's leg. He had no choice but to disengage.

To his surprise, he also heard a strange ringing in his ears. He glanced at his main monitor and saw the light from another explosion fill the screen. *Kusko!* he yelled. He knew the ringing in his ears was no ordinary ring, that Kusko had entered a state beyond his control, and that there was nothing more he could do. The ringing was also from the Gundam. There would be no retreat.

He began working feverishly to remove the Rick Dom's smashed leg from its socket.

KUSKO AL'S THOUGHTS HAD already been infiltrated by Amuro's. Her hatred and rage had escalated to the point where she was doing far more than controlling the Elmeth's twin mega particle cannon and remaining Bit units. Nearly half of her energy was radiating out into open space, like ripples spreading on the surface of a pond. But the accuracy of the three weapons she now controlled was increasing, rather than decreasing. And they were all trained on the Gundam.

Amuro had to depend on the Gundam's new magnetic coating to help him evade the attacks, but the Gundam was still a mechanical system—a machine—and he knew there were limits to its endurance. It simply wasn't capable of keeping up with the speed of his reflexes. And he knew the same was true of the Elmeth and its remote units. He projected an idea deep into Kusko Al's expanding wave of thought: <*If you want to stay alive, retreat!*>.

Amuro's thought jolted Kusko with far more force than he would ever realize. She felt something bordering on physical pain deep in her head, and such an intense chill ran through her that she felt as though her brain matter would explode through her nose and eyes. The psy-commu—which normally amplified and projected *her* thoughts—was now working in reverse, receiving and amplifying Amuro's.

<Retreat?!> She recoiled, resisting his demand with all her might. And her thoughts were broadcast back to him.

And then Amuro at last knew. <Kusko! It's *you*, isn't it?!> He remembered her chestnut hair and the seductive aura of her smile. But he was angry, and his anger was amplified by a twisted sense of shame. Why in the world should Kusko Al, of all people, be piloting the Elmeth? That question in turn triggered another thought in him, a lie, an attempt to erase his shame: <I never really wanted to sleep with you that time!>.

<You did!> she responded. <And you should have said so, boy. I would have said yes!>

The word "boy" caused Amuro to lose the final remnants of whatever self-control he had left. He screamed: <"*Boy?!*" You think we're playing kid's games here? This is for *keeps*!!> His beam saber sliced through the last surviving Bit unit, and the light from the explosion illuminated the Elmeth, its cockpit, and Kusko inside in her normal suit. Her smooth skin was covered in sweat and trembling with fear, but to Amuro, she seemed to be laughing at him.

<You're finished, Kusko!>

He sighted the Gundam's beam rifle on the front of the Elmeth, but then, to his shock, the same thing that had happened during his confrontation with Lalah Sune happened again. With what felt like a physical force, he was jolted by a thought wave from Char Aznable, trying to defend Kusko.

<No, she's not finished, Gundam!!>

<Char! Don't try to stop me!! If you do I'll have to kill you, too, just as your sister asked!>

<Artesia?!>

<Get out of here, Char! I've got a score to settle with Kusko!>

KUSKO AL HAD NOT laughed at Amuro. She had lost control of her bladder and bowels and vomited against the sun visor of her helmet. Yet through the horror of it all, there was something she realized—that she could give herself to Amuro completely, unconditionally. It was both a powerful thought radiating out from her and a premonition of her own destruction. The enemy energy pulsing from Amuro had ripped her psychic sense of balance to shreds, and left in its place an intense awareness of him as an individual.

<So it *was* you, wasn't it, Amuro?>

The thought of him gave her a second of peace that transcended the earlier moments of sheer hatred. To rush madly forward with the Elmeth and die in battle with the Gundam began to seem absurd. It would be preferable, somehow, to take the passive route, and let Amuro destroy her instantly with his beam rifle.

<*Goodbye, Amuro!*>

The same instant, a torrent of thought waves poured out of Amuro, and the muzzle of the Gundam's beam rifle exploded in flame.

The same instant Kusko Al saw the flash and confronted her own death, Amuro saw a mysterious light flow from her. It appeared silver in color. And then he could hear her singing. Singing something about London . . . *London*, of all things.

> <*London Bridge is . . .*
> *London Bridge is . . .*
> *London Bridge is down*
> *down, falling down*
> *London Bridge is falling down*
> *My fair lady.*
> *My . . . fair . . . lady. . . .*>

He heard a woman's voice overlaid on that of an infant. A beautiful woman. A "fair lady?" Could it be Kusko's mother? Then he heard an aria, and a violin being played. Was it her father? The hand of a strong

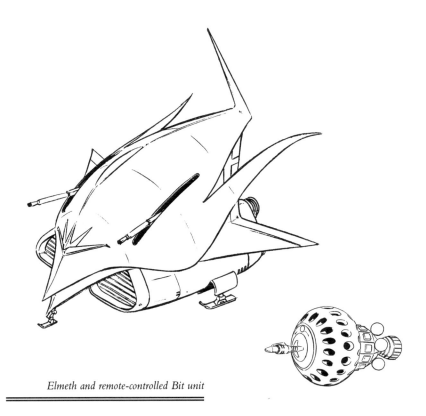

Elmeth and remote-controlled Bit unit

but gentle man touched the strings of the violin, saying, <Kusko, honey, that's not the way to do it. You're a half-tone off. You've got to push down harder with your pinky.> Her fingers ran up and down the neck of the violin. And Bach's *Air on a G String* formed a gentle curve and disappeared, wavering into the silver light.

> <*Build it up with wood and clay*
> *Wood and clay, wood and clay*
> *Build it up with wood and clay, wood and clay*
> *My fair lady. My . . . fair . . . lady.*
> *My . . . fair . . . lady. . . .*>

Then Amuro saw Kusko's pale fingers holding a pen and writing in a diary. He saw the letters she formed. They were distorted, and they, too, disappeared into the silver light, but he felt as if he had glimpsed her innermost, forbidden secrets.

<No! No! Stop!>

Kusko Al's gray pupils widened with terror and horror, and a young man's voice cried out, <I love you Kusko! I love you. You've got to believe me!>

<No! No! Stay away from me, you filthy pig!!>

> <*London Bridge is falling down*
> *Falling down, down*
> *London Bridge is falling down*
> *My fair lady. My fair lady.*>

<Stop! *Stop!*> It was almost a scream. And what Kusko Al saw, Amuro saw, too. A laughing man, a Federation soldier, plunged a bayonet into the belly of her beautiful mother. Her father lay bludgeoned to death in a pool of blood.

<You *swine*!!> As Kusko's scream spread out into the silver band of light and disappeared, Amuro again saw through her eyes—saw the face of the same Federation soldier, grinning, a cigarette clenched between his tar-stained teeth.

> <*Build it up with wood and clay*
> *Wood and clay, wood and clay*
> *Build it up with wood and clay, wood and clay*
> *My fair lady.*
> *My fair lady.*
> *My . . . fair . . . lady. . . .*>

It was then that Amuro finally realized the enormity of what he had done—he had committed the unpardonable sin of killing someone he normally would never have dreamed of hurting. He had lost control to the war, to the technology of the machines, to the whole situation. But it was no excuse. Kusko Al had already been incinerated. He wept and choked out the words, "*Kusko, my fair lady. . . .*"

After the Elmeth exploded in a giant ball of light, the Zeon and Federation MS units finally closed in on each other in full combat, and the Federation ships—*Pegasus, Cyprus,* and *Greyden,* began dueling with Zeon's Gattle fighter-bombers. It was an equal match in terms of firepower. The *Madagascar* was a mobile cruiser, and it and the Gattle squadron were not about to fall easy prey to anyone. Lt. Commander McVery and his six surviving Tomahawk fighters, for their part, braved the raging barrages and made a lightning strike on the enemy.

Meanwhile Amuro avoided two blasts from Char's Rick Dom and unleashed a few rounds with his own Vulcan cannon, but then he was forced to start retreating from the area. The other Rick Dom's were closing in on the *Pegasus*, and he had to stop them. But Char wasn't about to let him.

<*Why did you do it?!*>

As Char charged toward him, leaping around some of the space debris in the area, Amuro finally regained his presence of mind. He knew the enemy Suits would have a hard time destroying the *Pegasus* on their own. If he turned around, he was confident he could take on Char, but he knew Rick Doms were different from Zakus in terms of both speed and firepower. And he could feel Char's own energy, targeted straight at him.

Over his receiver, Amuro thought he faintly heard a woman's voice somewhere crying, "*Sarkus!! Sarkus!!*" Had Sarkus McGovern, the GM pilot, been destroyed?

Then he heard a roar and a *wham* inside his cockpit. The beams used by the Rick Doms formed slowly, and were so broad and powerful that even a near-miss could make his Suit shake violently and throw off his sighting. But it wasn't a beam. Looking out from the Corregidor shoal area, he saw what appeared to be a large nuclear explosion in the distance.

And then he heard Char Aznable, saying, <Is it true, Amuro?!>

Amuro was incredulous. Federation and Zeon MS pilots were battling to the death, yet here they were, still capable of "talking" to each other. Even in the midst of his duel to the death with Kusko Al, he had had verbal communication with her—and he had allowed a personal grudge to violate his belief that combat should always be depersonalized. His comment about Char's sister had also been on a private level; not the sort of thing one normally tossed at an enemy in the heat of combat. And he had no way of knowing how much his words affected Char.

<It's not possible to lie on this level, Char! If you don't believe me, ask your sister, Artesia!>

He had no way of knowing if Char received his thought, but the Rick Dom's remaining leg rose up and turned. Amuro fired his rifle. The blast went wild and he aimed again. And then it happened. His entire beam rifle destructed in a flash of light.

Damn! he thought. Another, different Rick Dom that had fired at him was coming at him, floating upward out of the darkness from below and to his right. Realizing it was trying to cut him off, he again put his Suit into retreat.

LT. COMMANDER MCVERY AND three of his Tomahawks never returned from their heroic mission. Nor did Ensign Sarkus McGovern in his GM. The *Greyden* was destroyed, as were all four of the Ball machines.

Back on the *Pegasus II*, Bright Noa looked up at the ship's screens at the expanse of the Corregidor shoals unfolding before him. "'We took quite a beating," he muttered.

"But sir," Sayla commented from behind him, as if to console him, "at least we destroyed the Elmeth and three of the enemy's new skirted Suits. We also annihilated the Gattle squadron and inflicted heavy damage on their warship."

"She's right, skipper," Mirai added while still manning the helm, "I'd say it was a draw, and that we held our own."

"And we collected quite a bit of data on Zeon's new Elmeth machine, sir," Marker, seated, chimed in from the boom crane chair above Bright. "Don't you think," he continued, looking down at Hayato, "that for all intents and purposes we've wiped out half their Newtype Unit?"

"If Zeon has two or three more units like that one," Hayato answered, "the entire Federation's in big trouble. We wouldn't have been able to stop the Elmeth attack this time if it hadn't been for Amuro."

"I see your point . . . " Bright said softly, gazing at his crew.

When Amuro finally spoke, it was with bitterness: "No! That was Zeon's *only* Newtype unit!"

Bright looked at him and frowned. "It's time for some rest, pilot," he ordered. "You'd better ask the medic for a tranquilizer."

"Yessir . . . " Amuro saluted. Then he turned around and asked Sayla for the battle report. She walked over to him and handed him a large file. None of the other pilots were yet interested in it—they were simply happy to be alive, to have survived, and in groups of twos and threes they started filing out of the bridge area toward their quarters. Amuro, still holding the unopened file, watched his friends leave and then turned toward Sayla.

"You knew the Red Comet was out there, didn't you?" he said.

"I knew," she said. "I could see him."

"I told him what you had asked. I think he understood."

Without warning, Sayla slapped Amuro across the face.

THE *PEGASUS II* AND the *Cyprus* rested briefly outside Corregidor. In a few hours the code words for the final attack on *A Baoa Qu*—"*play the Cembalo*"—would be signaled to the entire Federation armada.

CONFRONTATION

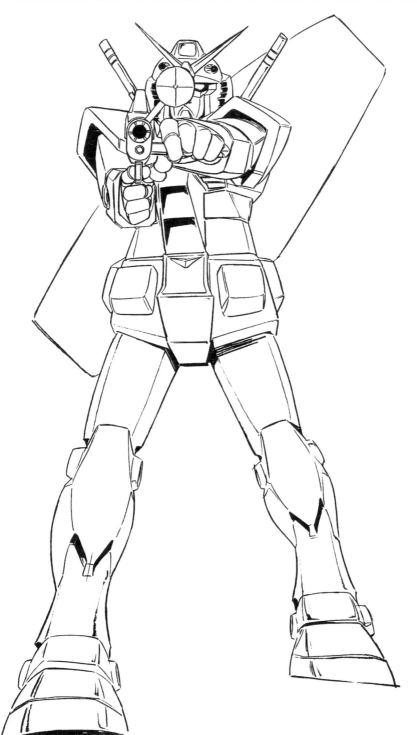

POWER AND AMBITION

"I'M JUST SPECULATING, BUT if we could be absolutely certain the Federation Forces really *were* going to converge around *A Baoa Qu*, then I, I . . . "

To Admiral Chapman Jirom's surprise, his superior—Gihren Zabi, the Supreme Commander of the Principality of Zeon—faltered in midsentence. For a man who normally spoke with unswerving conviction, even when the two of them were alone, it was utterly out of character.

"I've been thinking," Gihren finally continued, "that we could make *A Baoa Qu* one of the targets for the System plan. Well? What do you think?" His last words were rushed, as if he were overly self-conscious.

Chapman was horrified. "If, if I understand you correctly, Excellency," he said, tentatively, "you're ordering me to employ the System in our current campaign. If so, sir, I beg to reply that it is impossible . . . "

Gihren twisted his head and popped the joints in his neck. "What's the matter, Admiral?" he said, his voice suddenly hardening. "You're not worried about Dozle, Kycilia, and Randolph, are you?"

Chapman knew Gihren was angry at him for his weak-kneed response. But he knew what Gihren was really suggesting: targeting *A Baoa Qu* as part of a plan to annihilate Dozle and Kycilia Zabi—Gihren's own brother and sister—so he could rule unchallenged in a new postwar era. And because no witnesses could be permitted to survive such a dastardly attack, Vice Admiral Randolph Weigelman—Gihren's own right-hand man and the commanding officer on *A Baoa Qu*—would also have to be sacrificed. There was no other way to explain the earlier hesitation and tone. But Chapman wasn't completely surprised. He had long suspected Gihren might someday cook up such a diabolical scheme.

"They ought to be able to hold off the Federation forces long enough for us to complete the project," Gihren added. "Don't you agree?"

"Why, yessir." Chapman stroked his mustache with his ring finger and stared down at some notes on Gihren's desk in front of him. "You're quite right, I'm sure, sir. The parties you mention, after all, do command some of our crack units." He wished he had never heard Gihren's words. And he wished he knew nothing about Gihren's plans. But it was too late. He knew. And now his own position was in danger. Gihren would be watching every move he made, listening to every word he uttered. And eventually he, Chapman, would have no choice except to execute Gihren's crazy idea. Nonetheless, he raised his gaze to meet Gihren's and finally managed to blurt out, "But the . . . the . . . conditions are too difficult, sir . . . "

Gihren stood up and pushed a button on his expansive office desk. The left and right wall panels rose up, revealing giant four-meter-square screens that showed the universe unfolding before them. "Well? Why? Speak frankly, Admiral."

"We can't control where the Federation armada is finally going to concentrate its strength, sir. And we have no guarantee that use of the System will terminate the war. As long as that is true, I believe your plan is impossible to carry out, sir."

"Hmph. I see your point. But surely it's possible to use the System for something less than a single-point attack? Can't we use it to sort of rake their forces? Eh, Chapman?"

"Well . . . I, er, suppose so . . . "

"SYSTEM" WAS THE CODE name of a top-secret Zeon project to convert a cylindrical space colony over six kilometers in diameter into a giant laser cannon. Using this "Solar Ray" to rake the enemy presented several technical problems, not the least of which was the fact that the angle of fire could be tweaked only between three and five degrees. But as long as the target was tens of thousands of kilometers removed, even that would easily cover an entire combat zone. It would not even be necessary to wait for *all* the Federation ships to converge at one point. If, however, as Gihren seemed to imply, the goal was also to annihilate certain friendly forces—Zeon forces—and make it look like an accident, the plan would have to be perfectly executed. They would need double, even triple guarantees that it would work as designed.

GIHREN CONTINUED. "I'VE ALREADY had Rank Kiprodon, the president of Side 6, which as you know is ostensibly neutral, sound out the possibility of a negotiated peace settlement afterward with the Federation."

"And is there such a possibility, sir?" Chapman immediately regretted asking the question so soon. Gihren would probably pounce on him for it.

"You could say so," Gihren answered mysteriously. He then turned away from the wall screens and walked in front of Chapman. He smiled thinly, and Chapman instinctively stood at attention, holding his files at his side. He knew Gihren had made a decision.

"I'll leave the timing of the attack up to you," Gihren said, casually sitting down at his desk again. "Can you do it?"

"With . . . with one condition, sir," Chapman haltingly replied. "I need at least three days to bring the System up to eighty percent of its power potential. I need you to wait till then."

"Our campaign, Operation Revol I, has already begun. If the tides of war go against us, we may need to fire the System as early as this afternoon."

"But, *sir!!*" Chapman closed his eyes, raised his voice, and lodged the strongest protest he was capable of. The System was only fifty percent powered up, and to make up the difference he would have to do rush work on the over five hundred microchannels that linked *Mahal* with the solar batteries. It was obviously impossible. But that was just a technical issue. The moral issue was more complex.

Chapman Jirom was, however, an admiral with considerable personal ambition. He had been given a chance to win the favor and trust of the Supreme Commander, and he knew that if he succeeded his future would be bright. If the war could be concluded on favorable terms, he would probably be treated like one of the Zabi family. In fact, without Dozle and Kycilia Zabi around to interfere, he would probably be given a position in power second only to the Supreme Commander himself.

At the same time, Chapman was a fairly rational man, fully aware of what could happen to him if he linked himself too closely to Gihren's fate. Gihren had, after all, just decided to sacrifice one of his most trusted men, not to mention thousands of his troops and his own sister. But if he, Chapman, worked fast now to help Gihren eradicate potential future problems such as Dozle and Kycilia, he was convinced he could avoid Randolph's impending fate. Going along with Gihren, he quickly concluded, was a gamble, but it would be worth it. *The only obstacle left,* he suddenly thought, *will be Gihren's father, Degwin, and he's just a puppet.* In the end, his naive optimism in his own future and his limited understanding of the political scheming in Zeon won out.

"I know this plan entails an element of risk, Admiral," Gihren said. "That's why I wanted to consult with you first. I don't have a hot line to General Revil on the Federation side and can't call him up and tell him to slow down, but I think I can spare some ships now dedicated to the defense of the fatherland, and thus gain you another forty-eight hours."

"*Th-thank* you, sir!" Chapman gushed. "With two days I'm sure we can bring the System power output up to at least seventy percent. If you can just hold the targets in place, it'll work!"

"Good. I'm depending on you, Chapman."

Gihren whispered his final sentence, but Chapman understood its significance. Gihren, Supreme Commander Gihren Zabi, had called him—Chapman Jirom—not by rank but by name. It meant he had become the Supreme Commander's friend. He clicked the heels of his boots together, saluted, and exited his superior's office.

GIHREN WATCHED AS CHAPMAN departed. Chapman was around forty-five and, he congratulated himself, probably just the right age and temperament for the job. Then he turned and looked at the wall displays he had activated earlier. They showed an enlarged real image of the space colonies that comprised the Principality of Zeon, silhouetted by the sun.

Most Zeon colonies were of the sealed-cylinder type, and on their periphery had from six to eight giant solar-cell panels that supplied the residents inside with all the energy they needed. There were two reasons Zeon did not use the type of cylinder common elsewhere in space—the type with three or more giant mirrors to reflect natural light inside—and instead used sealed cylinders. First, the centrifugal force generated by colony rotation simulated Earth gravity on the enormous inside walls of the cylinder and made it possible to use them for living space. A closed cylinder, with no transparent glass sections to let in light, meant that the entire wall area could be used as "ground," and that the colonies could house far more people; most Zeon colonies held up to twenty million people in seventy-kilometer-long cylinders as wide as eighteen kilometers in diameter. Second, it was believed that even the old models of sealed-cylinder colonies gave residents superior protection from harmful radiation during solar storms. Enough time had passed so that the third generation of colony residents was now emerging, and they appeared healthy, but there was still no guarantee that people in space would be safe forever.

The sealed cylinders of Side 3, or what became the Principality of Zeon, had been built as a type of experiment. Instead of natural sunlight, a configuration of pipe-like structures resembling old-fashioned fluorescent lights ran through the core of the Zeon colony cylinders, serving as an artificial sun and providing a regulated twenty-four-hour cycle of day and night. As in Federation colonies, in the Principality adjustments were made in the length of the day to replicate Earth-style seasons and form a human "mean time" among the various cylinders. It was a system that had proved quite successful and there was little likelihood of change in the future. Sometimes people who emigrated to Side 3 complained because the seasons approximated those of the temperate zones in Earth's northern hemisphere, and in the early days, whenever an immigrant from a tropical region or from the southern hemisphere became an official of the Mean Time Control Agency, he or she would ritually propose a change. But in recent years the populations seemed to have accepted the status quo, or forgotten the difference.

Gihren loved to look at the display of Zeon's colonies. From such a distant perspective, everything seemed so peaceful. As those around him often cautiously joked behind his back, their Supreme Commander acted like a feudal lord, gazing with self-satisfaction at the happy, productive lives of the lowly subjects in his dominion. "He acts high and mighty, his head in the clouds," some whispered, "even though his feet are still in the gutter."

But he also loved to gaze at the sight of the Milky Way. If he squinted his eyes just right when he looked at the wall displays, the millions of stars blurred into a mysterious, beautiful glowing river through the sky and made him marvel at its vastness and ponder the meaning of life. That he was capable of such philosophical introspection would have surprised his aides, for Gihren was often assumed to be plotting what military-civilian ratio should exist on a specific colony or whom to reshuffle or demote. But as far as Gihren was concerned, those were mere details to be decided with a glance at the appropriate forms or the information regularly appearing on his monitor screens. He didn't need to gaze at the universe to make such mundane decisions. The gazing was done for the sake of gazing. Any thoughts generated by it were far more vast in scope.

Gihren was fascinated with what could be accomplished with hundreds of colonies and with what they implied about human potential.

If, as people said, the universe was infinite in size, men should act more boldly and assert themselves on a far grander scale than they had on Earth.

"There's no physical population problem out here," Gihren muttered to himself, looking out at the universe. "Ten or twenty billion people are no threat to the natural order of things. But we can do without the baser element. They only hold the rest of us back. They're worse than scum."

Then he suddenly started to worry about *Mahal*. He made the display cameras pan until the full moon came into view on the screens. He couldn't see *Mahal* yet, but he could discern a few other colonies rotating in space with their huge solar cells deployed. Regularly scheduled transports plied their way between them, their red and green lights blinking in the blackness. Then he spotted it.

Mahal was one of the earliest and therefore smallest sealed colonies built. Six kilometers in diameter and thirty kilometers in length, it had been specially chosen for the System project. Its citizens had all been evacuated, its inner walls had been coated with aluminum, and it had been turned into a giant carbon dioxide laser cannon. Because the power requirements for the project were staggering and because there was so little time, Gihren had used emergency measures to harness energy from nearly one third of all the solar cells in the Principality. But doing so had required appeals to the masses to conserve energy and make yet further sacrifices. He knew he had to keep appealing to their pride and reinforce in them the idea that they were a chosen, blessed people. If not, he ran the risk of creating fear and dissension, even fostering an antiwar movement. Governing might become difficult, and the last thing he wanted to do was sow the seeds of his own destruction by encouraging factions that opposed him. It was imperative that the System strategy lead to quick victory in the war against the Federation.

"Hmph," he muttered. "Here's hoping Kycilia, Dozle, and Randolph can hold off the Federation attack as long as possible."

Gihren liked to believe anything was possible, but at the same time, and in his own way, he knew the dangers of complacency and overconfidence. He knew he was no Napoleon, yet it bothered him that his own father—a puppet whom the Zeon citizenry still fawned upon as the "Sovereign"—had once referred to him as a second-rate "Hitler." But his father, he reassured himself, had probably said it out of jealousy more than anything else. He, Gihren, had gone to great lengths to maintain his objectivity. For example, he had placed Vice Admiral Randolph Weigelman, a trusted lieutenant, in charge of the *A Baoa Qu* space for-

Gihren Zabi

tress and regularly listened to his advice, respecting him as a friend who could always provide it. It was, in fact, Randolph who had provided the inspiration for the idea of destroying Kycilia. "I'm not saying there's not enough room in the solar system for both of you," Randolph had casually said several years earlier, "but your sister's too smart for her own good. She's the type that, if she'd been raised on Earth, would probably have revolted and formed her own Earth Federation."

It had been hard for Gihren to realize that his baby sister was so clever and scheming. But as Randolph had pointed out, throughout the war she had always tried to promote her own agenda. Not too long ago, for example, he had learned that she was lavishing public funds on the mysterious Flanagan Institute. And around the same time he had begun hearing rumors of Newtypes. Indeed, in the last few months the rumors had begun to take a more tangible form, and among both Federation and Zeon frontline troops it was increasingly said that Newtypes were not just enlightened Space Age men and women, as Zeon Zum Deikun had once prophesied, but extraordinary military warriors capable of finally bringing an end to the war. He had already received a battlefield report to the effect that the Federation had formed its own Newtype unit, centered on a new mobile suit called a Gundam. And from the reports he received once every three days from Lt. Challia Bull, he knew that Kycilia had formed a small unit of Rick Doms to be her Newtype unit, that she had put Commander Char Aznable in charge of it, and that she was already preparing to reinforce it. Clearly, Kycilia was ready for whatever was going to happen.

These aren't the Newtypes Zeon talked about, Gihren thought. *They must have some sort of superpowers.*

If Gihren had begun to overestimate Newtypes, it was partly because of Lt. Challia Bull. He had deliberately planted Challia in Kycilia's command as a spy without telling him he wanted to destroy Kycilia, but in the course of one meeting the lieutenant seemed to have read his mind. To Gihren, it had seemed like a form of telepathy and had made him start to believe the rumors about Newtypes. He recalled what the young revolutionary, Zeon Zum Deikun, had once said.

> *The universe is a new environment, which will compel mankind to change. If the first stage in mankind's evolution was his evolution from an ape to a human, and the second stage was his breakthrough from feudalism to the rational science of the Renaissance, then the third will be his transformation into a new type of human, a man with profound sensitivity and insight and a far greater awareness of the vastness of time and space.*
>
> *The transition to Newtypes will be a natural one. The act of walking increased man's range of movement and helped the concept of tribe and nation-state to develop. Powered vehicles expanded man's awareness to a global level. And now civilization is advancing into outer space. By living and working in space, man's consciousness will transcend the boundaries of Earth and become truly universal. The vastness of space will be "home." And as man's consciousness expands, he will begin to tap the unutilized portions of his cerebrum—the over half of his brain cells unused since time immemorial, the enormous untapped mental reserves given by God precisely for the new environment of space. And when this happens, man will change. Man will become a more enlightened, refined, and compassionate being. It is space—the act of living in an extraterrestrial environment—that will act as the trigger.*
>
> *O people of space! Now is the time to awaken! To realize your*

*latent potential! We are at the dawn of a transformation of mankind. A
true enlightenment of the human race. And we may finally be poised,
ready to transcend what has always been thought the impossible—
infinite space, and time itself. This is no idle dream. To live in a new
universe, man must transcend the psychological limitations of his old
environment!*

The memory of Zeon Deikun's speech was etched into Gihren Zabi's
brain. His father, Degwin Zabi, had financially backed the young revolutionary's activities. And when a true political movement had coalesced
around Zeon Deikun, culminating in the formation of a political party,
Gihren had been influenced by his father and had thrown himself into
the movement. But after several years of working with Zeon Deikun,
both he and his father had eventually reached the same conclusion: the
man's true talents were limited to those of a political agitator.

By the time the "Zeon movement" had begun advocating the autonomy of space colonies in the Earth Federation, Degwin Zabi and
Gihren had secretly usurped most of its true power, but Zeon Zum
Deikun remained a star. He was handsome, impassioned, and the type
of man with whom young women fell in love immediately; his charisma
was essential to turn the movement into a true political force. As public
opinion began to coalesce, and to advocate the right of Sides to exist
as independent states and the sacredness of Earth as mankind's original
home, Degwin and Gihren emerged as leaders of the Zeon faction.

As Zeon Zum Deikun had often said,

> *It is the height of arrogance for those who remain on Earth to look
> up at the heavens and believe they can continue to rule over all its
> inhabitants. It is true that we—the space colonists—were largely
> shipped from Earth against our will as a population-control measure.
> But now we are developing a new identity and awareness. We are a
> new people. We live, eat, and sleep among the stars. We live in infinite
> space, and we will have access to infinite energy until the sun burns
> out fifty billion years from now. Our consciousness will expand, and
> infinite space will be our true home. God has given us the stars to live
> among.*
>
> *We are the people of the universe. We have struggled to survive
> in a harsh environment, and new generations of colonists testify to our
> success. Now, when we gaze back at Earth, we see a sacred blue and
> green orb—the cradle of civilization and a sacred home that we must
> eternally preserve and protect. Our new consciousness as people of the*

*universe tells us that Earth was not created to be abused and polluted
by a few members of an elite, privileged class. Men and women who
have never been into outer space still believe Earth belongs to them
and still continue to rape and plunder it, but their time has passed.
Earth must be preserved as the sacred homeland of all mankind.
It does not belong solely to an Earthbound elite! By continuing to
dream of controlling all of mankind, they forever deny mankind its
true destiny.*

*Autonomy for the Sides, sovereignty for the colonies, does not
simply mean a revolt against sovereignty on Earth. It means that every
human should move into space, that the government of the Earth and
the area around it should be placed in the hands of an alliance of all
Sides, and that the Earth itself should be preserved and protected as the
sacred birthplace of all mankind. It is easy to expand the number of
colonies required to accomplish this.*

*In ancient times the Christians fought bloody battles for control
over the birthplace of their religion, but there is no need for humanity
to repeat this mistake over Earth.*

Zeon Zum Deikun's ideas struck a sympathetic chord among the
colonists on each Side, but the "absolute democracy" of the Earth Federation government also worked in his favor. The internal contradictions of
a dictatorship of the majority created endless parliamentary procedures,
which resulted in a rash of irresponsible legislation and an obfuscation of
responsibility among individual politicians. Even minor policy initiatives
invariably resulted in factional fighting among competing bureaucracies.
It became impossible to satisfy anyone. Dissatisfaction spread throughout
the system.

Some agencies of the Earth Federation government were aware of
the seriousness of the problems developing and were sympathetic to the
Sides, but when a hard-line Earth faction took over de facto control of
the entire Federation system, its members' prejudices inflamed the desire
for autonomy among the Sides and eventually created the conditions for
a direct challenge to the authority of the Federation government. By the
time the Earth Federation government tried to exercise control over the
situation, it was too late. Their actions succeeded only in derailing the
emerging Side 3 republican system.

On Side 3, already worsening relations between Degwin Zabi
and Zeon Zum Deikun were aggravated when Degwin and Gihren
conducted a massive purge of their opposition. In U.C. 0065, which
came to be known as the Black Year, a special Secret Service under the

control of Gihren eliminated two hundred thousand members of the anti-Deikun faction.

The purge was carried out in a draconian way entirely contrary to the beliefs of Zeon Zum Deikun. It even created a rift between Degwin and his son, but it did make it possible for Side 3 to successfully declare its independence from the Earth Federation two years later and to officially form a republic. It did not, however, mean that the power struggles within the Republic of Zeon itself were over yet, for five years after Side 3's declaration of independence, Zeon Zum Deikun died suddenly of what was reported as an illness—although rumors persisted that his death might not have been entirely natural. And three years after Zeon's death, Degwin declared Side 3 a "Principality" and installed himself at its head.

Instead of acting resolutely, the Earth Federation government chose to sit back and watch the power struggle unfolding between the ruling Zabi family and the surviving Deikun faction, and to naively wait for the new Zeon state to collapse of its own accord. But that approach backfired, for it gave the Zabi family time to consolidate its grip on Side 3 and turn what had been a republic into a powerful dictatorship.

Why did Side 3 turn into such a different system from what its founder, Zeon Zum Deikun, had envisioned? Top officials in the Earth Federation government were aghast and perplexed. But it was really the result of Gihren Zabi and his skillful use of the Secret Service. Gihren had his own maniacal vision of how mankind should evolve in space, and to realize it he knew that simple autonomy for Side 3 would not be enough. He believed the Earth Federation government itself would have to be destroyed, despite the fact that doing so would require overcoming an enormous disadvantage in military and logistical strength. And to that end, he knew that he had to transform Side 3 into a military pow-erhouse, that he would need not a vacillating democracy or republican government but a totalitarian system. Still, since his originally stated goal was to fulfill the vision of Zeon Zum Deikun, it was convenient to keep using Zeon Zum Deikun's name. Thus the new state became the Principality of Zeon.

Whether Degwin Zabi was aware of all of his son's machinations at the time was unclear, but Gihren Zabi soon became Supreme Com-mander and managed to gain control of both the Zeon military and police, placing his brother, Dozle, and sister, Kycilia, in positions of power. In the few years since the founding of the Principality, he had finally come within sight of achieving all his immediate ambitions. If he regretted anything, it was that his younger brother, Sasro, had been assassinated in the early struggles with the Deikun faction, for Sasro would have been ideally suited to work in government administration.

Inevitably, Gihren began to contemplate mankind's longer-term future. He possessed a brilliant, highly analytical mind and had an uncanny ability, even when grappling with particularly knotty problems, to think beyond it toward a larger goal. And having a larger goal always seemed to give him the power to break through whatever short-term problem he might confront.

FIVE MINUTES AFTER ADMIRAL Chapman Jirom left his office, Gihren began a meeting with another two officials, but then over his intercom speaker his secretary announced the arrival of Lt. Ramba Ral of the Secret Service.

"Tell him I'll meet him next door," Gihren replied into his desk mike. He stood up, excused himself, loosened the collar of his uniform, and headed for the smaller reception room that he always used for more intimate discussions. Ramba Ral was standing, waiting for him by the door. As Gihren entered, he noted with satisfaction that his secretary, Cecilia Irene, had readied tea for both of them.

"Good to see you again, Ramba. Have a seat."

"Thank you, Excellency," Ramba replied, bowing slightly and sitting by the table. He seemed unusually nervous.

"How about a shot," Gihren suggested.

"Don't mind if I do, sir," Ramba replied. As if on cue, Cecilia appeared with a little liquor cart, from which she produced a bottle of brandy and dispensed one shot into each teacup.

Ramba immediately lifted his cup to his lips and began to sip, but he did it with enough grace that Gihren was willing to overlook the violation of etiquette it represented. Gihren was a finicky man who normally hated meetings that involved eating and drinking with his men; at banquets, there was always someone who rubbed him the wrong way with his boorish manners. That most of his guests were visibly nervous when eating with him bothered him even more.

Slowly lowering his cup to the table, Ramba said, "I've scanned all of Challia Bull's reports up to yesterday. Frankly, sir, his writing isn't what one would expect from a man of his caliber. His observations seem extremely shallow."

"Hmph," Gihren said, savoring the brandy flavor in his tea.

"When he's simply reporting facts, I think he's quite objective and accurate even on minor details. The only personal, subjective statement he makes is to lament the death in action of Junior Grade Lieutenant

Kusko Al. As far as your sister Kycilia is concerned, he says he's only met her once and makes no mention of his impression. In summary, I can only say that he produces very run-of-the-mill, superficial reports."

"Perhaps he wants to avoid speculation."

"That's probably correct and would certainly be in character for him, but I must nonetheless confess I'm rather worried." When Ramba Ral finished his sentence he coughed softly and looked up at Gihren.

Noting Ramba's unusual demeanor, Gihren decided to probe. "Lieutenant Challia Bull always seemed an extremely cautious and conservative man. But I also trust your intuition, Ramba. You seem troubled. What is it?"

"Well, sir," Ramba began. His entire body, including the manly mustache he sported, trembled slightly. "It's about Commander Char Aznable, sir. I've learned something that affects me personally, sir. He's . . . he's one of the two orphaned children of Zeon Zum Deikun that my father, Jimba Ral, took with him when he fled to Earth years ago."

Supreme Commander Gihren Zabi lowered his teacup to the tabletop and stared transfixed at Ramba. He had never dreamed of such a connection. Ramba Ral was an important official in the Secret Service, which he, Gihren, directly controlled. He knew about Ramba's father, and precisely _because_ he knew, he had been convinced when Ramba joined the service that he would never waver in his allegiance. And thus far he had never been disappointed. Ramba was the type of military man he intuitively liked—broad-minded, devoted, and appropriately modest.

"You're seriously trying to tell me that our Commander Char Aznable, the star of Zeon's MS forces, is really Casval Rem Deikun?" he asked, heaving a sigh of exasperation.

"That's correct, sir," Ramba gingerly replied. "Apparently, after my father fled the Principality, he bought the family name of Mass for the Deikun children and changed Casval's name to Edward Mass. Then in U.C. 0070, Casval, aka Edward, managed to infiltrate back into Zeon and register himself under the Aznable family name. At age eighteen, he was accepted into the Military Academy and graduated at the top of his class. Because of an emergency call-up, he graduated six months ahead of schedule."

"Any idea of his motive?"

"Not really, sir. It's awfully hard to get good intelligence from Earth, sir."

"What about Jimba Ral, your father?"

"I've seen a report that he's still alive, sir." Ramba Ral kept his head bowed slightly when he answered, as if unable to look Gihren straight in the eye.

Gihren, for his part, was still reeling from the unexpected news, but at the same time he didn't want Ramba to take too much of the blame for this on himself. No matter what happened, he knew he could trust Ramba. He suddenly changed the subject. "Well, what about Crowley? Have you both signed the papers yet?"

It was such an out-of-the-blue question that Ramba at first had no idea what his superior was talking about.

"You know. Crowley Hamon. Your fiancée. It would be a better example to your men if you had an official marriage ceremony performed."

"Sir!" the startled Ramba replied as his mind recovered. "She hasn't consented yet. She says she'll only consider if the war ends and I'm still alive."

"Ha, ha, ha. I like that. A strong-willed girl. Well, her wish is about to be fulfilled, because we're about to settle this thing soon. Tell her I ordered you to get hitched. I shouldn't get involved in matchmaking, but I did tell her I'd find her a good man."

"Er . . . thank you, sir. I'll do everything I can to persuade her."

Ramba knew Gihren was trying to make him feel more at ease, but he was unable to stop a sinking feeling of despair in his gut.

"Don't worry so much, Ramba," Gihren added. "I'll take care of Kycilia's Newtype Corps in my own fashion. Frankly, I agree with your opinion on Lieutenant Challia Bull. I think he might be a turncoat. His reports are far too superficial. He's not following my instructions."

"Yessir," Ramba replied in near-whisper.

"If my sister has really put Casval Deikun in charge of her Newtype unit without knowing his true identity, it means I'll have to put my original plan into effect even earlier than I thought."

Ramba said nothing. He had no way of knowing what Gihren had ordered Admiral Chapman Jirom to do, but he could sense something big was going to happen. And Gihren's next words seemed to confirm it.

"I told you we were about to settle this thing for once and for all, right? You and the Secret Service, Ramba, are going to become busy in the next few days. I hope you're ready."

Ramba detected an odd twinkle in Gihren's eye when he spoke.

"Don't worry about what happened with Casval Deikun," Gihren continued. "I'm going to create a whole new postwar order."

Ramba watched Gihren drain the last drops from his teacup. Then, he suddenly understood. Gihren had something up his sleeve, something so drastic that it could create a new world order and eliminate the problem with Casval Deikun at the same time. But he couldn't imagine what that something might be.

"We need to make sure you can have your wedding soon, Ramba," Gihren said with a smile. "There's just one more thing I want to know. Tell me what kind of man this Commander Char Aznable really is."

In response, Ramba proffered a voluminous file and said, "We've got several tapes on him. This is the result of our investigation, sir."

Gihren glanced at the materials and marveled at Ramba's thoroughness. "Thanks," he said. "Good work. You're dismissed now, Lieutenant."

Ramba saluted smartly and left the office. Gihren pressed a special button in a little drawer underneath the table, and his secretary entered from the door to the left. Cecilia Irene was a buxom young woman dressed in a moss-green pantsuit outfit, the chic cut of which highlighted her long legs. Her long hair was brown, almost black, like her eyes. She had a heavy layer of lipstick on.

"I'm not very good at situations like this, Cecilia," Gihren said.

"But sir, Lieutenant Ramba Ral seems like a very forthright man. The kind who can be trusted."

Gihren nodded in agreement, and Cecilia smiled at him. Then she left the room. She was doing her job well. Two years earlier he had hired her specifically for her ability to size people up, and she hadn't disappointed him. But he wasn't about to let her observe him now. He flicked a switch on the intercom panel, deactivating the miniature observation camera built into it, and then pulled a video card from the file Lt. Ramba had left. It was a standard shirt-pocket-sized card with around three hours of images recorded on it. He plugged it in a slot, and an image began moving on a wall monitor.

The card appeared to be a copy of an amateur tape of Char Aznable, and the images were of poor resolution. First Gihren saw a young couple walking down a path on the campus of the Military Academy. The man—apparently Char—was blond, wearing sunglasses and walking arm-in-arm with a girl, laughing. The girl seemed to notice the camera first. Then the man walked directly over toward it, waving his hand and saying, "Hey! Who gave you permission to film us?"

Then a voice, apparently the cameraman, came from off camera. "Heck, Lulush asked me to."

The girl came closer, inquiring in an irritated tone, "Why are you always so uptight, Char?" But the young man continued to confront the camera, threatening, "Stop it or else . . . "

At that point the screen went blank for several seconds, and then a different image appeared of a party at the academy. This time the video seemed to have been shot by a professional. After a panoramic view of the dance floor, the camera zoomed in on one couple, showing a close-up of a man wearing regular untinted glasses, his blond forelocks shaking above their frames in time to the music. It was Char Aznable. He was an excellent dancer, and his partner was trying hard to keep up.

To Gihren's surprise, he suddenly noted a shadowlike scar on Char's forehead and wondered where it had come from. The dance sequence continued for several more minutes and then switched to scenes from the graduation ceremony at the Military Academy. Gihren saw himself presenting Garma Zabi—his own younger half brother—with the special dagger given to the cadet with top graduating honors. The camera then moved to the next officer in line after Garma—to Char Aznable—and lingered briefly on him. It was then that Gihren remembered. Garma had not really been the top in his class, but since he was a Zabi family member, the ceremony had been tailored so he would receive the dagger anyway.

Hmph, Gihren thought. *I should've given the dagger to Char, after all. If I had, I would've gotten a better look at him, and I might have recognized him as the son of Zeon Zum Deikun just by his bearing—it's uncannily similar.*

After graduation, Char had performed spectacularly in battle, and Gihren had received steady reports of his promotions. Garma, for his part, had also always recommended Char highly to him. It was just like Garma to have done so, Gihren recalled. He had always seemed a little guilty over having stolen the graduating dagger from Char. *Such a baby,* Gihren thought, remembering the finely chiseled jaw of his half sibling.

The monitor next showed scenes of Char Aznable as a lieutenant in the Principality of Zeon's military, wearing his distinctive face mask. According to one story Gihren had heard, the mask had been specially allowed because Char's eyes had been damaged when the automatic protective filter on his helmet had failed in battle. But while looking closely at the image on the screen, Garma realized the true reason Char had taken to wearing the mask: he had infiltrated Zeon and begun wearing it to get nearer to the Zabi family without being recognized as Casval Deikun! It was the only plausible explanation for wearing something that covered half his face all the time. As an infant, Casval had often played with both Gihren and Kycilia Zabi, and Jimba Ral had surely reminded him of it many times as he grew up. It was entirely conceivable that Jimba had in fact specifically raised Casval, the son of Zeon Zum Deikun, to infiltrate the Principality one day and destroy the

Zabi family and thus avenge his father's death. In fact, that was probably why Jimba Ral had left the care of his own son, Ramba Ral, with a foster parent and defected to the Earth Federation with Zeon Zum Deikun's two young children. He would have had no way of knowing how difficult this would eventually make life for his own son later, but he would simply raise Casval to fulfill Zeon Zum Deikun's original goal and once the lad was old enough, let him loose to perform his task. It had obviously been a long-term gamble, but Jimba Ral was a crafty old fox and probably knew Casval would be toughened by challenges along the way, and turn into a seasoned warrior with a mission. As Gihren all too well knew, it was Char's internalized sense of mission off or on the battlefield that made him a real threat.

Hmm, he next thought, *I could have sworn Casval's sister was named Artesia, or something like that.* He began poring through the other documents in the file that Ramba Ral had given him, searching for her name. Finally he came across a reference to the fact that she had emigrated voluntarily to Side 7 and hoped to become a physician. There was nothing else on her, but that wasn't a problem. The problem was Casval and the fact that he clearly was becoming an increasingly formidable enemy. The more Gihren thought about it, the more he realized that Casval was slowly closing in on *him*, Gihren Zabi. Casval had made enormous progress toward his goal in a relatively short time, befriending Garma Zabi, graduating at the top of his class, and being steadily promoted in the ranks until he had won the confidence of Kycilia—without her ever learning of his true identity. If Kycilia *had* known, Gihren was convinced, she never would have taken him under her wing.

Now the real question was whether Casval Rem Deikun, aka Char Aznable, was really a true Newtype. *Maybe Char's use of the nickname "Red Comet,"* Supreme Commander Gihren Zabi thought, *is less of a conceit than it seems.* Suddenly he imagined the vengeful spirit of Zeon Zum Deikun reincarnated in his young son.

DOZLE ZABI

BEING SLAPPED BY A girl didn't really hurt much, but the pain lingered a long time. Lt. (jg) Amuro Ray pondered this mystery briefly and then fell into a deep, dreamless sleep.

Five hours later he was jolted awake by an alarm. He thought about changing his underwear but remembered he'd done so before hitting the sack. Perhaps, he speculated, he was unconsciously preparing for the possibility of death. He got up, dabbed some lotion on his curly, reddish hair, massaged it vigorously, and ran a brush across his head. Then he donned his dog tags, pulled on his trousers and jacket, and dashed out of his room. In the hallway he grabbed the available first lift-grip and let it pull him horizontally through the weightless air. When he reached the pilots' room he found his comrades—Kai Shiden, Hayato Kobayashi, and Kria Maja—already changing into their lemon-yellow combat suits.

"Yo, Romeo," Kai joked. "You owe me a dinner after the way you moved in on her, man!"

"Sorry, but you'll have to wait till this campaign's over," Amuro retorted. Then, turning to Hayato, he said, "Next thing I know, you'll want one, too."

"You bet," Hayato replied. "And it'll cost you an arm and a leg. You stole our fave Wave!"

CHAPTER EIGHTEEN

Neither Hayato nor Kai knew that the woman they referred to, Petty Officer First Class Sayla Mass, had slapped Amuro earlier. They just knew he had slept with someone they both had designs on, and they were determined to extract a penalty from him. It was an unwritten rule among young men on Federation ships that the perpetrator of such a deed had to pay a penalty, either in the form of treating his comrades or forfeiting the right to visit the canteen for a month. There was a price to pay for being a Romeo.

It was ironic, Amuro thought, because he had lost some of his physical interest in Sayla when she had told him that Char Aznable—the faceless enemy he knew only from combat—was really her brother. He had been attracted to Sayla at first mainly because he knew she could give him something Lalah Sune couldn't; something, it was safe to say, that was mainly physical love. And she hadn't disappointed him. In the process, they had established a "relationship," but that had been more of an accident than anything else. They hadn't come together to become soul mates or to build a life together. He had sought something that he couldn't get from Lalah Sune. She had sought something her brother—Char, or Casval—couldn't give her. They had both sought substitutes for something else, and their love was therefore a simulated love, incapable of satisfying the true hunger in their souls. In the end, the spirits of both Char and Lalah Sune had formed a barrier between them.

When Sayla had told Amuro earlier that she wanted him to "kill" her brother if they met again in combat, she hadn't really meant it. She had been perversely motivated, not by hate, but by frustrated love for her brother. But Amuro had been unable to forgive her. He had tried not to let his feelings for Lalah Sune come between them, but she had not tried to do the same with her brother. She had naively assumed he would be able to understand her inner feelings simply because he seemed to be a Newtype.

As far as he was concerned, if it hadn't been for Char Aznable, he wouldn't have had to kill Lalah Sune or even Kusko Al; that he had met them because of Char was a thought too painful to contemplate. He placed enormous, almost naive weight on sincerity, and since he simply couldn't comprehend Sayla's statement, it remained between them like a festering wound.

During his duel with Kusko Al's Elmeth, he had confronted Char with Sayla's statement, hoping to throw him off balance and destroy him. Projecting in his thoughts, <Char! Don't try to stop me!> he had added, <If you do, I'll have to kill you, too, just as your sister asked.>

To his astonishment, it had worked. Char had reflexively projected back, <Is it true?>, clearly acknowledging receipt of his message and proving that sworn enemies—MS pilots—could communicate in the midst of combat. Partially out of spite, Amuro had replied, <It's not possible to lie on this level, Char. If you don't believe me, ask your sister, Artesia!>

The enemy red Rick Dom had seemed to shudder, and then a scream, accompanied by a gush of rage, had reverberated through his cerebrum, astonishing him with its intensity. But by hesitating a few seconds for an answer in the heat of emotion, he had also given Char an opportunity. The Rick Dom had evaded him, and disappeared into the Corregidor shoal zone. He knew he had damaged it, but he also knew that in MS combat anything short of a mortal blow was useless. He had hesitated, and he had lost Char. Only another Newtype in the area could possibly have understood what had transpired between them.

Now, IN THE PILOTS' room on the *Pegasus II*, as Amuro zipped shut the triple layer of fasteners connecting his helmet to his jacket, he bitterly regretted not having killed Char when he had had the chance. He felt he had failed as a military pilot, and as an only child he also felt a weird jealousy over the intensity of Sayla's relationship with her brother. And that had perversely propelled him to tell her about the interchange. He knew now that he never should have mentioned it. She had tried hard in her own way to apologize after making her impetuous, crazy request about killing Char. She had tried hard to bridge the distance her words had created between them. And he had ignored her efforts. When she had slapped him after he told her what had happened, he had known why.

He rotated a knob on the left ear of his helmet and lowered his sun-visor. He wondered if he were rushing too much, but he was still the last one out of the pilots' room. On the wide-range helmet receiver, he immediately heard the chatter going on between both Kai and Hayato and, mixed in with it, Sayla Mass's voice. Pretty blond Sayla. Her voice was practically inside his head. He tried mouthing the words, *Sayla, I love you!* and was amazed at how beautiful they sounded.

HALF THE ENGINES IN the *Madagascar*—the flagship of Commander Char Aznable's newly formed 300th Autonomous Squadron—had been disabled from damage received in the fight with Amuro Ray's unit. Char had been out in space at the time in his Rick Dom, but it had been his judgment call rather than that of Lt. Commander Bruce Marshall, the captain of the ship, that had saved it from total destruction. As soon as Char had

witnessed the Gundam destroy Kusko Al's Elmeth, he had ordered all survivors in his unit to retreat. With Lt. Challia Bull bravely supporting him,
he had engaged the Gundam Suit once more in order to gain time, and it
had retreated of its own accord, clearly fearing a pincer attack. Then, after
shepherding three surviving but heavily damaged Gattle fighter-bombers to safety, he and Challia had finally returned to the *Madagascar*. The
300th had then withdrawn from the area, using the Corregidor shoals as a
screen. With the Gattle fighter-bombers effectively out of action, its only
remaining viable forces were four surviving Rick Doms.

IN THE PILOTS' ROOM on the *Madagascar*, student recruit Lt. (jg) Leroy Gilliam hung a coffee tube on the holder next to him, turned to Char and
Challia, and choked, "I . . . I can't believe I survived and Cramble died."

"There's a reason you're alive, Leroy," Char said, trying to console
him. "You got two gold stars for sinking two enemy battleships before,
right? And you're young. It's an advantage." Char removed his helmet as
he spoke, and it temporarily muffled his voice.

As an astonished Challia Bull watched, Char also proceeded to
remove the face mask he always wore. He had a far more gentle expression beneath it than Challia had ever imagined. It was odd. Char had
a pessimistic side to him but he also had an ability to think beyond the
immediate present to the future. Most such people Challia had known
had an almost piercing expression, a look of excessive cleverness. It was
true of Gihren and Kycilia Zabi, and it had even been true of Kusko Al.
But Char was different. He radiated youthful energy and had the aura of
a genuinely refined individual. Perhaps, Challia thought, it was from his
upbringing, but that should have been more than canceled out by years
of hardship in the military. Even Leroy was astounded. Char seemed far
too youthful and too dignified at the same time.

As if suddenly aware of the reaction he had created, Char turned and
grinned. "Don't tell me this is the first time I ever took my mask off in
front of you," he said. "If it is, don't let it bother you. I never take this
thing off in public, not even in front of the Supreme Commander. But
there's no point in hiding anything from you men anymore."

Leroy felt a thrill when he heard Char's words. He had long ago
overcome any resistance to having such a young leader, and now he felt
genuine respect and trust. Char had an almost princely quality to him.

He and his comrades had often discussed Newtypes among themselves, and they had unanimously recognized Kusko Al as someone with
Newtype pilot skills, but Char, they often felt, was the more evolved as
a Newtype human. The problem, of course, was that no one had re-

ally defined a true Newtype yet. Was it someone who simply had extra sensory perception? Or was it someone who might help transform the human race? If the latter, as the late Zeon Zum Deikun had seemed to indicate in his speeches, then Kusko Al's paranormal abilities were clearly too predominant and she was not well-rounded enough as a human. The MS pilots had therefore secretly pinned their hopes on Char.

Most people, Leroy knew, were ordinary. And if the true Newtype concept could apply to ordinary people, then Newtype characteristics should also manifest themselves in a very ordinary way. Before joining the 300th Autonomous, he himself had been tested and identified as someone with Newtype powers, but he certainly didn't think of himself as an esper or a paranormal or anything like that. Before the war he had excelled in gymnastics and for the last five years he had worked out just to stay fit. He had also wanted to become a painter, and he was proud of the fact that his artistic ability was above average. He liked to think, in fact, that he had the emotional sensitivity of an artist and the detached, objective makeup of a philosopher. But that was all. Then, when he saw his commander's uncovered face, he believed he finally understood: *Ordinary people* can *be Newtypes*.

Ultimately, his opinion was based on the reaction of one normal person to another. He might have felt differently if Char's hair had been a little less blond or if the scar on his brow had extended more toward the bridge of his nose. But he was a budding artist who secretly idolized Michelangelo, and when he looked at Char, except for a slightly more average, less imposing physique, he noted a resemblance to Michelangelo's statue of David. It was a subjective opinion but one that clinched the issue for him. Char's uncovered face and aura of nobility finally convinced him that he was in the presence of a true Newtype.

THE TINY BRIEFING ROOM on the *Madagascar*, once filled with MS pilots, now held only three. The space seemed enormous, and cold.

"I've ordered the captain to rejoin the *Swamel*," Char commented, referring to Kycilia Zabi's flagship as he sipped from a coffee tube.

"Does that mean we're retreating, sir?" Leroy asked.

"How can we possibly go forward?" Char quickly fired back. "Where would we go, anyway?" He knew Leroy was cursing himself for asking such a dumb question, but he deliberately refrained from being too hard on him. "Listen, Lieutenant," he said with a smile. "I'm all in favor of a better idea if you have one. Let me know if you do, okay?"

"No, sir," Leroy answered. "You're absolutely right. We should link up with Her Excellency Kycilia and then decide what our next move will be. The way we have our forces deployed under Operation Revol I should make it difficult for the Federation to attack us."

"What makes you say that?"

"Because we're pretty evenly matched in terms of local strength, and because Revil seems to be severely underestimating Excellency Dozle Zabi's true power."

"But Revil's the type who'd do a structural analysis of a bridge before crossing it. What makes you think he's underestimating anything?"

"Well, you're right, sir. But he seems too preoccupied with our System project. Obsessed with its being some sort of secret weapon. I think he's rushing to try and destroy *A Baoa Qu* as a result."

"I know you're speculating, Lieutenant, but I still think your logic's a little weak . . . "

"Of course it is, sir. But there's something else to consider. It's true the Federation mobile suit unit has been running all over us, but even if the Gundam model MS were specifically created for a Newtype pilot, and even if it were equipped with something like the Elmeth's psycommu interface, it still wouldn't be enough to tip the balance of power in this war. And that's true on our side, too. Throughout military history, I don't think a single super weapon has ever been enough to end an entire war. I also don't think a single individual with paranormal powers has ever done anything spectacular enough to go down in history before. History isn't decided by solitary individuals anyway, but by a horde of them. So unless one strikes at the core of the problem—"

"The core of the problem, eh? So how does that apply to the Earth Federation?"

"Well, sir. The Jaburo command post on Earth's already an empty shell. It's not even worth trying to annihilate. I'm not even sure the problem's just the Federation."

Char said nothing. He put down his coffee tube, stood up, and stared at the dozen or more intercom monitors on the wall of the room, his back to the other two men. Leroy watched him, then turned and glanced at Challia Bull, whispering, "Think the commander's going to tell us what to do?"

Challia laughed gruffly and said, "Maybe, but don't hold your breath. The situation's too complex to predict an outcome yet. We don't have enough time, and we don't have enough people on our side, either."

Char heard Challia's words behind him, imagined a smug look on the man's face, and felt mild disgust. There was no way Challia could have known unless he were a paranormal freak, but when he had said that he was looking for a better idea, he actually had also been thinking about the earlier interchange between himself and the Gundam pilot and about his sister, Artesia.

He was more sensitive than he had originally thought. In fact, during his last battle with the Gundam, if he hadn't experienced a burst of sensation in the midst of all the killing, his consciousness and that of the Gundam MS pilot would never have linked and their communication would never have been possible. From what the upstart young Gundam pilot had conveyed to him during their confrontation, it was clear that he knew Sayla Mass was really Artesia Som Deikun, a secret only Jimba Ral, who had raised the Deikun children, was supposed to know. And there was only one way the Gundam pilot could have known, and that was if he were close to, or involved with, Artesia. Bitterly, he remembered how the Gundam pilot had destroyed both Lalah Sune and Kusko Al. At least his sister hadn't fallen for a wimp.

He turned and looked at the two men behind him. "You're probably wishing someone like the Gundam pilot was on our side," he said. "But he's not."

"Well, he would have made a nice addition to our team," an unfazed Challia replied. "Assuming he didn't hate the Principality too much."

"No. I don't detect that in him," Char said.

"Do you think maybe he's a real Newtype, sir?" Leroy asked tentatively.

"Probably," Char answered. "At least in the sense that Zeon Zum Deikun once referred to. I think he's probably a harbinger of true Newtypes."

"A *harbinger*," Leroy said, "I like the sound of that word, Commander. The world was changed by the Renaissance of ancient Europe. With Newtypes, maybe mankind's about to experience another renaissance."

"Who knows?" Char replied, coolly. "Words like 'renaissance' or 'enlightenment' are just abstractions coined by historians, aren't they? Who knows what the people of the time really thought? The point is to not get too carried away."

"But, sir," Leroy protested, "the ancient artists and philosophers were surely aware of what they were doing. Think of Dante, da Vinci, and even Raphael."

"Sorry to disappoint you," Char answered curtly, "but I've never even heard of them. And I'm just not certain how evolved we can claim to be ourselves at this point in time."

"I . . . I see," Leroy replied almost wistfully. He had left out Michelangelo's name, but it was probably a good thing. If his superior had said he had never heard of him either, he would have been crushed.

Challia quietly spoke up. "I still think we've touched on something important here. We need to change the status quo. We need to change the whole system of doing things."

One of the wall monitors suddenly flickered to life, showing the captain of the *Madagascar* making a report. Fighting had broken out again in the region through which they were retreating.

Char turned to Challia and Leroy. "Just between you, me, and the stars," he said with a wink, "we will."

VICE ADMIRAL DOZLE ZABI'S assignment suited his character: he was in command of the Principality of Zeon's Mobile Assault Force. Dozle had a personality utterly different from that of his half brother, Supreme Commander Gihren Zabi, and he was often described as both manly and coarse. He had the physique of a born soldier but, as his closest confidants knew, he had a complex about his appearance and feared it was too intimidating. Perhaps in reaction, he was extremely kind and gentle to his wife and children and to his troops. He was famous for always recommending his men to Gihren for promotion, usually with some sympathetic remark about their difficult family situation. Those who knew his true nature were intensely loyal and would follow him anywhere.

Right now, however, the normally calm Dozle was furious. General Revil, leading the Earth Federation armada, appeared to be ignoring *Solomon*, where Dozle and his forces were based.

"I don't know what the man's got up his sleeve," Dozle grumbled, "but he grates on my nerves. He doesn't seem to think we're worthy opponents." Until twelve hours earlier, Dozle had planned to keep most of his ships in close to *Solomon* for its defense. But now because Revil appeared to be concentrating his attack on *A Baoa Qu*, he had decided to take a gamble and move his forces out, even if it left *Solomon* exposed.

Dozle was a true warrior, the kind of man who liked to be where the action was. He had once personally piloted a Zaku MS to the front during the Battle of Loum, ostensibly to "observe" the situation firsthand but actually to engage in combat. His aides had panicked and even sent out three squads of Suits to guard him. Gihren Zabi had laughed when he heard about his younger brother's exploits and reproached him for his foolishness, but Dozle's bravery had only won him greater respect from his men. They were convinced that even if Dozle was an admiral and a Zabi family member, he was with them all the way. They would have followed him into hell.

Dozle had even commissioned the development of a new model mobile suit-like machine for himself. Currently undergoing field and

Dozle Zabi

flight tests, the Big Zam, as it was called, was heavily armored and, because it had legs but no arms, only vaguely humanoid.

If mobile suits often resembled giant infantry soldiers, the Big Zam looked more like a tank. It was many times larger, and with sixteen mega-particle cannons deployed around the periphery of its fuselage, which looked like two soup bowls welded together, it was capable of blasting anything in a 360-degree radius. Because Zeon engineers had succeeded in developing a particle accelerator mechanism of unprecedented compactness, the cannons had virtually no barrels and thus had difficulty covering the area immediately above and below the Big Zam fuselage, but that was more than compensated by the machine's fundamental agility.

Like mobile suits, the Big Zam was not yet perfect. Before most Suits were formally deployed they underwent rigorous prototype and field tests to identify and solve potential problems, but after two years of operation they still needed many improvements. Engineers were desperately trying to make them more compact, give them more power, and find a way to enhance their performance in formation.

The Big Zam, however, was a product of Dozle Zabi's character and the Zeon military organization. Whatever his scientists and engineers came up with, he wanted to try out himself; if something didn't work, he would demand a modification. And in pushing the Big Zam to its technical limits, he and his engineers were following in the tradition established by their brilliant Nazi German counterparts in another age. In totalitarian political systems where nearly everything was decided according to the whim of a leader, individual initiative was often crushed. But under the wing of the military in the same system, science and technology often flourished, even if the individual engineers and scientists involved originally had utterly different agendas and goals. As history had shown, if the possibility of technological progress existed, regardless of its application, few scientists were capable of resisting a summons to work by their political leaders.

In the beginning Principality scientists made excuses for their cooperation with the military, extolling the benefits of spin-offs to the civilian sector and emphasizing that the technologies they were developing were morally neutral and could be used for peaceful purposes as well as for war. But when war actually came, they fervently sought to ensure their nation's victory and gave their all to developing pure weapons of destruction.

Vice Admiral Dozle Zabi took off in his flagship, the *Gandow*, with the Big Zam in tow. His total force, divided into three battle groups, consisted of over one hundred ships. Fortunately for Dozle, the battle group clustered around the *Dolos*-class carrier *Midro*, normally assigned to the defense of *Solomon*, arrived at its staging point late and was therefore able to strike a wing of the Federation armada. In a one-sided battle, fifty combat-seasoned Zakus, accompanied by Jicco attack ships and Gattle fighter-bombers from the *Midro* group, easily annihilated over twenty Federation ships. The Zeon pilots had boasted prior to the battle that the Federation Flying Manta fighter-bombers would be no match for them, and they were proven correct.

Dozle himself had no such luck with the 127th Autonomous. Several hours after leaving the Corregidor shoals, the 127th had linked up with the 203rd and the 165th and, with them, was approaching *A Baoa Qu* from above. Both the 203rd and the 165th each consisted of a battleship and five cruisers, heavy and light, while the 127th included the *Pegasus II* and the *Cyprus*. Dozle's group consisted of the *Gandow*, accompanied by eight heavy and light cruisers, and a guard of thirty Zakus.

Up against thirty Zakus, the Federation group's twenty "Mister Ball" machines and ten GM suits were clearly outclassed. The Balls were an early, rudimentary version of mobile armor and toy-like compared to Zakus. The GMs were mass-produced mobile suits, but they were really an interim model manufactured while the Gundam and Guncannons were still in prototype phase, and hardly of a finalized design. On paper they had specs comparable to Zakus, but in actual performance they were outclassed because Zeon pilots were far more experienced. The Federation group's ace-in-the-hole was Amuro's little unit, consisting of junior grade lieutenants Kria Maja in his GM 325, Hayato Kobayashi in his C109 Guncannon, Kai Shiden in his C108 Guncannon, and Amuro Ray in his G3 Gundam. It was immediately clear that Amuro's unit was more than capable of holding its own against the Zeon force. It had, in fact, begun to demonstrate an astoundingly high level of performance.

"NORMAL SUITS" WERE LIGHTWEIGHT space suits—independently functioning life-support systems, pressurized and temperature-controlled—and no matter how well made they would always be an awkward fit. "Pilot suits" were far easier to wear. They used a high-grade, five-layer woven blend of glass fiber and flexible plastic and were worn close to the skin. They had roughly the same fit as the pressurized suits once worn by fighter pilots on Earth.

To Amuro, even his pilot suit seemed to interfere with his reflexes. He had never thought of himself as being particularly well coordinated, but during training he had demonstrated better than average ability, and in combat his strengths had been mysteriously amplified. And the more he improved, the more the pilot suit seemed to get in his way. It irritated him. He wished he could operate the MS naked. And if only his skin could withstand absolute zero temperatures, and if only he didn't need to breathe, he would have loved to get rid of the MS altogether. Then, he fantasized in a moment of overconfidence, he would easily be able to detect all the alien forces in the battlefield of space before him.

The next instant his left monitor showed a Zaku coming toward him. He put the Gundam into a sharp turn and fired a blast from his beam rifle. It was his third Zaku in the battle. Kai and Hayato, riding in their Guncannons fifty kilometers out on either side, were doing a good job of driving the enemy Suits straight toward him, and Kria, holding the rear in his GM, was giving him the room he needed to fire. His little unit, he proudly realized, had already evolved into a highly effective fighting team.

Then he heard Hayato yell at him again from his port side. Beams of light streaked through the blackness, and through them an enemy Zaku with a squad leader's antenna-like insignia swooped toward him. It was the fourth Zaku.

Amuro fired and scored a hit. He was dazzled for a second by the explosion that followed, and another Zaku took advantage of it to slip into his blind spot. He panicked, pulled his beam rifle trigger too fast, and missed. The Zaku veered sharply to the right, spinning in Kai's direction, but seconds later was enveloped in blasts from the Guncannon's shoulder guns and exploded in a ball of light. Working as a team, Amuro and his three comrades had already bagged seven enemy Zakus, an unprecedented number of continuous kills.

To Amuro's profound embarrassment, his preoccupation with his pilot suit and his overconfidence had allowed a Zaku to blindside him. Worse yet, the Zaku pilot had been a young hotshot and clearly not a seasoned veteran.

Amuro's situation resembled that of the ancient samurai swordsmen he had once read about. When two samurai of relatively equal standing faced off, they were often able to divine a certain logic to each other's moves and adopt an appropriate counterstrategy. But this became exceedingly difficult if one of the warriors was extremely skilled, as a true master rarely revealed any pattern to his opponent. Normally, however, with practice there were ways of dealing with even the most unpredictable opponent. The biggest threat to the expert swordsman was an opponent who had already mentally resigned himself to death and was attacking in a suicidal rage. Then it was usually better to avoid a frontal attack, avoid seeking an immediate kill, and instead work to weaken and isolate the opponent first.

Amuro knew he was no samurai. He was riding in a sixteen-meter-tall Gundam mobile suit. But his situation resembled that of the samurai in that his enemies could conceivably plunge out of the blackness toward him from any direction, at random. He knew that if only he could put his mind into a Zen-like state of nothingness, he would be able to detect the presence of an approaching enemy. His real enemy now was overconfidence, not his pilot suit. It was functioning as designed, protecting his physical body. And whatever irritation he felt was shared by the Zeon pilots.

The moment he finally regained his mental equilibrium, he detected an enemy presence. *This is the gift!* he thought, exulting in his good fortune. *The gift of Newtypes!* He thanked the stars that his powers of insight and intuition seemed to be increasing, for he knew that true victory wouldn't be achieved by merely eliminating a few Zakus in the battle zone. True victory, military theory went, could only be obtained by destroying the enemy fleet flagship—in this case Dozle Zabi's *Gandow*—and Amuro knew it was located somewhere thirty degrees below and to his left.

It was one thing to understand the theory. It was another to try to put it into action and identify the true center of the enemy's strength. He was operating in the real world of space, not the world of fantasy films and holoscopes. Pilots had to visually identify the enemy, but against a background of black space, with its millions of burning stars, visually sighting and identifying an object over one hundred kilometers away was no mean feat. It was especially hard to distinguish between enemy and friendly ships. Harder than in a confused dogfight on Earth. Harder, some old-timers said, than locating a single grain of sand on a long beach.

Amuro nonetheless intuitively detected a force capable of controlling the entire combat zone. *What is it?* he immediately wondered. It was more powerful than anything he had ever encountered, so strong that it flowed through the Gundam's armor as a heavy, insistent, undulating wave. He shifted his Gundam onto a slightly lower vector and turned on his laser oscillator for a few milliseconds, signaling in a burst to his left, right, and rear, trying to tell Kai, Hayato, and Kria to follow him. In a diamond formation separated by twenty kilometers, the four Suits then dropped toward the sun. And along the way they took out two more Zakus and a *Musai*-class Zeon cosmo cruiser.

VICE ADMIRAL DOZLE ZABI donned his pilot suit and strapped himself into the captain's seat in the Big Zam's cockpit. The machine's nuclear fusion engine fired with a pleasing sound.

"What's the delay?!" he demanded of the pilot and copilot seated in front of him. "Let's get those Federation Suits!!"

"There's something odd about them, sir," one pilot replied. "Two or three are streaking toward the *Gandow* right now, just like the Red Comet does!"

"Don't mention Char to me now!" Dozle barked, infuriated, as he donned his helmet. "Red Comet"—Char Aznable's nickname—was the last thing he wanted to hear. He had cashiered Char earlier for failing to protect his younger brother, Garma, in battle. And afterward his sister, Kycilia Zabi, for some weird reason had reinstated him in her unit. Now the mention of Char's nickname only served to remind Dozle of the irritating fact that he had dismissed Char too soon. It felt like a personal criticism.

"Tell the *Gandow* we don't need an escort," Dozle barked. "We'll destroy the entire Federation MS unit with this Big Zam. Cut this machine loose!" Dozle was getting more and more emotional and reacting more and more impetuously.

The *Gandow* released the Big Zam's tow line as commanded. With three rocket nozzles in its underbelly belching flame, the machine leapt into space, accelerating as fast as a heavy cruiser under full power as it climbed to meet the approaching enemy MS unit.

"I don't care if we *are* being attacked by some prissy Newtype unit," an enraged Dozle shouted. "McLaughlin's group and the *Midro* should be smashing through the Federation line from the rear right now. If this Federation unit thinks it can run over us the way they have the others, well, let 'em *try!*"

Dozle had every right to be angry. His *Gandow*-led fleet from *Solomon* represented the cream of the Principality's mobile forces in the area, but in the last twenty minutes a tiny force of enemy Suits had been wreaking havoc with his plans, destroying half the forces thrown at them, cutting a swath like a scythe through a field of grain. Even worse, they were aiming straight for his own flagship, the *Gandow*. The more he thought about it, the more humiliated he felt, for he knew that if it weren't for the unit harassing him now, he could easily be smashing a hole in the entire Federation line.

"I don't believe this Newtype crap for a second," Dozle exclaimed. "Designing humans to function like machines in battle. Hah! Crank up the fear quotient, and at some point even the best human pilot'll pee in his pilot suit!"

"One o'clock, sir!" the Big Zam pilot yelled. "Up eleven degrees!" As Dozle watched, an image flickered two or three times across an upper right monitor and then stabilized. It showed a telephoto view of a light gray mobile suit.

"What happened to the white Suit I've heard so much about?!" Dozle demanded. "Is that it?"

"Yessir!" the Big Zam pilot yelled back, his voice trembling. "Looks like they've tried to camouflage it, sir." He was fast approaching the psychological state his commander had referred to. But he would never notice unless he survived and later checked the urine flask he was hooked up to.

Dozle kept yelling. "It can't possibly have more than one beam-cannon, and that means we've got over ten times more firepower than it does. Get him in our sights! Hurry!"

"*There are* four *enemy Suits!*" the Big Zam pilot screamed. In response, four beam cannon on the Big Zam's prow fired for several milliseconds, and the effect was like a curtain of light, for each cannon could be moved incrementally to create a diffused strafing effect. As they watched, the Federation Suits all swooped as if avoiding the blasts and then reformed again, heading straight for not the *Gandow* but the Big Zam.

"Four Suits?" Dozle shouted in disbelief. He could scarcely believe his eyes. The entire Federation MS unit was now bearing down on *him*! He felt the flesh on his back crawl in cold fear. He could understand how the enemy, out of sheer luck, could evade a beam blast. But he could not understand how, at nearly the same instant, they could have corrected course to attack *him*. He was no fool. He was battle-seasoned enough to know intuitively that this was no ordinary enemy. It was one with a terrifying resolve.

"Put up a barrage of defensive fire!" he commanded, shouting. "Initiate evasive action. Let me operate one of those cannons!" He grabbed the controls of a cannon in front of him, activated its sights, and saw a simulated model of the enemy approaching on the screen; Generated from data provided by laser sensors, at close range the model was fairly accurate. He got the lead enemy Suit in his sights, put his finger on the trigger, and fired three times. And the Suit somehow evaded each blast.

Another chill ran down his spine. With renewed horror, he knew his earlier hunch had been correct. There was no way to explain logically how the enemy could have possibly avoided his carefully aimed shots. For a second he wondered if the computer-generated sights on his display had been skewed, but he knew their electronics were so simple that it was out of the question.

Dozle yelled to no one in particular, "Does this mean they're operating the same way people say Char Aznable does?" In an attempt to evade the attacking Suits and to rise above them, he made the Big Zam accelerate in a full power climb. Six *g*'s forced the men back into their seats, but Dozle nonetheless managed to recheck the cockpit monitors to see how the enemy formation reacted. Again, the images were a simulation, a computer-generated extrapolation of data received from sensors over a ten second period. But they were better than nothing and at least gave an indication of the enemy's relative size and mass and the speed of its approach. "The Suit riding tail in the formation seems a little slower than the others," he mused aloud. Knowing he was rising "above" the enemy somehow made him feel better. In a weightless environment words like "above" and "below" were technically meaningless, but humans still adhered to spatial concepts relative to their own physical position. And in that context, being on "top" of the enemy meant a great deal. Unfortunately for Dozle, however, it was a two-way street.

ON AMURO RAY'S COCKPIT monitors the Big Zam appeared to be climbing up toward him from "below." He knew he couldn't count on his men
hearing him clearly, but he radioed his observations anyway: "*Some sort of
new Suit's coming at us fast! It's not a Zaku! It's not skirted! And it's not an
Elmeth! I've never seen the thing before!*"

Normally, making a radio call would have distracted him momentarily, but this time it didn't. He sensed another three beam blasts directed
at him, evaded them in the nick of time, and continued plunging toward
the enemy machine, restraining his fire until he was in effective range
for his beam rifle. Kai and Hayato, on either side of him, seemed to be
doing the same, but the twin shoulder guns on both of their Guncannons
erupted in flame. Explosions occurred near the enemy machine, indicating a near-miss.

Amuro suddenly knew he had to act fast. For some mysterious reason
the "force" that he had sensed controlling the battle zone no longer
emanated from the nearby Principality battleship, but from the machine
charging straight toward him. He swung his beam rifle scope in front
of him, lined up the sights with the legs of the approaching enemy, and
fired. A band of light leapt from the barrel of his gun.

IN THE COCKPIT OF the Big Zam, Dozle gasped in astonishment. The pilot
and copilot groaned in fear and did the only thing they could think of,
which was to keep the Big Zam steady on course. They knew no Zeon
MS pilot could have sniped at them with such precision on the first shot,
not even the Red Comet.

Dozle screamed. "*Roll this bird over!! Ignite reverse thrusters!!*" The pilot
obeyed, and an intense *g* force bore down on them, riveting them to their
seats and nearly snapping their collarbones. They felt the blood drain
from their heads, but there was no time to become dizzy. A second enemy
blast creased the "prow" of the Big Zam and some of the particles on its
periphery hit home, for along with an odd *whissh* sound that seemed to
emanate outside their helmets, they felt an intense pressure. Instinctively,
out of terror more than anything else, they began madly strafing the
enemy formation.

"Knock those bastards out of the sky!" Dozle yelled, at the same time
saying a silent prayer of thanks for the pressurization in his pilot suit.
He was remarkably fit, but he knew the suit had kept him from losing
consciousness.

THE BEAM BLAST FROM Kria Maja's GM 325 created a burst of light with
an unusually evanescent quality when it hit the enemy machine. Amuro

knew it wasn't a fatal blow, but he was grateful that Kria was on his team and not on the enemy's. "Nice follow-up, Kria!!" he barked into his mike. He was impressed. Kria had waited until Amuro had fired before initiating his own attack, just as he was supposed to. Kria had qualified at the same time as he had, but GMs were a mass-produced Gundam-type of Suit that had only recently been put into active service; he had joined the 127th only after the battle inside *Texas* and therefore had relatively little MS combat experience, but he was learning fast. He could already evaluate a combat situation instantly and, while supporting Amuro's Gundam, calmly carry out his assigned tasks.

The Zeon machine responded with wild beam blasts of greater and greater intensity. Amuro then knew it was time. He altered the Gundam's course vector 150 degrees to one that would take him "under" the enemy machine, all the while keeping his attention on the Zeon battleship in the area approaching from his left. He checked the sights on his beam rifle and fired first one, then five blasts. He saw the flash of a direct hit and exulted in the possibility of having destroyed the weird two-legged machine in front of him. And then he let out a curse: *Damn!*

Kria's GM, which had maneuvered to his left side, suddenly exploded in a ball of light. Amuro couldn't tell if the fire had come from the odd Zeon machine or the battleship; the computer in his Suit merely indicated in bright dispassionate yellow on his upper left monitor that a friendly Suit had been destroyed. Kria's last words, barely audible through the static, were, "*The bastards!*"

Using the light from Kria's explosion, the two Guncannons turned toward the Zeon battleship. Amuro instinctively knew his comrades were telling him to concentrate on the two-legged machine, and he immediately scanned for it. In the light, he soon spotted it again, minus a left leg. Sparks were intermittently flying from the severed stump like blood spurting from a fresh wound, but the main engine still seemed to be intact, and it was closing in on him nearly as fast as a Zaku.

He wasn't sure if he should aim for the engine or what he thought was the cockpit, for he had never seen any mobile armor like it before. And while he deliberated, the machine fired a cannon on its left side. In an instant the Gundam's shield melted, and its left arm was scorched by particles on the beam's periphery. Luckily, he had been able to make his MS leap upward, this time positioning himself above the enemy.

"Your time has come!" he screamed as he fired. A particle beam blasted a hole in the top of the machine, hitting what he thought must be the main engine. The fuselage shook and slowly tilted but did not explode.

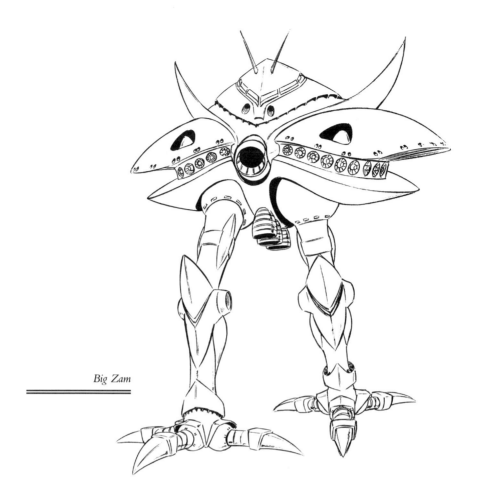

Big Zam

Suddenly he felt uneasy. What had happened? Hadn't his beam blast been powerful enough to pierce the machine? He sighted again, shifting his aim to the area where he assumed the cockpit should be. And then he saw such a bizarre sight that his trigger finger froze in terror. As he watched, paralyzed, a mysterious black mist suddenly roiled forth from the fuselage cockpit without diffusing completely into the vacuum of space. The mist seemed to be reaching out, trying to ensnare him. He instinctively knew he mustn't let it reach him and tried to maneuver the Gundam out of the area but, cursing, discovered that his own coordination seemed to have been affected. Luckily, the Gundam began a smooth retreat anyway.

For a moment he wondered if he were confronting some sort of supernatural apparition. Theoretically, gases were not supposed to be able to retain their shape so well in space. Perhaps, he tried to reassure himself, what he had witnessed had simply been unusual smoke from an explosion in the fuselage. He desperately *wanted* to believe his own theory, but seconds later, when the mist reformed in front of him again, his theory collapsed. For a few seconds he felt as though he were looking at what the old people had called "ghosts." Two eyes seemed to be staring out from the misty black form at the Gundam, at him. Perhaps they were background stars peeping through the mist, but for a second it was real. He shuddered and wondered if he were hallucinating. The eyes seemed filled with hate. What in heaven's name was happening? He was just an MS pilot and this was beyond the scope of his imagination.

The next instant he sensed a rapid sequence of pings, as if bullets from a machine gun or a rifle were striking the Gundam fuselage. Even his headset picked up the noise. He stared at the top of the enemy machine directly below him. It was still belching the strange mist and was so close that he could visually make out what looked like a Normal Suited figure, standing erect on the upper deck, firing away—with a *rifle,* of all things. The bullets were bouncing off the Gundam armor. It was an odd, almost comical scene. The man was tiny in relation to the machines, and there was no way in the world he could destroy a Gundam mobile suit with a rifle. But there he was, slapping in a new magazine and continuing to fire away brazenly.

Then Amuro finally knew. The mysterious force he had been sensing in the area belonged to this figure. Anger began to well up inside him. It was this man, he realized, who had been the source of the frightening black mist he had seen. The man was a fanatic. "These people are the cause of the war!" Amuro raged aloud.

VICE ADMIRAL DOZLE ZABI screamed in protest: "A single mobile suit can't determine an entire battle!" Then, as an image of his wife, Zenna, and infant daughter, Mineva, flashed through his mind, a blast from the Gundam's beam rifle vaporized both him and the Big Zam.

RETREAT

FROM GENERAL REVIL'S PERSPECTIVE, Operation Cembalo was not going well. The Federation armada, with himself and Vice Admiral Karel heading the primary battle groups, was steadily closing in on *A Baoa Qu*. The vanguard, including the 127th, continued to perform well. But several units following the 127th, which were scheduled to assault the top of the umbrella-shaped fortress, had already been roundly trounced. Should the armada lose even one of its remaining main fleets, he would be forced to rethink the entire campaign.

At least the 127th is still proceeding with its attack, he thought. He was worried. Was it really safe to stake so much on such a tiny unit? He believed in the *Pegasus II* and its three Suits, but he had to think about the entire armada. There was still a deep-rooted prejudice in the Forces against Suits, a belief that they were just another fighting machine with a weird humanoid shape.

"We'd better take *A Baoa Qu* quickly," he muttered. He wanted to avoid heavy losses, but the Zeon forces arrayed before him, including Weigelman's men on *A Baoa Qu*, were putting up an impressive defense. He was particularly disturbed by the use of "satellite missiles," or what were in effect huge chunks of asteroid material with old-fashioned recycled chemical rocket engines strapped to them. Like giant boulders hurled over huge distances, satellite missiles were relatively easy to avoid, but they were also cheap to assemble and thus could be used in vast numbers. They were a crude, comic-book approach to weaponry, yet they had already destroyed several state-of-the-art ships in the Earth Federation armada. They were an absolute victory for Zeon in terms of cost/performance.

ON *A BAOA QU*, after the first wave of satellite missiles was launched, the approaching Federation ships seemed to disperse their forces laterally, fanning the defender's fear of being surrounded. Vice Admiral Randolph Weigelman, in charge of the fortress defenses, nonetheless remained calm. "Hit each unit," he commanded. "Remember, they're most vulnerable where overextended!"

IN THE COMMAND CENTER of the Federation flagship *Drog*, General Revil was quick to detect the change in *A Baoa Qu* tactics. "Pull in our forces more," he ordered his officers. "Concentrate on a weak point in their defense and break it." His order was acknowledged and conveyed, but in a typical quirk of warfare it was also misinterpreted. The entire armada, instead of moving forward, began to retreat. Someone had misinterpreted his order to "pull in" as "pull back," and the code *The Cembalo strings are broken* had been transmitted from his flagship to the entire armada. And it meant not *attack* but *retreat*.

Revil secretly raged at whoever had botched his orders, but he was smart enough not to scream publicly in the command center. They were in the midst of a ferocious battle, and he knew what had happened. On displays throughout the command center, remote telescope cameras showed Zeon's space fortress, *A Baoa Qu*, and repeated flashes of missiles being fired. Only an utter idiot would fail to feel terror at the sight. Retreating was the logical thing to do.

Many of the other staff officers were also furious, especially since the enemy had only just been engaged and it was too early to declare a clear victor. But Revil's next order restored their spirits.

"We've no time to lose!" he barked. "Our group will move to destroy the *Solomon* forces in front of the Corregidor shoal zone. Vice Admiral Karel's group will support us."

On the *Pegasus II* Bright Noa felt the blood pound in his brain. "What the hell's going on?" he shouted to no one in particular. "If the others retreat and leave us behind in this area, we'll have the living daylights pounded out of us!" The two other vanguard units, the 203rd and the 165th, had already absorbed considerable damage in the earlier battles. But they were all still plunging straight for *A Baoa Qu.*

Sayla Mass, the comm officer, glanced up at the ship's operator, Ensign Marker Clan, and answered Bright. "There's no mistaking the signal, sir," she said. "It's in alpha gain code and it clearly reads *The Cembalo strings are broken.*"

"The code's correct, skipper," Marker called down from his perch on the bridge crane. "But it seems odd. There's no way to confirm the movements of Revil's group at this point, but the Fotofac squadron has already run into other Zeon forces out of *Solomon.* I can't believe Revil'd abandon them, sir."

"Looks like we're left guessing in the dark about our own armada," Bright grumbled, leaning back into his chair. As he watched from the bridge, he saw an explosion on yet another warship nearby. Two other Federation vessels, apparently from the 203rd, pulled alongside it, trying desperately to rescue the surviving crew. A monitor suspended above him flickered to life, and a man in a Federation captain's uniform appeared on the screen. "*Bright, this is Gror, commander of the 203rd. The 127th is to immediately proceed to support the Fotofac squadron. When we've completed taking in survivors, we'll follow. The strings do not all appear to be 'broken,' yet.*"

"Yessir!" Bright quickly answered with a snappy salute. He turned and looked at Sayla. She had her back to him but she seemed to understand what he wanted, for she immediately announced over the comm system, "C108, return to ship! Return to ship!"

Bright ordered the *Pegasus II* to turn around. Then he jumped out of his seat and barked, "I want the ship immediately inspected for damage and the pressure level rechecked." He looked somehow relieved.

Mirai, manning the ship's helm, took the time out to check its operation and gently scold her skipper while she did so. "I wouldn't relax too much," she said. "Trying to reach *A Baoa Qu* or joining up with the Fotofac squadron—both run the same level of risk."

"What kind of a comment is that, Mirai?" Bright retorted, walking over to her. "Do I look like I'm relaxing?"

"A little, sir. Don't forget, we just lost Kria Maja, one of our best MS pilots, and we only have three others left. It just seems to me we should try and maximize our chance of survival."

"Knock it off, Mirai," Bright angrily whispered in her ear. "You're starting to sound like my mother or my wife . . . "

"Sorry," she apologized, startled by his reaction. She turned and stared silently out the window of the bridge. Behind her, she could hear him angrily ordering the others about. She couldn't help smiling to herself. *You're getting too sensitive, Bright,* she thought.

THE *PEGASUS II* WAS depending more and more on Amuro Ray, Kai Shiden, Hayato Kobayashi, and their mobile suits. Immediately after returning to the ship, the young pilots had to prepare frantically for yet another sortie. While mechamen checked and resupplied their Suits, they changed their sweat-drenched underwear and redressed in the locker room. There was no time to mourn Kria's death.

"You think Kria had an amulet with him?" Kai wondered aloud.

"He always was a little careless about that stuff," Hayato answered. "Maybe he didn't believe in it."

"What about you, Amuro?" Kai asked. "You ever get an amulet from your favorite petty officer?"

Amuro was startled by the question. He had been thinking of Kria. Kria, so long and lanky, with a tinge of green in his eyes. He replied slowly, "Naw." He had never thought of asking her for one.

"Whoa, pardner," Kai said, suddenly looking very serious. "Cut the jokes. You're not trying to tell us you've made it this far without one, are you? If you were a certified Newtype, I wouldn't worry, but, hey, let's be realistic."

Hayato, donning his helmet behind Kai, chimed in. "Yeah. Don't forget, Amuro, we're the ones who'll be leading the final assault on *A Baoa Qu*. This sure as hell isn't the time and place to worry whether amulets work or not."

"Yeah," Kai added. "And don't give us this stuff about only trusting in your own intuition, blah, blah. It won't fly. We *need* you out there, pal. You're our shield, and don't get me wrong when I say it, but we're dead without you. If you weren't along, nobody in the world could get me to go on the next mission."

"Yeah, Amuro. She *must* have given you one," Hayato said mournfully.

"Sorry, guys. It just wasn't like that. I know it's hard to believe."

"'Wasn't like that?'" Kai retorted. "Hey, it's just like Sayla Mass to do something like that, to really screw things up for us in a big way. Tell you what, I'll go ask her myself. I'll be back in a second."

"Kai! Knock it off! We're launching again any minute."

"That's exactly why we've got to hurry. Right?!"

"AMULETS" WERE SNIPPETS OF pubic hair carried by pilots to ward off bad luck. Taken lightly for years, the superstition was now widely believed. To some outside the Forces it seemed a juvenile, even somewhat obscene practice, but to the pilots it had a simple, profound meaning. They were going into battle, and if a woman could give them something symbolizing her desire for them to return alive, it would somehow help the odds. Originally it was thought better to have an amulet from a woman living on Earth, but since Waves were now working and fighting in space, they were also potential donors. In the vast emptiness of the universe, the amulets were a tangible reminder of life. Among the military they were no laughing matter.

KAI SWITCHED ON THE comm link to the bridge, whereupon Sayla Mass appeared on the wall display, looking a little tired. "Requesting permission from the skipper," he demanded in a loud voice, "for Petty Officer Sayla Mass to come to the pilots' briefing room."

Sayla looked startled, but she did as asked and relayed the message to Bright behind her. Amuro, watching her over Kai's shoulder, couldn't help marveling at her beautiful profile.

Bright appeared. "What is it?" he demanded.

"Just do us a favor this once, skipper," Hayato pleaded. "Amuro needs to say good-bye to the Petty Officer."

"And we don't have much time, sir," interjected Kai.

Bright frowned but reluctantly consented. "Understood. But only for ten minutes." As they watched, he tapped Sayla on the shoulder and called for a stand-in for her at the comm console. When the other crewman arrived, Bright turned back to the monitor camera and said, "I don't want you boys to start thinking this is your final mission. Amuro! You there? You hear me, Amuro? You're to come back *alive*—not dead! Without you the *Pegasus II* is a sitting duck."

"Roger, sir," Amuro moved in view of the camera so Bright could see him. Kai, standing beside him, took a page out of the little notebook pilots carried and waved it in front of the comm camera so Bright could see. It had an amulet taped to it.

"Here's the problem, skipper," Kai said into the mike. "This idiot doesn't have one of these!"

"Hmph!" Bright exclaimed with genuine anger. "So Sayla bungled it again, eh?"

Kai quickly shut his notebook. Amuro couldn't resist ribbing him: "Hey, Kai, who'd you get that from, anyway?"

"I wouldn't tell you even if hell froze over," Kai retorted, quickly slipping it into an inner jacket pocket.

What had once seemed an amusing superstition, Amuro realized, was now a deadly serious ritual.

WHEN AMURO WAS FINALLY alone with Sayla in a corner of the briefing room, he tried to broach the subject as casually as possible.

"What?" Sayla said, puzzled. "What's this about an amulet?"

"Kai and Hayato are angry at me, Sayla. They say their lives are at risk unless I get one from you before we take off. They keep bugging me about asking you, so, you know, I thought—"

"But Amuro, I don't have any amulets. The closest thing I have is a locket with a photograph of my dad in it, and I can't give you that."

"No, no. That's not what I mean, Sayla. You know, the type women give to men going off to fight these days. The ones that're real popular."

"Popular?"

Sayla finally understood. Her expression hardened, and she stared directly at Amuro. "Do you mean to tell me you're asking me for *that*, just because Kai and Hayato want you to?! Are you serious?"

"Kai and Hayato are serious. It's not really that big a deal to me, personally."

"Well, tell them *no*, then."

"But Sayla. I, I know how they feel about it . . . "

"Well, I don't. For the life of me, I don't understand how you have the nerve to ask me just because they want you to."

"Well, I'm sorry," Amuro said.

"Why don't you just *pretend* I gave you one," she said, standing up and walking out the door of the room.

Amuro tried to follow her, but she had already grabbed a lift-grip in the passageway and rounded a corner several meters ahead of him. When he turned the corner, he could see her still traveling away from him, her blond hair intermittently highlighted by the emergency lamps lining the dimly lit passageway. It was too bad about the amulet, but he would have to forget it. He just wished they could have spent more time together. He wondered if Waves used amulets and if men normally presented them with one.

When Amuro reached the flight deck, he felt a familiar sensation—the tension before going into battle. The Gundam's left hand, scorched in the fight earlier, was apparently beyond repair.

"Weld the shield on the damn thing if you have to!" he shouted to one of the nearest mechamen. Then he jumped and sailed up to the gangway on the second floor of the flight deck hangar. All the talk about amulets had at least taken some of the tension out of him.

Feeling suddenly hungry, he decided to drop into the mess hall, where he ran into Kai. Hayato was still working on his Suit with the mechamen down on the flight deck. He ordered a hamburger, took a seat, and started to wolf it down.

"Well?" Kai demanded.

"Got 'em, Mack," he said, deliberately trying to imitate an old gangster movie he had once seen. "Three, to be exact. But I can't show 'em to you. I cut a deal with the petty officer."

"Hmph," Kai said, peeved.

"Hey, look, if she thinks you're going to leer over something that private, do you really think she'd hand 'em over that easily? She's got her pride, you know."

"Heh heh heh . . . I know what's going on, Amuro. Basically, you're awfully naive when it comes to this stuff. You're just stuck on the girl, right?"

"What's it to you?"

"Nothing." Kai finished off his tube of coffee and prepared to return to the flight deck. "You've got a healthy attitude. Keep it up, boy scout!"

Out of the corner of his eye, Amuro watched Kai leave. He felt like he had cleared a big hurdle, but he wondered why he had not pushed Sayla harder. He had wanted the amulet. He had wanted it for himself. And yet he had only been able to tell her how Kai and Hayato had been pushing him to get it from her. He wished he had had more confidence. He wished he weren't always so sensitive and self-conscious around her. He wished he were older.

After strapping himself in the seat of the Gundam's cockpit, Amuro communicated with the ship's bridge several times and then finally got a channel all to himself with Sayla. Taking advantage of the opportunity, he quickly said, "I asked you because *I* wanted it, Sayla. *I* needed it."

"*Understood, G3. One minute before launch this line will be turned over to the flight deck controller.*"

She had acknowledged his statement without deviating from her official tone. He suddenly felt relieved, more relieved than he would have felt even if she actually had handed him an amulet. Even if it was all a lie—and he was prepared that it might be—he was overjoyed.

Then the tense voice of Callahan Slay, the flight deck supervisor, echoed in his helmet headphones: "*Junior Grade Lieutenant Amuro Ray, cleared for catapult!*"

"I read you loud and clear, Callahan! Take care of C108 and C109 for me!"

"Roger, sir!"

Amuro heard Hayato and Kai's steady voices echo in his ear: "We're counting on you, G3!" Then his main engine fired, and the *g* force suddenly pushed him upward. Once more the Gundam mobile suit plunged into the star-strewn blackness.

KYCILIA ZABI'S FORCES HAD been granted use of a small section of *A Baoa Qu* for their command center. It was a cramped area, and the room Commander Char Aznable, Lt. Challia Bull, and Lt. (jg) Leroy Gilliam were in—the armory—was no exception. It made Char feel even more irritated. In his drive for self-perfection Char was mature beyond his years, but his occasional inflexibility betrayed his youth. They were waiting for Commander Garcia Dowal of the Flanagan Institute, and he hated having to meet people he didn't particularly like.

Garcia, pallid as ever, rushed into the room with his files in hand. "Sorry to keep you waiting," he blurted, ignoring the salutes from Challia and Leroy, seated behind Char. He then sat in the chair facing Char.

"Please allow me to be frank, Commander," Garcia said to Char, speaking with more courtesy than normal.

Char merely nodded, wondering what in heaven could have made the former clerk so agitated.

"The overall battle seems to be going in our favor," Garcia said. "Revil's mysterious change of course has effectively led most of the armada to retreat into the Corregidor shoal zone. Losses at this point are fairly evenly divided between us and the Federation. *A Baoa Qu* still survives. At one point things were going so well for us that the General Staff thought we might have been able to conclude the entire war. There is one major problem, however." Garcia suddenly stopped talking and glared at Challia and Leroy seated behind Char.

"Don't worry, these are the Newtype candidates your institute recommended," Char said. "They may even know what's going on better than you do. And by the way, you can forget about rank in here."

"Aha. Now I see. Sorry. Well, let me be frank, Commander," Garcia said, repeating his earlier intro. "To tell you the truth, until I heard that His Excellency Dozle Zabi's unit had been annihilated, I didn't really believe you were qualified to lead true Newtypes."

"What's this about Dozle?" Char demanded, suddenly startled. "Did you say 'annihilated'?"

"That's right. Apparently by the white Federation MS. I'm sure you know what's going on. You're in charge of our own elite, experimental Newtype unit, complete with Rick Doms and mobile armor—a unit, I might add, Her Excellency Kycilia thinks of as the centerpiece of her forces. Frankly, when you came back from the last battle with the Federation MS unit, having lost over half your men, I thought you were simply incompetent. But now I know I was wrong."

"What makes you say that?" Char asked, wishing Garcia would hurry up and get to the point.

"His Excellency Dozle was in a new, state-of-the-art type of mobile armor called a Big Zam, but even that didn't help him. And that's not all. Another fleet out of _Solomon_ had the Federation forces in its area on the run. But then two hours later the same Newtype unit arrived and destroyed over forty of its ships."

Char turned and looked at Challia in disbelief.

With a pained expression, Challia remarked, "They're raising their level of performance with every battle. It is possible. With just the Gundam and the two supporting red Suits."

"It still seems too much," Char said, still incredulous. Turning back to Garcia, he asked, "No one's double-checked this information yet, right?"

"Well, true. And we still don't know why General Revil abruptly detoured to the Corregidor shoal zone. But it's even odder that _all_ the ships in Dozle's unit were destroyed and that not a single Zaku survived. Normally in an engagement, even in what we call a 'defeat,' at least one-fourth of the Zakus are able to escape. Frankly, I don't know what's going on or if it's just because of the Gundam and its pilot. But whatever it is, the Federation Newtype unit has become terrifyingly powerful. That's why I have to apologize to you, Commander Char. I doubted you at one point, but you came back alive after encountering the same unit that annihilated everyone else. That means you're one of the few that can actually hold your own against it. Please forgive me."

"Hmm," Char said, ignoring the praise. "I think I get the picture. About Revil and his little 'detour,' though, until this last battle, I doubt if even he knew how powerful his 'Newtype' unit is. But just to change the subject, whatever happened to the request I put in to you?"

"For the extra Zakus?" Garcia said with a wry grin. "Well, I managed to procure five more for you. And we can pull pilots for them out of the second Newtype unit that Kycilia's planning. The order's already gone out, and they should be arriving here in a few hours."

"Good. And right now I really need the leg of my Rick Dom repaired. The Federation Gundam's going to arrive here soon."

"_Here?_"

"Correct. It still hasn't been destroyed, right?"

"True. Or at least we have no information to that effect."

"Then it's on its way," Char said. "And by the way," he added with a grin, "instead of those five Zakus you mentioned, we'd really prefer Rick Doms."

"I . . . I'd be glad to petition Her Excellency for you," Garcia said, gathering all of his notes together. Then, standing up, he announced, "I wish you the best, Commander."

"Don't worry. I'll do my best," Char replied with a smile and a snappy salute.

AFTER GARCIA DEPARTED, LEROY uneasily asked Char, "The Gundam pilot worries me, sir. I've never heard of anyone's performance increasing exponentially in such a short time. You really think it's possible?"

Leroy was expecting an answer, but he didn't get one because both Char and Challia Bull were too busy asking themselves the same question. They knew Garcia's report had to be taken with a grain of salt. Battlefield reports were often inflated thirty to fifty percent. If, for example, five mobile suits destroyed an enemy cruiser without confirming who would take credit for the kill, the reports sometimes listed five, instead of one, enemy ships annihilated. To prevent this problem, both Principality and Federation forces planted still and video cameras with panoramic views in combat zones and used them to record the action whenever possible. But it took hours to confirm later how many ships a specific Suit had bagged. Still, although Garcia's report certainly had had fuzzy areas, the urgent manner in which he had presented it suggested that a serious debacle had occurred. From the perspective of the intelligence experts on *A Baoa Qu*, at least, the Federation's Newtype unit had clearly pulled off an incredible feat.

Lt. Challia Bull was the first to break the silence. "I guess we can't afford to assume it was a onetime freak accomplishment, can we?" he muttered.

Challia stared at the ceiling as he spoke, and his gaze was so intense that Char wondered if he could see straight out into space. All he could see was the ceiling's shiny, spotless gray plastic finish. He turned around in his chair and, with his chin propped on his elbow, asked, "Tell me, Lieutenant, can you see through walls?"

"Are you kidding, sir? I'm not a superman . . . "

"Glad to hear it. It makes me feel better. But what the hell do you think's going on, anyway?"

"I don't know, but Kusko Al said a kid named Amuro Ray was piloting the Gundam, right? I wonder if we can't communicate with him somehow . . . "

"Forget it. Like you said, we're not supermen."

Leroy felt strange, watching his two superiors staring at the ceiling, conducting such a bizarre dialogue. "Seems to me it's important," he ventured, "not to overlook the fact that this same Amuro Ray had enough charisma to charm Kusko Al. And he was younger than her, if I recall."

"She was twenty-two, right?" Char said, suddenly turning to Leroy.

"Yes, sir," he answered reflexively. "And she wasn't always easy to get along with. I don't think she would've fallen for anyone a few years younger unless she was attracted to his innocence and sensitivity. But I'm sure there was something else about him that she found intellectually interesting. And I'll bet it was his Newtype potential. It's just possible that this Amuro Ray character's evolved enough to understand what we're trying to do. Maybe he *would* cooperate with us."

"Well," Char replied, "we can't exactly arrange a powwow with him in the middle of a battlefield, can we? Don't forget, I saw what he did to Lalah Sune in combat. He can also be impulsive, rash. I'd hesitate before I'd put any trust in him."

"All I know about Ensign Lalah Sune is what I read in Commander Garcia Dowal's reports, sir. Maybe she's the one responsible for triggering Amuro Ray's Newtype abilities. After all, as I understand it, she was a real rarity—someone with outstanding, quantifiable Newtype potential."

"Hmph," Char muttered.

"If we locate the Gundam, sir," Leroy said, "I'd be glad to initiate communication."

Char turned around and didn't answer Leroy.

"I'm sure you know, Commander," Challia said, "that we don't need to spend much time in contact with him."

"I know," Char replied stonily.

"It's a little hard for me to say this," Challia continued, "but with all due respect, maybe you've got too much of a grudge against him to appreciate the possibilities. You've already encountered him before. Don't you think he'd answer if you approached him point-blank?"

Leroy was so astounded by Challia's bluntness that he nearly fell out of his chair. He remained silent and waited to see what would happen.

"Sure," Char said. "I admit I don't like him. Ever since Lalah Sune, ever since I first met him, I've had nothing but embarrassing defeats. And you know what happened in our last encounter."

"You think he plays dirty, right?"

"No. I just think he's a little too single-minded," Char answered with a low, self-deprecating laugh. He hadn't told anyone how Amuro Ray, the Gundam pilot, had somehow communicated with him in combat, suddenly bringing up his sister Artesia's name and claiming that he had been asked by her to kill him. The Gundam pilot's effrontery had been bad enough. Even worse had been the thought that his sister might want to resolve her feelings toward him in such a way. It was almost too much to bear, because he also knew that the physical distance between them was gradually shrinking, that she was coming closer and closer. It made him feel profound self-disgust—disgust over the way he had treated her long ago, deserting her when she had needed him most.

"Sorry to have brought that up, Commander," said Challia. "On another tack, there is one variable in the equation that even makes me nervous. We won't know unless we do a thorough check of his combat history, of course, but if this kid's *too* developed as a Newtype, we may not be able to deal with him at all . . . "

"You're referring to what Leroy was suggesting earlier, about his Newtype potential?"

"Right, sir. If, for example, he's so developed he's already become some sort of esper, then he's also probably on his way to becoming a Newtype military freak, a killing machine. We'd be slaughtered, and the only thing left would be Amuro Ray."

"Any way to prevent that?"

"I don't know. But we'd better find out whether he's a real Newtype or a monster in a hurry. If the latter, we'd better do everything in our power to destroy him. We may even have to use some real dirty tricks to do it."

"Dirty tricks? You mean something like using Artesia?" Char had uttered his sister's name, but not specifically for Challia Bull. Challia ignored it, and Leroy was left to wonder if "Artesia" were some sort of spy. The atmosphere was too strained for him to want to pursue the matter. When it was important for him to know more about this mystery woman, he was sure the others would tell him.

LIGHTS FLARED THREE OR four hundred kilometers ahead of the *L-3* like fireworks on a distant shore, indicating the destruction of more Zeon and Federation ships. A *Columbus*-type transport, the *L-3* was built with a skeletal structure, and designed to carry containers; its only defenses were six missile tubes gracing its prow, stern, top, bottom, and sides. After carefully wending its way through debris in the Corregidor shoal zone, it finally made visual contact with *Pegasus II*.

IT USED TO BE commonly assumed that gravity-free conditions existed uniformly throughout the open areas of space, but around Earth there is actually a constant interplay between the gravitational forces of the Sun, the Earth, and its moon. With the Earth revolving around the Sun, and the moon revolving around both, there are in fact points in space where the gravity of all three neutralize each other, the most dramatic being Lagrange points—where the Earth Federation built its groups of space colonies called Sides. And just as there are regional differences in tides on Earth, in space, in addition to Lagrange points, there are also other, smaller gravity-neutral areas, many of which are poorly defined and difficult to measure. In the Space Age, a great deal of debris—mainly landfill—from decades of colony construction had collected in them, creating what were called shoal zones. Occasionally old satellites were even found in them, relics from the early days of space exploration.

ON THE BRIDGE OF the *L-3*, Lt. (jg) Matilda Ajan watched as the oddly shaped *Pegasus II* came into view. Then she grabbed the ship phone and announced, "*Prepare to unload the Number 14 starboard container block immediately!*" She began thinking of Amuro Ray, the young pilot whom she had last run into on the Federation's *LH* moon base. She knew he was attached to the *Pegasus II*. He had always seemed incurably naive and romantic, but she felt indebted to him.

Her fiancee, Lt. Woody Malden, was a straightlaced military engineer with whom she had fallen in love at first sight, but she had a contrary streak in her that never allowed her to admit it. Just when she had been frantically trying to figure out a way to get him to propose to her, Amuro had happened to be around, and luckier yet, Woody had noticed him. After she had mentioned Amuro's name in an offhanded way several times, Woody—the stalwart, reserved Woody—had become visibly jealous. Eventually, he had gotten the message and asked her to spend the rest of her life with him.

"*You mean you want me to be your wife?*" she had asked.

"*Damn straight!*" he had replied.

When the current campaign was over, Matilda planned to have a real wedding, and she hoped Amuro Ray would come. "I wonder how he's doing?" she whispered to herself, only to be overheard by the young skipper of the *L-3*, standing behind her.

"You say something?" he grumbled.

"I was just wondering if we were going to tie up alongside the *Pegasus II*, that's all."

"Now how the hell do you think we'd have time to do that?" the skipper said, irritated. "If we had time to socialize, we sure as hell wouldn't do it here. This is the Corregidor shoal zone, for godssake, and we could be hit by floating debris any moment!"

"Yessir! Yessir!" Matilda replied with a slightly sarcastic smile. She carefully watched as containers from the *L-3*'s cargo bays were ejected from the ship and floated into the *Pegasus*'s open stern hatch. Then she turned and looked at the skipper again. He was in the process of communicating with the *Pegasus*.

"You mind?" she asked.

He slammed a magnetized file he had been holding down on the metal console panel in front of him and made an odd motion with his chin. She knew it indicated "no," and took the bridge mike in hand.

"Junior Grade Lieutenant Matilda Ajan of the 28th Supply Division, wishing to leave a message for Junior Grade Lieutenant Amuro Ray of the *Pegasus II*."

Behind her, the *L-3* skipper muttered something about private communications being punishable under ship's regulations, but she ignored him. On a monitor before her she could see a pleasant-looking Wave from the *Pegasus* busily preparing to record her message.

"Tell him," she said, "that I'm getting married when this campaign's over and that he's invited to the wedding."

"Did you say '*wedding*'?" the blond comm tech on the *Pegasus* asked reflexively. "Wedding" was such an unexpected word, given the environment they were in, that it didn't register at first.

"Yes. Give him my greetings. And wish him good hunting!"

"*Understood! Consider it done!*"

Matilda smiled when she heard the chipper reply. She had encountered the petty officer twice before but didn't remember her name or much about her. She knew intuitively, however, that Amuro Ray probably had fond thoughts for her.

"Hey," the *L-3* skipper behind her yelled. "No private chitchat, remember!?" He angrily grabbed her shoulder and tried to turn her in his direction, but she was faster than he was and brushed off his hand. Her cheeks were flushed with indignation.

"The *Pegasus II* is directly under General Revil's command, and Amuro Ray is the key pilot on the warship!" she admonished him. "I frankly consider it my duty to establish friendly communications with him!" It wasn't a very logical response, but she said it with enough emotion to throw the skipper off, and for the moment her performance had won out. On the monitor, the *Pegasus*'s blond comm tech chuckled, and then the screen went blank. The *L-3* skipper, humiliated on both sides by two attractive women, just sulked.

"Don't worry, Captain," Matilda said, tapping his arm as if to console him, "you look great." She then walked over to the other side of the bridge.

He stared at her shapely back and for a second almost forgot about being angry. Then he shouted, "Rules aren't created just to be broken, you know!"

"I'll remember that," Matilda replied softly.

ON THE *PEGASUS II*, the pilots and core crew—those with the most Newtype potential—spontaneously gathered together in the briefing room for a brainstorming session led by Bright Noa. Lt. (jg) Sleggar Law, true to form, barged in on them, joking, "Maybe you guys are all just hallucinating, again."

"Sleggar," Bright said, sounding very much like the ship's captain, "if you're just here to make trouble, you'd better leave."

"I don't know what Amuro saw out there," Kai was saying, "but when we contacted Dozle's fleet I really felt the presence of something powerful. How 'bout you, Hayato?"

"I'll say," Hayato immediately responded. "I'm not sure it was really from the mobile armor Amuro told us to aim at. But whatever it was, the closer we got, the more powerful it felt and the more I knew we had to destroy it. Kai and I never actually established visual contact because we had to train our sights on the *Gandow* flagship and cover for Amuro. But I don't think that contradicts what Amuro says about a 'specter-like' force out there. It's just that I was in a combat zone right behind Dozle's unit, and I didn't sense anything *that* powerful. I'm sure it could exist, though."

"I felt something," Mirai said, then turning to Sayla and adding, "you did, too, didn't you?"

"Yes," Sayla answered, choosing her words carefully. "I think I know what Kai's talking about. There are 'forces' out there that are concentrated, and those that are not. And I can understand how Amuro would have sensed them in Dozle's unit."

Bright turned to Amuro. "Maybe this requires a leap of the imagination," he said, "but do you suppose Dozle Zabi himself—Dozle, the individual—could have been the source of what you saw?"

"But sir," Amuro protested, "do you really think a commander—a vice admiral—in the Principality of Zeon would expose himself at the front in mobile armor?"

"From everything we know about Dozle Zabi, Amuro, it sounds exactly like the sort of thing he'd do."

"He's one of the top Zabi family leaders, right?" Amuro said, clasping his hands together on the desktop in front of him and laughing in bewilderment. "You mean to say that maybe the apparition, or whatever it was that I saw, was generated by some sort of weird Zabi psychospasm of rage and frustration? Sounds a little too far-fetched to me."

No one in the room responded.

In a typically boorish attempt to grab Sayla's attention, Sleggar Law leaned over her and grumbled, "Hey, you really believe all this stuff?"

"It could all be real," Sayla answered, trying to signal for help from Kai by raising her voice, "if not, I'm sure Kai *would do something about it.*"

Kai came to her defense immediately. "Knock it off, Sleggar. Amuro's already proposed having a party tonight."

"A what?"

"A party," Amuro interjected. "It's a way for me to repay my fellow pilots for something."

Sleggar glanced at Amuro and Sayla. Sayla met his gaze for a second and then smiled as if to confirm what Amuro had just said.

"Hey, hey, sweet Sayla," Sleggar persisted, in his typically crude fashion. "Did you really let the kid do that to you? Where's that leave me? Baby! Tell me it's not true!"

"Sleggar! Kai! Amuro!" Bright finally yelled. "Cut the yapping. We've got important things to discuss. The *Pegasus II* may take independent action soon, so what we decide here now may have life-and-death significance for us later. Time's not on our side, guys, so can the jokes."

"'Jokes?'" Sleggar said. "Whoa . . . that's below the belt. We're not joking here, skipper . . . "

Amuro and Kai looked at each other. Both of them had noted Bright's words with alarm. Amuro shot a questioning expression in Mirai's direction. She understood what it meant, gently tapped Bright's hand and asked, "'Scuse me, sir, but what are you talking about? What do you mean by 'independent action?' Did you get new instructions from General Revil?"

"No," Bright said, as if surprised she had asked. "Not at all. I was just speculating. It just sort of suddenly occurred to me, that's all."

"Really?" said Sleggar. "It didn't sound that way . . . "

"Hey, Sleggar," Kai added in a clipped tone. "He can say anything he wants to here. This is a brainstorming session, right? And it may be our last . . . "

Sleggar adjusted the collar of his uniform and turned toward Bright. "Sorry, skipper. Speculate all you want."

"Well," Bright continued, "considering how much we've already accomplished on the *Pegasus II* this far, I'm beginning to wonder what our true potential is. It's just a fantasy, but I've been thinking maybe we could even take on Supreme Commander Gihren Zabi ourselves, without the rest of the armada. And do it soon. Like tomorrow, or the day after . . . "

Amuro let out a low whistle.

Mirai, shocked, nonetheless managed to quip, "I never knew you had such a vivid imagination, skipper. I'm going to have to rethink my whole impression of you."

"I know it sounds crazy," Bright added with a sheepish grin. "As I said, I'm just speculating. I guess I'm trying to make two points. First, if it's true that Amuro's Newtype abilities actually allowed him to detect a specter-like 'malevolent force' emanating from Dozle Zabi, then we seriously have to rethink the root cause of the entire conflict. If specific individuals are responsible for its continuation, then Gihren Zabi's a logical candidate, and if so, maybe our main mission should be to eliminate him. Second, I think the current Earth Federation's position—that *A Baoa Qu* is Zeon's final line of defense—is a little naive. I don't know about you guys, but it's even occurred to me that maybe Zeon's *deliberately* letting us get this close. If nothing else, the confusion among our own forces has given them valuable breathing room. And frankly, I'm worried that the rumors we've heard are true—that they've prepared some sort of ultimate, secret weapon. What do you all think?"

It took Amuro to express the sentiments of the others: "So *that's* why you're in a hurry," he said in a near whisper.

Bright knew that during peacetime it usually took the collective will of the people to transform a system of government. But the *Pegasus* was at war, and in war a successful localized military action could fundamentally alter the balance of power, even topple the existing order. The Earth Federation Forces had been able to resist Gihren Zabi thus far simply because of their material superiority, but if they were really only a lumbering aggregate of individuals with no overarching philosophy, no basic values and no vision, as many complained, then all Gihren Zabi would need to achieve his dreams would be a single dramatic victory. It was entirely possible that, as Bright had tried to imply, they were already ensnared by his consciousness. In fact, Bright had wanted to say it—that it *was* all a matter of consciousness. He started to speak again, hesitated for a second, and to his surprise Amuro spoke for him.

"We've enjoyed General Revil's support," Amuro said. "But never that of the entire Earth Federation. And without it we'll lose the war.

But if Gihren Zabi is the main force behind this war, and if he really does have such a powerful presence, we'd be able to detect it even easier than we did with Dozle."

"A *malevolent* force," Kai added, only half joking. "We're dealing with a monster . . ."

"And what the skipper's saying isn't all speculation," Mirai chimed in.

"Exactly," Amuro answered. "If we have the ability to detect such a force, I say we should go ahead and capture Gihren Zabi. If it'd end the war, I think maybe we should do it." The word "maybe" betrayed the doubt behind his otherwise-confident expression.

"Think we could persuade General Revil to help?" Sleggar asked, as it slowly dawned on him what his mysterious crewmates were really suggesting. "And if we could, you seriously think there's a snowball's chance in hell of us partying over to the *Drog* today and having the brass that surround Revil actually let us see him? Let's be realistic, guys. We've got the most powerful warship in the entire Earth Federation Forces. If they think we've got enough time to screw around with ideas like this, the first thing they'd tell us to do'd be to destroy *A Baoa Qu.*"

Sleggar was right, but Amuro's next observation startled everyone even more. "Actually, something else that worries me even more that," he said. "Say, for the sake of argument, we did as the skipper's thinking, and *did* succeed in deposing Gihren and ending the war? What would happen then? Well, for starters, we'd probably be punished for violating military discipline. But an even bigger problem is that the Earth Federation's General Staff Headquarters—Jaburo—would still be around. That's an idea I don't like."

"You mean it might take ten or twenty years to get promoted in the military," Bright said with a wink, "and eventually be given high-ranking government positions?"

"No," Amuro said with an unexpectedly serious look on his face. "I think you can assume that whatever happens to us might not be that positive."

"Why?"

Amuro turned and looked at everyone in the room. "Don't get me wrong," he said. "It's not that I don't believe in democracy. It's just that using simple majority rule to decide everything makes me a little nervous, especially because in the Federation government the final decisions really represent a consensus of the interests of the politicians themselves. I can imagine a scenario where we succeed in destroying Gihren, only to have people start asking, 'Why? Why, out of all the Federation Forces, was the *Pegasus II* able to do it?' The answer, of course, would be that we're Newtypes. A bunch of paranormal espers. A bunch of professional killers. They'd even start to question whether Newtypes and normal people can coexist. They'd say we'd dominate normal people and threaten everything they value. Just think of the possibilities. Everybody fibs once in a while in the real world, but they'd say that Newtypes can see right through normal people, read their thoughts like a book. They'd say that we're a supernatural phenomenon, that we're not humans in the normal sense of the word, that we're freaks who should be banished from normal human society. What are we going to do if people start talking this way? Forget about being promoted. Hell, we should worry about *surviving.*"

"Not the most eloquent speech I've ever heard," Kai muttered, nodding and looking at the others. "But not bad. I think Amuro's right."

Sleggar, always trying to look as informed as possible, turned in his seat and asked Sayla, "Listen, you know Zeon Zum Deikun, the guy who first talked about Newtypes and founded the republic that became the Principality of Zeon? Wasn't he murdered by the Zabi family?"

"Zeon Deikun?" Sayla replied cautiously. "I don't know about that, but I do know he was a good man. And he wasn't talking about the kind of Newtypes Amuro's been referring to. He was talking about an enlightenment that *all* mankind would experience. But I can see Amuro's point about society possibly wanting to purge itself of Newtypes."

"Amuro's right," Bright added. "The Earth Federation needs us as long as there's a war on, but who knows what'll happen when the war's over? The average person may usually know what's right and wrong, but usually he also winds up going along with what his government says."

"Let's not deal in generalizations," Mirai said suddenly. "Don't forget we may be forced to make some decisions on our own real soon. We'd better have a clear idea what we're going to do then."

"Well, we could always fight just hard enough to stay alive," Kai interjected.

"No," Bright answered firmly. "If we did that, we'd probably be targeted by some final weapon Zeon's developing, and that'd be the end of us."

"How do you know that, Skipper?" Amuro asked.

"I *don't* know," Bright shot back. "I'm just hazarding a guess, based on some highly circumstantial evidence."

There had to be more to it than that, Amuro thought. He suddenly realized that Bright's own intuition and awareness were increasing. It all made sense. "You were right," he said. "We *should* get rid of Gihren Zabi."

"How?"

Amuro grinned and said, "Well, we obviously can't pull off a frontal assault, but maybe there's someone close to him who would cooperate with us, say, be a coconspirator. That would help." He really had no idea what he was trying to say. He was just fantasizing, letting his mind go, and relying on his own intuition.

"Coconspirator?"

"Right. I'm thinking along the same lines as you, skipper. Someone, for example, like Char Aznable, the Red Comet."

"You mean initiate contact with their Newtypes? But Char was under Dozle Zabi's command."

"That's why I say, sir, maybe the whole thing's a fantasy."

"I think we'd better take a break from this discussion," Bright finally announced. "We'll be staying at level three battle stations until we get further operational orders."

As the group dispersed, it was Sleggar, of all people, who summed up things with unexpected brilliance: "Hmph. Maybe I'm a little slow compared to the rest of you Newtype candidates, but I fail to see how anyone here could be a freak. Seems like the ultimate criterion for a normal human is to be able to fall in love, and that's already happened."

AMURO SLIPPED OFF THE lift-grip, and looked back at the ship's passageway he had just traversed. At the other end, under one of the emergency combat lights, he could see Sayla standing and talking with Mirai. He felt awkward because he hadn't invited her to join him in his room.

A gulf had existed between them ever since she had made her crazy statement about killing her brother, but he still wanted her. He was a male with normal desires, and his nerves were frayed from combat. He thought about inviting her. He thought of how nice it would be to spend even ten minutes alone with her and feel her touch, and he wondered if she felt the same way, if she missed him, too. He felt a pang of guilt at his thoughts, at his desire to wait for her, after all. But he was unable to turn and walk away.

Only a few minutes earlier he had been having philosophical discussions about Newtypes. Now he was hoping for some physical attention from a woman. The contrast made him wonder how anyone in a normal human body could really become a true Newtype. Standing and waiting for Sayla, he felt like an utter fool.

He waited for a minute and it seemed like an eternity. He suddenly resolved to forget her for the time being. He loosened the collar of his pilot suit, turned around, and started to head for his quarters.

To his astonishment, Sayla skipped off the floor and grabbed onto a lift-grip running down the passageway toward him. From his perspective, she was flying through the air. She was headed in his direction, coming toward him. In his rational mind he hesitated, fearing he was expecting too much, but then he saw her float away from the lift-grip right at him, her blond hair shining so beautifully in the light. He wondered if other men felt the way he felt now and suspected they would have been more cool, confident, and detached.

Sayla floated up to him and stopped with her soft breasts against his chest. "Well, what happened, Mister Amuro Ray?"

"I. . . . I was afraid you wouldn't come . . . that's all . . . "

"You didn't ask me, so I thought I'd probably better not come. But Mirai said I should. And there's something I wanted to tell you, anyway."

Amuro was no longer listening. He put his lips over hers. He knew from her response that she wanted him to touch her, that he could feel free to be with her. And he felt happy.

"Amuro," Sayla said, playfully turning her head and pulling away from his embrace. "You're violating military regulations, you know."

With the wonderful sensation of her kiss lingering in his mind, he opened the door to his quarters, entered, and turned on the light. "By the way, you took that message from Lieutenant Matilda Ajan, right? Do I really have to attend her wedding ceremony?" he asked.

"Well, maybe she likes you, Amuro," Sayla said with a giggle. "She probably thinks you're cute."

"Cute" was the last word he wanted to hear. He had never really expected anything of Matilda. She was an awfully attractive Wave, and he had always enjoyed seeing her. To her, however, he had just been another earnest pilot cadet.

"She said she's having a military wedding, Amuro. And I'm sure she just wants to invite a few people who've been nice to her. I'm sure she has lots of friends outside her immediate coworkers."

"No need to reassure me. Either way, I won't have to decide whether to go or not until this campaign's over."

"But that's just it, Amuro. For a woman, a wedding's important. It's like an affirmation of life. Course, I don't really go along with that stuff myself. Matilda's a little too feminine for me." Sayla put her hair up, stood up, and crossed the room toward the shower. It was a joy just to watch her move, Amuro concluded; she looked fantastic even in a khaki military-issue bath towel. But he also knew they would never have enough time together, for the war was still on.

He began to ponder some of the things said at the meeting earlier. He was irritated by his own fickleness. It seemed that as soon as one problem was solved, he immediately started thinking of another. He was just glad that he hadn't raised the issue of Char again, or Sayla would have thought that was the only reason he had invited her to join him. It would be better to interact with her on only one level now, and that was physical.

When Sayla came out of the shower she gave him a quizzical look, but he didn't respond, and entered the shower room himself. In order to compensate for the weightless environment, showers on board ship used pressurized steam blasted from all angles. To prevent drowning there was a barrier in the shower that isolated the head and kept it dry. He rested his head on a chin rest, and resolved to discuss the matter of Char with Sayla later, after all.

When he emerged, to his surprise he found she wanted to talk about her brother. She had come to Amuro's room partly because she, too, had been unable to stop thinking about what Bright had said and partly, since Amuro had brought up Char's name, because she felt the need to resolve the issue between them.

"Casval always said he was going to avenge Father's death," she began. "But that was seven or eight years ago, before we parted. We were both still kids then. I received a few letters from him after he entered Military Academy on Zeon—not the usual video cards but old-fashioned typed letters. He never wrote anything beyond the usual pleasantries, but I got the sense he was maturing, and that he wasn't just in the academy to carry out his crazy plan for revenge. I really felt he was growing wiser and wiser. And you know what? He told me one of his classmates was Garma Zabi, the youngest son of 'Sovereign' Degwin Zabi. He said they were really good friends. Can you believe that?"

"You know what, Sayla? Garma Zabi was piloting the Gaw bomber we ran into after leaving Side 7 and your brother was probably in the same area. I wonder what it all means?"

"I don't know. I didn't have the same awareness of him then that I do now. The official combat reports I read were all so rough, it was impossible to really tell anything from them. What do you think?"

"Seems to me, if I recall rightly, that he didn't defend the Gaw bomber. I'm sure it wasn't intentional. I think he just wasn't in a position to do anything about it."

"Maybe some people in the Principality think he's responsible for the death of a Zabi family member, but I don't think my brother's that careless."

"Let's hope not. But tell me, Sayla, getting back to the discussion we all had earlier, how do you think we could contact your brother? That's our main problem. The second problem is deciding whether or not he's actually approachable."

"I don't think my brother's basically changed much, Amuro. But you know, there's something else I've never told you about him. Remember the *Texas* colony? Actually, I met my brother there before it blew . . . "

"You *what*?!" Amuro practically gasped. Sayla had her face turned to the side and was staring into space, as if embarrassed.

"I . . . I'm sorry," she said.

"'Sorry?!' You don't need to feel sorry, Sayla. I don't care if you met him. I just want to know *how*, in heaven's name, you managed to meet him. There was a pitched battle going on inside the colony!"

Sayla shrugged. "I felt as if Casval were calling me," she said. "But you know what? When we actually came face to face, he seemed just like the brother I remembered. He had never even sent me a photograph of him all those years, but I recognized him right away. He warned me not to get involved in the war. I could get emotional about it, but he was my *brother*. Tough, and gentle at the same time."

Sayla's information was extremely important to Amuro, for it gave him a new insight into Char Aznable's character. If both Char and Sayla had the same Newtype attributes, then perhaps Char's feelings toward his own sister could be exploited. It was a dangerous, naive idea, but everything he had heard about Char so far seemed to confirm his rapidly forming opinions.

Both Amuro and Sayla were being sentimental. But it made both of them happy.

A STIRRING

LOOKING AT CROWLEY HAMON made Kycilia Zabi wish she hadn't been born with such a long face and beady eyes. Crowley was two or three years older than she was but looked considerably younger. She wore her hair up, with the beautiful nape of her neck exposed, and exuded femininity.

"Well?" Kycilia icily asked. "Where have I met *you*?" She couldn't quite place the woman but knew she'd seen her before somewhere.

"I went to a couple of the Supreme Commander's parties a long time ago, Excellency. Perhaps we met then."

And you were probably one of the party girls Gihren loved to invite, Kycilia thought. The letter in front of her from Prime Minister Darcia Bakharov formally introduced Crowley, but something about it bothered her. Why was such a person being presented this way, by the Prime Minister?

"You were a friend of Gihren?" she asked.

"It was many years ago, Excellency."

"Does Darcia know this?"

"Yes."

Crowley Hamon then proceeded to claim that her past was a major reason Darcia had given her the assignment. "When the war's over," she said in a hushed voice, "I plan to marry Lieutenant Ramba Ral of

378

the Secret Service. I'm sure you know, but he's the eldest son of Jimba Ral."

"Aha. I see." The woman had a complex background, and it irritated Kycilia that she had neither the time nor the means to investigate it further. "Tell me, Miss Crowley," she asked, "if you're responsible for obtaining the information presented in this letter, shall I assume you're also the one who sold it to Darcia? Do you have a grudge against my brother Gihren?"

"Forgive me, Excellency, but that's a question I'd rather not answer. I wish I could say no."

"Well, that certainly makes it hard for me to trust you, doesn't it?" Kycilia picked up the letter from her desk and walked over toward the giant aquarium in her office. The red sword tails, as usual, were swimming around and around in a school, their scales flashing in the light. The fact that Darcia's letter hadn't come through official channels was definitely odd, but it also made her suspect it was genuine.

After the Federation armada had mysteriously shifted its offensive away from *A Baoa Qu* to the Corregidor shoal zone, several regular transports from the Principality had arrived at the fortress, and Crowley Hamon had been aboard one. She carried false identity papers listing herself as one of Kycilia's household servants and brought several trunks of Kycilia's personal effects, trunks that had been hand-packed by one of Kycilia's senior domestics. Unknown even to Crowley, her elaborate cover had been arranged not only by Prime Minister Darcia Bakharov but by none other than Sovereign Degwin Zabi himself. She had been dispatched as a special emissary, but without Degwin's help she never would have made it past Gihren Zabi's Secret Service agents.

Kycilia's natural suspicions were aroused by the mysterious machinations behind Crowley's mission. That Darcia had tried so hard to protect her suggested that his own position had been compromised. He had written the letter on special paper that would dissolve immediately in stomach acid and hidden it in Crowley's belt buckle. If Crowley had been caught by one of Gihren's operatives, all she would have had to do was to swallow the letter.

The letter appeared to be entirely in Darcia's handwriting and even concluded with his signature. But its contents were so horrifying that Kycilia immediately wished she could double-check its authenticity with computer analysis. It was too bad the equipment for that was under the control of the commander of *A Baoa Qu*, Vice Admiral Randolph Weigelman, a fanatical supporter of Gihren.

The letter contained a warning. The Earth Federation armada would soon reach *A Baoa Qu*, Darcia wrote, and when it did, Gihren Zabi planned to activate the System strategy, probably targeting *A Baoa Qu* itself. That meant, Kycilia realized, that Gihren not only was willing to sacrifice his own troops and one of his most faithful admirals, but that he wanted to eliminate her as well.

"Tell me, Crowley," she asked, "do you think Darcia's fully aware of the implications of this information? And, equally important, is Lieutenant Ramba Ral informed of your assignment?" Then she remembered something about Crowley Hamon. Several years ago, she recalled, Crowley had been one of several women with whom Gihren had consorted.

"Two days after I first reported to the Prime Minister," Crowley answered, "he summoned me and ordered me to convey this information to Your Excellency at all costs. I was also ordered to explain the circumstances in which the information was obtained. The Prime Minister told me I was the most qualified person for this assignment. As for your question about Lieutenant Ramba Ral, no, I don't see him every day, and he doesn't know what I'm doing here today."

Crowley continued talking, and Kycilia learned that because the authorities were rushing to perform a final check on the System project, security was being heavily enforced; that the Secret Service was inspecting every military ship leaving the Principality and all troops involved in the System project had been prohibited from leaving their stations. Ramba Ral had apparently complained to Crowley that he was too overwhelmed with work to move freely, and that he also had to look extra busy simply to maintain Gihren's trust. Kycilia made a mental note of this final comment, and concluded that Ramba Ral was unusually insecure in his relationship with Gihren.

"Didn't you say just a minute ago that Ramba Ral was the son of Jimba Ral?"

"Yes, Excellency."

"And Jimba Ral, as I recall, was one of the central figures in the old Deikun faction."

"That's correct, Excellency. Ramba never told me the whole story, but he did mention he had recently obtained information on the whereabouts of Casval and Artesia Deikun."

"Casval and Artesia? You mean he uncovered information on Zeon Zum Deikun's two children, who were reported to have been taken from the Principality by Jimba Ral? So the rumor was true?"

Crowley said nothing, and Kycilia didn't waste time pursuing the matter. She was sure Crowley herself didn't have the answer. The strange thing was that Gihren would let any man near him who confided in his girlfriend so easily; Gihren was fanatical about secrecy, but from what Crowley had said, Ramba Ral obviously blabbed far too much. What, she wondered, could a lieutenant in the Secret Service—and a man Gihren certainly knew was the son of Jimba Ral—be thinking? What could his real motivation be?

The names of Casval and Artesia Deikun brought back strong memories for Kycilia. In the old days, when Zeon Zum Deikun and her father, Degwin Zabi, had struggled to establish the Republic of Zeon, she had often played with the two young Deikun children. They both had looked like they had stepped out of an illustrated children's storybook—lovable, fair-haired, perfect infants—and she had been extremely fond of both of them. She practically blushed at the memory, but around the time she had reached puberty, she had secretly fantasized of one day meeting a fair-haired man and having children like Casval and Artesia.

"Thanks for the information," she said. "You're dismissed for now, Crowley." There were gaps in what Crowley had said, but she knew they could be filled in later. And even if Zeon Deikun's two orphaned children were still alive, it was inconceivable that they could have any effect on her current situation.

The instant Crowley Hamon's purple suit disappeared behind her office door, Kycilia suddenly thought of something. Perhaps Ramba Ral felt nervous about his relationship with Gihren precisely because of the information about the Deikun children. Perhaps they could affect what was going on.

She stared at her office door and suddenly realized young Casval's presence was much stronger in her subconscious than she had believed. She could almost imagine him walking through the door in front of her. *Perhaps,* she mused, *it has something to do with my having taken Char Aznable under my wing.*

Then, in a revelation, she made the connection. *Could Char Aznable actually be Casval Deikun?* The thought was so shocking that she bit down hard on her lower lip. But the next instant she smiled, and a warm feeling welled up inside her. *If so, what a fine man little Casval has grown up to be.* She felt an almost maternal instinct. Char sometimes became involved with the women around him, but he always did it with tact and lived honestly, devoting his entire being to his work and his profession. He was, in fact, one of her favorite young men. If he was actually the little Casval she had once known, she couldn't think of any reason not to rejoice at the thought.

She turned her gaze to the red sword tails swimming clockwise in her aquarium and tried hard to regain her composure. *I wonder why he changed his name when he returned to Zeon,* she thought. Char had always seemed a little unusual, in a nice way, for a military officer, and now it all made sense. *What a surprise,* she thought with a slightly hysterical laugh.

With her mind so fixated on the image of the little Casval she had adored, it was hard not to feel proud of him now, even if he had infiltrated the Principality under an alias. She did not condone his actions, but neither did she blame him entirely. After all, she was also partly responsible; something in her subconscious had merely prevented her from making the connection between Char and Casval. Perhaps she had instinctively known she could better use Char for her own purposes if she did *not* know his true background.

She reflected on the fact that Casval had surreptitiously obtained the Aznable family register, that he had been at the top of his class in the Military Academy, and that he had distinguished himself with valor in combat as someone with Newtype potential. In doing so, she found herself respecting him all the more. He had taken a roundabout way, but what pluck he had! If he had merely wanted revenge, it would have been far easier for him simply to rally the remaining progressive forces on Zeon and use them to carry out an assassination plan. His methodology was beyond her comprehension, but she admired his idealism intensely. It reminded her of his father, Zeon Zum Deikun, who had tried to obtain power through the will of the people. Char, she thought, must be a true Newtype, a product of the Space Age.

If she was incapable of objectively analyzing the situation and realizing how dangerous Char had actually become, she was nonetheless on guard. *I can understand it in a way, Casval,* she thought, as though addressing the lad of her memory, *but you're still naive. Watch out. The real world—the adult world—is far more cunning than you imagine.*

KYCILIA RESOLVED TO CONFRONT reality and act immediately on the information in Darcia's letter. She drank some coffee and issued several commands to her forces. Then she steeled herself and sent for Char Aznable.

She knew she could still use him for her own ends. After all, he had sworn allegiance to her. If he pulled out his pistol and shot her on the spot, that would be her destiny, but he would be destroyed with her, which was an almost romantic notion. If, on the other hand, nothing happened, she was also prepared. She had always believed Newtypes were like double-edged swords and had to be handled with extreme caution. In wartime they could be used as weapons; in peacetime they could be made into heroes or scapegoats, depending on the need. When the war was over, she planned to see how the general public felt about Newtypes and champion the popular mood. Char Aznable would be an important asset for her then. But for now, as long as the war continued, she would let him be the hero. She would let him develop, and the stronger he became, the greater his destructive power would become. He would be her own personal weapon.

Char, meanwhile, was not oblivious to his position. He knew Kycilia was a schemer and he knew why she had taken him under her wing. To protect himself, he had deliberately cultivated a mysterious air. She had often said, "Simply possessing paranormal abilities is unlikely to affect a person's basic personality. The persona and the paranormal potential are separate." And as far as he was concerned, he wanted her to continue thinking that way. It was safer for him.

MARGARET RING BLAIR HAD no idea of the level of deception in which Kycilia and Char were engaged. As one of Kycilia's lower-ranking "secretaries," she was privy to little important information and her actual work mainly consisted of receiving mail deliveries and ushering people in and out of Kycilia's office. But after Crowley Hamon had visited Kycilia's office, even Margaret could tell that something big was happening. It was evident from the way the head secretary rushed into the office and the way Char Aznable briskly walked right by her, ignoring her presence. He was radiating nervous energy.

"I'LL FINISH REORGANIZING MY unit in an hour, Excellency," Char carefully announced. "Of course, we'd ideally like to have two Elmeths at our disposal." He knew it was out of the question. He had mentioned the Elmeths half in jest, hoping to defuse the strange tension he felt in Kycilia.

"Don't ask for the moon, Commander," she admonished him, interpreting him literally. "We do, however, have a Braw Bro available, a type of mobile armor developed at the same time as the Elmeth. It's still in the prototype stage, but would you like to try one out? As far as I know there are two in the assembly hangar here on *A Baoa Qu*."

She turned on her intercom and casually ordered her secretary to arrange a visit to the hangar for Char. He detected both nervousness and condescension in her manner; she was acting overly flippant about the whole matter. He knew something was wrong. And then he heard her words:

"*By the way, dear Casval . . .*"

Char understood immediately.

He had long dreaded the day when his cover would be blown. But meeting Challia Bull had changed him, and what once had seemed terrifying was now merely an irritation and a disappointment, for if he had been a true Newtype, he ruefully realized, he would have been able to anticipate it. But he had not. He had had no idea that Kycilia knew. So much, he thought, for his own Newtype potential!

The disappointment was tempered by the fact that he had never totally convinced himself that he *had* Newtype potential. Nor, for that matter, had he ever completely believed the prevailing view in the Principality military, that Newtypes were ordinary people who suddenly manifested paranormal abilities. To him, true Newtypes were the people his father, Zeon Zum Deikun, had prophesied would appear, ordinary people with an uncommonly developed sense of intuition and a unique sense of humanity. People who, in adapting to a new concept of time and space in an extraterrestrial environment, would be transformed and develop a new communion with others. People who would, in effect, learn to transcend traditional concepts of time and space in order to survive. Recently, several of the people he had met seemed to confirm his ideas.

Lalah Sune, Kusko Al, and others had been thoroughly investigated by the Flanagan Institute for Newtype potential, and they did not support Kycilia Zabi's theory that possessing Newtype ability did not affect one's basic persona. They had been evolving, and it had been changing them. And if this experience could ever be shared by all of humanity, then, as his father had predicted, mankind itself could truly undergo a transformation.

It was too bad that the unusual abilities of Newtypes had first manifested themselves in combat situations, for Newtypes were now becoming disposable tools of the military—they were used, and then they died. Char knew that was one reason Challia Bull had broached the idea of enlisting the Federation Gundam pilot as an ally; he had wanted to put a stop to it. It was a brilliant idea and required a leap in imagination so vast that it was reassuring. Perhaps Newtypes already *were* attempting to transcend the old thinking that had dragged the world into war. Perhaps, subconsciously, he had really infiltrated the Principality years ago, not just in a petty act of revenge for his father's death but as part of a larger, subconscious movement to reform the entire world. It was a notion that made him less fearful of Kycilia. But in that context, his failure to predict her suddenly seeing through his disguise earlier was all the more disappointing, for again, it meant he was not a true Newtype.

"SO TELL ME, COMMANDER," Kycilia asked, "was the mask just an attempt to cloak your identity?"

"It was, Excellency," he replied with a touch of embarrassment. "It seems silly even to me now, but I intend to keep wearing it. Just as people started calling me the 'Red Comet' sometime back, it's become something of a trademark."

"And are all your endeavors really part of an attempt to rebuild the Deikun faction on Zeon?"

"That's why I infiltrated the Principality in the first place when I was fifteen, and that's what I believed until recently."

"I must say, I'm impressed by your courage and tenacity. And frankly, I don't care what your goals were when you were fifteen or even what they were when you first joined my command. I'm only worried about the Char Aznable I see standing before me now. And related to that, I have a favor to ask. Take off that silly mask and show me what you really look like. I want to see what kind of man little Casval grew up to be."

As Kycilia watched, Char removed his mask. The scar on his forehead wasn't very pleasant to look at, but his face still had the refined look that she remembered. She smiled, but then her expression turned serious.

Char had no idea what she was thinking and was frustrated with himself because of it. He was an ordinary human and responded as one. "I'm prepared for punishment, Your Excellency. You may do with me as you please."

To his surprise, she laughed. "I admire your gallantry, Char, but it's not necessary," she said. "Don't you remember what I said? I *need* you and your unit. That's why I called you here. After we escape from *A Baoa Qu* you can tell me all you want about your feud with my family. But right now I'm inclined to believe your goal is more than vengeance."

"Thank you, Excellency. I'm relieved to hear you say that. I am, after all, the son of Zeon Zum Deikun. I have no idea what to tell you in this situation. I don't know why, but my hands are shaking . . . " He was half-pretending. He wanted to wait to see how Kycilia reacted before deciding what to do next. Acting slightly emotional would give him a screen behind which to plan his next moves.

"My brother Gihren doesn't trust me, Commander," Kycilia said. "Nor do I trust him. Frankly, I'd feel a lot more comfortable facing a frontal attack from General Revil than a showdown with Gihren, but it seems inevitable. I'm planning to leave *A Baoa Qu* and head immediately for the Principality."

"Excellency, are you sure . . . ?"

"Yes, and I need your help. I need you to guard my ship."

"I understand. As I said, my unit needs to prepare before we can leave. When do you plan to depart?"

"Probably in five or six hours. I've got to get out of here before Revil hits us, and I'm not going alone. I'm going to take some of my forces with me."

"But Excellency . . . "

If Kycilia were seriously thinking of staging a revolt against her brother, it would be far easier said than done. The central colony of the Principality of Zeon, Zum City, had a defensive perimeter around it. And Char knew the Principality was capable of using the System project laser cannon for more than one blast. If Kycilia succeeded in escaping from *A Baoa Qu*, the authorities in Zum City would know about it almost instantly, and it was just possible, he surmised, that they might even make her a direct target of the cannon.

At last, he thought he understood why she was acting in such haste: she was probably included in the target Gihren had selected. There was no other way to explain her decision to abandon *A Baoa Qu*. But from the skirmish with Federation forces he had experienced earlier, he had learned one thing. The Principality had had a seventy percent chance of losing, but with the System project its victory now seemed almost guaranteed.

"It's the System project, isn't it Excellency?" Char said. "Forgive me for saying so, but don't you think you're rushing your decision?"

"You don't know what you're talking about. Can you imagine being hit by a laser beam six kilometers in diameter?"

"I can imagine, but if the tide of war clearly shifts in our favor, I can't believe the Supreme Commander would act so irrationally."

"You're naive! Put your Casval Deikun identity back on for a second and remember the way your own life has been consumed by the desire for revenge. Then remember what kind of man Gihren is."

"A painful point, well taken. But don't you think you're acting a little irrationally yourself?"

"What are you suggesting? Are you trying to tell me that I should let Gihren get away with this? Let him live?!"

"No. There's no chance of *us* winning if we're caught between *A Baoa Qu* and the Principality. I think we should try to escape from *A Baoa Qu* just as Revil hits the fortress. It might be difficult, but at least that way we won't have to worry about the guns of *A Baoa Qu* being turned on us—they'll be preoccupied with Revil. We should probably take the forces at your disposal, diffuse them in space, and then proceed on a course that lets us converge on the Principality. We'll need all your forces, I suppose."

"It's a long shot, Commander. I'm attempting something fraught with danger, and that's why I'm telling you the facts and asking for your help. I want your unit to be in the vanguard."

"I'm flattered, Excellency, and I know I've no choice in the matter, anyway. I'll cast my lot with you. But let's wait a little, at least until Revil closes in, before we stage our 'strategic retreat,' so-to-speak. We don't want it to look like another *Granada*, when you pulled out too soon."

"How *dare* you mention *Granada*! Leave the planning to me. Just busy yourself readying your unit and the new Braw Bros. I may even put an entire regular battalion under your command. We need as many ships and machines as possible."

"Thanks, Excellency, but as I stated once before, my unit, the 300th Autonomous, is supposed to be a strictly Newtype unit. As the Federation's White Base-class ship has so clearly demonstrated, in this new type of combat numbers are irrelevant."

"Understood. I'll leave it up to you, then."

Char saluted, and then Kycilia added, "Perhaps you pity me because of my current situation. But despite what's transpired between us today, I'd still like to consider you my ally, at least for the time being."

Char said nothing at first. Kycilia was a politician who helped prop up the Zabi family, and she was far too clever to pity very much. But he answered straight from the heart—"I don't pity you. Nor will I belittle you. Everyone is dealt a different hand in life. My own life has been filled with contradictions, too."

"Casval Deikun, if it came down to a choice of being shot by Gihren Zabi or you, I'd choose you. I can't guarantee your future, and I expect you can't guarantee mine, either. Correct?"

"Correct, Excellency." He saluted again lightly, and straightened his cape. Their conversation was over. At some point he might have to kill Kycilia Zabi. Or she might kill him. They would proceed with their own individual destinies. It would be an interesting game. A game, he realized, at which he would have to get much better if he wanted to take power someday.

AFTER EXITING KYCILIA'S OFFICE, Char stopped by Margaret Ring Blair's desk. She looked up at him with fear in her eyes. "Things are taking a turn for the worse," he whispered. "But no matter what happens, I want you to stay alive. I want you to bear my child someday."

It was an impulsive, radical statement, and completely out of character for Char, but Margaret accepted it and smiled. She was afraid for their future, but there was a limit to how much she could worry. Somehow, in Char, she was at least certain that there was a future.

LT. RAMBA RAL STARED at the image on his vid-phone screen. On the other end of the connection the camera panned back and forth sixty degrees, showing him Crowley Hamon's entire living room. Normally, vid-phones never displayed images unless the other party answered the phone, but because of Ramba Ral's Secret Service connections and the fact that Crowley's apartment was essentially in his name, it hadn't been all that difficult for him to activate the camera remotely.

Crowley's living room looked the way it always did when she wasn't around, but two scarves had been carelessly tossed on a sofa. And that was unlike her. And on a rack underneath the TV monitor he could also see a handbag with a handkerchief poking awkwardly out of it. Again, it wasn't like her. This was the third time he had checked her apartment in the last ten hours.

Maybe she did it, he thought, feeling relieved.

AFTER INFORMING THE SUPREME Commander of Char Aznable's real identity, Ramba Ral's Secret Service unit had been ordered to inspect all ships leaving the Principality. The order had come so unexpectedly that some of his men had questioned the motive behind it, but they were in the Secret Service and always obeyed their orders. He, however, still wanted to know what was going on. He knew that many Zeon military units in the *Mahal* colony area had suddenly been prohibited from leaving the Principality, which meant it had something to do with the System project. He also remembered something Gihren had said at their last meeting that had puzzled him: "*I've been thinking about settling matters for once and for all. Don't worry about what happened with Casval Deikun.*"

At first Ramba had thought that Gihren was simply planning to assassinate Char Aznable, and he had been prepared to carry out such an order if necessary. But with the emergency order to inspect all ships leaving the Principality, there suddenly appeared to be far more going on than apparent on the surface. Gihren's overblown ego was clearly acting up again.

Ramba thought of Crowley Hamon. She was a fine woman from a good Principality family and loved him deeply, but she had been passed along to him from Gihren, and he had never completely been able to shake off a sense of humiliation. She seemed to know how he felt, perhaps because she, too, had been humiliated by Gihren. In fact, it wouldn't have surprised him if she harbored a desire for revenge of her own. Ironically, their bond was strengthened by their relationship to Gihren.

To find out what was really going on, two nights earlier Ramba had decided to contact an old comrade of his who worked as an S.S. unit leader in the *Mahal* area; to his surprise, he had easily been able to obtain the information he needed. The man in charge of the *Mahal* project, Admiral Chapman Jirom, trusted the Secret Service unit attached to him and, in a moment of candor, had apparently let his guard down with them, telling them of the plan to change the *Mahal* axis so it could directly attack *A Baoa Qu*, even boasting of a plan to get rid of Kycilia Zabi.

The friend with whom Ramba had spoken, moreover, had been equally candid. "Whatever you do, Ramba," he had said, "don't mention this to anyone on *A Baoa Qu* before we put our plan into action. We serve the Supreme Commander, so I frankly couldn't care less about squabbles in the Zabi family. But this'll make Sovereign Degwin Zabi powerless and make it easy to get rid of Prime Minister Darcia Bakharov. Then Zeon will be ours. Things are starting to look good for us, Ramba."

Ramba, going along with the mood, had smiled, saying, "Right. Maybe we'll both get to visit Earth someday, after all . . . "

Now, Ramba thought, perhaps the Fates were presenting him with an opportunity. It was almost as if Crowley had come to him as part of a larger design, had understood what he was thinking, and had put his thoughts into action. The only proof he had was the fact that Crowley was not in her living room. But he wanted to believe it.

Neither Crowley nor Kycilia are stupid, he thought. He took a sip of coffee. Then he glanced at the schedule of ships leaving port that day, made sure none were leaving Zum City for *A Baoa Qu*, and stood up. One of his subordinates entered his office.

"Sir, we heard a rumor that Crowley Hamon was spotted on a ship that left last night. Is it true, sir?"

"*Crowley?*" he said, feigning surprise. "Surely, there must be some mistake."

"Well, sir, apparently someone who looks *exactly* like her boarded the ship, posing as one of Her Excellency Kycilia's personal staff."

"What?! Why in the world would Crowley do that? She said she was going to Island Park for three days. What's going on? Why are you idiots telling me this now? Can't you get your reports to me earlier? If only you'd told me!"

"Sorry, sir. We had three ships leave at the same time last night. And besides, we were told anyone with a pass from Her Excellency Kycilia should be allowed to leave, so we didn't feel the matter needed to be reported."

"And who was watching the ships?" Ramba asked.

"Ensign Tom Nishimura, sir."

"Hmph. Just the sort of thing that damn fool would do. Well, what the hell. When Crowley comes back, I'll have a few words with her."

"Yessir!"

RAMBA RAL KNEW CROWLEY could not have gone by herself to Kycilia Zabi unless she had also had contact with Darcia Bakharov. Furthermore, if she had posed as one of Kycilia's household members, it meant she was not operating alone but with the backing of a powerful organization. The main thing he worried about now was her safety—whether she would be able to escape from *A Baoa Qu* before being ensnared in Supreme Commander Gihren Zabi's plot.

SEVERAL HOURS BEFORE THE *Pegasus II* left the Corregidor shoal zone, General Revil visited on a launch from his flagship, the *Drog*. His normally calm face was flushed with excitement as he spoke to the core crew in the briefing room.

"What you have accomplished," he said, "is next to miraculous. In one battle the *Pegasus II* and its three mobile suits have done what normally requires a force twenty times larger. Frankly, I'm absolutely astonished."

For the *Pegasus* crew, these were powerful words. After all, they were spoken by the man who, after being captured during the Battle of Loum, had managed to escape from the Principality of Zeon, the man who had given the provocative, now famous speech, *Zeon is Exhausted!* and provided the rallying cry for the Federation in its darkest hour. Some people called Revil a brilliant strategist. Others, behind his back, called him an agitator. Given Revil's tactical talents, the Federation might have better employed him as a strategist away from the front, but he had never been fully trusted in the higher levels of the Federation government, and he had therefore always been assigned to the front. Ironically, he probably preferred it. To the crew of the *Pegasus,* General Revil was a hero.

"I'm convinced you are true Newtypes," he told them. "And when this mission's finally over, I'll see that you're all advanced two ranks. But right now promotions aren't enough. I want you to fight for something even larger, something the Federation can't possibly reward with a mere promotion. The success or failure of Operation Cembalo hinges on your performance. This may sound strange, but I've realized that it's in the best interest of the entire world that you folks—*even more than the Federation itself*—succeed. I don't wish to indulge in pie-in-the-sky dreaming in the midst of a war, but I came to visit the *Pegasus II* today because I believe in you, and because you have made me believe mankind may be capable of fundamental change. History may show that might makes right in war, but I believe the real victors in this conflict will not be the strongest, but those with the most just cause. It must be true. I came here today to ask your opinion, to see if you agreed with my ideas. Well? What do you—as Newtypes—think?"

Amuro felt awkward and embarrassed. He and the other *Pegasus II* crew members were all in their late teens or early twenties—Sleggar Law was the oldest—and they had always been in awe of Revil. Now, they felt like children suddenly asked advice by their grandfather. Bright, realizing their discomfort, stood up and answered first.

"It may be true, sir," he said, "that we have achieved unprecedented results in a short time. But if I understand your use of the word Newtype to be similar to that advocated by Zeon Zum Deikun—in other words, to represent a new step in the evolution of mankind—then I must disappoint you. We're just ordinary people, sir, and not really qualified to answer your question. But I think we'd all agree that the pilot of the Gundam mobile suit—Junior Grade Lieutenant Amuro Ray—has accomplished the most in combat, and if any change is occurring in us, it appears to be the most advanced in him. May I suggest we ignore rank here, sir, and ask him to answer your question first, and to speak his mind frankly?"

Amuro flushed when he heard Bright's words. He knew Revil's comments about promotions had been more of a gesture than anything else. Perhaps he had been promoted to junior grade lieutenant, but the Federation military organization was so short of people and so in danger of collapse that everyone knew ranks meant little anymore. Still, to be addressed in such respectful terms by Bright made him feel as though he had finally crossed the threshold into true adulthood. It was the doubts about his own ability that made him feel embarrassed.

Revil shifted his gaze to Amuro and nodded approvingly, as did several of his aides. "I've heard a lot about you, young man," he began, "and I'd love to know how you managed to pull off such a feat out there. But first, what do you think of what I said?"

Amuro stood up, shifted awkwardly, then straightened and tried to meet Revil's gaze directly. It wasn't easy speaking in front of the brass. But then he felt the stares of his comrades and turned around. Sayla was looking at him with a warm, encouraging expression. He felt inspired, and turned to face General Revil again.

"Thanks for the compliments, sir," he began. "To start with, even I'm not sure what's going on, but you did say you thought the victors in this war would be those with the most just cause, and to be blunt, I have a problem with that. In all the war stories I was raised on, the authors extolled the merits of a just cause but the authors already knew the outcome of the conflict. They started with the conclusion and adapted the record to fit it."

"A point well taken," Revil quickly replied with a chuckle. Everyone in the room smiled.

"Yessir," Amuro answered. "I've already discussed my theories on tactics many times with those in this room, so I'm going to spare them the repetition, but let me speak frankly about three things I've experienced, things I haven't told even my closest friends, things that might help you understand what's going on." He then proceeded to recount the story of his contact with Lalah Sune on the *Texas* colony and with Char Aznable and Kusko Al in the Corregidor shoal zone.

"Both Lalah Sune and Kusko Al were operating a rounded, flame-shaped type of mobile armor called an Elmeth, machines specifically designed for Newtypes, with some sort of thought-activated control system that can amplify consciousness, even project it at another human. But when I encountered Lalah Sune, the pilot of the first one, I had absolutely no knowledge of the system, and I was able to communicate with her *without* it.

"Char Aznable's another case in point. I ran into him around the same time I contacted Lalah Sune and sensed him as an interruption, a static-like sound in the midst of my communication with her. But later, during the skirmish in Corregidor, I was actually able to 'talk' with him. His communication to me was simple, like a threat to kill me, but it was as clear as if he had spoken out loud. There was no mistaking it. He was reacting spontaneously to the thoughts I was emitting.

"And then, finally, during the battle in Corregidor, nearly all the crew on the *Pegasus II* bridge were able to detect the presence of Kusko Al. We were all operating on the same wavelength. If there's anything else to add, it's—"

" . . . *Dozle's unit*," Kai interjected.

"Right. I almost forgot. When we ran into Dozle's fleet, we were able to destroy his new model machine because our awareness had been

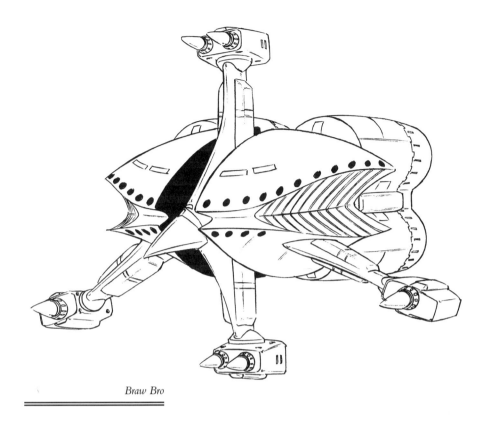

Braw Bro

amplified after encountering Kusko Al in Corregidor. And after Dozle
we were able intercept and destroy other, smaller prey because we could
feel the waves of fear and aggression emanating from them. Let me try
to describe it . . . "

Amuro continued talking for over thirty minutes, sharing his experiences and opinions in detail with everyone present for the first time.

Sleggar Law, as if representing the others, sighed hard and long and
said, "Wow. The part about contacting Kusko Al and the heartbeat, the
London Bridge tune . . . it's pretty incredible."

Revil and his officers were too amazed to comment at first, so Mirai
Yashima took the opportunity to speak up. "Of those of us on the bridge,
sir, Petty Officer First Class Sayla Mass seems to have become the most
sensitive. Sayla, why don't you tell them what you've experienced?"

"Me?" Sayla looked up, shocked on hearing her name. She hesitated,
glancing first at Revil as if to ask permission to speak.

One of Revil's aides quickly bent over and whispered in the general's
ear. "Let's hear her out, sir. She's the petty officer who saved the *Pegasus*
crew on *Texas*. I'm damned curious about what she has to say, sir."

"Curious?" Sayla echoed, overhearing.

"That's right. We did a background check on you," the officer announced.

"Oh, I see," she said softly, suddenly realizing that her secret was out. Steeling herself, she continued. "Then let me preface what I'm going to tell you. I joined this ship as a civilian, but I'm proud of the fact that I'm pulling my weight around here."

Revil gently interrupted. "We're aware of that, *Artesia Som Deikun*. And let me add, it pleases me to be able to address you by your true name."

Sayla's fellow crewmates were the most shocked. Except for Amuro, despite living and working with her day in and day out, they had never realized her true identity. Kai, unable to remain silent, summed up everyone's thoughts when he exclaimed in disbelief, "*Deikun*?! The same Deikun as in Zeon Zum Deikun? You've gotta be *kidding!*"

Sayla just smiled, but Bright gently reprimanded Kai for speaking out of turn. Then he nodded at her, encouraging her to continue.

As Amuro watched, Sayla straightened and thanked the general for his kindness. He felt so proud of her that he wanted to proclaim to all present that she was *his* woman! But then he realized with embarrassment that their level of involvement gave him no right to such a claim. It was still mostly physical.

"I am the child of Zeon Zum Deikun, sir," Sayla began again, "but my father was not a Newtype. He only proposed and advocated the Newtype concept. And like him, unless something indicates otherwise, I'll always believe I'm an ordinary person, too. I think the same thing's true of Amuro Ray. What he's accomplished is a fact, but we still don't know what it means in the larger scope of things. We're not in a position to control the abilities emerging in ourselves. There's just one thing I'd like to say, sir. Personally, if you really believe we're emerging Newtypes and you really believe Newtypes are going to help transform mankind, then I think you should stop using us as some sort of secret weapon, stop using us to wage war."

Revil replied slowly, as if mulling over her words. "Let me congratulate you on your bluntness, Miss Artesia Som Deikun," he said. "But from what I've heard here today, it would seem that if someone like young Amuro Ray here can actually see into another's past and future, it would indeed indicate a dramatically raised consciousness. And if, as we also assume, he's just an ordinary human, that would indicate *anyone's* capable of the same thing. Unfortunately, I'm not smart enough to be able to predict how this ability would affect people or the world. Perhaps our junior grade lieutenant could again tell us what he thinks."

Amuro noted that Revil had finally relaxed in front of everyone. His eyes had a new youthfulness to them, and his gaze was more clear and direct. If all leaders were like him, he surmised, mankind might not have made so many colossal blunders throughout history.

"Sometimes I feel terrible," he began, "because I can't control what's happening to me. But there's something even more important than control. As my abilities increase, I wish I could become a better person, too, but it's not happening. And that scares me. For example, we're part of a military organization, with all its constraints, hierarchies, and limited perspectives; I'd like to be able to transcend that as an individual, but I don't think I ever can. We live in a real world dominated by political organizations, governments, and the military, and as long as these exist, there'll always be conflicts. Even if Zeon Zum Deikun's theory's true, I don't think people'll ever evolve to the point where they no longer need conflicts. Maybe a special group of Newtypes, living in some sort of hermetically sealed environment, could. But we don't live in an isolated world. We live in a real world where we'll always have to interact with a variety of people. To transcend that'd require a superhuman effort. And we'd probably still be used as weapons. To be perfectly honest, it's depressing. I wish we had more power. I wish we had more support. If I were a true Newtype, I'd love to achieve some sort of total psychic breakthrough, to achieve total harmony with others—if universal harmony with all mankind, regardless of background or station in life, were really possible, I'd feel ecstatic—but right now I'm having enough trouble just harmonizing with myself. One of the main reasons I want to stay alive is that I want to see what's possible. In fact, I'm willing to do almost anything to survive. But that's probably an 'old type' concept. It's frustrating."

General Revil merely nodded in understanding, but the officer who had earlier whispered in his ear answered, "Don't worry, lad. A lot of us, myself included, would give their right arm to experience what you have, even for an instant, even if it was totally accidental. To be able to literally fuse your mind with that of another human seems like an incredible experience. It's something you should treasure."

"*No!*" Amuro responded emphatically. "You miss the point."

"*What?*" His attempt at sympathy rejected, the officer was suddenly angered.

"As long as the experience is random and accidental," Amuro continued, "then the Newtype concept isn't real. It's only a dream. And dreaming's not going to end the war or bring about some idealized transformation of mankind. As long as the experience is random, the people with real power in this world are going to ridicule us and classify us as paranormal freaks. They'll use us to justify their own dogmas and prejudices, just like the Jaburo bureaucrats on Earth use the entire Earth Federation Space Force as a big shield to hide behind."

To Amuro's surprise, General Revil seemed to agree. "A very astute observation, Mister Amuro Ray," he said. "I understand your feelings perfectly. The Newtype concept *is* a double-edged sword, with both positive and negative potential. But having said that, I'm going to give all of you an order based on my own 'old type' logic. The 127th Autonomous, centered around the *Pegasus II*, is to continue proceeding in the vanguard of the attack on *A Baoa Qu*. I'll have three squadrons accompany you, but I'm not sure how much protection they can provide. As the conflict escalates, I want you all to evaluate the situation autonomously and to take independent action as you see fit. I want *victories*! But remember, I also want you all to return *alive*. That's all I have to say."

And with that, General Revil stood up and left.

A BLUISH-WHITE ROCKET ENGINE flare streaked through the blackness as the *Pegasus II* continued at full speed toward *A Baoa Qu*. Even after they cleared the Corregidor shoal zone, the path to *A Baoa Qu* was by no means unobstructed. Giant boulders and fragments of old colonies—debris from the destruction of war—remained. But this time the ship tried to use the obstacles as cover, zigzagging forward from one to the other after identifying them with laser sensors.

At the helm of the ship, Mirai Yashima understood why her skipper had decided to employ such an unorthodox tactic and marveled at the way human psychology worked. The debris couldn't afford complete protection, and there was even a possibility of enemy Zakus lurking in ambush, but the crew nonetheless clung to the meager security it afforded.

When she looked out at space, at first nothing would seem to be moving. Then she would suddenly spot a huge rock or a fragment of an old colony bearing down on her, and it would fill her entire field of vision. She would quickly check the laser-sensor monitor built into the wall, get a reading on the size of the obstacle, and then, while coming so close that she could see the details on its surface, start to maneuver around it and head for the next one.

It was a frightening responsibility. The *Pegasus II* had an automatic avoidance system but it was often necessary to override it manually, and that decision and job was left entirely to her. Aggravating the problem, the debris was all backlit, and in the vacuum of space it was hard to deduce size visually. On Earth, the atmosphere tended to blur shapes in the distance but also to create a sense of distance. Without atmosphere, there was almost no way to get a true perspective. Laser sensors gave readings of size and distance, but in combat zones with a high concentration of Minovsky particles, they were often inaccurate.

THE ENTIRE CREW OF the *Pegasus II* was dressed for combat. All officers wore pistols strapped on top of their normal suits—what had once been called space suits before mobile suits were developed—and life-support kits. None of them knew when, if ever, they would be able to take the uncomfortable suits off again.

Mirai felt a chill. It started around her waist, crawled up her spine, passed her neck, and made her scalp tingle. She felt strangely out of place and wondered what in the world she was doing, piloting the ship through such an absurd situation. *Too bad I can't quit,* she thought. *I'd feel a lot safer farther back.* She didn't mean the rear of the unit. She meant someplace far, far removed from the world of combat. She wasn't even sure if such a place existed anymore.

She had left her home in Earth's Far East at the age of ten with her father. He was a second-generation politician from a family famous throughout the Federation, but he was also a self-righteous idealist who had nothing but loathing for the Federation. Unable to stand the machinations that were part of normal government in the Federation, he had volunteered for life as a colonist and left with her to live in space on Side 2.

Just before war broke out between the Principality of Zeon and the Earth Federation, Mirai had returned to her birthplace on Earth for a visit. But then war had erupted, and her entire family had been destroyed along with most of Side 2. In reaction, Mirai had volunteered for service and been assigned to the Earth Federation Space Force. Because of her name and connections she could have easily asked for a post in the rear, away from the action, but she had refused. She had known an Earth-bound assignment would have been against her father's wishes, and she had loved him, as idealistic as he was. Besides, her brother and sister had also died in space. She was in no frame of mind to be left behind on Earth, even if it were safer.

Mirai's situation was hardly unique on *Pegasus II.* Almost all the crew, including those who had joined the military before the war erupted, had a strong bond to space. They came from colonies that had been targeted by Zeon forces, and most of them had lost relatives. Hardly anyone had come from Side 6 or, like Amuro, from the uncompleted Side 7, both of which were relatively unscathed. Nearly a third of the crew had volunteered for service after the war began. Most, like many of the officers and enlisted men throughout the Earth Federation Space Force, had every reason to hate the enemy. And this set them apart from the politicians and bureaucrats on Earth, even from the General Staff sheltered in its underground complex in Jaburo, South America.

The gap in consciousness between those on Earth and those on the front lines in space was probably inevitable, but it didn't seem right to Mirai. She had inherited her father's idealistic streak and she abhorred the current makeup of the Earth Federation establishment. She knew the fear she felt standing on the bridge of the *Pegasus* was something the officials sheltered underground in Jaburo would never understand. The vastness of space created an enormous potential for error and mistake. And if it overamplified the fundamental misunderstandings that normally occurred between men, it might fundamentally, permanently, tear the human race apart. Perhaps, she thought, that was why humanity so yearned for the transformation the Newtype concept symbolized.

She stood steady at the helm, mustering every ounce of strength in her arms to counter the fear that surged through her body. She was thankful for the weightlessness because it made it easier to stand; in fact, it made it just as easy as sitting or lying down. All she had to do to hold her position on the floor was to turn the electromagnets on her boot soles on max.

SUDDENLY, AN ENORMOUS FRAGMENT of a space colony wall—perhaps one third of the original structure—soared into view, and in her earphones Mirai heard the skipper yell out her name. For a second she wondered if she had been dreaming. The port side of the ship shuddered as the *Pegasus* heaved up and over the colony fragment, barely clearing it. Bright's voice echoed again: "*Don't think about it, Mirai! Just look straight ahead and steer! Ignore the laser sensors—turn the damn things off! Put your mind on autopilot!*"

She knew everyone on the bridge was getting nervous. Then she heard Ensign Marker Clan's angry, reprimanding voice cut in on top of the skipper's. "*We've broken through the second combat line! Mobile suits launch in five minutes!*"

"All right, all right!" Bright grumbled, irritated. "So I was a little excited. You can turn the sensors back on now!"

Through her helmet sunvisor, Mirai could see Bright, nervously fiddling in the captain's seat in his normal suit. She glanced at him and laughed.

"Skipper!" she said.

"What?!"

"It'll work out. Have faith."

"Have *faith*?! You were shaking back there like a leaf yourself."

"I was. I admit it. But the *Pegasus*'ll make it, sir."

"This one of your 'Newtype' premonitions?"

"Interpret it any way you want," Mirai answered. Then, turning to Sayla, she said, "*You* agree with me, don't you?"

Sayla swallowed hard and replied, "Yes, but we might have to make a few sacrifices . . . "

Something about her response was unsettling to Bright. "You all right, Sayla?" he asked.

"Yes, sir," she answered, softly. "I'm just a little scared, too, that's all."

Mirai knew it was more than that.

"What's going on?" Bright demanded, pushing the issue. "Mirai just said we ought to have faith. I believe what Amuro said to General Revil earlier. But if we don't get through the jam we're in now and work to end this war fast, what he said'll *never* come true. If Gihren Zabi wins, forget about the whole Newtype concept, at least as Zeon Zum Deikun believed in it."

"But skipper," Mirai cautioned. "You can say the same thing if the Federation wins. The Federation's not all that different in its attitude to Newtypes."

"But if the Federation wins, we'll at least have some more time to think about what to do next. Not so if Gihren Zabi does," Bright retorted.

It was an idea with which Mirai found it hard to disagree.

TEST FIRING

ONLY THREE FEDERATION WARSHIPS of the White Base-class had been built: the *Pegasus,* destroyed in the conflagration on *Texas*; the *Thoroughbred*; and the *Pegasus II*. Because their solar panels, special hangars, and protruding bridge gave them a winged equine profile, the Zeon military had code-named them all *Trojan Horse*. They were the only ships in either the Federation or Principality forces specifically designed for joint operations with mobile suits.

The Gundam G3 and the two Guncannons, C108 and C109, stood on the *Pegasus II* foredecks, beam rifles in hands, like pilots on ancient sailing ships. But in this case the real pilots—Amuro Ray, Kai Shiden, and Hayato Kobayashi—were inside the giant Suits, and not on the lookout for reefs. The *Pegasus II* had just come in effective range of missiles and mega-particle beam-cannons from *A Baoa Qu*.

AS AMURO WATCHED, FLASHES appeared in the sky where the space fortress was located and then instantly forked into multiple streaks. The pattern was repeated, each time from a different spot, and each time the streaks seemed synchronized. Missile barrages were coming at them from at least fifteen different sites on the giant umbrella-shaped fortress and its periphery, creating a deadly crossfire.

Because homing missiles were impractical in regions with high Minovsky saturation, it was common to launch large numbers of conventional missiles in a hit-or-miss approach, but Amuro was certain he was witnessing a new record for the war. Thousands, not hundreds, of missiles were streaking toward them. While adjusting the sights of the beam rifle in the Gundam's left hand, he drew the hyperbazooka on its hip with the right hand. Then he kicked off the deck. On his rearview monitor he saw the two Guncannons with their twin shoulder guns launch after him from the ship's starboard deck. Both Kai and Hayato had developed more and more confidence in their support role and their basic combat skills, and as soon as they assumed their positions on either side of him, they all plunged ahead in formation into the fire-streaked heavens.

KAI AND HAYATO WEREN'T particularly worried about the incoming missiles hitting them. The missiles were unintelligent, randomly aimed, and traveling in a straight line, so there was no need for the young men to try to intuit or predict complex course changes; they just had to avoid the missiles in time, and that wasn't too difficult. They enjoyed a 280-degree field of vision, and ever since the last battle their emerging Newtype skills had allowed them to work in an increasingly coordinated fashion. As they advanced, they occasionally picked off missiles on a course that appeared to threaten the *Pegasus II*. And every time the mother ship safely made it through the ball of light from the explosions, they cheered inside their cockpits.

"*Hey*, Mister *Hayato! It's working!*"

"*Not bad, not bad! At this rate we'll land on the core of* A Baoa Qu *and eliminate its commander in no time! Whaddya say, pardner?*"

"*Better happen soon. The longer this continues, the worse the odds are for us. My nerves and body aren't gonna hold out forever. Let's go, Hayato! Let's go!*"

They were both excited and primed for action, but they made certain they stayed close to the Gundam.

IT WAS EASIER FOR Amuro to sight the line of approach of the missiles and evade them visually, so he was able to concentrate most of his mind on the panorama unfolding before them. He knew he needed to locate a dominating "presence" in the A Baoa Qu region, similar to what he had sensed before in his encounter with Dozle Zabi's unit in the Corregidor shoal zone. Then he had felt a strange, oppressive sensation, interpreted it as a powerful enemy force, and pursued it; to his surprise it had turned out to be psychic waves emanating from Dozle himself. Now, if he could just detect the same thing again, he could move in, destroy the source, and in the process help fatally weaken *A Baoa Qu*. Unfortunately, such manifestations of energy were apparently not always well defined, for although he could detect a diffused, seething mental energy emanating in swirls from the fortress itself, he could not isolate a single, dominating force.

Perhaps I'm still too far away, he thought. There had to be some other reason that the force was not as strong or defined as when he had encountered Dozle Zabi.

Then, in the vast area around *A Baoa Qu*, he abruptly sensed a second attacking force, and his eyes widened. He knew they still hadn't cleared *A Baoa Qu's* primary missile defense, but sure enough, there were suddenly more satellite missiles being lobbed at them. These crude projectiles were camouflaged black to avoid detection, and they could attain a speed equivalent to that of modern missiles, but they had a head diameter from ten to two hundred meters. At least a third of the Federation armada behind him was directly exposed. Sure enough, in his rearview monitor he soon saw explosions flowering like fireworks.

"We're coming to get you bastards!" he yelled at the enemy before him. It felt good to yell something. He thought about the destruction occurring behind him among his own forces, but restrained his impulse to shoot as many of the attacking missiles as possible. He had to save his ammunition for what he expected would soon be a Newtype showdown—with Char Aznable.

Then, while evading a barrage of missiles, he suddenly thought, *Uh, oh.* Behind one huge chunk of asteroid he saw a brief glint of sunlight on a metal surface and realized he was staring at an entire formation of Gattle fighter-bombers with camouflaged fuselages, approaching under cover. Behind them, in a textbook pattern, was a formation of Jicco attack ships. And following the Jiccos was the main force of Gaw bombers, reinforcing the defensive wall of Zeon mobile suits and the cross fire from the *A Baoa Qu* fortress itself.

GENERAL REVIL KNEW THE Federation armada could never take *A Baoa Qu* unless it could find or create a weak link in the fortress's defenses. There were therefore three options: to try a feint maneuver and cause the enemy to overconcentrate its strength in one area (and thus weaken its defenses in another), to stage a broad frontal assault and attempt to find a weak spot while doing so, or to focus all strength on one area and bore a hole right through the defenses.

He knew the third option would yield the heaviest losses, but he chose it because he believed it had the highest likelihood of success.

The vanguard of the armada would first assault the "stem" section of the umbrella-shaped fortress where the defensive cross fire was at its weakest, and the *Pegasus II*, as one of the point ships, would be given maximum flexibility; as the attack proceeded, if an opportunity to make a breakthrough presented itself, it would be allowed to make autonomous decisions and act on them independently.

It was a gamble, but he knew what he was doing. After having heard Amuro, Kai, Hayato, and the rest of the *Pegasus II* crew give their accounts of sensing Dozle Zabi in the midst of battle, he was convinced his plan would work. Even if the enemy were able to muster its own Newtype unit in defense of *A Baoa Qu*, in the end he was certain the same Newtype unit would help lead the Federation fleet to the core of the fortress.

AMURO HAD BEEN FULLY briefed on the plan. Taking care not to let anyone pick him off along the way, he kept his senses focused on the area the enemy fortress occupied and tried to identify the nucleus of its defenses. He switched his main monitor to high-power telescopic mode for a few seconds, and in the distance he could easily see the fortress's silhouette; from his perspective, he was looking "up" at the umbrella portion of its superstructure. He could almost smell the stench of battle—the stench of impending death.

❑ ❑ ❑

SUPREME COMMANDER GIHREN ZABI's face was intimidating even on good days, but judging from Cecilia Irene's reaction, he knew he must have just scowled particularly hard. Even she—his personal secretary, a strong woman who knew his innermost secrets and his private predilections—was terrified. He stopped reading the letter he had just received and glanced at her trembling form.

Cecilia was one of the few women in the world he totally trusted. He had a legal wife, but he considered her beneath him intellectually and treated her more like a domestic, never appearing with her in public. Cecilia was only one of many women with whom he had consorted in the past, but she had proved the most outstanding. Of lower-class background, she had developed a strong independent streak at an early age, studying to become a professional secretary while still a teenager. He had first been attracted to her shapely figure, but he had soon grown to appreciate her ability to understand people and her intuitive skepticism of their true motivations—both traits he valued highly. After she had worked in his office for over two years, he had made her his personal secretary.

Cecilia was so accurate in her evaluations of people that Gihren sometimes wondered if she might not be one of the Newtypes his sister Kycilia often referred to. She had begun to function more like a counsel or advisor than a secretary, and he in turn had begun to trust in her more and more. He loved her for her ability. Cecilia, for that matter, seemed to like his personality and style, and he liked to think her affection for him was aided by the fact that he had managed to alleviate a long-standing sexual frustration of hers. She always tried hard to understand his emotional makeup and ways of thinking, and she rationalized whatever he did by borrowing from his system of logic. Several days earlier she had learned of his plot and seemed to have approved.

"Hmph," Gihren grumbled. "Imagine these nit-picking numskull clerks writing code numbers on letters and worrying about format at a time like this. Makes my blood boil. I just want the facts reported. Especially for something like this."

Cecilia smiled. It was the last thing she had expected Gihren to say, but she knew it was his attempt to make her feel relaxed. He, for his part, knew her smile had another meaning: he wasn't supposed to worry about her. He grinned.

"Did my expression really look *that* bad?"

"Worse."

"Hmph," he grumbled. "Well, I never thought things would proceed *exactly* as planned." He again scanned the letter that had been delivered to him. It was from Vice Admiral Randolph Weigelman, the commanding officer on *A Baoa Qu*, and in the upper left hand corner was the source of his displeasure: the code name for his plan was displayed in elegant capital letters, followed by the communication number. It therefore made a relatively short message—that he wanted as few people as possible to notice—far too conspicuous.

The message itself was clear and concise, and merely stated that the Earth Federation Forces had recommenced their attack and gave the time. But this information was critical. Earlier, the Federation armada had bypassed *A Baoa Qu* and appeared headed in the direction of *Solomon*. When one unit had reached the Corregidor shoal zone between *A Baoa Qu* and *Solomon*, Gihren had staked his hopes on his brother Dozle. But then Dozle's attack had collapsed, far too easily.

Gihren's confidence had been shaken to the core by Dozle's defeat. What had happened? What had caused it? Even if Dozle's unit had been surrounded and attacked by the entire Federation armada, he should have been able to hold out half a day before being annihilated. That he could at least have understood. At the beginning of the battle, Dozle was supposed to have smashed into the wing of the Federation armada headed for *A Baoa Qu* and routed it. Then the Federation armada would have been at a severe disadvantage; it could have been bombarded broadside from *A Baoa Qu*, and special *A Baoa Qu* units could have been sent out in hot pursuit. In space warfare, an attack from the rear during retreat was to be avoided at all costs; in theory, it could be repulsed with twice the firepower of the pursuers, especially now that ECM (Electronic Counter Measure) tactics were so refined. Dozle's forces could have been expected to encounter heavy resistance, but at a minimum they should have been able to throw the enemy armada into absolute chaos. And that had not happened.

Dozle was defeated too easily. And Kycilia's forces don't seem to have helped him. Gihren's doubts began to gnaw in his mind, making him wonder if his secret plot was in danger of unraveling. Surely, he thought, the Federation Forces must also have incurred heavy losses. After all, hadn't that been why they had suddenly moved away from the space fortress and retreated to the Corregidor shoal zone in the first place?

"I HOPE VICE ADMIRAL Randolph Weigelman can hold up. Think I'm expecting too much?" Gihren stared at Cecilia's ample bosom as he spoke, but his mind was focused on something else. It was a habit of his. As he watched, her chest suddenly heaved and then shook softly. Wondering what had happened, he looked up at her soft, full lips.

"I . . . I'd say so," she said. She was trembling, and Gihren knew it wasn't an act.

Normally Cecilia enjoyed watching Gihren plot and manipulate his subordinates to achieve a desired goal. It seemed like a thrilling game, and after the humiliations of her own life she even derived a perverse pleasure from it. But this time he was going too far. Using the System plan to annihilate both his own sister Kycilia and Randolph Weigelman was too inhuman, even for her. And the loss, she feared, would be too great, even to Zeon.

"I'm not going to be angry with you, Cecilia," Gihren said. "I understand your fears. But look, I know what I'm doing. Everything, including acting as a behind-the-scenes dictator here on Zeon, is merely a means to an end in a long historical process. You know, my father often accuses me of being a poor clone of Adolf Hitler, but it's not true. I know what I'm doing. Most people are by nature stupid and weak. They need to fall as far as they can before they can be saved. If Zeon

Kai Shiden

Zum Deikun's prophecy of a new human enlightenment is anything more than a dream, then I'm going to be the one to make it possible. I swing the ax. Those with true Newtype potential will avoid it. Those without it, won't. It's that simple."

Gihren finished talking, stood up, and walked around his desk to Cecilia.

"I think you're going a little too far this time, sir." She had finally dared to say it. Gihren's use of the System represented far too big an ax for any single individual to swing.

Gihren was stung by her remark. "You're getting out of line, Cecilia," he said. He suddenly looked humiliated.

"Sorry, sir," she replied with a pained expression. "Please, forgive me."

Then he leaned over her, and with his lips began gently caressing the nape of her neck.

Cecilia felt a sudden chill. A chill of fear. She knew Gihren was irritated. She always prided herself on the fact that she never put undue pressure on him and that she served him well. She knew he kept only capable people around him, and she was always prepared for the moment when he would no longer need her. She knew what had happened in the past to women who knew too much and of whom he had then tired. They wound up ruined. Or dead. To avoid either fate she had tried extra hard to develop her skills and make herself indispensable, both as a woman and as his executive secretary. She was, in a sense, constantly engaged in a subtle competition with him, a competition that, since her life was at stake, always had an element of danger in it. And in a perverse psychosexual way, she always enjoyed that. She felt his lips trace the nape of her neck and imagined what life would be like without him. She would lose her biggest competitor, her most worthy competitor. But she knew right now he was just trying to butter her up. She pulled away.

"Did, did I do something wrong?" he gingerly asked.

Cecilia could hardly believe what she had just heard. For a second the Supreme Commander of the Principality of Zeon, none other than Gihren Zabi himself, had almost sounded contrite. She quickly recovered and smiled at him.

"You're being sweeter than usual. I just wish you'd act naturally."

A frown creased Gihren's brow. "What are you getting at?" he said, suddenly upset.

"Well . . . maybe you shouldn't be in such haste with the project," she said. Her heart was pounding, and she practically bit her lip when she spoke.

"Are you trying to provoke me, Cecilia? Don't you understand? If I can just void the Antarctic Treaty, a lot of problems will be solved. If the System works as it's supposed to, then we can nuke the Federation's Jaburo headquarters. After that, it'll be all over. The war'll end in a week."

CECILIA UNDERSTOOD THE LOGIC of what Gihren was trying to do. Within a month after Zeon had begun its war on the Federation, both the Principality and the Federation had lost nearly half their entire populations. It had been a terrifying loss of not only lives but also human resources, for losing such a huge number of people in such a short time nearly destroyed most vital social organizations. Civilization had tottered on the brink of total collapse, but then, in a testimony to mankind's resilience, most organizations had been recreated on a new, scaled-down size.

The Earth Federation had initially lost far more people than the Principality had, but it had managed to recover faster. It possessed far more people and resources to begin with, and it also possessed a far more flexible political system. But because the human losses had been so horrendous, after the Battle of Loum both the Principality and the Federation had agreed to sign the Antarctic Treaty, a far-reaching agreement that stipulated the way prisoners were to be treated and—in a move that had broad implications for the rest of the conflict—prohibited all use of poison gas and nuclear weapons as well as attempts to totally destroy each other's colonies. The treaty even confirmed possible procedures for terminating the war, but that was as far as the talks had gotten. After all the killing, the two adversaries were simply incapable of resolving their differences over a negotiating table; their views of each other were poisoned by distrust, and in a world where ideals and realities coexisted, the realities won out. The whole negotiating process was, as Gihren Zabi often claimed, a classic example of human stupidity. The paradox of history, he liked to say, was that in nations of laws, even bad laws had to be obeyed, but the laws themselves were made to be broken. Nonetheless, men still legislated, generated endless fancy legal documents, and promulgated worthless treaties.

"IN THE TWENTIETH CENTURY of the old calendar system," Gihren continued, "the Earth's total population was around four and a half billion. Do you know what that means, Cecilia?"

"Well, I suppose you're trying to suggest that even after losing half our population, we still have more than they did then, right?"

"Right. More people are alive now than there ever were at the end of the twentieth century, when modern science and technology made their most dramatic progress. So any talk about too many people having been killed thus far in the war is utter nonsense. The bureaucrats on Earth running the Federation's stupid system aren't helping prepare us for a Newtype age, they're just getting in the way. They're useless. And so's the Antarctic Treaty. If all it takes to destroy the Federation's Jaburo complex is a couple of nuclear warheads, I say they ought to be used. Someone has to do it."

"You're quite right, as usual, sir."

"Once I've accomplished my goals, I intend to retire. I'm just thinking of the interests of the survivors of this conflict." Gihren put his arms around her waist as if measuring her size. "I'm not just doing this for power and glory, you know," he said softly.

Cecilia noted Gihren's expression. He appeared utterly sincere.

Then he whispered, "Get me Admiral Chapman Jirom."

"WELL? THINK THIS THING'S okay, Lieutenant?" Commander Char Aznable looked over the new model of mobile armor, the Braw Bro, and wondered if Challia Bull would be able to pilot it. It was utterly unlike any machine he had worked with before. It was huge, with four protruding turrets topped with mega-particle cannon. The turrets could be detached from the main fuselage and used as wire-guided weapons, controlled by gunners inside the cockpit. Normally, it took four gunners to operate all the cannon, but the Braw Bro also had a prototype version of the Elmeth's psycommu interface built into it. As a result, while the Braw Bro, unlike the Elmeth, could not amplify and project human brain waves through open space, it could nonetheless transmit them to the cannon units via wire. One advanced Newtype pilot, hooked up to the interface, could therefore control all the system's cannon over a two kilometer radius and use them to attack a bewildered enemy. In fact, the scientists from the Flanagan Institute had left the Braw Bro on *A Baoa Qu* only because the Elmeth had shown so much more potential.

"I don't foresee any problem, Commander," Challia said, grinning and looking a little embarrassed as he stroked a two-day growth of beard. "The psycommu on this thing's one of the first ever made, but it's easy to operate. I can even do it all by myself."

"Leroy!" Char ordered young Lt. (jg) Leroy Gilliam behind him. "Bring this man a razor, will you?" Then he turned back to Challia and asked, "Why don't you just take another Rick Dom?"

"Because I want to stay alive," Challia replied. "The Braw Bro fuselage separates into left and right modules, which allows the cockpit to function as an escape capsule. It'll be easier for me to get out of in a jam."

"You're joking, I assume."

"Think so?" Challia said, as Leroy handed him a razor. "I want to contact the Gundam as early as possible. The Braw Bro psycommu interface actually *does* emit a small amount of brain waves, and I think it'll help."

"Hmm. Well, I'm not in a position to question your judgment in this matter, Lieutenant, so I guess I'll just have to take your word for it."

Char knew full well that Challia had been sent to his unit by Gihren Zabi to spy on him, and that Challia was still superficially carrying out his duties for the Supreme Commander. But he also knew Challia was now on his side. Both men believed in the Newtype vision and would do whatever they could to make it come true. Both men had also come to realize the need to stop the insane war going on around them. But to do that they would first have to escape from *A Baoa Qu*, and there was not a minute to lose.

The Federation Gundam MS was becoming too powerful for them, and after leaving *A Baoa Qu* they were determined to avoid engaging it in direct combat. They had agreed earlier that if, as they suspected, they were unable to destroy it quickly, they should try to enlist its pilot in their cause. In their next encounter they would make the decision. Challia Bull, at great personal risk, had volunteered to try to contact the Gundam.

"I just wish I could say this plan'd work with more certainty," Challia said, sighing.

"The most difficult thing," Char added, "is to get close enough to communicate with the pilot. Think he'll let us?"

Leroy Gilliam interjected. "I'll try to help make it possible," he said. "But can I also assume it's okay to destroy him if I have to?"

Leroy sounded too eager. He had what Char and Challia recognized as youthful overconfidence.

"If you can get a bead on him, good," Char said, "but make sure you aim for his backpack." Then, looking up at the newly delivered Zakus cramped together in the narrow hatchway of the hangar, he added, "At least we'll have some company out there."

"*Yessir!*" Leroy answered with a snappy salute. Then he kicked off the deck and floated up to the hatch of his Rick Dom, climbed in, and began strapping himself in the cockpit.

Char turned to Challia Bull. Since the two of them were finally alone, he told him what he had learned from Kycilia of Gihren's plot.

"Holy cow, sir," Challia said after hearing Char's description. "What'll these politicians think of next?"

"I don't know, but Gihren's gone too far this time. He's an intellectual anachronism."

"It's not a new problem, sir. He's just following his own flawed ideology."

"Think so?"

"I *know* so. He's an idealist, in a twisted way, and he thinks he's laying the foundation for a glorious new age. Unfortunately, he's convinced it can only be accomplished by power, by him dominating all of mankind. What he doesn't realize is that there's another way. He's just stuck in old-think mode. He's part of an old problem. Two thousand years of human history prove it."

"So why are there people like him?"

"Because individual humans are too isolated, too busy thinking about themselves to see the big picture. It's their karma."

"Same with us, right?"

"Right. It's a big problem. But I think we're on the right track. If I really believed something I was doing would help create a better world for future generations, well, frankly, I'd be ready to die for it. Wouldn't you?"

"Whoa, Lieutenant! Hold on a second! Don't be in such a hurry to vaporize yourself. Think of all the people you'd leave behind in tears."

"No parents, Commander. No wife. No girlfriend. No children. I don't have much keeping me here. But I need something to believe in, and right now I'm ready to follow you. The most important thing for us now is to time our escape right, so we aren't annihilated by Gihren. And we need to contact the Gundam and its pilot before it's too late, and either destroy him or enlist him as an ally."

"There you go. We've got to watch out for the Gundam. The thing's turned into an over-efficient killing machine. We've both got to stay alive."

"Hmph. Amuro Ray's the pilot, right? I think you once called him 'single-minded,' or 'straightforward,' right? Well, frankly, sir, I'm a little envious of him."

"Sometimes it's not a good idea to be too single-minded, Lieutenant."

"I know, sir. I agree," Challia said. "We're too complicated ourselves, Commander Char . . . er . . . or should I say Casval Deikun . . . "

The men shook hands, and climbed into the cockpits of their respective machines. Thirty minutes later the 300th Autonomous—Char's Newtype unit composed of one Braw Bro, four Rick Doms, and five Zakus—launched from the stem of *A Baoa Qu* and soared toward the combat zone.

A NEWTYPE UNIT, CHAR thought as his Rick Dom led the way. *It sounds nice, but who knows what it really means? There's no precedent for this.*

From that point on, he had no time for philosophizing. The entire area in front of him was laced with stabbing beams of light, and he had to concentrate with his whole being simply to stay alive. He even forgot about Margaret Ring Blair. He wasn't piloting a Zaku anymore, but he was still the Red Comet.

ALONG WITH THE SENIOR members of Kycilia Zabi's staff, Margaret Ring Blair boarded the *Swamel*. She knew a military showdown was approaching, for the crew shoved them into the ship's armory like cattle, shouting something about defending *A Baoa Qu* to the death. It didn't make sense to her. If they were going out to defend the space fortress, she didn't understand why so many of the officials associated with Kycilia were also being taken away. As she watched, the last senior secretary entered, accompanied by Crowley Hamon.

One of the ship's younger officers addressed them: "We may see action any minute now, so until ordered otherwise you must all remain here in this room. There are normal suits in the locker over in the corner. I advise checking them right now." With that, he left, closing the hatch behind him. Margaret made her way across the room past her colleagues, to Crowley.

"Hi," she said. "Tell me if it's my imagination, but things seem to have changed awfully fast around here ever since you walked into Her Excellency's office. What's going on?"

Crowley pulled back with a shocked look. "How should I know?" she said. "And why don't you mind your own business, anyway . . . "

Despite the rude rebuff, Margaret stared at Crowley's profile and couldn't help admiring her beautifully-shaped nose.

ON THE BRIDGE OF the *Swamel*, Kycilia Zabi issued the order to leave port. She had been assigned the task of defending the *S* field around the stem section of the *A Baoa Qu* fortress, and she had boarded the *Swamel* with every appearance of personally supervising the fortress's defense from the front. Technically, since she had informed neither Gihren nor the fortress commander, Vice Admiral Randolph Weigelman, she was still supposed to be in the *S* sector commander center, but none of the men who served her objected. They were relieved to see her with them. They much preferred to have her risk her life with them than to have her yelling out orders from the safety of the rear. None, needless to say, were aware she had really boarded the ship in a desperate attempt to avoid being vaporized in Gihren Zabi's diabolical plot.

Kycilia turned to the comm officer on the *Swamel* bridge and sternly ordered, "The vice admiral's in the *N* sector command center, but I want you to make absolutely sure all communications between me and him are routed through the *S* sector command center." Then she tried to send a message to Randolph inquiring about the position of *Mahal*. After several abortive attempts she finally received a reply.

"*Ten minutes from now we'll receive supporting fire from* Mahal, *Excellency,*" Randolph said, unaware of what was really being planned, "*with the first blast at thirty percent of potential output. The second will occur twenty minutes after the first.*"

"The first one comes ten minutes from now?" Kycilia asked.

"*We expect the Federation attackers will be routed after the first blast. The* Mahal *cylinder will be on the Gel Dorva target coordinates.*"

From his comments, Kycilia deduced that the first blast was for calibration purposes only. That meant that the second was intended for her.

"*If the second blast thirty minutes from now doesn't attain target output and doesn't do the job, Excellency, the Supreme Commander has promised to send us reinforcements. An entire fleet of ships is apparently launching right now.*"

"*Ha!*" Kycilia retorted. "I hope they have a lot of firepower. Surely you don't think he's going to send us help that arrives two or three hours late, and then expect us to thank him, do you?"

She asked the young vice admiral to continue sending her information on *Mahal* and then unilaterally signed off. *The fool,* she thought. *He doesn't even know what Gihren has in store for him!* Randolph Weigelman was a somewhat naive officer, and she knew there was no way in the world he could be acting. She ordered her comm officer to keep the laser channel with the *S* sector command center open.

Then, with several supporting ships following in its wake, the *Swamel* pulled away from the *A Baoa Qu* port.

AMURO HAD FINALLY LOCATED what he was looking for. From the area in front of him, slightly to his right, he felt a weak force flowing out toward him. Something was approaching at high speed. *I hope I'm not emitting the same sort of energy,* he thought. If he were, he wished he could somehow turn it off, for he knew that anyone else in the area with Newtype potential—someone like Char Aznable, for example—would easily be able to detect him.

He knew from books that some legendary samurai warriors had been capable of detecting another's presence, and, conversely, of stilling their own minds in order to mask their own presence. But he lived in the real world, where things were more complicated, where scientists had never even defined human consciousness. It was ridiculous to assume that psychic vibrations, or even the complex "presence" of Newtypes, could be intentionally controlled or suppressed. He did not want to believe, for example, that Dozle Zabi had some unique ability to generate the eerie, specter-like aura that he, Amuro, had detected oozing from his machine. If that was what a Newtype represented, he didn't want to have anything to do with it. As far as he was concerned, Newtypes who emitted frenzied, crazed auras were freaks.

To be a true Newtype, he realized, meant far more than merely possessing a simple ability, or a talent that others could exploit. It meant being an integral part of humanity. Newtypes were above all human. And humans were living beings. They were all inseparable.

He began to wonder. When an individual's consciousness was raised and expanded, could it exist independently from a physical form at some point? If the ability to generate an independent, free-floating consciousness was a survival advantage in the harsh environment of space, and if only the spirit, consciousness, or some form of thought-energy could transcend time and space, would anyone need a physical form? Was the physical body merely a vehicle, or a means of generating an independent consciousness? Even if it required enormous effort and training, Amuro at least wanted to believe that he could somehow control the development of his own consciousness. He had long ago realized that having a special gift did not guarantee a superior or moral character, although people tended to excuse nearly every action of someone they deemed gifted. In his own case, his own much ballyhooed Newtype potential was escalating, becoming increasingly independent, assertive, and even dangerous. His insights and his sense of prescience could help him win battles, and help him survive. But they were taking him in a totally different direction from the profound, shared empathy and spiritual communion that both Lalah Sune and Kusko Al had taught him were possible.

The more he thought about it, the more confusing it all seemed. Sayla Mass appeared to have some traits similar to his. But was he really interacting with her the way he should? Wasn't he just playing the typical male? Did the two of them really wish to have a relationship that went beyond the physical? Were they not simply two healthy young people of the opposite sex, caught up in the time compression that occurs in war, seeking temporary distraction and solace?

Ultimately, Amuro knew that he was only a military pilot and that there was a limit to what he could do. It made him feel impotent and trapped. Philosophize as he might, he had to fight to survive. His only reward was survival. Someone else, he knew, would reap the rewards of his victories. Someone like the Earth Federation leaders, secure in the safety of their underground headquarters in Jaburo.

AMURO'S THOUGHTS TRANSPIRED IN seconds, but their intensity fueled a new anger in his body that threatened to explode. He cursed, and then suddenly an enemy Zaku came at him from his upper right.

"Whoa!" he yelled. He fired, and a single blast from his beam rifle destroyed the enemy machine. The same instant, he spotted over a dozen

Jicco attack ships plunging forth in tight formation from behind the shelter of another satellite missile. He fired two blasts from his hyper-bazooka, and hit the two lead ships on either side; miraculously, the ensuing explosions took out several other ships in the formation. The other Jiccos slipped away to the rear, and he knew he wouldn't have to worry about them anymore. They were moving into a zone where battles were raging, but where their likelihood of survival was far greater than it would be against the Gundam. "See you later," he yelled after them.

The satellite missiles from *A Baoa Qu* were now providing both interference and cover for all combatants in the area. Several Zakus approached from behind one, but Amuro drove them toward Kai and Hayato. At the same time, he was careful to keep his attention focused on the "presence" approaching from his right. But then a *Musai*-class ship on his left suddenly turned toward him and fired a volley of beam blasts at him with astonishing accuracy. He was moving through space at maximum combat speed, and because of the magnetic coating on the Gundam's mechanical system, he had over twice the agility of a Zaku. Nonetheless, the beams kept getting closer and closer. It was extremely difficult to knock out a ship with a single shot unless it turned its prow directly toward him, so he aimed his rifle at its main engine. With all the blasts from its cannons, the ship was enveloped in light and hard to see clearly. But he knew what he had to do, and fired.

With a *WHOMP* the *Musai* exploded like a giant incendiary flare. The light spread throughout the combat zone, illuminating the nearby enemy Suits and smaller ships. And in the few seconds before the glow faded, Kai and Hayato were able to pinpoint most of the enemy Suits and destroy them.

In a superbly coordinated performance, the Gundam and the two Guncannons had virtually eliminated any effective resistance in their immediate area.

ON KYCILIA ZABI'S WARSHIP, the *Swamel*, the comm officer received a transmission from the Principality: "*System now in operation! Thirty seconds 'til firing. Line of elevation, ZZ-32XX22, Gel Dorva coordinates!*"

The operator on the *Swamel* bridge yelled, "*A Baoa Qu*, field NE! 323, 664! Distance, fifty kilometers!"

"Think we can clear the area on time?" Kycilia asked. From the perspective of the *Swamel*'s bridge, *A Baoa Qu* was fifty kilometers starboard to the stern.

The captain of the *Swamel* looked up anxiously at Kycilia. "All ships in the area have received the transmission," he said, "but there's such a high concentration of Minovsky particles in the area that radio is largely unintelligible. I don't know how much of the laser communications have gotten through . . . "

Kycilia was nervous, but convinced Gihren wouldn't use the first blast on her. When the war was over, if he were impeached and investigated because of the System project, he would need to somehow justify what he had done. He would need to establish that he had intended to use the laser cannon to destroy the Federation fleets and support *A Baoa Qu*. The first blast would help establish his alibi.

IN THE OPERATIONS ROOM of Zeon's General Staff Headquarters in Zum City, Gihren Zabi sat down in the spacious leather recliner reserved for the commanding officer. It was his job to push the button to activate what had now been dubbed the 'Solar Ray' laser cannon. And he took his job seriously. It was, in a sense, the final weapon.

"*Output twenty-eight percent. Approaching thirty-five percent. Start countdown.*"

"*Ten, nine, eight. . . .*"

A giant display in the center of the room showed a full view of the *Mahal* colony. On the right, over a dozen monitors showed the operations room of the battleship Guild, from which the entire *Mahal* cylinder was controlled. On one of the screens the strained face of Admiral Chapman Jirom appeared, looking in Gihren's direction. Gihren acknowledged him with a nod, while noting what a cowardly expression he wore. He had clearly overestimated the man's mettle and would have to reconsider whatever assignments he entrusted to him in the future.

"*Zero!!*" the operator yelled, a little late. Gihren pushed the special ignition button in front of him.

WHOOSH.

Gihren reflexively shielded his eyes with his hands and yelled in a mini panic, "This is what we get at *only thirty-five percent*? Is the colony cylinder going to hold up?!" Despite an automatic exposure control filter, the main display had turned sheer white, and as he stared at it, his first concern was that the cannon might not last long enough to be used in the next step of his plan. Then, as the screen gradually returned to a more normal exposure, the men in the operations room saw the unimaginable. One end of an entire sealed-cylinder colony had opened and spit out a laser beam six kilometers in diameter into space, creating residual flashes and sparks that illuminated the entire area. The beam was at less than half the output for which the system was designed. But never before in history, Gihren suspected, had man generated one so powerful.

IT TOOK ONLY A fraction of a second for the Solar Ray beam to reach the Earth Federation armada, but Amuro Ray detected it before it struck. The "force" that had been bearing directly down on him earlier was suddenly overwhelmed by an immense pressure from his right. He turned his head and in the same instant saw a beam of light split the heavens. Immediately, he knew something horrible had happened. In space, even in heavily contaminated areas, laser beams were usually invisible unless they reflected off debris and dust. But he had seen the beam.

Behind him, enormous balls of light began to mushroom, as Federation ships in the beam's path exploded. First he counted twelve flashes, then more and more . . . eighteen, twenty, twenty-three . . . Could twenty-three ships really have been destroyed? He was unable to confirm their size, but judging by the magnitude of the explosions he knew most were at least cruiser-class.

Then, as the light slowly dissipated, he sensed another, different force pushing at him from behind. It had the same oppressive quality he had experienced once before in his encounter with Dozle Zabi, but it was a compound, overlapping, merging cluster of forces. It was like an enormous howl from thousands of souls on the cusp of death; one that welled outward, disturbing the basic elements of the universe.

Amuro gasped in awe. He felt he was directly witnessing a physical manifestation of pure hate, something so intense that it could shake the heavens. He began to tremble, and then, to his astonishment, he felt, or heard, an enormous reverberation. It was a force that was not physically supposed to exist. It came out of nothing, and it resonated through a vacuum. It was like the roar of a giant tremor. Even the Gundam fuselage seemed to shake.

Where is it?! Where is it? He opened his mouth to scream and, the moment he did so, lost sight of the presence he had locked onto earlier. But he was still unable to lose the sensation that had built up in both his ears and his cerebrum. It permeated every pore in his body and threatened to tear him apart. In a futile attempt to ignore it, all he could do was scream over and over again. "*Where is it?! Where is it?!*"

Over his headphones he heard Hayato calling, "*Amuro! Amuro! What happened?!*" but he couldn't answer. Kai followed immediately, barely audible with all the static in the area, yelling, "*Hayato! Can you read me? This is Kai! Where's Amuro!? I . . . I can't see him!*" Both men were disturbed and experiencing the same reaction he was, but their voices helped him get a grip on himself.

He had to notify them of his position. The three of them needed to stay together, stay in tune with each other, if only to help detect approaching threats. He knew that turning on his 360-degree IFF laser sensors in a combat zone could cost him his life. Hoping the enemy wasn't watching, he nonetheless hit the switch for a second.

It worked. Both Kai and Hayato were now seasoned combat veterans, and the instant they detected his IFF signal, they moved to assume their normal formation on either side of him. With the shorter distance separating them, radio communications suddenly became dramatically clearer.

"*The flashes came from the area where the main Federation force's supposed to be!*" Hayato yelled. "*What the hell happened!*"

"I think it was some sort of laser attack," Amuro said. "I'm not sure, but it seemed like it came from the direction of the Principality. I could almost see it!" He was only guessing. He had no idea what had really happened. But the sensation that had made his flesh crawl a moment earlier was now slowly starting to dissipate.

"*Amuro!*" Kai yelled. "*It felt like a cold blast right through my body! What was it?!*"

"How the hell should I know?" Amuro retorted. "Concentrate on what the enemy's doing now! Not on what happened! They're starting to swarm around here!!"

He wasn't kidding. Suddenly, more and more rocket flares were visible, indicating more enemy ships and Suits launching into the darkness out of *A Baoa Qu*. And judging by their coordinated movements, none of the Zeon pilots seemed affected by the terrifying force Amuro and his comrades had just experienced.

Kai was frantic. "*Dammit! What the hell's going on?*"

"Maybe you felt it 'cuz you're a Newtype, Kai," Amuro said, sardonically. "But don't let it go to your head!"

"*Amuro! I'm serious!*" Kai was shocked by his comrade's tone, but he intuitively knew what he meant. And he also suspected that Amuro, in his ability to sense what was really happening, was evolving far beyond either himself or Hayato. "Wish I'd seen the look on your face when you said that," he added, trying to put up a good front.

"I'm not joking, Kai," Amuro added. "Once you let your abilities go to your head, it's like filtering reality—and the filter gets in the way. For most people it's better to not be aware of the kind of force we just felt." His tone was half-scolding now, but then he suddenly interrupted his speech and turned the Gundam's head to the side. A formation of Gattle fighter-bombers was bearing down on them. "Here they come!" he yelled as he aligned the sights on his beam rifle.

"Sir! Vice Admiral Karel's entire fleet has been wiped out!" a staff officer announced to an ashen-faced General Revil, seated at his desk in the rear of the *Drog*'s joint operations center. "We suspect a sneak attack with some sort of giant laser weapon, sir. Over forty craft have suddenly vanished. We've contacted only two surviving *Coral*-class ships, and they're linking up with us now. We're still conducting an investigation, but there appears to be a strong possibility that the attack originated from Zeon itself."

"Check what's happening with the *Mahal* colony immediately!" Revil ordered. His white-gloved hands kept trembling even though he had clasped them together. He moved them out of sight under his desk and tried desperately to maintain an aura of control.

My God! he thought, staring at the top of his desk. *What if we lose the war? I suppose Gihren would spare the average citizen. And if he got rid of the Jaburo bureaucrats, it'd be no big loss, I suppose. But what if all mankind has to grovel before the maniac for eternity?*

Then the same officer spoke again, and Revil heard the words, "But there's some good news, sir. I'm pleased to report that some of our units, centered around the 127th Autonomous, have reached the first combat line around *A Baoa Qu*."

Revil finally raised his face and tried to sweep his earlier defeatist notions out of his mind. *As long as those kids are still fighting,* he thought, *I've got to be here for them.* He stood up, and with a light pen on a holographic operations map indicated the course they should take.

"Our surviving fleets," he announced, after regaining his composure, "will try to breech *A Baoa Qu* defenses after the 127th has created an opening for us. We can assume the Principality has finally fired the secret weapon we've been hearing rumors of—the thing they code-named the System. It must require enormous amounts of power, so I can't imagine they'll fire it again right away, especially if we use *A Baoa Qu* as a shield. I want an all-out attack on the fortress immediately!"

Revil knew that if, as he suspected, Zeon had actually activated a colony-scale laser cannon, it would be futile to try to flee. They would probably be destroyed by another blast even before any Zeon pursuers caught up with them. On the other hand, although the cannon was powerful, it was indiscriminate. During the last blast, several Zeon ships in the wrong area at the wrong time had certainly been vaporized. It would therefore be impractical for the Zeon military to target an area where too many of its own craft were currently engaged with the enemy. The risk of destroying friendly ships would be too great.

Why, Revil wondered, hadn't Zeon fired its cannon before the Federation Forces reached the *A Baoa Qu* area? It was a mystery to him, and the only explanation he could think of was that the device had malfunctioned. *That's what always happens with new technology*, he thought. *Preparations probably took longer than planned.*

The odds in the battle had clearly shifted in Zeon's favor. And now, because of the laser cannon, there could be no retreat. There was only one thing to do, Revil concluded, and that was to stake everything on a final assault on *A Baoa Qu* and hope to occupy it. The prospects for success were bleak, but there was one ray of hope, and that was the 127th. It had already advanced far faster and farther than he had ever thought possible.

It's time, he thought. *It's time to stake everything on the* Pegasus II *and its young crew.*

Lt. Challia Bull had known the laser cannon was about to fire. But when Vice Admiral Karel's fleet was vaporized, he had nonetheless experienced a sensation as terrifying as that felt by Amuro Ray.

His Braw Bro had far more powerful engines than either a Rick Dom or a Zaku, so when he detected the presence of the Gundam and two other enemy Suits in the combat zone, he quickly moved out in front of Char Aznable.

Char made no attempt to stop him. He knew Challia wasn't hurrying simply because he wanted to engage the enemy. He knew Challia was operating on another level and following something that he—Char—couldn't detect. He also instinctively knew that the time had come for him to support Challia in combat, rather than the other way around. It was time to follow the Braw Bro. He felt connected to Challia by a thread of consciousness that enabled them to work together as a team. He felt joined by a conviction, a belief in a common goal. They were headed straight toward a dark force that even he could somehow detect.

Just when Challia sensed a faint presence ahead of him and wondered if it might be the young Gundam pilot, the *Mahal* laser cannon fired.

From Challia's perspective, hell suddenly broke loose. A curdling mass of blackness roared toward him, and he felt his Braw Bro shudder. As with the Federation pilots in the area, the sensation he perceived was real, even if his machine did not react physically. He instinctively initiated an evasive maneuver, but the force was greater than anything he had ever experienced before. It swept through his entire being, from his brain to his tailbone, rushing like a wall of black static and threatening to rip his vital organs out of his body. He could scarcely believe he was still alive, for the sensation of living, of awareness of the external world, rode precariously atop a thin layer of skin, which in turn rode atop his flesh and bones, and they were shaking uncontrollably. He burst into sweat, and pools formed around his feet inside his normal suit. His psyche rocked with waves of rage and grief.

I hope I come out of this intact, he thought vaguely, as he stared transfixed at the exploding Federation fleet in the darkness. *If I don't start moving, the Gundam'll destroy me. I've got to move! But if I die now, the terror will vanish, and what's wrong with that?! That might be better!* Then there emerged a more sobering thought, that even death might not be an escape. If there were an afterlife and his soul survived, it would be permanently scarred. His thoughts were an internal scream of despair, and an attempt to dispel his growing fear.

The next instant, he returned to his senses and became acutely aware of the sweat-caked underwear clinging to his skin. He did a quick 360-degree scan of the area in which his Braw Bro was drifting and decided he was in no immediate danger of being sniped at by the Gundam. But he knew he had to hurry before another blast came from the laser cannon. He had some business to take care of, and its importance transcended everything else. It was not yet time to die.

He checked the area once more and then heard, amid the static generated by Minovsky interference, a near-scream from his commander.

"*Challia Bull! Hurry!*" Char Aznable yelled from his Rick Dom.

Challia knew then that Char, too, had experienced it.

"ALL CREW CONCENTRATE ON *assigned tasks! No wavering now! The enemy's in front of us! Not behind!*" Bright, standing erect on the bridge of the *Pegasus II*, scolded Mirai and Sayla on either side of him, and when he did so his mike—still switched to "shipwide"—picked up and broadcast his words throughout the entire craft.

Immediately after the laser cannon attack several of the crew had experienced the same force as Amuro, Challia, and others. Some had been literally thrown out of their seats. Sayla Mass had clung to her comm panel for dear life, trembling in sheer terror. Mirai Yashima had managed to hold the ship's helm steady but had nearly vomited on it. Others, such as ship's operators Marker Clan and Oscar Dublin, and Bright himself, had felt the force but had not been affected so directly.

Mirai, with spittle flying, yelled back at her skipper. "That felt like a wind from hell, but it's not the sort of presence a true Newtype would generate!" Behind her normal suit visor she looked deathly pale, with her eyes starting to roll upward. She looked half-crazed.

"Some didn't feel a thing," Bright shouted, swallowing hard. "They're the ones in real danger now! We don't have a moment to lose. Just keep your eyes on the area we're heading into."

"*OH, MY GOD*," MIRAI groaned. Bright had been right. A formation of six Gattle fighter-bombers had already slipped through their starboard side defenses. She spun the helm and the ship heaved to port. She knew intuitively that fear was her worst enemy, that it could kill her, and she desperately tried to separate her paranoia from reality. She wished she could wipe off the spittle spattered on her face, but to do so she would have had to remove her helmet. Then she heard a *whomp!*

On a central monitor, the officer of the deck screamed: "*We've taken a hit in sector 362! Wait! Looks like a Gattle fighter-bomber crashed into us!*" Following his words, a computer graphics simulation of the damage appeared on screen.

"*On the double!*" Bright yelled, sounding slightly hysterical. "I want wall film applied immediately! Sayla! Double-check the lines to all anti-air observation posts!" He knew he had to calm down. His psyche had been rattled by the force earlier, perhaps not as much as Sayla and Mirai, but it had nonetheless slammed into his mind and rocked him. He knew the most important thing now was to help the core crew regain their senses, and that the best way to do that was to bark orders at them.

"Yessir!" Sayla shakily answered in response to his order. Her pupils were still dilated and trembling. She had suddenly become incontinent.

"Char's on his way!" Bright shouted. "Think of something we can do!" His words seemed to have an effect.

"Yessir!" she replied. "Checking anti-air observation posts." She turned to her comm console, suddenly looking very frail.

"Mark!" Bright yelled out to the ship's operator. "Find out what happened behind us! Immediately!"

"Yessir!" Marker replied. "Working on that right now! I know it sounds incredible, but it looks like Vice Admiral Karel's fleet was hit by some sort of laser blast!"

"Sayla!" Bright barked. "Open a radio channel for me!"

"Yessir! Channel open!" She switched an all-range radio channel over to the receiver on the captain's seat and out of the corner of her eye saw Bright fiddle with some controls on the front of his normal suit. Turning to Mirai, she quickly asked, "Can you feel it? Is it Char?"

Looking doll-like in her normal suit, Mirai replied, "No . . . not yet."

Sayla leaned over and stared out the bridge window at the panorama of open space. In the center, beam blasts from the *Pegasus II*'s main cannons were pulsing toward *A Baoa Qu*, and on either side, beams and regular fire from other ships and the fortress crisscrossed through the blackness, punctuated by explosions. And in the midst of this visual chaos, she sensed an enormous upheaval of the human psyche. Instinctively she knew: *Someone else, not just the men and women of the Karel fleet, will die! Someone else!* But much to her chagrin, she had no idea who it would be.

A BAOA QU

THE SOUTHERN SECTOR OF the Earth Federation Space Forces' frontline base, *Luna II*, was used to house refugees, almost all of whom had been mobilized to work in support of the military. Fraw Bow, Amuro Ray's childhood sweetheart from Side 7, was degreasing the critical parts of over a dozen ele-cars when she suddenly felt a chill surge through her body. It was so strong, and her limbs shook so hard, that she nearly lost her grip on the equipment she was operating.

For a second she wondered if she had contracted a particularly virulent form of the flu, but she quickly decided otherwise, for it was too intense. With lips trembling, she turned to Ryum, her aging coworker on the line, and asked, "Er . . . 'scuse me, but would you mind taking over for me for a minute?" Ryum took one look, instantly knew something was wrong, and told her to go lie down.

The dozen meters or so from the degreasing machinery to the employee rec room seemed to take forever. Fraw's heart began to pound, and she gasped loudly, gulping in the dusty factory air, which only aggravated her burning throat. As if in a dream, she heard someone behind her yell "*She needs a doctor!*" and only faintly realized it was Ryum. She reached the rec room door, groped for it, opened it, and staggered over to the vid-phone in the corner. *I've got to talk to someone,* she thought, as

424

she collapsed on the sofa beside the vid-phone, receiver in hand, shivering and feeling weaker and weaker. "Katz!" she groaned, calling out the name of the eldest of the three young war orphans she cared for.

Later, she would hardly remember if she had even made the call or not, for both her mind and her body seemed to have been temporarily paralyzed. But she did hear the voice of a child with a healthy pair of lungs, calling out to her, saying, "*Hey, Fraw! What's going on? Fraw! Fraw?! What happened?*" After what seemed an eternity, she mustered up enough strength to respond.

"Katz," she whispered. "I need you to come here. Just be with me for a minute . . . I'm in the factory rec room area . . . Katz . . . "

Out of the vid-phone speaker she faintly heard the young boy's voice calling once more, saying, "*Fraw? What's wrong? Fraw? I can't see your face . . .*" And then, as he apparently turned to his day care worker, "*Teacher! Something's wrong with my mom!*"

Amuro . . . Amuro, Fraw thought, *Why aren't you here with me?* She wondered if she would ever be able to understand everything he and his crewmates were going through. And then she drifted into unconsciousness. *Amuro . . . I'm wearing some lipstick today. For you, Amuro, for you. I've been trying it for you. Funny, huh?* She felt indescribably lonely. And suddenly she desperately missed the warm touch of her young charges with their soft, smooth, alive skin.

A BAOA QU. ELEVEN o'clock. Down twenty-three degrees. Relative speed, zero. Amuro knew they were getting close.

"*Damn!*" he spat, as he pulled the trigger of his bazooka one more time. In a fraction of a second a shell tore into yet another Zaku's armor and ripped it apart in the nick of time. The combat was so close-in now that he had to disengage immediately or risk being caught in the ensuing blast.

What?!

Suddenly, he heard a high-pitched sound, as if something were calling him. He looked up over his right shoulder and to his astonishment beheld the fiercest looking model of mobile armor he had ever encountered. And he was alone. Kai and Hayato were deployed off to his right and left, but at that very moment their thoughts were not linked, and he knew it would be several seconds before they realized what had happened.

Seen from the front, at a distance of three hundred meters, the Braw Bro appeared to have one twin mega particle cannon atop its fuselage and three underneath. But that, he quickly surmised, was probably deceiving; in reality it might have even more. The machine looked as if it had been there all along, just waiting for him to turn around and notice.

Why didn't I sense it come up on me? he wondered. There was no time to hesitate. He yanked his right-hand lever and put the verniers in the Gundam's legs on maximum thrust. He had to get out of the enemy machine's line of fire as soon as possible. On his monitors he saw the Braw Bro fuselage shudder and take off in pursuit of him. Then he suddenly heard it.

<*AMURO!*>

He had his normal suit headphones set to combat range, but with the Minovsky interference he could usually hear only static. The voice he heard now was clear as a bell, and not coming across on radio. And neither Kai nor Hayato appeared to have noticed it. Then he heard it again:

<*Answer if you are Amuro Ray!*>

CHALLIA BULL DETECTED SHOCK from Amuro and immediately knew he had made a mistake. He had approached the Federation pilot too abruptly, in a combat zone where MS pilots had to expect to be attacked from any direction at any time. But it was too late to turn back now. He projected his thoughts toward Amuro in a torrent.

<Fighting here is pointless. We must leave here immediately. We have other work to do. We need your help. We want to enlist your Newtype talents in our cause.>

Almost immediately, Challia picked up a sharp, reflexive response, but he overinterpreted its true meaning. He mistakenly assumed the response came because Amuro was far more advanced as a Newtype than either Char Aznable or Kusko Al. In the process, he forgot that people have both rational and emotive components to their beings, and that Amuro might not have been in a position to ponder the meaning of his words, and might only be sensing angry garbled thoughts. Challia simply knew there was no time to spare, for the laser cannon might fire again in ten minutes and take everything in its path with it.

He tried again. <We are both MS pilots, but this war won't be settled by us killing each other! We must bring it to a resolution, and we need your skills to do it. Commander Char Aznable and I are about to leave this combat area in an attempt to overthrow the Zabi family. We need your help. If we can destroy Gihren Zabi, we can end the entire war. All other problems we can deal with later. Amuro Ray! You and your comrades are like us. Follow us out of this area toward Zeon. Follow us before we're all destroyed by the System and the Solar Ray cannon!>

HAD CHALLIA'S THOUGHTS ARRIVED as concrete, audible speech, Amuro would no doubt have understood and responded as Challia hoped. Sayla, after all, had told him her brother could be trusted. Moreover, Amuro and other members of the *Pegasus II* crew had even discussed something similar to Challia's proposal among themselves previously. And General Revil, albeit in a rather oblique way, had given him and the others a virtual carte blanche to conduct the war as they saw fit. But to Amuro, Challia's thoughts were merely alien. Challia's words were based on Challia's own logic, which was in turn based on Challia's personal reality, and when they were compressed into a torrent of pure thought instead of speech the logical integrity of the statements was lost. To digest another individual's unique reality took time. To convert understanding into action took even more time. To expect it to happen in seconds was to expect the impossible.

The problem was compounded by two factors. First, thousands of Amuro's Earth Federation comrades had just been incinerated by Zeon's attack, and their souls remained unavenged. The emotive component of Amuro's personality was thus nearly frozen with terror, blocking and warping his logical thought processes. Second, Amuro was infinitely more advanced than Challia, and during his encounters with Newtypes such as Lalah Sune and Kusko Al a discrete part of his mind had been activated, making him hyper-sensitive. The intense, urgent tone of Challia's delivery felt like a violent assault on his psyche. Therefore, the more urgently Challia tried to communicate, the more Amuro was overwhelmed, and the more it felt like his mind was being raped.

Why did Challia attempt such an untested form of communication? He excelled at intuition and insight and, with Char Aznable, had occasionally succeeded in communicating his thoughts. But above all, he was desperate. <I know you're a Federation Newtype! We need your help!> he projected again.

AMURO CURSED IN RAGE and with computer-like reflexes turned his hyperbazooka toward the Braw Bro and fired twice. With the aid of the new magnetic coating on the Gundam's moving parts he was able to move faster than ever before, firing again before confirming how his first shot had performed. But somehow the Braw Bro managed to evade his attacks. It slowly dawned on him that his opponent also possessed an extraordinary ability.

The next instant he was caught off guard when a volley of megaparticle beam blasts stabbed forth at him from a point several hundred meters away from the Braw Bro. He fired the jets in the Gundam's backpack and feet and spun his MS to the left. *He hasn't perfected his aim yet,* he thought.

He's still wavering. But where will he fire from next? Could there be another machine around here?"

He intuitively sensed that the megaparticle blasts had been fired by the same person whose thoughts had assaulted him earlier. But because he did not know the mechanism that the Braw Bro employed, he had to assume the possibility of another machine. And then it dawned on him: it was like the Elmeth, with remote units it could control. The only problem was that he could not detect the crisscrossing brain waves that normally would accompany such a system.

What's going on? he wondered.

THE BRAW BRO INITIATED a zigzag evasive action, with Challia Bull still emitting powerful thought waves in Amuro's direction, trying to establish direct contact.

<I am Challia Bull. An ally of Commander Char Aznable! You must help us! We must not fight each other!>

To protect himself, Challia kept firing restraining blasts in the gray-colored Suit's direction, but it kept tearing toward him, weaving in and out in an utterly random pattern. And from the powerful psychic waves being discharged, he knew the elusive young pilot inside was highly disturbed. What he did not know was that his thoughts registered on Amuro merely as angry screams and amplified his growing outrage. Nor did he know that Amuro was desperately trying to comprehend the mechanism of the Braw Bro from its silhouette.

<Why? Why are you so angry? Calm yourself and listen to me!>

Then Challia fired two more restraining blasts from the megaparticle guns on his remote right unit and accidentally revealed his secret.

AMURO FINALLY REALIZED WHY the beams were coming at him from different directions. The machine in front of him was connected by wire to remote auxiliary cannon units. The units, separated from the main fuselage by several hundred meters, were independently aimed but not emitting psychic energy on their own, as with the Elmeth-Bits system. That was why the psychic force directed at him was focused and coming only from the main machine. And that was why, Amuro also realized, the system was so dangerous. Unlike the Elmeth-Bits system, these remote units could approach and attack him unnoticed. Amazingly, whoever was piloting the machine was trying to contact him, Amuro, at the same time he was operating the units.

Amuro lashed out at his enemy with a mental scream. <Don't let it go to your head, Newtype!>

CHALLIA WAS STUNNED. HAD he had too much faith, he wondered, in his ability to communicate with the Gundam? Had he made a colossal mistake? The young enemy Newtype was far more sensitive and emotional than he had ever imagined. Bitter and angry at himself, he began to edge away in his Braw Bro. And then it happened.

HAYATO NOTICED THE BRAW Bro and took off after it in his Guncannon in hot pursuit, firing his beam rifle. "Where'd that thing come from?" he yelled. "I never saw anything like it!"

Kai also spotted the new enemy, but he had to take care of an attacking Zaku first. He knew his buddy probably couldn't hear him, but he yelled, "Watch out, Hayato! It's a new model of mobile armor!"

Hayato closed in on the Braw Bro, carefully aiming his Suit's twin 28-centimeter shoulder cannons. The Braw Bro appeared to see him and began sighting its four cannons. Then Hayato fired and the near-impossible happened. The blast from his guns met head on with a beam from one of the Braw Bro's remote megaparticle cannons, and a huge ball of light erupted between the two machines and swirled into space.

Stunned, Hayato put his Guncannon into retreat, but the flames from the exploding unit overtook him, scorching his Suit and blowing it backward.

Amuro also took evasive action, but knew he had to stay in range of the Braw Bro. Somehow he had to find a weak point in the enemy system. He wanted desperately to warn Kai, Hayato, and his crewmates on the *Pegasus II* about what was really going on. He knew his radio transmitter wouldn't work, but somehow, he thought, if his comrades had Newtype potential, they just might understand him. He screamed.

"*Watch out! There's a Newtype out here!*"

Instead of peaceful psychic communion and universal awareness, Amuro's Newtype reality had become one of confusion and contradiction, of space combat fatigue. His scream was one of terror. Had he been a soldier in another age, fighting in the trenches on Earth, he might have had a few seconds to ponder the significance of Challia Bull's actions. And then things might have taken a different course. But he was surrounded by 360-degrees of wide-open space.

"*THE RED COMET'S OUT there!*"

Sayla's clear, urgent voice echoed in the headphones of Lt. (jg) Sleggar Law's normal suit. But try as hard as he might, he couldn't see anything in front of him other than the lines of fire he was directing toward *A Baoa Qu*. Nonetheless, he yelled at his men manning the laser sensors. "Keep your eyes open!" he barked. "If you see anything moving superfast out there, it's the Red Comet!"

Sometimes Sleggar had to slap his men. Sometimes he even kicked them. But he always made sure the ship's guns kept firing. The monitors above the scopes had a super-telescopic mode to monitor hits scored on the enemy, and although the images were of fuzzy resolution he knew the guns were reaching their target; what he could not tell was whether they were inflicting any significant damage. The more he thought about it, the more Sayla's ability mystified him. He still couldn't see a trace of the Red Comet.

On the *Pegasus*, Sleggar usually played the obnoxious boor, but he prided himself on his own common sense. After the meeting with General Revil, when Sayla had revealed her connection to the Deikun family, he had been careful not to broadcast her secret to the rest of the crew. He would have liked to, of course. He didn't feel comfortable with the idea of someone with her background not being under surveillance. But he knew that his suspicions also stemmed from a perverse curiosity. Deep down inside, he *believed* she could be trusted.

By nature, Sleggar always empathized with the misfits in any group. No matter what Sayla had done in the past, no matter how diffidently she occasionally acted toward him, he knew she could handle just about any situation. If not, she never would have hooked up with someone still as wet behind the ears as Amuro Ray. She was an adult and knew what she was doing. If they got through this battle without being betrayed by her, he fantasized, he might steal her from Amuro and bed her himself. In a rare moment of serious reflection, he decided she would be worth it. *But if you turn out to be a traitor, Sayla,* he thought with a chuckle, *I'll strip you naked and feed you to the cold black vacuum of space.*

Then, suddenly, Sleggar felt a strange sensation pierce his forehead. *Char?* He quickly scanned the heavens once more with his scope monitors. Something was still reverberating in his mind, leaving an almost visible trail behind it.

Is this it? he wondered. *Is this what Mirai and Sayla have been talking about? The "presence" or "force" they mentioned?* To his astonishment, there, in an area where nothing had been visible before, he saw something flash with a reddish hue.

If he could have, he would have fired the *Pegasus's* main cannons at it, but he knew the light was coming from a combat zone where their own Suits were involved in a melée with the enemy. He felt helpless.

"WHAT'S GOING ON WITH the Gundam?" Bright yelled in Sayla's direction.

She was dressed in her normal suit, monitoring the comm console, and from her position she couldn't easily tell what was worrying her skipper. "No change, sir," she reported. "At least it seems that way . . ." She was carrying out her assigned task to the letter, her voice clear and steady, without betraying the slightest hint of her own feelings.

"Operators!" Bright barked. "What's happening?"

"Both C108 and C109 appear to be doing fine, sir," Ensign Oscar Dublin replied, checking the left and right displays he always monitored from his perch.

Then a near-scream suddenly came from Mirai Yashima, startling everyone on the bridge. "*Red Comet!*" she yelled, staring out the window. "Closing in on us!"

Ensign Marker Clan, the ship's other operator, answered right after her: "Portside! Two Suits! Eleven o'clock, two minutes! Up twenty-seven degrees!"

For a moment the *Pegasus* crew feared their ship was finally about to fall prey to the Red Comet, but Mirai had overreacted. The two Suits approaching were Rick Doms belonging to Lt. (jg) Leroy Gilliam and a fellow pilot.

AFTER WEAVING THROUGH THE *Pegasus*'s defensive fire, Leroy finally got his first close look at the ship's unique shape. He could understand why Zeon pilots called it a Trojan Horse, but it was far more elegant than he had imagined. Compared to the videos that Zeon scouts had brought back in the past, the real ship looked delicate, ethereal, almost fantastic.

Leroy was an artist by training, and the *Pegasus* aroused mixed feelings in him. He was envious of its beauty and felt enormous respect for the Earth Federation for having adopted such an incongruous design for its Newtype unit. Suddenly, the enemy seemed far more creative to him than the Principality of Zeon. *How can we possibly win against the Federation?* he wondered, as he fired a blast from his beam bazooka and immediately initiated evasive maneuvers.

Damn! His blast seemed to have had no effect. The ship was still steady on course. Perhaps he had aimed at the wrong spot. His job was to gain time so Char Aznable and Challia Bull could approach the Gundam, and he had interpreted his orders to mean that he should avoid hitting the ship's bridge. The crew of the "Trojan Horse," after all, might be the very Newtypes they would want to enlist in their cause. There was no concrete evidence to support this theory, but he wanted to believe it. The ship's defensive fire was so intense, he couldn't get any closer.

"Jeez! What am I gonna do?" Leroy cried inside his Suit. "If the Commander doesn't decide what *he's* gonna do soon, I'm gonna be fried!"

TAILING THE BRAW BRO in his Rick Dom, Char Aznable realized his plans were starting to unravel. He began to worry that he might have put too much faith in Challia. The initial contact with the Gundam hadn't gone well, and Amuro Ray's reaction had been far too intense. Char hadn't been prepared for that. He had been stunned himself by the Solar Ray attack, in much the same way Amuro Ray must have been. He, too, had trembled in fear. But he had thought that the attack would have made enlisting the Federation Newtypes in his cause easier, rather than more difficult.

The combat zone where the Braw Bro and the Gundam now faced off was interlaced with bands of fire and waves of psychic confusion. *What the hell's going on?* Char thought with irritation. He jammed his Rick Dom's power levers for maximum thrust, and the flares from the rocket engines in its skirted base suddenly widened dramatically, sending him accelerating toward the Gundam so fast that for a moment the four Zakus following him imagined he might enter a sci-fi warp speed. They didn't try to keep up, but instead deployed themselves in the battle zone to keep hostile Suits and ships from entering the area.

THE *SWAMEL* AND THREE escorts waited on standby alert ten kilometers out from *A Baoa Qu*. From Kycilia Zabi's perspective, on the bridge of the *Swamel*, it looked as if the Earth Federation Forces were going to make a suicidal attack on the space fortress. Warships under Vice Admiral Randolph Weigelman's command, she therefore assumed, would converge along the first combat line in the *S* field, which, in the three dimensionality of space, meant that her unit would be assigned the top of a cone-shaped defensive perimeter.

"Now's our chance," she muttered to herself. "But where's that damned Char Aznable? It's been over five minutes since the first Solar Ray attack."

A communications officer handed her an envelope and announced, "We've received a communication from the *S* field command center, Excellency. It's been forwarded from Randolph Weigelman. He's requesting acknowledgment . . . "

Kycilia carefully read the message. She knew the vice admiral was still unaware she had left her command post and boarded the *Swamel*. She turned to her ship's captain and ordered, "Send five squads of Zakus

out in front of the *Swamel*. This ship is to be part of the final defense
line and is supposed to move forward another ten kilometers. That's an
order from the command center, understand? Take us forward slowly.
As slowly as possible!"

She sent a reply to Randolph indicating she understood his communication but sent it via the *S* field command post to make sure he
would think she was still there. Then she performed an urgent check on
the progress of the 300th—Char Aznable's unit. *I wish I knew what my
damn brother's plotting now*, she thought. She still had no concrete proof
that Gihren was planning to hit *A Baoa Qu* next time.

A young lieutenant from General Staff then brought her news of
Federation losses. "We have almost certain reports that two Earth Federation divisions were annihilated in the earlier attack, Excellency."

"And what about our losses?"

"Two battleships, seven heavy cruisers, six light cruisers, and an
unknown number of other ships missing, Excellency."

If the reports were true, Kycilia knew Revil had lost nearly one-third
of his entire armada. But in spite of that, his forces were pursuing their attack with equal if not greater ferocity. With their rear escape route cut off
and fearful of next being broadsided by another blast, they were probably
desperate, and hoping to occupy and use *A Baoa Qu* itself as cover.

"And General Revil?" she asked. "Was he eliminated, too?"

"We have no confirmation of that yet."

"Any evidence of long-range nuclear weapons being used by the
Federation?"

"Not yet, Excellency. We consider it highly unlikely that Revil
himself would violate the Antarctic Treaty."

Something about the soft tone of the young man's voice angered
Kycilia. "We're at war, Lieutenant," she reprimanded him. "We're not
playing games. Never assume *anyone* will follow *any* rules!"

"Y-Yes, Excellency!" the officer stammered in reply, his face redden-
ing. "We simply have no indication any missiles have been intercepted
in the mine fields protecting the fatherland." It was a feeble attempt at
self-justification.

"And have you personally verified this?" Kycilia yelled. "If not, get
out!!" Some of the officers from General Staff seemed to have no idea
how much Minovsky particles, which absorbed radar and radio waves,
could distort all information. It was depressing to think how many men
like him there were around her.

"Well?" she demanded of the ship's starboard operator. "Any contact
with Char yet?!"

"N-not yet, Excellency," came a nervous reply. The operator was having a hard time. The area in front of field E was now bathed in dazzling light from a full moon and the explosions of combat, which made using a telescopic lens to search for the enemy extremely difficult. This was one time Kycilia wished for a layer of air, which, by blurring far-off objects, would at least provide a better sense of distance.

Things are going too well for Gihren, she thought. Because General Revil's attack was advancing too fast, Gihren could use the second Solar Ray blast to "aid" *A Baoa Qu.* If it so much as creased the space fortress, there would be huge Principality losses and Kycilia and her forces would probably be destroyed, but Gihren could claim it had been necessary to "save" the fortress. Revil was handing Gihren a golden opportunity to execute his diabolical plot without having to incur an iota of guilt.

"Damn you, Revil!" Kycilia cursed under her breath. "Disperse your forces, or you're digging your own grave, and mine, too!" She turned to the ship's operator again, shook her fist, and screamed, "*Where's Commander Char!?*"

"OMNI-DIRECTIONAL ATTACK" DESCRIBED THE Braw Bro when it deployed its four wire-guided cannon units the maximum distance and then struck the enemy. Lt. Challia Bull had already lost one of the lower cannon to the Gundam, but he still had three left. Only a few seconds earlier he had appealed to Amuro to flee the area and help him in the campaign to destroy Gihren. But now his mind was filled with murderous thoughts. Instead of restraining blasts, he was desperately trying to destroy the enemy Suit.

IRONICALLY, CHALLIA'S CHANGE OF mind helped shock Amuro out of his confusion and helped him suddenly concentrate on the reality of combat. He saw an apparition-like cloud ooze out of the enemy machine, just as he had from Dozle Zabi's Big Zam. It was not as dark, but he knew it was a manifestation of the pilot's combative mindset.

"You *bastard!*" he screamed inside his cockpit. "What the hell do you think you're doing? Trying to kill me with black magic?" In spite of the deliberate randomness of the enemy machine's movements, he had already deduced a pattern in them and realized how the "omnidirectional" attack system worked.

CHALLIA BULL WAS MOMENTARILY distracted. Two enemy Suits—Guncannons—suddenly assumed positions above and below the Gundam. Then one swept up at him from below with its shoulder guns blazing, while the other attacked from above. Had the three enemy pilots been of ordinary ability, he could have destroyed them easily with his remaining independent, wire-guided cannons. But these were Newtypes.

AMURO'S NERVOUS SYSTEM WENT into action. And because he was a Newtype, he was capable of moving with blinding speed. Taking immediate advantage of the confusion he sensed in the Zeon pilot, he instantly drew a bead with his beam rifle and fired. A narrow beam of light zapped out of the rifle barrel and seared a gaping hole in the enemy machine's cockpit.

IN THE INSTANT BEFORE he evaporated from the full force of billions of searing mega particles, Challia Bull's last thought was one of pure shock, and a belief that he had been shot by a mentally deranged Newtype. Then the Braw Bro's main engines blew, and the entire machine flowered into a ball of light.

KAI SCREAMED, "*CHAR!*" BUT neither his words nor the thought behind them reached Amuro.

The instant Amuro's shot hit the Braw Bro, his nervous system had virtually shut down. In the frenzy of combat, his hypersensitive nervous system had temporarily overloaded, blocking his comprehension of Challia's thoughts. But now, in a delayed reaction, he had finally realized what Challia had been trying to do and had been seized with profound self-loathing. True, he had been stunned by the Solar Ray attack just before encountering the Braw Bro, but he had been grossly mistaken in thinking Challia's attempt at communication was an attack, and in then destroying him.

My God! What have I done?!

Memories of Lalah Sune and Kusko Al immediately returned. Perhaps it had all been an illusion, a hallucination, but he truly believed they had shown him a vision beyond time, encompassing both the past and the future. If he were truly worthy of them, and if he understood what their lives had meant, then he surely should have been able to understand what Challia Bull, risking his very life and soul, had tried to convey to him in their brief encounter. It seemed he had learned nothing.

Slowly, the significance of what had happened began to sink home. *And he said we had to get out of here.* Amuro sank into a deep, paralyzing despair. The Gundam continued traveling on inertia in a straight line through space.

CHAR AZNABLE WAS STUNNED. *"Damn it, Challia!"* he screamed in grief. *"It was too soon!"* The unthinkable had happened, and Challia had been destroyed because of his haste. But was their plan destroyed, too? Could they still not ensnare the Gundam's pilot? The enemy mobile suit looked as though it had been mortally damaged in the showdown with the Braw Bro. It was drifting seemingly frozen, and the pilot, from all appearances, was unconscious. For a second Char was torn by confusion. Should he abandon his idea and merely follow Kycilia out of the area? If they left such a powerful Suit alone, he worried, it would surely come after them, and destroy them.

The seconds Char wavered gave his enemies an opening. With a *wham*, a shell from a red Guncannon exploded next to his Rick Dom. Then another. And another. His Suit shuddered and miraculously survived, yet he felt a sound like that of a howl of wind go through his mind and knew it was not a hallucination; he knew it came from the Guncannon pilot. He maneuvered his Suit to cross in front of the enemy and then spotted yet another Guncannon closing in on him with breathtaking speed. Instinctively, he knew its rifle was sighted directly on his chest. In a flash he twisted away, turned back, aimed his beam bazooka, and fired before the Guncannon pilot could adjust.

Char's bazooka belched fire. A light suddenly illuminated Hayato Kobayashi's Guncannon. It turned white hot, melted, and dissolved in a ball of light that spread through the black sky in huge rings.

AMURO RAY SUDDENLY WOKE from his semiconscious state. A terrible scream pierced his mind and he instantly knew it was Hayato's death cry. He gritted his teeth and experienced his friend's death as if it were his own. But the shock focused his mind again on the battlefield before him. As the light from Hayato's exploding Guncannon swirled into the vacuum of space, expanding farther and farther, he knew what he had to do.

He screamed in rage, stomped on the accelerator pedals, jammed the left and right control levers forward, and leapt over the explosion. In his earphones he could hear Kai weeping. When he checked, he realized the surviving Guncannon was only fifty meters away, below and to his left, but positioned so that the light would blind him to an enemy approach.

"Kai!" Amuro yelled. "The Red Comet's on the other side of the explosion! But he's not the enemy! He's on our side! We've got to help him!"

"What?!" Kai screamed. *"But he just killed Hayato!"*

Ignoring Kai, Amuro turned his Gundam around toward the *Pegasus II* in the distance and plunged toward it. He activated his front laser sensors and temporarily locked his course. He knew if the Gundam wavered at all they would never be able to read the message he was about to send.

"G3 to *Pegasus II*! This is the Gundam! The Red Comet is trying to enlist our help! This area has been targeted for the next laser attack by Gihren Zabi! Leave here immediately. Follow Char Aznable!" And then it happened.

AFTER EVADING THE GUNCANNON'S explosion, Char again sighted the Gundam and by its movement realized the pilot had suddenly revived. But so did two other Rick Doms in his unit. Lt. (jg) Leroy Gilliam and his partner, in charge of maintaining diversionary fire against the *Pegasus*, had spotted the Gundam's laser sensor signals and targeted their source. As Char watched in horror, they fired their beam bazookas and scored direct hits on the Federation Suit.

"*Leroy!*" Char screamed.

The Gundam fuselage straightened and then, like hundreds of other Suits and ships he had seen before, exploded in a ball of light. But at the same moment, an enormous dark cloud permeated his mind. "The Gundam finally realized what we're trying to do, Leroy!" he screamed, but Leroy, of course, never heard him. He was left to curse his own carelessness. He had put too much faith in Challia Bull's ability and too much trust in the young Leroy. He was supposed to be a commander, a leader of men, and now he felt like an utter idiot. His curses echoed in his cockpit as he fell into a paroxysm of self-loathing.

Suddenly, in the midst of Char's mental chaos and confusion, an alien thought appeared.

Amuro?!

It lasted only a second, but he instinctively knew it had come from the Gundam pilot. And in the same instant, another awareness welled up in him, churning through old memories, echoing over and over again, deep in his soul.

Lalah?

Incredibly, he felt as though he had entered another dimension of communication. He could "hear" her.

<Commander, I'm so happy to be with you again. I'm grateful to Amuro Ray, because this never would have been possible without him. But most of all, I'm grateful to you. You made the connection, you

helped me realize my true potential, to realize how far human awareness can expand.>

Then Char "heard" the Gundam pilot again.

<I know I was naive, Char. Char Aznable. Or should I say Casval Deikun? I'm the one who hung around your sister. The one who killed Lalah Sune and Kusko Al. The one who was unable to figure out what you were trying to do and screwed up your plans as a result. What can I say? I'm sorry.>

Next Char felt the presence of someone else and to his astonishment realized it was Kusko Al. Somehow Amuro Ray, Lalah Sune, and Kusko Al were all alive, and distinct entities in his consciousness. Their presence assaulted his brain like a giant flare.

<You were always cute, Commander, because you always tried so hard. You tried so hard to be in control, to be mature, to be a schemer. Compared to you, Amuro was too well-behaved. Oh, he was *too* good. Ha ha ha . . . >

CHAR'S EXPERIENCE WAS REAL, unique, and transcendent. But he knew it was not a result of his own expanded consciousness. Rather, it resulted from the intensity of the psychic waves that Amuro Ray himself had emitted. Amuro's stored psychic potential had literally exploded.

In the midst of this shower of psychic waves, Char was still able to question his own actions objectively. He was enraged by his own weakness and failure to have helped Lalah, Kusko, or even Amuro. To his shock, Amuro's consciousness continued communicating, with Lalah Sune and Kusko Al interjecting comments.

<Ah, I can see why you'd feel that way, Char. After all, at one point you wanted to kill me even if it meant betraying your own sister. Frankly, I was always frustrated myself. I felt like I was light-years away from Lalah Sune or Kusko Al in terms of my development. And I killed them both.>

<They called him 'wet behind the ears,' Commander.>

<That's right, Commander. He was just a kid. I should teach him the words to "London Bridge.">

<So anyway, Char Aznable. My advice to you is to work for a world where people don't die pathetic deaths like I did. For starters, for the sake of all mankind, someone has to get rid of Gihren Zabi. I know you can do it. If anyone can, you can.>

CHAR WAS OVERWHELMED. "AMURO Ray! You're already *dead!*" he exclaimed. "What gives you the right to say anything? If you're so enlightened, why were you so afraid of what Challia was trying to tell you? Why'd you let yourself be killed by someone as green as Leroy?" Then, in a moment of pure perversity, he yelled, "You may be in some sort of spirit Nirvana now, Amuro Ray, but you'll never get either Lalah Sune or Kusko Al!!" It was his ultimate insult, and he regretted it the moment he said it. Amuro never had time to answer, for his consciousness had already diffused into the cosmos.

LT. (JG) LEROY GILLIAM was also contacted.

Psychic waves flowed into his cerebrum, mixed with fleeting, undefined images of two women. The thoughts never formed a solid, logical continuum. As with Amuro when he had first encountered Lalah Sune, Leroy Gilliam's mind was overwhelmed by the utter newness of the experience.

"Is this the Gundam pilot?" he said out loud, sensing Amuro's presence.

<Laugh if you want, Lieutenant. It is. Don't ever forget, you're like me. You're young. And you make mistakes. But there's no room for mistakes in this game. So be careful. Sometimes, even when the combat's intense, you have to be aware of what's going on outside yourself. Don't be rash. Don't be too self-absorbed. Don't make the same mistakes I made.>

For some reason, Leroy was later left with a single, burning impression that he knew had come directly from Amuro. Later, after everything blurred, he would think, *Char's a Newtype.*

AS KAI SHIDEN WATCHED, Amuro's Suit was enveloped in an explosion even bigger than that which had swallowed Hayato. He raged and wept. But the same psychic resonance that had affected both Char Aznable and Leroy Gilliam seeped into his consciousness, too. And it left an even more clearly defined impression. In his mind, Amuro spoke clearly.

<Hayato was killed, but now you've got to help Char Aznable, Kai. You've got to look beyond the immediate tragedy or everyone will die. Gihren Zabi's the real enemy! Then, after Gihren, *Jaburo!*>

"Damn you, Amuro!" Kai sobbed bitterly. "Why'd you go off and get killed? Why'd you leave us?! Prob'ly 'cuz you didn't have an amulet, that's why! Why should I listen to you now?" He knew he couldn't possibly carry out Amuro's wishes alone. He continued raging, but he knew the things Amuro and the other MS pilots had speculated about were more than a dream. They were gradually coming true. The world they knew *was* changing. Amuro's exploding consciousness had affected everyone in the immediate area with Newtype potential, subtly creating a thread of common awareness even among sworn enemies. Kai instinctively knew that he was now linked by a new consciousness with Char. The universe, which for the last few seconds seemed to have frozen, was about to change. With bloodshot eyes, he scanned the space in front of him.

IN THE *PEGASUS II*'s main gun turret, Lt. (jg) Sleggar Law suddenly tapped the headset built into his normal suit helmet. A voice, or a thought, had suddenly slipped into his consciousness.

<The Red Comet's different from the others, Sleggar! You have to follow him now! If you stay here, you're all finished. You must escape from this area. Turn your guns on the true enemy.>

Sleggar turned around and exclaimed to his men, "Somebody say this area's dangerous?" When no one replied, he checked the space in front of the ship and to his astonishment saw a huge ring of light spreading through the blackness. Immediately, he knew. It was Amuro.

So that, a speechless Sleggar realized, *was a true Newtype.*

MIRAI YASHIMA WAS MANNING the helm as usual when she heard the voice.

<Mirai! Char Aznable's not who you think he is. He's got a plan to end the war. Follow him out of this area immediately. Understand? Gihren Zabi's next laser attack's intended to take the entire *A Baoa Qu* space fortress with it. You've gotta escape. Go with Char, Mirai. He's right. Concentrate on destroying Gihren Zabi. Then Jaburo. That'll end the war. Newtypes have to work together!>

"*Amuro!*" Mirai screamed. "*Amuro—!*"

"THAT WAS AMURO?" BRIGHT said, staring in shock at the light in the sky.

As if in answer, Sayla reported over the comm system in a muffled voice, "It was a direct hit." Amuro's consciousness had already pierced her mind like a storm, and to her embarrassment, she had again lost control of her bladder.

<Have more confidence in yourself, Sayla. You always pretend to be strong, but you still depend psychologically on your brother. That's not the real you, Sayla. You've made it this far on your own. Without Casval. Casval is now Char. You're Sayla. You're an adult. Heck, you even initiated me into adulthood, Sayla . . . >

Sayla detected sadness in his message. She felt her body and mind relax. If only, she wished, it were possible to erase the pain the physical body remembered.

<Sayla! I don't want to die alone. I want you! If only I could feel your warmth again. If only you could love me again. Forever. I wish I could take you with me . . . I don't want to go alone. I don't want to die alone. Sayla . . . >

Not all of Amuro's last thoughts were dedicated to Sayla. There was one other person he had to communicate with, and she knew it and tried to accept it.

<It's . . . it's not like you think, Sayla . . . >

FRAW BOW LAY SEMICONSCIOUS in a ten-bed ward of the *Luna II* military hospital. The night lamp beside her illuminated her trembling form, curled up under her blankets. Suddenly she saw Amuro, standing next to her.

<Fraw. Did the fever go away?>

<Yes, Amuro, it did. You look so tired. What happened? What are you doing here? The war's not over yet, is it?>

<No, Fraw. I'm here to tell you I won't be able to see you again.>

<But why? Why now? I thought you'd forgotten about me.>

<I never forgot you, Fraw. Really. I never did.>

When Fraw raised her head from her bed and looked at Amuro, his pilot suit seemed to be glowing gently. He looked almost translucent, but nonetheless real.

<How are the kids? It's awful quiet around here without them.>

<Forget about them, Amuro, they're fine. You don't have much time, right? You're going away forever, and we'll never meet again, right? Just tell me about yourself.>

<There's nothing to say, really. I just came 'cause I wanted to see you. I was worried. And I hoped you were all right. I'm glad your fever finally went down.>

<Amuro.>

Fraw held out both arms as if to welcome Amuro and he bent over and hugged her. She could feel his weight and his warmth throughout her body. It was the first time, she realized, she had ever embraced him like this. Amuro was with her! Amuro was in her heart!

<I'll never let you go, Amuro. Never! You're mine, Amuro!>

And then she heard words that wrenched her soul:

<I'm sorry, Fraw. But I'm already dead.>

<No! No! You *can't* be!> Fraw nearly screamed. Her arms, clinging to thin air, suddenly collapsed on her chest. <Please, Amuro. Don't go! What'll I do? *Please* . . . >

JUST AS FRAW REALIZED she was communicating with neither thoughts nor words, Amuro's last message swept over her numbed psyche. <Don't worry, Fraw. You'll be all right. Those little kids'll keep you busy. They're a gift from God.>

Fraw Bow finally lost control. Tears streamed down her cheeks, and she burst into sobs.

THERE WERE OTHER THINGS Amuro tried to convey. He tried to explain the first leap in consciousness he had experienced in his encounter with Lalah Sune. He tried to demonstrate how one individual's consciousness could fuse with that of another, how in the process his consciousness had nearly exploded. His message did not register on everyone, for his thousands of thoughts transpired in an instant, and to separate them into discrete ideas required the ability to interpret vast quantities of information simultaneously—in short, the ability of a potential Newtype. Without that ability, Amuro's explosion of ideas was merely perceived as thought garbled beyond recognition, like the farewell cry of the thousands of individuals incinerated by the Solar Ray attack earlier, whose collective thoughts had been felt as a solid wave of terror.

But there *were* potential Newtypes in the area. And they picked up the information relevant to them and sensed the living consciousness of Lalah Sune and Kusko Al that existed in Amuro's mind.

ON THE PEGASUS II, Lt. Bright Noa switched the bridge phone to ship-wide and commanded, "We shall henceforth evacuate the area and proceed directly to the Zeon heartland. All forces are ordered to be on the alert for attacks from *A Baoa Qu* but to refrain from firing on the skirted Suits and the Zakus accompanying us. Full speed ahead!"

Mirai, hands on the helm, energetically replied "Yessir!" in acknowledgment. She now trusted her skipper implicitly; he had made precisely the same decision she would have made.

"Sayla!" Bright ordered. "Open a comm channel for Char Aznable. And let General Revil know immediately why we have to leave the area. He's got us under observation from the main armada."

"Yessir," Sayla replied, her still trembling hands resting on the switches of the comm console in front of her.

"Hurry!" Bright barked. "We don't have a minute to lose!"

CHAR AZNABLE, OUT IN space in his Rick Dom, lined up his laser sensor sights on the *Pegasus II* while Leroy and his other men covered for him. When the laser was correctly calibrated, a voice issued from his headphones saying, "*Commander Char Aznable. This is the* Pegasus II. *We have decided to leave the area with you. We await your instructions.*" The voice was official-sounding, but he immediately knew it was that of his sister, Artesia. After a second of stunned silence, he replied with the information she wanted, telling her the best course to take to avoid the next Solar Ray attack. Then he added, "But don't expect all your ships to be able to make it. The Solar Ray's fully capable of strafing us along the way."

"We read you, Commander," Sayla answered.

"And I request that the *Pegasus* follow the *Swamel.*"

"*Your request is understood,*" Sayla replied firmly.

When Char heard how clear and strong his sister's voice was, he felt somehow reassured. They had been separated for years, but he knew she had developed the strength of character to survive.

Then Char notified the *Swamel* that he was leaving the combat area and joining it.

IN THE MIDST OF a raging, Armageddon-sized space battle, a warning from a single ship stood a high probability of being overlooked, especially when both radio and laser transmissions were highly unreliable and there was no guarantee of the integrity of the information.

On General Revil's flagship, the *Drog*, the crew received a strange, confusing message from the *Pegasus II*. It eluded Revil's comprehension, for he lacked enough knowledge to put it into its proper context.

"It says here, sir, '*LEAVE AREA*' but I'm not sure what that means, sir. What do you think?"

"I don't know, either," Revil, answered. "It's possible they're leaving in order to avoid another attack from the Principality's laser cannon, but it's hard to see how retreating or changing course would help us at this point. We have to move to a point where *A Baoa Qu*'ll provide some cover for us in case another laser attack comes. It's just that we don't know when it'll come."

"I don't see how they could try and fire so close to *A Baoa Qu*, sir," said one of his aides. "It'd be a real mess. They'd never dare."

Revil laughed at his staff officer. "You're being way too optimistic," he said. "Don't forget there's a man sitting in an easy chair in a room in Zeon with his finger on the button. And all he has to do is move that finger a centimeter, and *wham*, the laser cannon goes off. It'll go off even if he sneezes. And besides, in a life-and-death struggle, he's not going to worry if things get a little messy. If I were in Gihren Zabi's shoes and thought I had a chance of annihilating most of the Federation Force, heck, I'd push the button even if it would generate a few casualties on my own side. Gihren can always shed a tear and mourn the Zeon losses later. He can always claim they were for a greater cause—for total victory."

"I, I see your point, sir."

THE SPECTER OF DEATH hung over the entire area around *A Baoa Qu*. The *Pegasus II* slipped by the space fortress and began following the *Swamel*. Between Kycilia's fleet and the *Pegasus II* were Char Aznable and the seven mobile suits under his command. The pilots were all silent. All were beginning to understand the true significance of their mission. One, Leroy Gilliam, opened the visor of his pilot suit and wiped tears from his eyes. And he uttered the same words Amuro Ray had uttered before him.

"My God. What have I done?"

ZUM CITY

ZUM CITY DERIVED ITS name from the late Zeon Zum Deikun's middle name and served as the Principality of Zeon's capital—its military, political and administrative center. The port sector of the giant sealed-cylinder colony held the branch offices of the Secret Service, whose personnel worked hand in hand with the customs and immigration authorities.

Looking out a giant window in his office, Lt. Ramba Ral could clearly see *Mahal* some 180 kilometers in the distance. The work shifts on the immigration check were not scheduled to change yet, but he had put a stop to inspections of embarking passengers two hours earlier. He and the dozen men in his command all knew *Mahal* was about to fire, and they watched and waited with bated breath.

"It's time . . . "

Before Ramba Ral finished his sentence, an enormous flare of light burst out of the end of the distant cylinder. The entire colony, six kilometers wide and thirty kilometers long, had been turned into a giant laser cannon, but the flare had come from the residual matter in the cylinder that had incinerated on ignition; the actual laser beam itself was invisible. Nonetheless, despite a five-layer window with built-in filters, Ramba and his men were overwhelmed by the intensity of light.

CHAPTER TWENTY-THREE

One of the younger men exclaimed nervously, "If that thing were aimed at the moon, it'd blow it out of the sky!"

"And that's not even at full power!" another marveled.

"The Federation attack on *A Baoa Qu*'s proceeding too fast," Ramba calmly said. "That's why they had to use it." Then the vid-phone next to him rang, and he grabbed the receiver.

"*This is the Communications division of the 58th Battalion on the System project. Admiral Chapman Jirom has a message for you and your men in the S.S. The second blast will take place twenty minutes from now. Until it is over you are ordered to stop any and all ships leaving Zum City.*"

"Instructions understood," Ramba replied.

The men around him who overheard the interchange suddenly began whispering among themselves.

"That was a *test*. They say the *next* blast's for real."

"That means the war's over, right? Twenty minutes from now."

Ramba pressed a button to lower the shutters on the outside wall of windows, turned around, and strolled over to pick up a coffee tube from a machine in the corner of the room. *So this is what the Supreme Commander meant by "settling this thing for once and for all,"* he thought. He could understand Gihren's mind-set, but at the same time he worried about Crowley. He knew the first blast had missed her, but there was a strong possibility the second would not. The real question was how Kycilia would interpret and react to whatever information Crowley had brought her. *Her life's hanging in the balance,* he concluded, *unless she can get away from the front lines or unless Revil changes his strategy.*

Ramba rarely thought about the fact that Gihren Zabi might be suspicious of Crowley's activities. He knew it was possible but never lost any sleep over it. And as for himself, his integrity and fatalistic attitude ultimately formed a veil that even Gihren's secretary, Cecilia Irene, was unable to see through. He was the type of man who served his master loyally no matter what. And it was not a charade. He simply had no idea that the little seed he had planted in Crowley's mind might eventually cause Gihren's death. Crowley Hamon was already working on another, more independent level.

As voices echoed through the Zum City Joint Command Operations room during the technical check, Gihren Zabi found he enjoyed watching the tension building on the faces of those around him. Pictures from observation satellites already indicated the test blast had achieved everything he had hoped for. The *Mahal* colony cylinder, in its new role as a laser oscillator, had performed exactly as designed. Only half the energy supplied by the solar batteries installed in the area around the colony had been used. It would not even be necessary to wait another twenty minutes for the next blast.

Suddenly, a terminal in front of Gihren indicated a problem, and several technicians dashed up and gathered before it. "What's this?" he demanded. "Two faulty microcircuits?"

He knew any equipment put in place so rapidly was likely to develop some problems. They were also in an area that was not entirely devoid of Minovsky particles, and there was bound to be some interference. But at least the effectiveness of the System had been proven. The Federation armada was part of Earth's last-ditch effort, and if the armada could be annihilated, it would inevitably mean the defeat of the Earth Federation. And if, in the process of ending the war, he could also eliminate his sister on *A Baoa Qu*, it would be like bagging two birds with one stone.

Captain Hasebe of the Engineers Corps was standing in front of him with his back turned.

"*Well*, Captain?" Gihren casually asked.

Hasebe spun around and said in a strained voice, "We can do the job at seventy-eight percent of power, Excellency. But the surviving Federation Forces seem to be regrouping slowly, sir. I think it's still too early to fire again."

Gihren turned to a General Staff officer standing behind him to his left. "Do you agree?" he asked.

"Yes, sir," the officer replied. "The forces under Vice Admiral Randolph Weigelman's command, and also those of Her Excellency Kycilia Zabi, are gradually closing in on the enemy, sir. If we fire the cannon now the losses to our own forces will be enormous. I suggest that using it immediately is out of the question. But I think we might win anyway."

"Don't ever use the word 'might' in front of me, Officer," Gihren suddenly hissed.

"Yessir! Beg your pardon, Excellency!" the man apologized.

"You don't think we should just sit back and *watch*, do you?"

"No, *sir*! Not at all, sir!"

"Good," Gihren replied calmly. He had just decided to wait another two or three minutes before making his final decision, when one of his aides in the room announced, "Admiral Chapman Jirom's on the hot line, sir."

Chapman hopefully wasn't going to create a problem, Gihren thought. The man was starting to grate on his nerves. The console in front of him was reserved for the commanding officer of the operations center, and it had a special box built into it with a secure comm line for confidential conversations. He lifted the lid on the box and took out a bright red receiver, whereupon an image appeared on the display directly above it, showing Chapman standing at attention holding a similar receiver.

"*In ten minutes we'll be ready for the second blast, Excellency. We await your decision on timing and the, er, final target.*" Chapman's voice was low and restrained, as if he were afraid someone would overhear him. Gihren wished he were more forthright.

"I've decided to wait a few minutes and see how things develop, Chapman. But there'll be no change in the final target. As soon as we fire up the laser cannon, we'll also start strafing on the Zig line as planned."

"Yes, *sir!*" Chapman answered, saluting.

"We'll say it was an accident. Understand, Chapman? An accident. I'll let you know as soon as I decide."

Gihren was trying to be easy on the man but wondered if it were a mistake. Perhaps he should have been more firm. Nothing was going to affect the situation very much at this point. As long as it appeared Revil was going to reach *A Baoa Qu*, then the space fortress would be included in the attack. Even if the Federation armada had been dealt a nearly fatal blow with the first blast, and even if Revil's forces had dispersed or retreated, he would still have carried out the strafing operation. It just would have been a little harder to come up with a plausible excuse to justify it. Revil, in his desperation, was now making things easier for him.

"Revil's an awfully determined bastard, that's all I can say," he mused aloud.

"It's quite possible, Excellency," an aide replied, "that he was killed in the first firing. It certainly would make sense to assume so."

"What makes you say that?" Gihren suddenly demanded. "Any normal fleet admiral would have turned tail and run right after being fired upon by a laser cannon of that magnitude. The Federation armada's plowing ahead precisely because Revil's still in command. He's probably trying to reach *A Baoa Qu* to use it as a shield. Don't forget, sometimes in war a bullheaded approach is the key to victory."

"Using *A Baoa Qu* as a shield?" The aide, along with the other staff members in the operations room, had never thought of that possibility. Suddenly he felt new respect for his leader.

The feeling was not mutual, however. Gihren loathed signs of weakness among his men. He looked up at the giant overhead operations display on which they relied so heavily. It wasn't radar-based and was only a computer simulation generated from unreliable laser sensor readings. *Hmph*, he thought. *And they believe in this junk . . .*

An official-sounding voice echoed from the operation room's speakers: *"Five minutes left until the second firing. Countdown now commencing."*

"Good," Gihren grunted, reaching again for the hot line receiver to contact Chapman and inform him of his decision. Then he heard a shout behind him and turned around.

"The Federation Forces have *what?!*" an excited officer was exclaiming.

"What's going on?" Gihren demanded.

"There seems to have been a change, Excellency!"

"Are you sure?"

"We're double-checking right now, sir!"

There had been no change in the operations display. It took time for information from laser sensors to be analyzed and extrapolated, and physical interference from Minovsky particles often blocked and distorted much of the data that did arrive.

"Countdown stopped. Countdown on hold. Ignition on standby."

Gihren put the hot line receiver back in its box and closed the lid. Then he spun his chair around to better see what was going on in the center of the operations room. On a special holoscopic monitor that generated a 3D image with coordinate lines for reference, computer data from a dozen regular terminals throughout the room was being collected and displayed. As Gihren watched, scores of red and green lights, used to differentiate friendly from enemy craft, began to wink on and off.

"It does appear, Excellency," one the staff officers announced, "that the Federation Forces are detouring to get around to the other side of *A Baoa Qu*. There's an eighty-two percent probability they're using it as a shield."

It was a mystery to Gihren how anyone in his right mind could put so much faith in numerical projections. Those who believed in such a sophisticated form of speculation, he concluded, were idiots. They lacked, he reminded himself, the very quality he so prided himself on—an acute sensitivity to the complexity of the issues at hand. And that thought helped him make his next decision.

"Order all *A Baoa Qu* ships to leave the area along the Gel Dorva line," he announced. "Restart the Solar Ray countdown! Now!"

Everything was going according to plan. His mind began to turn to ways of wrapping up business after the war was finally concluded. *If I threatened to decelerate* Luna II *and make it crash on their heads,* he thought, *the idiots underground in Jaburo would probably give up. But maybe that won't even be necessary.*

Gihren grabbed the hot line receiver once more, and Chapman's image immediately appeared on the dedicated monitor.

"Chapman here, sir."

"Good, Chapman. We'll proceed as planned." Then, in a low voice, he confirmed the true target. "I want you to strafe from Gel Dorva all the way to the Zig line of fire. As planned. Repeat. *As planned.*"

On the monitor screen, Chapman's eyes appeared to be closed. "Yessir," he replied softly.

Gihren slammed the receiver down and immediately grabbed another. "Give me Lieutenant Ramba Ral of the S.S. immediately," he barked to the comm officer.

"Lieutenant Ramba Ral appearing on screen, sir," the officer announced.

Gihren waited a second and then spoke. "Lieutenant. This is your Supreme Commander. I want you to be ready to leave immediately for *Mahal.* Wait in the port area till I give you your next orders."

"*Yes, sir!*"

Ramba's eager response made Gihren feel mild disgust. The man was destined to spend the rest of his life in a pathetic attempt to make amends for the fact that his father, Jimba Ral, had fled the Principality with the children of Zeon Zum Deikun.

FROM THE MOMENT THE Solar Ray system reached maximum power for the second blast, the staff officers in operations had held their breath in anticipation. They knew the Federation fleet was being targeted, but none of them knew what Gihren had just secretly ordered Chapman to do.

"*Thirty seconds remaining! Twenty-seven . . . Twenty-five . . . Twenty-three.*"

To Gihren's surprise, the final countdown was performed with the computer-simulated voice of an attractive young woman. Someone— probably Chapman—had apparently decided a female voice would register better on his ears. It was a nice touch, but it irritated him. It made him think that his men were trying too hard to please him, perhaps out of fear. He shut his eyes and contemplated a more serious matter.

Don't worry, Kycilia, he thought. *When the Solar Ray cannon hits* A Baoa Qu, *you won't feel a thing. Even if you're in the most sheltered, protected part of the fortress, the whole process'll only take a few seconds. Then you'll rest in peace. The real problem will be what to do with our father, the Sovereign . . .*

The countdown continued: "*three, two, one . . .*" Filters were activated on all monitors in the room linked to *Mahal.* And then the laser cannon fired with a FWOOSH. It was clearly a more powerful blast than the first. A colossal flare of light suddenly appeared around the opening as an invisible laser beam again split the heavens.

THE SAME INSTANT, CHAPMAN, in the *Mahal* control center on the *Guild*, turned the switch to ignite fifty-eight thruster rockets on the "top" side of the colony cylinder.

"Fire jets ninety-eight through one hundred and fifty-six!"

"Number ninety-eight has fired!"

"One hundred through one hundred and ten have fired! One hundred and ten through twenty have fired!"

IN ZUM CITY, IN the background on his secure hot line monitor, Gihren could hear the personnel in charge of adjusting the *Mahal* firing angle relay their commands throughout the center, linking up the system. Chapman, after his orders had been conveyed, looked ashen. Only a few men in his command were capable of understanding the basic operation of the laser cannon and its retargeting mechanism, and most had no time to question what they were doing. Those who had doubts probably were too tense to vocalize them, or so stunned by the magnitude of the giant flare of light that they never even noticed the correction in the firing angle.

The staff in the operations room of the Joint Command Headquarters at Zum City were the first to detect it, and the cry went up, *"Change in angle!* Mahal *now switching to Zig line of fire!"*

IN THE OPERATIONS ROOM of the *Guild*, the officer in charge of trajectory was the first to protest to Admiral Chapman Jirom. "Firing any jets over number one hundred and forty, sir, will make us deviate from the Gel Dorva line! We've got to stop immediately!"

"What?" Chapman screamed. "Who gave you permission to fire over one-forty? You say they've already fired? Stop the procedure instantly! Use reverse thrust and return the cylinder at once to position on the Gel Dorva line."

It was a masterpiece of acting. It was already too late to execute his request, for over ten seconds had already elapsed since he had hit the switch. The giant colony's inertia was far too great to stop suddenly.

The hot line phone in front of Chapman rang.

"Chapman! This is Gihren! What's going on? Mahal's *angle of fire is skewed! Are you trying to fry* A Baoa Qu*?!"*

"We're working on the problem, Excellency! The laser oscillation has ceased. But . . . but . . . " Chapman answered with as loud and panicked a voice as Gihren. In reality, he was overjoyed. The deception had worked. He and Gihren Zabi were carrying out a little charade that no one else was privy to. He congratulated himself: *The Supreme Commander and I are coconspirators . . .*

GIHREN ORDERED THE HOT line phone with Chapman disconnected. He knew the giant laser beam should have incinerated most of the Earth Federation Forces and melted the stem of *A Baoa Qu*. As far as he was concerned, the operation was over. He next contacted Lt. Ramba Ral, about to leave the Zum City port for the *Mahal* area.

"Ramba, this is Gihren. I want you to proceed directly to the *Guild*. Someone changed the laser cannon's angle of fire. I want you to find out who's responsible and arrest them. If anyone resists, execute them on the spot. That's an order."

"*Sir?*"

On the monitor, Lt. Ramba Ral appeared confused, as did the other officers in the operations room who overheard.

"Someone shifted the *Mahal* cylinder so its line of fire included the S sector of *A Baoa Qu*. I'm worried about my sister Kycilia. If anything has happened to her, I'm holding Admiral Chapman Jirom personally accountable, even if it was an accident. I want you to deal with him. Do you understand me, Ramba?"

"*Yes . . . yes, yessir! Supreme Commander, sir.*"

Without bothering to watch Ramba salute, Gihren turned to his aides and ordered, "I want a survey done on the level of damage to *A Baoa Qu* right away, and the results conveyed to Lieutenant Ramba Ral." He was secretly thrilled. Here he was, impersonating himself in an elaborate charade and doing such an excellent job. "I also want to know how extensive the Federation losses are," he added with just the right tone. "We can't be too careful!"

Then Gihren sat back in the upholstered chair provided him and thought, *Now I'll wait to see how well my plan really worked.* For some reason, he suddenly began thinking of Cecilia and her curvaceous form.

SEVERAL MINUTES BEFORE THE *Mahal* laser cannon fired its second blast, chaos erupted in the operations room on the Federation armada's flagship, *Drog*. The *Pegasus II* had paved the way for the Federation vanguard by weakening the bottom of *A Baoa Qu*'s defense perimeter, and with a little more effort the lead ships might have been able to smash through and land on the stem of the fortress itself. But now something bizarre was happening. Scouts had detected odd movements in the Principality defenders, seemingly unrelated to the Federation attack. And the cryptic communication received from *Pegasus II* was even more puzzling. The graying fleet admirals and staff officers around General Revil argued bitterly over its meaning and whether it meant they should change their strategy.

"The word from *Pegasus II* is that Gihren Zabi's planning to eliminate a few of his own forces, too!"

"That's *preposterous!* I want to know where that information comes from. I don't care how fanatical Gihren Zabi is, I simply refuse to believe he'd destroy his own crack units."

"Is this some sort of Newtype intuition? Or are we dealing with fortune-tellers? How can we possibly act on unconfirmed information and give up all we've gained?"

The staff officers debated furiously, knowing the success of the entire campaign depended on their correct interpretation of the situation. They tried to be as rational and objective as possible, but lacking concrete information they were ultimately reduced to speculating. And since they were staring directly into the maw of death, every minute spent on discussion was a minute squandered.

General Revil finally stood up and raised his hands to silence his agitated officers. "Gentlemen!" he announced. "I've given all your opinions careful consideration. Debates have their time and place, but we've wasted precious minutes, and now we need a decision."

A hush fell over the room, and the men turned toward him.

"I've decided we should immediately abandon our position and proceed in the direction the *Pegasus II* has indicated. Each fleet will continue to fire at the enemy but reverse course and disperse. After we've avoided the next laser cannon blast, we can immediately regroup again. This order is effective immediately, and I want it transmitted to all units. On the double!"

"Sir," asked the comm officer, "er, is radio transmission acceptable?"

"Anything!" Revil barked angrily. "Just get the message out. Immediately!" He waited until the man made his way through the cluster of staff officers to the comm console and then ordered the *Drog* captain: "Put *A Baoa Qu* between us and the sun and immediately reverse course."

THE *DROG* BRIDGE SPRANG to life and the ship's prow started turning around, while the upper and lower deck twin megaparticle cannons maintained a constant barrage on the stem of *A Baoa Qu*. The rest of the armada also began to react as soon as it received its new orders from the flagship. Three *Chivvay*-class heavy cruisers came up on the *Drog*'s port side, nearly grazing its prow, and joined in an intense barrage. Squadrons of Federation Flying Manta fighters plunged into melees with their Zeon Gattle counterparts in front of the ships. And when a nearby GM Suit was hit, fragments from the explosion rained on the *Drog*'s bridge.

What Revil and his staff officers feared most appeared to be coming true. The armada was like a giant with legs of clay, trying to turn on a dime. Disarray was already appearing in the ranks. With its weaknesses exposed, and nearly surrounded by the enemy, the armada was attempting a maneuver normally considered madness in space warfare.

With a worried look, Revil glanced at computer-simulated combat status displays on either side of him. "Well?" he asked the officer in charge. "Any sign of Zeon forces breaking through our lines?"

"No, sir. Their rear guard seems to have begun to disperse, sir. I don't know what it means, though . . . "

Suddenly, they were interrupted by the comm tech. "Sir! We've intercepted a communication from Zeon. It looks like an order's gone out for all fleets on the Gel Dorva line to retreat."

"The Gel Dorva line?! Can you tell what course they're on?"

"No, sir . . . Sorry, sir."

Revil was puzzled. Why was the Principality issuing an order to retreat? And why all fleets? There was no evidence they had done so earlier, before the first laser cannon blast had occurred. There was no way he could have known the order was merely Gihren Zabi's sop to his own conscience, a too-late attempt to atone for his diabolical plot.

"This is odd," Revil muttered.

AND THEN IT HAPPENED. Thousands of flashes occurred to the rear of both forces, turning the area into chaos, and an enormous ring of light spread out toward the core of the Earth Federation armada.

The final image that registered on General Revil's retina was that of the stem portion of Zeon's *A Baoa Qu* space fortress turning white hot and melting. Then his flesh and blood turned into dust and scattered into a jet-black cosmos.

IN THE COMMAND CENTER atop the giant *A Baoa Qu* fortress, Vice Admiral Randolph Weigelman's last words were a scream:

"My God! Have the men on Mahal *lost their minds?"*

Along with a third of his men, he had survived the initial attack, but after the fortress stem disintegrated, the entire superstructure began to shudder, sending him ricocheting between the floor and ceiling a dozen times, snapping his neck and killing him instantly. Others were killed in the weightless conditions when ordinary machinery and equipment became deadly projectiles. Then *A Baoa Qu* heaved mightily and exploded, spewing rock and metal fragments into space.

Gihren Zabi

THE EARTH FEDERATION SPACE armada had been destroyed.

Zeon's forces had been crippled, for Gihren Zabi had sacrificed many of his best units and people and a strategically vital final defense outpost.

The war, to all appearances, had virtually ended. But reality was not so simple.

UNBEKNOWNST TO GIHREN ZABI, his sister Kycilia had survived the attack on *A Baoa Qu* and was making a beeline for Zeon's heartland in the *Swamel*, accompanied by two heavy and three light cruisers. At secondary combat distance she was also followed by the *Pegasus II* and a pair of Federation *Salamis*-class cruisers. The shortest route normally took less than two hours, and after seeing what the Solar Ray laser cannon had done to *A Baoa Qu*, Kycilia ordered her engineers to wring every ounce of speed possible out of her ship.

On the bridge, one of her aides announced, "There seems to be no doubt, Excellency, that the *S* sector of the fortress was targeted." Like the other officers, he was still incredulous. And, being well aware of his superior's tendency for blind rages, he trembled to think what she might attempt for revenge.

Kycilia assembled her crew and addressed them. "I'm asking you to join me on a new and dangerous mission. This is not an order but a request. Those of you who disagree with what I am about to do are free to leave this ship. I will even provide one of the cruisers for your safe passage. You may surrender to the Federation or, when all is over, return to Zeon. All I ask is that you do not interfere with my plans."

The assembled officers and men waited nervously, wondering what she would say next.

"I've decided to use whatever force I have at my disposal to destroy the Supreme Commander of the Principality, Gihren Zabi. For your information, Commander Char Aznable has agreed to join me. I await your decision."

Kycilia knew that few of her crew would oppose her. She had, after all, just saved their lives; if not for her, they would have been roasted in the Solar Ray blast. And besides, she had the support of Char Aznable and the 300th Autonomous. While small in number, they were reputed to be the Principality's most powerful unit of all.

AFTER A FEW MOMENTS of deliberation, Captain Forsythe, representing all those assembled on the bridge, stepped up to Kycilia. "Excellency," he said, "the vote is unanimous. Some of us have questions, but we've all decided to cast our lot with you."

"Good," she answered. "Just for your information, we also have a Federation Trojan Horse and two *Salamis* cruisers following us. They're on our side."

"On our side? You mean they'll *help* us?"

"That's correct, Forsythe."

Then one of the younger officers blurted out in disbelief: "But . . . but why?!"

"The Earth Federation Space Force," Kycilia explained, "has for all intents and purposes been destroyed. These surviving ships are virtual orphans in the area and their only real chance for survival is to follow us to Zeon and surrender. When they realized the horror of what Gihren Zabi has really done, they decided to join us and try to eliminate him."

"But Excellency," the officer continued, apoplectic in his questioning, "how can you be sure? We still don't know exactly what happened. The damage to *A Baoa Qu* must have been the result of some sort of accident on *Mahal*. How can you unilaterally conclude we must eliminate the Supreme Commander!?"

Kycilia was suddenly seized by an impulse to scream at the man for his stupidity. "Because I know my own brother, Supreme Commander Gihren Zabi, deliberately targeted *A Baoa Qu's* S sector in an attempt to kill me. *That's* why!"

"The Supreme Commander tried to kill Your Excellency?!" The young man was incredulous as a new reality sank in. He and the other officers in the room had long heard rumors of Zabi family intrigues, and now they at last knew.

"Tell me one other thing, though," he ventured to ask. "How did the enemy ship—the Trojan Horse—know what was going on?"

"I don't know myself," Kycilia replied, glancing at Captain Forsythe. "As you all know, Commander Char Aznable's recent battle report was extremely vague."

She knew it was possible that Char had been in secret communication with the Federation White Base-class ship all along, but she doubted it. If he had been passing highly detailed information about her plans, she was certain it would have fled the area or turned around and attacked her squadron. She suspected something far more subtle was going on, something beyond her immediate comprehension.

Her suspicions had been reinforced earlier with verification of the Gundam mobile suit's destruction. Around the same time Char Aznable's report stated that the destruction had occurred, she had mysteriously "heard" the words <*Destroy Gihren.*> It was almost as if they had suddenly slipped into her mind, and at the time she had even wondered if they were a figment of her imagination. But then she had remembered the few times she had heard Char talk about his experiences in battle with Newtypes. She herself knew little about them and merely assumed they had a slightly more evolved consciousness. But if the pilot of the Gundam were a true Newtype and she herself had some of the same potential, then, she realized, she actually might have received some message from him. It was a tiny revelation, but it had swayed her.

"I believe," she continued, "it has something to do with the fact that they're a Newtype unit. I think they've joined us because they intuitively know Gihren Zabi's an enemy, not just of the Federation, but of all mankind."

"Even after we just destroyed their Gundam MS?" Forsythe asked, still doubting.

"The Gundam pilot wasn't their only Newtype," Kycilia snapped, irritated. "As far as I can tell, Newtypes aren't supermen but ordinary people with a unique sensitivity or awareness. They're people capable of seeing the totality of things. I'm sure there's more than one Newtype aboard that ship, and I'm sure that's why they've decided to join us."

"So now they're our comrades-in-arms?"

"Hmph. I don't like the sound of 'comrades,' frankly. Think of them as temporary allies. But enough talk. I want all crew members to stay at their posts but to try and rest. When we approach Zum City we'll probably encounter resistance. We'll assume battle formation as soon as we reach the third combat line."

Kycilia ended the session with a final exhortation to her troops, her shrill voice echoing throughout the bridge of the *Swamel*.

On the bridge of the *Pegasus II*, Bright Noa and the core crew members greeted an unusual visitor.

"We bear you no personal grudge, Commander Char Aznable," Bright said. "If we'd stayed in the area, we would've all been vaporized." It irritated him that he couldn't see the man's eyes clearly behind his protective mask.

"I am relieved to hear that," Char answered stiffly, "especially from the skipper of such a distinguished warship. It's a profound honor for me to be here, and as you know, it's not a mere accident. Frankly, without Amuro Ray, it never would have been possible. And without you and your crew, Amuro Ray would never have been able to develop his potential to the extent that he did."

Sayla continued to man the comm console on the bridge, but she could see and hear everything going on. Only a few steps away from her, standing with impeccable bearing, was her brother—tall and magnificent, with a warm voice, resplendent in his red Zeon military uniform, with his protective mask and platinum-colored helmet. His personal charisma was already helping to put the *Pegasus* crew at ease. Yet as she watched him discuss strategies with her skipper, she knew he had changed. He was her brother Casval Deikun, yet he was also Commander Char Aznable of the Principality of Zeon military, and the latter persona had by now nearly eclipsed the former. As much as she wanted to get up out of her seat and run to him, she couldn't. Her brother was a memory, a memory treasured by her own other persona, Artesia Deikun, which was also fading within her. Amuro had been right. And his words now helped her stay in control, helped her prepare for the inevitable parting she knew she would again experience. *He killed the man I loved*, she thought. As she watched, Kai Shiden extended his hand in greeting to Char.

"I'm the Guncannon pilot, Commander," Kai said, "and I'm sorry, but I'm not the forgiving type. Someday, you may have to pay a price."

"I understand. But remember that the situation's changing and that there's a time and place for everything. Right now all I ask is that you don't shoot me in the back until we get through this mess."

Sleggar Law answered for Kai. "It's a deal, Commander. But after it's all over, we may demand, as they say, satisfaction."

"Fine," Char replied with a crooked smile at Sleggar, Kai, and Bright. "That'll give me something to look forward to. Here's hoping we all survive till then."

Then Mirai stepped forward. "If we're going to be allies," she said,

"I've got one favor to ask. There's something that still makes me feel uncomfortable around you."

"Uncomfortable?"

"Yes. That weird mask. Why do you always wear it?"

"This thing?" Char said, taken aback. "It's sort of a personal statement, you might say. A trademark." Then, without hesitating, he doffed his helmet, handed it to Sleggar, and casually removed the mask. "Sorry to keep wearing it," he said with a shy grin. "It's just hard to break an old habit."

Bright extended his right hand and said, "Allies, Commander Char Aznable. *Allies.*"

Char took his hand and in a soft voice answered: "I want to believe in the communion among people that Amuro believed in."

"Let's work toward it then, Commander."

CHAR SPOTTED SAYLA, AND immediately walked over to her. He stopped in front of her and looked straight at her.

Sayla stood up. Her brother's arms seemed to be inviting her, ever so subtly. A rush of childhood memories surged through her body, and she embraced him gently.

"Artesia," Char said. "Can you forgive me?"

"Amuro was young, Casval, and I loved him."

Char bent down and looked at her closely, his chin brushing against her blond hair. "That's all I wanted to know," he said. "Because we may never meet again."

"I know," she replied, pulling away from him. She wasn't crying. She simply felt the Artesia persona within her becoming weaker and weaker. "Just try and stay out of trouble," she said.

Char chuckled at her subtle humor. "You've grown into quite a woman, sister."

Sayla smiled back at him and then noticed the rest of the crew members staring at them with an embarrassed look, like spectators at an intimate interchange.

Char turned and spoke to the assembled crew. "Petty Officer First Class Sayla Mass," he said, "is my sister, Artesia Deikun. She's my only sister, and she will always be my sister." He then bent over, kissed Sayla on the cheek, and put his mask back on. And Casval Rem Deikun once again disappeared behind it.

WHEN LT. RAMBA RAL arrived on the battleship *Guild,* he was accompanied by thirty members of the Zeon Secret Service. He immediately confronted the military men in the operations command center of the System project.

"We have instructions to arrest all those responsible for skewing *Mahal's* angle of fire," he announced. "Everyone here is a suspect."

A chorus of voices rose in protest: "But . . . but we were just following orders!" "You can't arrest us for that!" "The Admiral specifically ordered that thruster jets up to number one hundred and fifty-six be fired!" "I heard him!"

Ramba walked over to Chapman Jirom. "Admiral," he said, "I'm Lieutenant Ramba Ral of the Principality of Zeon's Secret Service. I regret to inform you that you're under arrest until given further notice."

"You can't arrest me, Lieutenant," Chapman said, smiling thinly at the tall young man. "We're still carrying out our own investigation into the cause of the accident." He had been prepared for the fact that some eager beavers from the S.S. might arrive after the "accident," but he felt secure in his own position. After all, he thought, he was protected by none other than the Supreme Commander of the Principality, Gihren Zabi.

Chapman was naive. An aging officer, he had in effect placed himself in a situation where he could be used, and disposed of, at whim. With no powerful connections outside his organizational relationship to Gihren Zabi, he had no one to support him in case the relationship soured. Even Ramba Ral was better positioned than Chapman Jirom was.

"Ah, but as I understand it, sir," Ramba continued, "*you* are the one who issued the order to change the angle of fire. Am I not right?"

"You must be mad . . . "

"Someone gave the order. Are you suggesting, sir, that it was not you but one of your trusted lieutenants?"

Ramba looked around the room at the assembled men. He knew that in command centers surveillance cameras normally recorded everything in triplicate, on videotapes and cards, and he ordered them played back. As he suspected, they contained useless noise. "Hmm," he said. "This appears to be the result of more than simple Minovsky interference . . . "

Chapman protested indignantly. "Listen, Lieutenant—Ramba Ral, isn't it?—What makes you think you have the authority to interrogate us like this, anyway?"

"Admiral, sir. I have been directly ordered to do so by His Excellency, Supreme Commander Gihren Zabi."

"You what?"

Instinctively, Chapman knew he was doomed. Lt. Ramba Ral had been sent to destroy him. "But, but I was issued the order from above," he sputtered. "My men here are my witnesses. How dare you accuse me!"

Chapman never saw what was coming. Ramba's left hand moved with blinding speed, drawing an old-fashioned automatic pistol from his hip and firing a bullet through the admiral's forehead, spattering his brains out the other side. Ramba slowly slid the gun back into its holster. The mood in the command center turned to ice.

"The will of the Supreme Commander has been carried out," he announced to the stunned crowd. "For the time being the *Guild* will be under the direct command of the Secret Service. You shall all return to your current posts and await orders." Then he had one of his own men search the admiral's pockets for the key to unlock the hot line vid-phone.

AFTER LISTENING TO RAMBA Ral's report on the hot line, Gihren Zabi said, "I'll send a special investigation team out immediately. As soon as they arrive, you can return to your regular duties." Then he hung up and reached for a cup of coffee sitting on a console in front of him. His scheme had worked beautifully. The "accident" had resulted in heavy losses of Zeon ships, but it was nothing compared to those of the Federation. Their entire armada appeared to have evaporated.

The operations room at Joint Command Headquarters in Zum City was suddenly bustling with activity. Military men rushed to check the displays used to monitor each battle zone, and as it became apparent that the Principality had achieved a resounding victory everywhere, the atmosphere turned party-like. Special food and drinks were delivered to all present. Here and there, curls of smoke rose from officers who had decided to sit back and enjoy a cigarette. Others continued to relay orders to the field but did so in a relaxed, boisterous mood: "Hurry up and contact the remaining *A Baoa Qu* forces." "Send scout ships out to monitor Federation supply lines." "Tell all fleets from *Solomon* to demand the surrender of any fleeing Federation ships."

Gihren turned his back on the clamor. "Hmph," he grumbled. "I wonder what the Jaburo moles are going to say now?" Then he turned to the comm officer in the room and in a loud voice ordered, "I want a line to Jaburo kept open round-the-clock from now on!"

"Yessir," the man replied with a smile.

Then, as his staff officers cheered and saluted, Gihren started striding toward the room exit. Because of the enthusiastic din on his way out, he missed hearing the shocked voice of another officer monitoring a comm line.

"What? You're from the *Swamel*, you say? You've captured three Federation ships? And you want to enter the Zum City port?"

THE ZUM CITY PORT was on the shady end of the mammoth colony cylinder. The sunny end was used primarily for agriculture and to collect solar energy for internal power requirements. The ships in Kycilia Zabi's unit, deployed in a circle around the *Pegasus II* and its consorts, were immediately ordered to stop their engines and wait outside the port module, but they kept them idling and drifted on inertia toward the giant entry hatches. A special patrol vessel came out to inspect the new arrivals.

On the *Swamel*, an intelligence officer turned to Kycilia and reported: "There are seven heavy cruisers in the area, one of which is now in port. A squadron from *Mahal* will arrive soon."

After a moment's hesitation, Kycilia decided to crush all resistance in Zum City immediately, before Gihren could mobilize his forces and before other warships could arrive on the scene.

"We'll go with Plan One," she announced. "We'll force our way in." Then she turned and hurried from the bridge area to the *Swamel's* hangar, where a red Rick Dom waited for her, its cockpit hatch open. Slightly behind and to the left of the pilot seat, she had ordered an auxiliary seat installed. Char would be the pilot but, despite the personal risk, she would accompany him. She was determined to exact revenge on Gihren Zabi herself.

"Ready?" Char asked after she boarded.

As was her custom before battle, Kycilia unrolled the scarf-like collar around her neck and raised it up over her mouth. "Take it away, Commander," she said in a muffled but confident voice. "Don't worry about me."

Ah, but I do, Char thought, knowing Kycilia was too busy thinking about her brother to sense his true intent.

The other MS pilots, including Leroy Gilliam, had positioned their Suits on the upper deck of the *Swamel* and were waiting for Char to launch. Then the hangar doors opened and the red Rick Dom slipped into space, signaling the start of the entire operation.

"Think we can find him?" Kycilia asked.

"Probably," Char answered, turning his main engine on full thrust. In his rearview monitor he saw three other Rick Doms and three Zakus follow him off the *Swamel's* decks. And then, from the *Pegasus II*, he saw the flare of an engine streak out of a hatch into black space and knew it was Kai Shiden's Guncannon. The eight Suits immediately assumed formation and plunged toward the Zum City port module. And following them, with flames belching from their main engines, came the newly allied force of eight Zeon and Federation ships.

THE *SWAMEL* TURNED ITS main cannon on the port module and fired once. A white-hot light leapt from the barrel and directly hit the giant exterior hatch doors, piercing two layers. The doors suddenly swelled, flashed, and then blew up, spewing forth metal shrapnel toward the Suits and ships, but they continued charging ahead.

Kai kept his eyes on the red Rick Dom in front of him. He felt uneasy. He was the only one in the MS formation who knew nothing about Zum City. He just hoped Char would lead them directly to Gihren Zabi, wherever he was.

When the Suits arrived at the colony port, two layers of the hatch doors were still intact, so they fired bazooka shells and tried to blow the third wide open. The fourth door they would have to leave intact, since destroying it would cause far too much damage to the inside of the Zum City colony. While they were working on the hatch doors, the *Swamel* and the *Pegasus II* left the other ships to stand guard outside and entered the port area.

Zeon ships loyal to Gihren Zabi in the Zum City area noticed something odd, but they failed to realize that a full-scale rebellion was under way because of the cover message constantly broadcast on all wavelengths by Kycilia's forces:

> *This is Her Excellency Kycilia Zabi's task force. This is not an insurrection, but an authorized military action. Any resistance will be crushed. This is Her Excellency Kycilia Zabi . . .*

Kai was prepared to encounter several Zeon Suits on guard inside the port module, and sure enough, while his new comrades busied themselves demolishing the remaining hatch doors, he put two out of action. In the meantime, Char's Rick Dom slipped through the hole in the third hatch door and reached the fourth and last. Guards on either side of the door began firing, but Char apparently located the manual lever that opened it, for the top and bottom halves slowly began to recede into the walls. As soon as they had enough clearance, the team of eight Suits dashed into the open space of the Zum City colony, fighting a fierce gale from the escaping air. Behind them, when the giant doors opened fully, came the *Swamel* and the *Pegasus II*. As soon as it cleared, the *Swamel* immediately broadcast a warning to the port authorities and the Zeon Joint Command Headquarters:

This is Her Excellency Kycilia Zabi. You are ordered to close the fourth hatch immediately. We are henceforth occupying Zum City! We intend no harm to civilians. Any resistance will only cause needless suffering to the colony and its inhabitants. Cease all resistance!

The MS unit quickly reformed and began descending from the port module toward the area where the government officials maintained their residences. Kai watched on his cockpit monitors as artificially generated clouds streamed by and then to his astonishment saw a vast green plain. He knew it was completely man-made, but it was the first Earth-like environment he had seen in months, and he could hardly contain his delight. People lived there. They led normal lives. He thought about something Char had said to the effect that the more artificial an environment, the more people deluded themselves into a sense of omnipotence, but he decided it wasn't true. Even if surrounded by a synthetic world, people tended to live and abide by the basic laws of real nature. He was an example himself, he thought with a touch of pride. But it was an issue he decided to shelve until later. He had to concentrate on where he was going.

The inside walls of the colony—the ground—had gravity generated by centrifugal force, so the middle of the cylinder was in a virtually weightless state. That made it easy to fly even in a machine with a humanoid configuration, but he had to be careful not to use too much power. They were inside one of the largest colony cylinders in the solar system—thirty kilometers wide and one hundred and fifty kilometers long—but they still had limited room to maneuver.

It was six-thirty in the morning, colony time, and certainly the first time any of the colony residents had ever seen a formation of eight huge mobile suits roaring over their heads. Thousands of civilians, mobilized for the war, were on their way to work, and when they looked up, they must have thought it was either a victory fly-by or a sign of something terrible about to happen.

"Anyone detect anything?" Char said into his mike to the MS formation. His voice was a little impatient, but it went over the radio channel loud and clear. There was almost no Minovsky interference.

"*No! Not yet!*" came a nervous reply from Leroy Gilliam.

Kycilia, seated next to Char, said, "He's got to be over at the Joint Command Headquarters," and checked the beam rifle by her side.

Then Kai Shiden's voice nearly jumped from Char's cockpit speaker: "*Got it! It's right in front of us! I sense a presence!*"

"Good work, Guncannon! Lead the way!" Char barked, and in response Kai's Suit immediately moved out in front of the formation, dropping faster and faster.

"He's a Federation pilot, isn't he . . . " Kycilia said, stating the obvious.

"Kai Shiden. A junior grade lieutenant," Char told her.

FOLLOWING THE FORMATION OF Suits, the *Swamel* and *Pegasus II* surged through the cloud cover, carefully maintaining a constant altitude. In the proscribed space of the colony cylinder, their incongruous appearance alone was enough to discourage resistance. The *Swamel* was jet-black with a beak-like prow and a round tank-like stern; the *Pegasus* was a brilliant white, almost delicate structure that true to its name resembled a horse. To the colonists, who had never seen Suits or ships inside their artificial environment, they seemed like apparitions from another world.

GIHREN ZABI SLIPPED HIS hand inside Cecilia Irene's blouse and fondled her ample left breast. But then she suddenly announced, "Sir, your sister Kycilia's coming here." The teacup in his other hand began to shake, and he looked at her in shock.

"*What?*" he choked. "Did you say *Kycilia?*"

"Yes, sir . . . "

Gihren's fingers went into a spasm and clutched at her breast, but she didn't even flinch. She was terrified herself. She had awakened that morning and waited for Gihren to return to his residence from the Joint Command Headquarters. As usual they would have a cup of their favorite tea together, and then, while Gihren catnapped in his study, she would monitor any emergency messages from headquarters.

"I don't know why, sir," Cecilia said nervously, "but I suddenly sensed her voice and felt that she was here. Maybe I'm hallucinating or something." What she didn't tell Gihren was that she had actually "heard" a voice—a thought from Kycilia, saying, <*I'm going to kill him.*>

Gihren finally came to his senses. "Hah. Some hallucination. Even Kycilia couldn't pull off a stunt like that." Then, noticing his hand still on Cecilia's breast, he squeezed the mound of her flesh even harder.

"Please, sir . . . " she said, wincing.

A comm monitor in the room flickered to life, and over an image of panicking staff officers at the Joint Command Headquarters Gihren heard an announcement: "*Sir! The Zum port area has just been bombarded by the* Swamel. *We appear to have an insurrection on our hands!*"

Cecilia had been right.

Gihren commanded with his most authoritative voice into a microphone, "Keep updating me as more information comes in." Then, leaving the monitor on, he walked back over to Cecilia. She quickly stood up and draped his jacket over his shoulders. He reached out and gently touched her left nipple through her blouse. One of his great strengths was his ability to quickly reconcile himself to a new situation.

"Sorry, Cecilia," he said. Then he added, "I wonder what my horoscope would say now?"

"I wish I knew . . . " she replied, with as much empathy as possible.

In the background, on the monitor, they could both hear an official-sounding voice continuing to relay information: "*The fourth hatch door in the port module has been breached. A squadron of mobile suits appears to have entered the colony. We need information on their number! Immediately!*"

Gihren left his study and headed for the front door of his residence. *This just shows I made the right decision,* he thought. *Kycilia couldn't be trusted. That's why I had to get rid of her.*

In front of the building, an ele-car limousine with a chauffeur and staff officer was waiting for him. He climbed in the back seat and barked, "Take me to the Joint Command Headquarters immediately!" Then he turned to the officer in front of him and demanded, "What sort of defense have we sent up?"

The officer, a receiver in hand, never took his eyes off a small monitor on the dash-board in front of him. "We've ordered our troops into action, sir," he replied.

"How many enemy Suits are there?"

"Looks like seven or eight, sir. The *Swamel*'s already infiltrated into the colony interior, and we have reports it's accompanied by a Federation White Base-class ship. The one our men call the Trojan Horse."

"You mean the one that's supposed to be carrying their Newtype unit?"

Just then the Staff officer suddenly exclaimed into his receiver, "What? You say the Red Comet's with them?"

Instantly, Gihren knew. Char Aznable, Kycilia, the Federation Newtypes. It could mean only one thing. Now that the Earth Federation Forces were on their last legs and the Principality had badly depleted its military strength, Kycilia had decided to use every means at her disposal to eliminate him in a full-scale coup d'etat.

As his limousine sped down the highway at full speed, he thought, *Kycilia, you're worse than I am.*

IN THE MIDST OF chaos and confusion, Kai Shiden detected Gihren's presence. Just as Amuro Ray had once detected Dozle Zabi's aura, it appeared to Kai as a swirling black psychic mist.

"I see it," he exclaimed inside his cockpit. "I see it! Just like Amuro said!" He almost thought he heard a voice—Amuro's voice—reply calmly, congratulating him.

Below him, he could see an unescorted limousine barreling down a six-lane highway, scattering civilian ele-cars on their way to work before it. He fired his retrorockets and put his Guncannon down on the road a hundred meters in front of the limousine, landing on the asphalt with a thud and creating huge cracks in the road. Then the seven other Suits of the combined MS unit landed around him. Together, they completely blocked the road.

GIHREN ZABI'S DRIVER SCREAMED as he slammed on the brakes of the limousine. Gihren craned his neck out the window, saw the Suits, and instantly realized he was surrounded. Then he heard the amplified voice of his sister Kycilia emerge from a red Rick Dom to the left.

"*Supreme Commander Gihren Zabi. Get out of your ele-car!*"

The Rick Dom held a beam bazooka in its right hand, and its sights were trained on his limousine. Directly in front of him was another red Suit of slightly different design.

"The, the *Red Comet?!*" Gihren sputtered in disbelief.

The humiliation of having eight mobile suits peering down at him was too much to bear. He knew there was no way to escape, but in a rage he opened the right-hand door of the limousine and stepped out. The Rick Dom's mono-eye glowered ominously down at him. The Suit directly in front, he suddenly realized, was a Federation Suit, proudly wearing its scratches and dents the way a seasoned warrior bore his scars.

ON THE MAIN MONITOR of Kai's Guncannon, the Supreme Commander of the Principality of Zeon looked like a dwarf. To Kai, somehow everything suddenly seemed anticlimactic but, he reflected, that was probably the way things were supposed to be. Then the red Rick Dom next to him moved its left hand horizontally around to the cockpit hatch. The hatch opened, and Kycilia Zabi stepped out onto the Suit's open palm, carrying a beam rifle. The hand gently lowered her to waist level so she could better confront Gihren, but she was still nine meters off the ground.

Behind the curtain of Suits, ele-cars belonging to the Principality military and equipped with wire-guided missiles began to collect, but when they saw that their Supreme Commander was being held hostage at gunpoint they were forced to watch, helpless. Seconds later, several hundred armed soldiers also arrived on the scene from the Joint Command Headquarters half a kilometer away, but they, too, became mere spectators at the standoff.

"Kycilia!" Gihren called out. "What are you trying to do?"

Kycilia had her mask drawn up over her chin. "The same thing you tried to do to me, brother. You tried to kill me!" she answered.

"How do you know that?"

"Ever hear of Lieutenant Ramba Ral and Crowley Hamon?" she said, training her gun on his private parts.

Gihren sputtered in disbelief, but at the same moment Kycilia fired. Gihren caught the full blast of the beam, and his body disintegrated before he even had time to cry out.

"Well, that's that," Kycilia said coolly.

Then Char suddenly flicked the Rick Dom's left wrist, and Kycilia flew through the air, her finger still on her beam rifle trigger. "*Char!*" she screamed, as her body fell with a thud on the scorched asphalt beside Gihren's limousine. A few fragments of Gihren's seared flesh, scattered high into the air, fell on top of her. Then it was all over.

CHAR'S RED RICK DOM spun around and headed toward the Joint Command Headquarters, striding down the asphalt road past Kai's Guncannon. Kai stared at the back of the Rick Dom. Then he stared at Kycilia. Her body lay motionless, trails of purple smoke rising in the air around her from where her beam rifle had scorched the pavement. *How easily people die*, he thought.

In the sky above, the *Pegasus II* and the *Swamel* approached with guns trained threateningly on the Joint Command Headquarters. Char, in his Rick Dom, had arrived on the steps of the building and appeared to be delivering some sort of speech to the troops there, but Kai couldn't hear what he was saying.

Amuro, he thought, *this is the way it turned out* . . . Suddenly, he realized that he hated Char Aznable.

❏ ❏ ❏

THE SURF FROTHED AROUND Sayla's bare feet. It was both white and transparent at the same time, and it felt warm. The southern European sun was getting stronger and soon would bring all the delights of summer. Her blond hair, wet from the tidal air, rustled against her shoulders.

On Zeon, Degwin Zabi had been dethroned, the Principality had reverted to a republic with Prime Minister Darcia Bakharov at its helm, and a peace treaty had been concluded with the Earth Federation government. The *Pegasus II* and its two consorts had been seized by Zeon forces, and nearly half the crews had voluntarily taken Zeon citizenship. Char Aznable remained in the Zeon military as a captain, helping in its reconstruction, and he was joined by Bright Noa, Mirai Yashima, and several dozen other members of the *Pegasus II* crew. Kai Shiden was not among them; he stayed with the Earth Federation Forces.

Luna II was placed under the jurisdiction of the Republic of Zeon, and Fraw Bow and her three charges lived peacefully thereafter.

Only Sayla Mass chose to return to Earth, to the place she had once lived. When she left, Char had said, "I'm staying here, but I'm not in it just for Zeon, Sayla. It's a lot bigger than that. Amuro was ahead of his time. And my work isn't over yet."

On Earth, Sayla began living a normal, uneventful life. As far as she was concerned, her brother Casval Deikun no longer existed. People in space continued to look down on those who chose to remain in the ravaged environment of Earth and derisively called them "moles," but she didn't care. She finally felt rested, as if after a long fatigue.

It was early summer, the most peaceful and beautiful time in the Mediterranean.

<Want to go swimming, Sayla?>

She slowly lowered her naked young body into the surf. A wave swelled over her, and she was surrounded by indigo blue. Amuro was gone, but he was with her. She began swimming with bold strokes, alone.

A WORD FROM THE TRANSLATOR

YOSHIYUKI TOMINO'S ORIGINAL TRILOGY of the *Mobile Suit Gundam* novels has stood the test of time. Boosted by the huge success of the ever-expanding, multimedia *Gundam* universe, the books have remained popular in Japan since their initial publication in 1979. They were Tomino's first foray into the world of novels, and helped him not only express a different, more fleshed-out version of the original *Gundam* story, but also launch a side career—in addition to that of anime director—as a popular science fiction and fantasy novelist.

This English-language translation of the original *Gundam* trilogy first appeared in the United States between 1990 and 1991. It was originally issued by Ballantine Books (a subsidiary of the giant publisher, Random House), under their popular Del Rey imprint. Prior to *Gundam*, Ballantine had previously issued the *Star Wars* and *Robotech* line of novels, the latter based on the popular *Robotech* TV series (which was in turn extremely loosely based on multiple Japanese TV anime series). Both of these series had been very successful, in part because they were supported by the huge name recognition of the properties themselves, and by the exposure that had been generated in advance by movies and sales of merchandise, etc.

I was first approached to translate the *Gundam* series around 1988 by a veteran sci-fi editor at Ballantine. As I recall, she had learned of me from people at Lucasfilm, where I sometimes worked as an interpreter, and also from my non-fiction books on *manga* and Japanese robotics. She was clearly looking for something that would fit with her company's line of *Star Wars* and *Robotech* books, and, on hearing about the huge *Gundam* phenomenon in Japan, thought Mr. Tomino's novels would be ideal candidates.

Although honored to be asked, I was at first reluctant to work on such a huge project, particularly since the publisher's expectations of the translator seemed particularly high, and an almost literal translation was demanded. But I liked the story, and felt that it could be faithfully rendered into English and still work as a novel, which is not always the case with Japanese popular literature.

Mr. Tomino wrote the *Gundam* novels in a fairly elaborate style, but in retrospect my biggest problem was not translating the meaning of his prose. Rather, it was figuring out what to do with his made-up terminology; since for his complex sci-fi saga, he had to invent scores of names for people and places and mecha. These names were mostly rendered in a Japanese phonetic script called *katakana,* usually used for foreign words, but they had no fixed English spellings because the original readers were, obviously, all Japanese. I therefore had to transliterate them into English, to assign them spellings. This in itself was not particularly difficult, but there was a somewhat amusing, political aspect to the problem.

With the success of *Gundam* merchandise in Japan, some local designers of plastic model kits and other items had already rendered many of the story's terms in English. Unfortunately, however, they had often done so with little regard for the spellings or sound, since they had little knowledge of English and were mainly trying to achieve an artistic effect. As a result, in the early days in Japan some English spellings of the terminology were rather unorthodox, if not awkward, and often there were multiple variants of the same terms. And around the same time, even before the *Gundam* videos and films and merchandise became officially available in the United States, a small group of dedicated fans there had already emerged. They, too, had begun to transliterate the story's complicated terminology, using their own preferred spellings, but like the designers in Japan they had no way of enforcing any unity outside of their own small group. In both Japan and the United States, therefore, *Gundam* spellings were in considerable disarray. Thus, the rebel nation pronounced *Jion* in Japanese was variously spelled in English-language articles or advertisements as "Zion," "Jion," "Xeon," and so forth.

I therefore went back to the original Japanese and tried to come up with spellings which I felt (1) sounded like the original and reflected the author's intent, (2) enhanced rather than detracted from the mood of the story, and (3) would be acceptable to American readers unfamiliar with the animation. I thus spelled "Jion" as "Zeon," because "Z" has strong overtones (think of all the "z"s used in US muscle car names). "Zion" was unacceptable because some readers might think Mr. Tomino is making a religious statement, when he is not. The antagonist of the story, whose name is pronounced in Japanese as *Sha Azunaburu*, I rendered as "Sha Aznable." I had seen this spelled variously as "Char Aznable" or even "Char Aznavour," but "Char Aznavour" didn't sound at all like the original Japanese. To me, it also had odd overtones of "charcoal" and "charwoman," etc., and seemed too close to the French chanson singer, Charles Aznavour.

I had no way of predicting it, but by the time I finally finished work on the series in 1991 the number of North American *Gundam* anime fans attached to specific spellings—especially to "Char"—had grown considerably. One email I received from an irate American fan (and early user of the Internet) opened with, "I eagerly awaited the release of *Gundam*, and literally rushed out to buy the book . . . I must say, you ruined my whole day. Your decision to change the names of the characters, chiefly Char, left me with a single question: Why?"

The English *Gundam* novels have now been out of print for over a decade. When first issued, they appeared with no advertising and promotion and almost no name recognition. Sales, while stellar by the standards of a small publisher, were not, it is safe to say, what Ballantine had probably expected. But in the fourteen years since the books first appeared, *Gundam* anime and merchandise have begun to appear in volume in the United States, with the result that the environment for these novels has changed radically. There is an exponentially larger fan community and market for English-language *Gundam* material than there was in 1990. As a result, more and more fans have recently been asking about the translated trilogy, despite the fact that (or perhaps partly because of it) it has a shockingly different ending than the animation with which most are familiar.

After long and arduous negotiations with both Ballantine and the Japanese rights-holders, it has finally become possible for Stone Bridge Press to reissue my translation in this new, single-volume format. At the same time, in recognition of the fact that they control a now-huge, global entertainment property, the rights-holders in Japan have finally created a unified list of English spellings of the characters and mecha, for all animation and merchandise sold overseas.

Therefore, although Mr. Tomino's trilogy should ideally be read as a story independent from the animation series, for this edition I have gone back and changed the names of familiar characters and mecha, to make them conform to now-official English spellings for the animated story. I have retained my original transliterations only when the characters and mecha are unique to the novels, and do not also appear in animation or other formats. In addition, I have taken the opportunity to smooth out the now quite old, original translation in a few places. I hope the result will allow modern readers the opportunity to enjoy Mr. Tomino's novels as they are supposed to be enjoyed, as pure entertainment.

In conclusion, I would like to give a tip of the hat to Mark Simmons for reading over my translation manuscript, and especially to Yoshiyuki Tomino and Yasuo Watanabe of Sunrise, Inc., for their support and encouragement in making this republication possible.

Frederik L. Schodt
San Francisco, April, 2004

ABOUT THE AUTHOR

Yoshiyuki Tomino is the principal creator of *Gundam*, beginning with the first animated television series of the same name in 1979, in Japan. His career in animation dates back to production work on *Tetsuwan Atomu* ("Astro Boy"), which was Japan's first animated television series. He has authored numerous novels using the characters he has developed, as well as other film and television projects in and outside the *Gundam* universe. One of his more recent creations is the 1999 TV series, *Turn A Gundam*, which was also made into a two-part theatrical feature in early 2002. A household name in Japan today, he lives in Tokyo.

ABOUT THE TRANSLATOR

Frederik L. Schodt is a writer, translator, and interpreter who lives in San Francisco, California. He is the author of numerous non-fiction books on Japanese manga, robotics, and history. His latest book is *Native American in the Land of the Shogun: Ranald MacDonald and the Opening of Japan*, published by Stone Bridge Press in 2003.

ABOUT MARK SIMMONS

As Bandai Entertainment's resident *Gundam* expert, Mark Simmons advises on the company's English adaptations of animated Gundam works and writes for its GundamOfficial.com website. He is also a contributor to *Animerica* magazine and the principal author of the *Gundam Official Guide*, published by Viz LLC in 2002.

Stone Bridge Press publishes fine books about Japan and Asia.
We welcome your comments and suggestions.
Write to us at sbp@stonebridge.com.

Stone Bridge Press • *P. O. Box 8208* • *Berkeley, California 94707*